Alfred Hitchcock presents

STORIES FOR LATE AT NIGHT

Alfred Hitchcock
presents

STORIES
FOR
LATE AT NIGHT

RANDOM HOUSE · New York

The editor gratefully acknowledges
the invaluable assistance of Robert Arthur
in the preparation of this volume.

Acknowledgments

DEATH IS A DREAM, Robert Arthur. Reprinted by permission of the Author and *Alfred Hitchcock's Mystery Magazine*. Copyright, 1957, by H. S. D. Publications, Inc.

IT'S A GOOD LIFE, Jerome Bixby. Reprinted by permission of the Author. Copyright, 1953, by Ballantine Books, Inc.

THE WHOLE TOWN'S SLEEPING, Ray Bradbury. Reprinted by permission of Harold Matson Company. Copyright, 1950, by Ray Bradbury.

LADY'S MAN, Ruth Chatterton. Reprinted by permission of the Author. Copyright ©, 1961, by Random House, Inc.

EVENING PRIMROSE, John Collier. Reprinted by permission of Harold Matson Company. From *Fancies and Goodnights*, by John Collier. Copyright, 1941, by John Collier.

THE SOUND MACHINE, Roald Dahl. Reprinted by permission of Alfred A. Knopf, Inc., from *Someone Like You*, by Roald Dahl. Originally published in *The New Yorker*. Copyright, 1949, 1953, by Roald Dahl.

THE COCOON, John B. L. Goodwin. Reprinted by permission of Story Magazine, Inc. From *Story* Magazine. Copyright, 1946, by Story Magazine, Inc.

VINTAGE SEASON, C. L. Moore. Reprinted by permission of Harold Matson Company. Originally published in *Astounding Science Fiction*. Copyright, 1946, by Street & Smith Publications, Inc.

PIECES OF SILVER, Brett Halliday. Reprinted by permission of the Author. Copyright, 1938, by David Dresser.

THE WHISTLING ROOM, William Hope Hodgson. Reprinted by permission of Arkham House: Publishers, from *Carnacki, The Ghost Finder*, by William Hope Hodgson. Copyright, 1947, by August Derleth.

TOLD FOR THE TRUTH, Cyril Hume. Reprinted by permission of A. Watkins, Inc. Copyright, 1927, 1954, by Cyril Hume.

THE ASH TREE, M. R. James. Reprinted by permission of and Copyright, 1931, by Edward Arnold (Publishers) Ltd., London, from *The Collected Ghost Stories of M. R. James.*

SIDE BET, Will F. Jenkins. Reprinted by permission of the Author. Copyright, 1937, by The Crowell-Collier Publishing Company.

SECOND NIGHT OUT, Frank Belknap Long. Reprinted by permission of Arkham House: Publishers, from *The Hounds of Tindalos,* by Frank Belknap Long. Copyright, 1933, by The Popular Fiction Publishing Company; 1946, by Frank Belknap Long.

OUR FEATHERED FRIENDS, Philip MacDonald. Reprinted by permission of the Author.

THE FLY, George Langelaan. Reprinted by permission of the Author. Originally published in *Playboy.* Copyright ©, 1957, by George Langelaan.

BACK THERE IN THE GRASS, Gouverneur Morris. Reprinted by permission of Charles Scribner's Sons, from *It and Other Stories,* by Gouverneur Morris. Copyright, 1912, by Charles Scribner's Sons; renewal copyright, 1940, by Gouverneur Morris.

THE MUGGING, Edward L. Perry. Reprinted by permission of the Author. From *Murder.* Originally titled, "A Mugging at Midnight." Copyright, 1956, by Flying Eagle Publishing Co.

FINGER, FINGER, Margaret Ronan. Reprinted by permission of the Copyright Owners. Copyright, 1941, by Street & Smith Publications, Inc.

A CRY FROM THE PENTHOUSE, Henry Slesar. Reprinted by permission of Ann Elmo Agency, Inc. Originally published in *Playboy.* Copyright ©, 1959, by Henry Slesar.

THE PEOPLE NEXT DOOR, Pauline Smith. Reprinted by permission of the Copyright Owner. Copyright, 1952, by Grace Publishing Co., Inc.

D-DAY, Robert Trout. Reprinted by permission of *Saturday Review.* Copyright, 1945, by The Saturday Review of Literature, Inc.

THE MAN WHO LIKED DICKENS, Evelyn Waugh. Reprinted by permission of Little, Brown & Company and William Morris Agency, Inc. From *A Handful of Dust,* by Evelyn Waugh. Copyright, 1934, by Evelyn Waugh.

THE IRON GATES, Margaret Millar. Reprinted by permission of Random House, Inc. Copyright, 1945, by Margaret Millar.

Contents

NOVELETTE

STORIES

NOVEL

Alfred Hitchcock presents

STORIES FOR LATE AT NIGHT

DEATH IS A DREAM

Robert Arthur

YOU'RE asleep now, David.

Yes, I'm asleep.

I want you to rest for a minute while I talk to your wife.

All right, Doctor, I'll rest.

Your husband is under light hypnosis now, Mrs. Carpenter. We can talk without disturbing him.

I understand, Dr. Manson.

Now tell me about these nightmares he's been having. You say they started the night you were married?

Yes, Doctor, a week ago. We came directly here to our new house after the ceremony. We had a small wedding supper here and didn't retire until midnight. It was just dawn when David woke me by crying out in his sleep. He was twisting and struggling and saying something unintelligible. I woke him. He was pale and trembling and said he'd been having a nightmare.

But he couldn't remember any of the details?

No, nothing. He took a seconal and went back to sleep. But the next night the same thing happened—and the next. It's happened every night.

A recurrent nightmare. I see. But you mustn't be alarmed. I've known David since he was a boy, and I think we can rid him of this nightmare without difficulty.

Oh, Doctor, I hope so!

Possibly Richard is trying to break through into his consciousness again.

3

Richard? Who's Richard?

Richard is David's other self, his other personality.

I don't think I understand.

When David was twelve, he was in an automobile accident. This gave him a severe nervous shock and resulted in a form of schizophrenia in which he developed two distinct personalities. One personality was David's normal self. The other, the second personality, was reckless and mischievous, completely uninhibited. David called this personality Richard and said it was his twin brother, who lived in his mind.

How strange!

There are many such cases in medical history. When David was tired or worried, Richard was able to take over control of his actions. Then Richard did things like making David walk in his sleep and setting fire to the bedclothes. David couldn't help himself when Richard was in control. Sometimes he couldn't remember what happened. Other times he thought it had been only a nightmare.

How upsetting!

I handled David's case at the time and I thought we had made a complete cure and banished Richard for good. But it's possible that— Well, I'll question David now about this recurrent dream. The details will probably tell us what we need to know . . . David!

Yes, Doctor?

I want you to tell me about the dream that's been bothering you. You can remember it now, can't you?

The dream! Yes, yes, I can remember it now!

You mustn't get excited. Just be perfectly calm and tell me all about the dream.

All right, I'll be calm. I'll be quite calm.

That's fine. Now tell me about the first time you had this dream.

The first time—that was the night Ann and I were married. No, no, that's wrong. It was the night before we were married.

You're sure of that?

Yes. I'd spent the whole day arranging my law practice so I could take a few days off. In the evening I came out to this new house we'd bought here in Riverdale, to make sure everything was ready. I wanted everything to be perfect for Ann. It was nearly eleven before I got back downtown to my bachelor apartment. I was terribly tired.

I went to bed, but I was too tired, I couldn't sleep. I took a seconal tablet. But I'd hardly fallen asleep before the dream began.

How did it begin, David?

I dreamed the telephone rang. The telephone actually was on the table beside my bed, and in my dream I sat up and answered it. For the moment, it seemed real to me—I thought I actually had answered the phone. Then I realized I was dreaming.

What made you realize that, David?

Because it was Louise who spoke to me, and even in my sleep I knew that Louise was dead.

When did Louise die, David?

A year ago. She was driving through the mountains of West Virginia to visit her parents when her car went off the road. She was burned to death.

So of course, when you heard her voice, you knew you were dreaming.

Yes, of course. She said, "David, this is Louise . . . David, what's the matter, why don't you answer?"

For a moment I couldn't speak. Then in my dream I answered, "It can't be Louise. Louise is dead."

"I know, David." Louise's voice had the same mocking note I learned to know so well when she was alive. "Why, of course."

"This is just a dream," I told her. "In a minute I'm going to wake up."

"Oh yes, indeed, darling," Louise answered me. "I want you to be awake when I call on you. I'm leaving the cemetery now. I'll be there soon."

Then I suppose she hung up, I don't know. Suddenly it changed the way dreams do and I was sitting up, fully dressed, smoking a cigarette, waiting. Waiting for Louise to leave the cemetery and come to my apartment. I knew she couldn't, but as one accepts the impossible in a dream I sat waiting for her.

I had smoked two cigarettes when the apartment doorbell rang. Mechanically I crossed the room and opened the door. But it wasn't Louise who stood there. It was Richard.

"Your twin brother, Richard?"

Yes, my twin brother, but taller than I, stronger, handsomer. He stood looking at me, smiling, self-assured, the old recklessness in his eyes.

"Well, David," he asked, "aren't you going to invite me in? And after we haven't seen each other for fifteen years?"

"No, Richard!" I cried. "You can't come back!"

"But I am back," he said, and pushed past me into the room. "I've been planning to visit you for a long time, and tonight seemed like a good occasion."

"Why have you come?" I demanded. "You're dead. Dr. Manson and I killed you."

"Louise is dead too," Richard said. "But she's coming back to-night. Why shouldn't I?"

"What do you want?"

"Only to help you, David. You need somebody to stand by you tonight. You're much too nervous to face a dead wife by yourself."

"Go away, Richard," I begged him.

"There's someone at the door," he answered. "It must be Louise. I'll leave you alone to talk to her. But remember, I'm here if you need me."

He strolled into the next room. The doorbell sounded again, impatiently, and I opened the door. Louise stood there. She was dressed all in white, just as I had buried her, and the veil, that had hidden the terribly burned face, made a little swirling movement about her head as she brushed past me silently into the room and settled, ever so slowly, into a chair.

For a long moment Louise said nothing. Then she said, "Why, David, you seem quite stricken dumb. Do shut the door. It's causing a draft and I'm not used to drafts. I've been shut up in a stuffy coffin for almost a year, you know."

I closed the door and words burst from me.

"What do you want here? Why have you come? You're dead."

She burst into laughter. "Why, David, you really believe that, don't you? I'm not dead. I've been having a little fun with you."

"Fun with me?" I repeated, and she laughed until I thought she was having hysterics.

"Yes, David," she gibed. "You've always reacted to a crisis by getting jumpy, so I couldn't resist playing the role of a ghost to see what you'd do."

"You're lying!" I shouted at her, "You are dead. I saw you buried."

"For heaven's sake, David." She was annoyed now. "Do I look dead?"

She flung back her veil and showed me her face. Her cheeks were flushed, her eyes bright, her teeth showing in a small, feline smile. "The body you buried was a girl I picked up and was giving a ride to. After the accident I saw she was dead, and on an impulse I put my rings on her fingers and slipped my handbag under her body. Then I set fire to the wreckage."

"But why?" I groaned, sinking into another chair. "Why did you do it?"

"Because it amused me. I was more tired of you than you of me, and I liked the idea of living as another person. Besides, I knew that when I got tired of the game I could always come back. And now that I've run out of money, I'm back."

"But I'm getting married tomorrow. To Ann."

"I know, I read the papers. It occurred to me you might not want me to stay around. All right, David darling, I'll go away and play dead some more. You can go ahead and marry the daughter of your best client. But of course I'll need money."

"No! I won't give you any money. You're dead."

"I can just see the headlines tomorrow night," Louise said. "Prominent Young Lawyer's Wife Returns From Grave—Supposedly Dead Wife Interrupts Wedding."

"No!" I shouted. "I won't let you!"

"Really, all I need is ten thousand dollars. I'll get a very quiet divorce and your new marriage can be legalized again later. You see, it'll work out very simply."

I could not answer. My mind was whirling. I felt weak, confused, uncertain. Only the deep-seated realization I was having a nightmare saved me from collapsing. Louise rose.

"Think it over. I'll go powder my nose. I'll give you five minutes —then I'll expect a check."

She walked out of the room. I covered my face in an agony of indecision, wishing I could wake up. When I looked up again, Richard, my twin brother, was standing before me.

"I must say you handled that rather badly, David. You let her scare you with her ridiculous joke about being dead. Now she knows she has you beaten."

"But she *is* dead!" I cried. "This is all just a dream."

"Who can say what's a dream and what's real? My advice to you is, don't take any chances. If you give her the money, she'll just come back for more."

"But there's nothing I can do," I said in despair.

"Of course there is. Louise died once. She must die again."

"No! I won't listen to you."

"Then I see I shall have to take matters into my own hands, as I did when we were boys . . . Look at me, David."

"No!" I tried to turn my eyes away, but his gaze held me, brilliant, mesmeric.

"Look into my eyes, David."

"I won't. I won't."

But I could not turn away. I felt as I had, years ago when we were boys. Richard's eyes grew bigger and bigger until they were pools of dark water in which I was about to be swallowed up.

"Now, David, I'm going to take charge of your body as I used to. And you'll have to go where I've been all this time—deep down in our brain."

I struggled for an instant longer. But his eyes, like enormous pools into which I was falling, came closer and closer. Then there was a wrenching feeling and Richard vanished. I knew he had won. *He* was real now—he controlled our body. And I was helpless. I could look and listen with our eyes and ears, but I could not interfere with anything he chose to do.

Louise reëntered the room. Her eyes were bright and self-assured.

"Well, David," she asked, "have you made up your mind yet?"

"Yes, Louise, I have."

Richard spoke in a voice deeper than mine, stronger, more confident. Louise seemed puzzled by the change.

"Make the check to cash," she said in a moment. "I'll get the divorce in Las Vegas. No one will associate my name with yours. Carpenter is a fairly common name."

"There will be no check and no divorce," Richard told her.

"Then there will be publicity. Rather lurid and unpleasant. It will hardly do your career any good."

"There will be no publicity either. And just for your information, I'm not David. I'm Richard."

"Richard?" Louise's face mirrored uncertainty. "What on earth are you talking about?"

"I'm David's twin brother. The one who does the things David doesn't dare do for himself."

"You're being ridiculous! Now I'm going. I'll give you until nine tomorrow to change your mind about that check."

"There will be no check. You have no intention of keeping any agreement, and I know it."

Richard took a step forward. For the first time Louise seemed alarmed. She turned, as if to run. He caught her arm, spun her around, then with both hands seized her around the throat.

I had to watch, helpless, as his hands pressed more and more tightly into her throat, while her face changed color and her eyes became enormous. She struggled for perhaps thirty seconds, trying to kick and scratch. Then her struggles ceased. That was unconsciousness. Her face became livid. Saliva streamed from the corners of her slack mouth. Her eyes seemed to be forced from their sockets, glaring and open. Calmly Richard continued the pressure on her throat until she was unmistakably dead. Then he let her fall in a heap on my floor.

"All right, David," he said, "you may speak now."

"You've killed her!"

Richard wiped his lips with my handkerchief.

"An interesting point. Have I or haven't I killed her? Was she alive, or was she really dead all the time?"

"You're confusing me!" I complained. "Of course she was dead. This is only a dream. But—"

"But even in a dream we can't leave a body lying on your apartment rug, can we? It seems we must take her back where she belongs. To Fairfield Cemetery."

"But that's impossible!"

"It would be impossible for you. Not for me. I'm simply going to carry Louise down in the elevator, get into a taxi, and drive to the cemetery. And now you are to be silent until I permit you to speak."

Calmly he proceeded to carry out his insane scheme. First he put on my hat and gloves. Then he took Louise's veil from her purse and he pinned it to her hat. He brushed her coat and smoothed back her hair, which had become disarranged in the struggle. Then he picked up her body in his arms, carrying her as if she were a sleepy child, and strode to the elevator.

He rang the bell and stood there, Louise's dead body cradled in his arms, humming to himself. The elevator came after a moment and Jimmy, the night attendant, opened the door.

"A little trouble, Jimmy," Richard said as he stepped in. He had to turn sideways to get Louise through the elevator door and the movement made her purse slip from her lap, where he had placed it. Jimmy stooped for it and put it back.

"The young lady"—Richard's tone was man-to-man—"apparently started drinking before she got here. I gave her one cocktail and she was out like a light. Now I've got to get her back home. Can you get me a taxi at the side entrance?"

"Sure thing, Mr. Carpenter." It was apparent that Jimmy understood perfectly.

I had expected detection, exposure, arrest. Instead Jimmy brought a taxi, Richard stepped into it with Louise, and we started off as if it were perfectly natural for a man to carry a dead woman about New York at midnight. But clever though Richard was, such a mad scheme could not go without a hitch. The hitch occurred when the taxi driver turned and asked the address.

"Fairfield Cemetery," Richard answered.

"Fairfield Cemetery?" the driver said. "At this time of night? You're kidding, mister."

"Not at all." Richard always became annoyed when anyone wouldn't take him seriously. "This lady is dead and I'm going to bury her."

"Listen, mister!" The driver turned all the way around—a small, truculent little man whose face was red with anger. "I don't like you society mugs and your funny stuff. Now tell me where you want to go or get out of my cab."

Richard hesitated, then shrugged. "Sorry," he said. "It wasn't a very good joke, was it? Take us to Riverdale—937 West 235th Street."

"Okay, that's better." A moment later we were threading our way through New York's busy after-theatre traffic. Richard, still cradling Louise's body in his arms as if she were a child, leaned back and hummed "Waltz me around again, Willie."

The ride that followed could only have happened in a dream. Through Times Square we went, and the bright lights danced and flickered on Louise's face beneath her veil. Sometimes we stopped for traffic lights and pedestrians surged about us, peering in and snickering. Traffic policemen stared briefly and were not interested. Through the busy heart of the world's greatest city, Richard carried a corpse, and no flicker of suspicion passed through the mind of a single individual.

Presently we swung off onto the Henry Hudson Highway and sped along it to Riverdale, where we drew up at the address Richard had given—this house, the house I bought for Ann and me to live in. Cautiously Richard eased Louise out of the cab, managed to get his hand into his pocket and pull out a bill, paid off the driver and sent him away. The night was dark, the street was still. No one saw Richard as he unceremoniously dumped Louise on the cold stone steps, found the key and carried her inside.

He did not turn on the lights. Instead he dropped Louise onto a couch in the living room, then sat down opposite her and lit a cigarette.

"All right, David, you may speak now," he said.

"Richard," I said in anguish, "are you mad? Bringing Louise here is no better than leaving her in my apartment. Now what are we going to do?"

"I'm considering that point now." Richard sounded petulant. He hated for obstacles to arise to balk his plans. "Too bad that silly driver wouldn't go to the cemetery."

And then Louise sat up.

She sat up, swaying like one who is ill. Her hand went to her throat and when she spoke, her voice was hoarse, her words thick.

"David," she said, "you—you tried to kill me."

Richard turned to look at her. In the darkness she was a blur, ghostly, remote.

"It seems I didn't do a very complete job," he remarked, and sounded annoyed.

"You tried to kill me," she repeated, as if finding the fact impossible to believe. "You'll go to jail for this, I promise you you will."

"Nothing of the sort." He rose to his feet and towered dangerously over her. "I merely have to do the job over again, that's all."

Louise shrank away from him.

"No, for God's sake!" she cried out. "I'm sorry, David, I didn't mean it. I shouldn't have come back. I'll go away again, really I will. I'll never bother you again, David."

"I'm Richard, not David," he told her, his voice sulky. "You're very hard to kill, aren't you, Louise? You've died twice now and still you aren't dead. Perhaps the third time will make it final."

"Richard, stop!" I shouted at him. "Let her go. She means it. She'll go away and never—"

"You don't know much about women like Louise," Richard sneered. "Anyway, this is between her and me now. You're becoming a nuisance. Go to sleep, David . . . to sleep . . ."

I felt myself becoming faint. Darkness overwhelmed me. In my dream it happened as it happened those times when I was a boy— Richard banished me completely and was free to do just as he pleased. I knew nothing more until I found myself in my pajamas in my own bed. Richard stood in the center of the room, smiling at me.

"Well David, here you are, safe and sound again," he said. "And I'm off. I'll be back, though. You can count on that."

"Louise!" I exclaimed. "What have you done with her?"

Richard yawned. "Forget Louise," he said. "She won't trouble you again. I persuaded her to see your point of view in the matter, David."

"How? What did you do to her?"

Richard merely smiled. "Good night, David," he said. "Oh, in the morning, I don't want you to be distressed by anything. So remember, this has just been a dream. Just an interesting dream."

With that he was gone. An instant later I opened my eyes to find it was nine in the morning and the alarm clock was ringing. And that's what my dream was, Doctor.

Thank you, David. I understand now. I'm going to explain your dream to you and then you'll never have it again.

Yes, Doctor.

Before your first wife, Louise, died, you wished her dead, didn't you?

Yes. I wanted her to die.

Exactly. Then when she did die, you felt an unconscious sense of guilt as if you'd murdered her. On the eve of your marriage to Ann, that sense of guilt manifested itself as a nightmare in which Louise was alive again. Probably the ringing of your alarm clock made you think of a telephone and that started off the whole dream —Louise, Richard, everything. Do you understand?

Yes, Doctor. I understand.

Now you're going to rest for a moment. When I next say wake up, you will do so. You'll have forgotten the dream utterly. It'll never trouble you again. Now rest, David.

Yes, Doctor.

Oh, Dr. Manson—

Yes, Mrs. Carpenter?

You're sure he won't ever have the dream again?

Quite sure. His unconscious guilt feeling has been brought to the surface, if I may put it that way, and so removed.

I'm so glad. Poor David was on the point of a breakdown. Oh, excuse me, there's the doorbell.

Of course.

. . . It was the man with our blankets. A wedding present from David's sister. I sent them to be monogrammed. Aren't they lovely?

Very beautiful indeed.

I'll put them right away. David had a cedar chest built in beneath this window seat. It's airtight and completely moth-proof, the builder said. I certainly hope it is—I'd hate to have any moths get into blankets like these.

David, you may wake up now . . . Good. How do you feel?

I feel fine, Doctor. Only I'm Richard, not David. I'm surprised at you for thinking David was just telling you about a dream. You should know that's only David's way of hiding the truth from himself. That first time there really was a phone call and—Ann! Stay away from that cedar chest! I warn you, don't open it! . . . . All right, I warned you. But you had to go ahead and open it. Now, there's no use in your standing there screaming, you know.

IT'S A *GOOD LIFE*

Jerome Bixby

AUNT AMY was out on the front porch, rocking back and forth in the highbacked chair and fanning herself, when Bill Soames rode his bicycle up the road and stopped in front of the house.

Perspiring under the afternoon "sun," Bill lifted the box of groceries out of the big basket over the front wheel of the bike, and came up the front walk.

Little Anthony was sitting on the lawn, playing with a rat. He had caught the rat down in the basement—he had made it think that it smelled cheese, the most rich-smelling and crumbly-delicious cheese a rat had ever thought it smelled, and it had come out of its hole, and now Anthony had hold of it with his mind and was making it do tricks.

When the rat saw Bill Soames coming, it tried to run, but Anthony thought at it, and it turned a flip-flop on the grass and lay trembling, its eyes gleaming in small black terror.

Bill Soames hurried past Anthony and reached the front steps, mumbling. He always mumbled when he came to the Fremont house, or passed it by, or even thought of it. Everybody did. They thought about silly things, things that didn't mean very much, like two-and-two-is-four-and-twice-is-eight and so on; they tried to jumble up their thoughts and keep them skipping back and forth, so Anthony couldn't read their minds. The mumbling helped. Because if Anthony got anything strong out of your thought, he might take a notion to do something about it—like curing your wife's sick headaches or your kid's mumps, or getting your old milk cow back on

13

schedule, or fixing the privy. And while Anthony mightn't actually mean any harm, he couldn't be expected to have much notion of what was the right thing to do in such cases.

That was if he liked you. He might try to help you, in his way. And that could be pretty horrible.

If he didn't like you . . . well, that could be worse.

Bill Soames set the box of groceries on the porch railing, and stopped his mumbling long enough to say, "Everythin' you wanted, Miss Amy."

"Oh, fine, William," Amy Fremont said lightly. "My ain't it terrible hot today?"

Bill Soames almost cringed. His eyes pleaded with her. He shook his head violently *no,* and then interrupted his mumbling again, though obviously he didn't want to: "Oh, don't say that, Miss Amy . . . it's fine, just fine. A real *good* day!"

Amy Fremont got up from the rocking chair, and came across the porch. She was a tall woman, thin, a smiling vacancy in her eyes. About a year ago, Anthony had gotten mad at her, because she'd told him he shouldn't have turned the cat into a cat-rug, and although he had always obeyed her more than anyone else, which was hardly at all, this time he'd snapped at her. With his mind. And that had been the end of Amy Fremont's bright eyes, and the end of Amy Fremont as everyone had known her. And that was when word got around in Peaksville (population: 46) that even the members of Anthony's own family weren't safe. After that, everyone was twice as careful.

Someday Anthony might undo what he'd done to Aunt Amy. Anthony's Mom and Pop hoped he would. When he was older, and maybe sorry. If it was possible, that is. Because Aunt Amy had changed a lot, and besides, now Anthony wouldn't obey anyone.

"Land alive, William," Aunt Amy said, "you don't have to mumble like that. Anthony wouldn't hurt you. My goodness, Anthony likes you!" She raised her voice and called to Anthony, who had tired of the rat and was making it eat itself. "Don't you, dear? Don't you like Mr. Soames?"

Anthony looked across the lawn at the grocery man—a bright, wet, purple gaze. He didn't say anything. Bill Soames tried to smile at him. After a second Anthony returned his attention to the rat. It had already devoured its tail, or at least chewed it off—for Anthony had made it bite faster than it could swallow, and little pink and red furry pieces lay around it on the green grass. Now the rat was having trouble reaching its hindquarters.

Mumbling silently, thinking of nothing in particular as hard as he could, Bill Soames went stiff-legged down the walk, mounted his bicycle and pedalled off.

"We'll see you tonight, William," Aunt Amy called after him.

As Bill Soames pumped the pedals, he was wishing deep down that he could pump twice as fast, to get away from Anthony all the faster, and away from Aunt Amy, who sometimes just forgot how *careful* you had to be. And he shouldn't have thought that. Because Anthony caught it. He caught the desire to get away from the Fremont house as if it was something *bad,* and his purple gaze blinked, and he snapped a small, sulky thought after Bill Soames—just a small one, because he was in a good mood today, and besides, he liked Bill Soames, or at least didn't dislike him, at least today. Bill Soames wanted to go away—so, petulantly, Anthony helped him.

Pedalling with superhuman speed—or rather, appearing to, because in reality the bicycle was pedalling *him*—Bill Soames vanished down the road in a cloud of dust, his thin, terrified wail drifting back across the summerlike heat.

Anthony looked at the rat. It had devoured half its belly, and had died from pain. He thought it into a grave out deep in the cornfield—his father had once said, smiling, that he might as well do that with the things he killed—and went around the house, casting his odd shadow in the hot, brassy light from above.

In the kitchen, Aunt Amy was unpacking the groceries. She put the Mason-jarred goods on the shelves, and the meat and milk in the icebox, and the beet sugar and coarse flour in big cans under the sink. She put the cardboard box in the corner, by the door, for Mr. Soames to pick up next time he came. It was stained and battered and torn and worn fuzzy, but it was one of the few left in Peaksville. In faded red letters it said *Campbell's Soup.* The last cans of soup, or of anything else, had been eaten long ago, except for a small communal hoard which the villagers dipped into for special occasions—but the box lingered on, like a coffin, and when it and the other boxes were gone, the men would have to make some out of wood.

Aunt Amy went out in back, where Anthony's Mom—Aunt Amy's sister—sat in the shade of the house, shelling peas. The peas, every time Mom ran a finger along a pod, went *lollop-lollop-lollop* into the pan on her lap.

"William brought the groceries," Aunt Amy said. She sat down wearily in the straight-backed chair beside Mom, and began fanning herself again. She wasn't really old; but ever since Anthony had snapped at her with his mind, something had seemed to be wrong with her body as well as her mind, and she was tired all the time.

"Oh, good," said Mom. *Lollop* went the fat peas into the pan.

Everybody in Peaksville always said "Oh fine," or "Good," or "Say, that's swell!" when almost anything happened or was mentioned—even unhappy things like accidents or even deaths. They'd always say "Good," because if they didn't try to cover up how they really felt, Anthony might overhear with his mind and then nobody knew what might happen. Like the time Mrs. Kent's husband, Sam, had come walking back from the graveyard, because Anthony liked Mrs. Kent and had heard her mourning.

Lollop.

"Tonight's television night," said Aunt Amy. "I'm glad. I look forward to it so much every week. I wonder what we'll see tonight?"

"Did Bill bring the meat?" asked Mom.

"Yes." Aunt Amy fanned herself, looking up at the featureless brassy glare of the sky. "Goodness, it's so hot! I wish Anthony would make it just a little cooler—"

"Amy!"

"Oh!" Mom's sharp tone had penetrated, where Bill Soames' agonized expression had failed. Aunt Amy put one thin hand to her mouth in exaggerated alarm. "Oh . . . I'm sorry, dear." Her pale blue eyes shuttled around, right and left, to see if Anthony was in sight. Not that it would make any difference if he was or wasn't—he didn't have to be near you to know what you were thinking. Usually, though, unless he had his attention on somebody, he would be occupied with thoughts of his own.

But some things attracted his attention—you could never be sure just what.

"This weather's just *fine*," Mom said.

Lollop.

"Oh, yes," Aunt Amy said. "It's a wonderful day. I wouldn't want it changed for the world!"

Lollop.

Lollop.

"What time is it?" Mom asked.

Aunt Amy was sitting where she could see through the kitchen window to the alarm clock on the shelf above the stove. "Four-thirty," she said.

Lollop.

"I want tonight to be something special," Mom said. "Did Bill bring a good lean roast?"

"Good and lean, dear. They butchered just today, you know, and sent us over the best piece."

"Dan Hollis will be *so* surprised when he finds out that tonight's television party is a birthday party for him too!"

"Oh *I* think he will! Are you sure nobody's told him?"

"Everybody swore they wouldn't."

"That'll be real nice," Aunt Amy nodded, looking off across the cornfield. "A birthday party."

"Well—" Mom put the pan of peas down beside her, stood up and brushed her apron. "I'd better get the roast on. Then we can set the table." She picked up the peas.

Anthony came around the corner of the house. He didn't look at them, but continued on down through the carefully kept garden— *all* the gardens in Peaksville were carefully kept, very carefully kept —and went past the rusting, useless hulk that had been the Fremont family car, and went smoothly over the fence and out into the cornfield.

"Isn't this a lovely day!" said Mom, a little loudly, as they went toward the back door.

Aunt Amy fanned herself. "A beautiful day, dear. Just *fine!*"

Out in the cornfield, Anthony walked between the tall, rustling rows of green stalks. He liked to smell the corn. The alive corn overhead, and the old dead corn underfoot. Rich Ohio earth, thick with weeds and brown, dry-rotting ears of corn, pressed between his bare toes with every step—he had made it rain last night so everything would smell and feel nice today.

He walked clear to the edge of the cornfield, and over to where a grove of shadowy green trees covered cool, moist, dark ground and lots of leafy undergrowth and jumbled moss-covered rocks and a small spring that made a clear, clean pool. Here Anthony liked to rest and watch the birds and insects and small animals that rustled and scampered and chirped about. He liked to lie on the cool ground and look up through the moving greenness overhead, and watch the insects flit in the hazy soft sunbeams that stood like slanting, glowing bars between ground and treetops. Somehow, he liked the thoughts of the little creatures in this place better than the thoughts outside; and while the thoughts he picked up here weren't very strong or very clear, he could get enough out of them to know what the little creatures liked and wanted, and he spent a lot of time making the grove more like what they wanted it to be. The spring hadn't always been here; but one time he had found thirst in one small furry mind, and had brought subterranean water to the surface in a clear cold flow, and had watched blinking as the creature drank, feeling its pleasure. Later he had made the pool, when he found a small urge to swim.

He had made rocks and trees and bushes and caves, and sunlight here and shadows there, because he had felt in all the tiny minds around him the desire—or the instinctive want—for this kind of resting place, and that kind of mating place, and this kind of place to play, and that kind of home.

And somehow the creatures from all the fields and pastures around the grove had seemed to know that this was a good place, for there were always more of them coming in—every time Anthony came out here there were more creatures than the last time, and more desires and needs to be tended to. Every time there would be some kind of creature he had never seen before, and he would find its mind, and see what it wanted, and then give it to it.

He liked to help them. He liked to feel their simple gratification.

Today, he rested beneath a thick elm, and lifted his purple gaze to a red and black bird that had just come to the grove. It twittered on a branch over his head, and hopped back and forth, and thought its tiny thoughts, and Anthony made a big, soft nest for it, and pretty soon it hopped in.

A long, brown, sleek-furred animal was drinking at the pool. Anthony found its mind next. The animal was thinking about a smaller creature that was scurrying along the ground on the other side of the pool, grubbing for insects. The little creature didn't know that it was in danger. The long, brown animal finished drinking and tensed its legs to leap, and Anthony thought it into a grave in the cornfield.

He didn't like those kinds of thoughts. They reminded him of the thoughts outside the grove. A long time ago some of the people outside had thought that way about *him,* and one night they'd hidden and waited for him to come back from the grove—and he'd just thought them all into the cornfield. Since then, the rest of the people hadn't thought that way—at least, very clearly. Now their thoughts were all mixed up and confusing whenever they thought about him or near him, so he didn't pay much attention.

He liked to help them, too, sometimes—but it wasn't simple, or very gratifying either. They never thought happy thoughts when he did—just the jumble. So he spent more time out here.

He watched all the birds and insects and furry creatures for a while, and played with a bird, making it soar and dip and streak madly around tree trunks until, accidentally, when another bird caught his attention for a moment, he ran it into a rock. Petulantly, he thought the rock into a grave in the cornfield; but he couldn't do anything more with the bird. Not because it was dead, though it was; but because it had a broken wing. So he went back to the house. He didn't feel like walking back through the cornfield, so he just *went* to the house, right down into the basement.

It was nice down here. Nice and dark and damp and sort of fragrant, because once Mom had been making preserves in a rack along the far wall and then she'd stopped coming down ever since Anthony had started spending time here, and the preserves had spoiled and leaked down and spread over the dirt floor, and Anthony liked the smell.

He caught another rat, making it smell cheese, and after he played with it, he thought it into a grave right beside the long animal he'd killed in the grove. Aunt Amy hated rats, and so he killed a lot of them, because he liked Aunt Amy most of all and sometimes did things that Aunt Amy wanted. Her mind was more like the little furry minds out in the grove. She hadn't thought anything bad at all about him for a long time.

After the rat, he played with a big black spider in the corner under the stairs, making it run back and forth until its web shook and shimmered in the light from the cellar window like a reflection in silvery water. Then he drove fruit flies into the web until the spider was frantic trying to wind them all up. The spider liked flies, and its thoughts were stronger than theirs, so he did it. There was something bad in the way it liked flies, but it wasn't clear—and besides, Aunt Amy hated flies too.

He heard footsteps overhead—Mom moving around in the kitchen. He blinked his purple gaze, and almost decided to make her hold still—but instead he went up to the attic, and, after looking out the circular window for a while at the front lawn and the dusty road and Henderson's tip-waving wheatfield beyond, he curled into an unlikely shape and went partly to sleep.

Soon people would be coming for television, he heard Mom think.

He went more to sleep. He liked television night. Aunt Amy had always liked television a lot, so one time he had thought some for her, and a few other people had been there at the time, and Aunt Amy had felt disappointed when they wanted to leave. He'd done something to them for that—and now everybody came to television.

He liked all the attention he got when they did.

Anthony's father came home around six-thirty, looking tired and dirty and bloody. He'd been over in Dunn's pasture with the other men, helping pick out the cow to be slaughtered this month and doing the job, and then butchering the meat and salting it away in Soames's icehouse. Not a job he cared for, but every man had his turn. Yesterday, he had helped scythe down old McIntyre's wheat. Tomorrow, they would start threshing. By hand. Everything in Peaksville had to be done by hand.

He kissed his wife on the cheek and sat down at the kitchen table. He smiled and said, "Where's Anthony?"

"Around someplace," Mom said.

Aunt Amy was over at the wood-burning stove, stirring the big pot of peas. Mom went back to the oven and opened it and basted the roast.

"Well, it's been a *good* day," Dad said. By rote. Then he looked at the mixing bowl and breadboard on the table. He sniffed at the dough. "M'm," he said. "I could eat a loaf all by myself, I'm so hungry."

"No one told Dan Hollis about its being a birthday party, did they?" his wife asked.

"Nope. We kept as quiet as mummies."

"We've fixed up such a lovely surprise!"

"Um? What?"

"Well . . . you know how much Dan likes music. Well, last week Thelma Dunn found a *record* in her attic!"

"No!"

"Yes! And we had Ethel sort of ask—you know, without really *asking*—if he had that one. And he said no. Isn't that a wonderful surprise?"

"Well, now, it sure is. A record, imagine! That's a real nice thing to find! What record is it?"

"Perry Como, singing *You Are My Sunshine*."

"Well, I'll be darned. I always liked that tune." Some raw carrots were lying on the table. Dad picked up a small one, scrubbed it on his chest, and took a bite. "How did Thelma happen to find it?"

"Oh, you know—just looking around for new things."

"M'm." Dad chewed the carrot. "Say, who has that picture we found a while back? I kind of liked it—that old clipper sailing along—"

"The Smiths. Next week the Sipichs get it and they give the Smiths old McIntyre's music-box, and we give the Sipichs—" And she went down the tentative order of things that would exchange hands among the women at church this Sunday.

He nodded. "Looks like we can't have the picture for a while, I guess. Look, honey, you might try to get that detective book back from the Reillys. I was so busy the week we had it, I never got to finish all the stories."

"I'll try," his wife said doubtfully. "But I hear the van Husens have a stereoscope they found in the cellar." Her voice was just a little accusing. "They had it two whole months before they told anybody about it—"

"Say," Dad said, looking interested. "That'd be nice, too. Lots of pictures?"

"I suppose so. I'll see on Sunday. I'd like to have it—but we still owe the van Husens for their canary. I don't know why that bird had to pick *our* house to die . . . it must have been sick when we got it. Now there's just no satisfying Betty van Husen—she even hinted she'd like our *piano* for a while!"

"Well, honey, you try for the stereoscope—or just anything you think we'll like." At last he swallowed the carrot. It had been a little young and tough. Anthony's whims about the weather made it so that people never knew what crops would come up, or what shape they'd be in if they did. All they could do was plant a lot; and always enough of something came up any one season to live on. Just once there had been a grain surplus; tons of it had been hauled to the edge of Peaksville and dumped off into the nothingness. Otherwise, nobody could have breathed when it started to spoil.

"You know," Dad went on. "It's nice to have the new things around. "It's nice to think that there's probably still a lot of stuff nobody's found yet, in cellars and attics and barns and down behind things. They help, somehow. As much as anything can help—"

"Sh-h!" Mom glanced nervously around.

"Oh," Dad said, smiling hastily. "It's all right! The new things are *good!* It's *nice* to be able to have something around you've never seen before, and know that something you've given somebody else is making them happy . . . that's a real *good* thing."

"A good thing," his wife echoed.

"Pretty soon," Aunt Amy said, from the stove, "there won't be any more new things. We'll have found everything there is to find. Goodness, that'll be too bad—"

"*Amy!*"

"Well—" Her pale eyes were shallow and fixed, a sign of her recurrent vagueness. "It will be kind of a shame—no new things—"

"Don't *talk* like that," Mom said, trembling. "Amy, be *quiet!*"

"It's *good,*" said Dad, in the loud, familiar, wanting-to-be-overheard tone of voice. "Such talk is *good.* It's okay, honey—don't you see? It's good for Amy to talk any way she wants. It's good for her to feel bad. Everything's good. Everything *has* to be good . . ."

Anthony's mother was pale. And so was Aunt Amy—the peril of the moment had suddenly penetrated the clouds surrounding her mind. Sometimes it was difficult to handle words so that they might not prove disastrous. You just never *knew.* There were so many things it was wise not to say, or even think—but remonstration for saying or thinking them might be just as bad, if Anthony heard and decided to do anything about it. You could just never tell what Anthony was liable to do.

Everything had to be good. Had to be fine just as it was, even if it wasn't. Always. Because any change might be worse. So terribly much worse.

"Oh, my goodness, yes, of course it's good," Mom said. "You talk any way you want to, Amy, and it's just fine. Of course, you want to remember that some ways are *better* than others . . ."

Aunt Amy stirred the peas, fright in her pale eyes.

"Oh, yes," she said. "But I don't feel like talking right now. It . . . it's *good* that I don't feel like talking."

Dad said tiredly, smiling, "I'm going out and wash up."

They started arriving around eight o'clock. By that time, Mom and Aunt Amy had the big table in the dining room set, and two more tables off to the side. The candles were burning, and the chairs situated, and Dad had a big fire going in the fireplace.

The first to arrive were the Sipichs, John and Mary. John wore his best suit, and was well-scrubbed and pink-faced after his day in

McIntyre's pasture. The suit was neatly pressed, but getting thread-bare at elbows and cuffs. Old McIntyre was working on a loom, designing it out of schoolbooks, but so far it was slow going. Mc-Intyre was a capable man with wood and tools, but a loom was a big order when you couldn't get metal parts. McIntyre had been one of the ones who, at first, had wanted to try to get Anthony to make things the villagers needed, like clothes and canned goods and medical supplies and gasoline. Since then, he felt that what had happened to the whole Terrance family and Joe Kinney was his fault, and he worked hard trying to make it up to the rest of them. And since then, no one had tried to get Anthony to do anything.

Mary Sipich was a small, cheerful woman in a simple dress. She immediately set about helping Mom and Aunt Amy put the finishing touches on the dinner.

The next arrivals were the Smiths and Dunns, who lived right next to each other down the road, only a few yards from the nothingness. They drove up in the Smiths' wagon, drawn by their old horse.

Then the Reillys showed up, from across the darkened wheatfield, and the evening really began. Pat Reilly sat down at the big upright in the front room, and began to play from the popular sheet music on the rack. He played softly, as expressively as he could—and nobody sang. Anthony liked piano playing a whole lot, but not singing; often he would come up from the basement, or down from the attic, or just *come,* and sit on top of the piano, nodding his head as Pat played *Lover* or *Boulevard of Broken Dreams* or *Night and Day*. He seemed to prefer ballads, sweet-sounding songs—but the one time somebody had started to sing, Anthony had looked over from the top of the piano and done something that made everybody afraid of singing from then on. Later they'd decided that the piano was what Anthony had heard first, before anybody had ever tried to sing, and now any-thing else added to it didn't sound right and distracted him from his pleasure.

So, every television night, Pat would play the piano, and that was the beginning of the evening. Wherever Anthony was, the music would make him happy, and put him in a good mood, and he would know that they were gathering for television and waiting for him.

By eight-thirty everybody had shown up, except for the seventeen children and Mrs. Soames who was off watching them in the school-house at the far end of town. The children of Peaksville were never, never allowed near the Fremont house—not since little Fred Smith had tried to play with Anthony on a dare. The younger children weren't even told about Anthony. The others had mostly forgotten about him, or were told that he was a nice, nice goblin but they must never go near him.

Dan and Ethel Hollis came late, and Dan walked in not suspecting a thing. Pat Reilly had played the piano until his hands ached—he'd worked pretty hard with them today—and now he got up, and everybody gathered around to wish Dan Hollis a happy birthday.

"Well, I'll be darned," Dan grinned. "This is swell, I wasn't expecting this at all . . . gosh, this is *swell!*"

They gave him his presents—mostly things they had made by hand, though some were things that people had possessed as their own and now gave him as his. John Sipich gave him a watch charm, hand-carved out of a piece of hickory wood. Dan's watch had broken down a year or so ago, and there was nobody in the village who knew how to fix it, but he still carried it around because it had been his grandfather's and was a fine old heavy thing of gold and silver. He attached the charm to the chain, while everybody laughed and said John had done a nice job of carving. Then Mary Sipich gave him a knitted necktie, which he put on, removing the one he'd worn.

The Reillys gave him a little box they had made, to keep things in. They didn't say what things, but Dan said he'd keep his personal jewelry in it. The Reillys had made it out of a cigar box, carefully peeled of its paper and lined on the inside with velvet. The outside had been polished, and carefully if not expertly carved by Pat—but his carving got complimented too. Dan Hollis received many other gifts—a pipe, a pair of shoelaces, a tie pin, a knit pair of socks, some fudge, a pair of garters made from old suspenders.

He unwrapped each gift with vast pleasure, and wore as many of them as he could right there, even the garters. He lit up the pipe, and said he'd never had a better smoke, which wasn't quite true, because the pipe wasn't broken in yet. Pete Manners had had it lying around ever since he'd received it as a gift four years ago from an out-of-town relative who hadn't known he'd stopped smoking.

Dan put the tobacco into the bowl very carefully. Tobacco was precious. It was only pure luck that Pat Reilly had decided to try to grow some in his backyard just before what had happened to Peaksville had happened. It didn't grow very well, and then they had to cure it and shred it and all, and it was just precious stuff. Everybody in town used wooden holders old McIntyre had made, to save on butts.

Last of all, Thelma Dunn gave Dan Hollis the record she had found.

Dan's eyes misted even before he opened the package. He knew it was a record.

"Gosh," he said softly. "What one is it? I'm almost afraid to look . . ."

"You haven't got it, darling," Ethel Hollis smiled. "Don't you remember, I asked about *You Are My Sunshine?*"

"Oh, gosh," Dan said again. Carefully he removed the wrapping and stood there fondling the record, running his big hands over the worn grooves with their tiny, dulling crosswise scratches. He looked around the room, eyes shining, and they all smiled back, knowing how delighted he was.

"Happy birthday, darling!" Ethel said, throwing her arms around him and kissing him.

He clutched the record in both hands, holding it off to one side as she pressed against him. "Hey," he laughed, pulling back his head. "Be careful . . . I'm holding a priceless object!" He looked around again, over his wife's arms, which were still around his neck. His eyes were hungry. "Look . . . do you think we could play it? Lord, what I'd give to hear some new music . . . just the first part, the orchestra part, before Como sings?"

Faces sobered. After a minute, John Sipich said, "I don't think we'd better, Dan. After all, we don't know just where the singer comes in—it'd be taking too much of a chance. Better wait till you get home."

Dan Hollis reluctantly put the record on the buffet with all his other presents. "It's *good*," he said automatically, but disappointedly, "that I can't play it here."

"Oh, yes," said Sipich. "It's good." To compensate for Dan's disappointed tone, he repeated, "It's *good*."

They ate dinner, the candles lighting their smiling faces, and ate it all right down to the last delicious drop of gravy. They complimented Mom and Aunt Amy on the roast beef, and the peas and carrots, and the tender corn on the cob. The corn hadn't come from the Fremont's cornfield, naturally—everybody knew what was out there, and the field was going to weeds.

Then they polished off the dessert—homemade ice cream and cookies. And then they sat back, in the flickering light of the candles, and chatted waiting for television.

There never was a lot of mumbling on television night—everybody came and had a good dinner at the Fremonts', and that was nice, and afterwards there was television, and nobody really thought much about that—it just had to be put up with. So it was a pleasant enough get-together, aside from your having to watch what you said just as carefully as you always did everyplace. If a dangerous thought came into your mind, you just started mumbling, even right in the middle of a sentence. When you did that, the others just ignored you until you felt happier again and stopped.

Anthony liked television night. He had done only two or three awful things on television night in the whole past year.

Mom had put a bottle of brandy on the table, and they each had a tiny glass of it. Liquor was even more precious than tobacco. The villagers could make wine, but the grapes weren't right, and certainly the techniques weren't, and it wasn't very good wine. There were only a few bottles of real liquor left in the village—four rye, three Scotch, three brandy, nine real wine and half a bottle of Drambuie belonging to old McIntyre (only for marriages)—and when those were gone, that was it.

Afterward, everybody wished that the brandy hadn't been brought out. Because Dan Hollis drank more of it than he should have, and mixed it with a lot of the home-made wine. Nobody thought anything about it at first, because he didn't show it much outside, and it was his birthday party and a happy party, and Anthony liked these get-togethers and shouldn't see any reason to do anything even if he was listening.

But Dan Hollis got high, and did a fool thing. If they'd seen it coming, they'd have taken him outside and walked him around.

The first thing they knew, Dan stopped laughing right in the middle of the story about how Thelma Dunn had found the Perry Como record and dropped it and it hadn't broken because she'd moved faster than she ever had before in her life and caught it. He was fondling the record again, and looking longingly at the Fremonts' gramophone over in the corner, and suddenly he stopped laughing and his face got slack, and then it got ugly, and he said, "Oh, *Christ!*"

Immediately the room was still. So still they could hear the whirring movement of the grandfather's clock out in the hall. Pat Reilly had been playing the piano, softly. He stopped, his hands poised over the yellowed keys.

The candles on the dining-room table flickered in a cool breeze that blew through the lace curtains over the bay window.

"Keep playing, Pat," Anthony's father said softly.

Pat started again. He played *Night and Day*, but his eyes were sidewise on Dan Hollis, and he missed notes.

Dan stood in the middle of the room, holding the record. In his other hand he held a glass of brandy so hard his hand shook.

They were all looking at him.

"Christ," he said again, and he made it sound like a dirty word.

Reverend Younger, who had been talking with Mom and Aunt Amy by the dining-room door, said "Christ" too—but he was using it in a prayer. His hands were clasped, and his eyes were closed.

John Sipich moved forward. "Now, Dan . . . it's *good* for you to talk that way. But you don't want to talk too much, you know."

Dan shook off the hand Sipich put on his arm.

"Can't even play my record," he said loudly. He looked down at the record, and then around at their faces. "Oh, my *God* . . ."

He threw the glassful of brandy against the wall. It splattered and ran down the wallpaper in streaks.

Some of the women gasped.

"Dan," Sipich said in a whisper. "Dan, cut it out—"

Pat Reilly was playing *Night and Day* louder, to cover up the sounds of the talk. It wouldn't do any good, though, if Anthony was listening.

Dan Hollis went over to the piano and stood by Pat's shoulder, swaying a little.

"Pat," he said. "Don't play *that*. Play *this*." And he began to sing. Softly, hoarsely, miserably: "Happy birthday to me. . . . Happy birthday to me . . ."

"Dan!" Ethel Hollis screamed. She tried to run across the room to him. Mary Sipich grabbed her arm and held her back. "Dan," Ethel screamed again. "Stop—"

"My God, be quiet!" hissed Mary Sipich, and pushed her toward one of the men, who put his hand over her mouth and held her still.

"—Happy Birthday, dear Danny," Dan sang. "Happy birthday to me!" He stopped and looked down at Pat Reilly. "Play it, Pat. Play it, so I can sing right . . . you know I can't carry a tune unless somebody plays it!"

Pat Reilly put his hands on the keys and began *Lover*—in a low waltz tempo, the way Anthony liked it. Pat's face was white. His hands fumbled.

Dan Hollis stared over at the dining-room door. At Anthony's mother, and at Anthony's father who had gone to join her.

"You had him," he said. Tears gleamed on his cheeks as the candlelight caught them. "*You* had to go and *have* him . . ."

He closed his eyes, and the tears squeezed out. He sang loudly, "You are my sunshine . . . my only sunshine . . . you make me happy . . . when I am blue . . ."

Anthony came into the room.

Pat stopped playing. He froze. Everybody froze. The breeze rippled the curtains. Ethel Hollis couldn't even try to scream—she had fainted.

"Please don't take my sunshine . . . away . . ." Dan's voice faltered into silence. His eyes widened. He put both hands out in front of him, the empty glass in one, the record in the other. He hiccupped, and said, "*No*—"

"Bad man," Anthony said, and thought Dan Hollis into something like nothing anyone would have believed possible, and then he thought the thing into a grave deep, deep in the cornfield.

The glass and record thumped on the rug. Neither broke.

Anthony's purple gaze went around the room.

Some of the people began mumbling. They all tried to smile. The sound of mumbling filled the room like a far-off approval. Out of the murmuring came one or two clear voices:

"Oh, it's a very *good* thing," said John Sipich.

"A good thing," said Anthony's father, smiling. He'd had more practice in smiling than most of them. "A wonderful thing."

"It's swell . . . just swell," said Pat Reilly, tears leaking from eyes and nose, and he began to play the piano again, softly, his trembling hands feeling for *Night and Day*.

Anthony climbed up on top of the piano, and Pat played for two hours.

Afterward, they watched television. They all went into the front room, and lit just a few candles, and pulled up chairs around the set. It was a small-screen set, and they couldn't all sit close enough to it to see, but that didn't matter. They didn't even turn the set on. It wouldn't have worked anyway, there being no electricity in Peaksville.

They just sat silently, and watched the twisting, writhing shapes on the screen, and listened to the sounds that came out of the speaker, and none of them had any idea of what it was all about. They never did. It was always the same.

"It's real nice," Aunt Amy said once, her pale eyes on the meaningless flickers and shadows. "But I liked it a little better when there were cities outside and we could get real—"

"Why, Amy!" said Mom. "It's good for you to say such a thing. Very good. But how can you mean it? Why, this television is *much* better than anything we ever used to get!"

"Yes," chimed in John Sipich. "It's fine. It's the best show we've ever seen!"

He sat on the couch, with two other men, holding Ethel Hollis flat against the cushions, holding her arms and legs and putting their hands over her mouth, so she couldn't start screaming again.

"It's really *good!*" he said again.

Mom looked out of the front window, across the darkened road, across Henderson's darkened wheat field to the vast, endless, gray nothingness in which the little village of Peaksville floated like a soul —the huge nothingness that was most evident at night, when Anthony's brassy day had gone.

It did no good to wonder where they were . . . no good at all. Peaksville was just someplace. Someplace away from the world. It was wherever it had been since that day three years ago when Anthony had crept from her womb and old Doc Bates—God rest him—had screamed and dropped him and tried to kill him, and Anthony had whined and done the thing. Had taken the village someplace. Or had destroyed the world and left only the village, nobody knew which.

It did no good to wonder about it. Nothing at all did any good— except to live as they must live. Must always, always live, if Anthony would let them.

These thoughts were dangerous, she thought.

She began to mumble. The others started mumbling too. They had all been thinking, evidently.

The men on the couch whispered and whispered to Ethel Hollis and when they took their hands away, she mumbled too.

While Anthony sat on top of the set and made television, they sat around and mumbled and watched the meaningless, flickering shapes far into the night.

Next day it snowed, and killed off half the crops—but it was a *good* day.

THE WHOLE TOWN'S SLEEPING

Ray Bradbury

IT WAS a warm summer night in the middle of Illinois country. The little town was deep far away from everything, kept to itself by a river and a forest and a ravine. In the town the sidewalks were still scorched. The stores were closing and the streets were turning dark. There were two moons: a clock moon with four faces in four night directions above the solemn black courthouse, and the real moon that was slowly rising in vanilla whiteness from the dark east.

In the downtown drugstore, fans whispered in the high ceiling air. In the rococo shade of porches, invisible people sat. On the purple bricks of the summer twilight streets, children ran. Screen doors whined their springs and banged. The heat was breathing from the dry lawns and trees.

On her solitary porch, Lavinia Nebbs, aged thirty-seven, very straight and slim, sat with a tinkling lemonade in her white fingers, tapping it to her lips, waiting.

"Here I am, Lavinia."

Lavinia turned. There was Francine, at the bottom porch step, in the smell of zinnias and hibiscus. Francine was all in snow white and didn't look thirty-five.

Miss Lavinia Nebbs rose and locked her front door, leaving her lemonade glass standing empty on the porch rail. "It's a fine night for the movie."

"Where you going, ladies?" cried Grandma Hanlon from her shadowy porch across the street.

They called back through the soft ocean of darkness: "To the Elite Theater to see Harold Lloyd in *Welcome, Danger!*"

"Won't catch *me* out on no night like this," wailed Grandma Hanlon. "Not with the Lonely One strangling women. Lock myself in with my *gun!*"

Grandma's door slammed and locked.

The two maiden ladies drifted on. Lavinia felt the warm breath of the summer night shimmering off the oven-baked sidewalk. It was like walking on a hard crust of freshly warmed bread. The heat pulsed under your dress and along your legs with a stealthy sense of invasion.

"Lavinia, you don't believe all that gossip about the Lonely One, do you?"

"Those women like to see their tongues dance."

"Just the same, Hattie McDollis was killed a month ago. And Roberta Ferry the month before. And now Eliza Ramsell has disappeared . . ."

"Hattie McDollis walked off with a traveling man, I bet."

"But the others—strangled—four of them, their tongues sticking out their mouths, they say."

They stood upon the edge of the ravine that cut the town in two. Behind them were the lighted houses and faint radio music; ahead was deepness, moistness, fireflies and dark.

"Maybe we shouldn't go to the movie," said Francine. "The Lonely One might follow and kill us. I don't like that ravine. Look how black, smell it, and *listen*."

The ravine was a dynamo that never stopped running, night or day: there was a great moving hum among the secret mists and washed shales and the odors of a rank greenhouse. Always the black dynamo was humming, with green electric sparkles where fireflies hovered.

"And it won't be *me*," said Francine, "coming back through this terrible dark ravine tonight, late. It'll be you, Lavinia, you down the steps and over that rickety bridge and maybe the Lonely One standing behind a tree. I'd never have gone over to church this afternoon if I had to walk through here all alone, even in daylight."

"Bosh," said Lavinia Nebbs.

"It'll be you alone on the path, listening to your shoes, not me. And shadows. You *all alone* on the way back home. Lavinia, don't you get lonely living by yourself in that house?"

"Old maids love to live alone," said Lavinia. She pointed to a hot shadowy path. "Let's walk the short cut."

"I'm afraid."

"It's early. The Lonely One won't be out till late." Lavinia, as cool as mint ice cream, took the other woman's arm and led her down the dark winding path into cricket-warmth and frog-sound, and mosquito-delicate silence.

"Let's run," gasped Francine.

"No."

If Lavinia hadn't turned her head just then, she wouldn't have seen it. But she did turn her head, and it was there. And then Francine looked over and she saw it too, and they stood there on the path, not believing what they saw.

In the singing deep night, back among a clump of bushes—half hidden, but laid out as if she had put herself down there to enjoy the soft stars—lay Eliza Ramsell.

Francine screamed.

The woman lay as if she were floating there, her face moon-freckled, her eyes like white marble, her tongue clamped in her lips.

Lavinia felt the ravine turning like a gigantic black merry-go-round underfoot. Francine was gasping and choking, and a long while later Lavinia heard herself say, "We'd better get the police."

"Hold me, Lavinia, please hold me, I'm cold. Oh, I've never been so cold since winter."

Lavinia held Francine and the policemen were all around in the ravine grass. Flashlights darted about, voices mingled, and the night grew toward eight-thirty.

"It's like December, I need a sweater," said Francine, eyes shut against Lavinia's shoulder.

The policeman said, "I guess you can go now, ladies. You might drop by the station tomorrow for a little more questioning."

Lavinia and Francine walked away from the police and the delicate sheet-covered thing upon the ravine grass.

Lavinia felt her heart going loudly within her and she was cold, too, with a February cold. There were bits of sudden snow all over her flesh and the moon washed her brittle fingers whiter, and she remembered doing all the talking while Francine just sobbed.

A police voice called, "You want an escort, ladies?"

"No, we'll make it," said Lavinia, and they walked on. I can't remember anything now, she thought. I can't remember how she looked lying there, or anything. I don't believe it happened. Already I'm forgetting, I'm making myself forget.

"I've never *seen* a dead person before," said Francine.

Lavinia looked at her wristwatch, which seemed impossibly far away. "It's only eight-thirty. We'll pick up Helen and get on to the show."

"The show!"

"It's what we *need*."

"Lavinia, you don't *mean* it!"

"We've got to forget this. It's not good to remember."

"But Eliza's back there now and—"

"We need to laugh. We'll go to the show as if nothing happened."

"But Eliza was once your friend, *my* friend—"

"We can't help her; we can only help ourselves forget. I insist. I won't go home and brood over it. I won't *think* of it. I'll fill my mind with everything else *but*."

They started up the side of the ravine on a stony path in the dark. They heard voices and stopped.

Below, near the creek waters, a voice was murmuring, "I am the Lonely One. I am the Lonely One. I *kill* people."

"And I'm Eliza Ramsell. Look. And I'm dead, see my tongue out my mouth, see!"

Francine shrieked. "You, there! Children, you nasty children! Get home, get out of the ravine, you hear me? Get home, get home, get home!"

The children fled from their game. The night swallowed their laughter away up the distant hills into the warm darkness.

Francine sobbed again and walked on.

"I thought you ladies'd never come!" Helen Greer tapped her foot atop her porch steps. "You're only an hour late, that's all."

"We—" started Francine.

Lavinia clutched her arm. "There was a commotion. Someone found Eliza Ramsell dead in the ravine."

Helen gasped. "Who found her?"

"We don't know."

The three maiden ladies stood in the summer night looking at one another. "I've a notion to lock myself in my house," said Helen at last.

But finally she went to fetch a sweater, and while she was gone Francine whispered frantically, "Why didn't you *tell* her?"

"Why upset her? Time enough tomorrow," replied Lavina.

The three women moved along the street under the black trees through a town that was slamming and locking doors, pulling down windows and shades and turning on blazing lights. They saw eyes peering out at them from curtained windows.

How strange, thought Lavinia Nebbs, the Popsicle night, the ice-cream night with the children thrown like jackstones on the streets, now turned in behind wood and glass, the Popsicles dropped in puddles of lime and chocolate where they fell when the children were scooped indoors. Baseballs and bats lie on the unfootprinted lawns. A half-drawn white chalk hopscotch line is there on the steamed sidewalk.

"We're crazy out on a night like this," said Helen.

"Lonely One can't kill three ladies," said Lavinia. "There's safety in numbers. Besides, it's too soon. The murders come a month separated."

A shadow fell across their faces. A figure loomed. As if someone had struck an organ a terrible blow, the three women shrieked.

"*Got* you!" The man jumped from behind a tree. Rearing into the moonlight, he laughed. Leaning on the tree, he laughed again.

"Hey, I'm the Lonely One!"

"Tom Dillon!"

"Tom!"

"Tom," said Lavinia. "If you ever do a childish thing like that again, may you be riddled with bullets by mistake!"

Francine began to cry.

Tom Dillon stopped smiling. "Hey, I'm sorry."

"Haven't you heard about Eliza Ramsell?" snapped Lavinia. "She's dead, and you scaring women. You should be ashamed. Don't speak to us again."

"Aw—"

He moved to follow them.

"Stay right there, Mr. Lonely One, and scare yourself," said Lavinia. "Go see Eliza Ramsell's face and see if its funny!" She pushed the other two on along the street of trees and stars, Francine holding a handkerchief to her face.

"Francine," pleaded Helen, "it was only a joke. Why's she crying so hard?"

"I guess we better tell you, Helen. *We* found Eliza. And it wasn't pretty. And we're trying to forget. We're going to the show to help and let's not talk about it. Enough's enough. Get your ticket money ready, we're almost downtown."

The drugstore was a small pool of sluggish air which the great wooden fans stirred in tides of arnica and tonic and soda-smell out into the brick streets.

"A nickel's worth of green mint chews," said Lavinia to the druggist. His face was set and pale, like all the faces they had seen on the half-empty streets. "For eating in the show," she explained, as the druggist dropped the mints into a sack with a silver shovel.

"Sure look pretty tonight," said the druggist. "You looked cool this noon, Miss Lavinia, when you was in here for chocolates. So cool and nice that someone asked after you."

"Oh?"

"You're getting popular. Man sitting at the counter—" he rustled a few more mints in the sack—"watched you walk out and he said to me. 'Say, who's *that?*' Man in a dark suit, thin pale face. 'Why, that's Lavinia Nebbs, prettiest maiden lady in town,' *I* said. 'Beautiful,' *he* said. 'Where's she live?'" Here the druggist paused and looked away.

"You *didn't?*" wailed Francine. "You didn't give him her address, I hope? You *didn't!*"

"Sorry, guess I didn't think. I said. 'Oh, over on Park Street, you know, near the ravine.' Casual remark. But now, tonight, them finding the body. I heard a minute ago, I suddenly thought, what've I *done!*" He handed over the package, much too full.

"You fool!" cried Francine, and tears were in her eyes.

"I'm sorry. 'Course maybe it was nothing."

"Nothing, nothing!" said Francine.

Lavinia stood with the three people looking at her, staring at her. She didn't know what or how to feel. She felt nothing—except perhaps the slightest prickle of excitement in her throat. She held out her money automatically.

"No charge for those pepperiments." The druggist turned down his eyes and shuffled some papers.

"Well, I know what we're going to do right *now!*" Helen stalked out of the drug shop. "We're going right straight home. I'm not going to be part of any hunting party for you, Lavinia. That man asking for you. You're *next!* You want to be dead in that ravine?"

"It was just a man," said Lavinia slowly, eyes on the streets.

"So's Tom Dillon a man, but maybe he's the Lonely One!"

"We're all overwrought," said Lavinia reasonably. "I won't miss the movie now. If I'm the next victim, let me *be* the next victim. A lady has all too little excitement in her life, especially an old maid, a lady thirty-seven like me, so don't you mind if I enjoy it. And I'm being sensible. Stands to reason he won't be out tonight, so soon after a murder. A month from now, yes, when the police've relaxed and when he *feels* like another murder. You've got to *feel* like murdering people, you know. At least that kind of murderer does. And he's just resting up now. And anyway I'm not going home to stew in my juices."

"But Eliza's face, there in the ravine!"

"After the first look I never looked again. I didn't *drink* it in, if that's what you mean. I can see a thing and tell myself I never saw it, that's how strong *I* am. And the whole argument's silly anyhow, because I'm not beautiful."

"Oh, but you are, Lavinia. You're the loveliest maiden lady in town, now that Eliza's—" Francine stopped. "If you'd only relaxed, you'd been married years ago—"

"Stop sniveling, Francine. Here's the box office. You and Helen go on home. I'll sit alone and go home alone."

"Lavinia, you're crazy. We can't leave you here—"

They argued for five minutes. Helen started to walk away but came back when she saw Lavinia thump down her money for a solitary movie ticket. Helen and Francine followed her silently into the theater.

The first show was over. In the dim auditorium, as they sat in the odor of ancient brass polish, the manager appeared before the worn red velvet curtains for an announcement:

"The police have asked for an early closing tonight. So everyone can be home at a decent hour. So we're cutting our short subjects and putting on our feature film again now. The show will be over at eleven. Everyone's advised to go straight home and not linger on the streets. Our police force is pretty small and will be spread around pretty thin."

"That means us, Lavinia. *Us!*" Lavinia felt the hands tugging at her elbows on either side.

Harold Lloyd in Welcome, Danger! said the screen in the dark.

"Lavinia," Helen whispered.

"What?"

"As we came in, a man in a dark suit, across the street, crossed over. He just came in. He just sat in the row behind us."

"Oh, Helen."

"He's right behind us *now*."

Lavinia looked at the screen.

Helen turned slowly and glanced back. "I'm calling the manager!" she cried and leaped up. "Stop the film! Lights!"

"Helen, come back!" said Lavinia, eyes shut.

When they set down their empty soda glasses, each of the ladies had a chocolate moustache on her upper lip. They removed them with their tongues, laughing.

"You see how *silly* it was?" said Lavinia. "All that riot for nothing. How embarrassing!"

The drugstore clock said eleven twenty-five. They had come out of the theater and the laughter and the enjoyment feeling new. And now they were laughing at Helen and Helen was laughing at herself.

Lavina said, "When you ran up that aisle crying 'Lights!' I thought I'd die!"

"That poor man!"

"The theater manager's brother from Racine!"

"I apologized," said Helen.

"You *see* what a panic can do?"

The great fans still whirled and whirled in the warm night air, stirring and restirring the smells of vanilla, raspberry, peppermint and disinfectant in the drugstore.

"We shouldn't have stopped for these sodas. The police said——"

"Oh, bosh the police." Lavinia laughed. "I'm not afraid of anything. The Lonely One is a million miles away now. He won't be back for weeks, and the police'll get him then, just wait. Wasn't the film *funny!*"

The streets were clean and empty. Not a car or a truck or a person was in sight. The bright lights were still lit in the small store windows where the hot wax dummies stood. Their blank blue eyes watched as the ladies walked past them, down the night street.

"Do you suppose if we screamed they'd do anything?"

"Who?"

"The dummies, the window-people."

"Oh, Fran*cine*."

"Well . . ."

There were a thousand people in the windows, stiff and silent, and three people on the street, the echoes following like gunshots when they tapped their heels on the baked pavement.

A red neon sign flickered dimly, buzzing like a dying insect. They walked past it.

Baked and white, the long avenue lay ahead. Blowing and tall in a wind that touched only their leafy summits, the trees stood on either side of the three small women.

"First we'll walk you home, Francine."

"No, I'll walk *you* home."

"Don't be silly. You live the nearest. If you walked me home, you'd have to come back across the ravine alone yourself. And if so much as a leaf fell on you, you'd drop dead."

Francine said, "I can stay the night at your house. You're the *pretty* one!"

"No."

So they drifted like three prim clothes-forms over a moonlit sea of lawn and concrete and tree. To Lavinia, watching the black trees flit by, listening to the voices of her friends, the night seemed to quicken. They seemed to be running while walking slowly. Everything seemed fast, and the color of hot snow.

"Let's sing," said Lavinia.

They sang sweetly and quietly, arm in arm, not looking back. They felt the hot sidewalk cooling underfoot, moving, moving.

"Listen," said Lavinia.

They listened to the summer night, to the crickets and the far-off tone of the courthouse clock making it fifteen minutes to twelve.

"Listen."

A porch swing creaked in the dark. And there was Mr. Terle, silent, alone on his porch as they passed, having a last cigar. They could see the pink cigar fire idling to and fro.

Now the lights were going, going, gone. The little house lights and big house lights, the yellow lights and green hurricane lights, the candles and oil lamps and porch lights, and everything felt locked up in brass and iron and steel. Everything, thought Lavinia, is boxed and wrapped and shaded. She imagined the people in their moonlit beds, and their breathing in the summer night rooms, safe and together. And here we are, she thought, listening to our solitary footsteps on the baked summer evening sidewalk. And above us the lonely street lights shining down, making a million wild shadows.

"Here's your house, Francine. Good night."

"Lavinia, Helen, stay here tonight. It's late, almost midnight now. Mrs. Murdock has an extra room. I'll make hot chocolate. It'd be ever such fun!" Francine was holding them both close to her.

"No, thanks," said Lavinia.

And Francine began to cry.

"Oh, not *again,* Francine," said Lavinia.

"I don't want you dead," sobbed Francine, the tears running straight down her cheeks. "You're so fine and nice, I want you alive. Please, oh, please."

"Francine, I didn't realize how much this has affected you. But I promise you I'll phone when I get home, right away."

"Oh, *will* you?"

"And tell you I'm safe, yes. And tomorrow we'll have a picnic lunch at Electric Park, all right? With ham sandwiches I'll make myself. How's that? You'll see; I'm going to live forever!"

"You'll phone?"

"I promised, didn't I?"

"Good night, good night!" Francine was gone behind her door, locked tight in an instant.

"Now," said Lavinia to Helen, "I'll walk *you* home."

The courthouse clock struck the hour. The sounds went across a town that was empty, emptier than it had ever been before. Over empty streets and empty lots and empty lawns the sound went.

"Ten, eleven, *twelve,*" counted Lavinia, with Helen on her arm.

"Don't you feel *funny?*" asked Helen.

"How do you mean?"

"When you think of us being out here on the sidewalk, under the trees, and all those people safe behind locked doors lying in their beds. We're practically the only walking people out in the open in a thousand miles, I bet." The sound of the deep warm dark ravine came near.

In a minute they stood before Helen's house, looking at each other for a long time. The wind blew the odor of cut grass and wet lilacs between them. The moon was high in a sky that was beginning to cloud over. "I don't suppose it's any use asking you to stay, Lavinia?"

"I'll be going on."

"Sometimes . . ."

"Sometimes what?"

"Sometimes I think people *want* to die. You've certainly acted odd all evening."

"I'm just not afraid," said Lavinia. "And I'm curious, I suppose. And I'm using my head. Logically, the Lonely One can't be around. The police and all."

"*Our* police? *Our* little old force? They're home in bed too, the covers up over their ears."

"Let's just say I'm enjoying myself, precariously but safely. If there were any *real* chance of anything happening to me, I'd stay here with you, you can be sure of that."

"Maybe your subconscious doesn't want you to live any more."

"You and Francine, honestly."

"I feel so guilty. I'll be drinking hot coffee just as you reach the ravine bottom and walk on the bridge in the dark."

"Drink a cup for me. Good night."

Lavinia Nebbs walked down the midnight street, down the late summer night silence. She saw the houses with their dark windows and far away she heard a dog barking. In five minutes, she thought, I'll be safe home. In five minutes I'll be phoning silly little Francine. I'll—

She heard a man's voice singing far away among the trees.

She walked a little faster.

Coming down the street toward her in the dimming moonlight was a man. He was walking casually.

I can run and knock on one of these doors, thought Lavinia. If necessary.

The man was singing, "Shine On, Harvest Moon," and he carried a long club in his hand. "Well, look who's here! What a time of night for you to be out, Miss Nebbs!"

"Officer Kennedy!"

And that's who it was, of course—Officer Kennedy on his beat.

"I'd better see you home."

"Never mind, I'll make it."

"But you live across the ravine."

Yes, she thought, but I won't walk the ravine with *any* man. How do I know *who* the Lonely One is? "No, thanks," she said.

"I'll wait right here then," he said. "If you need help give a yell. I'll come running."

She went on, leaving him under a light humming to himself, alone.

Here I am, she thought.

The ravine.

She stood on the top of the one hundred and thirteen steps down the steep, brambled bank that led across the creaking bridge one hundred yards and up through the black hills to Park Street. And only one lantern to see by. Three minutes from now, she thought, I'll be putting my key in my house door. Nothing can happen in just one hundred and eighty seconds.

She started down the dark green steps into the deep ravine night.

"One, two, three, four, five, six, seven, eight, nine steps" she whispered.

She felt she was running but she was not running.

"Fifteen, sixteen, seventen, eighteen, nineteen steps," she counted aloud.

"One fifth of the way!" she announced to herself.

The ravine was deep, deep and black, black. And the world was gone, the world of safe people in bed. The locked doors, the town, the drugstore, the theater, the lights, everything was gone. Only the ravine existed and lived, black and huge about her.

"Nothing's happened, has it? No one around, *is* there? Twenty-four, twenty-five steps. Remember that old ghost story you told each other when you were children?"

She listened to her feet on the steps.

"The story about the dark man coming in your house and you upstairs in bed. And now he's at the *first* step coming up to your room. Now he's at the second step. Now he's at the third and the fourth and the *fifth* step! Oh, how you laughed and screamed at that story! And now the horrid dark man is at the twelfth step, opening your door, and now he's standing by your bed. I *got you!*"

She screamed. It was like nothing she had ever heard, that scream. She had never screamed that loud in her life. She stopped, she froze, she clung to the wooden banister. Her heart exploded in her. The sound of its terrified beating filled the universe.

"There, there!" she screamed to herself. "At the bottom of the steps. A man, under the light! No, now he's gone! He was *waiting* there!"

She listened.

Silence. The bridge was empty.

Nothing, she thought, holding her heart. Nothing. Fool. That story I told myself. How silly. What shall I do?

Her heartbeats faded.

Shall I call the officer, did he hear my scream? Or was it only loud to *me*. Was it really just a small scream after all?

She listened. Nothing. Nothing.

I'll go back to Helen's and sleep the night. But even while she thought this she moved down again. No, it's nearer home now. Thirty-eight, thirty-nine steps, careful, don't fall. Oh, I *am* a fool. Forty steps. Forty-one. Almost half way now. She froze again.

"Wait," she told herself. She took a step.

There was an echo.

She took another step. Another echo—just a fraction of a moment later.

"Someone's following me," she whispered to the ravine, to the black crickets and dark green frogs and the black steam. "Someone's on the steps behind me. I don't dare turn around."

Another step, another echo.

Every time I take a step, *they* take one.

A step and an echo.

Weakly she asked of the ravine, "Officer Kennedy? Is that *you?*"

The crickets were suddenly still. The crickets were listening. The night was listening to *her*. For a moment, all of the far summer night meadows and close summer night trees were suspending motion. Leaf, shrub, star and meadowgrass had ceased their particular tremors and were listening to Lavinia Nebbs's heart. And perhaps a thousand miles away, across locomotive-lonely country, in an empty way station a lonely night traveler reading a dim newspaper under a naked light-bulb might raise his head, listen, and think, What's that! and decide, Only a woodchuck, surely, beating a hollow log. But it was Lavinia Nebbs, it was most surely the heart of Lavinia Nebbs.

Faster. Faster. She went down the steps.

Run!

She heard music. In a mad way, a silly way, she heard the huge surge of music that pounded at her, and she realized as she ran— as she ran in panic and terror—that some part of her mind was dramatizing, borrowing from the turbulent score of some private film. The music was rushing and plunging her faster, faster, plummeting and scurrying, down and down into the pit of the ravine!

"Only a little way," she prayed. "One hundred ten, eleven, twelve, thirteen steps! The bottom! Now, run! Across the bridge!"

She spoke to her legs, her arms, her body, her terror; she advised all parts of herself in this white and terrible instant. Over the roaring creek waters, on the hollow, swaying, almost-alive bridge planks she ran, followed by the wild footsteps behind, with the music following too, the music shrieking and babbling!

He's following. Don't turn, don't look—if you see him, you'll not be able to move! You'll be frightened, you'll freeze! Just run, run, *run!*

She ran across the bridge.

Oh, God! God, please, please let me get up the hill! Now up, up the path, now between the hills. Oh, God, it's dark, and everything so far away! If I screamed now it wouldn't help; I can't scream anyway! Here's the top of the path, here's the street. Thank God I wore my low-heeled shoes. I can run, I can run! Oh, God, please let me be safe! If I get home safe I'll never go out alone, I was a fool, let me admit it, a fool! I didn't know what terror was, I wouldn't let myself think, but if you let me get home from this I'll never go out without Helen or Francine again! Across the street now!

She crossed the street and rushed up the sidewalk.

Oh, God, the porch! My house!

In the middle of her running, she saw the empty lemonade glass where she had left it hours before, in the good, easy, lazy time, left it on the railing. She wished she were back in that time now, drinking from it, the night still young and not begun.

"Oh, please, please, give me time to get inside and lock the door and I'll be safe!"

She heard her clumsy feet on the porch, felt her hands scrabbling and ripping at the lock with the key. She heard her heart. She heard her inner voice shrieking.

The key fitted.

"Unlock the door, quick, quick!"

The door opened.

"Now inside. *Slam* it!"

She slammed the door.

"Now lock it, bar it, lock it!" she cried wretchedly. "Lock it *tight!*"

The door was locked and barred and bolted.

The music stopped.

She listened to her heart again and the sound of it diminishing into silence.

Home. Oh, safe at home. Safe, safe and safe at home! She slumped against the door. Safe, safe. Listen. Not a sound. Safe, safe, oh, thank God, safe at home. I'll never go out at night again. Safe, oh safe, safe, home, so good, so good, safe. Safe inside, the door locked. *Wait.* Look out the window.

She looked. She gazed out the window for a full half-minute.

"Why there's no one there at all! Nobody! There was no one following me at all. Nobody running after me." She caught her breath and almost laughed at herself. "It stands to reason. If a man *had* been following me, he'd have *caught* me. I'm not a fast runner. There's no one on the porch or in the yard. How silly of me. I wasn't running from anything except *me*. That ravine was safer than safe. Just the same, though, it's nice to be home. Home's the really good warm safe place, the *only* place to be."

She put her hand out to the light switch and stopped.

"What?" she asked. "What? *What?*"

Behind her, in the black living room, someone cleared his throat . . .

LADY'S MAN

Ruth Chatterton

IT HAPPENED in the soft stillness of a June night in England, just before World War II.

I had motored down from London the afternoon before to spend the week-end with Noel Coward at Goldenhurst, his lovely country house in Kent. I had rented a car and then spent a tense hour and a half behind a chauffeur I had never seen before in my life who snaked his way recklessly through the thick country-bound traffic. When at last we circled the driveway in front of the house, Noël's slim figure on the front step looked very comforting. A few feet away, his man was waiting to carry in my luggage.

With that usual sweet, sardonic grin of his, Noel stepped forward and gave me a hug.

"Everybody's having tea in the drawing room," he said as we went, arm in arm into the house. "You don't want to be bothered going to your room first, do you?"

It was too hot a day for a coat, I don't own a hat, and I had worn gloves to keep my hands clean, so we went straight away to join the others. One quick glance showed me that I knew practically all his other guests. I smiled at them, said a general hello, and went across the room to greet Noel's mother who was pouring tea. Mrs. Coward was a small and very merry woman and I had always been devoted to her.

As I bent down to give her a smacking kiss on her cheek, I caught a glimpse of the man servant carrying my bags through a small door which led from the drawing room into another wing of the house.

45

I vaguely wondered why he was taking my luggage to the kitchen, then I automatically dismissed it from my mind.

Noel's friends were a charming, heterogeneous lot, for Noel is gregarious and great-hearted and he likes to be amused. The nimble and graceful conversation went on and on, until the path of the sun through the west window became more and more oblique. Whiskeys and sodas replaced the tea, and little by little the room darkened. When I realized that the long English twilight was setting in, I got up from my chair.

Noel's eagle eye saw me start for the stairs. "Where do you think you're going?" he said.

"Upstairs to change for dinner. It's after eight."

"We're not changing."

"Oh," I said. "Then I'll just wash up a bit."

"No you don't, my girl. We've voted to keep this a dirty week-end." He grinned wickedly. "If Nature insists, use the thing in the hall. You know where it is."

I knew where it was—and I did.

Dinner was very gay, the food very English. We were given a roast of beef, boiled potatoes, Brussels sprouts, and the sweet was a trifle. Then came a nasty little savory of cold scrambled eggs on a bit of soggy toast, topped by a limp anchovy. I sneered at that little horror and left it untouched on my plate. Afterwards we had coffee in the drawing room and again, conversation. And the rest of the evening? Conversation—and more conversation. And, happily, music. There is always music wherever Noel Coward happens to be.

As it came on to midnight the shafts of ridicule were less acute, the wit not so swift, the laughter not quite so merry. From one corner of the room I heard a stifled yawn; then little by little the other guests departed for their downy couches until Noel and I were the only two left. At last, I, too, stretched and struggled to my feet.

"Think I'll go along, too, Noel," I said. "Isn't it a pleasant feeling to be sleepy in the country?"

"I'm not," he said. "Don't you want to talk?"

"Not any more tonight, if you don't mind," I said, trying not to yawn. "Bed and book beckon. I've got *Present Indicative* . . ." it was his autobiography. "I've been dying to read it."

I started for the stairs. "Aren't you coming up, Noel?"

"Eventually," came his clipped voice, "but you're not."

I wheeled around and looked at him. "What are you talking about?"

Noel smiled that rueful little smile of his, the one where the corners of his mouth turn down and his lips tremble.

"Darling, I'm most frightfully sorry," he said quite cheerfully, "but I'm afraid this damned week-end got a bit out of hand. We're really full-up upstairs. You know how it is—too few guest rooms sort of thing . . ."

"And your week-ends are always inclined to swell . . ."

He put his arm around my shoulders and steered me towards the little door through which I had seen my bags disappear that afternoon.

"You've never slept down here before, have you?" he asked me.

"No. I didn't even know there was a bedroom downstairs. Well, out with it, where is it?" I asked as he opened the door to the dining room wing. "No, no, don't tell me! I'm Cinderella, and I'm off to the kitchen to sleep among the ashes!"

"The stove's electric," Noel said solemnly.

I laughed.

"Are you afraid?"

"Of what?" I said scornfully. But it was a curious question and I wondered a little.

"To sleep down here by yourself."

"Good Lord, no!"

"It's really not a bad room, you know. It's next door to Mother's sitting room."

"A fat lot of good that would do me if I *were* afraid," I said. "She sits in it—she doesn't sleep in it!"

"And even if she did, she couldn't hear you if you yelled bloody murder," said Noel. "The old girl's as deaf as a post."

Inside the passage, Noel opened a door to our right. "Here we are, darling."

I leaned against the jamb of the door and looked around me. The room was square with white walls and dark beams supporting a rather low ceiling. Directly opposite the door where we stood there were casement windows with small diamond panes which went from wall to wall; and in its bay was a dressing table with a sheer white organdy petticoat. On top of it was a small standing mirror with two wings, and either side of it, a shaded candlestick. At right angles to the door, a bed with delicately fluted posts of rosewood stood between two small tables, each of them having a fairly large, rose-shaded lamp for reading purposes. There were two or three comfortable, chintz-covered chairs; the glass curtains at the windows were crisp and white; the carpet, pale gray, was of a soft, thick pile, and on the walls hung several old English prints in charming mirrored frames.

"Why, Noel, it's a perfectly lovely room!" I said. "Why haven't you ever put me in here before?"

"It's cozier upstairs," he said. "Think you'll be all right?"

Again I was aware of that unusual, serious note. "Of course I'll be all right."

"Then I think I'll toddle off. Goodnight, darling. Pleasant dreams," and he gave me a lovely hard hug. At the door, he turned. "I hope you won't be wanting anything during the night, my pretty. Because if you rang, there isn't a soul who could hear the bell."

"Don't worry, darling—I shan't."

"By the way, your bathroom is just across the hall," he said. "The light switch is on the wall, to your left."

"Oh, goodie!" I said. "I was going to use the thing in the other hall again."

"Don't try it, duckie. You might get lost in the dark." He was about to close the door when he pushed his head in again. "Are you quite sure you'll be all right?"

"Oh—shut up!"

"That's my brave girl!" He smiled at me, and pulled the door shut behind him.

When I had finished with my usual nightly routine, I snapped off the light in the little bathroom and went back to my room. After I closed the door, I paused for a moment, wondering whether or not to lock it. It looked like a very old door, white like the walls, with a black metal latch. When you press down the catch, the latch lifts and slips into a metal slot. There was a key in the door, but I finally decided it was silly to lock doors way out here in the English country. However, I gave it an extra little push just to be sure it was quite closed.

I threw open the windows a little wider and stood there a moment looking out into the night. There was no moon and only a few stars winked in the cloudless sky. Through the window came the damp, sweet smell of country air, but there was no breeze of any kind, no rustling of leaves. Nothing broke the stillness except the sleepy conversation of a few frogs from some far-distant pond.

I put out all the lights but the lamps either side of my bed and climbed in. As I slid down between the cool linen sheets, I thought how very pleasant it was to be alone in this quiet, peaceful room, much as I had enjoyed the hectic garrulity of the day. I sighed contentedly, settled back in my pillows and picked up Noel's book. The little clock at my bedside said 12:40, so I promised myself I'd just skim through a few pages of it.

However, I soon became completely absorbed in the sad, serious, funny little boy who was to become the brilliant man upstairs. After a while my eyes began to smart a bit, and instinctively, I glanced at the clock again. What? Ten minutes to three? It couldn't be—I was wide awake! Why wasn't I sleepy? I had been three hours before. I knew I ought to put the book away at once, but I was right in the middle of a chapter; so I decided that I'd just finish the chapter and then I'd try to get some sleep.

At that moment, he called me.

I sat up immediately and fixed my eye on the door. My first thought was one of guilt, because I had made the excuse of being sleepy when he wanted to sit up and talk, and here I was, still wide awake and reading happily. He must have seen my light and decided to come downstairs and chat for a while. What ailed Noel? Was there something really wrong?

It takes time to put these thoughts down on paper, but, actually they raced through my brain with the speed of ICBM missiles. I answered immediately.

"Yes?" I raised my voice so I could be heard through the door. "Who is it? Come in!"

Before I got the last word out the latch was silently lifted out of its slot, and swiftly the door opened wide and stayed there.

Someone did come in—but it wasn't Noel! He came in quickly—and I couldn't see him! All I could see was a yawning black void where the closed door had been. And what's more, whoever he was, he was still in the room, because I could sense the presence of some-one—or something.

How long I remained in that one position, my weight suspended on one finger, I don't know. The only thing I could move was my eyes. They searched stealthily among the shadows, but I could see nothing.

So, I was Noel's brave girl, was I? Why, I was so petrified that I felt as though my body had turned into granite, except for the fact that every pulse was pounding unbearably.

Well—everything has to come to an end sometime, even pure unadulterated terror—particularly if there is nothing whatever to be done about it; so at long last, I relaxed a little, lay back in my pillows and tried to think.

It wasn't a woman; that much was certain. The voice had been that of a man; a light, muted voice, as though he were loth to disturb the rest of the household.

"Ru . . . th!" the voice had called with that sing-song inflexion that children use when they call to another child, making two syllables of my name. But perhaps it hadn't been my name at all. Perhaps I had only thought it was. Perhaps he had been calling . . . *who*?

I gave the bedclothes a vicious kick. What was I implying? That it hadn't been a living man who had called me; who had lifted the latch and opened the door? Not a human being who had come in? Stuff and nonsense! Was I turning into a psychopath? No—of course I wasn't! I just *thought* someone called me. It undoubtedly had been the wind which had . . .

But there hadn't been any wind—not even a breeze! There still wasn't!

I shut my eyes but they wouldn't stay shut. Even though I tried not to look, they kept wandering to that inky vacuum beyond the wide-open door. That was when the noise began, or when I became aware of it. Tap-tap-tap, as if a fingernail were tapping on the glass of the pictures on the wall, one after the other. Then the floor boards began to creak. Someone seemed to be pacing back and forth beside my bed. I could hear it plainly.

I kept on telling myself that it was nothing but my imagination, that naturally there was some simple explanation for it; I really must get some sleep. Again and again I tried hard to swallow my heart which persisted in coming up in my throat, but it wouldn't stay down. If only I could turn over on my side I knew I could sleep, but I couldn't do that either; I was too scared. Well, I'd try to shut my eyes once more, and this time I would keep them shut tight—come hell or high water, until . . .

The next time I opened them, the sun was high in the heavens and pouring a golden stream through my window. There were great patches of sunlight on the gray carpet, but my bed lamps were still on.

For a few seconds I tried to think what I was doing in this strange room; then, very slowly, it began to come back to me. For a few minutes I lay there very still, once more searching for some logical explanation of the whole silly business of last night. After all, it had been very late and I must have been more tired than I thought—the tense drive, the long day and night; or, something in the book I was reading had touched off my imagination without my being aware of it; fear must have taken over, and I went the way of all hen-headed females. Well, that was the end of it. I would shoo it away and forget it.

I slipped into my dressing gown and made for the bathroom across the hall. As I opened the bedroom door, I was surprised to see how thick the carpet was, and how obviously it interfered with the easy opening and closing of the door. It would take superhuman strength to push it open wide . . .

When I stepped through the French window of the drawing room onto the lawn, I found all of my fellow guests standing about or relaxing in long garden chairs.

"You're late!" It was Noel's voice and it had his friendly grin in it. He was half-sitting, half-lying in the most comfortable chair of all a few yards away from the shady wall of the house, and Joyce Carey was in a chair beside him.

"Do you know what time it is? It's twelve o'clock. You certainly had a good sleep, didn't you?"

"Yes—heavenly!" Now why on earth did I have to use that word?

Noel got up and pulled a chair over so it faced his. "Sit down, darling; I'll go get you some coffee."

Joyce Carey is a tall slim woman with black hair and big dark eyes which are straightforward and intelligent. Joyce is a brilliant actress and a darling person. I think she comes close to being Noel's best friend. I have known her quite a while and have always been devoted to her.

"Have a good night?" she asked casually, making morning conversation.

"Why—yes. Didn't you hear me tell Noel?"

"Of course. How silly of me." She gave me a quick, friendly smile. "I thought that perhaps sleeping in a strange room . . ." she said. "You've never slept down there before, have you?"

"No." I glanced at her quickly, but she was looking off across the lush English countryside. "Have you, Joyce?"

Her eyes came back to me. "Have I what?"

"Slept in that room?"

"Once."

Her eyes wandered away again, and for a time both of us were silent.

"It's a pretty room," I said.

"Yes, isn't it?" This time her eyes were on Noel who was ·cautiously making his way across the grass, trying not to spill the coffee he was carrying.

"Here you are, my pet. It will warm your tummy until lunch." Then he threw himself in his chair again and shut his eyes against the sun.

Joyce was thumbing lazily through a *Tatler* and she began to hum softly one of the songs from Noel's operetta: *Bittersweet*. "I'll-see-you-again, whenever . . ." She would have to hum *that* one, I thought crossly. Then, as if she had read my mind, she looked up from her magazine and smiled at me. The humming stopped.

For a few moments none of us spoke. Then before I realized it, out came the thing I had meant not to say: "Noel, did you know your house was haunted?"

Once it was out, I hoped it had sounded careless and light-hearted. God alone knows what I expected from him in the way of an answer. "Pooh-pooh to you, woman! You really are an ass!" or something-or-other thoroughly disdainful, but it wasn't anything at all like that.

It may have been my over-worked imagination, or perhaps the sun was in my eyes, but I swear that all the color drained from his face and he said quietly: "What did you see?"

"Is it haunted?" It was more of a wail than a question.

He didn't answer that; he just gave Joyce a funny look.

I was so shocked . . . well, anyway, surprised, that all I could think of to say was: "Oh, dear." So I said it again. "Oh, dear!"

"Tell me, darling, what did you see?"

I shook my head miserably. "You knew all the time and you didn't tell me," I said in a small voice.

Noel ignored that. "What did you see?" he repeated.

"Oh, why do you keep on asking me that?" I said irritably. My heart wasn't pounding; it was spinning around inside me like a top.

"Because I want to know. Well?"

"Why don't you sleep in that room and see for yourself?"

"I have," he said quietly, and shrugged his shoulders. "Nothing."

"Nothing? *Ha!*"

"Nothing," he said firmly. Then he leaned forward and looked searchingly into my eyes. "Now, please tell me what you saw."

"I didn't see anything . . ."

"What's that?"

"That's right," I said, "but I heard plenty!"

Again that look passed between him and Joyce. "Well, go on," he said cautiously. "What did you hear?"

So, in detail, I told them everything about the ghastly night, and I stressed the fact that I was wide awake at all times and that the lights were on. "And I lay there all night, just staring at the awful blackness of the passage."

"You left the door open all night?" Noel asked me.

"Naturally!" I said indignantly. "You don't suppose I got up and shut it, do you? I was so . . ." I stopped and clapped my hand over my mouth ". . . oh, dear God!" I muttered through my fingers.

"Something else?"

"When I went to the bathroom this morning, that door was tight shut! That . . . that . . . whatever-it-was must have shut it!"

"Extraordinary!" Noel frowned. "No, it isn't," he added quickly. "Turnbull must have closed it this morning." Seeing the skeptical look on my face, he said: "Turnbull's a most frightful prude, you know."

Again we were silent. Finally I said: "Noel, what is it?"

"What's what?"

"*It!* the Thing, Noel! The Thing that called me and then opened my door and came into my room!"

"I wish to God I knew!"

"But, Noel, you just said the house was haunted . . ."

"It is. But why and by what, I don't know. All I can tell you," he said earnestly, "is that the entire wing—the kitchen, pantry, dining room, Mother's sitting room and the room you are in are all part of the original house—sixteenth century, it was."

"What about the rest?"

"The rest of it I built on to the old part. It's odd, but do you know he's never been seen anywhere in the house except in that wing?"

"*He?*"

"Oh, it's a man—we know that," he said. "Two people have seen him there and a third saw a material manifestation of his being in the room. All three were women." He smiled grimly. "Apparently he only calls on the female sex."

"So," I said indignantly, "you put me, another woman, in that damned room as one more victim for the gentleman from outer space."

Noel gave my hand an affectionate and placating pat. "He hasn't been around for some time, darling. And as there was no room upstairs, I remembered that you were always . . ."

". . . *your brave girl?*" I said, interrupting him rudely. "Yes, you called me that last night just before my disembodied visitor paralyzed me with fright! All right, go ahead if you like and believe that flying

airplanes and liking to ride obstreperous horses are signs of courage.
I know better! And anyway, ghosts are quite a different category!"

Well—I knew now. There would be no more searching for explanations, no more having to admit I was a coward. The house
was haunted, and that was that. And because I now knew the worst,
a delicious calm began to flow through me and I managed to give
Noel a little smile. "Very well, now that I have accepted the fact that
my room is ghost-ridden, tell me about my fellow victims."

"All right," he said. "As far as I know, Gladdie Henson was the
first to make the gentleman's acquaintance. You know Glad, don't
you?"

I nodded. Gladys was the wife of a well-known English comedian,
Leslie Henson. She's a dear, funny, hard-headed woman whom everybody likes a lot—including me.

"That particular night, Gladdie said she couldn't get to sleep because her bedroom door kept opening and closing," Noel went on.
"She thought it was the wind, naturally . . ."

"Naturally," I repeated, "but I'll bet you there's never any wind!"

"Be that as it may," said Noel, "she thought it was! Well, finally
she made herself get up and lock the door; but she had no more than
got back into bed when one of the casement windows began the
same goings-on. Poor Gladdie climbed in and out of bed and trotted
back and forth to the window until she was so mad she could hardly
spit! First the damned thing would open wide, then Glad would get
up and close it—she latched it, too. After she had gone through this
insane business about six times and was on her way to it for the
seventh, the old girl didn't have to bother. The window quietly closed
itself—and she only two feet away from it! It was when she saw the
latch slip into place that she screamed the place down. However,
when those of us who heard the screams got to her, whatever-it-was
had gone, leaving behind it a whimpering, quaking woman."

"Poor Glad!" I said. "I know just how she felt."

"At the time," Noel continued, "we all thought it was a burglar
who ran when she screamed. Glad didn't, though."

"What did she think?"

"She didn't say," his was an odd little smile, "but she wouldn't
ever sleep down there again."

"I should rather think not," I said a bit smugly, hoping he would
get my point. "Don't stop *there*. Who was the next?"

"Alicia Warwick. Know her?"

(I have used a fictitious name here, because, although I knew who she was, I had never met her personally; consequently, I never checked with her.)

I said I didn't, and he went on with the story. "It was a year or so after Gladdie's experience. I, stupidly, had completely forgotten that episode. After all, the room happens to be the nicest bedroom in the house, so I put Alicia in it. The next morning when she told me what had happened in the night, she said she had awakened —not as though some strange sound had aroused her—but quite serenely, and very wide awake. She opened her eyes and at that moment she saw a man throw one leg over the sill and then climb through the window. She was terrified. Her first instinct was to scream, but she managed to stifle it. She lay there, holding her breath and trying not to move, but she kept her eyes open and watched the intruder. He moved directly to the dressing table and stood there looking down at it. In a flash she remembered that her jewels were on top of the dressing case where she had tossed them when she undressed. Alicia's jewels are priceless, and she had a second seizure of panic. There was no moon that night, so she could only make out his outline, and then only when he was near the window. As far as she could see, he didn't touch the jewels. But she was convinced that he would discover that she was awake and kill her. Well, he didn't kill her, but she couldn't tell whether or not he was still in the room. It was too dark for her to see, and she couldn't hear anything—he walked like a cat, she said. She told me she didn't go back to sleep, but I presume she did—sometime."

I presumed she did, too, because I had. But I didn't say anything.

"In the morning, when she found her door still locked and the key on the inside, she was sick with fright. Naturally there was no sign of him and she nearly went mad trying to think how he could have got out of the room . . ." Noel smiled that funny smile again. "Dear Alicia never worked that one out. You see, she is still convinced he was a burglar."

"And you're not?"

"No, I'm not," he said quietly.

He had slid down in his chair again and was resting his head against its back.

"You said there was another woman, didn't you, Noel?" I wanted to hear the whole gruesome story.

"Oh, yes, there was another woman."

Perhaps I was suspicious but I seemed to detect a sly look in his eye. "Well—go on, please. Tell me about the third one."

Noel hesitated for just a moment. Finally he said: "All right, but if you don't mind, I think I won't tell you her name." My eyebrows went up a little. "Well, after all, duckie, she might not want anybody to know." After another brief pause, he went on with it. "Her experience was very like Alicia's except that when she awoke out of an apparently dreamless sleep, the Thing—as you call *it*—was already seated at the dressing table. *Its* hands moving about as if it were fingering bits and pieces on the table, or perhaps searching for some particular object—" Noel's eyes twinkled—"not the lady's jewels; this one hasn't got any, poor darling! After a time, *It* got up and walked around behind the dressing table and stood between it and the windows, raising *its* arms high as if to pull the drapes over them. Only it didn't; there were no drapes for *It* to pull. Then *It* came out from behind the dressing case and started towards the bed—and her, or so she thought! Sick with terror, she quickly shut her eyes, squeezing the lids together so tightly that her eyes began to ache, and prayed *It* wouldn't discover she was awake. She told me she had no idea how long she lay there with her eyes closed, but when she got the courage to open them, it was dawn, and through the murky whiteness she could just see the sun beginning to rise behind the trees. Then, just as Alicia had done, she found the key on the inside and her door locked. He—I mean *It*—was gone, leaving no trace."

"Hmmmm . . ." I murmured while I thought about it, "I wonder if . . ." then I stopped.

"What?" asked Noel.

"Nothing." I thought about it some more. "I say, Noel, did either of these women tell you what the—er—Thing looked like?"

"Oh, yes, both of them gave me the same description," he said. "It didn't seem to be wearing the type of jacket we men wear today. Don't forget all they could see was the outline, but whatever the garment was, it hugged the Thing's torso much as, well—much as a knitted pullover would—or a coat of mail . . ." he smiled somewhat apologetically. "They both told me that *It* had some kind of peculiar hat or cap on *Its* head; it was high on top and tight around the forehead with a large peak or visor. It might very well have been a helmet. Not much to go on, is it?"

"Didn't it clank?" I said, trying not to sound too sarcastic.

"No clanks. They saw—*you* heard."

I gulped. "Perhaps those women made it up," I said perversely. I guess I didn't want to believe it, really.

"Not a chance of that," he said. "They didn't even know each other. Each one told me her story at different times."

"I see," I said thoughtfully. I didn't see at all.

"Now you have the whole story—but without an exciting ending; because, you see, there isn't any. We're still in the dark."

"Not me—thank God!" and I looked straight up into the blinding sunlight.

"I'll tell you what," said Noel, "I'm going to let you sleep up in my untidy room tonight. I'll chance the ghostly visitor."

"Mmm—well, we'll see. Perhaps if I can muster up a little courage —or *bravado*," I said, "I might try it again. But thanks anyway."

Then Noel got up, came over to me and took both my hands in his. "Do something for me, will you, duckie?"

"I'll try, you know that. Just the same, you don't deserve it."

"I know, and I'm sorry," he said. "But be a darling, and if Mother happens to be around, keep very hush-hush about the whole ghost business, will you?"

I stared at him in astonishment. "Doesn't she *know*?"

He shook his head. "No, and I'd rather she didn't. The old girl's getting on, bless her, and she's a frail little thing, you know." Then he laughed gently. "Want to know something?" he said. "I believe the Thing must have been a great gentleman a few centuries ago, because undoubtedly, he—pardon me—*It*—seems to have considered Mother's age and frailty the way we have. As you pointed out to me last night, Mother doesn't *sleep* in her sitting room, she just *sits* there!"

"Well?" I said, a little puzzled.

"Darling, it's only in the night that the apparition pays his respects to the living." He let go my hands. "Want a drink? I'm going to have one."

"Thank you, Noel, I think I shall. And make it a martini—I need something that will give me that 'I don't care' feeling."

"Joycie?"

Joyce just smiled and shook her head.

While Noel went to fetch the drinks, I mulled the whole business over. Automatically my mind went back to my first impression when I heard my name called in the passage. It was then that the nasty doubts began to creep in. Of course it was Noel! But could he have opened my door and sneaked back upstairs again without my seeing him? Seems almost impossible.

Perhaps I imagined the whole thing! Yes, that was the answer.

Noel listened very carefully while I was telling him about it. He probably thought it would be great fun to play on my stupid imagination; so he began spinning me a tall tale—an old wives' tale if you ask me! Why not? Noel was a consummate actor and a fine writer. He made his protagonists women because I was a woman, and put them all in that room. And he'd make sure to name women who weren't around to be questioned. And that one about not telling his mother! Naturally if I told her what had happened to me, she would spoil it all by spilling the truth. Yes, that was it; just another of Noel's silly pranks—the stinker! Why there's no such thing as a ghost! All intelligent people know that . . . All right, if he wanted to play games, I'd play right along with him . . .

"Here you are, darling," and he handed me my martini.

"Thank you, Noel." I took a sip of my martini. "Mmmmm— tastes good! Look here . . ." I watched him closely ". . . I'm not so sure that the Thing is a supernatural being after all. Want to know what I think? I think it may be a psychopathic thief who lives in the village, and who, every now and then gets a compulsion to break into the house. Or it might be . . ."

"For God's sake, shut up!" said Joyce. It was the first word she had uttered since Noel and I began our ghastly conversation.

"Hello, Joyce!" I said, "have you come up for air?"

"No, darling. I've 'come up' to suggest that you stop expounding silly platitudes and plausible explanations about last night," she said pleasantly. "Forgive me, but you don't know what you're talking about."

" 'Ark at 'er!" I said to Noel, trying to be funny.

"Listen to me," she said earnestly, "do you remember at all Noel's telling you that the apparition went *behind* the dressing table to pull the curtains together, and that *It* stood *between* the dressing table and the windows?"

"Yes, I remember that. But what of it?"

"Just this, my girl! No human being could possibly have stood between the windows and the dressing table, because that dressing table was pushed up so close against the windows that there wasn't an inch to spare. Of course, one couldn't tell about that in the dark, but when the dawn came up it was easy to see that it had to be something supernatural."

"Joyce, darling, surely you, of all people, don't believe all that rot. Noel's taken you in just as he tried to do with me."

She shook her head. "Stop being pompous, and don't try to explain away the supernatural according to your own mortal logic. It's silly."

"But Joyce, I don't believe in . . ."

She stopped me. "Hear this! Hear this!" she chanted sardonically, "there *is* a ghost at Goldenhurst who returns to that room again and again, although what it is searching for, I can't imagine. Up to now it has done no one any harm but . . ." with a shrug of her shoulders, "who knows?"

My heart gave a painful thump. "*You* seem to know, Joyce, but . . ."

She didn't let me finish. "That the ghost really exists? Well, why shouldn't I?" and she gave me a strange little smile, "I was the third woman."

EVENING PRIMROSE

John Collier

MARCH 21   Today I made my decision. I would turn my back for good and all upon the *bourgeois* world that hates a poet. I would leave, get out, break away—

And I have done it. I am free! Free as the mote that dances in the sunbeam! Free as a house-fly crossing first-class in the largest of luxury liners! Free as my verse! Free as the food I shall eat, the paper I write upon, the lamb's-wool-lined softly slithering slippers I shall wear.

This morning I had not so much as a car-fare. Now I am here, on velvet. You are itching to learn of this haven; you would like to organize trips here, spoil it, send your relations-in-law, perhaps even come yourself. After all, this journal will hardly fall into your hands till I am dead. I'll tell you.

I am at Bracey's Giant Emporium, as happy as a mouse in the middle of an immense cheese, and the world shall know me no more.

Merrily, merrily shall I live now secure behind a towering pile of carpets, in a corner-nook which I propose to line with eider-downs, angora vestments, and the Cleopatrean tops in pillows. I shall be cosy.

I nipped into this sanctuary late this afternoon, and soon heard the dying footfalls of closing time. From now on, my only effort will be to dodge the night-watchman. Poets can dodge.

I have already made my first mouse-like exploration. I tiptoed as far as the stationery department, and, timid, darted back with

only these writing materials, the poet's first need. Now I shall lay
them aside, and seek other necessities: food, wine, the soft furniture
of my couch, and a natty smoking-jacket. This place stimulates me.
I shall write here.

DAWN, NEXT DAY I suppose no one in the world was ever more
astonished and overwhelmed than I have been tonight. It is unbelievable. Yet I believe it. How interesting life is when things get
like that!

I crept out, as I said I would, and found the great shop in mingled
light and gloom. The central well was half illuminated; the circling
galleries towered in a pansy Piranesi of toppling light and shade.
The spidery stairways and flying bridges had passed from purpose
into fantasy. Silks and velvets glimmered like ghosts, a hundred
pantie-clad models offered simpers and embraces to the desert air.
Rings, clips, and bracelets glittered frostily in a desolate absence of
Honey and Daddy.

Creeping along the transverse aisles, which were in deeper darkness, I felt like a wandering thought in the dreaming brain of a
chorus girl down on her luck. Only, of course, their brains are not
as big as Bracey's Giant Emporium. And there was no man there.

None, that is, except the night-watchman. I had forgotten him.
As I crossed an open space on the mezzanine floor, hugging the
lee of a display of sultry shawls, I became aware of a regular
thudding, which might almost have been that of my own heart.
Suddenly it burst upon me that it came from outside. It was footsteps, and they were only a few paces away. Quick as a flash I seized
a flamboyant mantilla, whirled it about me and stood with one arm
outflung, like a Carmen petrified in a gesture of disdain.

I was successful. He passed me, jingling his little machine on its
chain, humming his little tune, his eyes scaled with refractions of the
blaring day. "Go, worldling!" I whispered, and permitted myself a
soundless laugh.

It froze on my lips. My heart faltered. A new fear seized me.

I was afraid to move. I was afraid to look around. I felt I was
being watched, by something that could see right through me. This
was a very different feeling from the ordinary emergency caused by
the very ordinary night-watchman. My conscious impulse was the
obvious one: to glance behind me. But my eyes knew better. I remained absolutely petrified, staring straight ahead.

My eyes were trying to tell me something that my brain refused to believe. They made their point. I was looking straight into another pair of eyes, human eyes, but large, flat, luminous. I have seen such eyes among the nocturnal creatures, which creep out under the artificial blue moonlight in the zoo.

The owner was only a dozen feet away from me. The watchman had passed between us, nearer him than me. Yet he had not seen him. I must have been looking straight at him for several minutes at a stretch. I had not seen him either.

He was half reclining against a low dais where, on a floor of russet leaves, and flanked by billows of glowing home-spun, the fresh-faced waxen girls modeled spectator sports suits in herringbones, checks, and plaids. He leaned against the skirt of one of these Dianas; its folds concealed perhaps his ear, his shoulder, and a little of his right side. He, himself, was clad in dim but large-patterned Shetland tweeds of the latest cut, suède shoes, a shirt of a rather broad *motif* in olive, pink, and grey. He was as pale as a creature found under a stone. His long thin arms ended in hands that hung floatingly, more like trailing, transparent fins, or wisps of chiffon, than ordinary hands.

He spoke. His voice was not a voice; it was a mere whistling under the tongue. "Not bad, for a beginner!"

I grasped that he was complimenting me, rather satirically, on my own, more amateurish, feat of camouflage. I stuttered. I said, "I'm sorry. I didn't know anyone else lived here." I noticed, even as I spoke, that I was imitating his own whistling sibilant utterance.

"Oh, yes," he said. "*We* live here. It's delightful."

"We?"

"Yes, all of us. Look!"

We were near the edge of the first gallery. He swept his long hand round, indicating the whole well of the shop. I looked. I saw nothing. I could hear nothing, except the watchman's thudding step receding infinitely far along some basement aisle.

"Don't you see?"

You know the sensation one has, peering into the half-light of a vivarium? One sees bark, pebbles, a few leaves, nothing more. And then, suddenly, a stone breathes—it is a toad; there is a chameleon, another, a coiled adder, a mantis among the leaves. The whole case seems crepitant with life. Perhaps the whole world is. One glances at one's sleeve, one's feet.

So it was with the shop. I looked, and it was empty. I looked, and there was an old lady, clambering out from behind the monstrous clock. There were three girls, elderly *ingénues*, incredibly emaciated, simpering at the entrance of the perfumery. Their hair was a fine floss, pale as gossamer. Equally brittle and colourless was a man with the appearance of a colonel of southern extraction, who stood regarding me while he caressed mustachios that would have done credit to a crystal shrimp. A chintzy woman, possibly of literary tastes, swam forward from the curtains and drapes.

They came thick about me, fluttering, whistling, like a waving of gauze in the wind. Their eyes were wide and flatly bright. I saw there was no colour to the iris.

"How raw he looks!"

"A detective! Send for the Dark Men!"

"I'm not a detective. I am a poet. I have renounced the world."

"He is a poet. He has come over to us. Mr. Roscoe found him."

"He admires us."

"He must meet Mrs. Vanderpant."

I was taken to meet Mrs. Vanderpant. She proved to be the Grand Old Lady of the store, almost entirely transparent.

"So you are a poet, Mr. Snell? You will find inspiration here. I am quite the oldest inhabitant. Three mergers and a complete rebuilding, but they didn't get rid of me!"

"Tell how you went out by daylight, dear Mrs. Vanderpant, and nearly got bought for Whistler's *Mother!*"

"That was in pre-war days. I was more robust then. But at the cash desk they suddenly remembered there was no frame. And when they came back to look at me—"

"—She was gone."

Their laughter was like the stridulation of the ghosts of grasshoppers.

"Where is Ella? Where is my broth?"

"She is bringing it, Mrs. Vanderpant. It will come."

"Tiresome little creature! She is our foundling, Mr. Snell. She is not quite our sort."

"Is that so, Mrs. Vanderpant? Dear, dear!"

"I lived alone here, Mr. Snell, for many years. I took refuge here in the terrible times in the eighties. I was a young girl then, a beauty, people were kind enough to say, but poor Papa lost his money. Bracey's meant a lot to a young girl, in the New York of those days, Mr. Snell. It seemed to me terrible that I should not be able to come here in the ordinary way. So I came here for good. I was quite alarmed when others began to come in, after the crash of 1907. But it was the dear Judge, the Colonel, Mrs. Bilbee—"

I bowed. I was being introduced.

"Mrs. Bilbee writes plays. *And* of a very old Philadelphia family. You will find us quite *nice* here, Mr. Snell."

"I feel it a great privilege, Mrs. Vanderpant."

"And of course, all our dear *young* people came in '29. *Their* poor papas jumped from skyscrapers."

I did a great deal of bowing and whistling. The introductions took a long time. Who would have thought so many people lived in Bracey's?

"And here at last is Ella with by broth."

It was then I noticed that the young people were not so young after all, in spite of their smiles, their little ways, their *ingénue* dress. Ella was in her teens. Clad only in something from the shop-soiled counter, she nevertheless had the appearance of a living flower in a French cemetery, or a mermaid among polyps.

"Come, you stupid thing!"

"Mrs. Vanderpant is waiting."

Her pallor was not like theirs; not like the pallor of something that glistens or scuttles when you turn over a stone. Hers was that of a pearl.

Ella! Pearl of this remotest, most fantastic cave! Little mermaid, brushed over, pressed down by objects of a deadlier white—tentacles—! I can write no more.

MARCH 28   Well, I am rapidly becoming used to my new and half-lit world, to my strange company. I am learning the intricate laws of silence and camouflage which dominate the apparently casual strollings and gatherings of the midnight clan. How they detest the night-watchman, whose existence imposes these laws on their idle festivals!

"Odious, vulgar creature! He reeks of the coarse sun!"

Actually, he is quite a personable young man, very young for a night-watchman, so young that I think he must have been wounded in the war. But they would like to tear him to pieces.

They are very pleasant to me, though. They are pleased that a poet should have come among them. Yet I cannot like them entirely. My blood is a little chilled by the uncanny ease with which even the old ladies can clamber spider-like from balcony to balcony. Or is it because they are unkind to Ella?

Yesterday we had a bridge party. Tonight, Mrs. Bilbee's little play, *Love in Shadowland,* is going to be presented. Would you believe it?—another colony, from Wanamaker's, is coming over *en masse* to attend. Apparently people live in all the great stores. This visit is considered a great honour, for there is an intense snobbery in these creatures. They speak with horror of a social outcast who left a highclass Madison Avenue establishment, and now leads a wallowing, beachcomberish life in a delicatessen. And they relate with tragic emotion the story of the man in Altman's, who conceived such a passion for a model plaid dressing jacket that he emerged and wrested it from the hands of a purchaser. It seems that all the Altman colony, dreading an investigation, were forced to remove beyond the social pale, into a five-and-dime. Well, I must get ready to attend the play.

APRIL 14   I have found an opportunity to speak to Ella, I dared not before; here one has a sense always of pale eyes secretly watching. But last night, at the play, I developed a fit of hiccups. I was somewhat sternly told to go and secrete myself in the basement, among the garbage cans, where the watchman never comes.

There, in the rat-haunted darkness, I heard a stifled sob. "What's that? Is it you? Is it Ella? What ails you, child? Why do you cry?"

"They wouldn't even let me see the play."

"Is that all? Let me console you."

"I am so unhappy."

She told me her tragic little story. What do you think? When she was a child, a little tiny child of only six, she strayed away and fell asleep behind a counter, while her mother tried on a new hat. When she awoke, the store was in darkness.

"And I cried, and they all came around, and took hold of me. 'She will tell, if we let her go,' they said. Some said, 'Call in the Dark Men.' 'Let her stay here,' said Mrs. Vanderpant. 'She will make me a nice little maid.'"

"Who are these Dark Men, Ella? They spoke of them when I came here."

"Don't you know? Oh, it's horrible! It's horrible!"

"Tell me, Ella. Let me share it."

She trembled. "You know the morticians, 'Journey's End,' who go to houses when people die?"

"Yes, Ella."

"Well, in that shop, just like here, and at Gimbel's, and at Bloomingdale's, there are people living, people like these."

"How disgusting! But what can they live upon, Ella, in a funeral home?"

"Don't ask me! Dead people are sent there, to be embalmed. Oh, they are terrible creatures! Even the people here are terrified of them. But if anyone dies, or if some poor burglar breaks in, and sees these people, and might tell—"

"Yes? Go on."

"Then they send for the others, the Dark Men."

"Good heavens!"

"Yes, and they put the body in Surgical Supplies—or the burglar, all tied up, if it's a burglar—and they send for these others, and then they all hide, and in they come, the others—Oh! they're like pieces of blackness. I saw them once. It was terrible."

"And then?"

"They go in, to where the dead person is, or the poor burglar. And they have wax there—and all sorts of things. And when they're gone there's just one of these wax models left, on the table. And then our people put a dress on it, or a bathing suit, and they mix it up with all the others, and nobody never knows."

"But aren't they heavier than the others, these wax models? You would think they'd be heavier."

"No. They're not heavier. I think there's a lot of them—gone."

"Oh, dear! So they were going to do that to you, when you were a little child?"

"Yes, only Mrs. Vanderpant said I was to be her maid."

"I don't like these people, Ella."

"Nor do I. I wish I could see a bird."

"Why don't you go into the pet shop?"

"It wouldn't be the same. I want to see it on a twig, with leaves."

"Ella, let us meet often. Let us creep away down here and meet. I will tell you about birds, and twigs and leaves."

MAY 1   For the last few nights the store has been feverish with the shivering whisper of a huge crush at Bloomingdale's. Tonight was the night.

"Not changed yet? We leave on the stroke of two." Roscoe has appointed himself, or been appointed, my guide or my guard.

"Roscoe, I am still a greenhorn. I dread the streets."

"Nonsense! There's nothing to it. We slip out by two's and three's, stand on the sidewalk, pick up a taxi. Were you never out late in the old days? If so, you must have seen us, many a time."

"Good heavens, I believe I have! And often wondered where you came from. And it was from here! But, Roscoe, my brow is burning. I find it hard to breathe. I fear a cold."

"In that case you must certainly remain behind. Our whole party would be disgraced in the unfortunate event of a sneeze."

I had relied on their rigid etiquette, so largely based on fear of discovery, and I was right. Soon they were gone, drifting out like leaves aslant on the wind. At once I dressed in flannel slacks, canvas shoes, and a tasteful sport shirt, all new in stock today. I found a quiet spot, safely off the track beaten by the night-watchman. There in a model's lifted hand, I set a wide fern frond culled from the florist's shop, and at once had a young, spring tree. The carpet was sandy, sandy as a lake-side beach. A snowy napkin; two cakes, each with a cherry on it; I had only to imagine the lake and to find Ella.

"Why, Charles, what's this?"

"I'm a poet, Ella, and when a poet meets a girl like you he thinks of a day in the country. Do you see this tree? Let's call it *our* tree. There's the lake—the prettiest lake imaginable. Here is grass, and there are flowers. There are birds, too, Ella. You told me you like birds."

"Oh, Charles, you're so sweet. I feel I hear them singing."

"And here's our lunch. But before we eat, go behind the rock there, and see what you find."

I heard her cry out in delight when she saw the summer dress I had put there for her. When she came back the spring day smiled to see her, and the lake shone brighter than before. "Ella, let us have lunch. Let us have fun. Let us have a swim. I can just imagine you in one of those new bathing suits."

"Let's just sit there, Charles, and talk."

So we sat and talked, and the time was gone like a dream. We might have stayed there, forgetful of everything, had it not been for the spider.

"Charles, what are you doing?"

"Nothing, my dear. Just a naughty little spider, crawling over your knee. Purely imaginary, of course, but that sort are sometimes the worst. I had to try to catch him."

"Don't, Charles! It's late. It's terribly late. They'll be back any minute. I'd better go home."

I took her home to the kitchenware on the sub-ground floor, and kissed her good-day. She offered me her cheek. This troubles me.

MAY 10   "Ella, I love you."

I said it to her just like that. We have met many times. I have dreamt of her by day. I have not even kept up my journal. Verse has been out of the question.

"Ella, I love you. Let us move into the trousseau department. Don't look so dismayed, darling. If you like, we will go right away from here. We will live in that little restaurant in Central Park. There are thousands of birds there."

"Please—please don't talk like that!"

"But I love you with all my heart."

"You mustn't."

"But I find I must. I can't help it. Ella, you don't love another?"

She wept a little. "Oh, Charles, I do."

"Love another, Ella? One of these? I thought you dreaded them all. It must be Roscoe. He is the only one that's any way human. We talk of art, life, and such things. And he has stolen your heart!"

"No, Charles, no. He's just like the rest, really. I hate them all. They make me shutter."

"Who is it, then?"

"It's him."

"Who?"

"The night-watchman."

"Impossible!"

"No. He smells of the sun."

"Oh, Ella, you have broken my heart."

"Be my friend, though."

"I will. I'll be your brother. How did you fall in love with him."

"Oh, Charles, it was so wonderful. I was thinking of birds, and I was careless. Don't tell on me, Charles. They'll punish me."

"No. No. Go on."

"I was careless, and there he was, coming round the corner. And there was no place for me; I had this blue dress on. There were only some wax models in their underthings."

"Please go on."

"I couldn't help it. I slipped off my dress, and stood still."

"I see."

"And he stopped just by me, Charles. And he looked at me. And he touched my cheek."

"Did he notice nothing?"

"No. It was cold. But Charles, he said—he said—'Say, honey, I wish they made 'em like you on Eighth Avenue.' Charles, wasn't that a lovely thing to say?"

"Personally, I should have said Park Avenue."

"Oh, Charles, don't get like these people here. Sometimes I think you're getting like them. It doesn't matter what street, Charles; it was a lovely thing to say."

"Yes, but my heart's broken. And what can you do about him? Ella, he belongs to another world."

"Yes, Charles, Eighth Avenue. I want to go there. Charles, are you truly my friend?"

"I'm your brother, only my heart's broken."

"I'll tell you. I will. I'm going to stand there again. So he'll see me."

"And then?"

"Perhaps he'll speak to me again."

"My dearest Ella, you are torturing yourself. You are making it worse."

"No, Charles. Because I shall answer him. He will take me away."

"Ella, I can't bear it."

"Ssh! There is someone coming. I shall see the birds—real birds, Charles—and flowers growing. They're coming. You must go."

MAY 13   The last three days have been torture. This evening I broke. Roscoe had joined me. He sat eying me for a long time. He put his hand on my shoulder.

He said, "You're looking seedy, old fellow. Why don't you go over to Wanamaker's for some skiing?"

His kindness compelled a frank response. "It's deeper than that, Roscoe. I'm done for. I can't eat, I can't sleep. I can't write, man, I can't even write."

"What is it? Day starvation?"

"Roscoe—it's love."

"Not one of the staff, Charles, or the customers? That's absolutely forbidden."

"No, it's not that, Roscoe. But just as hopeless."

"My dear fellow, I can't bear to see you like this. Let me help you. Let me share your trouble."

Then it all came out. It burst out. I trusted him. I think I trusted him. I really think I had no intention of betraying Ella, of spoiling her escape, of keeping her here till her heart turned towards me. If I had, it was subconscious, I swear it.

But I told him all. All! He was sympathetic, but I detected a sly reserve in his sympathy. "You will respect my confidence, Roscoe? This is to be a secret between us."

"As secret as the grave, old chap."

And he must have gone straight to Mrs. Vanderpant. This evening the atmosphere has changed. People flicker to and fro, smiling nervously, horribly, with a sort of frightened sadistic exaltation. When I speak to them they answer evasively, fidget, and disappear. An informal dance has been called off. I cannot find Ella. I will creep out. I will look for her again.

LATER   Heaven! It has happened. I went in desperation to the manager's office, whose glass front overlooks the whole shop. I watched till midnight. Then I saw a little group of them, like ants bearing a victim. They were carrying Ella. They took her to the surgical department. They took other things.

And, coming back here, I was passed by a flittering, whispering horde of them, glancing over their shoulders in a thrilled ecstacy of panic, making for their hiding places. I, too, hid myself. How can I describe the dark inhuman creatures that passed me, silent as shadows? They went there—where Ella is.

What can I do? There is only one thing. I will find the watchman. I will tell him. He and I will have her. And if we are overpowered— Well, I will leave this on a counter. Tomorrow, if we live, I can recover it.

If not, look in the windows. Look for three new figures: two men, one rather sensitive-looking, and a girl. She has blue eyes, like periwinkle flowers, and her upper lip is lifted a little.

Look for us.

Smoke them out! Obliterate them! Avenge us!

THE SOUND MACHINE

Roald Dahl

IT WAS a summer evening and Klausner walked quickly through the front gate and around the side of the house and into the garden at the back. He went on down the garden until he came to a wooden shed and he unlocked the door, went inside and closed the door behind him.

The interior of the shed was an unpainted room. Against one wall, on the left, there was a long wooden workbench, and on it, among a littering of wires and batteries and small sharp tools, there stood a black box about three feet long, the shape of a child's coffin.

Klausner moved across the room to the box. The top of the box was open, and he bent down and began to poke and peer inside it among a mass of different-colored wires and silver tubes. He picked up a piece of paper that lay beside the box, studied it carefully, put it down, peered inside the box and started running his fingers along the wires, tugging gently at them to test the connections, glancing back at the paper, then into the box, then at the paper again, checking each wire. He did this for perhaps an hour.

Then he put a hand around to the front of the box where there were three dials, and he began to twiddle them, watching at the same time the movement of the mechanism inside the box. All the while he kept speaking softly to himself, nodding his head, smiling sometimes, his hands always moving, the fingers moving swiftly, deftly, inside the box, his mouth twisting into curious shapes when a thing was delicate or difficult to do, speaking to himself, saying, "Yes. . . . Yes. . . . And now this one. . . . Yes. . . . Yes. . . . . But

71

is this right? . . . Is it—where's my diagram? . . . Ah, yes. . . . Of course. . . . Yes, yes. . . . That's right. . . . And now. . . . Good. . . . Good. . . . Yes. . . . Yes, yes, yes." His concentration was intense; his movements were quick; there was an air of urgency about the way he worked, of breathlessness, of strong suppressed excitement.

Suddenly he heard footsteps on the gravel path outside and he straightened and turned swiftly as the door opened and a tall man came in. It was Scott. It was only Scott, the doctor.

"Well, well, well," the Doctor said. "So this is where you hide yourself in the evenings."

"Hullo, Scott," Klausner said.

"I happened to be passing," the Doctor told him, "so I dropped in to see how you were. There was no one in the house, so I came down here. How's that throat of yours been behaving?"

"It's all right. It's fine."

"Now I'm here I might as well have a look at it."

"Please don't trouble. I'm quite cured. I'm fine."

The Doctor began to feel the tension in the room. He looked at the black box on the bench; then he looked at the man. "You've got your hat on," he said.

"Oh, have I?" Klausner reached up, removed the hat, and put it on the bench.

The Doctor came up closer and bent down to look into the box. "What's this?" he said. "Making a radio?"

"No. Just fooling around."

"It's got rather complicated-looking innards."

"Yes." Klausner seemed tense and distracted.

"What is it?" the Doctor asked. "It's rather a frightening-looking thing, isn't it?"

"It's just an idea."

"Yes?"

"It has to do with sound, that's all."

"Good heavens, man! Don't you get enough of that sort of thing all day in your work?"

"I like sound."

"So it seems." The Doctor went to the door, turned, and said, "Well, I won't disturb you. Glad your throat's not worrying you any more." But he kept standing there, looking at the box, intrigued by the remarkable complexity of its insides, curious to know what this strange patient of his was up to. "What's it really for?" he asked. "You've made me inquisitive."

Klausner looked down at the box, then at the Doctor, and he reached up and began gently to scratch the lobe of his right ear. There was a pause. The Doctor stood by the door, waiting, smiling.

"All right, I'll tell you, if you're interested." There was another pause, and the Doctor could see that Klausner was having trouble about how to begin. He was shifting from one foot to the other, tugging at the lobe of his ear, looking at his feet, and then at last, slowly, he said, "Well, it's like this. . . . It's . . . the theory is very simple, really. The human ear . . . You know that it can't hear everything. There are sounds that are so low-pitched or so high-pitched that it can't hear them."

"Yes," the Doctor said. "Yes."

"Well, speaking very roughly, any note so high that it has more than fifteen thousand vibrations a second—we can't hear it. Dogs have better ears than us. You know you can buy a whistle whose note is so high-pitched that you can't hear it at all. But a dog can hear it."

"Yes, I've seen one," the Doctor said.

"Of course you have. And up the scale, higher than the note of that whistle, there is another note—a vibration, if you like, but I prefer to think of it as a note. You can't hear that one either. And above that there is another and another rising right up the scale forever and ever and ever, an endless succession of notes . . . an infinity of notes . . . there is a note—if only our ears could hear it—so high that it vibrates a million times a second . . . and another a million times as high as that . . . and on and on, higher and higher, as far as numbers go, which is . . . infinity . . . eternity . . . beyond the stars. . . ."

Klausner stood next to the workbench, fluttering his hands, becoming more animated every moment. He was a small, frail man, nervous and twitchy, with always moving hands. His large head inclined toward his left shoulder, as though his neck were not quite strong enough to support it rigidly. His face was smooth and pale, almost white, and the pale-gray eyes that blinked and peered from behind a pair of thick-lensed steel spectacles were bewildered, unfocussed, remote. He was a frail, nervous, twitchy little man, a moth of a man, dreamy and distracted, suddenly fluttering and animated; and now the Doctor, looking at that strange pale face and those pale gray eyes, felt that somehow there was about this little person a quality of distance, of immense, immeasurable distance, as though the mind were far away from where the body was.

The Doctor waited for him to go on. Klausner sighed and clasped his hands tightly together. "I believe," he said, speaking more slowly now, "that there is a whole world of sound about us all the time that we cannot hear. It is possible that up there in those high-pitched, inaudible regions there is a new, exciting music being made, with subtle harmonies and fierce grinding discords, a music so powerful that it would drive us mad if only our ears were tuned to hear the sound of it. There may be anything . . . for all we know there may—"

"Yes," the Doctor said. "But it's not very probable."

"Why not? Why not?" Klausner pointed to a fly sitting on a small roll of copper wire on the workbench. "You see that fly? What sort of a noise is that fly making now? None—that one can hear. But for all we know the creature may be whistling like mad on a very high note, or barking or croaking or singing a song. It's got a mouth, hasn't it? It's got a throat!"

The Doctor looked at the fly and he smiled. He was still standing by the door with his hand on the doorknob. "Well," he said. "So you're going to check up on that?"

"Some time ago," Klausner said, "I made a simple instrument that proved to me the existence of many odd, inaudible sounds. Often I have sat and watched the needle of my instrument recording the presence of sound vibrations in the air when I myself could hear nothing. And *those* are the sounds I want to listen to. I want to know where they come from and who or what is making them."

"And that machine on the table, there," the Doctor said, "is that going to allow you to hear these noises?"

"It may. Who knows? So far, I've had no luck. But I've made some changes in it, and tonight I'm ready for another trial. This machine," he said, touching it with his hands, "is designed to pick up sound vibrations that are too high-pitched for reception by the human ear and to convert them to a scale of audible tones. I tune it in, almost like a radio."

"How d'you mean?"

"It isn't complicated. Say I wish to listen to the squeak of a bat. That's a fairly high-pitched sound—about thirty thousand vibrations a second. The average human ear can't quite hear it. Now, if there were a bat flying around this room and I tuned in to thirty thousand on my machine, I would hear the squeaking of that bat very clearly. I would even hear the correct note—F sharp, or B flat, or whatever it might be—but merely at a much *lower pitch*. Don't you understand?"

The Doctor looked at the long, black coffin-box. "And you're going to try it tonight?"

"Yes."

"Well, I wish you luck." He glanced at his watch. "My goodness!" he said. "I must fly. Goodbye, and thank you for telling me. I must call again sometime and find out what happened." The Doctor went out and closed the door behind him.

For a while longer, Klausner fussed about with the wires in the black box; then he straightened up and, in a soft, excited whisper, said, "Now we'll try again. . . . We'll take it out into the garden this time . . . and then perhaps . . . perhaps . . . the reception will be better. Lift it up now . . . carefully. . . . Oh, my God, it's heavy!" He carried the box to the door, found that he couldn't open the door without putting it down, carried it back, put it on the bench, opened the door, and then carried it with some difficulty into the garden. He placed the box carefully on a small wooden table that stood on the lawn. He returned to the shed and fetched a pair of earphones. He plugged the wire connections from the earphones into the machine and put the earphones over his ears. The movements of his hands were quick and precise. He was excited, and breathed loudly and quickly through his mouth. He kept on talking to himself with little words of comfort and encouragement, as though he were afraid—afraid that the machine might not work and afraid also of what might happen if it did.

He stood there in the garden beside the wooden table, so pale, small, and thin that he looked like an ancient, consumptive, bespectacled child. The sun had gone down. There was no wind, no sound at all. From where he stood, he could see over a low fence into the next garden, and there was a woman walking down the garden with a flower basket on her arm. He watched her for a while without thinking about her at all. Then he turned to the box on the table and pressed a switch on its front. He put his left hand on the volume control and his right hand on the knob that moved a needle across a large central dial, like the wave-length dial of a radio. The dial was marked with many numbers, in a series of bands, starting at 15,000 and going on up to 1,000,000.

And now he was bending forward over the machine. His head

was cocked to one side in a tense, listening attitude. His right hand was beginning to turn the knob. The needle was travelling slowly across the dial, so slowly that he could hardly see it move, and in the earphones he could hear a faint, spasmodic crackling.

Behind this crackling sound, he could hear a distant humming tone, which was the noise of the machine itself, but that was all. As he listened, he became conscious of a curious sensation, a feeling that his ears were stretching out away from his head, that each ear was connected to his head by a thin, stiff wire, like a tentacle, and that the wires were lengthening, that the ears were going up and up toward a secret and forbidden territory, a danger-ous, ultrasonic region where ears had never been before and had no right to be.

The little needle crept slowly across the dial, and suddenly he heard a shriek, a frightful piercing shriek, and he jumped and dropped his hands, catching hold of the edge of the table. He stared around him as if expecting to see the person who had shrieked. There was no one in sight except the woman in the garden next door, and it was certainly not she. She was bending down, cutting yellow roses and putting them in her basket.

Again it came—a throatless, inhuman shriek, sharp and short, very clear and cold. The note itself possessed a minor, metallic quality that he had never heard before. Klausner looked around him, searching instinctively for the source of the noise. The woman next door was the only living thing in sight. He saw her reach down, take a rose stem in the fingers of one hand and snip the stem with a pair of scissors. Again he heard the scream.

It came at the exact moment when the rose stem was cut.

At this point, the woman straightened up, put the scissors in the basket with the roses and turned to walk away.

"Mrs. Saunders!" Klausner shouted, and his voice was high and shrill with excitement. "Oh, Mrs. Saunders!"

The woman looked around, and she saw her neighbor standing on his lawn—a fantastic, arm-waving little person with a pair of earphones on his head—calling to her in a voice so high and loud that she became alarmed.

"Cut another one! Please cut another one quickly!"

She stood still, staring at him. "Why, Mr. Klausner," she said, "what's the matter?"

"Please do as I ask," he said. "Cut just one more rose!"

Mrs. Saunders had always believed her neighbor to be a rather peculiar person; now it seemed . . . it seemed that he had gone completely crazy. She wondered whether she should run into the house and fetch her husband. No, she thought. No, he's harmless. I'll just humor him. "Certainly, Mr. Klausner, if you like," she said. She took her scissors from the basket, bent down, and snipped another rose.

Again Klausner heard that frightful throatless shriek in the earphones; again it came at the exact moment the rose stem was cut. He took off the earphones and ran to the fence that separated the two gardens. "All right," he said. "That's enough. No more. Please, no more."

The woman stood there holding the yellow rose that she had just cut, looking at him.

"I'm going to tell you something, Mrs. Saunders," he said, "something that you won't believe." He put his hands on the top of the fence and peered at her intently through his thick spectacles. "You have, this evening, cut a basketful of roses. You have, with a sharp pair of scissors, cut through the stems of living things, and each rose that you cut screamed in the most terrible way. Did you know that, Mrs. Saunders?"

"No," she said. "I certainly didn't know that."

"It happens to be true," he said. He was breathing rather rapidly, but he was trying to control his excitement. "I heard them shrieking. Each time you cut one I heard the cry of pain. A very high-pitched sound, approximately one hundred and thirty-two thousand vibrations a second. You couldn't possibly have heard it yourself. But I heard it."

"Did you really, Mr. Klausner?" She decided she would make a dash for the house in about five seconds.

"You might say," he went on, "that a rosebush has no nervous system to feel with, no throat to cry with. You'd be right. It hasn't. Not like ours, anyway. But *how do you know, Mrs. Saunders"*— and here he leaned far over the fence and spoke in a fierce whisper— *"how do you know* that a rosebush doesn't feel as much pain when someone cuts its stem in two as you would feel if someone cut your wrist off with a garden shears? *How do you know that?* It's alive, isn't it?"

"Yes, Mr. Klausner. Oh, yes—and good night," and quickly she turned and ran up the garden to her house. Klausner went back to the table. He put on the earphones and stood for a while listening. He could still hear the faint spasmodic crackling sound and the humming noise of the machine, but nothing more. Slowly he bent down and took hold of a small white daisy growing on the lawn. He took it between thumb and forefinger and slowly pulled it upward and sideways until the stem broke.

From the moment that he started pulling to the moment when the stem broke, he heard—he distinctly heard in the earphones— a faint, high-pitched cry, curiously inanimate. He took another daisy and did it again. Once more he heard the cry, but he wasn't so sure now that it expressed *pain*. No, it wasn't pain; it was surprise. Or was it? It didn't really express any of the feelings or emotions known to a human being. It was just crying, a neutral, stony cry— a single, emotionless note, expressing nothing. It had been the same with the roses. He had been wrong in calling it a cry of pain. A flower probably didn't feel pain. It felt something else which we didn't know about—something called toin or spurl or plinuckment, or anything you like.

He stood up and removed the earphones. It was getting dark and he could see pricks of light shining in the windows of the houses all around him. Carefully, he picked up the black box from the table, carried it into the shed and put it on the workbench. Then he went out, locked the door behind him and walked up to the house.

The next morning, Klausner was up as soon as it was light. He dressed and went straight to the shed. He picked the machine up and carried it outside, clasping it to his chest with both hands, walking unsteadily under its weight. He went past the house, out through the front gate, and across the road to the park. There he paused and looked around him; then he went on until he came to a large tree, a beech tree, and placed the machine on the ground, close to the trunk of the tree. Quickly he went back to the house and got an axe from the coal cellar and carried it across the road into the park. He put the axe on the ground beside the tree.

Then he looked around him again, peering nervously through his thick glasses in every direction. There was no one about. It was six in the morning.

He put the earphones on his head and switched on the machine. He listened for a moment to the faint familiar humming sound; then he picked up the axe, took a stance with his legs wide apart, and swung the axe as hard as he could at the base of the tree trunk. The blade cut deep into the wood and stuck there, and at the instant of impact he heard a most extraordinary noise in the earphones. It was a new noise, unlike any he had heard before—a harsh, noteless, enormous noise, a growling, low-pitched, screaming sound, not quick and short like the noise of the roses, but drawn out, like a sob, lasting for fully a minute, loudest at the moment when the axe struck, fading gradually, fainter and fainter, until it was gone.

Klausner stared in horror at the place where the blade of the axe had sunk into the woodflesh of the tree; then gently, he took the axe handle, worked the blade loose, and threw the thing on the ground. With his fingers he touched the gash that the axe had made in the wood, touching the edges of the gash, trying to press them together to close the wound, and he kept saying, "Tree . . . oh, tree . . . I am sorry . . . I am so sorry . . . but it will heal. . . . It will heal fine . . ."

For a while he stood there with his hands upon the trunk of the great tree; then suddenly he turned away and hurried off out of the park, across the road, through the front gate, and back into his house. He went to the telephone, consulted the book, dialled a number, and waited. He held the receiver tightly in his left hand and tapped the table impatiently with his right. He heard the telephone buzzing at the other end, and then the click of a lifted receiver and a man's voice, a sleepy voice, saying, "Hullo. Yes?"

"Dr. Scott?" he said.

"Yes. Speaking."

"Dr. Scott. You must come at once—quickly please."

"Who is it speaking?"

"Klausner here, and you remember what I told you last night about my experiments with sound and how I hoped I might—"

"Yes, yes, of course, but what's the matter? Are you ill?"

"No, I'm not ill, but—"

"It's half past six in the morning," said the Doctor, "and you call me, but you are not ill."

"Please come. Come quickly. I want someone to hear it. It's driving me mad! I can't believe it. . . ."

The Doctor heard the frantic, almost hysterical note in the man's voice, the same note he was used to hearing in the voices of people who called up and said, "There's been an accident. Come quickly." He said slowly, "You really want me to get out of bed and come over now?"

"Yes now. At once please."

"All right then, I'll come."

Klausner sat down beside the telephone and waited. He tried to remember what the shriek of the tree had sounded like, but he couldn't. He could remember only that it had made him feel sick with horror. He tried to imagine what sort of noise a human would make if he had to stand anchored to the ground while someone deliberately swung a small sharp thing at his leg so that the blade cut in deep and wedged itself in the cut. Same sort of noise perhaps? No. Quite different. The noise of the tree was worse than any known human noise, because of that frightening, toneless, throatless quality. He began to wonder about other living things, and he thought immediately of a field of wheat, a field of wheat standing up straight and yellow and alive, with the mower going through it, cutting the stems, five hundred stems a second, every second. Oh, my God, what would the noise be like? Five hundred wheat plants screaming together, and every second another five hundred being cut and screaming and no, he thought, no I do not want to go to a wheat field with my machine. I would never eat bread after that. But what about potatoes and cabbages and carrots and onions? And what about apples? Ah, no! Apples are all right. They fall off naturally when they are ripe. Apples are all right if you let them fall off instead of tearing them from the tree branch. But not vegetables. Not a potato for example. A potato would surely shriek; so would a carrot and an onion and a cabbage. . . .

He heard the click of the front-gate latch and he jumped up and went out and saw the tall doctor coming down the path, his little black bag in hand.

"Well," the Doctor said. "Well, what's all the trouble?"

"Come with me, Doctor. I want you to hear it. I called you because you're the only one I've told. It's over the road in the park. Will you come now?"

The Doctor looked at him. He seemed calmer now. There was no sign of madness or hysteria; he was merely disturbed and excited. "All right, I'll come," the Doctor said. They went across the road into the park, and Klausner led the way to the great beech tree at the foot of which stood the long, black coffin-box of the machine—and the axe.

"Why did you bring the machine out here?" asked the Doctor.

"I wanted a tree. There aren't any big trees in the garden."

"And why the axe?"

"You'll see in a moment. But now please put on these earphones and listen. Listen carefully and tell me afterwards precisely what you hear. I want to make quite sure. . . ."

The Doctor smiled and took the earphones, which he put over his ears.

Klausner bent down and flicked the switch on the panel of the machine; then he picked up the axe and took his stance with his legs apart, ready to swing. For a moment, he paused. "Can you hear anything?" he said to the Doctor.

"Can I what?"

"Can you *hear* anything?"

"Just a humming noise."

Klausner stood there with the axe in his hands, trying to bring himself to swing, but the thought of the noise that the tree would make made him pause again.

"What are you waiting for?" the Doctor asked.

"Nothing," Klausner answered, and then he lifted the axe and swung it at the tree; and as he swung, he thought he felt, he could swear he felt, a movement of the ground on which he stood. He felt a slight shifting of the earth beneath his feet, as though the roots of the tree were moving underneath the soil, but it was too late to check the blow, and the axe blade struck the tree and wedged deep into the wood. At that moment, high overhead, there was the cracking sound of wood splintering and the swishing sound of leaves brushing against other leaves and they both looked up and the Doctor cried, "Watch out! Run, man! Quickly run!"

The Doctor had ripped off the earphones and was running away fast, but Klausner stood spellbound, staring up at the great branch, sixty feet long at least, that was bending slowly downward, breaking and crackling and splintering at its thickest point, just where it joined the main trunk of the tree. The branch came crashing down, and Klausner leapt just in time. It fell upon the machine and smashed it into pieces.

"Great heavens!" shouted the Doctor as he came running back. "That was a near one! I thought it had got you!"

Klausner was staring at the tree. His large head was leaning to one side and upon his smooth white face there was a tense, horrified expression. Slowly he walked up to the tree and gently he pried the blade loose from the trunk.

"Did you hear it?" he said, turning to the Doctor. His voice was barely audible.

The Doctor was still out of breath from the running and the excitement. "Hear what?"

"In the earphones. Did you hear anything when the axe struck?"

The Doctor began to rub the back of his neck. "Well," he said, "as a matter of fact . . ." He paused and frowned and bit his lower lip. "No, I'm not sure. I couldn't be sure. I don't suppose I had the earphones on for more than a second after the axe struck."

"Yes, yes, but what did you hear?"

"I don't know," the Doctor said. "I don't know what I heard. Probably the noise of the branch breaking." He was speaking rapidly, rather irritably.

"What did it sound like?" Klausner leaned forward slightly, staring hard at the Doctor. "Exactly what did it sound like?"

"Oh hell!" the Doctor said. "I really don't know. I was more interested in getting out of the way. Let's leave it."

"Dr. Scott, what—did—it—sound—like?"

"For God's sake, how could I tell, what with half the tree falling on me and having to run for my life?" The Doctor certainly seemed nervous. Klausner had sensed it now. He stood quite still, staring at the Doctor, and for fully half a minute he didn't speak. The Doctor moved his feet, shrugged his shoulders, and half turned to go. "Well," he said, "we'd better get back."

"Look," said the little man, and now his smooth white face became suddenly suffused with color. "Look," he said, "you stitch this up." He pointed to the last gash the axe had made in the tree trunk. "You stitch this up quickly."

"Don't be silly," the Doctor said.

"You do as I say. Stitch it up." Klausner was gripping the axe handle and he spoke softly, in a curious, almost a threatening tone.

"Don't be silly," the Doctor said. "I can't stitch through wood. Come on. Let's get back."

"So you can't stitch through wood?"

"No, of course not."

"Have you got any iodine in your bag?"

"Yes, of course."

"Then paint the cut with iodine. It'll sting, but that can't be helped."

"Now, look," the Doctor said, and again he turned as if to go. "Let's not be ridiculous. Let's get back to the house and then . . ."

"Paint—the—cut—with—iodine."

The Doctor hesitated. He saw Klausner's hands tightening on the handle of the axe. He decided that his only alternative was to run away fast, and he certainly wasn't going to do that.

"All right," he said. "I'll paint it with iodine."

He got his black bag which was lying on the grass about ten yards away, opened it and took out a bottle of iodine and some cotton wool. He went up to the tree trunk, uncorked the bottle, tipped some of the iodine onto the cotton wool, bent down and began to dab it into the cut. He kept one eye on Klausner, who was standing motion-less, with the axe in his hands, watching the Doctor.

"Make sure you get it right in."

"Yes," the Doctor said.

"Now do the other one, the one just above it!"

The Doctor did as he was told. "There you are," he said. "It's done."

He straightened up and surveyed his work in a very serious man-ner. "That should do nicely."

Klausner came closer and gravely examined the two wounds.

"Yes," he said, nodding his huge head slowly up and down. "Yes, yes, yes, that will do nicely." He stepped back a pace. "You'll come and look at them tomorrow?"

"Oh, yes," the Doctor said. "Of course."

"And put some more iodine on?"

"If necessary, yes."

"Thank you, Doctor," Klausner said, and he nodded his head again and he dropped the axe and all at once he smiled, a wild, ex-cited smile, and quickly the Doctor went over to him and gently he took him by the arm and he said, "Come on, we must go now," and suddenly they were walking away, the two of them, walking silently, rather hurriedly, across the park, over the road, back to the house.

THE COCOON

John B. L. Goodwin

WHEREAS downstairs his father had a room the walls of which were studded with trophies of his aggressive quests: heads of ibex, chamois, eland, keitloa, peccary, and ounce, upstairs Denny had pinned upon his playroom walls the fragile bodies of Swallowtails, Nymphs, Fritillaries, Meadow Browns and Anglewings.

Although his father had maneuvered expeditions, experienced privation, waded through jungles, climbed upon crags for his specimens, Denny had blithely gathered his within the fields and gardens close to home. It was likely that his father's day as a collector was over; Denny's had just begun.

Danny was eleven and his father forty-six and the house in which they lived was a hundred or more years old though no one could be exact about it. Mr. Peatybog, the postmaster in the shriveled village, said as how he could recall when the circular window on the second-story landing hadn't been there and Mrs. Bliss said she knew that at one time what was now the kitchen had been a taproom because her father had told her about it. The heart of the house, as Denny's father put it, was very old but people had altered it and added on and covered up. Denny's father had added the room where his heads were hung, but Denny's playroom must have been the original attic because where the rafters of its high, abrupt ceiling were visible the nails in them were square-headed and here and there the timbers were still held together with wooden pegs.

But the playroom, where Denny also slept, appeared to the casual glance anything but old. The floor was carpeted in blue, and curtains were yellow and the bedspread blue and white. The wallpaper, which his mother had chosen for him before she left, was yellow willow trees on a pale blue ground and to an alien eye the butterflies pinned on the walls seemed part of the design. It had been a long time since Denny's father had been up in the room and although he knew that his son's collection of Lepidoptera, as he called them, was pinned upon the walls he did not know and therefore could not reprimand his son for the damage they had done the pretty wallpaper. Under each specimen a putty-colored blot was spreading over the blue paper. It was the oil exuding from the drying bodies of the dead insects.

In one corner of the room was a chintz-covered chest in which lay the remains of Denny's earlier loves: battered trains and sections of track, an old transformer, batteries covered with cavernlike crystals of zinc salts, trucks, and windmills no longer recognizable as much more than haphazard, wooden arrangements of fitted blocks and sticks, books crumpled and torn with Denny's name or current dream scrawled aggressively in crayon across the print and pictures, a gyroscope, a rubber ball, its cracked paint making a mosaic of antique red and gold around its sphere, and somewhere at the bottom weighed down with tin and lead and wood more than any corpse with earth and grass, lay a bear, a monkey, and a boy doll with a scar across one cheek where Denny had kicked it with a skate. In another corner the symbols of his present were proudly displayed. The butterfly net leaned against the wall, and close to the floor on a wooden box turned upside down stood Denny's cyanide bottle, tweezers, and pins, the last shining as dangerously bright as minute surgical instruments in their packet of black paper.

After almost a year of collecting butterflies, Denny had found that a certain equivocal quality could be added to his pursuit if he were to collect not only the butterflies but also the earlier stages of their mutations. By cramming milk bottles, shoe boxes, and whatever other receptacle the house might offer with caterpillars and pupae he was, in the case of those that survived, able to participate in a sort of alchemy. Intently he would squat on his haunches and gaze into the receptacles, studying the laborious transformations, the caterpillar shedding skin, the exudation that is used to hitch its shroudlike chrysalid to twigs or undersides of leaves, and then the final uupredictable attainment of the imago. It was like opening a surprise package, for as yet Denny had not learned to tell what color, size, or shape worm would turn into a Dog's Head Sulphur, Mourning Cloak, or Tiger Swallowtail.

As late summer approached, Denny insisted that the servant girl refrain from opening the windows wide in order to air out his room. The sudden change in temperature, he said, would disturb the caterpillars and pupae. Even though the girl reported to his father that Denny's room smelled unhealthily from all the bugs and things, the man did no more than mention it to Denny in an offhand manner. Denny grunted to show that he had heard and did no more about it, and as his father was writing a book on his jungles and crags and beasts, he had really very little concern about what went on upstairs.

So it was that an acrid smell of decaying vegetable matter resolving itself into insect flesh pervaded Denny's bright attic room and the oily blotches on the walls beneath his specimens spread over so slightly, discoloring the paper more and more.

In a book, *Butterflies You Ought to Know Better,* which an aunt had sent him for Christmas, Denny read that a suitable "castle" for a caterpillar could be made by placing a lamp chimney, closed at the top, upon a flowerpot filled with earth. He prepared this enclosure, purchasing the lamp chimney from the village store with his own money. It was such an elegant contrivance and yet so magical that he decided to save it for an especially unusual specimen. It was not until a late afternoon in October that Denny found one worthy of the "castle."

He was exploring a copse between two fields. Because of the stoniness of its ground it had never been cultivated and lay like a sword between the fertility of the fields on either side. Denny had never trespassed on it before and dared to now only because of his growing self-confidence in his power over nature. A month ago he would have shied away from the area entirely, even taking the precaution to circumvent the two fields enclosing it. But he felt a little now the way he thought God must feel when, abject within its glass and cardboard world, the life he watched took form, changed, and ceased. Protected from unpleasant touch or any unpredictable action, Denny watched the metamorphosis from worm to chrysalid to miraculously vibrant petal. It lay within his power to sever abruptly the magical chain of their evolution at any point he chose. In a little way he *was* a little like God. It was this conceit that now gave him the courage to climb over the stones of the old wall and enter the half acre of dense woodland.

The autumn sun, already low, ogled the brittle landscape like some improbable jack-o'-lantern hanging in the west. What birds were still in that country spoke in the rasping tone of the herd; the more mellifluous and prosperous had already gone south. Although the leaves on the trees displayed the incautious yellows of senility and ochres of decay, the underbrush such as cat briar and wild grape were mostly green. Armed with his forceps and his omnipotence, Denny explored each living leaf and twig.

Brambles tore his stockings and scratched his knees but, except for vulgar tent caterpillars in the wild cherry trees, Denny's efforts went unrewarded. It was dusk when, searching among the speculatively shaped leaves of a sassafras, Denny found a specimen beyond his most arrogant expectations. At first sight, due in part to the twilight, it looked more like some shriveled dragon than a caterpillar. Between it and the twig a filament stretched and this, added to the fact that when Denny touched it gingerly he could feel its puffy flesh contract the way caterpillars do, convinced him that it was no freak of nature or if it was it was a caterpillar freak and therefore nothing to fear. Tearing it cautiously with his tweezers from the twig, he put the monster in the Diamond Match box he always carried with him and, running breathlessly, blind to briar and brambles, Denny headed home.

It was suppertime when he got there and his father was already at the table, his left hand turning the pages of a book while with his right hand he ladled soup into his mouth. Denny had clattered up the stairs before his father was aware of his presence.

"You're late, son," he said in the moment between two printed sentences and two spoonfuls of soup.

"I know, Father," Denny replied without stopping, "but I got something."

Another sentence and another spoonful.

"How many times have I told you to be explicit? *Something* can be anything from a captive balloon to a case of mumps."

From the second landing Denny called down, "It's just *something*. I don't know what it is."

His father mumbled, and by the time he had finished a paragraph and scooped up the last nugget of meat out of his soup and had addressed his son with the words, "Whatever it is it will wait until you have your supper," Denny was peering at it through the glass of the lamp chimney.

Even in the bright electric glare it was reptilian. It was large for a caterpillar, between four and five inches long Denny guessed, and was a muddy purple color, its underside a yellowish black. At either extremity it bore a series of three horny protuberances of a vermilion shade; they were curved sharply inward and stiff little hairs grew from them. From its mouth there protruded a set of small grasping claws like those of a crustacean. Its skin was wrinkled like that of a tortoise and the abdominal segments were sharply defined. The feet lacked the usual suction-like apparatuses caterpillars have but were scaly and shaped like tiny claws.

It was indeed worthy of its "castle." It was not to be found in any of the illustrated books Denny had. He would guard it and keep it a secret and finally, when he presented its metamorphosis into a winged thing to the world, his father's renown as the captor of extraordinary beasts would pale beside his own. The only thing he could guess at, and that because of its size, was that it was the larva of a moth rather than that of a butterfly.

He was still peering at it when the servant girl brought up a tray. "Here," she said, "if you're such a busy little gentleman that you can't spare time for supper like an ordinary boy. If I had my way you'd go hungry." She set the tray down on the table. "Pugh!" she added. "The smell of this room is something awful. What have you got there now?" And she was about to peer over Denny's shoulder.

"Get out!" he shrieked, turning on her. "Get out!"

"I'm not so sure I will if you speak like that."

He arose and in his fury pushed her hulk out the door, slamming it and locking it after her.

She started to say something on the other side, but what it was Denny never knew or cared, for his own voice screaming, "And stay out!" sent the young girl scurrying down the stairs to his father.

It was typical of the man that he merely commiserated with the girl, agreed with her on the urgency of some sort of discipline for his son, and then, settling back to his pipe and his manuscript, dismissed the matter from his mind.

The following day Denny told the girl that henceforth she was not to enter his room, neither to make the bed nor to clean.

"We shall see about that," she said, "though it would be a pleasure such as I never hoped for this side of heaven were I never to enter that horrid smelling room again."

Again his father was approached and this time he reluctantly called his son to him.

"Ethel tells me something about you not wanting her to go into your room," he said, peering over his glasses.

"I'd rather she didn't, Father," Denny replied, humble as pie. "You see, she doesn't understand about caterpillars and cocoons and things and she messes everything up."

"But who will see to the making of your bed and dusting and such?"

"I will," asserted Denny. "There's no reason why if I don't want anyone to go into my room I shoudn't have to make up for it somehow, like making my own bed and clearing up."

"Spoken like a soldier, son," the father said. "I know the way you feel and if you're willing to pay the price in responsibility I see no reason why you shouldn't have your wish. But," and he pointed a paper knife of walrus tusk at the boy, "if it isn't kept neat and tidy we'll have to rescind the privilege; remember that."

His father, grateful that the interview had not been as tedious as he had anticipated, told his son he could go. From then on Denny always kept the key to his room in his pocket.

Because caterpillars cease to eat prior to their chrysalis stage and Denny's caterpillar refused to eat whatever assortment of leaves he tried to tempt it with, Denny knew that it had definitely been preparing its cocoon when he had plucked it from the sassafras branch. It was very restless, almost convulsive now, and within the lamp chimney it humped itself aimlessly from twig to twig, its scaly little claws searching for something to settle upon. After a day of such meanderings the caterpillar settled upon a particular crotch of the twig and commenced to spin its cocoon. By the end of twenty-four hours the silken alembic was complete.

Though there was now nothing for Denny to observe, he still squatted for hours on end staring at the cocoon that hung like some parasitic growth from the sassafras twig. His concentration upon the shape was so great as he sat hunched over it, that his eyes seemed to tear the silken shroud apart and to be intimately exploring the secret that was taking place within.

Now Denny spent less and less of the days out in the open searching for the more common types of chrysalid with which he was acquainted. Such were for him as garnets would be to a connoisseur of emeralds. His lean, tanned face became puffy and the palms of his hands were pale and moist.

The winter months dragged on and Denny was as listlessly impatient as what was inside the cocoon. His room was cold and airless, for a constant low temperature must be kept if the cocoon was to lie dormant until spring. His bed was seldom made and the floor was thick with dust and mud. Once a week the girl left the broom and dustpan along with the clean sheets outside his door, but Denny took only the sheets into his room where they would collect into a stack on the floor for weeks at a time. His father took no notice of his condition other than to write a postscript to what was otherwise a legal and splenetic letter to his wife that their son looked peaked and upon receiving an apprehensive reply he casually asked Denny if he was feeling all right. The boy's affirmative though noncommittal answer seemed to satisfy him and, dropping a card to his wife to the effect that their son professed to be in sound health, he considered himself released from any further responsibility.

When April was about gone Denny moved his treasure close to the window where the sun would induce the dormant thing within it into life. In a few days Denny was sure that it was struggling for release, for the cocoon seemed to dance up and down idiotically upon its thread. All that night he kept vigil, his red and swollen eyes focused on the cocoon as upon some hypnotic object. His father ate breakfast alone and by nine o'clock showed enough concern to send the servant girl up to see if everything was all right. She hurried back to report that his son was at least still alive enough to be rude to her. The father mumbled something in reply about the boy's mother having shirked her responsibilities. The girl said that if it pleased him, she would like to give notice. She was very willing to enumerate the reasons why, but the man dismissed her casually with the request that she stay until she found someone to take her place.

At ten Denny was positive that the cocoon was about to break; by ten-thirty there was no longer any doubt in his mind. Somewhat before eleven the eclosion took place. There was a convulsive moment inside and the cocoon opened at the top with the faint rustle of silk. The feathery antennae and the two forelegs issued forth, the legs clutching the cocoon in order to hoist the body through the narrow aperture. The furry and distended abdomen, upon which were hinged the crumpled wings, was drawn out with effort. Immediately the creature commenced awkwardly to climb the twig from which the cocoon was suspended. Denny watched the procedure in a trance. Having gained the tip of the branch and unable to proceed farther, the insect rested, its wings hanging moist and heavy from its bloated body. The abdomen with each pulsation shrank visibly and gradually, very gradually, the antennae unfurled and the wings expanded with the juices pumped into them from the body.

Within an hour the metamorphosis of many months was complete. The beast, its wings still slightly damp though fully spread, fluttered gently before the eyes of the boy. Though escaped from its cocoon, it lay imprisoned still behind the glass.

Denny's pallor was suddenly flushed. He grasped the lamp chimney as if he would hold the insect to him. This was his miracle, his alone. He watched with a possessive awe as the creature flexed its wings, although it was still too weak to attempt flight. Surely this specimen before him was unique. The wings were easily ten inches across and their color was so subtly graduated that it was impossible to say where black turned to purple and purple to green and green back to black. The only definite delineations were a crablike simulacrum centered on each hind wing and upon each fore wing, the imitation of an open mouth with teeth bared. Both the crabs and the mouths were chalked in white and vermillion.

By noon Denny was hungry, yet so overcome with nervous exhaustion that he almost decided to forego the midday meal. Aware, however, that an absence from two meals running would surely precipitate an intrusion by his father with the servant girl as proxy, he reluctantly left his room and went downstairs to face his father over luncheon.

Despite his compliance, the father was immediately aware of the transformation in his son.

"Spring seems to have put new life into the lad," he said, turning over the page of a book. "You're like your mother in that respect and in that respect only, thank God. She never did do well in cold weather."

It was the first time he had mentioned the mother to the son since he had been forced to explain her departure obliquely some five years before. The boy was shocked. But as the opportunity had arisen, he hastily decided to follow up the mention of his mother. It was unseemly that he should disclose any sentiment, so he hesitated and calculated before putting his question. "Why doesn't she write or send me presents?" he asked.

His father's pause made him almost unbearably aware of the

man's chagrin in having opened the subject. He didn't look up at the boy as he answered. "Because legally she is not allowed to."

The remainder of the meal was passed in silent and mutual embarrassment.

Denny returned to his room as soon as he could respectfully quit the table, and while unlocking the door for an awful moment the possibility that the moth might have escaped, might never really have been there, scorched Denny's mind. But it was there, almost as he had left it, only now it had changed its position; the spread of its wings being nearly horizontal and in this position Denny realized that the lamp chimney was too narrow to allow it free movement.

There was no receptacle in the room any larger and in Denny's mind there paraded the various jars, the vases, and other vessels in the house that had from time to time in the past served as enclosures for his specimens. None of them was large enough. Without sufficient room, the moth as soon as it attempted flight would in no time at all damage its wings. In a kind of frenzy Denny racked his brains for the memory of some container that would satisfy his need. Like a ferret his thoughts suddenly pounced on what had eluded them. In his father's room a huge crystal tobacco jar with a lid of repoussé silver stood on an ebony taboret beneath the smirking head of a tiger.

There was no time to lose; for within five hours after emerging from the cocoon a moth will try its wings in flight. Breathlessly Denny bounded down the stairs and for a moment only hesitated before he knocked upon his father's door.

"Yes?" his father asked querulously, and Denny turned the knob and walked in.

"Father—" he began, but he had not as yet caught his breath.

"Speak up, boy, and stop shaking. Why, even confronted by a rogue elephant I never shook so."

"I want to b-b-borrow something," the boy managed to stammer.

"Be more explicit! Be more explicit! What do you want? A ticket to Fall River? A hundred-dollar bill? A dose of ipecac? The last would seem the most logical to judge from your looks."

Hating his father as he had never hated him before, the boy spoke up. "I want to borrow your tobacco jar."

"Which one?" the father parried. "The elephant foot the President gave me? The Benares brass? The Dutch pottery one? The music box?"

The boy could bear this bantering no longer. "I want that one."
And he pointed directly where it stood half full of tobacco.

"What for?" his father asked.

The boy's bravura was suddenly extinguished.

"Speak up. If you make an extraordinary request you must be
ready to back it up with a motive."

"I want it for a specimen."

"What's wrong with all the containers you have already ap-
propriated from kitchen, pantry, and parlor?"

Denny would not say they were not big enough. It might arouse
sufficient interest within his father so that he would insist on seeing
for himself what this monster was. Denny had a vision of his father
grabbing the moth and hastening to impale it upon the study wall,
adding it to his other conquests.

"They won't do," Denny said.

"Why won't they do?"

"They just won't."

"Be explicit!' his father thundered at him.

"I want to put some stuff in it that won't fit in the others."

"You will stand where you are without moving until you can tell
me what you mean by 'stuff.' " His father laid down his glasses and
settled back in his chair to underscore the fact that he was prepared
to wait all day if need be.

"Chrysalids and dirt and sticks and food for them," the boy
mumbled.

The man stared at Denny as if he were an animal he had at bay.

"You intend to put *that* filth into *that* jar?"

Denny made no answer. His father continued.

"Are you by any chance aware that that jar was a gift from the
Maharana of Udaipur? Have you any faintest conception of its
intrinsic value aside from the sentimental one? And can you see
from where you stand that, besides any other objections I might have,
the jar is being employed for what it was intended for? And if for
one moment you think I am going to remove my best tobacco from
my best jar so that you can use it for a worm bowl you are, my lad,
very much mistaken."

The man waited for the effect of his speech and then added, "Go
and ask Ethel for a crock."

It was useless for Denny to attempt to explain that he wouldn't
be able to see through a crock. Without a word he turned and
walked out of the room, leaving the door open behind him.

His father called him back, but he paid no mind. As he reached the second landing Denny heard the door slam downstairs.

A half hour had been wasted and, as he had been sure it would, the moth, having gained control over itself, was in the first struggles of flight.

There was only one thing to do. Denny went to the corner where he kept his equipment. Returning, he lifted the lid from the lamp chimney and reaching inside with his forceps he clenched the moth with a certain brutality, though he took pains to avoid injury to its wings. Lifting it out, the beauty of so few hours, Denny once again felt his omnipotence. Without hesitation he plunged the moth into the cyanide jar and screwed down the lid.

The wings beat frantically with the effort that should have carried the moth on its first flight through the spring air. Breathless, Denny watched for fear the wings would be injured. The dusty abdomen throbbed faster and faster, the antennae twitched from side to side; with a spasm the abdomen formed a curve to meet the thorax. The eyes, still bearing the unenlightened glaze of birth, turned suddenly into the unknowing glaze of death. But in the moment that they turned Denny thought he saw his distorted image gleaming on their black, china surfaces as if in that instant the moth had stored his image in its memory.

Denny unscrewed the cap, plucked out the moth and, piercing its body with a pin from the black paper packet, he pinned the moth to the wall at the foot of his bed. He gave it a place of honor, centering it upon a yellow willow tree. From his bed he would see it first thing in the morning and last thing at night.

A few days and nights passed, and Denny, though still on edge, felt somewhat as a hero must returning from a labor. The untimely death of the moth had perhaps been fortuitous, because now in its death the creature was irrevocably his.

The meadows were already filled with cabbage butterflies, and Denny would go out with his net and catch them, but they were too common to preserve and so, having captured them, he would reach his hand into the net and squash them, wiping the mess in his palm off on the grass.

It was less than a week after the death of the moth when Denny was awakened in the night by a persistent beating on his windowpane. He jumped from bed, switched on the light, and peered outside. With the light on he could see nothing, and whatever it had been was gone.

Realizing that though the light made anything outside invisible to him it would also act as a lure to whatever had tried to come in, he went back to bed leaving the light on and the window open. He tried to stay awake but soon fell back into sleep.

In the morning he looked about the room, but there was no sign of anything having entered. It must have been a June bug or possibly a lunar moth though it had sounded too heavy for one, thought Denny. He went over to look at the moth on the wall, a morning ritual with him. Although he could not be sure, the dust of one wing seemed to be smudged and the oily stain from the body had soaked into the wallpaper considerably since the day before. He put his face close to the insect to inspect it more fully. Instinctively he drew back; the odor was unbearable.

The following night Denny left his window wide open and shortly before midnight he was awakened by a beating of wings upon his face. Terrified and not fully conscious, he hit out with his open hands. He touched something and it wasn't pleasant. It was yielding and at the same time viscid. And something scratched against the palm of his hand like a tiny spur or horn.

Leaping from bed, Denny switched on the light. There was nothing in the room. It must have been a bat and the distasteful thought made him shudder. Whatever it had been, it left a stench behind not unlike the stench of the spot on the wall. Denny slammed the window shut and went back to bed and tried to sleep.

In the morning his red-rimmed eyes inspecting the moth plainly saw that not only were the wings smudged but that the simulacra of crabs and mouths upon the wings seemed to have grown more definite. The oily spot had spread still farther and the smell was stronger.

That night Denny slept with his window closed, but in his dreams he was beset by horned and squashy things that pounded his flesh with their fragile wings, and awakening in fright he heard the same sound as he had heard the previous night; something beating against the windowpane. All night it beat against the closed window and Denny lay rigid and sleepless in his bed and the smell within the room grew into something almost tangible.

At dawn Denny arose and forced himself to look at the moth. He held his nose as he did so and with horror he saw the stain on the paper and the crabs and the mouths which now not only seemed more definite but also considerably enlarged.

For the first time in months Denny left his room and did not return to it until it was his bedtime. Even that hour he contrived to postpone a little by asking his father to read to him. It was the lesser of two evils.

The stench in the room was such that although Denny dared not leave the window open he was forced to leave the door from the landing into his room ajar. What was left of the light in the hall below, after it had wormed its way up and around the stairs, crawled exhaustedly into the room. For some perverse reason it shone most brightly upon the wall where the moth was transfixed. From his bed Denny could not take his eyes off it. Though they made no progress, the two crabs on the hind wings appeared to be attempting to climb up into the two mouths on the fore wings. The mouths seemed to be very open and ready for them.

That night no sooner had the beating of wings upon the window awakened Denny than it abruptly ceased. The light downstairs was out and the room was now in darkness. Curling himself up into a ball and pulling the sheet over his head, Denny at length went off to sleep.

Sometime shortly afterward something came through the door and half crawled and half fluttered to the bed. Denny awoke with a scream, but it was too muffled for either his father or Ethel to hear because what caused him to scream had wormed its way beneath the sheet and was resting like a sticky pulp upon Denny's mouth.

Floundering like a drowning person, the boy threw back the covers and managed to dislodge whatever had been upon his mouth. When he dared to, he reached out and turned on the light. There was nothing in the room, but upon his sheets there were smudges of glistening dust almost black, almost purple, almost green, but not quite any of them.

Denny went down to breakfast without looking at the moth.

"No wonder you look ghastly," his father said to him, "if the smell in this house is half of what it must be in your room, it's a wonder you're not suffocated. What are you running up there? A Potters' Field for Lepidoptera? I'll give you until noon to get them out."

All day Denny left the window of his room wide open. It was the first of May and the sun was bright. As a sop to his father he brought down a box of duplicate specimens. He showed them to his father before disposing of them.

"Pugh!" said his father. "Dump them far away from the house."

That night Denny went to bed with both the door and window locked tight in spite of the smell. The moon was bright and shone all night unimpaired upon the wall. Denny could not keep his eyes off the moth.

By now both crabs and mouths were nearly as large as the wings themselves and the crabs were moving, Denny could swear. They appeared in relief, perhaps through some trick of chiaroscuro induced by the moonlight upon the dusty white and red markings. The claws seemed upon the verge of attacking the mouths, or were the so terribly white teeth of the mouths waiting to clamp down upon the crabs? Denny shuddered and closed his eyes.

Sleep came eventually, only to be broken in upon by the beating of wings against the windowpane. And no sooner had that ceased and Denny become less rigid than the thing was at the door beating urgently as though it must be let in. The only relief from the tap-tapping was an occasional, more solid thud against the panel of the door. It was, Denny guessed, caused by the soft and fleshy body of the thing.

If he survived the night Denny vowed he would destroy the thing upon the wall or, better than losing it entirely, he would give it to his father and he in turn would present it to some museum in Denny's name. Denny for a moment was able to forget the persistent rapping which had now returned to the window, for in his mind he saw a glass case with the moth in it and a little card below upon which was printed

Unique specimen Lepidoptera. Gift of Mr. Denny Longwood, Aged 12.

All through the night, first at the window, then at the door, the beating of the wings continued, relieved only by the occasional plop of the soft, heavy body.

Though having dozed for only an hour or two, with the bright light of day Denny felt his decision of the night before indefensible. The moth smelled; that was undeniable. The matter of the crab and mouthlike markings seeming to expand and become more intense in their color could probably be explained by somebody who knew about such things. As for the beating against the window and the door, it was probably as he had at first surmised, a bat or, if need be, two bats. The moth on the wall was dead, was his. He had hatched it and he knew the limitations of a moth dead or alive. He looked at it. The stain had spread so that now its diameter was as great as the spread of the wings. It was no longer exactly a stain, either. It looked as if a spoonful of dirty cereal had adhered to the wall; it was just about the color of mush. It will stop in time like the others; just as soon as the abdomen dries up, thought Denny.

At breakfast his father remarked that the smell as yet hadn't left the house, that it was in fact stronger if anything. Denny admitted it might take a day or two more before it was completely gone.

Before the meal was over his father told Denny that he was looking so badly that he had better see Dr. Phipps.

"How much do you weigh?" he asked.

Denny didn't know.

"You look," his father said, "all dried up like one of those pupae you had upstairs."

The moon shone bright again that night. In spite of his logic of the morning Denny felt sure that the movement of the white and vermilion crabs up to the white teeth and vermilion lips was more than just hallucination. And the beating of wings started at the window again. Then at the door. Then back to the window. And, in a way, worse than that the plop now and then of the body against the barrier. Though he tried to rise and look out when it was at the window, his limbs would not obey him. Hopelessly his eyes turned to the wall again. The crablike spots clicked their tiny claws together each time the wings struck against the windowpane. And each time the plump, squashy body went plop, the teeth snapped together between the thin-lipped mouths.

All at once the stench within the room became nauseating. There was nothing for Denny to do but make for the door while whatever it was still pounded at the window. As much as he feared and hated him, his father's cynical disbelief was to be preferred to this terror.

Denny refrained from switching on the light for fear that it would reveal his movements to the thing outside. Halfway across the room and shivering, he involuntarily turned his head and for a moment his feverish eyes saw what was outside before it disappeared.

Denny rushed for the door and unlocked it, but as he twisted the knob something beat against the other side of the door, pushing it open before Denny could shut the door against it.

When luncheon was over Ethel was sent upstairs to see what had happened. She was so hysterical when she came down that Denny's father went up to see for himself.

Denny lay in his pajamas on the floor just inside the door. The skin of his lonely and somewhat arrogant face was marred by the marks of something pincerlike and from his nose, eyes, ears, and mouth a network of viscid filaments stretched across his face and to the floor as though something had tried to bind his head up in them. His father had some trouble in lifting him up because the threads adhered so stubbornly to the nap of the blue carpet.

The body was feather light in the father's arms. The thought that the boy had certainly been underweight passed inanely through his father's mind.

As he carried his son out his eyes fell upon a spot on the wall at the foot of the bed. The pattern of a willow tree was completely obliterated by a creeping growth that looked like fungus. Still carrying his son, the man crossed over to it. A pin protruded from its center and it was from this spot, Mr. Longwood could tell, that the terrible smell came.

VINTAGE SEASON

C. L. Moore

THREE people came up the walk to the old mansion just at dawn on a perfect May morning. Oliver Wilson in his pajamas watched them from an upper window through a haze of conflicting emotions, resentment predominant. He didn't want them there.

They were foreigners. He knew only that much about them. They had the curious name of Sancisco, and their first names, scrawled in loops on the lease, appeared to be Omerie, Kleph and Klia, though it was impossible as he looked down upon them now to sort them out by signature. He hadn't even been sure whether they would be men or women, and he had expected something a little less cosmopolitan.

Oliver's heart sank a little as he watched them follow the taxi driver up the walk. He had hoped for less self-assurance in his unwelcome tenants, because he meant to force them out of the house if he could. It didn't look very promising from here.

The man went first. He was tall and dark, and he wore his clothes and carried his body with that peculiar arrogant assurance that comes from perfect confidence in every phase of one's being. The two women were laughing as they followed him. Their voices were light and sweet, and their faces were beautiful, each in its own exotic way, but the first thing Oliver thought of when he looked at them was, Expensive!

It was not only that patina of perfection that seemed to dwell in every line of their incredibly flawless garments. There are degrees of wealth beyond which wealth itself ceases to have significance.

100

Oliver had seen before, on rare occasions, something like this assurance that the earth turning beneath their well-shod feet turned only to their whim.

It puzzled him a little in this case, because he had the feeling as the three came up the walk that the beautiful clothing they wore so confidently was not clothing they were accustomed to. There was a curious air of condescension in the way they moved. Like women in costume. They minced a little on their delicate high heels, held out an arm to stare at the cut of a sleeve, twisted now and then inside their garments as if the clothing sat strangely on them, as if they were accustomed to something entirely different.

And there was an elegance about the way the garments fitted them which even to Oliver looked strikingly unusual. Only an actress on the screen, who can stop time and the film to adjust every disarrayed fold so that she looks perpetually perfect, might appear thus elegantly clad. But let these women move as they liked, and each fold of their clothing followed perfectly with the movement and fell perfectly into place again. One might almost suspect the garments were not cut of ordinary cloth, or that they were cut according to some unknown, subtle scheme, with many artful hidden seams placed by a tailor incredibly skilled at his trade.

They seemed excited. They talked in high, clear, very sweet voices, looking up at the perfect blue and transparent sky in which dawn was still frankly pink. They looked at the trees on the lawn, the leaves translucently green with an undercolor of golden newness, the edges crimped from constriction in the recent bud.

Happily and with excitement in their voices they called to the man, and when he answered, his own voice blended so perfectly in cadence with theirs that it sounded like three people singing together. Their voices, like their clothing, seemed to have an elegance far beyond the ordinary, to be under a control such as Oliver Wilson had never dreamed of before this morning.

The taxi driver brought up the luggage, which was of a beautiful pale stuff that did not look quite like leather, and had curves in it so subtle it seemed square until you saw how two or three pieces of it fitted together when carried, into a perfectly balanced block. It was scuffed, as if from much use. And though there was a great deal of it, the taxi-man did not seem to find his burden heavy. Oliver saw him look down at it now and then and heft the weight incredulously.

One of the women had very black hair and skin like cream, and smoke-blue eyes heavy-lidded with the weight of her lashes. It was the other woman Oliver's gaze followed as she came up the walk. Her hair was a clear, pale red, and her face had a softness that he thought would be like velvet to touch. She was tanned to a warm amber darker than her hair.

Just as they reached the porch steps the fair woman lifted her head and looked up. She gazed straight into Oliver's eyes and he saw that hers were very blue, and just a little amused, as if she had known he was there all along. Also they were frankly admiring.

Feeling a bit dizzy, Oliver hurried back to his room to dress.

"We are here on a vacation," the dark man said, accepting the keys. "We will not wish to be disturbed, as I made clear in our correspondence. You have engaged a cook and housemaid for us, I understand? We will expect you to move your own belongings out of the house, then, and—"

"Wait," Oliver said uncomfortably. "Something's come up. I—" He hesitated, not sure just how to present it. These were such increasingly odd people. Even their speech was odd. They spoke so distinctly, not slurring any of the words into contractions. English seemed as familiar to them as a native tongue, but they all spoke as trained singers sing, with perfect breath control and voice placement.

And there was a coldness in the man's voice, as if some gulf lay between him and Oliver, so deep no feeling of human contact could bridge it.

"I wonder," Oliver said, "if I could find you better living quarters somewhere else in town. There's a place across the street that—"

The dark woman said, "Oh, no!" in a lightly horrified voice, and all three of them laughed. It was cool, distant laughter that did not include Oliver.

The dark man said, "We chose this house carefully, Mr. Wilson. We would not be interested in living anywhere else."

Oliver said desperately, "I don't see why. It isn't even a modern house. I have two others in much better condition. Even across the street you'd have a fine view of the city. Here there isn't anything. The other houses cut off the view, and—"

"We engaged rooms here, Mr. Wilson," the man said with finality. "We expect to use them. Now will you make arrangements to leave as soon as possible?"

Oliver said, "No," and looked stubborn. "That isn't in the lease. You can live here until next month, since you paid for it, but you can't put me out. I'm staying."

The man opened his mouth to say something. He looked coldly at Oliver and closed it again. The feeling of aloofness was chill between them. There was a moment's silence. Then the man said, "Very well. Be kind enough to stay out of our way."

It was a little odd that he didn't inquire into Oliver's motives. Oliver was not yet sure enough of the man to explain. He couldn't very well say, "Since the lease was signed, I've been offered three times what the house is worth if I'll sell it before the end of May." He couldn't say, "I want the money, and I'm going to use my own nuisance-value to annoy you until you're willing to move out." After all, there seemed no reason why they shouldn't. After seeing them, there seemed doubly no reason, for it was clear they must be accustomed to surroundings infinitely better than this timeworn old house.

It was very strange, the value this house had so suddenly acquired. There was no reason at all why two groups of semi-anonymous people should be so eager to possess it for the month of May.

In silence Oliver showed his tenants upstairs to the three big bedrooms across the front of the house. He was intensely conscious of the red-haired woman and the way she watched him with a sort of obviously covert interest, quite warmly, and with a curious undertone to her interest that he could not quite place. It was familiar, but elusive. He thought how pleasant it would be to talk to her alone, if only to try to capture that elusive attitude and put a name to it.

Afterward he went down to the telephone and called his fiancée.

Sue's voice squeaked a little with excitement over the wire.

"Oliver, so early? Why, it's hardly six yet. Did you tell them what I said? Are they going to go?"

"Can't tell yet. I doubt it. After all, Sue, I did take their money, you know."

"Oliver, they've got to go! You've got to do something!"

"I'm trying, Sue. But I don't like it."

"Well, there isn't any reason why they shouldn't stay somewhere else. And we're going to need that money. You'll just have to think of something, Oliver."

Oliver met his own worried eyes in the mirror above the telephone and scowled at himself. His straw-colored hair was tangled and there was a shining stubble on his pleasant, tanned face. He was sorry the red-haired woman had first seen him in his untidy condition. Then his conscience smote him at the sound of Sue's determined voice and he said:

"I'll try, darling. I'll try. But I did take their money."

They had, in fact, paid a great deal of money, considerably more than the rooms were worth even in that year of high prices and high wages. The country was just moving into one of those fabulous eras which are later referred to as the Gay Forties or the Golden Sixties— a pleasant period of national euphoria. It was a stimulating time to be alive—while it lasted.

"All right," Oliver said resignedly. "I'll do my best."

But he was conscious, as the next few days went by, that he was not doing his best. There were several reasons for that. From the beginning the idea of making himself a nuisance to his tenants had been Sue's, not Oliver's. And if Oliver had been a little less determined the whole project would never have got under way. Reason was on Sue's side, but—

For one thing, the tenants were so fascinating. All they said and did had a queer sort of inversion to it, as if a mirror had been held up to ordinary living and in the reflection showed strange variations from the norm. Their minds worked on a different basic premise, Oliver thought, from his own. They seemed to derive covert amusement from the most unamusing things; they patronized, they were aloof with a quality of cold detachment which did not prevent them from laughing inexplicably far too often for Oliver's comfort.

He saw them occasionally, on their way to and from their rooms. They were polite and distant, not, he suspected, from anger at his presence but from sheer indifference.

Most of the day they spent out of the house. The perfect May weather held unbroken and they seemed to give themselves up wholeheartedly to admiration of it, entirely confident that the warm, pale-gold sunshine and the scented air would not be interrupted by rain or cold. They were so sure of it that Oliver felt uneasy.

They took only one meal a day in the house, a late dinner. And their reactions to the meal were unpredictable. Laughter greeted some of the dishes, and a sort of delicate digust others. No one would touch the salad, for instance. And the fish seemed to cause a wave of queer embarrassment around the table.

They dressed elaborately for each dinner. The man—his name was Omerie—looked extremely handsome in his dinner clothes, but he seemed a little sulky and Oliver twice heard the women laughing because he had to wear black. Oliver entertained a sudden vision, for no reason, of the man in garments as bright and as subtly cut as the women's, and it seemed somehow very right for him. He wore even the dark clothing with a certain flamboyance, as if cloth-of-gold would be more normal for him.

When they were in the house at other mealtimes, they ate in their rooms. They must have brought a great deal of food with them, from whatever mysterious place they had come. Oliver wondered with increasing curiosity where it might be. Delicious odors drifted into the hall sometimes, at odd hours, from their closed doors. Oliver could not identify them, but almost always they smelled irresistible. A few times the food smell was rather shockingly unpleasant, almost nauseating. It takes a connoisseur, Oliver reflected, to appreciate the decadent. And these people, most certainly, were connoisseurs.

Why they lived so contentedly in this huge ramshackle old house was a question that disturbed his dreams at night. Or why they refused to move. He caught some fascinating glimpses into their rooms, which appeared to have been changed almost completely by additions he could not have defined very clearly from the brief sights he had of them. The feeling of luxury which his first glance at them had evoked was confirmed by the richness of the hangings they had apparently brought with them, the half-glimpsed ornaments, the pictures on the walls, even the whiffs of exotic perfume that floated from half-open doors.

He saw the women go by him in the halls, moving softly through the brown dimness in their gowns so uncannily perfect in fit, so lushly rich, so glowingly colored they seemed unreal. That poise born of confidence in the subservience of the world gave them an imperious aloofness, but more than once Oliver, meeting the blue gaze of the woman with the red hair and the soft, tanned skin, thought he saw quickened interest there. She smiled at him in the dimness and went by in a haze of fragrance and a halo of incredible richness, and the warmth of the smile lingered after she had gone.

He knew she did not mean this aloofness to last between them. From the very first he was sure of that. When the time came she would make the opportunity to be alone with him. The thought was confusing and tremendously exciting. There was nothing he could do but wait, knowing she would see him when it suited her.

On the third day he lunched with Sue in a little downtown restaurant overlooking the great sweep of the metropolis across the river far below. Sue had shining brown curls and brown eyes, and her chin was a bit more prominent than is strictly accordant with beauty.

From childhood Sue had known what she wanted and how to get it, and it seemed to Oliver just now that she had never wanted anything quite so much as the sale of this house.

"It's such a marvelous offer for the old mausoleum," she said, breaking into a roll with a gesture of violence. "We'll never have a chance like that again, and prices are so high we'll need the money to start housekeeping. Surely you can do *something,* Oliver!"

"I'm trying," Oliver assured her uncomfortably.

"Have you heard anything more from that madwoman who wants to buy it?"

Oliver shook his head. "Her attorney phoned again yesterday. Nothing new. I wonder who she is."

"I don't think even the attorney knows. All this mystery—I don't like it, Oliver. Even those Sancisco people—What did they do today?"

Oliver laughed. "They spent about an hour this morning telephoning movie theaters in the city, checking up on a lot of third-rate films they want to see parts of."

"Parts of? But why?"

"I don't know. I think . . . oh, nothing. More coffee?"

The trouble was, he thought he did know. It was too unlikely a guess to tell Sue about, and without familiarity with the Sancisco oddities she would only think Oliver was losing his mind. But he had from their talk, a definite impression that there was an actor in bit parts in all these films whose performances they mentioned with something very near to awe. They referred to him as Golconda, which didn't appear to be his name, so that Oliver had no way of guessing which obscure bit-player it was they admired so deeply. Golconda might have been the name of a character he had once played—and with superlative skill, judging by the comments of the Sanciscos—but to Oliver it meant nothing at all.

"They do funny things," he said, stirring his coffee reflectively. "Yesterday Omerie—that's the man—came in with a book of poems published about five years ago, and all of them handled it like a first edition of Shakespeare. I never even heard of the author, but he seems to be a tin god in their country, wherever that is."

"You still don't know? Haven't they even dropped any hints?"

"We don't do much talking," Oliver reminded her with some irony.

"I know, but—Oh, well, I guess it doesn't matter. Go on, what else do they do?"

"Well, this morning they were going to spend studying 'Golconda' and his great art, and this afternoon I think they're taking a trip up the river to some sort of shrine I never heard of. It isn't very far, wherever it is, because I know they're coming back for dinner. Some great man's birthplace, I think—they promised to take home souvenirs of the place if they could get any. They're typical tourists, all right—if I could only figure out what's behind the whole thing. It doesn't make sense."

"Nothing about that house makes sense any more. I do wish—"

She went on in a petulant voice, but Oliver ceased suddenly to hear her, because just outside the door, walking with imperial elegance on her high heels, a familiar figure passed. He did not see her face, but he thought he would know that poise, that richness of line and motion, anywhere on earth.

"Excuse me a minute," he muttered to Sue, and was out of his chair before she could speak. He made the door in half a dozen long strides, and the beautifully elegant passerby was only a few steps away when he got there. Then, with the words he had meant to speak already half-uttered, he fell silent and stood there staring.

It was not the red-haired woman. It was not her dark companion. It was a stranger. He watched, speechless, while the lovely, imperious creature moved on through the crowd and vanished, moving with familiar poise and assurance and an equally familiar strangeness as if the beautiful and exquisitely fitted garments she wore were an exotic costume to her, as they had always seemed to the Sancisco women. Every other woman on the street looked untidy and ill at ease beside her. Walking like a queen, she melted into the crowd and was gone.

She came from *their* country, Oliver told himself dizzily. So someone else nearby had mysterious tenants in this month of perfect May weather. Someone else was puzzling in vain today over the strangeness of the people from the nameless land.

In silence he went back to Sue.

The door stood invitingly ajar in the brown dimness of the upper hall. Oliver's steps slowed as he drew near it, and his heart began to quicken correspondingly. It was the red-haired woman's room, and he thought the door was not open by accident. Her name, he knew now, was Kleph.

The door creaked a little on its hinges and from within a very sweet voice said lazily, "Won't you come in?"

The room looked very different indeed. The big bed had been pushed back against the wall, and a cover thrown over it that brushed the floor all around looked like soft-haired fur except that it was a pale blue-green and sparkled as if every hair were tipped with invisible crystals. Three books lay open on the fur, and a very curious-looking magazine with faintly luminous printing and a page of pictures that at first glance appeared three-dimensional. Also a tiny porcelain pipe encrusted with porcelain flowers, and a thin wisp of smoke floating from the bowl.

Above the bed a broad picture hung, framing a square of blue water so real Oliver had to look twice to be sure it was not rippling gently from left to right. From the ceiling swung a crystal globe on a glass cord. It turned gently, the light from the windows making curved rectangles in its sides.

Under the center window a sort of chaise longue stood which Oliver had not seen before. He could only assume it was at least partly pneumatic and had been brought in the luggage. There was a very rich-looking quilted cloth covering and hiding it, embossed all over in shining metallic patterns.

Kleph moved slowly from the door and sank upon the chaise longue with a little sigh of content. The couch accommodated itself to her body with what looked like delightful comfort. Kleph wriggled a little and then smiled up at Oliver.

"Do come on in. Sit over there, where you can see out the window. I love your beautiful spring weather. You know, there never was a May like it in civilized times." She said that quite seriously, her blue eyes on Oliver's, and there was a hint of patronage in her voice, as if the weather had been arranged especially for her.

Oliver started across the room and then paused and looked down in amazement at the floor, which felt unstable. He had not noticed before that the carpet was pure white, unspotted, and sank about an inch under the pressure of the feet. He saw then that Kleph's feet were bare, or almost bare. She wore something like gossamer buskins of filmy net, fitting her feet exactly. The bare soles were pink as if they had been rouged, and the nails had a liquid gleam like tiny mirrors. He moved closer, and was not as surprised as he should have been to see that they really were tiny mirrors, painted with some lacquer that gave them reflecting surfaces.

"Do sit down," Kleph said again, waving a white-sleeved arm toward a chair by the window. She wore a garment that looked like short, soft down, loosely cut but following perfectly every motion she made. And there was something curiously different about her very shape today. When Oliver saw her in street clothes, she had the square-shouldered, slim-flanked figure that all women strove for, but here in her lounging robe she looked—well, different. There was an almost swanlike slope to her shoulders today, a roundness and softness to her body that looked unfamiliar and very appealing.

"Will you have some tea?" Kleph asked, and smiled charmingly.

A low table beside her held a tray and several small covered cups, lovely things with an inner glow like rose quartz, the color shining deeply as if from within layer upon layer of translucence. She took up one of the cups—there were no saucers—and offered it to Oliver.

It felt fragile and thin as paper in his hand. He could not see the contents because of the cup's cover, which seemed to be one with the cup itself and left only a thin open crescent at the rim. Steam rose from the opening.

Kleph took up a cup of her own and tilted it to her lips, smiling at Oliver over the rim. She was very beautiful. The pale red hair lay in shining loops against her head and the corona of curls like a halo above her forehead might have been pressed down like a wreath. Every hair kept order as perfectly as if it had been painted on, though the breeze from the window stirred now and then among the softly shining strands.

Oliver tried the tea. Its flavor was exquisite, very hot, and the taste that lingered upon his tongue was like the scent of flowers. It was an extremely feminine drink. He sipped again, surprised to find how much he liked it.

The scent of flowers seemed to increase as he drank, swirling through his head like smoke. After the third sip there was a faint buzzing in his ears. The bees among the flowers, perhaps, he thought incoherently—and sipped again.

Kleph watched him, smiling.

"The others will be out all afternoon," she told Oliver comfortably. "I thought it would give us a pleasant time to be acquainted." Oliver was rather horrified to hear himself saying, "What makes you talk like that?" He had had no idea of asking the question; something seemed to have loosened his control over his own tongue.

Kleph's smile deepened. She tipped the cup to her lips and there was indulgence in her voice when she said, "What do you mean 'like that?' "

He waved his hand vaguely, noting with some surprise that at a glance it seemed to have six or seven fingers as it moved past his face.

"I don't know—precision, I guess. Why don't you say 'don't,' for instance?"

"In our country we are trained to speak with precision," Kleph explained. "Just as we are trained to move and dress and think with precision. Any slovenliness is trained out of us in childhood. With you, of course—" She was polite. "With you, this does not happen to be a national fetish. With us, we have time for the amenities. We like them."

Her voice had grown sweeter and sweeter as she spoke, until by now it was almost indistinguishable from the sweetness of the flower-scent in Oliver's head, and the delicate flavor of the tea.

"What country do you come from?" he asked, and tilted the cup again to drink, mildly surprised to notice that it seemed inexhaustible.

Kleph's smile was definitely patronizing this time. It didn't irritate him. Nothing could irritate him just now. The whole room swam in a beautiful rosy glow as fragrant as the flowers.

"We must not speak of that, Mr. Wilson."

"But—" Oliver paused. After all, it was, of course, none of his business. "This is a vacation?" he asked vaguely.

"Call it a pilgrimage, perhaps."

"Pilgrimage?" Oliver was so interested that for an instant his mind came back into sharp focus. "To—what?"

"I should not have said that, Mr. Wilson. Please forget it. Do you like the tea?"

"Very much."

"You will have guessed by now that it is not only tea, but an euphoriac."

Oliver stared. "Euphoriac?"

Kleph made a descriptive circle in the air with one graceful hand, and laughed. "You do not feel the effects yet? Surely you do?"

"I feel," Oliver said, "the way I'd feel after four whiskeys."

Kleph shuddered delicately. "We get our euphoria less painfully. And without the aftereffects your barbarous alcohols used to have." She bit her lip. "Sorry. I must be euphoric myself to speak so freely. Please forgive me. Shall we have some music?"

Kleph leaned backward on the chaise longue and reached toward the wall beside her. The sleeve, falling away from her round tanned arm, left bare the inside of the wrist, and Oliver was startled to see there a long, rosy streak of fading scar. His inhibitions had dissolved in the fumes of the fragrant tea; he caught his breath and leaned forward to stare.

Kleph shook the sleeve back over the scar with a quick gesture. Color came into her face beneath the softly tinted tan and she would not meet Oliver's eyes. A queer shame seemed to have fallen upon her.

Oliver said tactlessly, "What is it? What's the matter?"

Still she would not look at him. Much later he understood that shame and knew she had reason for it. Now he listened blankly as she said:

"Nothing . . . nothing at all. A . . . an inoculation. All of us . . . oh, never mind. Listen to the music."

This time she reached out with the other arm. She touched nothing, but when she had held her hand near the wall a sound breathed through the room. It was the sound of water, the sighing of waves receding upon long, sloped beaches. Oliver followed Kleph's gaze toward the picture of the blue water above the bed.

The waves there were moving. More than that, the point of vision moved. Slowly the seascape drifted past, moving with the waves, following them toward shore. Oliver watched, half-hypnotized by a motion that seemed at the time quite acceptable and not in the least surprising.

The waves lifted and broke in creaming foam and ran seething up a sandy beach. Then through the sound of the water music began to breathe, and through the water itself a man's face dawned in the frame, smiling intimately into the room. He held an oddly archaic musical instrument, lute-shaped, its body striped light and dark like a melon and its long neck bent back over his shoulder. He was singing, and Oliver felt mildly astonished at the song. It was very familiar and very odd indeed. He groped through the unfamiliar rhythms and found at last a thread to catch the tune by—it was "Make-Believe," from *Showboat,* but certainly a showboat that had never steamed up the Mississippi.

"What's he doing to it?" he demanded after a few moments of outraged listening. "I never heard anything like it!"

Kleph laughed and stretched out her arm again. Enigmatically she said, "We call it kyling. Never mind. How do you like this?"

It was a comedian, a man in semi-clown make-up, his eyes exaggerated so that they seemed to cover half his face. He stood by a broad glass pillar before a dark curtain and sang a gay, staccato song interspersed with patter that sounded impromptu, and all the while his left hand did an intricate, musical tattoo of the nailtips on the glass of the column. He strolled around and around it as he sang. The rhythms of his fingernails blended with the song and swung widely away into patterns of their own, and blended again without a break.

It was confusing to follow. The song made even less sense than the monologue, which had something to do with a lost slipper and was full of allusions which made Kleph smile, but were utterly unintelligible to Oliver. The man had a dry, brittle style that was not very amusing, though Kleph seemed fascinated. Oliver was interested to see in him an extension and a variation of that extreme smooth confidence which marked all three of the Sanciscos. Clearly a racial trait, he thought.

Other performances followed, some of them fragmentary as if lifted out of a completer version. One he knew. The obvious, stirring melody struck his recognition before the figures—marching men against a haze, a great banner rolling backward above them in the smoke, foreground figures striding gigantically and shouting in rhythm, "Forward, forward the lily banners go!"

The music was tinny, the images blurred and poorly colored, but there was a gusto about the performance that caught at Oliver's imagination. He stared, remembering the old film from long ago. Dennis King and a ragged chorus, singing "The Song of the Vagabonds" from—was it "Vagabond King?"

"A very old one," Kleph said apologetically. "But I like it."

The steam of the intoxicating tea swirled between Oliver and the picture. Music swelled and sank through the room and the fragrant fumes and his own euphoric brain. Nothing seemed strange. He had discovered how to drink the tea. Like nitrous oxide, the effect was not cumulative. When you reached a peak of euphoria, you could not increase the peak. It was best to wait for a slight dip in the effect of the stimulant before taking more.

Otherwise it had most of the effects of alcohol—everything after awhile dissolved into a delightful fog through which all he saw was uniformly enchanting and partook of the qualities of a dream. He questioned nothing. Afterward he was not certain how much of it he really had dreamed.

There was the dancing doll, for instance. He remembered it quite clearly, in sharp focus—a tiny, slender woman with a long-nosed, dark-eyed face and a pointed chin. She moved delicately across the white rug—knee-high, exquisite. Her features were as mobile as her body, and she danced lightly, with resounding strokes of her toes, each echoing like a bell. It was a formalized sort of dance, and she sang breathlessly in accompaniment, making amusing little grimaces. Certainly it was a portrait-doll, animated to mimic the original perfectly in voice and motion. Afterward, Oliver knew he must have dreamed it.

What else happened he was quite unable to remember later. He knew Kleph had said some curious things, but they all made sense at the time, and afterward he couldn't remember a word. He knew he had been offered little glittering candies in a transparent dish, and that some of them had been delicious and one or two so bitter his tongue still curled the next day when he recalled them, and one— Kleph sucked luxuriantly on the same kind—of a taste that was actively nauseating.

As for Kleph herself—he was frantically uncertain the next day what had really happened. He thought he could remember the softness of her white-downed arms clasped at the back of his neck, while she laughed up at him and exhaled into his face the flowery fragrance of the tea. But beyond that he was totally unable to recall anything, for a while.

There was a brief interlude later, before the oblivion of sleep. He was almost sure he remembered a moment when the other two Sanciscos stood looking down at him, the man scowling, the smoky-eyed woman smiling a derisive smile.

The man said, from a vast distance, "Kleph, you know this is against every rule—" His voice began in a thin hum and soared in fantastic flight beyond the range of hearing. Oliver thought he remembered the dark woman's laughter, thin and distant too, and the hum of her voice like bees in flight.

"Kleph, Kleph, you silly little fool, can we never trust you out of sight?"

Kleph's voice then said something that seemed to make no sense. "What does it matter, *here*?"

The man answered in that buzzing, faraway hum. "The matter of giving your bond before you leave, not to interfere. You know you signed the rules—"

Kleph's voice, nearer and more intelligible: "But here the difference is . . . it does not matter *here*! You both know that. How could it matter?"

Oliver felt the downy brush of her sleeve against his cheek, but he saw nothing except the slow, smokelike ebb and flow of darkness past his eyes. He heard the voices wrangle musically from far away, and he heard them cease.

When he woke the next morning, alone in his own room, he woke with the memory of Kleph's eyes upon him very sorrowfully, her lovely tanned face looking down on him with the red hair falling fragrantly on each side of it and sadness and compassion in her eyes. He thought he had probably dreamed that. There was no reason why anyone should look at him with such sadness.

Sue telephoned that day.

"Oliver, the people who want to buy the house are here. That madwoman and her husband. Shall I bring them over?"

Oliver's mind all day had been hazy with the vague, bewildering memories of yesterday. Kleph's face kept floating before him, blotting out the room. He said, "What? I . . . oh, well, bring them if you want to. I don't see what good it'll do."

"Oliver, what's wrong with you? We agreed we needed the money, didn't we? I don't see how you can think of passing up such a wonderful bargain without even a struggle. We could get married and buy our own house right away, and you know we'll never get such an offer again for that old trash-heap. Wake up, Oliver!"

Oliver made an effort. "I know, Sue—I know. But—"

"Oliver, you've got to think of something!" Her voice was imperious.

He knew she was right. Kleph or no Kleph, the bargain shouldn't be ignored if there was any way at all of getting the tenants out. He wondered again what made the place so suddenly priceless to so many people. And what the last week in May had to do with the value of the house.

A sudden sharp curiosity pierced even the vagueness of his mind today. May's last week was so important that the whole sale of the house stood or fell upon occupancy by then. Why? *Why?*

What's going to happen next week?" he asked rhetorically of the telephone. "Why can't they wait till these people leave? I'd knock a couple of thousand off the price if they'd—"

"You would not, Oliver Wilson! I can buy all our refrigeration units with that extra money. You'll just have to work out some way to give possession by next week, and that's that. You hear me?"

"Keep your shirt on," Oliver said practically. "I'm only human, but I'll try."

"I'm bringing the people over right away," Sue told him. "While the Sanciscos are still out. Now you put your mind to work and think of something, Oliver." She paused, and her voice was reflective when she spoke again. "They're . . . awfully odd people, darling."

"Odd?"

"You'll see."

It was an elderly woman and a very young man who trailed Sue up the walk. Oliver knew immediately what had struck Sue about them. He was somehow not at all surprised to see that both wore their clothing with the familiar air of elegant self-consciousness he had come to know so well. They, too, looked around them at the beautiful, sunny afternoon with conscious enjoyment and an air of faint condescension. He knew before he heard them speak how musical their voices would be and how meticulously they would pronounce each word.

There was no doubt about it. The people of Kleph's mysterious country were arriving here in force—for something. For the last week of May? He shrugged mentally; there was no way of guessing —yet. One thing only was sure: all of them must come from that nameless land where people controlled their voices like singers and their garments like actors who could stop the reel of time itself to adjust every disordered fold.

The elderly woman took full charge of the conversation from the start. They stood together on the rickety, unpainted porch, and Sue had no chance even for introductions.

"Young man, I am Madame Hollia. This is my husband." Her voice had an underrunning current of harshness, which was perhaps age. And her face looked almost corsetted, the loose flesh coerced into something like firmness by some invisible method Oliver could not guess at. The make-up was so skillful he could not be certain it was make-up at all, but he had a definite feeling that she was much older than she looked. It would have taken a lifetime of command to put so much authority into the harsh, deep, musically controlled voice.

The young man said nothing. He was very handsome. His type, apparently, was one that does not change much no matter in what culture or country it may occur. He wore beautifully tailored garments and carried in one gloved hand a box of red leather, about the size and shape of a book.

Madame Hollia went on. "I understand your problem about the house. You wish to sell to me, but are legally bound by your lease with Omerie and his friends. Is that right?"

Oliver nodded. "But—"

"Let me finish. If Omerie can be forced to vacate before next week, you will accept our offer. Right? Very well. Hara!" She nodded to the young man beside her. He jumped to instant attention, bowed slightly, said, "Yes, Hollia," and slipped a gloved hand into his coat.

Madame Hollia took the little object offered on his palm, her gesture as she reached for it almost imperial, as if royal robes swept from her outstretched arm.

"Here," she said, "is something that may help us. My dear—" She held it out to Sue—"if you can hide this somewhere about the house, I believe your unwelcome tenants will not trouble you much longer."

Sue took the thing curiously. It looked like a tiny silver box, no more than an inch square, indented at the top and with no line to show it could be opened.

"Wait a minute," Oliver broke in uneasily. "What is it?"

"Nothing that will harm anyone, I assure you."

"Then what—"

Madame Hollia's imperious gesture at one sweep silenced him and commanded Sue forward. "Go on, my dear. Hurry, before Omerie comes back. I can assure you there is no danger to anyone."

Oliver broke in determinedly. "Madame Hollia, I'll have to know what your plans are. I—"

"Oh, Oliver, please!" Sue's fingers closed over the silver cube. "Don't worry about it. I'm sure Madame Hollia knows best. Don't you *want* to get those people out?"

"Of course I do. But I don't want the house blown up or—"

Madame Hollia's deep laughter was indulgent. "Nothing so crude, I promise you, Mr. Wilson. Remember, we want the house! Hurry, my dear."

Sue nodded and slipped hastily past Oliver into the hall. Outnumbered, he subsided uneasily. The young man, Hara, tapped a negligent foot and admired the sunlight as they waited. It was an afternoon as perfect as all of May had been, translucent gold, balmy with an edge of chill lingering in the air to point up a perfect contrast with the summer to come. Hara looked around him confidently, like a man paying just tribute to a stage-set provided wholly for himself. He even glanced up at a drone from above and followed the course of a big transcontinental plane half dissolved in golden haze high in the sun. "Quaint," he murmured in a gratified voice.

Sue came back and slipped her hand through Oliver's arm, squeezing excitedly. "There," she said. "How long will it take, Madame Hollia?"

"That will depend, my dear. Not very long. Now, Mr. Wilson, one word with you. You live here also, I understand? For your own comfort, take my advice and—".

Somewhere within the house a door slammed and a clear high voice rang wordlessly up a rippling scale. Then there was the sound of feet on the stairs, and a single line of song, *"Come hider, love, to me—"*

Hara started, almost dropping the red leather box he held.

"Kleph!" he said in a whisper. "Or Kial. I know they both just came on from Canterbury. But I thought—"

"Hush." Madame Hollia's features composed themselves into an imperious blank. She breathed triumphantly through her nose, drew back upon herself and turned an imposing facade to the door.

Kleph wore the same softly downy robe Oliver had seen before, except that today it was not white, but a pale, clear blue that gave her tan an apricot flush. She was smiling.

"Why, Hollia!" Her tone was at its most musical. "I thought I recognized voices from home. How nice to see you. No one knew you were coming to the—" She broke off and glanced at Oliver and then away again. "Hara, too," she said. "What a pleasant surprise."

Sue said flatly, "When did *you* get back?"

Kleph smiled at her. "You must be the little Miss Johnson. Why, I did not go out at all. I was tired of sightseeing. I have been napping in my room."

Sue drew in her breath in something that just escaped being a disbelieving sniff. A look flashed between the two women, and for an instant held—and that instant was timeless. It was an extraordinary pause in which a great deal of wordless interplay took place in the space of a second.

Oliver saw the quality of Kleph's smile at Sue, that same look of quiet confidence he had noticed so often about all of these strange people. He saw Sue's quick inventory of the other woman, and he saw how Sue squared her shoulders and stood up straight, smoothing down her summer frock over her flat hips so that for an instant she stood posed consciously, looking down on Kleph. It was deliberate. Bewildered, he glanced again at Kleph.

Kleph's shoulders sloped softly, her robe was belted to a tiny waist and hung in deep folds over frankly rounded hips. Sue's was the fashionable figure—but Sue was the first to surrender.

Kleph's smile did not falter. But in the silence there was an abrupt reversal of values, based on no more than the measureless quality of Kleph's confidence in herself, the quiet, assured smile. It was suddenly made very clear that fashion is not a constant. Kleph's curious, out-of-mode curves without warning became the norm, and Sue was a queer, angular, half-masculine creature beside her.

Oliver had no idea how it was done. Somehow the authority passed in a breath from one woman to the other. Beauty is almost wholly a matter of fashion; what is beautiful today would have been grotesque a couple of generations ago and will be grotesque a hundred years ahead. It will be worse than grotesque; it will be outmoded and therefore faintly ridiculous.

Sue was that. Kleph had only to exert her authority to make it clear to everyone on the porch. Kleph was a beauty, suddenly and very convincingly, beautiful in the accepted mode, and Sue was amusingly old-fashioned, an anachronism in her lithe, square-shouldered slimness. She did not belong. She was grotesque among these strangely immaculate people.

Sue's collapse was complete. But pride sustained her, and bewilderment. Probably she never did grasp entirely what was wrong. She gave Kleph one glance of burning resentment and when her eyes came back to Oliver there was suspicion in them, and mistrust.

Looking backward later, Oliver thought that in that moment, for the first time clearly, he began to suspect the truth. But he had no time to ponder it, for after the brief instant of enmity the three people from—elsewhere—began to speak all at once, as if in a belated attempt to cover something they did not want noticed.

Kleph said, "This beautiful weather—" and Madame Hollia said, "So fortunate to have this house—" and Hara, holding up the red leather box, said loudest of all, "Cenbe sent you this, Kleph. His latest."

Kleph put out both hands for it eagerly, the eiderdown sleeves falling back from her rounded arms. Oliver had a quick glimpse of that mysterious scar before the sleeve fell back, and it seemed to him that there was the faintest trace of a similar scar vanishing into Hara's cuff as he let his own arm drop.

"Cenbe!" Kleph cried, her voice high and sweet and delighted. "How wonderful! What period?"

"From November, 1664," Hara said. "London, of course, though I think there may be some counterpoint from the 1347 November. He hasn't finished—of course." He glanced almost nervously at Oliver and Sue. "A wonderful example," he said quickly. "Marvelous. If you have the taste for it, of course."

Madame Hollia shuddered with ponderous delicacy. "That man!" she said. "Fascinating, of course—a great man. But—so *advanced!*"

"It takes a connoisseur to appreciate Cenbe's work fully," Kleph said in a slightly tart voice. "We all admit that."

"Oh yes, we all bow to Cenbe," Hollia conceded. "I confess the man terrifies me a little, my dear. Do we expect him to join us?"

"I suppose so," Kleph said. "If his—work—is not yet finished, then of course. You know Cenbe's tastes."

Hollia and Hara laughed together "I know when to look for him, then," Hollia said. She glanced at the staring Oliver and the subdued but angry Sue, and with a commanding effort brought the subject back into line.

"So fortunate, my dear Kleph, to have this house," she declared heavily. "I saw a tridimensional of it—afterward—and it was still quite perfect. Such a fortunate coincidence. Would you consider parting with your lease, for a consideration? Say, a coronation seat at—"

"Nothing could buy us, Hollia," Kleph told her gaily, clasping the red box to her bosom.

Hollia gave her a cool stare. "You may change your mind, my dear Kleph," she said pontifically. "There is still time. You can always reach us through Mr. Wilson here. We have rooms up the street in the Montgomery House—nothing like yours, of course, but they will do. For us, they will do."

Oliver blinked. The Montgomery House was the most expensive hotel in town. Compared to this collapsing old ruin, it was a palace. There was no understanding these people. Their values seemed to have suffered a complete reversal.

Madame Hollia moved majestically toward the steps.

"Very pleasant to see you, my dear," she said over one well-padded shoulder. "Enjoy your stay. My regards to Omerie and Klia. Mr. Wilson—" she nodded toward the walk. "A word with you."

Oliver followed her down toward the street. Madame Hollia paused halfway there and touched his arm.

"One word of advice," she said huskily. "You say you sleep here? Move out, young man. Move out before tonight."

Oliver was searching in a half-desultory fashion for the hiding place Sue had found for the mysterious silver cube, when the first sounds from above began to drift down the stairwell toward him. Kleph had closed her door, but the house was old, and strange qualities in the noise overhead seemed to seep through the woodwork like an almost visible stain.

It was music, in a way. But much more than music. And it was a terrible sound, the sounds of calamity and of all human reaction to calamity, everything from hysteria to heartbreak, from irrational joy to rationalized acceptance.

The calamity was—single. The music did not attempt to correlate all human sorrows; it focused sharply upon one and followed the ramifications out and out. Oliver recognized these basics to the sounds in a very brief moment. They were essentials, and they seemed to beat into his brain with the first strains of the music which was so much more than music.

But when he lifted his head to listen he lost all grasp upon the meaning of the noise and it was sheer medley and confusion. To think of it was to blur it hopelessly in the mind, and he could not recapture that first instant of unreasoning acceptance.

He went upstairs almost in a daze, hardly knowing what he was doing. He pushed Kleph's door open. He looked inside—

What he saw there he could not afterward remember except in a blurring as vague as the blurred ideas the music roused in his brain. Half the room had vanished behind a mist, and the mist was a three-dimensional screen upon which were projected— He had no words for them. He was not even sure if the projections were visual. The mist was spinning with motion and sound, but essentially it was neither sound nor motion that Oliver saw.

This was a work of art. Oliver knew no name for it. It transcended all art-forms he knew, blended them, and out of the blend produced subtleties his mind could not begin to grasp. Basically, this was the attempt of a master composer to correlate every essential aspect of a vast human experience into something that could be conveyed in a few moments to every sense at once.

The shifting visions on the screen were not pictures in themselves, but hints of pictures, subtly selected outlines that plucked at the mind and with one deft touch set whole chords ringing through the memory. Perhaps each beholder reacted differently, since it was in the eye and the mind of the beholder that the truth of the picture lay. No two would be aware of the same symphonic panorama, but each would see essentially the same terrible story unfold.

Every sense was touched by that deft and merciless genius. Color and shape and motion flickered in the screen, hinting much, evoking unbearable memories deep in the mind; odors floated from the screen and touched the heart of the beholder more poignantly than anything visual could do. The skin crawled sometimes as if to a tangible cold hand laid upon it. The tongue curled with remembered bitterness and remembered sweet.

It was outrageous. It violated the innermost privacies of a man's mind, called up secret things long ago walled off behind mental scar tissue, forced its terrible message upon the beholder relentlessly though the mind might threaten to crack beneath the stress of it.

And yet, in spite of all this vivid awareness, Oliver did not know what calamity the screen portrayed. That it was real, vast, overwhelmingly dreadful he could not doubt. That it had once happened was unmistakable. He caught flashing glimpses of human faces distorted with grief and disease and death—real faces, faces that had once lived and were seen now in the instant of dying. He saw men and women in rich clothing superimposed in panorama upon reeling thousands of ragged folk; great throngs of them swept past the sight in an instant, and he saw that death made no distinction among them.

He saw lovely women laugh and shake their curls, and the laughter shriek into hysteria and the hysteria into music. He saw one man's face, over and over—a long, dark, saturnine face, deeply lined, sorrowful, the face of a powerful man wise in worldliness, urbane—and helpless. That face was for awhile a recurring motif, always more tortured, more helpless than before.

The music broke off in the midst of a rising glide. The mist vanished and the room reappeared before him. The anguished dark face for an instant seemed to Oliver printed everywhere he looked, like after-vision on the eyelids. He knew that face. He had seen it before, not often, but he should know its name—

"Oliver, Oliver—" Kleph's sweet voice came out of a fog at him. He was leaning dizzily against the doorpost looking down into her eyes. She, too, had that dazed blankness he must show on his own face. The power of the dreadful symphony still held them both. But even in this confused moment Oliver saw that Kleph had been enjoying the experience.

He felt sickened to the depths of his mind, dizzy with sickness and revulsion because of the super-imposing of human miseries he had just beheld. But Kleph—only appreciation showed upon her face. To her it had been magnificence, and magnificence only.

Irrelevantly Oliver remembered the nauseating candies she had enjoyed, the nauseating odors of strange food that drifted sometimes through the hall from her room.

What was it she had said downstairs a little while ago? Connoisseur, that was it. Only a connoisseur could appreciate work as—as *advanced*—as the work of someone called Cenbe.

A whiff of intoxicating sweetness curled past Oliver's face. Something cool and smooth was pressed into his hand.

"Oh, Oliver, I am so sorry," Kleph's voice murmured contritely. "Here, drink the euphoriac and you will feel better. Please drink!"

The familiar fragrance of the hot sweet tea was on his tongue before he knew he had complied. Its relaxing fumes floated up through his brain and in a moment or two the world felt stable around him again. The room was as it had always been. And Kleph—

Her eyes were very bright. Sympathy showed in them for him, but for herself she was still brimmed with the high elation of what she had just been experiencing.

"Come and sit down," she said gently, tugging at his arm. "I am so sorry—I should not have played that over, where you could hear it. I have no excuse, really. It was only that I forgot what the effect might be on one who had never heard Cenbe's symphonies before. I was so impatient to see what he had done with . . . with his new subject. I am so very sorry, Oliver!"

"What was it?" His voice sounded steadier than he had expected. The tea was responsible for that. He sipped again, glad of the consoling euphoria its fragrance brought.

"A . . . a composite interpretation of . . . oh, Oliver, you know I must not answer questions!"

"But—"

"No—drink your tea and forget what it was you saw. Think of other things. Here, we will have music—another kind of music, something gay—"

She reached for the wall beside the window, and as before, Oliver saw the broad framed picture of blue water above the bed ripple and grow pale. Through it another scene began to dawn like shapes rising beneath the surface of the sea.

He had a glimpse of a dark-curtained stage upon which a man in a tight dark tunic and hose moved with a restless, sidelong pace, his hands and face startingly pale against the black about him. He limped; he had a crooked back and he spoke familiar lines. Oliver had seen John Barrymore once as the crook-backed Richard, and it seemed vaguely outrageous to him that any other actor should essay that difficult part. This one he had never seen before, but the man had a fascinatingly smooth manner and his interpretation of the Plantagenet king was quite new and something Shakespeare probably never dreamed of.

"No," Kleph said, "not this. Nothing gloomy." And she put out her hand again. The nameless new Richard faded and there was a swirl of changing pictures and changing voices, all blurred together, before the scene steadied upon a stageful of dancers in pastel ballet skirts, drifting effortlessly through some complicated pattern of motion. The music that went with it was light and effortless too. The room filled up with the clear, floating melody.

Oliver set down his cup. He felt much surer of himself now, and he thought the euphoriac had done all it could for him. He didn't want to blur again mentally. There were things he meant to learn about. Now. He considered how to begin.

Kleph was watching him. "That Hollia," she said suddenly. "She wants to buy the house?"

Oliver nodded. "She's offering a lot of money. Sue's going to be awfully disappointed if—" He hesitated. Perhaps, after all, Sue would not be disappointed. He remembered the little silver cube with the enigmatic function and he wondered if he should mention it to Kleph. But the euphoriac had not reached that level of his brain, and he remembered his duty to Sue and was silent.

Kleph shook her head, her eyes upon his warm with—was it sympathy?

"Believe me," she said, "you will not find that—important—after all. I promise you, Oliver."

He stared at her. "I wish you'd explain."

Kleph laughed on a note more sorrowful than amused. But it occurred to Oliver suddenly that there was no longer condescension in her voice. Imperceptibly that air of delicate amusement had vanished from her manner toward him. The cool detachment that still marked Omerie's attitude, and Klia's, was not in Kleph's any more. It was a subtlety he did not think she could assume. It had to come spontaneously or not at all. And for no reason he was willing to examine, it became suddenly very important to Oliver that Kleph should not condescend to him, that she should feel toward him as he felt toward her. He would not think of it.

He looked down at his cup, rose-quartz, exhaling a thin plume of steam from its crescent-slit opening. This time, he thought, maybe he could make the tea work for him. For he remembered how it loosened the tongue, and there was a great deal he needed to know. The idea that had come to him on the porch in the instant of silent rivalry between Kleph and Sue seemed now too fantastic to entertain. But some answer there must be.

Kleph herself gave him the opening.

"I must not take too much euphoriac this afternoon," she said, smiling at him over her pink cup. "It will make me drowsy, and we are going out this evening with friends."

"More friends?" Oliver asked. "From your country?"

Kleph nodded. "Very dear friends we have expected all this week."

"I wish you'd tell me," Oliver said bluntly, "where it is you come from. It isn't from here. Your culture is too different from ours— even your names—" He broke off as Kleph shook her head.

"I wish I could tell you. But that is against all the rules. It is even against the rules for me to be here talking to you now."

"What rules?"

She made a helpless gesture. "You must not ask me, Oliver." She leaned back on the chaise longue, which adjusted itself luxuriously to the motion, and smiled very sweetly at him. "We must not talk about things like that. Forget it, listen to the music, enjoy yourself if you can—" She closed her eyes and laid her head back against the cushions. Oliver saw the round tanned throat swell as she began to hum a tune. Eyes still closed, she sang again the words she had sung upon the stairs, *"Come hider, love, to me—"*

A memory clicked over suddenly in Oliver's mind. He had never heard the queer, lagging tune before, but he thought he knew the words. He remembered what Hollia's husband had said when he heard that line of song, and he leaned forward. She would not answer a direct question, but perhaps—

"Was the weather this warm in Canterbury?" he asked, and held his breath. Kleph hummed another line of the song and shook her head, eyes still closed.

"It was autumn there," she said. "But bright, wonderfully bright. Even their clothing, you know . . . everyone was singing that new song, and I can't get it out of my head." She sang another line, and the words were almost unintelligible—English, yet not an English Oliver could understand.

He stood up. "Wait," he said. "I want to find something. Back in a minute."

She opened her eyes and smiled mistily at him, still humming. He went downstairs as fast as he could—the stairway swayed a little, though his head was nearly clear now—and into the library. The book he wanted was old and battered, interlined with the penciled notes of his college days. He did not remember very clearly where the passage he wanted was, but he thumbed fast through the columns and by sheer luck found it within a few minutes. Then he went back upstairs, feeling a strange emptiness in his stomach because of what he almost believed now.

"Kleph," he said firmly, "I know that song. I know the year it was new."

Her lids rose slowly; she looked at him through a mist of euphoriac. He was not sure she had understood. For a long moment she held him with her gaze. Then she put out one downy-sleeved arm and spread her tanned fingers toward him. She laughed deep in her throat.

"Come hider, love, to me," she said.

He crossed the room slowly, took her hand. The fingers closed warmly about his. She pulled him down so that he had to kneel beside her. Her other arm lifted. Again she laughed, very softly, and closed her eyes, lifting her face to his.

The kiss was warm and long. He caught something of her own euphoria from the fragrance of the tea breathed into his face. And he was startled at the end of the kiss, when the clasp of her arms loosened about his neck, to feel the sudden rush of her breath against his cheek. There were tears on her face, and the sound she made was a sob.

He held her off and looked down in amazement. She sobbed once more, caught a deep breath, and said, "Oh, Oliver, Oliver—" Then she shook her head and pulled free, turning away to hide her face. "I . . . I am sorry," she said unevenly. "Please forgive me. It does not matter . . . I *know* it does not matter . . . but—"

"What's wrong? What doesn't matter?"

"Nothing. Nothing . . . please forget it. Nothing at all." She got a handkerchief from the table and blew her nose, smiling at him with an effect of radiance through the tears.

Suddenly he was very angry. He had heard enough evasions and mystifying half-truths. He said roughly, "Do you think I'm crazy? I know enough now to—"

"Oliver, please!" She held up her own cup, steaming fragrantly. "Please, no more questions. Here, euphoria is what you need, Oliver. Euphoria, not answers."

"What year was it when you heard that song in Canterbury?" he demanded, pushing the cup aside.

She blinked at him, tears bright on her lashes. "Why . . . what year do you think?"

"I know," Oliver told her grimly. "I know the year that song was popular. I know you just came from Canterbury—Hollia's husband said so. It's May now, but it was autumn in Canterbury, and you just came from there, so lately the song you heard is still running through your head. Chaucer's Pardoner sang that song some time around the end of the fourteenth century. Did you see Chaucer, Kleph? What was it like in England that long ago?"

Kleph's eyes fixed his for a silent moment. Then her shoulders drooped and her whole body went limp with resignation beneath the soft blue robe. "I am a fool," she said gently. "It must have been easy to trap me. You really believe—what you say?"

Oliver nodded.

She said in a low voice. "Few people do believe it. That is one of our maxims, when we travel. We are safe from much suspicion because people before The Travel began will not believe."

The emptiness in Oliver's stomach suddenly doubled in volume. For an instant the bottom dropped out of time itself and the universe was unsteady about him. He felt sick. He felt naked and helpless. There was a buzzing in his ears and the room dimmed before him.

He had not really believed—not until this instant. He had expected some rational explanation from her that would tidy all his wild half-thoughts and suspicions into something a man could accept as believable. Not this.

Kleph dabbed at her eyes with the pale-blue handkerchief and smiled tremulously.

"I know," she said. "It must be a terrible thing to accept. To have all your concepts turned upside down— We know it from childhood, of course, but for you . . . Here, Oliver, the euphoriac will make it easier."

He took the cup, the faint stain of her lip rouge still on the crescent opening. He drank, feeling the dizzy sweetness spiral through his head, and his brain turned a little in his skull as the volatile fragrance took effect. With that turning, focus shifted and all his values with it.

He began to feel better. The flesh settled on his bones again, and the warm clothing of temporal assurance settled upon his flesh, and he was no longer naked and in the vortex of unstable time.

"The story is very simple, really," Kleph said. "We—travel. Our own time is not terribly far ahead of yours. No. I must not say how far. But we still remember your songs and poets and some of your great actors. We are a people of much leisure, and we cultivate the art of enjoying ourselves.

"This is a tour we are making—a tour of a year's seasons. Vintage seasons. That autumn in Canterbury was the most magnificent autumn our researchers could discover anywhere. We rode in a pilgrimage to the shrine—it was a wonderful experience, though the clothing was a little hard to manage.

"Now this month of May is almost over—the loveliest May in recorded times. A perfect May in a wonderful period. You have no way of knowing what a good, gay period you live in, Oliver. The very feeling in the air of the cities—that wonderful national confidence and happiness—everything going as smoothly as a dream. There were other Mays with fine weather, but each of them had a war or a famine, or something else wrong." She hesitated, grimaced and went on rapidly. "In a few days we are to meet at a coronation in Rome," she said. "I think the year will be 800—Christmastime. We—"

"But why," Oliver interrupted, "did you insist on this house? Why do the others want to get it away from you?"

Kleph stared at him. He saw the tears rising again in small bright crescents that gathered above her lower lids. He saw the look of obstinacy that came upon her soft, tanned face. She shook her head.

"You must not ask me that." She held out the steaming cup. "Here, drink and forget what I have said. I can tell you no more. No more at all."

When he woke, for a little while he had no idea where he was. He did not remember leaving Kleph or coming to his own room. He didn't care, just then. For he woke to a sense of overwhelming terror. The dark was full of it. His brain rocked on waves of fear and pain. He lay motionless, too frightened to stir, some atavistic memory warning him to lie quiet until he knew from which direction the danger threatened. Reasonless panic broke over him in a tidal flow; his head ached with its violence and the dark throbbed to the same rhythms.

A knock sounded at the door. Omerie's deep voice said, "Wilson! Wilson, are you awake?"

Oliver tried twice before he had breath to answer. "Y-yes—what is it?"

The knob rattled. Omerie's dim figure groped for the light switch and the room sprang into visibility. Omerie's face was drawn with strain, and he held one hand to his head as if it ached in rhythm with Oliver's.

It was in that moment, before Omerie spoke again, that Oliver remembered Hollia's warning. "Move out, young man—move out before tonight." Wildly he wondered what threatened them all in this dark house that throbbed with the rhythms of pure terror.

Omerie in an angry voice answered the unspoken question.

"Someone has planted a subsonic in the house, Wilson. Kleph thinks you may know where it is."

"S-subsonic?"

"Call it a gadget," Omerie interpreted impatiently. "Probably a small metal box that—"

Oliver said, "Oh," in a tone that must have told Omerie everything. "Where is it?" he demanded. "Quick. Let's get this over."

"I don't know." With an effort Oliver controlled the chattering of his teeth. "Y-you mean all this—all this is just from the little box?"

"Of course. Now tell me how to find it before we all go crazy."

Oliver got shakily out of bed, groping for his robe with nerveless hands. "I s-suppose she hid it somewhere downstairs," he said. "S-she wasn't gone long."

Omerie got the story out of him in a few brief questions. He clicked his teeth in exasperation when Oliver had finished it.

"That stupid Hollia—"

"Omerie!" Kleph's plaintive voice wailed from the hall. "Please hurry, Omerie! This is too much to stand! Oh, Omerie, please!"

Oliver stood up abruptly. Then a redoubled wave of the inexplicable pain seemed to explode in his skull at the motion, and he clutched the bedpost and reeled.

"Go find the thing yourself," he heard himself saying dizzily. "I can't even walk—"

Omerie's own temper was drawn wire-tight by the pressure in the room. He seized Oliver's shoulder and shook him, saying in a tight voice, "You let it in—now help us get it out, or—"

"It's a gadget out of your world, not mine!" Oliver said furiously.

And then it seemed to him there was a sudden coldness and silence in the room. Even the pain and the senseless terror paused for a moment. Omerie's pale, cold eyes fixed upon Oliver a stare so chill he could almost feel the ice in it.

"What do you know about our—world?" Omerie demanded.

Oliver did not speak a word. He did not need to; his face must have betrayed what he knew. He was beyond concealment in the stress of this night-time terror he still could not understand.

Omerie bared his white teeth and said three perfectly unintelligible words. Then he stepped to the door and snapped, "Kleph!"

Oliver could see the two women huddled together in the hall, shaking violently with involuntary waves of that strange, synthetic terror. Klia, in a luminous green gown, was rigid with control, but Kleph made no effort whatever at repression. Her downy robe had turned soft gold tonight; she shivered in it and the tears ran down her face unchecked.

"Kleph," Omerie said in a dangerous voice, "you were euphoric again yesterday?"

Kleph darted a scared glance at Oliver and nodded guiltily.

"You talked too much." It was a complete indictment in one sentence. "You know the rules, Kleph. You will not be allowed to travel again if anyone reports this to the authorities."

Kleph's lovely creamy face creased suddenly into impenitent dimples.

"I know it was wrong. I am very sorry—but you will not stop me if Cenbe says no."

Klia flung out her arms in a gesture of helpless anger. Omerie shrugged. "In this case, as it happens, no great harm is done," he said, giving Oliver an unfathomable glance. "But it might have been serious. Next time perhaps it will be. I must have a talk with Cenbe."

"We must find the subsonic first of all," Klia reminded them, shivering. "If Kleph is afraid to help, she can go out for a while. I confess I am very sick of Kleph's company just now."

"We could give up the house!" Kleph cried wildly. "Let Hollia have it! How can you stand this long enough to hunt—"

"Give up the house?" Klia echoed. "You must be mad! With all our invitations out?"

"There will be no need for that," Omerie said. "We can find it if we all hunt. You feel able to help?" He looked at Oliver.

With an effort Oliver controlled his own senseless panic as the waves of it swept through the room. "Yes," he said. "But what about me? What are you going to do?"

"That should be obvious," Omerie said, his pale eyes in the dark face regarding Oliver impassively. "Keep you in the house until we go. We can certainly do no less. You understand that. And there is no reason for us to do more, as it happens. Silence is all we promised when we signed our travel papers."

"But——" Oliver groped for the fallacy in that reasoning. It was no use. He could not think clearly. Panic surged insanely through his mind from the very air around him. "All right," he said. "Let's hunt."

It was dawn before they found the box, tucked inside the ripped seam of a sofa cushion. Omerie took it upstairs without a word. Five minutes later the pressure in the air abruptly dropped and peace fell blissfully upon the house.

"They will try again," Omerie said to Oliver at the door of the back bedroom. "We must watch for that. As for you, I must see that you remain in the house until Friday. For your own comfort, I advise you to let me know if Hollia offers any further tricks. I confess I am not quite sure how to enforce your staying indoors. I could use methods that would make you very uncomfortable. I would prefer to accept your word on it."

Oliver hesitated. The relaxing of pressure upon his brain had left him exhausted and stupid, and he was not at all sure what to say.

Omerie went on after a moment. "It was partly our fault for not insuring that we had the house to ourselves," he said. "Living here with us, you could scarcely help suspecting. Shall we say that in return for your promise, I reimburse you in part for losing the sale price on this house?"

Oliver thought that over. It would pacify Sue a little. And it meant only two days indoors. Besides, what good would escaping do? What could he say to outsiders that would not lead him straight to a padded cell?

"All right," he said wearily. "I promise."

By Friday morning there was still no sign from Hollia. Sue telephoned at noon. Oliver knew the crackle of her voice over the wire when Kleph took the call. Even the crackle sounded hysterical; Sue saw her bargain slipping hopelessly through her grasping little fingers.

Kleph's voice was soothing. "I am sorry," she said many times, in the intervals when the voice paused. "I am truly sorry. Believe me, you will find it does not matter. I know . . . I am sorry—"

She turned from the phone at last. "The girl says Hollia has given up," she told the others.

"Not Hollia," Klia said firmly.

Omerie shrugged. "We have very little time left. If she intends anything more, it will be tonight. We must watch for it."

"Oh, not tonight!" Kleph's voice was horrified. "Not even Hollia would do that!"

"Hollia, my dear, in her own way is quite as unscrupulous as you are," Omerie told her with a smile.

"But—would she spoil things for us just because she can't be here?"

"What do you think?" Klia demanded.

Oliver ceased to listen. There was no making sense out of their talk, but he knew that by tonight whatever the secret was must surely come into the open at last. He was willing to wait and see.

For two days excitement had been building up in the house and the three who shared it with him. Even the servants felt it and were nervous and unsure of themselves. Oliver had given up asking questions—it only embarrassed his tenants—and watched.

All the chairs in the house were collected in the three front bedrooms. The furniture was rearranged to make room for them, and dozens of covered cups had been set out on trays. Oliver recognized Kleph's rose-quartz set among the rest. No steam rose from the thin crescent-openings, but the cups were full. Oliver lifted one and felt a heavy liquid move within it, like something half-solid, sluggishly.

Guests were obviously expected, but the regular dinner hour of nine came and went, and no one had yet arrived. Dinner was finished; the servants went home. The Sanciscos went to their rooms to dress, amid a feeling of mounting tension.

Oliver stepped out on the porch after dinner, trying in vain to guess what it was that had wrought such a pitch of expectancy in the house. There was a quarter moon swimming in haze on the horizon, but the stars which had made every night of May thus far a dazzling translucency, were very dim tonight. Clouds had begun to gather at sundown, and the undimmed weather of the whole month seemed ready to break at last.

Behind Oliver the door opened a little, and closed. He caught Kleph's fragrance before he turned, and a faint whiff of the fragrance of the euphoriac she was much too fond of drinking. She came to his side and slipped a hand into his, looking up into his face in the darkness.

"Oliver," she said very softly. "Promise me one thing. Promise me not to leave the house tonight."

"I've already promised that," he said a little irritably.

"I know. But tonight—I have a very particular reason for wanting you indoors tonight." She leaned her head against his shoulder for a moment, and despite himself his irritation softened. He had not seen Kleph alone since that last night of her revelations; he supposed he never would be alone with her again for more than a few minutes at a time. But he knew he would not forget those two bewildering evenings. He knew too, now, that she was very weak and foolish— but she was still Kleph and he had held her in his arms, and was not likely ever to forget it.

"You might be—hurt—if you went out tonight," she was saying in a muffled voice. "I know it will not matter, in the end, but— remember you promised, Oliver."

She was gone again, and the door had closed behind her before he could voice the futile questions in his mind.

The guests began to arrive just before midnight. From the head of the stairs Oliver saw them coming in by twos and threes, and was astonished at how many of these people from the future must have gathered here in the past weeks. He could see quite clearly now how they differed from the norm of his own period. Their physical elegance was what one noticed first—perfect grooming, meticulous manners, meticulously controlled voices. But because they were all idle, all, in a way, sensation-hunters, there was a certain shrillness underlying their voices, especially when heard all together. Petulance and self-indulgence showed beneath the good manners. And tonight, an all-pervasive excitement.

By one o'clock everyone had gathered in the front rooms. The teacups had begun to steam, apparently of themselves, around midnight, and the house was full of the faint, thin fragrance that induced a sort of euphoria all through the rooms, breathed in with the perfume of the tea.

It made Oliver feel light and drowsy. He was determined to sit up as long as the others did, but he must have dozed off in his own room, by the window, an unopened book in his lap.

For when it happened he was not sure for a few minutes whether or not it was a dream.

The vast, incredible crash was louder than sound. He felt the whole house shake under him, felt rather than heard the timbers grind upon one another like broken bones, while he was still in the borderland of sleep. When he woke fully he was on the floor among the shattered fragments of the window.

How long or short a time he had lain there he did not know. The world was still stunned with that tremendous noise, or his ears still deaf from it, for there was no sound anywhere.

He was halfway down the hall toward the front rooms when sound began to return from outside. It was a low, indescribable rumble at first, prickled with countless tiny distant screams. Oliver's eardrums ached from the terrible impact of the vast unheard noise, but the numbness was wearing off and he heard before he saw it the first voices of the stricken city.

The door to Kleph's room resisted him for a moment. The house had settled a little from the violence of the—the explosion?—and the frame was out of line. When he got the door open he could only stand blinking stupidly into the darkness within. All the lights were out, but there was a breathless sort of whispering going on in many voices.

The chairs were drawn around the broad front windows so that everyone could see out; the air swam with the fragrance of euphoria. There was light enough here from outside for Oliver to see that a few onlookers still had their hands to their ears, but all were craning eagerly forward to see.

Through a dreamlike haze Oliver saw the city spread out with impossible distinctness below the window. He knew quite well that a row of houses across the street blocked the view—yet he was looking over the city now, and he could see it in a limitless panorama from here to the horizon. The houses between had vanished.

On the far skyline fire was already a solid mass, painting the low clouds crimson. That sulphurous light reflecting back from the sky upon the city made clear the rows upon rows of flattened houses with flame beginning to lick up among them, and farther out the formless rubble of what had been houses a few minutes ago and was now nothing at all.

The city had begun to be vocal. The noise of the flames rose loudest, but you could hear a rumble of human voices like the beat of surf a long way off, and staccato noises of screaming made a sort of pattern that came and went continuously through the web of sound. Threading it in undulating waves the shrieks of sirens knit the web together into a terrible symphony that had, in its way, a strange, inhuman beauty.

Briefly through Oliver's stunned incredulity went the memory of that other symphony Kleph had played here one day, another catastrophe retold in terms of music and moving shapes.

He said hoarsely, "Kleph—"

The tableau by the window broke. Every head turned, and Oliver saw the faces of strangers staring at him, some few in embarrassment avoiding his eyes, but most seeking them out with that avid, inhuman curiosity which is common to a type in all crowds at accident scenes. But these people were here by design, audience at a vast disaster timed almost for their coming.

Kleph got up unsteadily, her velvet dinner gown tripping her as she rose. She set down a cup and swayed a little as she came toward the door, saying, "Oliver . . . Oliver—" in a sweet, uncertain voice. She was drunk, he saw, and wrought up by the catastrophe to a pitch of stimulation in which she was not very sure what she was doing.

Oliver heard himself saying in a thin voice not his own, "W-what was it, Kleph? What happened? What—" But *happened* seemed so inadequate a word for the incredible panorama below that he had to choke back hysterical laughter upon the struggling questions, and broke off entirely, trying to control the shaking that had seized his body.

Kleph made an unsteady stoop and seized a steaming cup. She came to him, swaying, holding it out—her panacea for all ills.

"Here, drink it, Oliver—we are all quite safe here, quite safe." She thrust the cup to his lips and he gulped automatically, grateful for the fumes that began their slow, coiling surcease in his brain with the first swallow.

"It was a meteor," Kleph was saying. "Quite a small meteor, really. We are perfectly safe here. This house was never touched."

Out of some cell of the unconscious Oliver heard himself saying incoherently, "Sue? Is Sue—" he could not finish.

Kleph thrust the cup at him again. "I think she may be safe—for awhile. Please, Oliver—forget about all that and drink."

"But you *knew!*" Realization of that came belatedly to his stunned brain. "You could have given warning, or—"

"How could we change the past?" Kleph asked. "We knew—but could we stop the meteor? Or warn the city? Before we come we must give our word never to interfere—"

Their voices had risen imperceptibly to be audible above the rising volume of sound from below. The city was roaring now, with flames and cries and the crash of falling buildings. Light in the room turned lurid and pulsed upon the walls and ceiling in red light and redder dark.

Downstairs, a door slammed. Someone laughed. It was high, hoarse, angry laughter. Then from the crowd in the room someone gasped and there was a chorus of dismayed cries. Oliver tried to focus upon the window and the terrible panorama beyond, and found he could not.

It took several seconds of determined blinking to prove that more than his own vision was at fault. Kleph whimpered softly and moved against him. His arms closed about her automatically, and he was grateful for the warm, solid flesh against him. This much at least he could touch and be sure of, though everything else that was happening might be a dream. Her perfume and the heady perfume of the tea rose together in his head, and for an instant, holding her in this embrace that must certainly be the last time he ever held her, he did not care that something had gone terribly wrong with the very air of the room.

It was blindness—not continuous, but a series of swift, widening ripples between which he could catch glimpses of the other faces in the room, strained and astonished in the flickering light from the city.

The ripples came faster. There was only a blink of sight between them now, and the blinks grew briefer and briefer, the intervals of darkness more broad.

From downstairs the laughter rose again up the stairwell. Oliver thought he knew the voice. He opened his mouth to speak, but a door nearby slammed open before he could find his tongue, and Omerie shouted down the stairs.

"Hollia?" he roared above the roaring of the city. "Hollia, is that you?"

She laughed again, triumphantly. "I warned you!" her hoarse, harsh voice called. "Now come out in the street with the rest of us if you want to see any more!"

"Hollia!" Omerie shouted desperately. "Stop this or—"

The laughter was derisive. "What will you do, Omerie? This time I hid it too well—come down in the street if you want to watch the rest."

There was angry silence in the house. Oliver could feel Kleph's quick, excited breathing light upon his cheek, feel the soft motions of her body in his arms. He tried consciously to make the moment last, stretch it out to infinity. Everything had happened too swiftly to impress very clearly on his mind anything except what he could touch and hold. He held her in an embrace made consciously light, though he wanted to clasp her in a tight, despairing grip, because he was sure this was the last embrace they would ever share.

The eye-straining blinks of light and blindness went on. From far away below, the roar of the burning city rolled on, threaded together by the long, looped cadences of the sirens that linked all sounds into one.

Then in the bewildering dark another voice sounded from the hall downstairs. A man's voice, very deep, very melodious, saying:

"What is this? What are you doing here? Hollia—is that you?"

Oliver felt Kleph stiffen in his arms. She caught her breath, but she said nothing in the instant while heavy feet began to mount the stairs, coming up with a solid, confident tread that shook the old house to each step.

Then Kleph thrust herself hard out of Oliver's arms. He heard her high, sweet, excited voice crying, "Cenbe! Cenbe!" and she ran to meet the newcomer through the waves of dark and light that swept the shaken house.

Oliver staggered a little and felt a chair seat catching the back of his legs. He sank into it and lifted to his lips the cup he still held. Its steam was warm and moist in his face, though he could scarcely make out the shape of the rim.

He lifted it with both hands and drank.

When he opened his eyes it was quite dark in the room. Also it was silent except for a thin, melodious humming almost below the threshold of sound. Oliver struggled with the memory of a monstrous nightmare. He put it resolutely out of his mind and sat up, feeling an unfamiliar bed creak and sway under him.

This was Kleph's room. But no—Kleph's no longer. Her shining hangings were gone from the walls, her white resilient rug, her pictures. The room looked as it had looked before she came, except for one thing.

In the far corner was a table—a block of translucent stuff—out of which light poured softly. A man sat on a low stool before it, leaning forward, his heavy shoulders outlined against the glow. He wore earphones and he was making quick, erratic notes upon a pad on his knee, swaying a little as if to the tune of unheard music.

The curtains were drawn, but from beyond them came a distant, muffled roaring that Oliver remembered from his nightmare. He put a hand to his face, aware of a feverish warmth and a dipping of the room before his eyes. His head ached, and there was a deep malaise in every limb and nerve.

As the bed creaked, the man in the corner turned, sliding the earphones down like a collar. He had a strong, sensitive face above a dark beard, trimmed short. Oliver had never seen him before, but he had that air Oliver knew so well by now, of remoteness which was the knowledge of time itself lying like a gulf between them.

When he spoke his deep voice was impersonally kind.

"You had too much euphoriac, Wilson," he said, aloofly sympathetic. "You slept a long while."

"How long?" Oliver's throat felt sticky when he spoke.

The man did not answer. Oliver shook his head experimentally. He said, "I thought Kleph said you don't get hangovers from—" Then another thought interrupted the first, and he said quickly, "Where is Kleph?" He looked confusedly toward the door.

"They should be in Rome by now. Watching Charlemagne's coronation at St. Peter's on Christmas Day more than a thousand years from here."

That was not a thought Oliver could grasp clearly. His aching brain sheered away from it; he found thinking at all was strangely difficult. Staring at the man, he traced an idea painfully to its conclusion.

"So they've gone on—but you stayed behind? Why? You . . . you're Cenbe? I heard your—symphonia, Kleph called it."

"You heard part of it. I have not finished yet. I needed—this." Cenbe inclined his head toward the curtains beyond which the subdued roaring still went on.

"You needed—the meteor?" The knowledge worked painfully through his dulled brain until it seemed to strike some area still untouched by the aching, an area still alive to implication. "The *meteor?* But—"

There was a power implicit in Cenbe's raised hand that seemed to push Oliver down upon the bed again. Cenbe said patiently, "The worst of it is past now, for a while. Forget if you can. That was days ago. I said you were asleep for some time. I let you rest. I knew this house would be safe—from the fire at least."

"Then—something more's to come?" Oliver only mumbled his question. He was not sure he wanted an answer. He had been curious so long, and now that knowledge lay almost within reach, something about his brain seemed to refuse to listen. Perhaps this weariness, this feverish, dizzy feeling would pass as the effect of the euphoriac wore off.

Cenbe's voice ran on smoothly, soothingly, almost as if Cenbe, too, did not want him to think. It was easiest to lie there and listen.

"I am a composer," Cenbe was saying. "I happen to be interested in interpreting certain forms of disaster into my own terms. That is why I stayed on. The others were dilettantes. They came for the May weather and the spectacle. The aftermath—well why should they wait for that? As for myself—I suppose I am a connoisseur. I find the aftermath rather fascinating. And I need it. I need to study it at first hand, for my own purposes."

His eyes dwelt upon Oliver for an instant very keenly, like a physician's eyes, impersonal and observing. Absently he reached for his stylus and the note pad. And as he moved, Oliver saw a familiar mark on the underside of the thick, tanned wrist.

"Kleph had that scar, too," he heard himself whisper. "And the others."

Cenbe nodded. "Inoculation. It was necessary, under the circumstances. We did not want disease to spread in our own time-world."

"Disease?"

Cenbe shrugged. "You would not recognize the name."

"But, if you can inoculate against disease—" Oliver thrust himself up on an aching arm. He had a half-grasp upon a thought now which he did not want to let go. Effort seemed to make the ideas come more clearly through his mounting confusion. With enormous effort he went on.

"I'm getting it now," he said. "Wait. I've been trying to work this out. You can change history? You can! I know you can. Kleph said she had to promise not to interfere. You all had to promise. Does that mean you really could change your own past—our time?"

Cenbe laid down his pad again. He looked at Oliver thoughtfully, a dark, intent look under heavy brows. "Yes," he said. "Yes, the past can be changed. But it is extremely difficult, and it has never been allowed." He shrugged. "A theoretical science. We do not change history, Wilson. If we changed our past, our present would be altered, too. And our time-world is entirely to our liking."

Oliver spoke louder against the roaring from beyond the windows. "But you've got the power! You could alter history, if you wanted to —wipe out all the pain and suffering and tragedy—"

"All of that passed away long ago," Cenbe said.

"Not—now! Not—this!"

Cenbe looked at him enigmatically for a while. Then—"This, too," he said.

And suddenly Oliver realized from across what distances Cenbe was watching him. A vast distance, as time is measured. The dying city outside, the whole world of *now* was not quite real to Cenbe. It was merely one of the building blocks that had gone to support the edifice on which Cenbe's culture stood in a misty, unknown, terrible future.

It seemed terrible to Oliver now. Even Kleph—all of them had been touched with a pettiness, the faculty that had enabled Hollia to concentrate on her malicious, small schemes to acquire a ringside seat while the meteor thundered in toward Earth's atmosphere. They were all dilettantes, Kleph and Omerie and the other. They toured time, but only as onlookers. Were they bored—sated—with their normal existence?

Not sated enough to wish change, basically. They dared not change the past—they could not risk flawing their own present.

Revulsion shook him. Remembering the touch of Kleph's lips, he felt a sour sickness on his tongue. Kleph—leaving him for the barbaric, splendid coronation at Rome a thousand years ago—*how had she seen him?* Not as a living, breathing man. He knew that, very certainly. Kleph's race were spectators.

He lay back on the bed letting the room swirl away into the darkness behind his closed and aching lids. The ache was implicit in every cell of his body, almost a second ego taking possession and driving him out of himself, a strong, sure ego taking over as he himself let go.

Why, he wondered dully, should Kleph have lied? She had said there was no aftermath to the drink she had given him. No aftermath

—and yet this painful possession was strong enough to edge him out of his own body.

Kleph had not lied. It was no aftermath to drink. He knew that— but the knowledge no longer touched his brain or his body. He lay still, giving them up to the power of the illness which was aftermath to something far stronger than the strongest drink. The illness that had no name—yet.

He hardly noticed when Cenbe left. He lay motionless for a long while, thinking feverishly—

I've got to find some way to tell people. If I'd known in advance, maybe something could have been done. We'd have forced them to tell us how to change the probabilities. We could have evacuated the city.

If I could leave a message—

Maybe not for today's people. But later. They visit all through time. If they could be recognized and caught somewhere, sometime, and made to change destiny—

It wasn't easy to stand up. The room kept tilting. But he managed it. He found pencil and paper and through the swaying of the shadows he wrote down what he could. Enough. Enough to warn, enough to save.

He put the sheets on the table, in plain sight, and weighted them down before he stumbled back to bed through closing darkness.

The house was dynamited six days later, part of the futile attempt to halt the relentless spread of the Blue Death.

PIECES OF SILVER

Brett Halliday

THE gringo Thurston? Si, senor. I remember him well. I was one of those who went with him on his trip into the hill country exploring for oil.

The trip, senor, from which he did not return.

You ask what became of him? That is a question no man may answer with certainty. Not even I, though I have the American education and am known through the Isthmus of Tejauntepec as the smartest man in Mexico.

I understand, senor. You are from the American insurance company and have come to Teluocan seeking proof of Thurston's death. I will tell you the story as I know it, and you will have to judge for yourself whether it is the proof you seek.

Seat yourself comfortably here on the veranda and listen well. It is not a long story, but it must begin when the gringo Thurston first stepped off the riverboat which comes up from Porto Blanco.

You knew him, perhaps? No? A big man, with broad shoulders and eyes holding the cold glitter of ice; a harsh voice, giving loud orders as though he spoke to dogs rather than to free men who have the blue blood of Spanish dons in their veins, mixed with that of native tribes who held this continent long before it was discovered by a wandering Italian sailor.

You comprehend, senor, that we of Mexico are a race slow to anger. Gringo Americans mistake this for weakness or fear, and sometimes do not learn their mistake until too late.

Patience, senor. It is the story of Thurston I am telling. To under-

141

stand his end, you must see him as he was when he came arrogantly among us with harsh words on his lips and contempt for us in his heart.

Ay, and with a look in his eyes when he gazed upon our women that was not good. He was a stranger to the tropics and he mistook a simplicity in the clothing of our women for an invitation to evil thoughts.

Be not impatient. I seek to make you see the gringo Thurston as we of Teluocan saw him . . . that you may have better understanding of what happened inside such a man when he stood face to face with Lolita Simpson in the jungle.

Si, senor, Senor Simpson is an American, but not a gringo like Thurston. A little man with no hair on his head, and a mild voice. Twenty years ago he came from *Los Estados Unidos* to Teluocan.

Perhaps with scorn you would say he is one who has gone native. It is true that he took a wife from the Jurillo tribe, Indians of the hill country. But she has been a loyal wife to him and I think Senor Simpson has not regretted his choice.

With her, he settled near the headwaters of the Rio Chico, cleared a small plantation and planted bananas, reared six fine children of which his daughter, Lolita, is eldest.

Senor Simpson was in town for supplies that day when Thurston came on the river boat.

I saw them meet upon this veranda, senor, as I stood close to them three nights later while Lolita danced the *fluencita* beneath the light of flaming torches and the warrant for the gringo Thurston's death was signed.

The gringo stood a head above Simpson, looking down at him with coldness, saying:

"They tell me you have a little two-by-four plantation up the river and could guide me that far on my journey into the hill country."

Senor Simpson looked up at the gringo, then away. It was as though the bad smell was in his nose. But he said:

"Yes. I am in Teluocan for supplies. I will be starting back in the cool of the morning."

"I'm pulling out up-river right after lunch. There's ten dollars in it for you to get together some Mex carriers and guide me as far as your place."

"After lunch is the siesta hour," Senor Simpson said. "They

have a saying down here that only mad dogs and gringo fools venture into the sun during siesta."

The gringo threw back his head and laughed loudly. "Let them call me a gringo fool. I've been called worse."

Senor Simpson shook his head. "It is too hot for men to travel with packs. Tomorrow will be soon enough."

"Damn your siesta and your mananas," said Thurston. He was like that, senor. With a curse for everything not his own way. "If you don't want to earn ten dollars, I'll go alone."

Without anger, Senor Simpson admitted he had use for ten dollars. In a land where pesos are scarce, American dollars are much valued. But why, asked Simpson, did the other Americans wish to go into the hills?

"My business is oil. The geological exploration. I've heard of oil seepages up there. Have you ever seen any?"

Senor Simpson shrugged his shoulders and said he did not know.

The gringo snorted with loudness. "That's the trouble with you Americans that go native. You settle down with some slobby-fat Spick woman and lose all your American push."

I was watching Senor Simpson and I saw the look on his face when Thurston said that to him. It was not a look good to see. For it is true that his wife is not as slender in the waist as when he took her to the priest.

But he rolled a corn-husk cigarillo and said nothing. One knew he was thinking it was useless to try to make the gringo Thurston understand . . . and ten American dollars do not drop into one's hands in Teluocan every day.

In the end the gringo had his way. At the beginning of the siesta hour we started up-river. Six of us with packs, Senor Simpson with his two burros carrying supplies for the plantation.

And, mark you, senor! The gringo going ahead on the trail carrying a pack heavier than any of the rest.

The midday heat on the Isthmus, you comprehend, is like no heat you will find elsewhere. There is a heaviness that crushes one. The breath comes hard into the lungs because it is steamy thick with vapors.

There is silence in the jungle with even the birds and monkeys retreating deep into shady places. And there is the heavy stink rising upward from damp decay which we of this country learn to endure but not to enjoy.

Through this, the gringo Thurston set such a pace as no man who knew the tropics would attempt. Such a man, senor, is a difficult leader. One who is in the pay of such a man cannot well lag behind.

For three hours we in the rear kept up the pace set by Thurston. It was too much, after three hours, for Alberto, the youngest among us.

He was sick in his stomach and could not keep up. His older brother, Pedro, pushed up the trail to tell Senor Simpson we must make the stop for Alberto to rest.

"I am not the *patron*," Senor Simpson told him with regret. "Senor Thurston goes on without resting."

"But he has not the sickness *en la estomacha*," Pedro said. "The other *patron* will stop if you tell him, senor."

With the wisdom of the country and of our people, Simpson knew it would be best to rest Alberto's *estomacha*. He stopped and called: "One of your carriers is sick, Thurston."

The gringo turned and came striding back with anger on his face.

"Which of you," asked the gringo with harshness, "pretends the sickness to get a rest?"

Alberto was not without spirit. He lifted his head and said, "It is I. In a little time the sickness will pass. It is the too much heat."

The gringo was not one to hear excuses from weaker men. "It is not hotter for you than for me," he told Alberto. "Get ahead of me on the trail where I may kick your pants when the sickness comes."

It was not the wise thing to say to a sick man. There was a look of hatred on every face, and behind the gringo Pedro's hand went inside his waistband where a sharp knife is always concealed.

It was, senor, what you Americans would call the showdown.

The insult brought a blaze to Alberto's eyes but he was too sick to defy the gringo. He shrugged his shoulders and let the pack slide off, saying simply: "I rest here until the sickness goes."

"Not," said the gringo, "while I'm paying you good money. Take your sick belly back to town."

There was heavy breathing and the dangerous silence of hate there on the trail. More than one hand itched for a knife, but the big gringo faced us with a snarl.

All but Pedro. Pedro was luckily behind him, crouched like a tiger of the jungle with hot sunlight gleaming on polished steel in his right hand.

Senor Simpson tried to save the gringo. He stepped forward and said: "You're making a mistake, Thurston. These men won't stand for talk like that."

To Senor Simpson, his own countryman, the gringo said: "Shut up," and it was as though the words were icicles dripping from his mouth.

It was not good to see Senor Simpson back away. One does not enjoy, you comprehend, to see fear soften the backbone of one's friend.

Behind the gringo, Pedro was moving closer. We waited in silence, the rest of us, for the quick death Pedro's knife is known to carry.

Something in our eyes, perhaps, warned the gringo.

He whirled with a quickness remarkable in a man so big . . . and he laughed at sight of Pedro's knife held low for the bellyrip.

A laugh, senor, that was more fearful than a curse.

He lunged forward with his fist that was like a kick of a shod mule. Pedro went down to the trail and his knife made a gleaming arc in the sunlight before it was buried in the muck.

There remained four of us . . . none unarmed. But the gringo faced us as we pressed forward, his hand going inside his shirt like a striking snake, coming out with one of your fast-shooting American pistols.

We have a saying in the tropics that hot lead is faster than cold steel. None of us were of a mind to put it to the proof. I hang my head, senor, recalling how like a pack of whipped curs we were as the gringo told Alberto to get out of sight down the trail while he ordered the rest of us to divide his pack and move ahead of him.

Pedro went with us, licking blood from his mouth, leaving his knife where it had fallen, and for the remaining hours of that day we stayed far in front of his *pistole*.

The sun was below the treetops before he gave the order to halt. Our rear-ends were dragging behind us, as you Americans would say, and none among us was of a mind for anything but food and rest.

Darkness comes swiftly to the jungle after the sun drops from sight, and the blackness of night was on the trail by the time we had a fire built.

The gringo gave no orders, said not a word to us. He settled himself downtrail with his back against a tree where the firelight flickered on his face.

There was something about that one that gave us pause before lifting a hand against him. We were not timid men, but five of us that night were held by a fear that was more than fear of the gringo's *pistole*.

How to explain it? There is no explanation for the way of a man like Thurston over other men. From him there came a feel of evil that took away our courage.

The same evil sense of fear drove us on the next day. It was a journey that men will speak of in hushed voices for many years to come. We in the lead, with the gringo striding behind us: Senor Simpson following behind his burros, prodding them with a sharp stick that they might not lag behind.

Mark you, senor. It is a trip of three days from Teluocan to the plantation of Senor Simpson and yet we sighted it late that afternoon . . . after a day and a half on the trail. Of a certainty, it is not strange that Americans die young.

A welcome sight the plantation was to us who were as dead men on our feet. Palm-thatched houses in the bend of the river, with rows of banana plants leading back into the jungle.

A dog came yapping to meet us, followed by the running figure of a girl who stopped by the side of the trail at sight of many pack-burdened men instead of only her father.

Si, senor. The girl was Lolita Simpson.

There was the coldness of ice in my veins when she stood for Thurston to look upon her with those eyes which I had seen lighted with unclean fire as he gazed on the innocent young of our village.

How to describe Lolita to you, senor?

Dias! but she was more beautiful than I can tell. Beneath her cotton dress were the soft young curves to quicken the heart-beat of any man. With the innocent questioning of childhood in her eyes, a virgin freshness of her cheeks; yet one knew that inside, the red blood of her mother's people ran hot and near the surface.

She was only sixteen, but the tropics make a woman at sixteen.

She did not look at us as we passed before her on the trail. Her gaze was for the broad figure of Thurston behind us. Senor, the sweat stood on my forehead as I turned my head to watch that meeting.

The gringo stopped in the trail and looked at her with that in his eyes which would have sent her flying for concealment if she had read it aright.

But she knew nothing of the evil lust of men. She was as un-awakened and unafraid as any wild young thing of the jungle. Yet, with this difference. American blood was half in her veins with that of the hill tribe.

I think Thurston was the first American she had seen except her father. Who knows what took place inside her? What secret longing was locked in her breast to be lighted to flame by the bold gaze of the gringo?

I saw it happen, senor. I saw her take one slow step toward him. Her face was blank like one who is hypnotized.

No one can say what might have happened had not Senor Simpson come up in time. He was panting and there were deep lines of more than weariness on his face.

I heard the gringo say to him: "You are not needed here. Go on . . . while the girl stays with me."

And Senor Simpson replied. "It is my daughter, Lolita." His voice was thin, like a tight wire singing in the wind.

Thurston laughed at him. "You don't need to tell me. I can spot a half-breed a mile away."

It would have not been so brutal, senor, if he had slapped Simpson on the face.

He turned to the girl and said two words: "Come here."

There was no sound except the heavy breathing of the father. A spell was on the jungle.

It was broken by Senor Simpson's voice shouting, "No!" at Lolita.

She had taken one step forward. She drew back with a frightened look, as though she had just wakened from sleep.

"Go back to the house," her father said in a hoarse voice. "Go quickly."

She went submissively without looking back. And Thurston said:

"You can't keep her away from me. She'll come when I crook my finger. It's the breed blood in her."

Murder blazed in Simpson's eyes. There was the feel of death in the air. His lips were back from his teeth and there was no longer the look of mildness on his face.

The gringo laughed. It would have pleased him to kill the man who stood between him and Lolita. His hand went inside his shirt and he waited.

I think, senor, I will never live as long a minute, until Senor Simpson turned his head away and began rolling a cigarillo. His fingers shook and he spilled tobacco on the trail. Then he went past the gringo toward his house.

He did not ask Thurston to stay at his house. He took his pay from the gringo and had no words for him.

Thurston understood, but he was a man who enjoyed feeling the hatred of other men.

He moved up the river two hundred paces and had us make camp there. He seemed not anxious to go on, telling us he might stay in camp for several days.

Senor Simpson came to me that night under the cover of darkness . . . taking me aside where Thurston could not hear.

He asked me first whether we went on in the morning, nodding with melancholy when I repeated what the gringo had said.

"I am afraid for my Lolita," he said in a sad voice. "She has been acting strangely since meeting Thurston."

I understood. I told him I would do what I could.

He asked me if I would ride into the hills that night bearing a message to Ruoey Urregan, son of the head man of the Jurillos to whom Lolita was promised in marriage.

I agreed, and the message was this: "The bethrothal ceremony between you and my Lolita must be at once instead of waiting until next month as planned. Come tomorrow night lest you come too late."

I understood, senor. It was the wise strategy to save the girl from herself. Among the Jurillos, the ceremony of betrothal is as binding as marriage. And they are a fierce, wild tribe, zealous of the purity of their maidens.

I slipped away from the gringo's camp while he slept, and rode one of Senor Simpson's mules into the hills.

I was proud to have a part in the undoing of the gringo.

I delivered the message and was back in camp before the sun rose again, and before the preparations began for the *baile* that would celebrate the ceremony that night.

Not knowing the reason for the stir Thurston sat three hours beneath a banyan tree waiting for Lolita to come to him.

True, senor, it is hard to understand the ways of such a man. Another might have tried by stealth to see the girl. That was not the gringo's way. It would have pleased him to humble the father by having her come to him openly. But Lolita did not come.

At noon Thurston went to Simpson's house and knocked.

I was in the yard with some others preparing a pit of charcoal for the roast pig on which the guests would feast that night.

Senor Simpson opened the door to the gringo's knock. He had a two-barreled shotgun in his hands which he held pointed at Thurston's belly. I do not know why he did not shoot. You Americans have many ways that are puzzling to us.

He stood in the doorway and told Thurston of the betrothal ceremony. Then he closed the door in the gringo's face.

Thurston went back to his camp on the bank of the river, saying no word to anyone. What his thoughts were, no one could guess.

He was forgotten as the noisy preparations went on. Messengers had gone out to spread news of the festivity and the guests began coming in the afternoon. Native planters riding on burros, with their women and children behind them on foot as was proper. Indians from the jungle, naked but for loin-cloths.

A platform on the wharf was cleared for dancing, banked with pink and white flowers of the mimosa mixed with the flaming blooms of hibiscus and with sprays of jasmine for fragrance. Wood that was heavy with pitch was gathered and tied in bundles with bamboo shoots to the tops of green poles for torches.

In the yard was the chatter of many women and the shrill cries of naked children running between the legs of their elders, the clean smell of wood smoke and the odor of pigs roasting over the charcoal pits.

Ay, a happy, festive scene, senor, bringing a smile even to the face of the host as he mingled with his guests and kept his eyes turned away from the camp on the river where Thurston sat motionless, watching.

It was dusk when a band of young bloods from the Jurillo tribe came down from the hills escorting Ruoey Urregan to his betrothal.

Mounted on shaggy native ponies and brandishing spears tipped with iron, they burst like a whirlwind into the clearing with young Urregan proudly in the lead.

Dios! but there was a man! A true son of many generations of tribal chieftains. Tall and slim of hip, with broad shoulders and muscles rippling beneath the skin.

The gringo, I think, got what you call the full-eye as he watched silently from his place on the river.

Their medicine man came with them to make the ceremony, a shrunken little man with piercing black eyes that were never quiet, and looking to have more than the hundred and fifty years he claims.

They made a half circle there in front of the house while dusk came on swiftly, the young men with their lances held before them, chanting low to the beat of a drum in the hands of the medicine man.

Rouey Urregan stepped to the front as the door opened and Lolita came out on the arm of her father.

Ay! they made a picture, senor, that one does not soon forget. Lolita, in a Spanish mantilla and a lace gown of black that had been her father's wedding gift to her mother; her tall Indian lover with tight-fitting white pants and a red sash above his waist.

They stood side by side before the medicine man, and there was a hush over the watchers.

I, senor, am educated and do not believe in the power of ill-smelling herbs burnt over coals and the sing-song of an old man to make magic. But I tell you, there was magic in the clearing as darkness came on.

Patience, senor. The end is near. I must tell the story my own way for each happening that night is burned upon my memory and has its proper place in what is to come.

Later, there was the dance, the *baile*. There were guitars to make the music, the torches flared in the night air above the platform casting light and shadows upon the moving couples.

Thurston's campfire burned in the darkness close by, but it was late in the evening before he showed his face at the *baile* to which he had no invitation. The guitars were in the slow rhythm of a tango and Lolita was dancing in the arms of her lover when I saw the gringo moving toward Senor Simpson who stood near the edge of the platform.

I stepped forward, my blood fired with fear for what was to come.

The gringo's eyes were upon Lolita, feasting themselves upon her young body yielding itself to the movements of her lover. Truly, Lolita dancing the tango was a sight to draw the eyes of any man.

The other dancers were stepping back, giving to the affianced couple the entire floor. The tango is the dance of youth, you comprehend, the dance of courtship.

The gringo's gaze clung to Lolita as he stood beside Simpson and said:

"I suppose her sweetheart will be going back into the hills after the *baile*. He's not allowed to hang around her until they're married, is he?"

There was a sneer in his voice, senor, but Simpson answered:

"Yes. Back to the hills . . . where you will be going."

Thurston's reply was not one to make Simpson happier: "I'm getting an early start in the morning. I'll finish my work and return soon . . . in time for a little vacation here before I go back to the states. Business before pleasure is my motto."

I was standing close behind Senor Simpson and I saw a trembling take hold of his body.

The gringo's tongue licked his lips. His eyes bulged, watching Lolita.

I moved a little closer, and I do not deny that my hand was on my knife. Senor Simpson was my friend and I did not know what was in his mind. He was a father, you comprehend, and the gringo was looking at his daughter.

But more than a tango was to come.

There was the clapping of hands when the dance ended. Lolita and her Jurillo lover faced each other breathlessly. In that moment of silence, a single guitar began tapping out a strange rhythm that was like the distant beat of a jungle drum.

The other guitars took it up one by one and Lolita swayed back in the torchlight, her young bosom lifting the lace of her mother's wedding gown, a look as of dreaminess on her upturned face.

From all about us there came excited cries: *"Ola Bravo. La fluencita. Aie. La fluencita!"*

Ruoey Urregan stood stiff in the center of the platform with his arms folded and his eyes bright. He turned slowly as Lolita circled about him with her arms curved above her head, fingers snapping like castanets.

It was the *fluencita,* senor. The passion-dance of the Jurillos. A sight for a man to carry locked in his memories until he grows old and has need of such memories. A dance, which none but an affianced maiden may dance for her lover.

Ay, there was the fever-heat of the jungle in the song of the guitars. A strange note of madness, which struck deep inside a man, to set the pulse drumming.

Faster and more fast was the beat of music, and Lolita circled faster and yet faster, stamping her right foot sharply, her eyes holding those of her lover, a strange quiver in every muscle of her young body that was bent backward like a drawn bow.

Ah, senor, to see Lolita dance the *fluencita* was to feel again the fierce fire of youth and of love in one's veins. Even now, I close my eyes and I stand again beside the platform . . .

But it ended suddenly. Over the heads of the watchers, half a dozen American dollars clattered at Lolita's feet.

The music stopped. Lolita looked down at the coins with round eyes, a flush of shame on her cheeks. Ruoey Urregan whirled about, his face black with anger.

Do you comprehend, senor? It was the insult supreme. A sign of contempt such as one makes to a cheap dancing girl who entertains men for pay.

The gringo had turned his back and was striding toward the circle of darkness beyond the torchlight. Urregan leaped forward, off the platform in pursuit, his hand going to a dagger in his sash.

But Senor Simpson caught his arm and held him back. I heard him say in the young man's ear:

"No. In his shirt is concealed a pistol. He goes into the hills tomorrow . . . exploring for oil."

That was the end of the *baile,* senor. There were black looks toward the gringo's camp, and muttered threats, but Ruoey Urregan whispered to his friends and they went back into the hills leaving the insult unavenged.

We broke camp before sunrise the next morning. Business before pleasure, you comprehend.

We traveled far that day and made dry camp at night, went upward into the hills until noon the next day when we were approached by two Indians on shaggy ponies. They had heard, they said, that the Americano sought for signs of black oil in the hills.

It was so, Thurston told them with excitement. Did they know of such?

They told him of a spring not far away which bubbled up with black scum upon it which would burn. He offered them money to take him there, and they agreed, senor.

He went with them eagerly telling us to make camp and await his return.

We stood together and watched while he and the Indians went from sight over a small hill. Pedro crossed himself and said *"Vas con Dios"* through lips that were bruised from the gringo's fist.

We then turned back, and no one has seen the gringo Thurston again.

No, senor. It would have been useless for us to wait there for him to return. The Indians who guided him away were Jurillos. They have a tribal law that one who insults a woman of their tribe must die before two suns go down.

And they obey that law.

But no, senor, it would be useless and perhaps dangerous to look for proof of his death. Even for the purpose of insurance, it would not be wise.

The tribal law of the Jurillos has to do with rubbing honey on the body of their victim and stretching him with grass ropes across a nest of ants. The ants, you comprehend, are without knowledge of American insurance rules and leave little that is recognizable.

He was a fool, you say, to throw money at the feet of Lolita while she danced the *fluencita* for her lover?

But yes senor, that indeed would have been a foolish thing for the gringo to do.

You have misunderstood me, senor. It was not the gringo Thurston who threw the money at Lolita's feet. Dias, no!

He was not that foolish. Indeed, he had already turned his back to leave when it happened.

But it was very unwise of him to pay Senor Simpson with American silver dollars.

THE WHISTLING ROOM

William Hope Hodgson

CARNACKI shook a friendly fist at me as I entered, late. Then he opened the door into the dining room and ushered the four of us—Jessop, Arkright, Taylor and myself—in to dinner.

We dined well, as usual, and equally as usual Carnacki was pretty silent during the meal. At the end we took our wine and cigars to our accustomed positions and Carnacki—having got himself comfortable in his big chair—began without any preliminary:

"I have just got back from Ireland, again," he said. "And I thought you chaps would be interested to hear my news. Besides, I fancy I shall see the thing clearer after I have told it all out straight. I must tell you this, though, at the beginning—up to the present moment I have been utterly and completely stumped. I have tumbled upon one of the most peculiar cases of haunting—or devilment of some sort—that I have come against. Now listen.

"I have been spending the last few weeks at Iastrae Castle, about twenty miles North-East of Galway. I got a letter about a month ago from a Mr. Sid K. Tassoc, who it seemed had bought the place lately and moved in, only to find that he had got a very peculiar piece of property.

"When I reached there he met me at the station and drove me up to the castle. I found that he was 'pigging it' there with his boy brother and another American who seemed to be half-servant and half-companion. It appears that all the servants had left the place, in a body as you might say, and now they were managing among themselves, assisted by some day-help.

"The three of them got together a scratch feed and Tassoc told

154

me all about the trouble whilst we were at table. It is most extraordinary and different from anything that I have had to do with, though that Buzzing Case was very queer too.

"Tassoc began right in the middle of his story. 'We've got a room in this shanty,' he said, 'which has got a most infernal whistling in it, sort of haunting it. The thing starts any time, you never know when, and it goes on until it frightens you. It's not ordinary whistling and it isn't the wind. Wait till you hear it.'

" 'We're all carrying guns,' said the boy, and slapped his coat pocket.

" 'As bad as that?' I said, and the older brother nodded. 'I may be soft,' he replied, 'but wait till you've heard it. Sometimes I think it's some infernal thing and the next moment I'm just as sure that someone's playing a trick on us.'

" 'Why?' I asked. 'What is to be gained?'

" 'You mean,' he said, 'that people usually have some good reason for playing tricks as elaborate as this. Well, I'll tell you. There's a lady in this province by the name of Miss Donnehue who's going to be my wife, this day two months. She's more beautiful than they make them, and so far as I can see, I've just stuck my head into an Irish hornet's nest. There's about a score of hot young Irishmen been courting her these two years gone and now that I've come along and cut them out they feel raw against me. Do you begin to understand the possibilities?'

" 'Yes,' I said. 'Perhaps I do in a vague sort of way, but I don't see how all this affects the room?'

" 'Like this,' he said. 'When I'd fixed it up with Miss Donnehue I looked out for a place and bought this one. Afterwards I told her, one evening during dinner, that I'd decided to tie up here. And then she asked me whether I wasn't afraid of the whistling room. I told her it must have been thrown in gratis, as I'd heard nothing about it. There were some of her men friends present and I saw a smile go round. I found out after a bit of questioning that several people have bought this place during the last twenty-odd years. And it was always on the market again, after a trial.

" 'Well, the chaps started to bait me a bit and offered to take bets after dinner that I'd not stay six months in this shanty. I looked once or twice at Miss Donnehue, but I could see that she didn't take it as a joke at all. Partly, I think, because there was a bit of a sneer in the way the men were tackling me and partly because she really believed there is something in this yarn of the whistling room.

" 'However, after dinner I did what I could to even things up with the others. I nailed all their bets and screwed them down good and safe. I guess some of them are going to be hard hit, unless I lose; which I don't mean to. Well, there you have practically the whole yarn.'

" 'Not quite,' I told him. 'All that I know is that you have bought a castle with a room in it that is in some way "queer," and that you've been doing some betting. Also, I know that your servants have got frightened and run away. Tell me something about the whistling.'

" 'O, that!' said Tassoc. 'That started the second night we were in. I'd had a good look round the room in the daytime, as you can understand; for the talk up at Arlestrae—Miss Donnehue's place— had me wonder a bit. But it seems just as usual as some of the other rooms in the old wing, only perhaps a bit more lonesome feeling. But that may be only because of the talk about it, you know.

" 'The whistling started about ten o'clock on the second night, as I said. Tom and I were in the library when we heard an awfully queer whistling coming along the East Corridor—the room is in the East Wing, you know.

" ' "That's that blessed ghost!" I said to Tom and we collared the lamps off the table and went up to have a look. I tell you, even as we dug along the corridor it took me a bit in the throat, it was so beastly queer. It was a sort of tune in a way, but more as if a devil or some rotten thing were laughing at you and going to get round at your back. That's how it makes you feel.

" 'When we got to the door we didn't wait, but rushed it open, and then I tell you the sound of the thing fairly hit me in the face. Tom said he got it the same way—sort of felt stunned and be-wildered. We looked all round and soon got so nervous we just cleared out and I locked the door.

" 'We came down here and had a stiff drink each. Then we felt better and began to feel we'd been nicely had. So we took sticks and went out into the grounds, thinking after all it must be some of these confounded Irishmen working the ghost-trick on us. But there was nothing stirring.

" 'We went back into the house and walked over it and then paid another visit to the room. But we simply couldn't stand it. We fairly ran out and locked the door again. I don't know how to put it into words, but I had a feeling of being up against something that was rottenly dangerous. You know! We've carried our guns ever since.

" 'Of course we had a real turnout of the room next day and the whole house-place, and we even hunted round the grounds but there was nothing queer. And now I don't know what to think, except that the sensible part of me tells me that it's some plan of these wild Irishmen to try to take a rise out of me.'

" 'Done anything since?' I asked him.

" 'Yes,' he said. 'Watched outside of the door of the room at night and chased round the grounds and sounded the walls and floor of the room. We've done everything we could think of and it's beginning to get on our nerves, so we sent for you.'

"By this we had finished eating. As we rose from the table Tassoc suddenly called out:—'Ssh! Listen!'

"We were instantly silent, listening. Then I heard it, an extraordinary hooning whistle, monstrous and inhuman, coming from far away through corridors to my right.

" 'By God!' said Tassoc, 'and it's scarcely dark yet! Collar those candles, both of you, and come along.'

"In a few moments we were all out of the door and racing up the stairs. Tassoc turned into a long corridor and we followed, shielding our candles as we ran. The sound seemed to fill all the passage as we drew near, until I had the feeling that the whole air throbbed under the power of some wanton Immense Force—a sense of an actual taint, as you might say, of monstrosity all about us.

"Tassoc unlocked the door then, giving it a push with his foot, jumped back and drew his revolver. As the door flew open the sound beat out at us with an effect impossible to explain to one who has not heard it—with a certain, horrible personal note in it, as if in the darkness you could picture the room rocking and creaking in a mad, vile glee to its own filthy piping and whistling and hooning, and yet all the time aware of you in particular. To stand there and listen was to be stunned by Realization. It was as if someone showed you the mouth of a vast pit suddenly and said: That's Hell. And you *knew* that they had spoken the truth. Do you get it, even a little bit?

"I stepped a pace into the room and held the candle over my head and looked quickly round. Tassoc and his brother joined me and the man came up at the back and we all held our candles high. I was deafened with the shrill, piping hoon of the whistling and then, clear in my ear something seemed to be saying to me:—'Get out of here—quick! Quick! Quick!'

" 'As you chaps know, I never neglect that sort of thing. Sometimes it may be nothing but nerves, but as you will remember, it was just such a warning that saved me in the 'Grey Dog' Case and in the 'Yellow Finger' Experiments, as well as other times. Well, I turned sharp round to the others: 'Out!' I said. 'For God's sake, *out* quick!' And in an instant I had them into the passage.

"There came an extraordinary yelling scream into the hideous whistling and then, like a clap of thunder, an utter silence. I slammed the door, and locked it. Then, taking the key, I looked round at the others. They were pretty white and I imagine I must have looked that way too. And there we stood a moment, silent.

" 'Come down out of this and have some whisky,' said Tassoc, at last, in a voice he tried to make ordinary; and he led the way. I was the back man and I knew we all kept looking over our shoulders. When we got downstairs Tassoc passed the bottle round. He took a drink himself and slapped his glass on to the table. Then sat down with a thud.

" 'That's a lovely thing to have in the house with you, isn't it!' he said. And directly afterwards:—'What on earth made you hustle us all out like that, Carnacki?'

" 'Something seemed to be telling me to get out, *quick*,' I said. 'Sounds a bit silly—superstitious, I know, but when you are meddling with this sort of thing you've got to take notice of queer fancies and risk being laughed at.'

"I told him then about the 'Grey Dog' business and he nodded a lot to that. 'Of course,' I said, 'this may be nothing more than those would-be rivals of yours playing some funny game, but personally, though I'm going to keep an open mind, I feel that there is something beastly and dangerous about this thing.'

"We talked for a while longer and then Tassoc suggested billiards, which we played in a pretty half-hearted fashion, and all the time cocking an ear to the door for sounds; but none came, and later after coffee he suggested early bed and a thorough overhaul of the room in the morning.

"My bedroom was in the newer part of the castle and the door opened into the picture gallery. At the East end of the gallery was the entrance to the corridor of the East Wing; this was shut off from the gallery by two old and heavy oak doors which looked rather odd and quaint beside the more modern doors of the various rooms.

"When I reached my room I did not go to bed, but began to unpack my instrument-trunk. I intended to take one or two preliminary steps at once in my investigation of the extraordinary whistling.

"Presently, when the castle had settled into quietness, I slipped out of my room and across to the entrance of the great corridor. I opened one of the low, squat doors and threw the beam of my pocket search-light down the passage. It was empty and I went through the doorway and pushed-to the oak behind me. Then along the great passage-way, throwing my light before and behind and keeping my revolver handy.

"I had hung a 'protection belt' of garlic round my neck and the smell of it seemed to fill the corridor and give me assurance; for as you all know, it is a wonderful 'protection' against the more usual Aeiirii forms of semi-materialization by which I supposed the whistling might be produced, though at that period of my investigation I was still quite prepared to find it due to some perfectly natural cause, for it is astonishing the enormous number of cases that prove to have nothing abnormal in them.

"In addition to wearing the necklet I had plugged my ears loosely with garlic and as I did not intend to stay more than a few minutes in the room, I hoped to be safe.

"When I reached the door and put my hand into my pocket for the key I had a sudden feeling of sickening funk. But I was not going to back out if I could help it. I unlocked the door and turned the handle. Then I gave the door a sharp push with my foot, as Tassoc had done, and drew my revolver, though I did not expect to have any use for it, really.

"I shone the searchlight all round the room and then stepped inside with a disgustingly horrible feeling of walking slap into a waiting danger. I stood a few seconds, expectant, and nothing happened and the empty room showed bare from corner to corner. And then, you know, I realized that the room was full of purposeful silence, just as sickening as any of the filthy noises the Things have power to make. Do you remember what I told you about the 'Silent Garden' business? Well this room had just that same *malevolent* silence—the beastly quietness of a thing that is looking at you and not seeable itself, and thinks that it has got you. Oh, I recognized it instantly and

I slipped the top off my lantern so as to have light over the *whole* room.

"Then I set to working like fury and keeping my glance all about me. I sealed the two windows with lengths of human hair, right across, and sealed them at every frame. As I worked a queer, scarcely perceptible tenseness stole into the air of the place and the silence seemed, if you can understand me, to grow more solid. I knew then that I had no business there without 'full protection,' for I was practically certain that this was no mere Aeiirii development, but one of the worse forms, such as the Saiitii; like that 'Grunting Man' Case—you remember.

"I finished the window and hurried over to the great fireplace. This is a huge affair and has a queer gallows-iron, I think they are called, projecting from the back of the arch. I sealed the opening with seven human hairs—the seventh crossing the six others.

"Then just as I was making an end, a low mocking whistle grew in the room. A cold, nervous prickling went up my spine and round my forehead from the back. The hideous sound filled the room with an extraordinary, grotesque parody of human whistling, too gigantic to be human—as if something gargantuan and monstrous made the sounds softly. As I stood there a last moment, pressing down the final seal, I had little doubt but that I had come across one of those rare and horrible cases of the *Inanimate* reproducing the functions of the *Animate*. I made a grab for my lamp and went quickly to the door, looking over my shoulder and listening for the thing that I expected. It came just as I got my hand upon the handle—a squeal of incredible, malevolent anger, piercing through the low hooning of the whistling. I dashed out, slamming the door and locking it.

"I leant a little against the opposite wall of the corridor, feeling rather funny for it had been a hideously narrow squeak . . . 'thyr be noe sayfetie to be gained bye gayrds of holieness when the monyster hath pow'r to speak throe woode and stoene.' So runs the passage in the Sigsand MS. and I proved it in that 'Nodding Door' business. There is no protection against this particular form of monster, except possibly for a fractional period of time; for it can reproduce itself in or take to its purposes the very protective material which you may use and has power to '*forme* wythine the pentycle,' though not immediately. There is, of course, the possibility of the Unknown Last Line of the Saaamaaa Ritual being uttered but it is too uncertain to count upon and the danger is too hideous, and even then it has no power to protect for more than 'maybe fyve beats of the harte' as the Sigsand has it.

"Inside of the room there was now a constant, meditative, hooning whistling, but presently this ceased and the silence seemed worse for there is such a sense of hidden mischief in a silence.

"After a little I sealed the door with crossed hairs and then cleared off down the great passage and so to bed.

"For a long time I lay awake, but managed eventually to get some sleep. Yet about two o'clock I was waked by the hooning whistling of the room coming to me, even through the closed doors. The sound was tremendous and seemed to beat through the whole house with a presiding sense of terror. As if (I remember thinking) some monstrous giant had been holding mad carnival with itself at the end of that great passage.

"I got up and sat on the edge of the bed, wondering whether to go along and have a look at the seal and suddenly there came a thump on my door and Tassoc walked in with his dressing-gown over his pyjamas.

" 'I thought it would have waked you so I came along to have a talk,' he said. 'I *can't* sleep. Beautiful! Isn't it?'

" 'Extraordinary!' I said, and tossed him my case.

"He lit a cigarette and we sat and talked for about an hour, and all the time that noise went on down at the end of the big corridor.

"Suddenly Tassoc stood up:

" 'Let's take our guns and go and examine the brute,' he said, and turned towards the door.

" 'No!' I said. 'By Jove—NO! I can't say anything definite yet but I believe that the room is about as dangerous as it well can be.'

" 'Haunted—*really* haunted?' he asked, keenly and without any of his frequent banter.

"I told him, of course, that I could not say a definite yes or no to such a question, but that I hoped to be able to make a statement soon. Then I gave him a little lecture on the False Re-Materialization of the Animate-Force through the Inanimate-Inert. He began then to understand the particular way in which the room might be dangerous, if it were really the subject of a manifestation.

"About an hour later the whistling ceased quite suddenly and Tassoc went off again to bed. I went back to mine also, and eventually got another spell of sleep.

"In the morning I walked along to the room. I found the seals on the door intact. Then I went in. The window seals and the hair were all right, but the seventh hair across the great fireplace was broken. This set me thinking. I knew that it might very possibly have snapped, through my having tensioned it too highly; but then, again, it might have been broken by something else. Yet it was scarcely possible that a man, for instance, could have passed between the six unbroken hairs for no one would ever have noticed them, entering the room that way, you see; but just walked through them, ignorant of their very existence.

"I removed the other hairs and the seals. Then I looked up the chimney. It went up straight and I could see blue sky at the top. It was a big, open flue and free from any suggestion of hiding places or corners. Yet, of course, I did not trust to any such casual examination and after breakfast I put on my overalls and climbed to the very top, sounding all the way, but I found nothing.

"Then I came down and went over the whole of the room—floor, ceiling and the walls, mapping them out in six-inch squares and sounding with both hammer and probe. But there was nothing unusual.

"Afterwards I made a three-weeks' search of the whole castle in the same thorough way, but found nothing. I went even further then for at night, when the whistling commenced, I made a microphone test. You see, if the whistling were mechanically produced this test would have made evident to me the working of the machinery if there were any such concealed within the walls. It certainly was an up-to-date method of examination, as you must allow.

"Of course I did not think that any of Tassoc's rivals had fixed up any mechanical contrivance, but I thought it just possible that there had been some such thing for producing the whistling made away back in the years, perhaps with the intention of giving the room a reputation that would insure its being free of inquisitive folk. You see what I mean? Well of course it was just possible, if this were the case, that someone knew the secret of the machinery and was utilizing the knowledge to play this devil of a prank on Tassoc. The microphone test of the walls would certainly have made this known to me, as I have said, but there was nothing of the sort in the castle so that I had practically no doubt at all now but that it was a genuine case of what is popularly termed 'haunting.'

"All this time, every night, and sometimes most of each night the hooning whistling of the Room was intolerable. It was as if an

Intelligence there knew that steps were being taken against it and piped and hooned in a sort of mad, mocking contempt. I tell you, it was as extraordinary as it was horrible. Time after time I went along—tiptoeing noiselessly on stockinged feet—to the sealed floor (for I always kept the room sealed.) I went at all hours of the night and often the whistling inside would seem to change to a brutally jeering note, as though the half-animate monster saw me plainly through the shut door. And all the time as I would stand, watching, the hooning of the whistling would seem to fill the whole corridor so that I used to feel a precious lonely chap messing about there with one of Hell's mysteries.

"And every morning I would enter the room and examine the different hairs and seals. You see, after the first week, I had stretched parallel hairs all along the walls of the room and along the ceiling, but over the floor, which was of polished stone, I had set out little colorless wafers, sticky-side uppermost. Each wafer was numbered and then arranged after a definite plan so that I should be able to trace the exact movements of any living thing that went across.

"You will see that no material being or creature could possibly have entered that room without leaving many signs to tell me about it. But nothing was ever disturbed and I began to think that I should have to risk an attempt to stay a night in the room in the Electric Pentacle. Mind you, I *knew* that it would be a crazy thing to do, but I was getting stumped and ready to try anything.

Once about midnight, I did break the seal on the door and have a quick look in, but I tell you, the whole Room gave one mad yell and seemed to come towards me in a great belly of shadows as if the walls had bellied in towards me. Of course, that must have been fancy. Anyway, the yell was sufficient and I slammed the door and locked it, feeling a bit weak down my spine. I wonder whether you know the feeling.

"And then when I had got to that state of readiness for anything I made what, at first, I thought was something of a discovery:

" 'Twas about one in the morning and I was walking slowly round the castle, keeping in the soft grass. I had come under the shadow of the East Front and far above me I could hear the vile, hooning whistling of the Room up in the darkness of the unlit wing. Then suddenly, a little in front of me, I heard a man's voice speaking low, but evidently in glee:—

"'By George! You chaps, but I wouldn't care to bring a wife home to that!' it said, in the tone of the cultured Irish.

"Someone started to reply, but there came a sharp exclamation and then a rush and I heard footsteps running in all directions. Evidently the men had spotted me.

"For a few seconds I stood there feeling an awful ass. After all, *they* were at the bottom of the haunting! Do you see what a big fool it made me seem? I had no doubt but that they were some of Tassoc's rivals and here I had been feeling in every bone that I had hit a genuine Case! And then, you know, there came the memory of hundreds of details that made me just as much in doubt again. Anyway, whether it was natural or abnatural, there was a great deal yet to be cleared up.

"I told Tassoc next morning what I had discovered and through the whole of every night for five nights we kept a close watch round the East Wing, but there was never a sign of anyone prowling about; and all this time, almost from evening to dawn, that grotesque whistling would hoon incredibly, far above us in the darkness.

"On the morning after the fifth night I received a wire from here which brought me home by the next boat. I explained to Tassoc that I was simply bound to come away for a few days, but told him to keep up the watch round the castle. One thing I was very careful to do and that was to make him absolutely promise never to go into the Room between sunset and sunrise. I made it clear to him that we knew nothing definite yet, one way or the other, and if the room were what I had first thought it to be, it might be a lot better for him to die first than enter it after dark.

"When I got here and had finished my business I thought you chaps would be interested and also I wanted to get it all spread out clear in my mind, so I rang you up. I am going over again tomorrow and when I get back I ought to have something pretty extraordinary to tell you. By the way, there is a curious thing I forgot to tell you. I tried to get a phonographic record of the whistling, but it simply produced no impression on the wax at all. That is one of the things that has made me feel queer.

"Another extraordinary thing is that the microphone will not magnify the sound—will not even transmit it, seems to take no account of it and acts as if it were nonexistent. I am absolutely and utterly stumped up to the present. I am a wee bit curious to see whether any of you dear clever heads can make daylight of it. *I* cannot—not yet."

He rose to his feet.

"Good-night, all," he said, and began to usher us out abruptly, but without offence, into the night.

A fortnight later he dropped us each a card and you can imagine that I was not late this time. When we arrived Carnacki took us straight in to dinner and when we had finished and all made ourselves comfortable he began again, where he had left off:

"Now just listen quietly, for I have got something very queer to tell you. I got back late at night and I had to walk up to the castle as I had not warned them that I was coming. It was bright moonlight, so that the walk was rather a pleasure than otherwise. When I got there the whole place was in darkness and I thought I would go round outside to see whether Tassoc or his brother was keeping watch. But I could not find them anywhere and concluded that they had got tired of it and gone off to bed.

"As I returned across the lawn that lies below the front of the East Wing I caught the hooning whistling of the Room coming down strangely clear through the stillness of the night. It had a peculiar note in it I remember—low and constant, queerly meditative. I looked up at the window, bright in the moonlight, and got a sudden thought to bring a ladder from the stable-yard and try to get a look into the Room from the outside.

"With this notion I hunted round at the back of the castle among the straggle of the office and presently found a long, fairly light ladder, though it was heavy enough for one, goodness knows! I thought at first that I should never get it reared. I managed at last and let the ends rest very quietly against the wall a little below the sill of the larger window. Then, going silently, I went up the ladder. Presently I had my face above the sill and was looking in, alone with the moonlight.

"Of course the queer whistling sounded louder up there, but it still conveyed that peculiar sense of something whistling quietly to itself —can you understand? Though for all the meditative lowness of the note, the horrible, gargantuan quality was distinct—a mighty parody of the human, as if I stood there and listened to the whistling from the lips of a monster with a man's soul.

"And then, you know, I saw something. The floor in the middle of the huge, empty room was puckered upwards in the center into a strange, soft-looking mound parted at the top into an everchanging hole that pulsated to that great, gentle hooning. At time, as I watched, I saw the heaving of the indented mound gap across with a queer, inward suction as with the drawing of an enormous breath, then the thing would dilate and pout once more to the incredible melody. And suddenly as I stared, dumb, it came to me that the thing was living. I was looking at two enormous, blackened lips, blistered and brutal, there in the pale moonlight . . .

"Abruptly they bulged out to a vast pouting mound of force and sound, stiffened and swollen and hugely massive and clean-cut in the moonbeams. And a great sweat lay heavy on the vast upper-lip. In the same moment of time the whistling had burst into a mad screaming note that seemed to stun me, even where I stood, outside of the window. And then the following moment I was staring blankly at the solid, undisturbed floor of the room—smooth, polished stone flooring from wall to wall. And there was an absolute silence.

"You can picture me staring into the quiet Room and knowing what I knew. I felt like a sick, frightened child and I wanted to slide *quietly* down the ladder and run away. But in that very instant I heard Tassoc's voice calling to me from within the Room for help, *help*. My God! but I got such an awful dazed feeling and I had a vague, bewildered notion that after all, it was the Irishmen who had got him in there and were taking it out of him. And then the call came again and I burst the window and jumped in to help him. I had a confused idea that the call had come from within the shadow of the great fireplace and I raced across to it, but there was no one there.

" 'Tassoc!' I shouted, and my voice went empty-sounding round the great apartment, and then in a flash *I knew that Tassoc had never called.* I whirled round, sick with fear, towards the window and as I did so a frightful, exultant whistling scream burst through the Room. On my left the end wall had bellied-in towards me in a pair of gargantuan lips, black and utterly monstrous, to within a yard of my face. I fumbled for a mad instant at my revolver; not for *it,* but myself, for the danger was a thousand times worse than death. And then suddenly the Unknown Last Line of the Saasmaaa Ritual was whispered quite audibly in the room. Instantly the thing happened that I have known once before. There came a sense as of dust falling continually and monotonously and I knew that my life hung uncertain and suspended for a flash in a brief, reeling vertigo of unseeable things. Then *that* ended and I knew that I might live. My soul and body blended again and life and power came to me. I dashed furiously at the window and hurled myself out head-foremost, for I can tell you that I had stopped being afraid of death. I crashed down on to the ladder and slithered, grabbing and grabbing and so came some way or other alive to the bottom. And there I sat in the soft, wet grass with the moonlight all about me and far above through the broken window of the Room, there was a low whistling.

"I was not hurt and went to the front and knocked. When they let me in we had a long yarn over some good whiskey—for I was shaken to pieces—and I explained things as much as I could. I told Tassoc that the room would have to come down and every fragment of it be burned in a blast-furnace erected within a pentacle. He nodded. There was nothing to say. Then I went to bed.

"We turned a small army on to the work and within ten days that lovely thing had gone up in smoke and what was left was calcined and clean.

"It was when the workmen were stripping the panelling that I got hold of a sound notion of the beginnings of that beastly development. Over the great fireplace, after the great oak panels had been torn down, I found that there was let into the masonry a scrollwork of stone with on it an old inscription in ancient Celtic, that here in this room was burned Dian Tiansay, Jester of King Alzof, who made the Song of Foolishness upon King Ernore of the Seventh Castle.

"When I got the translation clear I gave it to Tassoc. He was tremendously excited for he knew the old tale and took me down to the library to look at an old parchment that gave the story in detail. Afterwards I found that the incident was well-known about the countryside, but always regarded more as a legend than as history. And no one seemed ever to have dreamt that the old East Wing of Iastrae Castle was the remains of the ancient Seventh Castle.

"From the old parchment I gathered that there had been a pretty dirty job done, away back in the years. It seems that King Alzof and King Ernore had been enemies by birthright, as you might say truly, but that nothing more than a little raiding had occurred on either side for years until Dian Tiansay made the Song of Foolishness upon King Ernore and sang it before King Alzof, and so greatly was it appreciated that King Alzof gave the jester one of his ladies to wife.

"Presently all the people of the land had come to know the song and so it came at last to King Ernore who was so angered that he made war upon his old enemy and took and burned him and his castle; but Dian Tiansay, the jester, he brought with him to his own place and having torn his tongue out because of the song which he had made and sung, he imprisoned him in the Room in the East Wing (which was evidently used for unpleasant purposes), and the jester's wife he kept for himself, having a fancy for her prettiness.

"But one night Dian Tiansay's wife was not to be found and in the morning they discovered her lying dead in her husband's arms and he sitting, whistling the Song of Foolishness, for he had no longer the power to sing it.

"Then they roasted Dian Tiansay in the great fireplace—probably from the self-same 'gallows-iron' which I have already mentioned. And until he died Dian Tiansay 'ceased not to whistle' the Song of Foolishness which he could no longer sing. But afterwards 'in that room' there was often heard at night the sound of something whistling and there 'grew a power in that room' so that none dared to sleep in it. And presently, it would seem, the King went to another castle for the whistling troubled him.

"There you have it all. Of course, that is only a rough rendering of the translation from the parchment. It's a bit quaint! Don't you think so?"

"Yes," I said, answering for the lot. "But how did the thing grow to such a tremendous manifestation?"

"One of those cases of continuity of thought producing a positive action upon the immediate surrounding material," replied Carnacki. "The development must have been going forward through centuries, to have produced such a monstrosity. It was a true instance of Saiitii manifestation which I can best explain by likening it to a living spiritual fungus which involves the very structure of the aether-fibre itself and, of course, in so doing acquires an essential control over the 'material-substance' involved in it. It is impossible to make it plainer in a few words."

"Then you believe that the Room itself had become the material expression of the ancient Jester—that his soul, rotted with hatred had bred into a monster—eh?" I asked.

"Yes," said Carnacki, nodding. "I think you've put my thought rather neatly. It is a queer coincidence that Miss Donnehue is supposed to be descended (so I heard since) from the same King Ernore. It makes one think some rather curious thoughts, doesn't it? The marriage coming on and the Room waking to fresh life. If she had gone into that room, ever . . . eh? IT had waited a long time. Sins of the fathers. Yes, I've thought of that. They're to be married next week and I am to be best man, which is a thing I hate. And he won his bets, rather! Just think, *if* ever she had gone into that room, Pretty horrible, eh?"

He nodded his head, grimly, and we four nodded back. Then he rose and took us collectively to the door and presently thrust us forth in friendly fashion on to the Embankment and into the fresh night air.

"Good night," we called back and went to our various homes.

If she had, eh? If she had? That is what I kept thinking.

TOLD FOR THE TRUTH

Cyril Hume

THIS story was told me a year or two ago by an American doctor from Philadelphia. I met him in the American Express at Florence, and because I knew the city better than he, I was able to render him a slight service. As a result he had me to dine with him. We became acquainted over champagne.

He was a pleasant blondish man with thinning hair and a look of out-of-doors healthiness. He annoyed me a little at first. His smile was perhaps too charming. I could see him using it at the bedsides of his more fashionable lady patients. But over the second bottle of champagne he seemed a good fellow.

For a while the doctor told me many curious facts concerning the grim tricks nature plays with human flesh. He spoke quietly. I was reminded of an old biology instructor of mine who had used the same manner over my student microscope. ". . . Strange things. All of them strange. Some so strange that there are only two or three examples of them in the books. You'd think doctors would run into cases like that, wouldn't you? But there seems to be a sort of shame attached to them. They are kept hidden . . . Undertakers must come across amazing examples . . . I tell you it's a shock when one does run into a case, a completion and a fulfilment of what is only indicated by those rudimentary cases in the books."

Then I found myself listening to his story. It never occurred to me until later that he was a liar.

"This friend of mine—may as well call him Hunter—had been a kid with me. We lived next door for years in a suburb of Philadel-

170

phia. He and I went through the pet animal stage together. There was a disused shed on his place where we used to keep our menagerie of mice and turtles and rabbits and stray cats.

"I suppose that at one time or another we must have had twenty creatures in our crates and cages. Of course, there was nothing strange in that. All boys reach the pet-keeping stage. The strange thing was that Hunter never graduated from it. I went on to long trousers and cigarettes and girls, but Hunter stuck to his animals. After I broke up the partnership he began collecting snakes. Knots of them he had under glass. Then there was a big screen cage full of all kinds of spiders that used to devour each other. Finally somebody gave him a fox puppy. That was the time I nearly quit my girl-chasing to join him again.

"Hunter stuck. I don't remember ever seeing him even look at a girl. But cats would go to him in a way that would scare you.

"You mustn't think there was anything queer about Hunter, though. Except that his eyes used to go happy and soft whenever he saw an animal. At college his room whiffed of them. It was full of squeaks and scurries and whistles. He'd spend an evening with you, though, any time, and he'd let you name your bar. It was Hunter, for instance, who stole the safe out of the Dean's office in Junior year. There was nothing in any way queer about Hunter.

"Until he got himself a lemur. You know: one of those weezily monkeyish little creatures with a thick furry tail as long as itself. Hunter carried the thing everywhere with him. It would sit on his shoulder and wrap its tail around his throat and cling to his scalp with its nasty half-human hands. A wise little foxy face with big shining eyes that peered at you, and seemed to wonder and try to think . . . But all those years Hunter never had a girl.

"You can imagine then how surprised I was—I was doing my last year at Bellevue—when I got a letter from Hunter asking me to come down to Philadelphia to meet his fiancée. In his letter he tried to describe the girl to me, but all I could gather from his incoherencies was that she was from Georgia and he loved her crazily. He said— but you know how these woman-haters are once a woman gets hold of them.

"I could not get off to Philadelphia at once, but by the time I did go I was worried. I had heard things. You know the vague insinuating stories one hears sometimes. A person laughs when they're told. They seem to go in one ear and out the other. One can't even remember who told them. But they leave—cobwebs. Rotten stories.

Nothing actually against the girl. She was supposed to be right
enough. As a matter of fact, she was a member of one of the oldest
families in the South. The kind of family that is so old it has bona-fide
pre-Revolutionary history, and queer fables besides. These stories
hinted rather picturesquely at a vast uncultivated estate in Georgia
with not a single Negro on it. It seemed they refused to stay there,
and for generations all the servants in the great house had been
Finns.

"A race of warlocks, the Finns, silent people . . . Then there was
an even wilder yarn about the girl's brother. He was supposed to
be a great mathematician and chess-player whom no one ever saw.
He was kept locked up in a little shuttered brick library which was
detached from the main house. Now and then at night he'd break out,
and there would be trouble among the horses until the Finns captured
him again. Neighbors told stories of the Finns whooping through the
night with flashlights and ropes, and of a naked running man whose
monstrously long forearms ended in globes of bandage big as a man's
head . . . Gossip, of course, but the stories were queer. Suppose even
it was simple insanity. I worried a great deal when I was finally on
my way to Philadelphia.

"I can't say just what I thought the girl would be, but I'm quite
certain that in the back of my mind I was sure she'd be strange and
unwholesome in some way. I probably expected to be repelled by
her, so that when I met her the surprise was like a blow in the face.
Not that she was not strange enough and unwholesome enough, too.
But where I had looked for repulsiveness I found only danger. The
sort of danger that fascinates a man and challenges him and, unless
he is wonderfully self-controlled or very fortunate, makes a slave
of him. I looked at her with a kind of horror, and—do you know?—
the first thing I said to myself was, 'Good God! I've got to be loyal to
old Hunter!'

"She was a slender tall girl, very dark and vividly colored, but in
spite of her height she had the quick appearing grace of a little
woman. She had thoughtful and unreadable brown eyes. Her small
head was covered with dark childishly fine hair which fell naturally
into waves that somehow gave the impression of life and instability
like the photographed waves of running water.

"Perhaps I did not notice all these things in the moment when
we were introduced. I could not have, of course. However, I'm
certain I felt the resultant force of them. But in that first instant I

felt another force besides which had nothing at all to do with outward appearances. The force of her personality. Her soul, if you
prefer to call it that . . . Yes, when I met poor Hunter's fiancée I'm
sure I discerned something of her soul. And what I discerned chilled
me with a kind of Gothic fear, for it seemed to me that her soul
was entirely body . . .

"Perhaps I'm not clear. For example, certain thoroughbred
animals, fine horses or fine dogs, are so beautiful and alive, so proudly
conscious of their own beauty and vitality, that something radiates
out from them. Something that many humans lack, something one
feels and must venerate, an emanation, a soul. That was Hunter's
lovely passionate-lipped young fiancée.

"We shook hands. She looked steadily at me and said, 'How do
you do?' in a charming Southern voice which was not quite deep
enough rightly to be called contralto.

"Those are the only words I can remember her ever having said
to me. We must have spoken together a hundred times after that,
but I can actually remember only her first words.

"I stood holding her strange unwomanly hand, and I thought,
'God help me!' For in that moment I was whirled away on a wind
of longing and desire so overwhelming that even then I wondered at
it. In that moment, too, I had carried her off to a fury and a con-
summation of dream-perfect love-making. I vividly pictured the time
when I should look down bewilderedly close into her eyes and see
them as every man must long to see the eyes of the woman he loves.
With the under lid drawn upward at the corners in an expression almost of fierceness; with the upper lid drooping so heavily in a passive
drunkenness as to be pitiful; and between, the eyes themselves,
luminous, deep and soulless as the open eyes of a cataleptic.

"You see, I fell in love with the girl—all in an instant as I held
her hand. And so I said, 'God help me! I must be loyal.' But even
as I said that I was disloyal, for I looked at her and longed for
her . . . I can imagine no woman being quite unconscious of the
flood of emotion which poured out of me toward her just then. At
such moments a woman knows. She takes her hand away more
quickly or more slowly than usual. She does this or that with her
eyes. And she has answered you. But this quiet Southern girl made
no sign whatever. Her eyes remained steady and thoughtful. Her long
unwomanly hand neither hurried nor lingered. She felt nothing.

"I asked myself how had gentle simple old Hunter ever seized upon and held this girl, this dark flame more terrible than an army with banners. And I knew it had been the lemur. Don't ask me how I knew, or why. But I'm certain I was right. The lemur entirely deserted Hunter for the girl now, and I think Hunter was jealous. He would call, 'Chee-ki! Chee-ki!' and clap his hands. But the little animal that had been so obedient would only turn its face and look when Hunter called. It would cling tighter than ever to the girl, and the girl would smile. Hunter hated it, and I hated it. Chee-ki would perch on the girl's shoulder and curl his long tail close about her neck in a kind of embrace. Or it would sweep the thing over her body, as if appraising her. Softly, gropingly, tenderly. And she would smile. I hated it.

"But I must go back and tell you of the evening when I met her first. There was to be a small dinner. As Hunter's best friend I was to sit next to his fiancée. Hunter genially told us to get acquainted. That was the purpose of the dinner . . . After my first stunning surge of desire for the girl I managed to get myself a little in hand so that I was able to notice various things about her.

"She was stranger even than I had imagined she would be. This was back in 1920. You remember the clothes girls were wearing then, short knee-length affairs? Well, the first thing that surprised me about Hunter's fiancée was that her skirt reached to her ankles, and when I looked close I guessed that her gown had been made at home. I don't mean to give the impression that the girl looked shoddy.

"As a matter of fact the thing she was wearing seemed to me very lovely. It was made of some soft flesh-colored stuff, and there were silvery strips in the skirt. It clung about her with more amplitude than was the fashion then, in long folds of inevitable grace. She made a striking and, to me, an exquisite contrast to the rest of the women in the room. As I watched her I noticed with the tender and indulgent amusement of a man in love that she was extraordinarily careful of her Greek-like draperies. More careful even than a woman is likely to be. Careful with the meticulousness of a Persian cat. When she sat down or rose to her feet she arranged her skirt about herself almost with anxiety. It struck me at the time that in spite of her care its grace was marred now and then by an awkward gathering or a heavy fold.

"Dinner was announced and I followed her into the dining room with my eyes focused upon the nape of her slim neck. And I thought how I would kiss her neck just there where my eyes rested, and how I would encircle her throat with kisses like a chain to bind her to me. Then I had a shock. My eyes jumped to keener focus. Below the sharp line where her bobbed hair ended I could see, in spite of the powder that had been laid on so artfully, that the skin was faintly blue with subcutaneous hairs like the shaved chin of a dark man. This bluish sheen, which only the closest scrutiny such as a lover's could detect, ran out of sight below the rather high neck of her dinner gown. My mind put a fantastic and sickening question, so that for a moment I felt a bitter antagonism for this tall girl who walked so gracefully and so pliantly before me into the bright dining room. But when I held her chair for her at the dinner-table I forgot my resentment. I could only watch with an almost painful tenderness how childishly careful she was in arranging her long skirt.

"I might have been drunk for all I can remember of that dinner. None of its conversation comes back, and only a few of the faces that ringed the table. I can recall vaguely that all the women seemed constrained, and that I said to myself, 'I am imagining all this because she is so much more alive than they.' A perfume came from her, more disturbing than any I had ever known. I remember watching her hands. They were thin lovely hands. The nails were longer, more pointed and more highly polished than I suppose was quite good taste. But at the time my heart was bursting to kiss them.

"They were not a woman's hands. She did not use them as women use them, to supplement her beauty. When they were idle they lay in her lap or rested on the table edge, unaffected and relaxed as resting animals. What was most unusual, she was not, as is every newly engaged girl, even absently conscious of her blazing solitaire. When she stretched her hand out I saw that the ring had slipped around on her finger, and the stone was turned in.

"She seemed unaware of this and left it so. Strong hands. Once she took an almond in one of them, and removed the shell with a motion so deft and quick I could not see how she had done it. Afterward she seemed confused.

"I sat beside her in a trance-like abstraction . . . At the head of the table sat Hunter's mother, a large beautifully turned-out woman with the sort of personality that heads ladies' committees, and the sort of hair that is compared to platinum. Even in my abstraction I saw that she was tense like the rest of the women at the table, and that she seemed worried. These things are vague. I may have imagined them . . .

"A girl was sitting beside Hunter directly across the table from me. She was a pretty girl, with a cloud of golden hair and a patrician air. One could tell from her manner that her people must be socially prominent in Philadelphia. A fine courageous child, innocently arrogant, proud because of inexperience, assured because of her looks and her position. I watched her mistily and, if I recollect, almost regretfully, as a man might look back from fairyland into the dear ordinary world of unenchantment. And somehow I felt sorry for the child, and somewhat grateful, too. Soon I was aware that an antagonism had sprung to life between her and the dark woman beside me. Their eyes came to grips across the table. All the while, aloofly, wistfully, carelessly, I was admiring the fine unbroken arrogance of the girl opposite me. The woman at my side betrayed no arrogance, no heat. She was simply quiet and altogether attentive. All at once the girl across the table began to blush—painfully, conspicuously. Her blue eyes fell, as though they had looked inadvertently at something shameful. For a while she struggled with a confusion which brought her close to tears. When she had mastered it she gave her attention to Hunter with a forced and frightened vivacity.

"Next I realized that the woman beside me had become jealous, furiously jealous of Hunter and the girl next to him. Now there was no possible reason for this. His face was dull and vacuous with adoration. But surely I felt emanating from this woman so intense a current of jealous hatred that I was frightened of her, and stabbed with admiration. I watched out of the corners of my eyes, experiencing fear, desire, awe . . .

"Suddenly I felt a strong muffled blow on my calf, as though some hurrying animal had got entangled in the woman's dress and had blundered against me. A moment later the same thing again, so strong this time that I started and looked down. Mrs. Hunter's eyes must have been on us all through dinner, for she caught my start and called at once, 'What is it, Doctor?'

"I answered stupidly something about imagining that Chee-ki had run against my leg. Mrs. Hunter told one of the servants to see if Chee-ki had escaped from the sun porch. The man came back shortly with the reply that the creature was asleep in its basket. Everybody laughed, Hunter's fiancée with the rest. But when a new topic of conversation had distracted the other guests, she turned her head quick as an animal and gave me a look of fury that made me a little sick with terror. In an instant her face was calm again, and I might have thought I had imagined her look but that she moved slightly in her chair and sat further from me during the rest of the dinner.

"I remember Mrs. Hunter's eyes at the end of the table. Her face was the face of an assured and skilled hostess, but her eyes were puzzled and worried.

"Love for the girl took me irresistibly. After less than five hours in her presence I found myself loving her with an intensity which I had not imagined possible. I knew nothing about her. I had no especial sympathy or respect for her. In fact some instinct warned me that if I could see her once uncloaked in glamor I should find her hateful and repulsive. And yet I felt for her an almost insane tenderness, a more than insane hunger. She preoccupied me so completely that I was not even ashamed of making no attempt to combat my infatuation for her, the fiancée of a friend.

"I became a monomaniac, ruthless with desperation. After that first evening I began following her. I tried deliberately to make her see, to make her feel the thing that shook me. If I remember, I actually tried to speak of it once or twice.

"Hunter was quite blind to all this. In his infatuation with her he was as preoccupied as I was. But she herself understood me very well. I had no doubt of that. And I felt a demonic exultation that her understanding failed to trouble or to anger her. I sensed a conscienceless evil in her and my heart cried out to it . . . But except for this fact that she knew my mind and still tolerated me, she did nothing during those weeks to which even Hunter and his worried mother could take exception.

"Hunter and she were married shortly. I was best man. The memory of the pain I suffered that day affects me still with a faint nausea. To me everything that happened was like the slow formless ceremonial of a fever. I was desperate, crazy with a degrading and vivid physical jealousy. There were impulses in me toward violence and homicide . . .

"He took her away finally. I watched her little feet mount briskly into a waiting limousine, and through a silver haze I seemed to notice an ugly fold at the back of her skirt. Then she was gone. One thought alone kept me from running amuck among the guests. 'When they come back,' I said, 'I shall be invited to their house very often.'

My whole nature closed upon that thought like dull snake jaws over a stone.

"They returned from their honeymoon sooner than had been expected, and I had a telephone call from Hunter almost immediately. He asked me to lunch with him at his club on the following day. I went to the appointment speculating indifferently whether or not I should stab him where he sat at table. But when I saw him, there was something in his look which jumped my heart with a fear that everything was not well with his wife. It is hard to describe that look. I have seen it often and had to steel myself against it in hospital corridors where women wait in mortal terror and mortal pain outside closed doors, afraid to put into speech the question their eyes are shrieking.

"Hunter seemed older now, littler, utterly subdued. His naïve good nature had shriveled, like a fruit that rots without having ripened, into pain. I asked him quickly if his wife was well, and he assured me that she was very well, very well, indeed. But his manner only strengthened my sick misgivings.

"I went to their house for the first time, weak with the fear that I should find her ill. Then I saw her, and literally I was stunned by the blaze of vitality which seemed to spread out from her in dark swordlike rays.

"It was as though all her hidden energy of living had been realized at last, and released somehow to drench a world of lovers. And in that first instant when I saw her I had an intuition strong as a conviction that it was because she was to have a child.

"I sat in her presence adoring her and desiring her beauty, crying out silently in exultation to the living evil of her soul. Presently I glanced at Hunter and was struck to wild internal laughter. The idiot was treating this woman, this flaring nebula of energy, as though she were an invalid. His voice and all his gestures were soft. He kept trying to make her comfortable with cushions and footstools. (She, I thought, 'who might sit naked upon a throne of iron to be adored forever!') His eyes were sad and tender like those woman eyes in hospital corridors. His mouth was wistful, gentle and ineffably sad with smiles.

"She resented this tenderness, and repaid him with such fierce scorn that I could have shouted for pride in her. He would come close and bend over her and whisper anxiously, but she would turn away her dark head which seemed to me to be always crowned with rays. The lemur on her shoulder would show its little teeth and chatter angrily.

"I suppose you will despise me. I suppose I ought to despise myself for my behavior. Yet in retrospect I cannot blame myself any more than I could blame another person, one of my patients perhaps, who was suffering from some fever or brain disease. And actually all the events of those days are vague in my memory as the recollections of a sickness.

"I would come to the house of my old friend, sometimes as often as three times a week, with the definite intention of seducing his wife. When my last year of internship at Bellevue was over I moved to Philadelphia immediately so that I could be near her and see her every day . . . The three of us used to sit around in the evening after dinner, talking together. As I remember those evenings now it seems as though there must always have been two conversations going on simultaneously. For the life of me I can't be certain. But either we talked aloud, all three of us, of casual things while Hunter's wife and I addressed each other telepathically without words (I told you I can remember nothing she ever said), or else she and I had those amazing conversations aloud while Hunter sat by in silence, apathetic because of what he knew. Whether I actually spoke aloud or not, there is no doubt but that she understood. She would sit impassive, smiling a little and denying me.

"Again sometimes she would seem to withdraw into herself as into an immense silence and brood there over some secret thing which I knew was the child she was to bear. And every day the aura of her vitality grew in size and intensity. As she sat, the lemur would perch upon her or scramble over her. Occasionally it would scold at Hunter, Hunter would watch his wife, and his face was very tender and very sad.

"One day Hunter came to me and said that he was worried about his wife, that he had been worried for some time. He thought that I might, considering the fortunate circumstance that I came to the house often as a friend, take the opportunity of observing her professionally quite without her knowledge. I accepted quickly. Hunter thanked me. Had I noticed anything peculiar about her lately? I answered as calmly as I could that to me she seemed to be in exceptionally good health. But Hunter shook his head and looked harassed. It was not so much her bodily health he was speaking of, he said. He thought there was something of another sort wrong with her.

"But he would let me observe for myself. For he was worried. He was certain there was something in her mind which was dragging her apart, slowly away from the normal thoughts and motives of human beings. This, he admitted, might be due to a—a certain physical misfortune of hers . . . But no matter about that just now. It was her mind only that concerned him. She had become subject to odd and increasing fits of excitement during which she seemed . . . when it almost seemed to him that she was regressing toward something . . . something he didn't care to think about. Then there was this physical misfortune. Perhaps that . . . But he wanted me to see if I could reach the trouble through her mind before he spoke of that.

"I made nothing of this rigmarole. In my excitement I hardly paid any attention to it. After that I came to the house even more often than before, and when I was alone with Hunter I would pretend seriously to discuss his wife's condition with him. 'I wouldn't worry,' I'd say. 'It's nothing serious I'm sure. Still I'll watch. I have a notion, too, that I'm beginning to get at the trouble you mentioned. Just a little time. But in the meanwhile there's really no need of worrying.' And Hunter would be grateful.

"So more and more I continued to implore her, speaking madly and obscenely out of my unbalanced brain. And she sat impassive, always refusing me, beautiful in her draped and occasionally awkward clothes, terrible and compelling with the radiance of her vital force. She would only listen, saying no words that I can remember, smiling a little, and with her long inhuman hands caressing the agile clinging body of the lemur. And from week to week her invisible field of power expanded and grew in strength until I thought it must crack and explode presently, like an overcharged cloud, into destroying lightning. Hunter watched in deep sadness. For myself, I could only hold my breath and adore and wait almost in fear. Sometimes it seemed to me that the lemur waited also . . .

"I became filled with a kind of wincing expectancy during those last days. I have no idea what I expected. Anything, I suppose, which would relieve the constantly increasing tension. And my expectation produced in me that feeling of nervous exasperation one gets from watching a long cigar ash and waiting for it to fall. As I said, I felt that the lemur was waiting, too, waiting with more knowledge and more certainty than I. But that final afternoon I had no premonition, no idea at all . . .

"It had been a slightly overcast day late in March. I came to the house as usual shortly after five o'clock, expecting a talk and a cocktail or two before dinner. Now night was falling. There was a faint gleam of ugly color in the west, and it seemed as though a thin yellow glow clung in the upper branches of the bare trees along the street. I reached the house at twilight.

"As I climbed the front porch I was surprised to see no lights in any of the windows, and to hear no noise at all in the recesses of the house. The place was still and shadowy as though it had been empty for a decade. I listened with God knows what thoughts tearing through my mind. Then presently it seemed that after all there was a sound—high overhead inside the house. A squeaky creak, I thought, regular as the beat of a pendulum, but so faint I could not be sure I was really hearing it.

"I listened, with my hand poised irresolutely over the door-bell. Then for no particular reason I began remembering my own expectations of disaster—and wondering. 'Hunter has been so bothered,' I mused. Could there have been a reason after all? Then something said to me: There are no servants in this quiet house. They have left as they have always left . . . Sometimes I thought I heard that thin sound high under the house roof. Sometimes not. But in the intervals of doubt my memory kept time, and presently I would pick up the rhythm again . . . I peered through the glass of the front door. But there was a net curtain inside and I could distinguish nothing. As I peered, the silence of the house poured out to me, burdened faintly with that indefinable creaking which beat like a metronome above it.

"All at once I knew I must ring the bell without delay, or else turn away in the twilight from that door and run with fear under the bare trees. Suddenly, hysterically, I shot my thumb against the bell-button and held it there, held it there. Then as suddenly I drew back my hand in panic. Deep in the house the frightful clangor of the bell had summoned fear up from silence. Silence fell back, but that awakened fear came near to me, and crowded close behind the door. And now it seemed as though that squeaking sound beat faster because of the fear, just as my own heart beat . . .

"I heard light feet gallop down the stair inside. Behind the curtain I saw a dim motion, a blob of shadow that darted and bounded here and there, swift as a frightened captive bird. Then startlingly close against my eyes Chee-ki's face appeared upon the curtain. He clung for a moment, looking out at me with bright inscrutability. Then he was gone again, and I could see his moving shadow and hear him dashing softly about in the hall beyond the door. There was something unbearable in the reckless excitement of the small creature loose and alone in the still house. I thought I would be sick if it continued, so I tried the latch. The door was unlocked. I pushed it open and entered. 'Chee-ki!' I called in a queer voice. 'Chee-ki! Be still!'

"The lemur sprang up to the top of the newel-post and perched there with his long tail hanging. He sat quite still, looking with shining excited eyes alternately at me and toward the top of the shadowed stair. As though he beckoned. I advanced across the hall. Chee-ki leaped down from his perch and ran swiftly on all fours before me up the stair, carrying his tail high like a cat hurrying to be fed. I followed silently. As I climbed I heard, now unmistakably, that faint creak which beat on and on above the dark hush of the house.

"As I reached the landing of the second floor I saw Chee-ki scuttle down the hall and flash into the doorway of the room I knew to be Hunter's . . . Hunter's body lay twisted upon the bed. His face was toward the ceiling. It shone like silver in the dusk, except where a dark stain ran down from one corner of his mouth to form a small black fan upon the pillow. My nose stung with the faint reek of an acid, and when I searched I found an empty bottle on the floor. I went close and touched Hunter's hand. It was cold. I said, 'Oh!—Hunter!' Then Chee-ki, on the footboard of the bed, began chattering very loudly. 'Quiet!' I whispered. 'Chee-ki!'

"Chee-ki commenced chattering again, and again I whispered, 'Quiet!' For a little longer I stood listening to that thin regular sound above my head. My pulse shook with it. Hunter's big golf bag stood in one corner of the room. Hardly thinking what I did I went over to it and chose a heavy niblick with a stout shaft. Gripping this I went out into the hall. Chee-ki followed.

"I was certain now where the sound came from. I crept toward the attic stair. Once I stumbled, and looking down I saw one of her long dresses lying in a heap at my feet. Further on were a slipper and a stocking. The sound was very plain now, a heavy muffled creak such as wood might give out, complaining under some uneasy weight. Clutching the niblick I moved forward.

"It was almost dark in the attic. I blinked and peered. Then Chee-ki chattered and I heard the answer. Looking upward I saw that shadow swinging from the roof-beams. And I understood . . .

I shall not tell you, because you could not believe how she was swinging there, making the beam creak rhythmically under her weight. But I shall tell you that she hung head-downward, and that she chattered as the lemur also chattered.

"I think I did not move for a long time after I saw her, because it had become quite dark in the attic when the thought came which cut through my terror with a flash of anger: the thought of the child she would bring into the world. My fingers tightened upon the niblick handle . . .

"Afterward I came down from the attic and rummaged among poor Hunter's shaving things in the bathroom. Then, with a candle and the instrument I had sought, I climbed the stairs again. Considerably later I stumbled down through the darkness into the cellar of the house. I moved uncertainly because there was no light, and my hands were occupied so I could not feel my way.

"The weather had been mild so that the furnace was checked when I found it. The whole thing took some time, especially as I was careful to make no noise when I put on more coal. But at last it was over. I opened all the draughts and went upstairs again. I arranged Hunter's shaving things as I had found them. I removed certain spots from the attic floor. Then I telephoned the police.

"The coroner who investigated the case decided that Hunter had taken his wife to the attic and beaten in her skull with the heavy golf club which was discovered near the body, and that he had then immediately gone down to his room and drunk a pint of corrosive cleaning-fluid. The coroner offered no theory concerning a motive for the crime.

"A friend who had discovered the double tragedy had testified that as far as he knew the Hunters had been happy together. Insanity at once suggested itself, though an autopsy revealed no lesions in Hunter's brain. The coroner had no doubts as to the actual facts of the case (a murder followed by a suicide) though certain aspects of it puzzled him. First, the body of Hunter's pet lemur had been found in the upper hallway with its neck wrung. Second, although the weather was mild, the furnace had been burning furiously when the police arrived at the house.

"One of the officers had investigated this suspicious circumstance by dumping and extinguishing the fire, and had discovered among the embers what appeared to be the oxidized and scattered back-bone of some unidentified vertebrate. Third, when he had examined Mrs.

Hunter's body he had discovered a skilfully made incision at the base of the spine."

My companion rose suddenly. "I guess I've drunk too much," he muttered. He picked up his hat, and wandered away across the square . . . It did not occur to me until later that the man was an outrageous liar.

THE ASH TREE

M. R. James

EVERYONE who has traveled over Eastern England knows the smaller country-houses with which it is studded—the rather dank little buildings, usually in the Italian style, surrounded with parks of some eighty to a hundred acres. For me they have always had a very strong attraction: with the gray paling of split oak, the noble trees, the meres with their reed-beds, and the line of distant woods. Then, I like the pillared portico—perhaps stuck on to a red-brick Queen Anne house which has been faced with stucco to bring it into line with the "Grecian" taste of the end of the eighteenth century; the hall inside, going up to the roof, which hall ought always to be provided with a gallery and a small organ. I like the library, too, where you may find anything from a Psalter of the thirteenth century to a Shakespeare quarto. I like the pictures, of course; and perhaps most of all I like fancying what life in such a house was when it was first built, and in the piping times of landlords' prosperity, and not least now, when, if money is not so plentiful, taste is more varied and life quite as interesting. I wish to have one of these houses, and enough money to keep it together and entertain my friends in it modestly.

But this is a digression. I have to tell you of a curious series of events which happened in such a house as I have tried to describe. It is Castringham Hall in Suffolk. I think a good deal has been done to the building since the period of my story, but the essential features I have sketched are still there—Italian portico, square block of white house, older inside than out, park with fringe of woods, and mere. The one feature that marked out the house from a score of others is gone. As you looked at it from the park, you saw on the right a great old ash tree growing within half a dozen yards of the wall, and almost or quite touching the building with its branches. I suppose it had stood there ever since Castringham ceased to be a fortified place, and since the moat was filled in and the Elizabethan dwelling-house built. At any rate, it had well-nigh attained its full dimensions in the year 1690.

In that year the district in which the Hall is situated was the scene of a number of witch trials. It will be long, I think, before we arrive at a just estimate of the amount of solid reason—if there was any—which lay at the root of the universal fear of witches in old times. Whether the persons accused of this offense really did imagine that they were possessed of unusual powers of any kind; or whether they had the will at least, if not the power, of doing mischief to their neighbors; or whether all the confessions, of which there are so many, were extorted by the mere cruelty of the witch finders—these are questions which are not, I fancy, yet solved. And the present narrative gives me pause. I cannot altogether sweep it away as mere invention. The reader must judge for himself.

Castringham contributed a victim to the auto-da-fé. Mrs. Mothersole was her name, and she differed from the ordinary run of village witches only in being rather better off and in a more influential position. Efforts were made to save her by several reputable farmers of the parish. They did their best to testify to her character, and showed considerable anxiety as to the verdict of the jury.

But what seems to have been fatal to the woman was the evidence of the then proprietor of Castringham Hall—Sir Matthew Fell. He deposed to having watched her on three different occasions from his window, at the full of the moon, gathering sprigs "from the ash tree near my house." She had climbed into the branches, clad only in her shift, and was cutting off small twigs with a peculiarly curved knife, and as she did so she seemed to be talking to herself. On each occasion Sir Matthew had done his best to capture the woman, but she had always taken alarm at some accidental noise he had made, and all he could see when he got down to the garden was a hare running across the park in the direction of the village.

On the third night he had been at pains to follow at his best speed, and had gone straight to Mrs. Mothersole's house; but he had had to wait a quarter of an hour battering at her door, and then she had come out very cross, and apparently very sleepy, as if just out of bed; and he had no good explanation to offer of his visit.

Mainly on this evidence, though there was much more of a less striking and unusual kind from other parishioners, Mrs. Mothersole was found guilty and condemned to die. She was hanged a week after the trial, with five or six more unhappy creatures, at Bury St. Edmunds.

Sir Matthew Fell, then deputy sheriff, was present at the execution. It was a damp, drizzly March morning when the cart made its way up the rough grass hill outside Northgate, where the gallows stood. The other victims were apathetic or broken down with misery; but Mrs. Mothersole was, as in life so in death, of a very different temper. Her "poysonous Rage," as a reporter of the time puts it, "did so work upon the Bystanders—yea, even upon the Hangman—that it was constantly affirmed of all that saw her that she presented the living Aspect of a mad Divell. Yet she offer'd no Resistance to the Officers of the Law; onely she looked upon those that laid Hands upon her with so direfull and venomous an Aspect that—as one of them afterwards assured me—the meer Thought of it preyed inwardly upon his Mind for six Months after."

However, all that she is reported to have said was the seemingly meaningless words: "There will be guests at the Hall." Which she repeated more than once in an undertone.

Sir Matthew Fell was not unimpressed by the bearing of the woman. He had some talk upon the matter with the vicar of his parish, with whom he traveled home after the assize business was over. His evidence at the trial had not been very willingly given; he was not specially infected with the witch-finding mania, but he declared, then and afterwards, that he could not give any other account of the matter than that he had given, and that he could not possibly have been mistaken as to what he saw. The whole transaction had been repugnant to him, for he was a man who liked to be on pleasant terms with those about him; but he saw a duty to be done in this business, and he had done it. That seems to have been the gist of his sentiments, and the vicar applauded it, as any reasonable man must have done.

A few weeks after, when the moon of May was at the full, vicar and squire met again in the park, and walked to the Hall together. Lady Fell was with her mother, who was dangerously ill, and Sir Matthew was alone at home; so the vicar, Mr. Crome, was easily persuaded to take a late supper at the Hall.

Sir Matthew was not very good company this evening. The talk ran chiefly on family and parish matters, and, as luck would have it, Sir Matthew made a memorandum in writing of certain wishes or intentions of his regarding his estates, which afterwards proved exceedingly useful.

When Mr. Crome thought of starting for home, about half-past nine o'clock, Sir Matthew and he took a preliminary turn on the graveled walk at the back of the house. The only incident that struck Mr. Crome was this: they were in sight of the ash tree which I described as growing near the windows of the building, when Sir Matthew stopped and said:

"What is that that runs up and down the stem of the ash? It is never a squirrel? They will all be in their nests by now."

The vicar looked and saw the moving creature, but he could make nothing of its color in the moonlight. The sharp outline, however, seen for an instant, was imprinted on his brain, and he could have sworn, he said, though it sounded foolish, that, squirrel or not, it had more than four legs.

Still, not much was to be made of the momentary vision, and the two men parted. They may have met since then, but it was not for a score of years.

Next day Sir Matthew Fell was not downstairs at six in the morning, as was his custom, nor at seven, nor yet at eight. Hereupon the servants went and knocked at his chamber door. I need not prolong the description of their anxious listenings and renewed batterings on the panels. The door was opened at last from the outside, and they found their master dead and black. So much you have guessed. That there were any marks of violence did not at the moment appear; but the window was open.

One of the men went to fetch the parson, and then by his directions rode on to give notice to the coroner. Mr. Crome himself went as quick as he might to the Hall, and was shown to the room where the dead man lay. He has left some notes among his papers which show how genuine a respect and sorrow was felt for Sir Matthew, and there is also this passage, which I transcribe for the sake of the light it throws upon the course of events, and also upon the common beliefs of the time:

"There was not any the least Trace of an Entrance having been forc'd to the Chamber: but the Casement stood open, as my poor Friend would always have it in this Season. He had his Evening Drink of small Ale in a silver vessel of about a pint measure, and to-night had not drunk it out. This Drink was examined by the Physician from Bury, a Mr. Hodgkins, who could not, however, as he afterwards declar'd upon his Oath, before the Coroner's quest, discover that any matter of a venomous kind was present in it. For, as was natural, in the great Swelling and Blackness of the Corpse, there was talk made among the Neighbours of Poyson. The Body was very much Disorder'd as it laid in the Bed, being twisted after so extream a sort as gave too probable Conjecture that my worthy Friend and Patron had expir'd in great Pain and Agony. And what is as yet unexplain'd, and to myself the Argument of some Horrid and Artful Designe in the Perpetrators of this Barbarous Murther, was this, that the Women which were entrusted with the laying-out of the Corpse and washing it, being both sad Persons and very well Respected in their Mournful Profession, came to me in a great Pain and Distress both of Mind and Body, saying, what was indeed confirmed upon the first View, that they had no sooner touch'd the Breast of the Corpse with their naked Hands than they were sensible of a more than ordinary violent Smart and Acheing in their Palms, which, with their whole Forearms, in no long time swell'd so immoderately, the Pain still continuing, that, as afterwards proved, during many weeks they were forc'd to lay by the exercise of their Calling; and yet no mark seen on the Skin.

"Upon hearing this, I sent for the Physician, who was still in the House, and we made as careful a Proof as we were able by the Help of a small Magnifying Lens of Crystal of the condition of the Skinn on this Part of the Body: but could not detect with the Instrument we had any Matter of Importance beyond a couple of small Punctures or Pricks, which we then concluded were the Spotts by which the Poyson might be introduced, remembering that Ring of *Pope Borgia,* with other known Specimens of the Horrid Act of the Italian Poysoners of the last age.

"So much is to be said of the Symptoms seen on the Corpse. As to what I am to add, it is merely my own Experiment, and to be left to Posterity to judge whether there be anything of Value therein. There was on the Table by the Beddside a Bible of the small size, in which my Friend—punctuall as in Matters of less Moment, so in this more weighty one—used nightly, and upon his First

Rising, to read a sett Portion. And I taking it up—not without a Tear duly paid to him which from the Study of this poorer Adumbration was now pass'd to the contemplation of its great Originall—it came into my Thoughts, as at such moments of Helplessness we are prone to catch at any the least Glimmer that makes promise of Light, to make trial of that old and by many accounted Superstitious Practice of drawing the *Sortes*: of which a Principall Instance, in the case of his late Sacred Majesty the Blessed Martyr King *Charles* and my Lord *Falkland,* was now much talked of. I must needs admit that by my Trial not much Assistance was afforded me: yet, as the Cause and Origin of these Dreadful Events may hereafter be search'd out, I set down the Results, in the case it may be found that they pointed the true Quarter of the Mischief to a quicker Intelligence than my own.

"I made, then, three trials, opening the Book and placing my Finger upon certain Words: which gave in the first these words, from Luke xiii. 7, *Cut it down;* in the second, Isaiah xiii. 20, *It shall never be inhabited;* and upon the third Experiment, Job xxxix. 30, *Her young ones also suck up blood.*"

This is all that need be quoted from Mr. Crome's papers. Sir Matthew Fell was duly coffined and laid into the earth, and his funeral sermon, preached by Mr. Crome on the following Sunday, has been printed under the title of "The Unsearchable Way; or, England's Danger and the Malicious Dealings of Antichrist," it being the vicar's view, as well as that most commonly held in the neighborhood, that the squire was the victim of a recrudescence of the Popish Plot.

His son, Sir Matthew the second, succeeded to the title and estates. And so ends the first act of the Castringham tragedy. It is to be mentioned, though the fact is not surprising, that the new baronet did not occupy the room in which his father had died. Nor, indeed, was it slept in by anyone but an occasional visitor during the whole of his occupation. He died in 1735, and I do not find that anything particular marked his reign, save a curiously constant mortality among his cattle and livestock in general, which showed a tendency to increase slightly as time went on.

Those who are interested in the details will find a statistical account in a letter to the *Gentleman's Magazine* of 1772, which draws the facts from the baronet's own papers. He put an end to it at last by a very simple expedient, that of shutting up all his beasts in sheds at night, and keeping no sheep in his park. For he had noticed that nothing was ever attacked that spent the night indoors. After that the disorder confined itself to wild birds, and beasts of chase. But as we have no good account of the symptoms, and as all-night watching was quite unproductive of any clue, I do not dwell on what the Suffolk farmers called the "Castringham sickness."

The second Sir Matthew died in 1735, as I said, and was duly succeeded by his son, Sir Richard. It was in his time that the great family pew was built out on the north side of the parish church. So large were the squire's ideas that several of the graves on that unhallowed side of the building had to be disturbed to satisfy his requirements. Among them was that of Mrs. Mothersole, the position of which was accurately known, thanks to a note on a plan of the church and yard, both made by Mr. Crome.

A certain amount of interest was excited in the village when it was known that the famous witch, who was still remembered by a few, was to be exhumed. And the feeling of surprise, and indeed disquiet, was very strong when it was found that, though her coffin was fairly sound and unbroken, there was no trace whatever inside it of body, bones, or dust. Indeed, it is a curious phenomenon, for at the time of her burying no such things were dreamed of as resurrection men, and it is difficult to conceive any rational motive for stealing a body otherwise than for the uses of the dissecting room.

The incident revived for a time all the stories of witch trials and of the exploits of the witches, dormant for forty years, and Sir Richard's orders that the coffin should be burned were thought by a good many to be rather foolhardy, though they were duly carried out.

Sir Richard was a pestilent innovator, it is certain. Before his time the Hall had been a fine block of the mellowest red brick; but Sir Richard had traveled in Italy and become infected with the Italian taste, and, having more money than his predecessors, he determined to leave an Italian palace where he had found an English house. So stucco and ashlar masked the brick; some indifferent Roman marbles were planted about in the entrance hall and gardens; a reproduction of the Sibyl's temple at Tivoli was erected on the opposite bank of the mere; and Castringham took on an entirely new, and, I must say, a less engaging, aspect. But it was much admired, and served as a model to a good many of the neighboring gentry in after-years.

One morning (it was in 1754) Sir Richard woke after a night of discomfort. It had been windy, and his chimney had smoked persistently, and yet it was so cold that he must keep up a fire. Also something had so rattled about the window that no man could get a moment's peace. Further, there was the prospect of several guests of position arriving in the course of the day, who would expect sport of some kind, and the inroads of the distemper (which continued among his game) had been lately so serious that he was afraid for his reputation as a game preserver. But what really touched him most nearly was the other matter of his sleepless night. He could certainly not sleep in that room again.

That was the chief subject of his meditations at breakfast, and after it he began a systematic examination of the rooms to see which would suit his notions best. It was long before he found one. This had a window with an eastern aspect and that with a northern; this door the servants would be always passing, and he did not like the bedstead in that. No, he must have a room with a western lookout, so that the sun could not wake him early, and it must be out of the way of the business of the house. The housekeeper was at the end of her resources.

"Well, Sir Richard," she said, "you know that there is but one room like that in the house."

"Which may that be?" said Sir Richard.

"And that is Sir Matthew's—the west chamber."

"Well, put me in there, for there I'll lie tonight," said her master. "Which way is it? Here, to be sure," and he hurried off.

"Oh, Sir Richard, but no one has slept there these forty years. The air has hardly been changed since Sir Matthew died there."

Thus she spoke, and rustled after him.

"Come, open the door, Mrs. Chiddock. I'll see the chamber, at least."

So it was opened, and, indeed, the smell was very close and earthy. Sir Richard crossed to the window, and, impatiently, as was his wont, threw the shutters back, and flung open the casement. For this end of the house was one which the alterations had barely touched, grown up as it was with the great ash tree, and being otherwise concealed from view.

"Air it, Mrs. Chiddock, all today, and move my bed-furniture in in the afternoon. Put the Bishop of Kilmore in my old room."

"Pray, Sir Richard," said a new voice, breaking in on this speech, "might I have the favor of a moment's interview?"

Sir Richard turned round and saw a man in black in the doorway, who bowed.

"I must ask your indulgence for this intrusion, Sir Richard. You will, perhaps, hardly remember me. My name is William Crome, and my grandfather was vicar here in your grandfather's time."

"Well, sir," said Sir Richard, "the name of Crome is always a passport to Castringham. I am glad to renew a friendship of two generations' standing. In what can I serve you? For your hour of calling—and, if I do not mistake you, your bearing—shows you to be in some haste."

"That is no more than the truth, sir. I am riding from Norwich to Bury St. Edmunds with what haste I can make, and I have called in on my way to leave with you some papers which we have but just come upon in looking over what my grandfather left at his death. It is thought you may find some matters of family interest in them."

"You are mighty obliging, Mr. Crome, and, if you will be so good as to follow me to the parlor, and drink a glass of wine, we will take a first look at these same papers together. And you, Mrs. Chiddock, as I said, be about airing this chamber. . . . Yes, it is here my grandfather died. . . . Yes, the tree, perhaps, does make the place a little dampish. . . . No; I do not wish to listen to any more. Make no difficulties, I beg. You have your orders—go. Will you follow me, sir?"

They went to the study. The packet which young Mr. Crome had brought—he was then just become a Fellow of Clare Hall in Cambridge, I may say, and subsequently brought out a respectable edition of Polyænus—contained among other things the notes which the old vicar had made upon the occasion of Sir Matthew Fell's death. And for the first time Sir Richard was confronted with the enigmatical *Sortes Biblicæ* which you have heard. They amused him a good deal.

"Well," he said, "my grandfather's Bible gave one prudent piece of advice—*Cut it down*. If that stands for the ash tree, he may rest assured I shall not neglect it. Such a nest of catarrhs and agues was never seen."

The parlor contained the family books, which, pending the arrival of a collection which Sir Richard had made in Italy, and the building of a proper room to receive them, were not many in number.

Sir Richard looked up from the paper to the bookcase.

"I wonder," says he, "whether the old prophet is there yet? I fancy I see him."

Crossing the room, he took out a dumpy Bible, which, sure enough, bore on the flyleaf the inscription: "To Matthew Fell, from his Loving Godmother, Anne Aldous, 2 September, 1659."

"It would be no bad plan to test him again, Mr. Crome. I will wager we get a couple of names in the Chronicles. H'm! what have we here? 'Thou shalt seek me in the morning, and I shall not be.' Well, well! Your grandfather would have made a fine omen of that, hey? No more prophets for me! They are all in a tale. And now, Mr. Crome, I am infinitely obliged to you for your packet. You will, I fear, be impatient to get on. Pray allow me— another glass."

So with offers of hospitality, which were genuinely meant (for Sir Richard thought well of the young man's address and manner), they parted.

In the afternoon came the guests—the Bishop of Kilmore, Lady Mary Hervey, Sir William Kentfield, etc. Dinner at five, wine, cards, supper, and dispersal to bed.

Next morning Sir Richard is disinclined to take his gun with the rest. He talks with the Bishop of Kilmore. This prelate, unlike a good many of the Irish bishops of his day, had visited his see, and, indeed, resided there for some considerable time. This morning, as the two were walking along the terrace and talking over the alterations and improvements in the house, the bishop said, pointing to the window of the west room:

"You could never get one of my Irish flock to occupy that room, Sir Richard."

"Why is that, my lord? It is, in fact, my own."

"Well, our Irish peasantry will always have it that it brings the worst of luck to sleep near an ash tree, and you have a fine growth of ash not two yards from your chamber window. Perhaps," the bishop went on, with a smile, "it has given you a touch of its quality already, for you do not seem, if I may say it, so much the fresher for your night's rest as your friends would like to see you."

"That, or something else, it is true, cost me my sleep from twelve to four, my lord. But the tree is to come down tomorrow, so I shall not hear much more from it."

"I applaud your determination. It can hardly be wholesome

to have the air you breathe strained, as it were, through all that leafage."

"You lordship is right there, I think. But I had not my window open last night. It was rather the noise that went on—no doubt from the twigs sweeping the glass—that kept me open-eyed."

"I think that can hardly be, Sir Richard. Here—you see it from this point. None of these nearest branches even can touch your casement unless there were a gale, and there was none of that last night. They miss the panes by a foot."

"No, sir, true. What, then, will it be, I wonder, that scratched and rustled so—ay, and covered the dust on my sill with lines and marks?"

At last they agreed that the rats must have come up through the ivy. That was the bishop's idea, and Sir Richard jumped at it.

So the day passed quietly, and night came, and the party wished Sir Richard a better night and dispersed to their rooms.

And now we are in his bedroom, with the light out and the squire in bed. The room is over the kitchen, and the night outside still and warm, so the window stands open.

There is very little light about the bedstead, but there is a strange movement there; it seems as if Sir Richard were moving his head rapidly to and fro with only the slightest possible sound. And now you would guess, so deceptive is the half-darkness, that he had several heads, round and brownish, which move back and forward, even as low as his chest. It is a horrible illusion. Is it nothing more? There! something drops off the bed with a soft plump, like a kitten, and is out of the window in a flash; another —four—and after that there is quiet again.

"Thou shalt seek me in the morning, and I shall not be."

As with Sir Matthew, so with Sir Richard—dead and black in his bed!

A pale and silent party of guests and servants gathered under the window when the news was known. Italian poisoners, popish emissaries, infected air—all these and more guesses were hazarded, and the Bishop of Kilmore looked at the tree, in the fork of whose lower boughs a white tomcat was crouching, looking down the hollow which years had gnawed in the trunk. It was watching something inside the tree with great interest.

Suddenly it got up and craned over the hole. Then a bit of the edge on which it stood gave way, and it went slithering in. Everyone looked up at the noise of the fall.

It is known to most of us that a cat can cry; but few of us have heard, I hope, such a yell as came out of the trunk of the great ash. Two or three screams there were—the witnesses are not sure which—and then a slight and muffled noise of some commotion or struggling was all that came. But Lady Mary Hervey fainted outright, and the housekeeper stopped her ears and fled till she fell on the terrace.

The Bishop of Kilmore and Sir William Kentfield stayed. Yet even they were daunted, though it was only at the cry of a cat; and Sir William swallowed once or twice before he could say:

"There is something more than we know of in that tree, my lord. I am for an instant search."

And this was agreed upon. A ladder was brought, and one of the gardeners went up, and, looking down the hollow, could detect nothing but a few dim indications of something moving. They got a lantern, and let it down by a rope.

"We must get at the bottom of this. My life upon it, my lord, but the secret of these terrible deaths is there."

Up went the gardener again with the lantern, and let it down the hole cautiously. They saw the yellow light upon his face as he bent over, and saw his face struck with an incredulous terror and loathing before he cried out in a dreadful voice and fell back from the ladder—where, happily, he was caught by two of the men—letting the lantern fall inside the tree.

He was in a dead faint, and it was some time before any word could be got from him.

By then they had something else to look at. The lantern must have broken at the bottom, and the light in it caught upon dry leaves and rubbish that lay there, for in a few minutes a dense smoke began to come up, and then flame; and, to be short, the tree was in a blaze.

The bystanders made a ring at some yards' distance, and Sir William and the bishop sent men to get what weapons and tools they could; for, clearly, whatever might be using the tree as its lair would be forced out by the fire.

So it was. First, at the fork, they saw a round body covered with fire—the size of a man's head—appear very suddenly, then seem to collapse and fall back. This, five or six times; then a similar ball leaped into the air and fell on the grass, where after a moment it lay still. The bishop went as near as he dared to it, and saw—what but the remains of an enormous spider, veinous and seared! And, as the fire burned lower down, more terrible bodies like this began to break out from the trunk, and it was seen that these were covered with grayish hair.

All that day the ash burned, and until it fell to pieces the men stood about it, and from time to time killed the brutes as they darted out. At last there was a long interval when none appeared, and they cautiously closed in and examined the roots of the tree.

"They found," says the Bishop of Kilmore, "below it a rounded hollow place in the earth, wherein were two or three bodies of these creatures that had plainly been smothered by the smoke; and, what is to me more curious, at the side of this den, against the wall, was crouching the anatomy or skeleton of a human being, with the skin dried upon the bones, having some remains of black hair, which was pronounced by those that examined it to be undoubtedly the body of a woman, and clearly dead for a period of fifty years."

SIDE BET

Will F. Jenkins

THERE was a vast blue bowl which was the sky. Across it, with
agonizing slowness, there marched a brazen sun which poured
down light to dazzle and burn out the man's eyes, and heat to
broil the brains in his skull. At intervals the blue bowl grew dark
and was dotted with stars, which ranged themselves in pairs like
the eyes of snakes—unwinking and cold and maliciously amused
—and watched through the night while the man recovered strength
to endure the torture of another day. There was a sea of infinite
blueness, which heaved slowly up and down and up and down
and alternately reflected the blue bowl and the monstrous aggrega-
tion of star eyes. And there was the island, which was not more
than fifty by fifteen yards in extent.

Also, there was the rat, with which the man played a game with
rather high stakes, a game in which life was a side bet.

The man and the rat were not friends. No. When huge waves
flung the man scornfully upon the island he thought himself the
sole survivor of his ship, and for twenty-four hours he disregarded
every other thought or observation in trying to salvage as much
of the wreckage as he could. He could not do much. During all
that day and night colossal combers beat upon the shore, overwhelming two thirds of its length in sputtering spume. There was
then no sky or sea or any other thing but hurtling masses of water
and foam plunging upon and over and past the island. And the
island was only rock. There was no vegetation. There was no shelter.
There was barely more than a foothold behind a steep upcropping

198

of wet and slippery stone. But now and again some fragment of the ship was pounded senselessly upon that upcrop by the sea, and the man tried desperately to salvage it.

He saved but little. A dozen crates of fruit broke open and all their contents went to waste upon rockery so continuously wave-swept as to be past clinging to. Four separate times he saw masses of cargo—some of which must have been edible—surge past the island, infuriatingly near yet impossibly distant. And a life raft, floating high in the water, was deliberately smashed and maliciously pounded before his eyes into splintered wood and crumpled metal —and then the sea took that away too.

Before the waves abated the man made sure of some bits of wood and some cordage, and from the life raft as it went to pieces he rescued a keg of water and a canvas bag of hard sea bread— biscuit. But there was nothing on which he could hope to leave the island, nor canvas to make a shelter, and he had not even a stick long enough to make a mast on which to fly his confession of help-lessness and distress for the sea to look at.

But he did have a companion: the rat.

The rat was huge. It was a wise and resourceful ship rat and had all the cunning and ferocity of its race. Its body was almost a foot long. It had come ashore without help from the man; he never knew how. Perhaps clinging man-fashion to one of the two masses of spars and cordage now lodged securely on the island. Perhaps in some fashion only a rat could even imagine. But it had reached the island and it knew of the man's presence, and it knew exactly what the island offered of sustenance when the seas went down and the long, agonizing procession of days began in which the sky was a vast blue bowl and a brazen sun marched slowly across it.

When that happened, the man took account of his prospects, which were not bright. He counted his stores. He had twenty-two biscuits, all tainted with salt water, and a small keg of fresh water. There was a fairly impressive mass of lumber, mostly splintered and none suitable even for the manufacture of a raft if the man had possessed tools, which he did not. There was some rope, at-tached to shattered spars. In a money belt, the man had sixty dollars. That was all.

He had no matches but he found that with a small spike extracted from the wreckage he could strike a spark from the rock of the island. He had nothing to cook, and therefore a fire was needless.

But he picked cordage into oakum for tinder, and he arranged his stock of wood in a great pyre, the smaller splinters lowest, so that from a single spark he could send up a roaring beacon of flame and smoke to summon any ship he might sight from the island. His stock of food and water was so trivial that he rationed himself strictly. He could not actually live on such infinitesimal portions as he allotted himself for each day, but he would starve very slowly. He would live longer and suffer longer. The will to live is not a matter of reason. And then the days of waiting began as separate Gehennas of heat and thirst and hopelessness.

The sun by day was horrible. There was no shade. There was no shelter. There was no soil. There was only fissured, tumbled rock. The man scorched, panting in the baking heat, and gazed with smarting eyes at the horizon. He looked for a ship, though he could not really hope for one. In the morning he ate his strictly allotted ration and prepared to endure the day. In the evening he drank a little, a very little, water, and during the night he gathered strength to suffer through another day. From the amount of food and drink he possessed, he had calculated exactly how long he could live upon the island. He did not ask himself why he should wish to.

It was probably the seventh or eighth day when he learned that the rat was also on the island.

He had picked up the canvas bag which held the sea biscuits. It should have been nearly full. His daily ration was small. But as he lifted the bag, something fell at his feet. There was a hole in the bag. A fine white powder sifted out of it, spreading in the air. At his feet was half a biscuit, irregularly gnawed. The tooth marks were clearly those of a rat.

The man's heart tried to stop. He regarded the hole and the gnawed biscuit with a sort of stupefied horror. Then he swiftly counted the contents of the bag. He should have had nineteen of the biscuits. Instead, he had sixteen and the fragment which was less than a half. More than a week of life had been taken from him.

He had no real hope of rescue, of course. The island was a speck in a waste of sea. It might or might not be on the charts. He did not know. If it was charted, ships would avoid it as a danger to navigation. But the instinct to cling to life is too strong for mere reason to controvert. The man's hands shook. He carefully unraveled a strand of rope. He tied up the hole in the bag. And he had apportioned his supplies to keep him alive for a certain number

of days. He could not bring himself to surrender even one hour
of that scheduled time. Since a part of his food had been taken
from him, he desperately resolved to cut down his ration to make
up for the theft. And he did.

He chewed the reduced fraction of a sea biscuit, which was his
day's food, with exhaustive care. He made it last a very long time.
He watched the horizon with dazzled, reddened eyes. He was
already hungry all the time. He had hunger cramps in the night.
His knees felt oddly exhausted when he climbed about the wave-
rounded mass which was the island, but he resolutely made the
journey. He watched all day. He saw nothing. When night came
he drank the few swallows he allowed himself. He tied the bag to
a spliced stick and propped it up so that it hung in mid-air. He
slept.

In the morning the bag was on the ground again. The rat had
gnawed through the cord upholding it. There were only twelve biscuits left and the man saw a floury scraping on the rock, two
yards from the bag, which told him that the rat had carried off one
biscuit uneaten.

The man knew hatred, now. And he made a savage search of
every square inch of the island. It was not difficult. One hundred
and fifty feet in one direction. About forty-five in another. Nothing
of any size could hide, but there were cracks and crevices and
miniature caverns in which the rat could conceal itself during the
search. The man found one tiny, crumby place where the rat had
eaten, at leisure, food which was more than the man allowed himself for three days. And he came to have an inkling of how the rat
drank. Even now, the small crevices in the rocks were cool. Undoubtedly moisture condensed upon their surfaces during the night
and the rat licked it. It would serve a rat but no man could live
that way.

But he did not find the rat. He did not even catch a glimpse of it,
but by this time he hated it with an emotion far past any hatred
men ordinarily know.

That night the man's rage kept him from sleeping. He had a
section of splintered plank not too heavy to be a club. He put out
the bag of biscuits as bait and sat on guard beside it. The sun sank.
The vast blue bowl turned dark and very many pairs of malevolent
stars shone out, to look down upon him and watch him maliciously.
His hands shook with his hatred. The sea soughed and gurgled

among the irregular rocks about the shore line. The man waited, hating . . .

But he was very weak. He woke suddenly. His club, held ready, had fallen with a crash to the rock before him. The sound had roused him. He heard the scurrying of tiny feet. The rat, scuttling away.

The canvas bag was a good two feet from where it had been. The rat had been trying to drag it to its own hiding place.

The man made inarticulate noises of fury. He knew, now, that the rat would seek to prey upon him for food as long as the two of them lived upon the island. That is the instinct of rats. And in any case he would have tried to kill the rat if he saw it, because that is the instinct of men. But here the conflict of instincts became more than inevitable. It became deadly. Both the man and the rat could not live upon this island. If the man lived, the rat died. If the man died, the chance of the rat for survival would be directly and specifically increased.

But the man was too weak to think very clearly. He had found a rock with a hollow in it. He put the bag of biscuits there and lay down. His body formed a protecting lid over the receptacle for his food. The rat could not reach the biscuits without first gnawing the man. But the man slept fitfully and even through his dreams there moved, a hazy, groping thought. The rat must die, or he must . . .

In the morning the man chewed his ration for hours. It was the fraction of a sea biscuit. He savored every particle of flavor it possessed. The heat beat upon him. He panted, watching the unchanging horizon beneath a brazen sun. He kept his body wetted with seawater so that he would not need to drink. But already he suffered severely from thirst. And then, toward nightfall, he saw the rat.

It was swimming toward an outlying rock which was perhaps ten yards from the main island. The rock was certainly no more than five feet across and rose perhaps that much above the slow, smooth swells which forever swayed across the sea.

The rat reached the base of that rock. It swam about it, trying to find gripping places for its paws. The man watched in a passion of sheer hatred until it disappeared. Then he moved closer. He heard its paws scratching and scrambling, out of sight. Presently its pointed muzzle appeared on top of the small rock. It went sniffing here and there. Suddenly it stopped stock-still. It began to eat. And the man smelled something tainted. Perhaps a dead fish flung to the top of the rock by a wave or swell. Perhaps a gull or tern which had died there recently. Whatever it was, the rat ate it.

The man trembled all over with hatred. He could no longer compute the anguish he had suffered, of hunger with but a tantalizing morsel of food a day, and of thirst with but enough of luke-warm water barely to moisten his lips. But the rat had enough of water, somehow, and now it fed!

The man stumbled back to his utterly useless cache of shattered timbers and weathered cordage. He thought bitterly of the rat's smooth body. Of its unshrunken muscles. Of its sleek fur. And suddenly, as in his hatred he envisioned rending it limb from limb— suddenly he saw it in a new light. From a thing to be hated and destroyed, the rat suddenly became a fascinating, an infinitely desirable thing. The man was starving. As he thought of the rat his mouth watered.

The conditions of the game now were wholly clear. If the man died, the rat's chances of survival would be directly increased. If the rat died, the man would live longer at least by days. So the rat must die, or the man. They had played a deadly game before. Now the side bet—of life—was explicit.

Days passed. The sun rose and there was a vast blue bowl which was the sky. The sun sank and a multitude of stars gazed down. The man gave all his thought, now, to the game. He did not even glance at the horizon. He grew rapidly weaker, but his whole thought was fixed upon the construction of elaborate gins and traps by which the rat might be captured. He made them, and they failed, because he could not bring himself to risk even a scrap of food for bait.

When at last he risked a full quarter of his day's ration in hopes of luring the rat into capture, the rat cunningly sprang the trap and escaped with the bread. It was a morsel about half the size of a thimble. The man wept when he discovered his failure. But it was for the loss of the bread.

Then he made a bow and arrow. It was clumsy and crude and it would be hopelessly inaccurate, because he had no tools. When he had made the weapon, he spent three days stalking the rat over the uneven surface of the island. Most of the time he had to crawl, because of his weakness. Much of the time he knew where the rat was. Some of the time he even saw it, because the rat had grown bolder since the man's weakness had forced him to crawl rather than walk.

The first day's stalking brought no result. Nor the second. But on the third day—even the rat was starving, now—the man's persistence and infinite care took him to where he saw the rat clearly. It was sleeping. The man crept closer, inch by inch. He moved with breathless caution. He saw, though he did not realize, that the rat's ribs now showed through its fur. Its eyes were rimmed with red. It was no longer sleek and well-muscled. It was shabby and unkempt and almost as emaciated as the man.

The man drew his solitary arrow back. But he had not realized his weakness. His heart pounded hysterically. His eyes glared. His mouth slobbered in horrible anticipation. His hands shook. And when he had drawn back the arrow to the fullest extent of which he was capable, the arrow flicked forward, glanced off a rock—it would have missed—and by sheer ironic accident was deflected again into its true path. It struck the rat.

And the bow had been drawn so weakly that the arrow did not penetrate. The rat leaped upright, squeaking, and fled. And the useless arrow lay where it had fallen while the starving man wept. He saw, now, that it was the rat which would win the game and the stakes —and the side bet.

The rat knew it too. Two days later the man's rations, both of food and of water, came to an end. He regarded them both for a long time. Once gone, the rat won their deadly game.

The man ate the bread and drank the water. He lay down. He did not bother even to glance at the horizon, because the game was over and he had lost. He was not suffering at all when night came. He felt no hunger and even his thirst was not severe. He was peculiarly clearheaded and calm. His body was weak, to be sure, but there were no gripings in his belly. He lay and looked up at the stars and foresaw the rat's winning of game and stakes and side bet, and was unmoved by the foreknowledge. He was too weak for emotion.

But then he heard a little sound, and in the starlight he saw a movement. It was the rat.

It was still for a long time. The man did not move. It crept toward him. The man stirred. The rat stopped. Presently it sank down on all fours, watching the man with glowing eyes.

There was silence save for the gurgling of the long slow swells among the rocks. The man even laughed weakly. The rat waited with a quivering impatience. It had known nothing of rationing. It had eaten more fully than the man, but not as often. Its whole body was a clamoring, raging hunger. It quivered with a horrible desire to claim its winnings in the deadly game.

"No," said the man detachedly. His voice was a bare croak, but there was almost amusement in it. "Not yet! The one who dies first loses. I'm not dead yet . . ."

The rat quivered. It backed away when the man spoke, its eyes flaring hatred. But when he stopped it crept forward. A little closer than before. It stopped only when the man stirred.

Then the man thought of something. He was very weak indeed, but at the very beginning he had picked out some soft fiber from the cordage he had saved. He had worked out a small spike, and he tested it against the rock. He had even dried out a little seaweed, as more practical than hemp for the making of a blaze.

Now he struck the spike against the rock. It sparked. The rat retreated. Presently it crept forward again. The man struck the spike again upon the rock. The rat was checked.

It happened many times before the sparks struck in the improvised oakum tinder. Then it fatigued the man very much to blow it and sift dried and crumpled seaweed upon it—blowing the while—and later to transfer the small coal to the assembly of little splinters he had made ready long since. They were to kindle the signal fire he had intended to light if a ship should ever come into view. But now he lighted the kindling because the rat was no more than five feet from him and he could hear it panting in a desperate eagerness to claim its winnings. The flames caught and climbed.

The rat drew back slowly, his eyes desperate. The man watched.

Over his head malicious stars looked down, but now a huge and spreading column of smoke rose up, lighted from below by the blaze. It blotted out the stars. And the flames climbed higher and higher, crackling fiercely, and the fire roared. There was a leaping thicket of yellow flame beneath the smoke. Its topmost branches reared up for fifteen feet. Twenty. Long tongues of detached incandescence licked up into the thick smoke even higher still. And the reddish-yellow glare upon the smoke made it into a radiant mist.

"It would have been a pretty good signal," the man thought.

Then he thought of something else. If he could have contrived to be upon that heap of blazing timber, and had contrived that it should catch fire after he was dead, the rat would never collect its winnings from the game.

"But that wouldn't have been fair," said the man lightheartedly. "It, it would've been welshing . . ."

The rat had vanished, crept into some crack or crevice to hide from the glare and the heat of the fire. And the fire blazed up and up, and slowly died down, and when the dawn came the man saw smoke still rising from the ashes.

And again he saw the rat.

But he heard—he heard the rattle of an anchor chain. Which was that of a ship which had seen the flame-lit smoke of the fire during the dark hours, and had thought it another ship ablaze, and had come to offer help. Now a boat was on its way ashore.

When they carried the man to the small boat, he croaked out a request. They placed him as he wished in the boat, so that as it pulled toward the ship he saw the island. And he saw the rat upon it.

The rat ran crazily back and forth, squealing. The squeals were cries of rage. The rat was a bare skeleton covered with tight-stretched hide, and its rage was ghastly. Its disappointment was incredible. The man was being carried away and there was no other food upon the island . . .

"I—I've got a money belt on," croaked the man. "There's sixty dollars in it. I . . . I've lost a bet." He rested for a moment. "I want to buy some food and have it left on the island for that . . . rat. He won a game from me and I . . . don't want to welsh on a bet . . ."

They lifted him carefully to the steamer's deck. Weakly, he insisted on this final favor. The boat went back to the island. It left a great heap of more than a hundred pounds of ship's biscuit where the sea was not likely to wash any of it away. Before it had pulled out from the island, the rat had flung itself upon the heap and was eating.

They told the man. He grinned feebly . . . he had been fed . . . and went incontinently to sleep. They told him afterward that the rat was still eating when the ship sailed over the horizon.

What happened after that, the man never knew. But he felt that he had paid the side bet.

SECOND NIGHT OUT

Frank Belknap Long

IT WAS past midnight when I left my stateroom. The upper promenade deck was entirely deserted and thin wisps of fog hovered about
the deck chairs and curled and uncurled about the gleaming rails.
There was no air stirring. The ship moved forward sluggishly through
a quiet, fog-enshrouded sea.

But I did not object to the fog. I leaned against the rail and inhaled the damp, murky air with a positive greediness. The almost
unendurable nausea, the pervasive physical and mental misery had
departed, leaving me serene and at peace. I was again capable of
experiencing sensuous delight, and the aroma of the brine was not to
be exchanged for pearls and rubies. I had paid in exorbitant coinage
for what I was about to enjoy—for the five brief days of freedom
and exploration in glamorous, sea-splendid Havana which I had
been promised by an enterprising and, I hoped, reasonably honest
tourist agent. I am in all respects the antithesis of a wealthy man,
and I had drawn so heavily upon my bank balance to satisfy the
greedy demands of The Loriland Tours, Inc., that I had been compelled to renounce such really indispensable amenities as after-
dinner cigars and ocean-privileged sherry and chartreuse.

But I was enormously content. I paced the deck and inhaled the
moist, pungent air. For thirty hours I had been confined to my cabin
with a sea-illness more debilitating than bubonic plague or malignant
sepsis, but having at length managed to squirm from beneath its
iron heel I was free to enjoy my prospects. They were enviable and
glorious. Five days in Cuba, with the privilege of driving up and

207

down the sun-drenched Malecon in a flamboyantly upholstered limousine, and an opportunity to feast my discerning gaze on the pink walls of the Cabanas and the Columbus Cathedral and La Fuerza, the great storehouse of the Indies. Opportunity, also, to visit sunlit *patios,* and saunter by iron-barred *rejas,* and to sip *refrescos* by moonlight in open-air cafés, and to acquire, incidentally, a Spanish contempt for Big Business and the Strenuous Life. Then on to Haiti, dark and magical, and the Virgin Islands, and the quaint, incredible Old World harbor of Charlotte Amalie, with its chimneyless, red-roofed houses rising in tiers to the quiet stars; the natural Sargasso, the inevitable last port of call for rainbow fishes, diving boys and old ships with sun-bleached funnels and incurably drunken skippers. A flaming opal set in an amphitheater of malachite—its allure blazed forth through the gray fog and dispelled my northern spleen. I leaned against the rail and dreamed also of Martinique, which I would see in a few days, and of the Indian and Chinese wenches of Trinidad. And then, suddenly, a dizziness came upon me. The ancient and terrible malady had returned to plague me.

Sea-sickness, unlike all other major afflictions, is a disease of the individual. No two people are ever afflicted with precisely the same symptoms. The manifestations range from a slight malaise to a devastating impairment of all one's faculties. I was afflicted with the gravest symptoms imaginable. Choking and gasping, I left the rail and sank helplessly down into one of the three remaining deck chairs.

Why the steward had permitted the chairs to remain on deck was a mystery I couldn't fathom. He had obviously shirked a duty, for passengers did not habitually visit the promenade deck in the small hours, and foggy weather plays havoc with the wicker-work of steamer chairs. But I was too grateful for the benefits which his negligence had conferred upon me to be excessively critical. I lay sprawled at full length, grimacing and gasping and trying fervently to assure myself that I wasn't nearly as sick as I felt. And then, all at once, I became aware of an additional source of discomfiture.

The chair exuded an unwholesome odor. It was unmistakable. As I turned about, as my cheek came to rest against the damp, varnished wood my nostrils were assailed by an acrid and alien odor of a vehement, cloying potency. It was at once stimulating and indescribably repellent. In a measure, it assuaged my physical unease, but it also filled me with the most overpowering revulsion, with a sudden, hysterical and almost frenzied distaste.

I tried to rise from the chair, but the strength was gone from

my limbs. An intangible presence seemed to rest upon me and weigh
me down. And then the bottom seemed to drop out of everything.
I am not being facetious. Something of the sort actually occurred.
The *base* of the sane, familiar world vanished, was swallowed up.
I sank down. Limitless gulfs seemed open beneath me, and I was
immersed, lost in a gray void. The ship, however, did not vanish.
The ship, the deck, the chair continued to support me, and yet,
despite the retention of these outward symbols of reality, I was afloat
in an unfathomable void. I had the illusion of falling, of sinking
helplessly down through an eternity of space. It was as though the
chair which supported me had passed into another dimension without ceasing to leave the familiar world—as though it floated simultaneously both in our three-dimensional world and in another world
of alien, unknown dimensions. I became aware of strange shapes
and shadows all about me. I gazed through illimitable dark gulfs at
continents and islands, lagoons, atolls, vast gray waterspouts. I sank
down into the great deep. I was immersed in dark slime. The bounda-
ries of sense were dissolved away, and the breath of an active cor-
ruption blew through me, gnawing at my vitals and filling me with
extravagant torment. I was alone in the great deep. And the shapes
that accompanied me in my utter abysmal isolation were shriveled
and black and dead, and they cavorted deliriously with little monkey-
heads with streaming, sea-drenched viscera and putrid, pupilless
eyes.

And then, slowly, the unclean vision dissolved. I was back again
in my chair and the fog was as dense as ever, and the ship moved
forward steadily through the quiet sea. But the odor was still present
—acrid, overpowering, revolting. I leapt from the chair, in profound
alarm. . . . I experienced a sense of having emerged from the bowels
of some stupendous and unearthly *encroachment,* of having in a
single instant exhausted the resources of earth's malignity, and drawn
upon untapped and intolerable reserves.

I have gazed without flinching at the turbulent, demon-seething
utterly benighted infernos of the Italian and Flemish primitives. I
have endured with calm vision the major inflictions of Hieronymus
Bosch, and Lucas Cranach, and I have not quailed even before the
worst perversities of the elder Breughel, whose outrageous gargoyles
and ghouls and cacodemons are so self-contained that they fester
with an over-brimming malignancy, and seem about to burst asunder
and dissolve hideously in a black and intolerable froth. But not
even Signorelli's *Soul of the Damned,* or Goya's *Los Caprichos,* or

the hideous, ooze-encrusted sea-shapes with half-assembled bodies and dead, pupilless eyes which drag themselves sightlessly through Segrelles' blue worlds of fetor and decay were as unnerving and ghastly as the flickering visual sequence which had accompanied my perception of the odor. I was vastly and terribly shaken.

I got indoors somehow, into the warm and steamy interior of the upper saloon, and waited, gasping, for the deck steward to come to me. I had pressed a small button labeled "Deck Steward" in the wainscoting adjoining the central stairway, and I frantically hoped that he would arrive before it was too late, before the odor outside percolated into the vast, deserted saloon.

The steward was a daytime official, and it was a cardinal crime to fetch him from his berth at one in the morning, but I had to have some one to talk to, and as the steward was responsible for the chairs I naturally thought of him as the logical target for my interrogations. He would *know*. He would be able to explain. The odor would not be unfamiliar to him. He would be able to explain about the chairs . . . about the chairs . . . about the chairs . . . I was growing hysterical and confused.

I wiped the perspiration from my forehead with the back of my hand, and waited with relief for the steward to approach. He had come suddenly into view above the top of the central stairway, and he seemed to advance toward me through a blue mist.

He was extremely solicitous, extremely courteous. He bent above me and laid his hand concernedly upon my arm. "Yes, sir. What can I do for you, sir? A bit under the weather, perhaps. What can I do?"

Do? Do? It was horribly confusing. I could only stammer: "The chairs, steward. On the deck. Three chairs. Why did you leave them there? Why didn't you take them inside?"

It wasn't what I had intended asking him. I had intended questioning him about the odor. But the strain, the shock had confused me. The first thought that came into my mind on seeing the steward standing above me, so solicitous and concerned, was that he was a hypocrite and a scoundrel. He pretended to be concerned about me and yet out of sheer perversity he had prepared the snare which had reduced me to a pitiful and helpless wreck. He had left the chairs on deck deliberately, with a cruel and crafty malice, knowing all the time, no doubt, that *something* would occupy them.

But I wasn't prepared for the almost instant change in the man's demeanor. It was ghastly. Befuddled as I had become I could perceive at once that I had done him a grave, a terrible injustice. *He hadn't known.* All the blood drained out of his cheeks and his mouth fell open. He stood immobile before me, completely inarticulate, and for an instant I thought he was about to collapse, to sink helplessly down upon the floor.

"You saw—chairs?" he gasped at last.

I nodded.

The steward leaned toward me and gripped my arm. The flesh of his face was completely destitute of luster. From the parchment-white oval his two eyes, tumescent with fright, stared wildly down at me.

"It's the black, dead thing," he muttered. "The monkey-face. I *knew* it would come back. It always comes aboard at midnight on the second night out."

He gulped and his hand tightened on my arm.

"It's always on the second night out. It knows where I keep the chairs, and it takes them on deck and sits in them. I *saw* it last time. It was squirming about in the chair—lying stretched out and squirming horribly. Like an eel. It sits in all three of the chairs. When it saw me it got up and started toward me. But I got away. I came in here, and shut the door. But I saw it through the window."

The steward raised his arm and pointed.

"There. Through that window there. Its face was pressed against the glass. It was all black and shriveled and eaten away. A monkey-face, sir. So help me, the face of a dead, shriveled monkey. And wet—dripping. I was so frightened I couldn't breathe. I just stood and groaned, and then it went away."

He gulped.

"Doctor Blodgett was mangled, clawed to death at ten minutes to one. We heard his shrieks. The thing went back, I guess, and sat in the chairs for thirty or forty minutes after it left the window. Then it went down to Doctor Blodgett's stateroom and took his clothes. It was horrible. Doctor Blodgett's legs were missing, and his face was crushed to a pulp. There were claw-marks all over him. And the curtains of his berth were drenched with blood.

"The captain told me not to talk. But I've got to tell someone. I can't help myself, sir. I'm afraid—I've got to talk. This is the third time it's come aboard. It didn't take anybody the first time, but it sat in the chairs. It left them all wet and slimy, sir—all covered with black stinking slime."

I stared in bewilderment. What was the man trying to tell me?

Was he completely unhinged? Or was I too confused, too ill myself to catch all that he was saying?

He went on wildly: "It's hard to explain, sir, but this boat is *visited*. Every voyage, sir—on the second night out. And each time it sits in the chairs. Do you understand?"

I didn't understand, clearly, but I murmured a feeble assent. My voice was appallingly tremulous and it seemed to come from the opposite side of the saloon.

"Something out there," I gasped. "It was awful. Out there, you hear? An awful odor. My brain. I can't imagine what's come over me, but I feel as though something were pressing on my brain. Here."

I raised my fingers and passed them across my forehead.

"Something here—something—"

The steward appeared to understand perfectly. He nodded and helped me to my feet. He was still self-engrossed, still horribly wrought up, but I could sense that he was also anxious to reassure and assist me.

"Stateroom 16D? Yes, of course. Steady, sir."

The steward had taken my arm and was guiding me toward the central stairway. I could scarcely stand erect. My decrepitude was so apparent, in fact, that the steward was moved by compassion to the display of an almost heroic attentiveness. Twice I stumbled and would have fallen had not the guiding arm of my companion encircled my shoulders and levitated my sagging bulk.

"Just a few more steps, sir. That's it. Just take your time. There isn't anything will come of it, sir. You'll feel better when you're inside, with the fan going. Just take your time, sir."

At the door of my stateroom I spoke in a hoarse whisper to the man at my side. "I'm all right now. I'll ring if I need you. Just—let me—get inside. I want to lie down. Does this door lock from the inside?"

"Why, yes. Yes, of course. But maybe I'd better get you some water."

"No, don't bother. Just leave me—please."

"Well—all right, sir." Reluctantly the steward departed, after making certain that I had a firm grip on the handle of the door.

The stateroom was extremely dark. I was so weak that I was compelled to lean with all my weight against the door to close it. It shut with a slight click and the key fell out upon the floor. With a groan I went down on my knees and grovelled apprehensively with my fingers on the soft carpet. But the key eluded me.

I cursed and was about to rise when my hand encountered something fibrous and hard. I started back, gasping. Then, frantically, my fingers slid over it, in a hectic effort at appraisal. It was—yes, undoubtedly a shoe. And sprouting from it, an ankle. The shoe reposed firmly on the floor of the stateroom. The flesh of the ankle, beneath the sock which covered it, was very cold.

In an instant I was on my feet, circling like a caged animal about the narrow dimensions of the stateroom. My hands slid over the walls, the ceiling. If only, dear God, the electric light button would not continue to elude me!

Eventually my hands encountered a rubbery excresence on the smooth panels. I pressed, resolutely, and the darkness vanished to reveal a man sitting upright on a couch in the corner—a stout, well-dressed man holding a grip and looking perfectly composed. Only his face was invisible. His face was concealed by a handkerchief—a large handkerchief which had obviously been placed there intentionally, perhaps as a protection against the rather chilly air currents from the unshuttered port. The man was obviously asleep. He had not responded to the tugging of my hands on his ankles in the darkness, and even now he did not stir. The glare of the electric light bulbs above his head did not appear to annoy him in the least.

I experienced a sudden and overwhelming relief. I sat down beside the intruder and wiped the sweat from my forehead. I was still trembling in every limb, but the calm appearance of the man beside me was tremendously reassuring. A fellow-passenger, no doubt, who had entered the wrong compartment. It should not be difficult to get rid of him. A mere tap on the shoulder, followed by a courteous explanation, and the intruder would vanish. A simple procedure, if only I could summon the strength to act with decision. I was so horribly enfeebled, so incredibly weak and ill. But at last I mustered sufficient energy to reach out my hand and tap the intruder on the shoulder.

"I'm sorry, sir," I murmured, "but you've got into the wrong stateroom. If I wasn't a bit under the weather I'd ask you to stay and smoke a cigar with me, but you see I"—with a distorted effort at a smile I tapped the stranger again nervously—"I'd rather be alone, so if you don't mind—sorry I had to wake you."

Immediately I perceived that I was being premature. I had not waked the stranger. The stranger did not budge, did not so much as agitate by his breathing the handkerchief which concealed his features.

I experienced a resurgence of my alarm. Tremulously I stretched forth my hand and seized a corner of the handkerchief. It was an outrageous thing to do, but I had to know. If the intruder's face matched his body, if it was composed and familiar all would be well, but if for any reason—

The fragment of physiognomy revealed by the uplifted corner was not reassuring. With a gasp of affright I tore the handkerchief completely away. For a moment, a moment only, I stared at the dark and repulsive visage, with its stary, corpse-white eyes, viscid and malignant, its flat simian nose, hairy ears, and thick black tongue that seemed to leap up at me from out of the mouth. The face *moved* as I watched it, wriggled and squirmed revoltingly, while the head itself shifted its position, turning slightly to one side and revealing a profile more bestial and gangrenous and unclean than the brunt of his countenance.

I shrank back against the door, in frenzied dismay. I suffered as an animal suffers. My mind, deprived by shock of all capacity to form concepts, agonized instinctively, at a brutish level of consciousness. Yet through it all one mysterious part of myself remained horribly observant. I saw the tongue snap back into the mouth; saw the lines of the features shrivel and soften until presently from the slavering mouth and white sightless eyes there began to trickle thin streams of blood. In another moment the mouth was a red slit in a splotched horror of countenance—a red slit rapidly widening and dissolving in an amorphous crimson flood. The horror was hideously and repellently dissolving into the basal sustainer of all life.

It took the steward nearly ten minutes to restore me. He was compelled to force spoonfuls of brandy between my tightly-locked teeth, to bathe my forehead with ice-water and to massage almost savagely my wrists and ankles. And when, finally, I opened my eyes he refused to meet them. He quite obviously wanted me to rest, to remain quiet, and he appeared to distrust his own emotional equipment. He was good enough, however, to enumerate the measures which had contributed to my restoration, and to enlighten me in respect to the *remnants:*

"The clothes were all covered with blood—*drenched,* sir. I burned them."

On the following day he became more loquacious. "It was wearing the clothes of the gentleman who was killed last voyage, sir—it was wearing Doctor Blodgett's things. I recognized them instantly."

"But why—"

The steward shook his head. "I don't know, sir. Maybe your going up on deck saved you. Maybe it couldn't wait. It left a little after one the last time, sir, and it was later than that when I saw you to your stateroom. The ship may have passed out of its *zone,* sir. Or maybe it fell asleep and couldn't get back in time, and that's why it—dissolved. I don't think it's gone for good. There was blood on the curtains in Dr. Blodgett's cabin, and I'm afraid it always *goes* that way. It will come back next voyage, sir. I'm sure of it."

He cleared his throat.

"I'm glad you rang for me. If you'd gone right down to your stateroom it might be wearing your clothes next voyage."

Havana failed to restore me. Haiti was a black horror, a repellent quagmire of menacing shadows and alien desolation, and in Martinique I did not get a single hour of undisturbed sleep in my room at the hotel.

OUR FEATHERED FRIENDS

Philip MacDonald

THE hot, hard August sunshine poured its pale and blazing gold over the countryside. At the crest of the hill, which overlooked a county and a half, the tiny motorcar drawn up to the side of the dusty road which wound up the hill like a white riband looked not so much mechanical as insectile. It looked like a Brobdingnagian bee which, wings folded, had settled for a moment's sleepy basking in the fierce sunshine.

Beside the car, seeming almost ludicrously out of proportion with it, stood a man and a woman. The sum of their ages could not have exceeded forty-five. The dress of the girl, which was silken and slight, would not, at all events upon her charming body, have done aught save grace a car as large and costly as this one was minute and cheap. But the clothes of the boy, despite his youth and erect comeliness, were somehow eloquent of Norwood, a careful and not unintelligent clerkliness pursued in the city of London, and a pseudo-charitable arrangement whereby the bee-like motorcar should be purchased, for many pounds more than its actual worth, in small but almost eternal slices.

The girl was hatless, and her clipped golden poll glittered in the sunrays. She looked, and was, cool, despite the great heat of the afternoon. The boy, in his tweed jacket, thick flannel trousers, and over-tight collar, at whose front blazed a tie which hoped to look like that of some famous school or college, was hot, and very hot. He pulled his hat from his dark head and mopped at his brow with a vivid handkerchief.

"Coo!" he said. "Hot enough for you, Vi?"

216

She wriggled slim, half-covered shoulders. "It's a treat!" she said. She gazed about her with wide blue eyes; she looked down and round at the county-and-a-half. "Where's this, Jack?"

The boy continued to puff and mop. He said:

"Blessed if *I* know! . . . I lost me bearings after that big village place—what was it? . . ."

"Greyne, or some such," said the girl absently. Her gaze was now directed down the hillside to her right, where the emerald roof of a dense wood shone through the sun's gold. There was no breath of wind, even right up upon this hill, and the green of the leaves showed smooth and unbroken.

The boy put on his hat again. "Better be getting on, I s'pose. You've had that leg-stretch you were wanting."

"Ooh! Not *yet*, Jack. Don't let's yet!" She put her fingers on her left hand upon his sleeve. On the third of these fingers there sparkled a ring of doubtful brilliance. "Don't let's go on yet, Jack!" she said. She looked up into his face, her lips pouted in a way which was not the least of reasons for the flashing ring.

He slid an arm about the slim shoulders; he bent his head and kissed thoroughly the red mouth. "Just's *you* like Vi. . . . But what you want to do?" He looked about him with curling lip. "Sit around up here on this dusty grass and frizzle?"

"Silly!" she said, pulling herself away from him. She pointed down to the green roof, "I want to go down there. . . . Into that wood. Jest to see what its like. Haven't been in a reel wood since the summer holidays before last, when Effie an' me went to Hastings. . . . Cummon! Bet it's lovely and cool down there. . . ."

This last sentence floated up to him, for already she was off the narrow road and beginning a slipping descent of the short rough grass of the hillside's first twenty feet.

He went sliding and stumbling after her. But he could not catch up with the light, fragile little figure in its absurdly enchanting wisp of blue silk. The soles of his thick shoes were of leather, and, growing polished by the brushing of the close, arid grass, were treacherous. Forty feet down, on the suddenly jutting and only gently sloping plateau where the wood began, he did come up with her: he ended a stumbling, sliding rush with an imperfect and involuntary somersault which landed him asprawl at her feet.

He sat up, shouting with laughter. With a shock of surprise greater than any of his short life, he felt a little foot kick sharply—nearly savagely—at his arm, and heard a tensely whispered "SSH!"

He scrambled to his feet, to see that she was standing facing the trees, her shining golden head thrust forward, her whole body tense as that of a sprinter waiting for the pistol's crack. As, wonderingly, he shuffled to take his stand at her shoulder, she said:

"*Listen!* . . . Birds! . . . Jever hear the like? . . ." Her tone was a hushed yet clear whisper—like none he had ever heard her use before.

He said nothing. He stood scowling sulkily down at the grass beneath his feet and rubbing at the spot where her shoe had met his arm.

It seemed to him an hour before she turned. But turn at last she did. He still had his hand at the kicked arm, for all the world as if it really were causing him pain. From beneath his brows he watched her, covertly. He saw the odd rapt look leave the small face once more its pertly pretty self; saw the blue eyes suddenly widen with memory of what she had done. . . .

And then soft warm arms came about his neck and by their pressure pulled down his head so that, close pressed against him and standing upon tiptoe, she might smother his face with the kisses of contrition.

He said, in answer to the pleas for forgiveness with which the caresses were interspersed:

"Never known you do a thing like that before, Vi!"

"No," she said. "And you never won't again! Reely, Jack darling! . . . It . . . it . . ."—a cloud came over the blue eyes—"it . . . I don't rightly know what came over me. . . . I was listening to the birds. . . . I never heard the like . . . and . . . and I never heard you till you laughed . . . and I dunno *what* it was, but it seemed 's if I jest *had* to go on hearing what the birds were . . . 's if it was . . . was wrong to listen to anything else. . . . Oh, *I* dunno!"

The small face was troubled and the eyes desperate with the realization of explanation's impossibility. But the mouth pouted. The boy kissed it. He laughed and said:

"Funny kid, you!" He drew her arm through the crook of his and began to walk towards the first ranks of the trees. He put up his free hand and felt tenderly at the back of his neck. He said:

"Shan't be sorry for some shade. Neck's gettin' all sore."

They walked on, finding that the trees were strangely further away than they had seemed. They did not speak, but every now and then the slim, naked arm would squeeze the thick, clothed arm and have its pressure returned.

They had only some ten paces to go to reach the fringe of the wood when the girl halted. He turned his head to look down at her and found that once more she was tense in every muscle and thrusting the golden head forward as if the better to hear. He frowned; then smiled; then again bent his brows. He sensed that there was somewhere an oddnes which he knew he would never understand—a feeling abhorrent to him, as, indeed, to most men. He found that he, too, was straining to listen.

He supposed it must be birds that he was listening for. And quite suddenly he laughed. For he had realized that he was listening for something which had been for the last few moments so incessantly in his ears that he had forgotten he was hearing it. He explained this to the girl. She seemed to listen to him with only half an ear, and for a moment he came near to losing his temper. But only for a moment. He was a good-natured boy, with sensitive instincts serving him well in place of realized tact.

He felt a little tugging at his arm and fell into step with her as she began to go forward again. He went on with his theme, ignoring her patently half-hearted attention.

"Like at a dance," he said. "You know, Vi—you never hear the noise of the people's feet on the floor unless you happen to listen for it, an' when you do listen for it an' hear that sort of *shishing*—then you know you've been hearing it all the time, see? That's what we were doing about the birds. . . ." He became suddenly conscious that, in order to make himself clearly heard above the chattering, twittering flood of bird-song, he was speaking in a tone at least twice as loud as the normal. He said:

"Coo! . . . You're right, Vi. *I* never heard anything like it!"

They were passing now through the ranks of the outer line of trees. To the boy, a little worried by the strangeness of his adored, and more than a little discomfited by the truly abnormal heat of the sun, it seemed that he passed from an inferno to a paradise at one step. No more did the sun beat implacably down upon the world. In here, under the roof of green which no ray pierced but only a gentle, pervading, filtered softness of light, there was a cool peacefulness which seemed to bathe him, instantly, in a placid bath of contentment.

But the girl shivered a little. She said:

"Oh! It's almost cold in here!"

He did not catch the words. The chirping and carolling which was going on all about and above them seemed to catch up and absorb the sound of her voice.

"Drat the birds!" he said. "What you say?"

He saw her lips move, but though he bent his head, did not catch a sound. There had come, from immediately above their heads, the furious squeaks and flutterings of a bird-quarrel.

"Drat the birds!" he said again.

They were quite deep in the wood now. Looking round, he could not see at all the sun-drenched grass plateau from which they had come. He felt a tugging at his arm. The girl was pointing to a gently sloping bed of thick moss which was like a carpet spread at the foot of an old and twisted tree.

They sauntered to this carpet and sat down upon it, the boy sprawling at his ease, the girl very straight of back, with her hands clasped tightly about her raised knees. Had he been looking at her, rather than at the pipe he was filling, he would have seen again that craning forward of her head.

He did not finish the filling of his pipe. The singing of the birds went on. It seemed to gather volume until the whole world was filled with its chaotic whistling. The boy found, now that he had once consciously listened for and to it, that he could not again make his ears unconscious of the sound; the sound which, with its seemingly momentarily increased volume, was now so plucking at the nerves within his head—indeed over his whole body—that he felt he could not sit much longer to endure it. He thrust pipe and pouch savagely back into his pocket and turned to say to the girl that the quicker they got away from this blinking twittering the better he'd be pleased.

But the words died upon his lips. For even as he turned he became aware of a diminution of the reedy babel. He saw, too, calmer now with the decrease of irritation, that the girl was still in rapt attention.

So he held his tongue. The singing of the birds grew less and lesser with each moment. He began to feel drowsy, and once caught himself with a startled jerk from the edge of actual slumber. He peered sideways at his companion and saw that still she sat rigid; not by the breadth of a hair had she altered her first attentive pose. He felt again for pipe and pouch.

His fingers idle in the jacket-pocket, he found himself listening again. Only this time he listened because he wanted to listen. There was now but one bird who sang. And the boy was curiously conscious, hearing these liquid notes alone and in the fullness of their uninterrupted and almost unbearable beauty, that the reason for his hatred of that full and somehow discordant chorus which a few moments ago had nearly driven him from the trees and their lovely shelter had been his inability to hear more than an isolated note or two of this song whose existence then he had realized only subconsciously.

The full, deep notes ceased their rapid and incredible trilling, cutting their sound off sharply, almost in the manner of an operatic singer. There was, then, only silence in the wood. It lasted, for the town-bred boy and girl caught suddenly in this placid whirlpool of natural beauty, for moments which seemed strained and incalculable ages. And then into this pool of pregnant no-sound were dropped, one by one, six exquisite jewels of sound, each pause between these isolated lovelinesses being of twice the duration of its predecessor.

After the last of these notes—deep and varying and crystal-pure, yet misty with unimaginable beauties—the silence fell again; a silence not pregnant, as the last, with the vibrant foreshadowings of the magic to come, but a silence which had in it the utter and miserable quietness of endings and nothingness.

The boy's arm went up and wrapped itself gently about slim, barely covered shoulders. Two heads turned, and dark eyes looked into blue. The blue were abrim with unshed tears. She whispered:

"It was *him* I was listening to all the while. I could hear *that* all . . . all through the others. . . ."

A tear brimmed over and rolled down the pale cheek. The arm about her shoulders tightened, and at last she relaxed. The little body grew limp and lay against his strength.

"You lay quiet, darling," he said. His voice trembled a little. And he spoke in the hushed voice of a man who knows himself in a holy or enchanted place.

Then silence. Silence which weighed and pressed upon a man's soul. Silence which seemed a living deadness about them. From the boy's shoulder came a hushed, small voice which endeavoured to conceal its shaking. It said:

"I . . . I . . . felt all along . . . we shouldn't . . . shouldn't be here. . . . We didn't ought to 've come. . . ."

Despite its quietness there was something like panic in the voice.

He spoke reassuring words. To shake her from this queer, repressed hysteria, he said these words in a loud and virile tone. But this had only the effect of conveying to himself something of the odd disquiet which had possessed the girl.

"It's cold in here," she whispered suddenly. Her body pressed itself against him.

He laughed; an odd sound. He said hastily:

"Cold! You're talking out of the back of your neck, Vi."

"It is," she said. But her voice was more natural now. "We better be getting along, hadn't we?"

He nodded. "Think we had," he said. He stirred, as if to get to his feet. But a small hand suddenly gripped his arm, and her voice whispered:

"Look! *Look!*" It was her own voice again, so that, even while he started a little at her sudden clutch and the urgency of her tone, he felt a wave of relief and a sudden quietening of his own vague but discomfortable uneasiness.

His gaze followed the line of her pointing finger. He saw, upon the carpeting of rotten twigs and brown mouldering leaves, just at the point where this brown and the dark cool green of their moss-bank met, a small bird. It stood upon its slender sticks of legs and gazed up at them, over the plump bright-hued breast, with shining little eyes. Its head was cocked to one side.

"D'you know," said the girl's whisper, "that's the first one we've *seen!*"

The boy pondered for a moment. "Gosh!" he said at last. "So it is and all!"

They watched in silence. The bird hopped nearer.

"Isn't he *sweet*, Jack?" Her whisper was a delighted chuckle.

"Talk about tame!" said the boy softly. "Cunning little beggar!"

Her elbow nudged his ribs. She said, her lips barely moving:

"Keep still. If we don't move, I believe he'll come right up to us."

Almost on her words, the bird hopped nearer. Now he was actually upon the moss, and thus less than an inch from the toe of the girl's left shoe. His little pert head, which was of a shining green with a rather comically long beak of yellow, was still cocked to one side. His bright, small eyes still surveyed them with the unwinking stare of his kind.

The girl's fascinated eyes were upon the small creature. She saw nothing else. Not so the boy. There was a nudge, this time from his elbow.

"Look there!" he whispered, pointing. "And there!"

She took, reluctantly enough, her eyes from the small intruder by her foot. She gazed in the directions he had indicated. She gasped in wonder. She whispered:

"Why, they're *all* coming to see us!"

Everywhere between the boles of the close-growing trees were birds. Some stood singly, some in pairs, some in little clumps of four and more. Some seemed, even to urban eyes, patently of the same family as their first visitor, who still stood by the white shoe, staring up at the face of its owner. But there were many more families. There were very small birds, and birds of sparrow size but unsparrowlike plumage, and birds which were a little bigger than this, and birds which were twice and three times the size. But one and all faced the carpet of moss and stared with their shining eyes at the two humans who lay upon it.

"This," said the boy, "is the rummest start *I* ever . . ."

The girl's elbow nudged him to silence. He followed the nod of her head and, looking down, saw that the first visitor was now perched actually upon her instep. He seemed very much at his ease there. But he was no longer looking up at them with those bright little eyes. And his head was no longer cocked to one side: it was level, so that he appeared to be in contemplation of a silk-clad shin.

Something—perhaps it was a little whispering, pattering rustle among the rotting leaves of the wood's carpet—took the boy's fascinated eyes from this strange sight. He lifted them to see a stranger; a sight perhaps more fascinating, but with by no means the same fascination.

The birds were nearer. Much, much nearer. And their line was solid now; an unbroken semicircle with bounding-line so wide-flung that he felt rather than saw its extent. One little corner of his brain for an instant busied itself with wild essays at numerical computation, but reeled back defeated by the impossibility of the task. Even as he stared, his face pale now, and his eyes wide with something like terror, that semicircle drew yet nearer, each unit of it taking four hops and four hops only. Now, its line unmarred, it was close upon the edge of the moss.

But was it only a semicircle? A dread doubt of this flashed into his mind.

One horrified glance across his shoulder told him that semicircle it was not. Full circle it was.

Birds, birds, birds! Was it possible that the world itself should hold such numbers of birds?

Eyes! Small, shining, myriad button-points of glittering eyes. All fixed upon him . . . and—God!—upon *her*. . . .

In one wild glance he saw that as yet she had not seen. Still she was in rapt, silent ecstasy over her one bird. And this now sat upon the outspread palm of her hand. Close to her face she was holding this hand. . . .

Through the pall of silence he could feel those countless eyes upon him. Little eyes; bright, glittering eyes. . . .

His breath came in shuddering gasps. He tried to get himself in hand; tried, until the sweat ran off him with the intensity of his effort, to master his fear. To some extent he succeeded. He would no longer sit idle while the circle . . . while the circle . . .

The silence was again ruffled upon its surface by a rustling patter. . . . It was one hop this time. It brought the semicircle fronting him so near that there were birds within an inch of his feet.

He leapt up. He waved his arms and kicked out and uttered one shout which somehow cracked and was half-strangled in his throat.

Nothing happened. At the edge of the moss a small bird, crushed by his kick, lay in a soft, small heap.

Not one of the birds moved. Still their eyes were upon him.

The girl sat like a statue in living stone. She had seen, and terror held her. Her palm, the one bird still motionless upon it, still was outspread near her face.

From high above them there dropped slowly into the black depths of the silence one note of a sweetness ineffable. It lingered upon the breathless air, dying slowly until it fused with the silence.

And then the girl screamed. Suddenly and dreadfully. The small green poll had darted forward. The yellow beak had struck and sunk. A scarlet runnel coursed down the tender cheek.

Above the lingering echo of that scream there came another of those single notes from on high.

The silence died then. There was a whirring which filled the air. That circle was no more.

There were two feathered mounds which screamed and ran and leapt, and at last lay and were silent.

THE FLY

George Langelaan

TELEPHONES and telephone bells have always made me uneasy. Years ago, when they were mostly wall fixtures, I disliked them, but nowadays, when they are planted in every nook and corner, they are a downright intrusion. We have a saying in France that a coal-man is master in his own house; with the telephone that is no longer true, and I suspect that even the Englishman is no longer king in his own castle.

At the office, the sudden ringing of the telephone annoys me. It means that, no matter what I am doing, in spite of the switchboard operator, in spite of my secretary, in spite of doors and walls, some unknown person is coming into the room and onto my desk to talk right into my very ear, confidentially—and that whether I like it or not. At home, the feeling is still more disagreeable, but the worst is when the telephone rings in the dead of the night. If anyone could see me turn on the light and get up blinking to answer it, I suppose I would look like any other sleepy man annoyed at being disturbed. The truth in such a case, however, is that I am strug-gling against panic, fighting down a feeling that a stranger has broken into the house and is in my bedroom. By the time I manage to grab the receiver and say: *"Ici Monsieur Delambre. Je vous ecoute,"* I am outwardly calm, but I only get back to a more normal state when I recognize the voice at the other end and when I know what is wanted of me.

This effort at dominating a purely animal reaction and fear had become so effective that when my sister-in-law called me at two in the morning, asking me to come over, but first to warn the police that she had just killed my brother, I quietly asked her how and why she had killed Andre.

"But, Francois! . . . I can't explain all that over the telephone. Please call the police and come quickly."

"Maybe I had better see you first, Helene?"

"No, you'd better call the police first; otherwise they will start asking you all sorts of awkward questions. They'll have enough trouble as it is to believe that I did it alone . . . And, by the way, I suppose you ought to tell them that Andre . . . Andre's body, is down at the factory. They may want to go there first."

"Did you say that Andre is at the factory?"

"Yes . . . under the steam-hammer."

"Under the what!"

"The steam-hammer! But don't ask so many questions. Please come quickly Francois! Please understand that I'm afraid . . . that my nerves won't stand it much longer!"

Have you ever tried to explain to a sleepy police officer that your sister-in-law has just phoned to say that she has killed your brother with a steam-hammer? I repeated my explanation, but he would not let me.

"*Oui, Monsieur, oui,* I hear . . . but who are you? What is your name? Where do you live? I said, where do you live!"

It was then that Commissaire Charas took over the line and the whole business. He at least seemed to understand everything. Would I wait for him? Yes, he would pick me up and take me over to my brother's house. When? In five or 10 minutes.

I had just managed to pull on my trousers, wriggle into a sweater and grab a hat and coat, when a black Citroen, headlights blazing, pulled up at the door.

"I assume you have a night watchman at your factory, Monsieur Delambre. Has he called you?" asked Commissaire Charas letting in the clutch as I sat down beside him and slammed the door of the car.

"No, he hasn't. Though of course my brother could have entered the factory through his laboratory where he often works late at night . . . all night sometimes."

"Is Professor Delambre's work connected with your business?"

"No, my brother is, or was, doing research work for the Ministere de l'Air. As he wanted to be away from Paris and yet within reach of where skilled workmen could fix up or make gadgets big and small for his experiments, I offered him one of the old work-shops of the factory and he came to live in the first house built by our grandfather on the top of the hill at the back of the factory."

"Yes, I see. Did he talk about his work? What sort of research work?"

"He rarely talked about it, you know; I suppose the Air Ministry could tell you. I only know that he was about to carry out a num-ber of experiments he had been preparing for some months, some-thing to do with the disintegration of matter, he told me."

Barely slowing down, the Commissaire swung the car off the road, slid it through the open factory gate and pulled up sharp by a policeman apparently expecting him.

I did not need to hear the policeman's confirmation. I knew now that my brother was dead, it seemed that I had been told years ago. Shaking like a leaf, I scrambled out after the Commissaire.

Another policeman stepped out of a doorway and led us to-wards one of the shops where all the lights had been turned on. More policemen were standing by the hammer, watching two men setting up a camera. It was tilted downwards, and I made an effort to look.

It was far less horrid than I had expected. Though I had never seen my brother drunk, he looked just as if he were sleeping off a terrific binge, flat on his stomach across the narrow line on which the white-hot slabs of metal were rolled up to the hammer. I saw at a glance that his head and arm could only be a flattened mess, but that seemed quite impossible; it looked as if he had somehow pushed his head and arm right into the metallic mass of the ham-mer.

Having talked to his colleagues, the Commissaire turned to-wards me:

"How can we raise the hammer, Monsieur Delambre?"

"I'll raise it for you."

"Would you like us to get some of your men over?"

"No, I'll be all right. Look, here is the switchboard. It was originally a steam-hammer, but everything is worked electrically here now. Look Commissaire, the hammer has been set at 50 tons and its impact at zero."

"At zero . . . ?"

"Yes, level with the ground if your prefer. It is also set for single strokes, which means that it has to be raised after each blow. I don't know what Helene, my sister-in-law, will have to say about all this, but one thing I am sure of: she certainly did not know how to set and operate the hammer."

"Perhaps it was set that way last night when work stopped?"

"Certainly not. The drop is never set at zero, Monsieur le Commissaire."

"I see. Can it be raised gently?"

"No. The speed of the upstroke cannot be regulated. But in any case it is not very fast when the hammer is set for single strokes."

"Right. Will you show me what to do? It won't be very nice to watch, you know."

"No, no, Monsieur le Commissaire. I'll be all right."

"All set?" asked the Commissaire of the others. "All right then, Monsieur Delambre. Whenever you like."

Watching my brother's back, I slowly but firmly pushed the upstroke button.

The unusual silence of the factory was broken by the sigh of compressed air rushing into the cylinders, a sigh that always makes me think of a giant taking a deep breath before solemnly socking another giant, and the steel mass of the hammer shuddered and then rose swiftly. I also heard the sucking sound as it left the metal base and thought I was going to panic when I saw Andre's body heave forward as a sickly gush of blood poured all over the ghastly mess bared by the hammer.

"No danger of it coming down again, Monsieur Delambre?"

"No, none whatever," I mumbled as I threw the safety switch and, turning around, I was violently sick in front of a young green-faced policeman.

For weeks after, Commissaire Charas worked on the case, listening, questioning, running all over the place, making out reports, telegraphing and telephoning right and left. Later, we became quite friendly and he owned that he had for a long time considered me as suspect number one, but had finally given up that idea because, not only was there no clue of any sort, but not even a motive.

Helene, my sister-in-law, was so calm throughout the whole business that the doctors finally confirmed what I had long considered the only possible solution: that she was mad. That being the case, there was of course no trial.

My brother's wife never tried to defend herself in any way and even got quite annoyed when she realized that people thought her mad, and this of course was considered proof that she was indeed mad. She owned up to the murder of her husband and proved easily that she knew how to handle the hammer; but she would never say why, exactly how, or under what circumstances she had killed my brother. The great mystery was how and why had my brother so obligingly stuck his head under the hammer, the only possible explanation for his part in the drama.

The night watchman had heard the hammer all right; he had even heard it twice, he claimed. This was very strange, and the stroke-counter which was always set back to nought after a job, seemed to prove him right, since it marked the figure two. Also, the foreman in charge of the hammer confirmed that after cleaning up the day before the murder, he had as usual turned the stroke-counter back to nought. In spite of this, Helene maintained that she had only used the hammer once, and this seemed just another proof of her insanity.

Commissaire Charas who had been put in charge of the case at first wondered if the victim were really my brother. But of that there was no possible doubt, if only because of the great scar running from his knee to his thigh, the result of a shell that had landed within a few feet of him during the retreat in 1940; and there were also the fingerprints of his left hand which corresponded to those found all over his laboratory and his personal belongings up at the house.

A guard had been put on his laboratory and the next day half-a-dozen officials came down from the Air Ministry. They went through all his papers and took away some of his instruments, but before leaving, they told the Commissaire that the most interesting documents and instruments had been destroyed.

The Lyons police laboratory, one of the most famous in the world, reported that Andre's head had been wrapped up in a piece of velvet when it was crushed by the hammer, and one day Commissaire Charas showed me a tattered drapery which I immediately recognized as the brown velvet cloth I had seen on a table in my brother's laboratory, the one on which his meals were served when he could not leave his work.

After only a very few days in prison, Helene had been transferred to a nearby asylum, one of the three in France where insane criminals are taken care of. My nephew Henri, a boy of six, the very image of his father, was entrusted to me, and eventually all legal arrangements were made for me to become his guardian and tutor.

Helene, one of the quietest patients of the asylum, was allowed visitors and I went to see her on Sundays. Once or twice the Commissaire had accompanied me and, later, I learned that he had also visited Helene alone. But we were never able to obtain any information from my sister-in-law who seemed to have become utterly indifferent. She rarely answered my questions and hardly ever those of the Commissaire. She spent a lot of her time sewing, but her favorite pastime seemed to be catching flies which she invariably released unharmed after having examined them carefully.

Helene only had one fit of raving—more like a nervous breakdown than a fit said the doctor who had administered morphia to quieten her—the day she saw a nurse swatting flies.

The day after Helene's one and only fit, Commissaire Charas came to see me.

"I have a strange feeling that there lies the key to the whole business, Monsieur Delambre," he said.

I did not ask him how it was that he already knew all about Helene's fit.

"I do not follow you, Commissaire. Poor Madame Delambre could have shown an exceptional interest for anything else, really. Don't you think that flies just happen to be the border-subject of her tendency to raving?"

"Do you believe she is really mad?" he asked.

"My dear Commissaire, I don't see how there can be any doubt. Do you doubt it?"

"I don't know. In spite of all the doctors say, I have the impression that Madame Delambre has a very clear brain . . . even when catching flies."

"Supposing you were right, how would you explain her attitude with regard to her little boy? She never seems to consider him as her own child."

"You know, Monsieur Delambre, I have thought about that also. She may be trying to protect him. Perhaps she fears the boy or, for all we know, hates him?"

"I'm afraid I don't understand, my dear Commissaire."

"Have you noticed, for instance, that she never catches flies when the boy is there?"

"No. But come to think of it, you are quite right. Yes, that is strange . . . Still, I fail to understand."

"So do I, Monsieur Delambre. And I'm very much afraid that we shall never understand, unless perhaps your sister-in-law should *get better*."

"The doctors seem to think that there is no hope of any sort you know."

"Yes. Do you know if your brother ever experimented with flies?"

"I really don't know, but I shouldn't think so. Have you asked the Air Ministry people? They knew all about the work."

"Yes, and they laughed at me."

"I can understand that."

"You are very fortunate to understand anything, Monsieur Delambre. I do not . . . but I hope to some day."

"Tell me, Uncle, do flies live a long time?"

We were just finishing our lunch and, following an established tradition between us, I was just pouring some wine into Henri's glass for him to dip a biscuit in.

Had Henri not been staring at his glass gradually being filled to the brim, something in my look might have frightened him.

This was the first time that he had ever mentioned flies, and I shuddered at the thought that Commissaire Charas might quite easily have been present. I could imagine the glint in his eye as he would have answered my nephew's question with another question. I could almost hear him saying:

"I don't know, Henri. Why do you ask?"

"Because I have again seen the fly that *Maman* was looking for."

And it was only after drinking off Henri's own glass of wine that I realized that he had answered my spoken thought.

"I did not know that your mother was looking for a fly."

"Yes, she was. It has grown quite a lot, but I recognized it all right."

"Where did you see this fly, Henri, and . . . how did you recognize it?"

"This morning on your desk, Uncle Francois. Its head is white instead of black, and it has a funny sort of leg."

Feeling more and more like Commissaire Charas, but trying to look unconcerned, I went on:

"And when did you see this fly for the first time?"

"The day that Papa went away. I had caught it, but *Maman* made me let it go. And then after, she wanted me to find it again. She'd changed her mind," and shrugging his shoulders just as my brother used to, he added, "You know what women are."

"I think that fly must have died long ago, and you must be mistaken, Henri," I said, getting up and walking to the door.

But as soon as I was out of the dining room, I ran up the stairs to my study. There was no fly anywhere to be seen.

I was bothered, far more than I cared to even think about. Henri had just proved that Charas was really closer to a clue than had seemed when he told me about his thoughts concerning Helene's pastime.

For the first time I wondered if Charas did not really know much more than he let on. For the first time also, I wondered about Helene. Was she really insane? A strange, horrid feeling was growing on me, and the more I thought about it, the more I felt that, somehow, Charas was right: Helene was *getting away with it!*

What could possibly have been the reason for such a monstrous crime? What had led up to it? Just what had happened?

I thought of all the hundreds of questions that Charas had put to Helene, sometimes gently like a nurse trying to soothe, sometimes stern and cold, sometimes barking them furiously. Helene had answered very few, always in a calm quiet voice and never seeming to pay any attention to the way in which the question had been put. Though dazed, she had seemed perfectly sane then.

Refined, well-bred and well-read, Charas was more than just an intelligent police official. He was a keen psychologist and had an amazing way of smelling out a fib or an erroneous statement even before it was uttered. I knew that he had accepted as true the few answers she had given him. But then there had been all those questions which she had never answered: the most direct and important ones. From the very beginning, Helene had adopted a very simple system. "I cannot answer that question," she would say in her low quiet voice. And that was that! The repetition of the same question never seemed to annoy her. In all the hours of questioning that she underwent, Helene did not once point out to the Commissaire that he had already asked her this or that. She would simply say, "I cannot answer that question," as though it was the very first time that that particular question had been asked and the very first time she had made that answer.

This cliché had become the formidable barrier beyond which Commissaire Charas could not even get a glimpse, an idea of what Helene might be thinking. She had very willingly answered all questions about her life with my brother—which seemed a happy and uneventful one—up to the time of his end. About his death, however, all that she would say was that she had killed him with the steam-hammer, but she refused to say why, what had led up to the drama and how she got my brother to put his head under it. She never actually refused outright; she would just go blank and, with no apparent emotion, would switch over to, "I cannot answer that question."

Helene, as I have said, had shown the Commissaire that she knew how to set and operate the steam-hammer.

Charas could only find one single fact which did not coincide with Helene's declarations, the fact that the hammer had been used twice. Charas was no longer willing to attribute this to insanity. That evident flaw in Helene's stonewall defense seemed a crack which the Commissaire might possibly enlarge. But my sister-in-law finally cemented it by acknowledging:

"All right, I lied to you. I did use the hammer twice. But do not ask me why, because I cannot tell you."

"Is that your only . . . misstatement, Madame Delambre?" had asked the Commissaire, trying to follow up what looked at last like an advantage.

"It is . . . and you know it, Monsieur le Commissaire."

And, annoyed, Charas had seen that Helene could read him like an open book.

I had thought of calling on the Commissaire, but the knowledge that he would inevitably start questioning Henri made me hesitate. Another reason also made me hesitate, a vague sort of fear that he would look for and find the fly Henri had talked of. And that annoyed me a good deal because I could find no satisfactory explanation for that particular fear.

Andre was definitely not the absent-minded sort of professor who walks about in pouring rain with a rolled umbrella under his arm. He was human, had a keen sense of humor, loved children and animals and could not bear to see anyone suffer. I had often seen him drop his work to watch a parade of the local fire brigade, or see the *Tour de France* cyclists go by, or even follow a circus parade all around the village. He liked games of logic and precision, such as billiards and tennis, bridge and chess.

How was it then possible to explain his death? What could have made him put his head under that hammer? It could hardly have been the result of some stupid bet or a test of his courage. He hated betting and had no patience with those who indulged in it. Whenever he heard a bet proposed, he would invariably remind all present that, after all, a bet was but a contract between a fool and a swindler, even if it turned out to be a toss-up as to which was which.

It seemed there were only two possible explanations to Andre's death. Either he had gone mad, or else he had a reason for letting his wife kill him in such a strange and terrible way. And just what could have been his wife's role in all this? They surely could not have been both insane?

Having finally decided not to tell Charas about my nephew's innocent revelations, I thought I myself would try to question Helene.

She seemed to have been expecting my visit for she came into the parlor almost as soon as I had made myself known to the matron and been allowed inside.

"I wanted to show you my garden," explained Helene as I looked at the coat slung over her shoulders.

As one of the "reasonable" inmates, she was allowed to go into the garden during certain hours of the day. She had asked for and obtained the right to a little patch of ground where she could grow flowers, and I had sent her seeds and some rosebushes out of my garden.

She took me straight to a rustic wooden bench which had been made in the men's workshop and only just set up under a tree close to her little patch of ground.

Searching for the right way to broach the subject of Andre's death, I sat for a while tracing vague designs on the ground with the end of my umbrella.

"Francois, I want to ask you something," said Helene after a while.

"Anything I can do for you, Helene?"

"No, just something I want to know. Do flies live very long?"

Staring at her, I was about to say that her boy had asked the very same question a few hours earlier when I suddenly realized that here was the opening I had been searching for and perhaps even the possibility of striking a great blow, a blow perhaps powerful enough to shatter her stonewall defense, be it sane or insane.

Watching her carefully, I replied:

"I don't really know, Helene; but the fly you were looking for was in my study this morning."

No doubt about it, I had struck a shattering blow. She swung her head round with such force that I heard the bones crack in her neck. She opened her mouth, but said not a word; only her eyes seemed to be screaming with fear.

Yes, it was evident that I had crashed through something, but what? Undoubtedly, the Commissaire would have known what to do with such an advantage; I did not. All I knew was that he would never have given her time to think, to recuperate, but all I could do, and even that was a strain, was to maintain my best poker-face, hoping against hope that Helene's defenses would go on crumbling.

She must have been quite a while without breathing, because she suddenly gasped and put both her hands over her still open mouth.

"Francois . . . Did you kill it?" she whispered, her eyes no longer fixed, but searching every inch of my face.

"No."

"You have it then . . . You have it on you! Give it to me!" she almost shouted touching me with both her hands, and I knew that had she felt strong enough, she would have tried to search me.

"No, Helene, I haven't got it."

"But you know now . . . You have guessed, haven't you?"

"No, Helene. I only know one thing, and that is that you are not insane. But I mean to know all Helene and, somehow, I am going to find out. You can choose: either you tell me everything and I'll see what is to be done, or . . ."

"Or what? Say it!"

"I was going to say it, Helene . . . or I assure you that your friend the Commissaire will have that fly first thing tomorrow morning."

She remained quite still, looking down at the palms of her hands on her lap and, although it was getting chilly, her forehead and hands were moist.

Without even brushing aside a wisp of long brown hair blown across her mouth by the breeze, she murmured:

"If I tell you . . . will you promise to destroy that fly before doing anything else?"

"No, Helene. I can make no such promise before knowing."

"But Francois, you must understand. I promised Andre that fly would be destroyed. That promise must be kept and I can say nothing until it is."

I could sense the deadlock ahead. I was not yet losing ground, but I was losing the initiative. I tried a shot in the dark:

"Helene, of course you understand that as soon as the police examine that fly, they will know that you are not insane, and then . . ."

"Francois, no! For Henri's sake! Don't you see? I was expecting that fly; I was hoping it would find me here but it couldn't know what had become of me. What else could it do but go to others it loves, to Henri, to you . . . you who might know and understand what was to be done!"

Was she really mad, or was she simulating again? But mad or not, she was cornered. Wondering how to follow up and how to land the knockout blow without running the risk of seeing her slip away out of reach, I said very quietly:

"Tell me all, Helene. I can then protect your boy."

"Protect my boy from what? Don't you understand that if I am here, it is merely so that Henri won't be the son of a woman who was guillotined for having murdered his father? Don't you understand that I would by far prefer the guillotine to the living death of this lunatic asylum?"

"I understand Helene, and I'll do my best for the boy whether you tell me or not. If you refuse to tell me, I'll still do the best I can to protect Henri, but you must understand that the game will be out of my hands, because Commissaire Charas will have the fly."

"But why must you know?" said, rather than asked, my sister-in-law, struggling to control her temper.

"Because I must and will know how and why my brother died, Helene."

"All right. Take me back to the . . . house. I'll give you what your Commissaire would call my 'Confession.' "

"Do you mean to say that you have written it!"

"Yes. It was not really meant for you, but more likely for

your friend, the Commissaire. I had foreseen that, sooner or later, he would get too close to the truth."

"You then have no objection to his reading it?"

"You will act as you think fit, Francois. Wait for me a minute."

Leaving me at the door of the parlor, Helene ran upstairs to her room. In less than a minute she was back with a large brown envelope.

"Listen Francois; you are not nearly as bright as was your poor brother, but you are not unintelligent. All I ask is that you read this alone. After that, you may do as you wish."

"That I promise you, Helene," I said, taking the precious envelope. "I'll read it tonight and although tomorrow is not a visiting day, I'll come down to see you."

"Just as you like," said my sister-in-law without even saying good-bye as she went back upstairs.

It was only on reaching home, as I walked from the garage to the house, that I read the inscription on the envelope:

TO WHOM IT MAY CONCERN

(Probably Commissaire Charas)

Having told the servants that I would have only a light supper to be served immediately in my study and that I was not to be disturbed after, I ran upstairs, threw Helene's envelope on my desk and made another careful search of the room before closing the shutters and drawing the curtains. All I could find was a long since dead mosquito stuck to the wall near the ceiling.

Having motioned to the servant to put her tray down on a table by the fireplace, I poured myself a glass of wine and locked the door behind her. I then disconnected the telephone—I always did this now at night—and turned out all the lights but the lamp on my desk.

Slitting open Helene's fat envelope, I extracted a thick wad of closely written pages. I read the following lines neatly centered in the middle of the top page:

This is not a confession because, although I killed my husband, I am not a murderess. I simply and very faithfully carried out his last wish by crushing his head and right arm under the steam-hammer of his brother's factory.

Without even touching the glass of wine by my elbow, I turned the page and started reading.

For very nearly a year before his death (*the manuscript began*), my husband had told me of some of his experiments. He knew full well that his colleagues of the Air Ministry would have forbidden some of them as too dangerous, but he was keen on obtaining positive results before reporting his discovery.

Whereas only sound and pictures had been, so far, transmitted through space by radio and television, Andre claimed to have discovered a way of transmitting matter. Matter, any solid object, placed in his "transmitter" was instantly disintegrated and reintegrated in a special receiving set.

Andre considered his discovery as perhaps the most important since that of the wheel sawn off the end of a tree trunk. He reckoned that the transmission of matter by instantaneous "disintegration-reintegration" would completely change life as we had known it so far. It would mean the end of all means of transport, not only of goods, including food, but also of human beings. Andre, the practical scientist who never allowed theories or daydreams to get the better of him, already foresaw the time when there would no longer be any airplanes, ships, trains or cars and, therefore, no longer any roads or railway lines, ports, airports or stations. All that would be replaced by matter-transmitting and receiving stations throughout the world. Travelers and goods would be placed in special cabins and, at a given signal, would simply disappear and reappear almost immediately at the chosen receiving station.

Andre's receiving set was only a few feet away from his transmitter, in an adjoining room of his laboratory, and he at first ran into all sorts of snags. His first successful experiment was carried out with an ash tray taken from his desk, a souvenir we had brought back from a trip to London.

That was the first time he told me about his experiments and I had no idea of what he was talking about the day he came dashing into the house and threw the ash tray in my lap.

"Helene, look! For a fraction of a second, a bare 10-millionth of a second, that ash tray has been completely disintegrated. For one little moment it no longer existed! Gone! Nothing left, absolutely nothing! Only atoms traveling through space at the speed of light! And the moment after, the atoms were once more gathered together in the shape of an ash tray!"

"Andre, please . . . please! What on earth are you raving about?"

He started sketching all over a letter I had been writing. He laughed at my wry face, swept all my letters off the table and said:

"You don't understand? Right. Let's start all over again. Helene, do you remember I once read you an article about the mysterious flying stones that seem to come from nowhere in particular, and which are said to occasionally fall in certain houses in India? They come flying in as though thrown from outside and that, in spite of closed doors and windows."

"Yes, I remember. I also remember that Professor Augier, your friend of the College de France, who had come down for a few days, remarked that if there was no trickery about it, the only possible explanation was that the stones had been disintegrated after having been thrown from outside, come through the walls, and then been reintegrated before hitting the floor or the opposite walls."

"That's right. And I added that there was, of course, one other possibility, namely the momentary and partial disintegration of the walls as the stone or stones came through."

"Yes, Andre. I remember all that, and I suppose you also remember that I failed to understand, and that you got quite annoyed. Well, I still do not understand why and how, even disintegrated, stones should be able to come through a wall or a closed door."

"But it is possible, Helene, because the atoms that go to make up matter are not close together like the bricks of a wall. They are separated by relative immensities of space."

"Do you mean to say that you have disintegrated that ash tray, and then put it together again after pushing it through something?"

"Precisely, Helene. I projected it through the wall that separates my transmitter from my receiving set."

"And would it be foolish to ask how humanity is to benefit from ash trays that can go through walls?"

Andre seemed quite offended, but he soon saw that I was only teasing, and again waxing enthusiastic, he told me of some of the possibilities of his discovery.

"Isn't it wonderful, Helene?" he finally gasped, out of breath.

"Yes, Andre. But I hope you won't ever transmit me; I'd be too much afraid of coming out at the other end like your ash tray."

"What do you mean?"

"Do you remember what was written under that ash tray?"

"Yes, of course: MADE IN JAPAN. That was the great joke of our typically British souvenir."

"The words are still there Andre; but . . . look!"

He took the ash tray out of my hands, frowned, and walked over to the window. Then he went quite pale, and I knew that he had seen what had proved to me that he had indeed carried out a strange experiment.

The three words were still there, but reversed and reading:

Made in Japan

Without a word, having completely forgotten me, Andre rushed off to his laboratory. I only saw him the next morning, tired and unshaven after a whole night's work.

A few days later, Andre had a new reverse which put him out of sorts and made him fussy and grumpy for several weeks. I stood it patiently enough for a while, but being myself bad tempered one evening, we had a silly row over some futile thing, and I reproached him for his moroseness.

"I'm sorry, *cherie*. I've been working my way through a maze of problems and have given you all a very rough time. You see, my very first experiment with a live animal proved a complete fiasco."

"Andre! You tried that experiment with Dandelo, didn't you?"

"Yes. How did you know?" he answered sheepishly. "He disintegrated perfectly, but he never reappeared in the receiving set."

"Oh, Andre! What became of him then?"

"Nothing . . . there is just no more Dandelo; only the dispersed atoms of a cat wandering, God knows where, in the universe."

Dandelo was a small white cat the cook had found one morning in the garden and which we had promptly adopted. Now I knew how it had disappeared and was quite angry about the whole thing, but my husband was so miserable over it all that I said nothing.

I saw little of my husband during the next few weeks. He had most of his meals sent down to the laboratory. I would often wake up in the morning and find his bed unslept in. Sometimes, if he had come in very late, I would find that storm-swept appearance which only a man can give a bedroom by getting up very early and fumbling around in the dark.

One evening he came home to dinner all smiles, and I knew that his troubles were over. His face dropped, however, when he saw I was dressed for going out.

"Oh. Were you going out, Helene?"

"Yes, the Drillons invited me for a game of bridge, but I can easily phone them and put it off."

"No, it's all right."

"It isn't all right. Out with it, dear!"

"Well, I've at last got everything perfect and I wanted you to be the first to see the miracle."

"*Magnifique,* Andre! Of course I'll be delighted."

Having telephoned our neighbors to say how sorry I was and so forth, I ran down to the kitchen and told the cook that she had exactly 10 minutes in which to prepare a "celebration dinner."

"An excellent idea, Helene," said my husband when the maid appeared with the champagne after our candlelight dinner. "We'll celebrate with reintegrated champagne!" and taking the tray from the maid's hands, he led the way down to the laboratory.

"Do you think it will be as good as before its disintegration?" I asked, holding the tray while he opened the door and switched on the lights.

"Have no fear. You'll see! Just bring it here, will you," he said, opening the door of a telephone call-box he had bought and which had been transformed into what he called a transmitter. "Put it down on that now," he added, putting a stool inside the box.

Having carefully closed the door, he took me to the other end of the room and handed me a pair of very dark sun glasses. He put on another pair and walked back to a switchboard by the transmitter.

"Ready Helene?" said my husband turning out all the lights. "Don't remove your glasses till I give the word."

"I won't budge Andre, go on," I told him, my eyes fixed on the tray which I could just see in a greenish shimmering light through the glass paneled door of the telephone booth.

"Right," said Andre, throwing a switch.

The whole room was brilliantly illuminated by an orange flash. Inside the cabin I had seen a crackling ball of fire and felt its heat on my face, neck and hands. The whole thing lasted but the fraction of a second, and I found myself blinking at green-edged black holes like those one sees after having stared at the sun.

"*Et voilà!* You can take off your glasses, Helene."

A little theatrically perhaps, my husband opened the door of the cabin. Though Andre had told me what to expect, I was astonished to find that the champagne, glasses, tray and stool were no longer there.

Andre ceremoniously led me by the hand into the next room, in a corner of which stood a second telephone booth. Opening the door wide, he triumphantly lifted the champagne tray off the stool.

Feeling somewhat like the good natured kind-member-of-the audience that has been dragged onto the music hall stage by the magician, I repressed from saying, "All done with mirrors," which I knew would have annoyed my husband.

"Sure it's not dangerous to drink?" I asked as the cork popped.

"Absolutely sure, Helene," he said, handing me a glass. "But that was nothing. Drink this off and I'll show you something much more astounding."

We went back into the other room.

"Oh, Andre! Remember poor Dandelo!"

"This is only a guinea pig, Helene. But I'm positive it will go through all right."

He set the furry little beast down on the green enamelled floor of the booth and quickly closed the door. I again put on my dark glasses and saw and felt the vivid crackling flash.

Without waiting for Andre to open the door, I rushed into the next room where the lights were still on and looked into the receiving booth.

"Oh, Andre! *Cheri!* He's there all right!" I shouted excitedly watching the little animal trotting round and round. "It's wonderful Andre. It works! You've succeeded!"

"I hope so, but I must be patient. I'll know for sure in a few weeks' time."

"What do you mean? Look! He's as full of life as when you put him in the other cabin."

"Yes, so he seems. But we'll have to see if all his organs are intact, and that will take some time. If that little beast is still full of life in a month's time, we then consider the experiment a success."

I begged Andre to let me take care of the guinea pig.

"All right, but don't kill it by overfeeding," he agreed with a grin for my enthusiasm.

Though not allowed to take Hop-la—the name I had given the guinea pig—out of its box in the laboratory, I had tied a pink ribbon round its neck and was allowed to feed it twice a day.

Hop-la soon got used to its pink ribbon and became quite a tame little pet, but that month of waiting seemed a year.

And then one day, Andre put Miquette, our cocker spaniel, into his "transmitter." He had not told me beforehand, knowing full well that I would never have agreed to such an experiment with our dog. But when he did tell me, Miquette had been successfully transmitted half-a-dozen times and seemed to be enjoying the operation thoroughly; no sooner was she let out of the "reintegrator" than she dashed madly into the next room, scratching at the "transmitter" door to have "another go," as Andre called it.

I now expected that my husband would invite some of his colleagues and Air Ministry specialists to come down. He usually did this when he had finished a research job and, before handing them long detailed reports which he always typed himself, he would carry out an experiment or two before them. But this time, he just went on working. One morning I finally asked him when he intended throwing his usual "surprise party," as we called it.

"No, Helene; not for a long while yet. This discovery is much too important. I have an awful lot of work to do on it still. Do you realize that there are some parts of the transmission proper which I do not yet myself fully understand? It works all right, but you see, I can't just say to all these eminent professors that I do this and that and, poof, it works! I must be able to explain how and why it works. And what is even more important, I must be ready and able to refute every destructive argument they will not fail to trot out, as they usually do when faced with anything really good."

I was occasionally invited down to the laboratory to witness some new experiment, but I never went unless Andre invited me, and only talked about his work if he broached the subject first. Of course it never occurred to me that he would, at that stage at least, have tried an experiment with a human being; though, had I thought about it—knowing Andre—it would have been obvious that he would never have allowed anyone into the "transmitter" before he had been through to test it first. It was only after the accident that I discovered he had duplicated all his switches inside the disintegration booth, so that he could try it out by himself.

The morning Andre tried this terrible experiment, he did not show up for lunch. I sent the maid down with a tray, but she brought it back with a note she had found pinned outside the laboratory door: "Do not disturb me, I am working."

He did occasionally pin such notes on his door and, though I noticed it, I paid no particular attention to the unusually large handwriting of his note.

It was just after that, as I was drinking my coffee, that Henri came bouncing into the room to say that he had caught a funny fly, and would I like to see it. Refusing even to look at his closed fist, I ordered him to release it immediately.

"But, *Maman,* it has such a funny white head!"

Marching the boy over to the open window, I told him to release the fly immediately, which he did. I knew that Henri had caught the fly merely because he thought it looked curious or different from other flies, but I also knew that his father would never stand for any form of cruelty to animals, and that there would be a fuss should he discover that our son had put a fly in a box or a bottle.

At dinnertime that evening, Andre had still not shown up, and a little worried, I ran down to the laboratory and knocked at the door.

He did not answer my knock, but I heard him moving around and a moment later he slipped a note under the door. It was typewritten:

> Helene, I am having trouble. Put the boy to bed and come back in an hour's time. A.

Frightened, I knocked and called, but Andre did not seem to pay any attention and, vaguely reassured by the familiar noise of his typewriter, I went back to the house.

Having put Henri to bed, I returned to the laboratory where I found another note slipped under the door. My hand shook as I picked it up because I knew by then that something must be radically wrong. I read:

> Helene, first of all I count on you not to lose your nerve or do anything rash because you alone can help me. I have had a serious

accident. I am not in any particular danger for the time being though it is a matter of life and death. It is useless calling to me or saying anything. I cannot answer, I cannot speak. I want you to do exactly and very carefully all that I ask. After having knocked three times to show that you understand and agree, fetch me a bowl of milk laced with rum. I have had nothing all day and can do with it.

Shaking with fear, not knowing what to think and repressing a furious desire to call Andre and bang away until he opened, I knocked three times as requested and ran all the way home to fetch what he wanted.

In less than five minutes I was back. Another note had been slipped under the door:

Helene, follow these instructions carefully. When you knock I'll open the door. You are to walk over to my desk and put down the bowl of milk. You will then go into the other room where the receiver is. Look carefully and try to find a fly which ought to be there but which I am unable to find. Unfortunately I cannot see small things very easily.

Before you come in you must promise to obey me implicitly. Do not look at me and remember that talking is quite useless. I cannot answer. Knock again three times and that will mean I have your promise. My life depends entirely on the help you can give me.

I had to wait a while to pull myself together, and then I knocked slowly three times.

I heard Andre shuffling behind the door, then his hand fumbling with the lock, and the door opened.

Out of the corner of my eye, I saw that he was standing behind the door, but without looking round, I carried the bowl of milk to his desk. He was evidently watching me and I felt I must at all cost appear calm and collected.

"*Cheri,* you can count on me," I said gently, and putting the bowl down under his desk lamp, the only one alight, I walked into the next room where all the lights were blazing.

My first impression was that some sort of hurricane must have blown out of the receiving booth. Papers were scattered in every direction, a whole row of test tubes lay smashed in a corner, chairs and stools were upset and one of the window curtains hung half torn from its bent rod. In a large enamel basin on the floor a heap of burned documents was still smoldering.

I knew that I would not find the fly Andre wanted me to look for. Women know things that men only suppose by reasoning and deduction; it is a form of knowledge very rarely accessible to them and which they disparagingly call intuition. I already knew that the fly Andre wanted was the one which Henri had caught and which I had made him release.

I heard Andre shuffling around in the next room, and then a strange gurgling and sucking as though he had trouble in drinking his milk.

"Andre, there is no fly here. Can you give me any sort of indication that might help? If you can't speak, rap or something . . . you know: once for yes, twice for no."

I had tried to control my voice and speak as though perfectly calm, but I had to choke down a sob of desperation when he rapped twice for "no."

"May I come to you Andre? I don't know what can have happened, but whatever it is, I'll be courageous, dear."

After a moment of silent hesitation, he tapped once on his desk.

At the door I stopped aghast at the sight of Andre standing with his head and shoulders covered by the brown velvet cloth he had taken from a table by his desk, the table on which he usually ate when he did not want to leave his work. Suppressing a laugh that might easily have turned to sobbing, I said:

"Andre, we'll search thoroughly tomorrow, by daylight. Why don't you go to bed? I'll lead you to the guest room if you like, and won't let anyone else see you."

His left hand tapped the desk twice.

"Do you need a doctor, Andre?"

"No," he rapped.

"Would you like me to call up Professor Augier? He might be of more help . . ."

Twice he rapped "no" sharply. I did not know what to do or say. And then I told him:

"Henri caught a fly this morning which he wanted to show me, but I made him release it. Could it have been the one you are looking for? I didn't see it, but the boy said its head was white."

Andre emitted a strange metallic sigh, and I just had time to bite my fingers fiercely in order not to scream. He had let his right arm drop, and instead of his long-fingered muscular hand, a gray stick with little buds on it like the branch of a tree, hung out of his sleeve almost down to his knee.

"Andre, *mon cheri,* tell me what happened. I might be of more help to you if I knew. Andre . . . oh, it's terrible!" I sobbed, unable to control myself.

Having rapped once for yes, he pointed to the door with his left hand.

I stepped out and sank down crying as he locked the door behind me. He was typing again and I waited. At last he shuffled to the door and slid a sheet of paper under it.

> Helene, come back in the morning. I must think and will have typed out an explanation for you. Take one of my sleeping tablets and go straight to bed. I need you fresh and strong tomorrow, ma pauvre cherie. A.

"Do you want anything for the night, Andre?" I shouted through the door.

He knocked twice for no, and a little later I heard the typewriter again.

The sun full on my face woke me up with a start. I had set the alarm-clock for five but had not heard it, probably because of the sleeping tablets. I had indeed slept like a log, without a dream. Now I was back in my living nightmare and crying like a child I sprang out of bed. It was just on seven!

Rushing into the kitchen, without a word for the startled servants, I rapidly prepared a trayload of coffee, bread and butter with which I ran down to the laboratory.

Andre opened the door as soon as I knocked and closed it again as I carried the tray to his desk. His head was still covered, but I saw from his crumpled suit and his open camp-bed that he must have at least tried to rest.

On his desk lay a typewritten sheet for me which I picked up. Andre opened the other door, and taking this to mean that he wanted to be left alone, I walked into the next room. He pushed the door to and I heard him pouring out the coffee as I read:

> Do you remember the ash tray experiment? I have had a similar accident. I "transmitted" myself successfully the night before last. During a second experiment yesterday a fly which I did not see must have got into the "disintegrator." My only hope is to find that fly and go

through again with it. Please search for it carefully since, if it is not found, I shall have to find a way of putting an end to all this.

If only Andre had been more explicit! I shuddered at the thought that he must be terribly disfigured and then cried softly as I imagined his face inside-out, or perhaps his eyes in place of his ears, or his mouth at the back of his neck, or worse!

Andre must be saved! For that, the fly must be found!

Pulling myself together, I said:

"Andre, may I come in?"

He opened the door.

"Andre, don't despair; I am going to find that fly. It is no longer in the laboratory, but it cannot be very far. I suppose you're disfigured, perhaps terribly so, but there can be no question of putting an end to all this, as you say in your note; that I will never stand for. If necessary, if you do not wish to be seen, I'll make you a mask or a cowl so that you can go on with your work until you get well again. If you cannot work, I'll call Professor Augier, and he and all your other friends will save you, Andre."

Again I heard that curious metallic sigh as he rapped violently on his desk.

"Andre, don't be annoyed; please be calm. I won't do anything without first consulting you, but you must rely on me, have faith in me and let me help you as best I can. Are you terribly disfigured, dear? Can't you let me see your face? I won't be afraid . . . I am your wife you know."

But my husband again rapped a decisive "no" and pointed to the door.

"All right. I am going to search for the fly now, but promise me you won't do anything foolish; promise you won't do anything rash or dangerous without first letting me know all about it!"

He extended his left hand, and I knew I had his promise.

I will never forget that ceaseless day-long hunt for a fly. Back home, I turned the house inside-out and made all the servants join in the search. I told them that a fly had escaped from the Professor's laboratory and that it must be captured alive, but it was evident they already thought me crazy. They said so to the police later, and that day's hunt for a fly most probably saved me from the guillotine later.

I questioned Henri and as he failed to understand right away what I was talking about, I shook him and slapped him, and made him cry in front of the roundeyed maids. Realizing that I must not let myself go, I kissed and petted the poor boy and at last made him understand what I wanted of him. Yes, he remembered, he had found the fly just by the kitchen window; yes, he had released it immediately as told to.

Even in summer time we had very few flies because our house is on the top of a hill and the slightest breeze coming across the valley blows round it. In spite of that, I managed to catch dozens of flies that day. On all the window sills and all over the garden I had put saucers of milk, sugar, jam, meat—all the things likely to attract flies. Of all those we caught, and many others which we failed to catch but which I saw, none resembled the one Henri had caught the day before. One by one, with a magnifying glass, I examined every unusual fly, but none had anything like a white head.

At lunch time, I ran down to Andre with some milk and mashed potatoes. I also took some of the flies we had caught, but he gave me to understand that they could be of no possible use to him.

"If that fly has not been found tonight, Andre, we'll have to see what is to be done. And this is what I propose: I'll sit in the next room. When you can't answer by the yes-no method of rapping, you'll type out whatever you want to say and then slip it under the door. Agreed?"

"Yes," rapped Andre.

By nightfall we had still not found the fly. At dinner time, as I prepared Andre's tray, I broke down and sobbed in the kitchen in front of the silent servants. My maid thought that I had had a row with my husband, probably about the mislaid fly, but I learned later that the cook was already quite sure that I was out of my mind.

Without a word, I picked up the tray and then put it down again as I stopped by the telephone. That this was really a matter of life and death for Andre, I had no doubt. Neither did I doubt that he fully intended committing suicide, unless I could make him change his mind, or at least put off such a drastic decision. Would I be strong enough? He would never forgive me for not keeping a promise, but under the circumstances, did that really matter? To the devil with promises and honor! At all costs Andre must be saved! And having thus made up my mind, I looked up and dialed Professor Augier's number.

"The Professor is away and will not be back before the end of the week," said a polite neutral voice at the other end of the line.

That was that! I would have to fight alone and fight I would. I would save Andre come what may.

All my nervousness had disappeared as Andre let me in and, after putting the tray of food down on his desk, I went into the other room, as agreed.

"The first thing I want to know," I said as he closed the door behind me, "is what happened exactly. Can you please tell me, Andre?"

I waited patiently while he typed an answer which he pushed under the door a little later.

Helene, I would rather not tell you. Since go I must, I would rather you remember me as I was before. I must destroy myself in such a way that none can possibly know what has happened to me. I have of course thought of simply disintegrating myself in my transmitter, but I had better not because, sooner or later, I might find myself reintegrated. Some day, somewhere, some scientist is sure to make the same discovery. I have therefore thought of a way which is neither simple nor easy, but you can and will help me.

For several minutes I wondered if Andre had not simply gone stark raving mad.

"Andre," I said at last, "whatever you may have chosen or thought of, I cannot and will never accept such a cowardly solution. No matter how awful the result of your experiment or accident, you are alive, you are a man, a brain . . . and you have a soul. You have no right to destroy yourself! You know that!"

The answer was soon typed and pushed under the door.

I am alive all right, but I am already no longer a man. As to my brain or intelligence, it may disappear at any moment. As it is, it is no longer intact. And there can be no soul without intelligence . . . and you know that!

"Then you must tell the other scientists about your discovery. They will help you and save you, Andre!"

I staggered back frightened as he angrily thumped the door twice.

"Andre . . . why? Why do you refuse the aid you know they would give you with all their hearts?"

A dozen furious knocks shook the door and made me understand that my husband would never accept such a solution. I had to find other arguments.

For hours, it seemed, I talked to him about our boy, about me, about his family, about his duty to us and to the rest of humanity. He made no reply of any sort. At last I cried:

"Andre . . . do you hear me?"

"Yes," he knocked very gently.

"Well, listen then. I have another idea. You remember your first experiment with the ash tray? . . . Well, do you think that if you had put it through again a second time, it might possibly have come out with the letters turned back the right way?"

Before I had finished speaking, Andre was busily typing and a moment later I read his answer:

I have already thought of that. And that was why I needed the fly. It has got to go through with me. There is no hope otherwise.

"Try all the same, Andre. You never know!"

I have tried seven times already,

was the typewritten reply I got to that.

"Andre! Try again, please!"

The answer this time gave me a flutter of hope, because no woman has ever understood, or will ever understand, how a man about to die can possibly consider anything funny.

I deeply admire your delicious feminine logic. We could go on doing this experiment until doomsday. However, just to give you that pleasure, probably the very last I shall ever be able to give you, I will try once more. If you cannot find the dark glasses, turn your back to the machine and press your hands over your eyes. Let me know when you are ready.

"Ready Andre!" I shouted without even looking for the glasses and following his instructions.

I heard him move around and then open and close the door of his "disintegrator." After what seemed a very long wait, but probably was not more than a minute or so, I heard a violent crackling noise and perceived a bright flash through my eyelids and fingers.

I turned around as the cabin door opened.

His head and shoulders still covered with the brown velvet carpet, Andre was gingerly stepping out of it.

"How do you feel Andre? Any difference?" I asked touching his arm.

He tried to step away from me and caught his foot in one of the stools which I had not troubled to pick up. He made a violent effort to regain his balance, and the velvet carpet slowly slid off his shoulders and head as he fell heavily backwards.

The horror was too much for me, too unexpected. As a matter of fact, I am sure that, even had I known, the horror-impact could hardly have been less powerful. Trying to push both hands into my mouth to stifle my screams and although my fingers were bleeding, I screamed again and again. I could not take my eyes off him, I could not even close them, and yet I knew that if I looked at the horror much longer, I would go on screaming for the rest of my life.

Slowly, the monster, the thing that had been my husband, covered its head, got up and groped its way to the door and passed it. Though still screaming, I was able to close my eyes.

I who had ever been a true Catholic, who believed in God and another, better life hereafter, have today but one hope: that when I die, I really die, and that there may be no after-life of any sort because, if there is, then I shall never forget! Day and night, awake or asleep, I see it, and I know that I am condemned to see it forever, even perhaps into oblivion!

Until I am totally extinct, nothing can, nothing will ever make me forget that dreadful white hairy head with its low flat skull and its two pointed ears. Pink and moist, the nose was also that of a cat, a huge cat. But the eyes! Or rather, where the eyes should have been were two brown bumps the size of saucers. Instead of a mouth, animal or human, was a long hairy vertical slit from which hung a black quivering trunk that widened at the end, trumpet-like, and from which saliva kept dripping.

I must have fainted, because I found myself flat on my stomach on the cold cement floor of the laboratory, staring at the closed door behind which I could hear the noise of Andre's typewriter.

Numb, numb and empty. I must have looked as people do immediately after a terrible accident, before they fully understand what has happened. I could only think of a man I had once seen on the platform of a railway station, quite conscious, and looking stupidly at his leg still on the line where the train had just passed.

My throat was aching terribly, and that made me wonder if my vocal cords had not perhaps been torn, and whether I would ever be able to speak again.

The noise of the typewriter suddenly stopped and I felt I was going to scream again as something touched the door and a sheet of paper slid from under it.

Shivering with fear and disgust, I crawled over to where I could read it without touching it:

Now you understand. That last experiment was a new disaster my poor Helene. I suppose you recognized part of Dandelo's head. When I went into the disintegrator just now, my head was only that of a fly. I now only have its eyes and mouth left. The rest has been replaced by parts of the cat's head. Poor Dandelo whose atoms had never come together. You see now that there can only be one possible solution, don't you? I must disappear. Knock on the door when you are ready and I shall explain what you have to do.

Of course he was right, and it had been wrong and cruel of me to insist on a new experiment. And I knew that there was now no possible hope, that any further experiments could only bring about worse results.

Getting up dazed, I went to the door and tried to speak, but no sound came out of my throat . . . so I knocked once!

You can of course guess the rest. He explained his plan in short typewritten notes, and I agreed, I agreed to everything!

My head on fire, but shivering with cold, like an automaton, I followed him into the silent factory. In my hand was a full page of explanations: what I had to know about the steam-hammer.

Without stopping or looking back, he pointed to the switchboard that controlled the steam-hammer as he passed it. I went no further and watched him come to a halt before the terrible instrument.

He knelt down, carefully wrapped the carpet round his head, and then stretched out flat on the ground.

It was not difficult. I was not killing my husband. Andre, poor Andre, had gone long ago, years ago it seemed. I was merely carrying out his last wish . . . and mine.

Without hesitating, my eyes on the long still body, I firmly pushed the "stroke" button right in. The great metallic mass seemed to drop slowly. It was not so much the resounding clang of the hammer that made me jump as the sharp cracking which I had distinctly heard at the same time. My hus . . . the thing's body shook a second and then lay still.

It was then I noticed that he had forgotten to put his right arm, his fly-leg, under the hammer. The police would never understand but the scientists would, and they must not! That had been Andre's last wish, also!

I had to do it and quickly, too; the night watchman must have heard the hammer and would be round any moment. I pushed the other button and the hammer slowly rose. Seeing but trying not to look, I ran up, leaned down, lifted and moved forward the right arm which seemed terribly light. Back at the switchboard, again I pushed the red button, and down came the hammer a second time. Then I ran all the way home.

You know the rest and can now do whatever you think right.

So ended Helene's manuscript.

The following day I telephoned Commissaire Charas to invite him to dinner.

"With pleasure, Monsieur Delambre. Allow me, however to ask: is it the Commissaire you are inviting, or just Monsieur Charas?"

"Have you any preference?"

"No, not at the present moment."

"Well then, make it whichever you like. Will eight o'clock suit you?"

Although it was raining, the Commissaire arrived on foot that evening.

"Since you did not come tearing up to the door in your black Citroen, I take it you have opted for Monsieur Charas, off duty?"

"I left the car up a side-street," mumbled the Commissaire with a grin as the maid staggered under the weight of his raincoat.

"Merci," he said a minute later as I handed him a glass of Pernod into which he tipped a few drops of water, watching it turn the golden amber liquid to pale blue milk.

"You heard about my poor sister-in-law?"

"Yes, shortly after you telephoned me this morning. I am sorry, but perhaps it was all for the best. Being already in charge of your brother's case, the inquiry automatically comes to me."

"I suppose it was suicide."

"Without a doubt. Cyanide the doctors say quite rightly; I found a second tablet in the unstitched hem of her dress."

"Monsieur est servi," announced the maid.

"I would like to show you a very curious document afterwards, Charas."

"Ah, yes. I heard that Madame Delambre had been writing a lot, but we could find nothing beyond the short note informing us that she was committing suicide."

During our tête-à-tête dinner, we talked politics, books and films, and the local football club of which the Commissaire was a keen supporter.

After dinner, I took him up to my study where a bright fire—a habit I had picked up in England during the war—was burning.

Without even asking him, I handed him his brandy and mixed myself what he called "crushed-bug juice in soda water"—his appreciation of whiskey.

"I would like you to read this, Charas; first because it was partly intended for you and, secondly, because it will interest you. If you think Commissaire Charas has no objection, I would like to burn it after."

Without a word, he took the wad of sheets Helene had given me the day before and settled down to read them.

"What do you think of it all?" I asked some 20 minutes later as he carefully folded Helene's manuscript, slipped it into the brown envelope, and put it into the fire.

Charas watched the flames licking the envelope from which wisps of gray smoke were escaping, and it was only when it burst into flames that he said, slowly raising his eyes to mine:

"I think it proves very definitely that Madame Delambre was quite insane."

For a long while we watched the fire eating up Helene's "confession."

"A funny thing happened to me this morning, Charas. I went to the cemetery, where my brother is buried. It was quite empty and I was alone."

"Not quite, Monsieur Delambre. I was there, but I did not want to disturb you."

"Then you saw me . . ."

"Yes. I saw you bury a matchbox."

"Do you know what was in it?"

"A fly, I suppose."

"Yes. I had found it early this morning, caught in a spider's web in the garden."

"Was it dead?"

"No, not quite. I . . . crushed it . . . between two stones. Its head was . . . white . . . all white."

BACK THERE IN THE GRASS

Gouverneur Morris

IT WAS spring in the South Seas when, for the first time, I went ashore at Batengo, which is the Polynesian village, and the only one on the big grass island of the same name. There is a cable station just up the beach from the village, and a good-natured young chap named Graves had charge of it. He was an upstanding, clean-cut fellow, as the fact that he had been among the islands for three years without falling into any of their ways proved. The interior of the corrugated iron house in which he lived, for instance, was bachelor from A to Z. And if that wasn't a sufficient alibi, my pointer dog, Don, who dislikes anything Polynesian or Melanesian, took to him at once. And they established a romping friendship. He gave us lunch on the porch, and because he had not seen a white man for two months or a liver-and-white dog for years, he told us the entire story of his young life, with reminiscences of early childhood and plans for the future thrown in.

The future was very simple. There was a girl coming out to him from the States by the next steamer but one; the captain of that steamer would join them together in holy wedlock, and after that the Lord would provide.

"My dear fellow," he said, "you think I'm asking her to share a very lonely sort of life, but if you could imagine all the—the affection and gentleness, and thoughtfulness that I've got stored up to pour out at her feet for the rest of our lives, you wouldn't be a bit afraid for her happiness. If a man spends his whole time and imagination thinking up ways to make a girl happy and occupied, he can

256

think up a whole lot. . . . I'd like ever so much to show her to you."

He led the way to his bedroom, and stood in silent rapture before a large photograph that leaned against the wall over his dressing table.

She didn't look to me like the sort of girl a cable agent would happen to marry. She looked like a swell girl—the real thing—beautiful and simple and unaffected.

"Yes," he said, "isn't she?"

I hadn't spoken a word. Now I said:

"It's easy to see why you aren't lonely with that wonderful girl to look at. Is she really coming out by the next steamer but one? It's hard to believe because she's so much too good to be true."

"Yes," he said, "isn't she?"

"The usual cable agent," I said, "keeps from going mad by having a dog or a cat or some pet or other to talk to. But I can understand a photograph like this being all-sufficient to any man—even if he had never seen the original. Allow me to shake hands with you."

Then I got him away from the girl, because my time was short and I wanted to find out about some things that were important to *me*.

"You haven't asked me my busines in these parts," I said, "but I'll tell you. I'm collecting grasses for the Bronx Botanical Garden."

"Then, by Jove!" said Graves, "you have certainly come to the right place. There used to be a tree on this island, but the last man who saw it died in 1789—Grass! The place is all grass: there are fifty kinds right around my house here."

"I've noticed only eighteen," I said, "but that isn't the point. The point is: when do the Batengo Island grasses begin to go to seed?" And I smiled.

"You think you've got me stumped, don't you?" he said. "That a mere cable agent wouldn't notice such things. Well, that grass there," and he pointed—"beach nut we call it—is the first to ripen seed, and, as far as I know, it does it just six weeks from now."

"Are you just making things up to impress me?"

"No, sir, I am not. I know to the minute. You see, I'm a victim of hay-fever."

"In that case," I said, "expect me back about the time your nose begins to run."

"Really?" And his whole face lighted up. "I'm delighted. Only six weeks. Why, then, if you'll stay round for only five or six weeks *more* you'll be here for the wedding."

"I'll make it if I possibly can," I said. "I want to see if that girl's really true."

"Anything I can do to help you while you're gone? I've got loads of spare time——"

"If you knew anything about grasses——"

"I don't. But I'll blow back into the interior and look around. I've been meaning to right along, just for fun. But I can never get any of *them* to go with me."

"The natives?"

"Yes. Poor lot. They're committing race suicide as fast as they can. There are more wooden gods than people in Batengo village, and the superstition's so thick you could cut it with a knife. All the manly virtues have perished. . . . Aloiu!"

The boy who did Graves's chores for him came lazily out of the house.

"Aloiu," said Graves, "just run back into the island to the top of that hill—see?—that one over there—and fetch a handful of grass for this gentleman. He'll give you five dollars for it."

Aloiu grinned sheepishly and shook his head.

"Fifty dollars?"

Aloiu shook his head with even more firmness, and I whistled. Fifty dollars would have made him the Rockefeller-Carnegie-Morgan of those parts.

"All right, coward," said Graves cheerfully. "Run away and play with the other children. . . . Now, isn't that curious? Neither love, money, nor insult will drag one of them a mile from the beach. They say that if you go 'back there in the grass' something awful will happen to you."

"As what?" I asked.

"The last man to try it," said Graves, "in the memory of the oldest inhabitant was a woman. When they found her she was all black and swollen—at least that's what they say. Something had bitten her just above the ankle."

"Nonsense," I said, "there are no snakes in the whole Batengo group."

"They didn't say it was a snake," said Graves. "They said the marks of the bite were like those that would be made by the teeth of a very little—child."

Graves rose and stretched himself.

"What's the use of arguing with people that tell yarns like that! All the same, if you're bent on making expeditions back into the grass, you'll make 'em alone, unless the cable breaks and I'm free to make 'em with you."

Five weeks later I was once more coasting along the wavering hills of Batengo Island, with a sharp eye out for a first sight of the cable station and Graves. Five weeks with no company but Kanakas and a pointer dog makes one white man pretty keen for the society of another. Furthermore, at our one meeting I had taken a great shine to Graves and to the charming young lady who was to brave a life in the South Seas for his sake. If I was eager to get ashore, Don was more so. I had a shot-gun across my knees with which to salute the cable station, and the sight of that weapon, coupled with toothsome memories of a recent big hunt down on Forked Peak, had set the dog quivering from stem to stern, to crouching, wagging his tail till it disappeared, and beating sudden tattoos upon the deck with his forepaws. And when at last we rounded on the cable station and I let off both barrels, he began to bark and race about the schooner like a thing possessed.

The salute brought Graves out of his house. He stood on the porch waving a handkerchief, and I called to him through a megaphone, hoped that he was well, said how glad I was to see him, and asked him to meet me in Batengo village.

Even at that distance I detected something irresolute in his manner; and a few minutes later when he had fetched a hat out of the house, locked the door, and headed toward the village, he looked more like a soldier marching to battle than a man walking half a mile to greet a friend.

"That's funny," I said to Don. "He's coming to meet us in spite of the fact that he'd much rather not. Oh, well!"

I left the schooner while she was still under way, and reached the beach before Graves came up. There were too many strange brown men to suit Don, and he kept very close to my legs. When Graves arrived the natives fell away from him as if he had been a leper. He wore a sort of sickly smile, and when he spoke the dog stiffened his legs and growled menacingly.

"Don!" I exclaimed sternly, and the dog cowered, but the spines along his back bristled and he kept a menacing eye upon Graves. The man's face looked drawn and rather angry. The frank boyishness was clean out of it. He had been strained by something or other to the breaking-point—so much was evident.

"My dear fellow," I said, "what the devil is the matter?"

Graves looked to right and left, and the islanders shrank still farther away from him.

"You can see for yourself," he said curtly. "I'm taboo." And then, with a little break in his voice: "Even your dog feels it. Don, good boy! Come here, sir!"

Don growled quietly.

"You see!"

"Don," I said sharply, "this man is my friend and yours. Pat him, Graves."

Graves reached forward and patted Don's head and talked to him soothingly.

But although Don did not growl or menace, he shivered under the caress and was unhappy.

"So you're taboo!" I said cheerfully. "That's the result of anything, from stringing pink and yellow shells on the same string to murdering your uncle's grandmother-in-law. Which have *you* done?"

"I've been back there in the grass," he said, "and because—because nothing happened to me I'm taboo."

"Is that all?"

"As far as they know—yes."

"Well!" said I, "my business will take me back there for days at a time, so I'll be taboo, too. Then there'll be two of us. Did you find any curious grasses for me?"

"I don't know about grasses," he said, "but I found something very curious that I want to show you and ask your advice about. Are you going to share my house?"

"I think I'll keep headquarters on the schooner," I said, "but if you'll put me up now and then for a meal or for the night——"

"I'll put you up for lunch right now," he said, "if you'll come. I'm my own cook and bottle-washer since the taboo, but I must say the change isn't for the worse so far as food goes."

He was looking and speaking more cheerfully.

"May I bring Don?"

He hesitated.

"Why—yes—of course."

"If you'd rather not?"

"No, bring him. I want to make friends again if I can."

So we started for Graves's house, Don very close at my heels.

"Graves," I said, "surely a taboo by a lot of fool islanders hasn't upset you. There's something on your mind. Bad news?"

"Oh, no," he said. "She's coming. It's other things. I'll tell you by and by—everything. Don't mind me. I'm all right. Listen to the wind in the grass. That sound day and night is enough to put a man off his feed."

"You say you found something very curious back there in the grass?"

"I found, among other things, a stone monolith. It's fallen down, but it's almost as big as the Empire State Building in New York. It's ancient as days—all carved—it's a sort of woman, I think. But we'll go back one day and have a look at it. Then, of course, I saw all the different kinds of grasses in the world—they'd interest you more—but I'm such a punk botanist that I gave up trying to tell 'em apart. I like the flowers best—there's millions of 'em—down among the grass. . . . I tell you, old man, this island is the greatest curiosity-shop in the whole world."

He unlocked the door of his house and stood aside for me to go in first.

"Shut up, Don!"

The dog growled savagely, but I banged him with my open hand across the snout, and he quieted down and followed into the house, all tense and watchful.

On the shelf where Graves kept his books, with its legs hanging over, was what I took to be an idol of some light brownish wood—say sandalwood, with a touch of pink. But it was the most lifelike and astounding piece of carving I ever saw in the islands or out of them. It was about a foot high, and represented a Polynesian woman in the prime of life, say, fifteen or sixteen years old, only the features were finer and cleaner carved.

It was a nude, in an attitude of easy repose—the legs hanging, the toes dangling—the hands resting, palms downward, on the blotter, the trunk relaxed. The eyes, which were a kind of steely blue, seemed to have been made, depth upon depth, of some wonderful translucent enamel, and to make his work still more realistic the artist had planted the statuette's eyebrows, eyelashes, and scalp with real hair, very soft and silky, brown on the head and black for the lashes and eyebrows. The thing was so lifelike that it frightened me. And when Don began to growl like distant thunder I didn't blame him. But I leaned over and caught him by the collar, because it was evident that he wanted to get at that statuette and destroy it.

When I looked up the statuette's eyes had moved. They were

turned downward upon the dog, with cool curiosity and indifference. A kind of shudder went through me. And then, lo and be-
hold, the statuette's tiny brown breasts rose and fell slowly, and
a long breath came out of its nostrils.

I backed violently into Graves, dragging Don with me and half-
choking him. "My God Almighty!" I said. "It's alive!"

"Isn't she!" said he. "I caught her back there in the grass—
the little minx. And when I heard your signal I put her up there to
keep her out of mischief. It's too high for her to jump—and she's
very sore about it."

"You found her in the grass," I said. "For God's sake!—are
there more of them?"

"Thick as quail," said he, "but it's hard to get a sight of 'em.
But *you* were overcome by curiosity, weren't you, old girl? You
came out to have a look at the big white giant and he caught you
with his thumb and forefinger by the scruff of the neck—so you
couldn't bite him—and here you are."

The womankin's lips parted and I saw a flash of white teeth.
She looked up into Graves's face and the steely eyes softened. It
was evident that she was very fond of him.

"Rum sort of a pet," said Graves. "What?"

"Rum?" I said. "It's horrible—it isn't decent—it—it ought to
be taboo. Don's got it sized up right. He—he wants to kill it."

"Please don't keep calling her It," said Graves. "She wouldn't
like it—if she understood." Then he whispered words that were
Greek to me, and the womankin laughed aloud. Her laugh was
sweet and tinkly, like the upper notes of a spinet.

"You can speak her language?"

"A few words—Tog ma Lao?"

"Na!"

"Aba Ton sug ato."

"Nan Tane dom ud lon anea!"

It sounded like that—only all whispered and very soft. It
sounded a little like the wind in the grass.

"She says she isn't afraid of the dog," said Graves, "and that
he'd better let her alone."

"I almost hope he won't," said I. "Come outside. I don't like
her. I think I've got a touch of the horrors."

Graves remained behind a moment to lift the womankin down
from the shelf, and when he rejoined me I had made up my mind
to talk to him like a father.

"Graves," I said, "although that creature in there is only a foot high, it isn't a pig or a monkey, it's a woman and you're guilty of what's considered a pretty ugly crime at home—abduction. You've stolen this woman away from kith and kin, and the least you can do is to carry her back where you found her and turn her loose. Let me ask you one thing—what would Miss Chester think?"

"Oh, that doesn't worry me," said Graves. "But I *am* worried —worried sick. It's early—shall we talk now, or wait till after lunch?"

"Now," I said.

"Well," said he, "you left me pretty well enthused on the subject of botany—so I went back there twice to look up grasses for you. The second time I went I got to a deep sort of valley where the grass is waisthigh—that, by the way, is where the big monolith is—and that place was alive with things that were frightened and ran. I could see the directions they took by the way the grass tops acted. There were lots of loose stones about and I began to throw 'em to see if I could knock one of the things over. Suddenly all at once I saw a pair of bright little eyes peering out of a bunch of grass—I let fly at them, and something gave a sort of moan and thrashed about in the grass—and then lay still. I went to look, and found that I'd stunned—*her*.

She came to and tried to bite me, but I had her by the scruff of the neck and she couldn't. Further, she was sick with being hit in the chest with the stone, and first thing I knew she keeled over in the palm of my hand in a dead faint. I couldn't find any water or anything—and I didn't want her to die—so I brought her home. She was sick for a week—and I took care of her—as I would a sick pup—and she began to get well and want to play and romp and poke into everything. She'd get the lower drawer of my desk open and hide in it—or crawl into a rubber boot and play house. And she got to be right good company—same as any pet does—a cat or a dog—or a monkey—and naturally, she being so small, I couldn't think of her as anything but a sort of little beast that I'd caught and tamed. . . . You see how it all happened, don't you? Might have happened to anybody."

"Why, yes," I said. "If she didn't give a man the horrors right at the start—I can understand making a sort of pet of her—but, man, there's only one thing to do. Be persuaded. Take her back where you found her, and turn her loose."

"Well and good," said Graves. "I tried that, and next morning

I found her at my door, sobbing—horrible, dry sobs—no tears. . . . You've said one thing that's full of sense: she isn't a pig—or a monkey—she's a woman."

"You don't mean to say," said I, "that that mite of a thing is in love with you?"

"I don't know what else you'd call it."

"Graves," I said, "Miss Chester arrives by the next steamer. In the meanwhile something has got to be done."

"What?" said he hopelessly.

"I don't know," I said. "Let me think."

The dog Don laid his head heavily on my knee, as if he wished to offer a solution of the difficulty.

A week before Miss Chester's steamer was due the situation had not changed. Graves's pet was as much a fixture of Graves's house as the front door. And a man was never confronted with a more serious problem. Twice he carried her back into the grass and deserted her, and each time she returned and was found sobbing —horrible, dry sobs—on the porch. And a number of times we took her, or Graves did, in the pocket of his jacket, upon systematic searches for her people. Doubtless she could have helped us to find them, but she wouldn't. She was very sullen on these expeditions and frightened. When Graves tried to put her down she would cling to him, and it took real force to pry her loose.

In the open she could run like a rat; and in open country it would have been impossible to desert her; she would have followed at Graves's heels as fast as he could move them. But forcing through the thick grass tired her after a few hundred yards, and she would gradually drop farther and farther behind—sobbing. There was a pathetic side to it.

She hated me and made no bones about it, but there was an armed truce between us. She feared my influence over Graves, and I feared her—well, just as some people fear rats or snakes. Things utterly out of the normal always do worry me, and Bo, which was the name Graves had learned for her, was, so far as I know, unique in human experience. In appearance she was like an unusually good-looking island girl observed through the wrong end of an opera-glass, but in habit and action she was different. She would catch flies and little grasshoppers and eat them all alive and kicking, and if you teased her more than she liked her ears would flatten the way a cat's do, and she would hiss like a snapping-turtle, and show her teeth.

But one got accustomed to her. Even poor Don learned that it was not his duty to punish her with one bound and a snap. But he would never let her touch him, believing that in her case discretion was the better part of valor. If she approached him he withdrew, always with dignity, but equally with determination. He knew in his heart that something about her was horribly wrong and against nature. I knew it, too, and I think Graves began to suspect it.

Well, a day came when Graves, who had been up since dawn, saw the smoke of a steamer along the horizon, and began to fire off his revolver so that I, too, might wake and participate in his joy. I made tea and went ashore.

"It's *her* steamer," he said.

"Yes," said I, "and we've got to decide something."

"About Bo?"

"Suppose I take her off your hands—for a week or so—till you and Miss Chester have settled down and put your house in order. Then Miss Chester—Mrs. Graves, that is—can decide what is to be done. I admit that I'd rather wash my hands of the business—but I'm the only white man available, and I propose to stand by my race. Don't say a word to Bo—just bring her out to the schooner and leave her."

In the upshot Graves accepted my offer, and while Bo, fairly bristling with excitement and curiosity, was exploring the farther corners of my cabin, we slipped out and locked the door on her. The minute she knew what had happened she began to tear around and raise Cain. It sounded a little like a cat having a fit.

Graves was white and unhappy. "Let's get away quick," he said; "I feel like a skunk."

But Miss Chester was everything that her photograph said about her, and more too, so that the trick he had played Bo was very soon a negligible weight on Graves's mind.

If the wedding was quick and business-like, it was also jolly and romantic. The oldest passenger gave the bride away. All the crew came aft and sang "The Voice That Breathed O'er That Earliest Wedding-Day"—to the tune called "Blairgowrie." They had worked it up in secret for a surprise. And the bride's dove-brown eyes got a little teary. I was best man. The captain read the service, and choked occasionally. As for Graves—I had never thought him handsome—well, with his brown face and white linen suit, he made me think, and I'm sure I don't know why, of St. Michael—that time he overcame Lucifer. The captain blew us to breakfast, with champagne and a cake, and then the happy pair went ashore in a boat full of the bride's trousseau, and the crew manned the bulwarks and gave three cheers, and then something like twenty-seven more, and last thing of all the brass cannon was fired, and the little square flags that spell G-o-o-d L-u-c-k were run up on the signal halyards.

As for me, I went back to my schooner feeling blue and lonely. I knew little about women and less about love. It didn't seem quite fair. For once I hated my profession—seed-gatherer to a body of scientific gentlemen whom I had never seen. Well, there's nothing so good for the blues as putting things in order.

I cleaned my rifle and revolver. I wrote up my notebook. I developed some plates; I studied a brand-new book on South Sea grasses that had been sent out to me, and I found some mistakes. I went ashore with Don, and had a long walk on the beach—in the opposite direction from Graves's house, of course—and I sent Don into the water after sticks, and he seemed to enjoy it, and so I stripped and went in with him. Then I dried in the sun, and had a match with my hands to see which could find the tiniest shell. Toward dusk we returned to the schooner and had dinner, and after that I went into my cabin to see how Bo was getting on.

She flew at me like a cat, and if I hadn't jerked my foot back she would have bitten me. As it was, her teeth tore a piece out of my trousers. I'm afraid I kicked her. Anyway, I heard her land with a crash in a far corner. I struck a match and lighted candles—they are cooler than lamps—very warily, one eye on Bo. She had retreated under a chair and looked out—very sullen and angry. I sat down and began to talk to her.

"It's no use," I said, "your trying to bite and scratch, because you're only as big as a minute. So come out here and make friends. I don't like you and you don't like me; but we're going to be thrown together for quite some time, so we'd better make the best of it. You come out here and behave pretty and I'll give you a bit of gingersnap."

The last word was intelligible to her, and she came a little way out from under the chair. I had a bit of gingersnap in my pocket, left over from treating Don, and I tossed it on the floor midway between us. She darted forward and ate it with quick bites.

Well, then, she looked up, and her eyes asked—just as plain as day: "Why are things thus? Why have I come to live with you? I don't like you. I want to go back to Graves."

I couldn't explain very well, and just shook my head and then went on trying to make friends—it was no use. She hated me, and after a time I got bored. I threw a pillow on the floor for her to sleep on, and left her. Well, the minute the door was shut and locked she began to sob. You could hear her for quite a distance, and I couldn't stand it. So I went back—and talked to her as nicely and soothingly as I could. But she wouldn't even look at me—just lay face down—heaving and sobbing.

Now I don't like little creatures that snap—so when I picked her up it was by the scruff of the neck. She had to face me then, and I saw that in spite of all the sobbing her eyes were perfectly dry. That struck me as curious. I examined them through a pocket magnifying-glass, and discovered that they had no tear-ducts. Of course she couldn't cry. Perhaps I squeezed the back of her neck harder than I meant to—anyway, her lips began to draw back and her teeth to show.

It was exactly at that second that I recalled the legend Graves had told me about the island woman being found dead, and all black and swollen, back there in the grass, with teeth marks on her that looked as if they had been made by a very little child.

I forced Bo's mouth wide open and looked in. Then I reached for a candle and held it steadily between her face and mine. She struggled furiously so that I had to put down the candle and catch her legs together in my free hand. But I had seen enough. I felt wet and cold all over. For if the swollen glands at the base of the deeply grooved canines meant anything, that which I held between my hands was not a woman—but a snake.

I put her in a wooden box that had contained soap and nailed slats over the top. And, personally, I was quite willing to put scrap-iron in the box with her and fling it overboard. But I did not feel quite justified without consulting Graves.

As an extra precaution in case of accidents, I overhauled my medicine-chest and made up a little package for the breast pocket —a lancet, a rubber bandage, and a pill-box full of permanganate crystals. I had still much collecting to do, "back there in the grass," and I did not propose to step on any of Bo's cousins or her sisters or her aunts, without having some of the elementary first-aids to the snake-bitten handy.

It was a lovely starry night, and I determined to sleep on deck. Before turning in I went to have a look at Bo. Having nailed her in a box securely, as I thought, I must have left my cabin door ajar. Anyhow she was gone. She must have braced her back against one side of the box, her feet against the other and burst it open. I had most certainly underestimated her strength and resources.

The crew, warned of peril, searched the whole schooner over, slowly and methodically, lighted by lanterns. We could not find her. Well, swimming comes natural to snakes.

I went ashore as quickly as I could get a boat manned and rowed. I took Don on a leash, a shot-gun loaded, and both pockets of my jacket full of cartridges. We ran swiftly along the beach, Don and I, and then turned into the grass to make a short cut for Graves's house. All of a sudden Don began to tremble with eagerness and nuzzle and sniff among the roots of the grass. He was "making game."

"Good Don," I said, "good boy—hunt her up! Find her!"

The moon had risen. I saw two figures standing in the porch of Graves's house. I was about to call to them and warn Graves that Bo was loose and dangerous—when a scream—shrill and frightful—rang in my ears. I saw Graves turn to his bride and catch her in his arms.

When I came up she had collected her senses and was behaving splendidly. While Graves fetched a lantern and water she sat down on the porch, her back against the house, and undid her garter, so that I could pull the stocking off her bitten foot. Her instep, into which Bo's venomous teeth had sunk, was already swollen and discolored. I slashed the teethmarks this way and that with my lancelet. And Mrs. Graves kept saying: "All right—all right—don't mind me—do what's best."

Don's leash had wedged between two of the porch planks, and all the time we were working over Mrs. Graves he whined and struggled to get loose.

"Graves," I said, when we had done what we could, "if your wife begins to seem faint, give her brandy—just a very little at a time—and—I think we were in time—and for God's sake don't ever let her know *why* she was bitten—or by *what*—"

Then I turned and freed Don and took off his leash.

The moonlight was now very white and brilliant. In the sandy path that led from Graves's porch I saw the print of feet—shaped just like human feet—less than an inch long. I made Don smell them, and said:

"Hunt close, boy! Hunt close!"

Thus hunting, we moved slowly through the grass toward the interior of the island. The scent grew hotter—suddenly Don began to move more stiffly—as if he had the rheumatism—his eyes straight ahead saw something that I could not see—the tip of his tail vibrated furiously—he sank lower and lower—his legs worked more and more stiffly—his head was thrust forward to the full stretch of his neck toward a thick clump of grass. In the act of taking a wary step he came to a dead halt—his right forepaw just clear of the ground. The tip of his tail stopped vibrating. The tail of itself stood straight out behind him and became rigid like a bar of iron. I never saw a stancher point.

"Steady, boy!" I pushed forward the safety of my shot-gun and stood at attention . . .

"How is your wife?"

"Seems to be pulling through. I heard you fire both barrels. What luck?"

THE MUGGING

Edward L. Perry

IT WAS Tony's idea. We had just come out of the flicker. Me, him, and my deb Jane. It had cost us our last coin, and the picture had been lousy. It's late, close to midnight. And we have to figure a way to make some dough. Fast. Then we spot this crud.

He's standing in front of the flicker, goggling at the young chicks who come out. He's a fat, greasy slob with blubber hanging over his belt, but he's dressed to kill. Loud sport coat and flashy cufflinks. Real gold ones.

But you don't notice these things much. You only notice his face. It's a round white blot, with small, restless pig-eyes that strip you naked. There's beads of sweat on his upper lip, and he keeps mopping his forehead with a handkerchief. When a young chick walks by, he gives them a sickly grin and leans towards them like a dog sniffing at a bone.

I'd seen his type before; so I know what's churning around in that brain of his. He likes chicks. Real young ones.

Then he spots Jane, and he starts mopping his forehead like there's a furnace burning inside of him. I don't blame him. Jane's really decked out tonight. She's wearing a thin white skirt, so tight across the hips that their firmness is brought out in sharp relief, and a red blouse opened at the throat with a plunging V neckline. She's young and cute.

We walk to the end of the street and stop. Tony takes out a weed and lights up. He nods in Fatboy's direction.

"Let's take him," he says.

270

I don't think much of the idea and I say so.

"What's wrong with you, man?" he wants to know. "That fat guy looks really loaded. Did you get a look at them clothes?"

"I don't like his looks. He acts like a Horn Bug."

"You mean one of those sex maniacs? Man, what are you talking about, huh? He's just trying to pick up something. That's all."

"I still don't like it," I say.

"He's big. Real big." But I know Tony is going to talk me into it. He always does. I look at Jane. "What do you think?"

"I don't know—" she says slowly. "I don't like the way he looked at me. It sure gave me the creeps."

Tony exhales slowly and flips the butt into the gutter.

"Listen, man," he says, "the streets're emptying fast. And—and this crud is a pushover."

"I don't know, Tony. I just—"

"Listen, man. I wouldn't take no chances if I didn't know we could handle him. Now would I, huh?"

"No—no I guess not." I'm looking at Jane as I say this. She knows Tony is talking me into it, and she's scared. Real scared. Her face has gone pale, and she keeps shifting her weight from one foot to the other. She's new at this racket, but she'll do anything I ask her. I see how helpless she looks and I want to tell Tony to go to hell. But I ain't got the guts. He'd think I was scared, punking out.

"You sure we can handle him, Tony?"

"Easy, man, easy!"

I'm not looking at Jane now, but I hear her gulp hard. She reaches out and puts her hand on my arm. Her hand is shaking.

"You want to do it, Jane?" I ask.

For a moment she hesitates; then she nods her head slowly. But when she speaks, her voice trembles. "If you say so, Jake. I'll do anything you want."

Tony rubs his hands together. "Good, man. Then it's all settled, huh?"

"Yeah," I say, "I guess so."

"Now here's how we'll do it. Jane, you go back up the street and let Fatboy pick you up. Give him the eye, see. Then you waltz him up the street to a good dark alley. Me and Jake'll follow. Once you get him in the alley, we'll rush in, work lover boy over, and scram with the loot. It's simple."

I take out a butt and light up. I'm shaking like a leaf, but I try to laugh it off. Tell myself I'm getting chicken since I met Jane. We've done this kind a jig before. Lots of times. Nothing has ever gone wrong.

"Okay," Jane says in a small voice, "but promise you'll be right behind me and him. He scares me."

"We will be, kid." I promise, and I mean it. She gets up on tiptoes and kisses me right in front of Tony. It's a sweet one.

I lean back against the lamppost and watch her walk up the street and I get that sick feeling all over again. Something about Fatboy scares me, too.

The streets are deserted, now. Only Jane and Fatboy are in sight. He's watching her come towards him, and he starts mopping his forehead like mad. Yeah, man. He's getting all steamed up. He don't see Tony and me. We watch her make contact. She's young. Sixteen. But she knows the ropes. She stops, and for a moment they stand there talking. Then I see Fatboy reach over and hook his finger in the V of her blouse. I can hear him giggle and I want to kick his guts out.

"Easy, man, easy," Tony mutters, and I realize I've been cussing Fatboy out loud.

The crud wraps one arm around Jane's waist, and they start down the street away from us. I can see by the way she's lagging back that she's scared to death of the crud.

"Let's go, Tony," I say, and start up the street.

He grabs me by the arm. "Not yet, stupid! What's wrong with you, huh? You want to mess it up?"

I force myself to relax. I know he's right. We got to wait. If we're seen now Fatboy will catch on. I start puffing my weed like mad, but it don't do no good. I'm really keyed up.

Jane and Fatboy comes to an alley at the end of the block. They duck inside.

"Let's take him!" Tony says, and he don't have to repeat it a second time. We start up the street. Fast. I wanta run. I'm cold, freezing up. The alley's a hundred miles off. Seems like we're never going to reach it.

"Walk normal!" Tony snaps. "Walk normal!"

That's easy for him to say. It ain't his girl in the alley. Time's flying. I don't want to get there too late.

Next thing I know this police car pulls up to the curb and two bulls pile out of it.

"Hold up there, you two!" A graveled voice orders.

"What's the beef, Copper?" Tony wants to know.

"You'll find out, kid. Over against the wall."

"Listen, copper—" I began.

"You heard me, move!"

Something in his voice leaves no room for argument. We move against the side of the building. Palms out. The bull runs his hands up and down my body, searching. I'm clean.

"Where've you been?" Graveled Voice wants to know.

"To the flicker. We just got out."

"Yeah?"

"Sure, man. There ain't no law against that, is there?"

"How about the other one?" Graveled Voice asks.

"Clean as a whistle," the other bull reports. "Reckon we ought to take them in?"

Suddenly, I feel like I'm going to faint. My knees are shaking so hard I have to lean against the building to support myself. I'm tough. I don't like cops. I never did and I've let 'em know it. But not tonight. I keep thinking about what's going on in the alley, and I start pleading because the police station is a mile off and if they take us all the way there—

"Look, man, we've just come out of the flicker. Honest!"

Graveled Voice looks thoughtful. "Take that one on back to the theatre and check their alibi," he says after awhile.

The other bull starts down the street in the direction we've just covered. He takes Tony with him. I want to cry out.

Graveled Voice takes out a weed and lights up. He ain't in no hurry. He looks me over through narrowed eyes.

"You're mighty jumpy, kid. Anything wrong?"

I force a smile. "No—no, nothing's wrong. Why?"

"Just wondered."

I laugh uneasily. No. Nothing's wrong, I think. Nothing's wrong unless Fatboy *is* a Horn Bug. Nothing's wrong if we can just get to the alley in time. I cast a glance towards it. I can't see nothing. Just an empty street. No sound. Nothing. I turn my attention to the bull.

"Who are you looking for?" I ask. I couldn't care less.

"Couple of punks robbed a store down the block."

"It wasn't us." I say quickly.

The bull looks at his weed, studying it. "We'll find out soon enough, kid."

My eyes go back to the alley. Then I feel sweat popping out all over me and I start digging my fingers into the brick wall until they hurt like hell.

Fatboy has come out of the alley. For a moment, he stands on the street looking over his shoulder at something he's left behind. I see something fall out of his pocket and land on the sidewalk. He don't seem to notice. Then he catches sight of me and the bull and he starts cruising down the street in the opposite direction. Fast.

My tongue feels fuzzy, and I try to open my mouth to speak, but can't. I watch Fatboy disappear from sight. I don't even see Tony and the bull who was with him come back.

"They've got an alibi," the bull says. "The girl at the ticket window remembered this one."

"Okay, kids, get on home," we're told.

But I'm not listening. My feet start moving up the street. Tony's right behind me. The bulls climb back into the car. I walk faster, then break into a run. To hell with them!

We come to the alley. Tony leans down and picks something up off the sidewalk, the something Fatboy dropped. He holds it up to the street lamp. It's a shiv. The blade is covered with blood! For a moment Tony's eyes hold mine. Then we make a dive for the alley. I feel sick and I want to vomit. I know what we're going to find.

FINGER! FINGER!

Margaret Ronan

WHEN the tray was laid out, Carola took it from Mrs. Higginson and went out into the hall.

"Careful," Mrs. Higginson called after her. "The cream pitcher's too full."

It was. Some had already spilled on the cloth, but Carola did not stop now to wipe it up. Breakfast was late enough, and Miss Amanda, lying upstairs, would be hungry. That was all there was left for her to be, Higginson had remarked more than once.

Carola's shadow moved carefully to heel all the way upstairs. It was a stockily built shadow, like Carola herself, but it lacked her full white throat and the warm brown hair that smoothed her head with the iridescence of water. Elbows out to accent the balance of the tray, girl and shadow climbed with a self-conscious deliberation.

Just outside Miss Amanda's door, Carola stopped and put down the tray. She was more nervous now, her hand uncertain about rearranging her apron, smoothing her hair, setting the cap farther back. It was her first day. Her first place, she reminded herself with some severity. Taking a corner of the apron, she mopped at the spilt cream and set the pitcher over the spot it had left. Then, with the tray in one hand, she lifted her free hand to knock. But the voice, leaping as it did from the other side of the door, was too quick for her.

"Come in! I hear you out there!"

Carola got the door open awkwardly and closed it after her. She crossed the room and set the tray down on the night table. Her smile felt stiff as she turned toward the old woman who lay beneath the spread of quilts.

Miss Amanda. This was Miss Amanda. She was incredibly fat, this old woman, bloated. Higginson said she had not walked in forty-odd years. Her face had the bloodlessness of dough. It lay in bleached folds, as if there were no skull behind it, only pillows. Over her the bedclothes struggled into hills and gullies, and above this landscape she watched Carola with wicked, buried little eyes.

"You must be the new girl," she said. "What's your name?"

"Carola, ma'am."

"Oh." The little eyes were not amused, but Miss Amanda's mouth began to be. Out of the great, gross face a tiny smile came. "You're very young, aren't you?"

It was the look, the tone of voice, the whole stuffy bedroom which made Carola feel the question to be too personal, too prying. But that was silly. The old lady was only being kind. Carola fixed her eyes on a yellow patch in one of the quilts and answered, "Sixteen, ma'am."

Miss Amanda considered this in silence until the three china clocks stationed in the room gained a new resonance, and the yellow patch wavered before Carola's eyes. If she had been able, she would have gone about putting the tray on Miss Amanda's knees, plumping up the pillows behind the mountainous back. But that was the odd thing. Just now she could not think of the tray and do something about it at the same time. Her hands felt as if they had gone to sleep, and in spite of her brain's dull warning, she found her eyes pulling away from the yellow patch, up over the hills and gullies, to stop at last on Miss Amanda's face.

Then the crystal void snapped without warning. Sound and object leaped back into focus.

There was the patch on the quilt again, and other patches like it. There was Miss Amanda's faintly smiling face. Carola felt at once confused and angry. She heard herself repeating the word "breakfast" over and over like an idiot. She pulled at her apron, the blood hot and thick in her throat.

"I'm sorry, ma'am," she muttered. "I can't think what came over me."

Miss Amanda closed her eyes and opened them again slowly. She did not appear to have heard Carola's apology.

"Yes, you're young," she murmured. "Not pretty, but young. When I was your age I was a beauty. Black hair and a skin like flowers. I had more proposals than I could listen to." She struck her great, unfeeling body. "Slim, I was. Not thick-waisted, like you." Her smile seeped away into the flesh again. "But I was lying here, paralyzed, before I knew what it really meant to be young and lovely and strong."

Carola did not know what to say. She could feel no real pity for the old woman. At the moment she only wanted to get out of the room and back to Higginson and the kitchen. A pain had begun to throb in her head, pound at her ears. But Miss Amanda did not dismiss her.

"Have you a young man, Carola?"

"Yes, ma'am."

"Put the tray here, Carola. That's right. Now push up the pillows, will you? There, much better." She sank back against the linen and patted the curve of the sugar bowl languidly. "Two lumps."

Carola picked up the sugar tongs, and it was then that Miss Amanda caught her left arm, just above the wrist. The two women looked at each other for a long moment; Miss Amanda with a sly, reminiscent grin, Carola bewildered and uneasy. With her little finger held fastidiously away from its fellows, the old woman's right hand began to stroke Corola's arm. Up and down, up and down. Once she pinched it gently, and the smile deepened. Then the slow, heavy caress was resumed. It had the insinuating, boneless pressure of a snake's weight.

"I'm not like most old women, Carola," Miss Amanda murmured. "I'm not like you'd think. You can't put me off with food. There are other things, and I haven't forgotten those other things. You think because you're young you can have them all to yourself, but you mustn't be selfish."

Eagerness crystallized in the little eyes, lay like a film over the wet, sly grin.

"So you have a young man. What's his name?"

"Donald, ma'am."

"Donald, eh? Tell me about him. Is he tall? Strong? Very strong? Tell me how strong he is, Carola. Tell me how he makes love to you."

Carola forgot caution and jerked her arm away. She felt strangled. She felt she might be very sick unless she got away from the bed, the china clocks, the fastidious lifted little finger.

Miss Amanda seemed to lose interest. Her face grew blank, the eyelids drooped. She began to dissect an egg carefully, her little finger still held aloof.

"Get along, Carola, she said. "Come back in half an hour for the tray."

All the way down the stairs Carola fought back tears. Dirty-minded old beast! She wanted to scream, to break the hanging lamp above the lower landing—anything to ease the clotted tears behind her eyelids. Donald, Donald, Donald! She said the name over and over to herself like a kind of hysterical apology. She told herself she didn't care if the old woman sacked her that very day. Donald, Donald!

She went into the kitchen, brushing past Higginson before the older woman should see her eyes. At the sink she turned on the tap and began to wash her hands and arms, running the water over them in a clear, swift stream.

"Now what's eating you?" Higginson asked with mild interest.

"Nothing," Carola muttered.

"Have a set-to with the old lady?" said Higginson. "Well, she's not easy to work for. You've got to watch your step. She's a queer one! The girls that's been here and gone! We was without one for near six months until you come." She settled herself into a chair and prepared to elaborate. "That's the truth. Some of 'em, the younger ones, took to behaving queer themselves after they was here awhile. They'd go around imitating Miss Amanda, the cheeky bits! Crooking out their little fingers like she does, sliding their eyes around—even talking like her sometimes. It was enough to give a body the creeps. There was one—girl about your age, I'd say. She was the worst of the lot when it came to imitating the old lady. Kept it up for about a month or so, and then the first thing we knew she'd gone and hung herself down there in the orchard. No reason anyone could find, either. Stood on a kitchen chair to reach the branch, she did. This very chair!" Higginson slapped the chair back triumphantly. "Couldn't nobody, not even the police, make anything out of it, and they was here long enough about it, tracking up the place!"

Carola did not answer. She was crying quietly, but not for the girl Higginson was talking about.

"Well!" said Higginson. "Don't take on so. You can't be so queasy in this work. Old women will say their say, and it's your place to listen and keep still. And stop running that water! You've washed your hands so long that there's likely no hide left to them!"

With the growth of the day, her headache grew steadily worse. It made her absent-minded and nervous. She washed up the breakfast dishes, peeled vegetables, scrubbed out the pantry. Noon came, and the luncheon tray was taken up and brought back down. Miss Amanda scarcely spoke to her. Carola watched the afternoon hours crawl through aching eyes. She broke a dish, she forgot what Higginson had told her about the stove flue. Her hands shook like rags in a wind whenever she tried to lift anything. Four o'clock. Five thirty. Six o'clock. At eight, Donald would be by with his wagon and team to take her home. Behind her forehead the pain was a hot, tight band.

"You'd better mind what you're about, my girl," Higginson told her crossly.

Carola set her teeth against the sick pounding of her skull and took the supper tray from Higginson. She would be careful. She wouldn't spill anything. But when she entered the bedroom, the dumb feeling of outrage swept over her again so that the tray shook in her hands. For a moment she almost hoped the old woman would say something, would attempt to repeat her sly caress. Then, thought Carola, it would be time and cause for striking out—for hitting at that useless body, clawing the evil, bloated face to strips. She put down the tray with a sense of shock. What had come over her? She had never thought things like that in her life! And her head had never hurt so.

But the meal went off without incident, and Carola was through with the dishes and waiting in the kitchen when Donald came. As she buttoned her coat, she could see his wagon through the window, see him sitting atop it, lazily flicking flies from the horses with his whip. She thought with satisfaction of his quick temper. He would probably burn this house down if she told him what the old lady had said to her. She put on her hat, and then Miss Amanda's bell jangled. Twice.

"That's for you," Higginson said. "You'd better go up and see what she wants. Don't fidget. Your young man will wait. I'll tell him you've been held up."

Carola looked at the woman desperately and went. She felt she could not bear the sight of Miss Amanda again that day. But there was the bedroom door. She opened it and went in.

"Going, Carola?" asked Miss Amanda sweetly. "But of course! How stupid I'm getting. There's someone waiting for you, isn't there? I can see him through the window here if I pull myself up a little. There! Is that your Donald?"

"Yes, ma'am," Carola answered quickly. "Did you want something, ma'am?" She thought, "If you say anything more, I'll walk out. I'll tell Donald. I'll never come back."

But all Miss Amanda said was: "Very well. But before you go, I wish you'd take away one of these pillows. I can't sleep with all of them."

Carola might have been more wary. She might have run then, out of the room, away from the chiming of the china clocks and the twisting of the old, unquiet hands. But Miss Amanda's voice was fretful and complaining, the way an old woman's has a right to be. And Carola went up to the bed to do as she was told.

"That's better," said Miss Amanda. "Much better."

Suddenly her hands clamped over Carola's shoulders, forcing her down on the bed, holding her so that the girl's frightened face was only an inch from her own. Those hands were very strong. One of them alone was quite capable of keeping Carola where she was.

"Let me go!" Carola gasped. She could hardly force her voice out of her dry throbbing throat. The headache cut into her brain. It caught fire with what Miss Amanda was saying.

"Not just now, Carola. You see, you're not going to meet your lover, Carola. Never again. But he won't be disappointed. He won't ever know. How should he, when you aren't even Carola any more—Carolacarolacarola—"

The voice seemed to come now from the old eyes. It gathered about Carola and held her. It became part of the roaring pain within her, part of the silly china clocks scratching away at time. She heard the wind and the darkness, and then the old face vanished, leaving only the pits of eyes. Only two pits which became one, a pulling well of night in which she plunged down, down.

And then the room was quiet. The aching left her skull, became a weakness so intense that it was like fire. It spread down through her thighs, her ankles, her feet. They stretched out before her, massive, covered with quilts. Quilts that seemed to have no weight.

With a speechless fascination she watched herself, in a brown, high-buttoned coat, get up from the bed, cross the room, open the door and go out. The footsteps went swiftly down the stairs, but she could not follow them. She could not even get to the mirror to find out why the little finger of her right hand should be crooked out like that. She could not do any of these things because, as she realized with a slow horror, she had not walked in more than forty years, and would never walk again!

The room spun, then settled. She realized almost immediately that although she was imprisoned, she was not helpless. The bell rope hung from the head of her bed, just to the left. The alien, bloated arm moved to her will, sent peal after peal to halt the retreating feet on the stairs.

She remembered words the old, wet mouth had said: *"There's someone waiting for you, isn't there? I can see him through the window if I pull myself up a little."*

And Carola, at the thought of Donald and the Thing which wore her body, dragged the leaden weight up on the pillows, clung to the bedposts, and saw him also. Down there in the yard, slouched on the wagon seat, handsome, careless. His face turned to the light which streaked through the open kitchen door. He smiled at the girl who came through that door to the wagon.

"Well, Carola," he called to that girl, "you've kept me a time, you have." His voice stabbed clearly through the bedroom window and through Carola.

She saw the face which had been hers laughing up at Donald. She saw him put out his arms to lift the girl up beside him. But he never did, for with one heavy hand, Carola flung open the bedroom window and screamed at them in a voice she had never spoken with before.

"Stop, thief! Thief!"

She pulled herself around so that she hung over the window sill. Below, Higginson came running from the kitchen door to stare upward. Donald and the girl stared up at her also, their faces frozen with surprise. Words formed cool and whole in her brain. She knew exactly what to do.

"My rings!" she screamed to Higginson. "That girl's got my rings!"

The face below, which had been hers, arched its white neck in protest. Whatever the strength of Miss Amanda's will, the body it ruled now was no match for Higginson's strength. Outraged, the cook caught the girl's arm, jerked her out of Donald's reach and into the house. For a moment Donald sat stunned. Then he jumped to the ground. He looked more bewildered than angry.

"I don't know what this is all about," he shouted after Higginson, "but you're not taking her in there alone. I'm coming, too!"

He spoke prematurely. Higginson, having reached the house, shoved her prisoner inside. Then she waited in the doorway just long enough to give Donald a push which threw him off balance.

The door slammed in his face, and did not open again in response to his furious knocking.

Carola closed the window so that the knocking dulled and was no louder than her heart. She sank back against the pillows to wait. Higginson evidently had the girl in hand. She was attempting to force her up the stairs to the bedroom, and their footsteps came shuffled and uneven to Carola, broken once by scuffling. Then the door opened and Higginson pushed the girl inside.

"You can go, Higginson," said Carola. "I'll attend to this alone."

"Yes, ma'am. I'll send for the police if you say so, but she ought to be made to give up your rings first. I thought I could—"

"The police," Carola murmured. "Yes, the police. Call them and then come back."

"You can't keep me here forever, you know," she heard Amanda say in the warm, young voice. "When the police come, they'll find all the rings locked in that box on the bureau. They'll put you down for a trouble-making old woman and maybe leave it at that. But they'll let me go—and I'll take Donald with me! Your precious Donald!"

She said this over twice again, coming closer to the bed as she spoke. When she was near enough she leaned over and almost spat out the last words at the old, watchful face.

As if the scene had happened a hundred times before, Carola knew what she must do. Beneath the young face was a young, white neck. Carola had not known that the old hands could move so quickly, that the girl's throat would fit them so well. The strength of the fingers filled her with an almost unbearable pleasure.

Feet were coming up the stairs outside before Carola released the dead throat. A policeman's tread, heavy and impersonal. For a moment she only listened and waited, then her brain roused with alarm. Not only the old legs were paralyzed now. She could not take her eyes from the terrible strength of those fingers, hooked to fit a girl's neck. Nine hooked fingers. The tenth had thrust itself out fastidiously.

Higginson's voice preceded the policeman in the hall. It came clearly through the bedroom door.

"In here," she was saying, "and time you showed up. It's a pity honest folk have to go *looking* for you when there's trouble! The old lady's bedridden, too, and what's the law for if it's not to protect the likes of her, I want to know?"

A CRY FROM THE PENTHOUSE

Henry Slesar

THAT was Coombs for you; he had to pick a night like this to settle
his affairs. Chet Brander tightened the muffler around his throat and
dug his gloved hands into his overcoat pockets, but there was no way
of barricading his body from the subzero cold. The city streets seemed
glazed with ice, and the taxis rumbled past the corner with clouds
of frost billowing from their exhaust pipes. The wind carried knives;
Chet winced at every thrust, and was almost tempted to forget the
whole thing. But he couldn't afford it. Tonight was payoff night, and
he longed to get hands on the money that had lingered so long in
Frank Coombs' pocket.

Then he got lucky. A cab pulled up and a redcheeked matron got
out, he almost knocked her down in his haste to occupy the back
seat. He gave the hackie the address of Coombs' apartment house
on the river, and stepped out 10 minutes later into a night that had
grown even more insufferable. He fought the arctic river breeze all
the way to the entrance, and was grateful when the glass doors closed
behind him.

There was something eerie about the apartment house, an unearthly quiet that was a combination of overcarpeting and under-
occupancy. The building had been opened for rentals only two
months before, with plenty of fanfare and slick newspaper ads. But
the stampede of renters had never really gotten underway, the hun-
dred-dollar-a-room apartments remained largely untenanted. Nevertheless, Frank Coombs had been impressed. Frank Coombs had
been one of the first to sign a lease, and for nothing less than the
building penthouse. In the operatorless elevator, Chet Brander's

283

mouth twisted in a frown as he rode past eight unoccupied floors to reach the plush apartment that Coombs' borrowed money had bought him.

At the door of the penthouse, he stabbed the bell and muttered: "Big shot!"

Warmth flooded out of the doorway when Coombs answered. Pleasant steamheat-and-fireplace warmth, whiskey warmth, the warmth of geniality. That was Coombs for you: the perennial host, always ready to smile and clap you on the back and make you welcome, and all so smoothly that you hardly even noticed the hand dipping into your pocket to count the contents of your wallet. "Chester!" Coombs chortled. "Damn nice of you to come out on a lousy night like this. Come on in, fella!"

Brander went in, shedding his coat as he followed Coombs into the lavish front room. It was a room rich in textures: furry carpets and nubby upholstery, satiny drapes and grainy wood-paneling. Coombs had many textures himself: waxen smooth hair, silken cheeks, velvety smoking jacket, roughcut briar. He gestured with the pipe, and said:

"Well, what do you think, Chet? Does this place beat the pants off that old dump of mine or not? Minute I heard about this building I jumped for it—"

Brander grunted. "Nobody's killing themselves to get in. Half the apartments are empty."

"Only the top-floor apartments; they're the ones that cost real dough, you know." He gathered up his visitor's outer clothing. "Let me hang this stuff up. Maybe you want that jacket off? I keep it warm in here." He put his hand on Brander, and was shaken off.

"I'll hold on to it," he said, looking around. "Yeah, it's quite a place, Frank. Sure you can afford it?"

Coombs laughed. "Don't you worry about old Frankie. When I told you I knew my investments, I knew what I was talking about. You won't regret lending me that dough, Chet, take my word for it."

"Then the deal worked out?"

Coombs coughed. "Let's have a drink, pal. I'm ten fingers ahead of you."

"We can have the drink later. Look, Frank, I came out on a hell of a night for this. You made a lot of big promises about that dough, and now I have to know. Is it a payoff, or a stall?"

Coombs started to make himself a highball, and then ignored the soda. He downed the drink in three large gulps, and said: "It's a payoff, Chet, like I told you. Before you leave, I'll give you a check for every nickel you loaned me. Plus."

"Plus what?"

Coombs laughed again, and took a step forward, swaying slightly. "You'll see, Chet, you'll see. But come on, don't be so mercenary. We used to be pals, remember. I want you to see the place—"

"I saw it."

"You didn't see the best part." He swept his hand around the room, encompassing the wide, heavily draped windows. "I got three hundred feet of terrace out there, and it's all mine. Greatest view of the city you ever saw—" He strode over to the double doors and flung them open, admitting an inquisitive cloud of cold air.

"Hey," Chet Brander said.

"Come on, you won't freeze. Just take a look at this, will ya? You never saw anything like it in your life—"

Brander stood up. Through the open doors, the lights of Manhattan blinked and glowed. It was a hard sight to resist; city lights, like earthbound stars, had always compelled and excited him. Then, as if to tempt him further, Coombs gleefully pulled back the drapes from the window, enlarging the view.

"How about that, huh? Gets you right here, don't it?" Coombs touched the monogram on his velvet jacket.

"What are all the bars for?" Brander said.

"The window bars?" Coombs tittered. "You know me, Chet. Never trusted anybody. Burglars are always bustin' into penthouses, so I had the building bar all the windows. Even the door is made of steel; I don't take any chances. But come on, fella!"

Brander went forward, out onto the terrace, no longer feeling the cold or hearing the wind. Manhattan, obliterated in contours, was etched before him only in golden lights. He caught his breath.

"What do you say, Chet?" Coombs chuckled. "Is this living, Chet? Is this the life?"

"Yeah," he breathed.

"You feast your eyes, boy. I'm going to make us a drink. You just look at that, Chet," Coombs said, going back into the room.

Chet Brander looked, and felt strange and restless and exalted. As if in a dream, he looked, until he realized that he was coatless and hatless in the worst cold that had descended upon the city in seven years. Shivering, he turned back to the doorway of the warm apartment, just in time to see Coombs' grinning face, in time to see Coombs, calmly and without hurry, closing the terrace doors.

"Hey," he said, shaking the knob. "Open up, Frank."

Misty behind the small diamond-patch of glass set into the metal door, Coombs' face stopped grinning and became a silken mask. He lifted the drink in his hand, as if in salute, and took a long swallow. Then he moved away.

"Hey!" Chet Brander shouted, shaking the door harder but not causing a single rattle in its hinges. "Let me in, Frank! It's goddam cold out here!" He couldn't see Coombs any more, but he knew he must be there, enjoying his little prank. Brander thudded on the small pane of glass with his fist, and felt the solidity of it, saw the tiny octagonal wire mesh that made it unbreakable. He shoved against the door, and remembered that it was steel. "Frank! Goddam it, cut out the clowning, Frank! Let me in, will ya?"

Then the lights went out in the penthouse apartment.

It was only then that Chet Brander knew that Coombs had planned more than an impulsive prank. He wasn't going to reopen the sturdy door that led back into the warmth, not in the next minute, or the next hour. Maybe even—

"Frank!" Brander screamed, and realized that he could barely hear his own voice as the wind came by and swallowed the syllables greedily. *"Let me in!"* Brander yelled soundlessly, hammering and pounding and kicking at the door.

There was no telling how long he stood there, denying the fact that the entrance was closed to him. Finally, he moved away, toward the windows; one touch of his hand recalled that they had been barred against intruders, against the entry of strangers or friends. He was neatly sealed out of Coombs' penthouse, where the warmth was. He was alone, outside, with the cold.

Cold! So heated had been his exertions that Brander hadn't even been aware of the temperature. But he felt it now—a cold that gripped his flesh as if there hadn't been an ounce of clothing on him. Cold, and a howling, vicious wind that whirled the frost like an icy shroud around his body. Cold so terrible and so inescapable that Chet Brander had thoughts of death and the grave.

It was no prank. He knew that now. It was no coincidence that Coombs had chosen this night for his rendezvous. It was cold that Coombs had been waiting for, cold and the freezing wind and dark night, and the chance to leave his creditor shivering and alone outside the steel door of his penthouse apartment, to end his debt forever in death.

But how would Coombs explain it? What would he say when

they found Chet Brander's body, a victim of exposure in the middle of the city? . . .

Brander stopped thinking about it, and went to the terrace wall, to peer down at the terrifying distance between himself and the street.

"Help!" Chet Brander shrieked: *"Help me!"*

The wind took his words. He cried out again, but the lights were dark in the untenanted floors beneath him, and no one heard.

"They'll never hear me," he said aloud, the sobs beginning in his throat. "They'll never know I'm here. . . ."

He made a circuit of the terrace, round and round and round the penthouse, searching for some weakness in the fortress of Coombs' apartment. There was none. Already, his feet had become numb; he could barely feel his own footsteps. He clapped his hands together, and then pounded them over his body in an effort to keep the blood circulating.

"Got to keep moving," he muttered. "Keep moving. . . ."

He began to run. He ran wildly, staggering around the terrace, until his breath left him, and he fell, panting, to the frigid stone floor.

"Got to get help," he said to himself.

He began a frantic search of his pockets. His hands first touched the bulk of his wallet, but his fingers barely felt the leather. He looked at it stupidly for a moment, and then took it to the edge of the wall.

"Write a note," he said. But even as he said it, hopefully, he knew that he had discovered no solution. He carried no pen, no pencil, no tool that would help him tell the indifferent world below that he was a prisoner of cold 20 stories above the street.

He looked at his wallet, and then flung it over the wall. He lost sight of it at once, and there was no hope in his heart for rescue.

In his breast pocket, he found cigarettes and matches. He tossed the cigarettes aside, and then tried to light a match in his cupped hands, eager for even one pinpoint of warmth. The wind, capricious, wouldn't permit the luxury; in disgust, he hurled the matches over the wall.

In his right-hand jacket pocket, he found a key. He looked at it blankly for a moment, not recognizing it. It wasn't *his* key; he'd never seen it before. He almost threw it away, but then stopped when he realized what it was. It was a key to Coombs' apartment. Coombs must have slipped it into his pocket. But why?

Then he knew. If Coombs had given him a key, then Coombs could explain Chet Brander's mysterious death. If he were found with a key on his frozen body, then anyone would believe that he had used it to enter Coombs' apartment, and then had been locked out on the terrace by his own foolishness or misfortune. . . .

Clever! Brander wanted to laugh, but his features were like stone. Not so clever, he thought, getting ready to hurl the key out into the night. But then he stopped, clutching it in his hand, knowing that, though useless to him here on the terrace, it was a key to the warmth only a few tantalizing inches away. He couldn't part with it. . . .

He put the key into his trouser pocket, and went back to the penthouse door. He hammered on it until the skin of his hands cracked and bled. Then he fell in a heap and sobbed.

When he got to his feet again, he was in a delirium. For a moment, he thought that the cold had gone, that the weather had suddenly turned deliciously balmy. But it was only the delirium and a moment's surcease of wind. When the freezing wind came again, it was a kind of blessing: it woke him to his situation, filled him once more with the desire to help himself.

He leaned over the waist-high wall and shouted helplessly into the night.

"I'm here," he moaned. "Oh, my God! Don't you know I'm *here?*"

Then he thought of the roof.

The penthouse had a roof. If he could find access to it, he might find a door leading below, into the other floors of the building!

He took a handkerchief from his trouser pocket and wrapped it about his painful, bleeding right hand. Then he felt his way carefully along the wall.

A wire brushed his face.

At first, he didn't do more than touch it lightly. Then he gripped the wire between his numb hands and yanked. The wire held; it was thick, stout cable. If he could climb it. . . .

He tensed every muscle in his body, and held on. Then he leaped off the ground and swung his feet to the penthouse wall.

For a second, he was frozen in the posture, unable to move, willing to give up and die rather than force his aching, frozen body into action once more.

Then he thought of Coombs' silken smile, and the hate gave him strength. He inched upwards, slowly, the smooth wire cutting like a razor's edge into his palms.

It was an agony. He went upwards another inch, and then turned his eyes into the darkness. He saw the lights of the city, and now they seemed like the distant fires of hell.

Another inch. Another. He wanted to let go, and enjoy the luxury of falling, the tranquility of death, but he kept on.

He saw the edge of the roof.

With a last, gasping effort, he clambered up the wire, scraping his knees against the side of the masonry walls until the rough stone shredded cloth and skin. Then he flung himself over the side, to safety.

It was only some 10 feet above the terrace, but the wind and the cold seemed more terrible here. Along the rim, ghostly jutting shapes surrounded him. Television antennas. He blinked at them, as if they were curious spectators.

He staggered about in the darkness until he found the roof door. His hand touched a doorknob, and he cried out in relief. Then the cry became a moan.

The door was locked.

He screamed and raged at it in fury, but not for long. He put his hand in his trouser pocket, and felt the key to the penthouse. "You win, Frank," he tried to say aloud, but his lips couldn't move to form the words.

He moved back toward the edge, knowing no sensation in his limbs. He leaned against a tall antenna, limply.

"They say don't fall asleep," he thought, chuckling in his throat.

He began to slip to the roof floor, and held on to a trailing wire for support.

The wire!

The flat, broad, light wire lay in his numbed hand, and he remembered what this wire could do.

He tugged at it. He tugged harder. He tugged frantically, desperately, insanely. He found other broad, flat wires depending from the antennas of the roof, and tugged at them. One of them came loose in his hand, but he wasn't satisfied. He went to them all, tugging and yanking until he felt sure that the effects of his work had been seen or noticed somewhere below, that he had ripped or torn the metal ribbons from the bright, glowing instruments of the warm, unaware people in the fancy apartment house by the river. . . .

He began to laugh, through unmoving lips, as he went about his destructive labors. And then, when he was too exhausted to go on, he fell to his hands and knees and tried to remember how prayer went.

Minutes later, a light exploded on the rooftop.

"Hey, will you look at this?" he heard a voice say.

"Must be some kind of nut. . . ."

"I thought my picture was acting funny, but I thought it was just the wind. . . ."

"I haven't been getting *any* picture . . . and right in the middle of the show. . . ."

Hands touched him. Warm hands.

"Hey, this guy's in bad shape. . . ."

"Wouldn't be surprised if he froze to death out here. . . ."

"Better get him inside. . . ."

"Thanks," Chet Brander tried to say, but it was only an unspoken thought. When he felt the first touch of the warmth on the other side of the roof's door, he let himself enjoy the luxury of unconsciousness.

He was on a sofa. His mouth held a bitter, molten taste, and there was a furnace roaring in his stomach. His hands and feet were burning, and he began to squirm to avoid the tongues of the flames.

He opened his eyes, and saw the broad, fleshy face of an anxious, elderly man.

"You OK, son? What the hell were you doing out there, anyway?"

He couldn't answer.

"That's all right, don't try to talk. I'm Mr. Collyer, from Apartment 12-D. I found you up on the roof. Those other people wanted me to call the police, but I said, what for, all he needs is to get warm. That's why I brought you here, to my place."

Brander looked about him, and studied the new textures of the strange apartment. He forced himself to sit up, and recognized the alcohol taste in his mouth.

"I thought a little brandy'd help," the man said, watching him. "I guess you got locked out, eh? You live in the building?"

"No," Brander said, in a voice he didn't recognize. "I—I was just looking at the apartments upstairs. Thinking about renting, maybe. Then I remembered hearing something about a sundeck on the roof, and I went to have a look—"

"Hell of a night for sightseeing," the man grunted.

"Yes. But I went, just to see. The next thing I knew, the door slammed behind me."

"Quite a wind up there, all right. We all thought it was the wind that knocked the antennas out, until we found you." He chuckled.

"Lot of people in the building sore at you, son. 'Specially since they can't get a repair man till late tomorrow morning."

"I'm sorry."

"Never mind that; you did the smart thing. Hey, where're you going?"

Brander was on his feet, tightening the knot in his tie, moving unsteadily toward the doorway.

"You can't go out like that, mister—"

"It's OK, I'll get a cab. Got to be going."

"Let me lend you something. Coat or something—"

"No, I'll be all right," Brander said, turning the doorknob.

"Maybe you ought to see a doctor. . . ."

"I will, I will!" Brander said, and went out into the quiet, overcarpeted hallway.

He pressed the button that would bring the automatic elevator to the 12th floor, and then dug into his trouser pocket. It was still there, icy to his touch. The key to Coombs' penthouse.

When the elevator arrived, he stepped inside the car and punched P.

He didn't turn on the lights as he entered. He went to the closet and found his overcoat, his hat and his muffler.

He put them on, but felt no warmer.

Then he went to the double doors of the terrace, unlatched them, and opened them a scant two inches.

He returned to Coombs' sofa, and sat down in the dark to wait.

At 1:30, he heard the key in the lock. He rose unhurriedly, and went toward the doorway of Coombs' bedroom, concealing himself behind it.

The front door opened. Coombs, muttering, stepped inside. He stumbled about the darkened room, dropping his overcoat on the carpet before his hand found the light switch. Then, still mumbling, he looked blearily toward the terrace, and chuckled drunkenly. He went to the liquor cabinet, and poured himself something from a bottle, no ice. He downed it, still looking at the terrace.

Chet watched the glass come down slowly, and heard Coombs say, thickly:

"What the hell?"

Coombs went to the doors. When he found them unlatched, he opened them wide and stepped out onto the terrace.

"Brander!" he heard him shout, in chorus with the wind.

But Brander wasn't there. Brander was racing across the carpet of the penthouse living room, racing to reach the terrace doors before Coombs could return. He won the contest easily, slamming the steel portals shut even before Coombs was close enough to see his triumphant face. But he waited behind the wire-meshed diamond pane of glass, waiting for Coombs to get near enough to know, to understand.

"Brander!" he heard Coombs cry, his voice muffled and thin. "For God's sake, Brander, let me in!"

Chet smiled, and moved away. "Don't try messing with the antennas," he said, although he knew Coombs could not hear him. "Nobody's watching TV tonight. . . ."

"Chet! Chet, for the love of God! *Chet!*"

Outside, in the hallway, he could no longer hear the faintest sound of Coombs' pleas. He took the elevator to the ground floor and nodded pleasantly at the doorman, who was looking skyward with a frown.

"Bad night," Chet said, conversationally.

"And gettin' worse," the doorman answered, holding out a broad, flat palm. "See what's comin' now?"

"What?" Chet asked, looking at the sky.

"Snow," the doorman said.

Chet corrected him: "Sleet."

THE PEOPLE NEXT DOOR

Pauline C. Smith

"WELL, how are you getting along with your new neighbor?"
Ed asked.

Evelyn looked down at the knitting in her lap. "All right," she said.

"I talked with her a few minutes before dinner, while I was out
in the yard. They used to live in California, she said. Seemed like a
nice, ordinary woman."

Evelyn held up the wool, inspected it. "She did?"

"You like her all right, don't you?"

"I guess so."

"It gives you someone for company during the day. Keeps you
from thinking about yourself too much," he persisted.

"I don't see her much. Sometimes I talk to her when she's hanging the wash on the line."

"Well, it's good for you," he said briskly, the clinical look taking
over his face.

Evelyn picked up the wool again and clicked the needles. The
knitting was a form of prescription.

"She hangs out her washing as if she was angry at it," she said.
"She puts the clothespins on the shirts as if she were stabbing them."

"Evie!" His tone was sharp.

"Well, she does," Evelyn persisted. "Maybe it's because there's
so many shirts. Fourteen of them. Two clean shirts every day. Perhaps her husband has a phobia about clean shirts."

Ed rattled his newspaper as he lowered it.

"Evie," he said, "you mustn't imagine things! You mustn't try
to find phobias and neuroses in everything anybody does. It isn't

healthy. I should think you'd have had enough of analyzing and being analyzed all this last year since your breakdown."

Evie thought of the washing erupting convulsively onto the line as the woman next door hung up each garment with controlled violence.

"Maybe she's tired of washing and ironing so many shirts every week," she said. "Maybe she's sick to death of it. Maybe that's why she seems to be stabbing the shirts with the clothespins."

"Evie, you're almost well now!" Ed was speaking with forced calm. "You can't afford to let your imagination run away about every simple little thing. It isn't healthy. You'll have a relapse."

"I'm sorry, Ed." She picked up the wool again. "I won't imagine things."

"That's a good girl." He relaxed. "She tell you what her husband does?"

"He's a salesman," Evelyn said, needles clicking. "He sells cutlery to restaurants—knives and cleavers and things."

"You see?" Ed remarked. "Salesmen have to be neat. That's why he wears so many shirts."

"Is it?" Evelyn studied the sweater. The gray wool was very unexciting. She decided she would work a little pattern into it—red, maybe. "Have you ever seen him?"

"No." Ed removed his glasses and polished them. "Have you?"

"Every morning. He leaves for work a little while after you do. His car is parked in their driveway, right by our kitchen window. I see him while I'm doing the breakfast dishes."

Ed turned the pages of his newspaper to the sport section.

"What's he like?"

"He's very tall and thin. His mouth is thin, like a knife. He wears gray all the time. He makes me think of a gray snake."

"Evie!" Ed's voice was angry now. "Stop that!"

"All right." She stood up. "I guess I'll go to bed now."

In her bedroom, she stood for a moment at the window. There was a light on next door—one window was an orange oblong. She got into bed, took a nembutal, and fell asleep.

Over the clean suds of dishwater each morning she saw the man next door appear, stride quickly to his car and get in with his sample case—tall, his features as sharp as the knives he sold, his eyes hooded. Then the car would start, rattle off and he would be gone.

Through her brief appearances in the back yard, Evelyn grew to know the woman; by her long strides to the refuse can where she would clatter the lid off, throw in her paper-wrapped bundle with an over-arm motion, clang the lid back; by her short, fierce tussle with a garment on the clothesline; by her soliloquy as she talked to herself, the words inaudible but the tone clear—sometimes a grumbling complaint and sometimes a violently fierce monolog. Evelyn grew to know her, she felt, quite well. And sometimes at night she would hear sounds from next door. Not very loud sounds; not conversation. Muffled sounds. You would have to use imagination to say they were sounds of anger, or perhaps of pain. And she had promised Ed not to let herself imagine things . . .

When the car had been sitting in the driveway for two days, she mentioned it to Ed. He lowered his paper.

"Oh?" he said politely. "Is he sick?"

"Maybe he is. I haven't seen her, either."

"You'd better go over, hadn't you? Maybe they're both sick."

"No. I don't want to go over there."

He glanced at his paper, then at his wife. "Why not? You've talked to her. It would be the kind thing to do."

Evelyn bent over her occupational therapy, the knitting on her lap. "She might think I was snooping."

Aggravation and indulgence struggled in Ed's face. At last, he said mildly, "I don't think she'd think that."

"She might."

Through one more day without backyard clangor, Evelyn listened and watched while the house next door slept.

On the next day the woman next door emerged to hang out her washing. She no longer moved with a controlled fury. She handled the pieces of wash, even the shirts, as if they were fabric, inanimate and impersonal—no longer as if she wrestled a hated opponent.

Stepping to the dividing fence, Evelyn rested her hands on the palings. She leaned over. "I see your husband's car in the driveway . . ." she began.

The words seemed to filter slowly through the other woman's mind, to arrange themselves in her brain to make a sense which startled her. She looked at the car, then back at Evelyn.

"He took a trip." Her expression was suddenly veiled and withdrawn. She wet her lips with the tip of her tongue. "He's gone off to a convention. It was too far to drive. He took the train and left the car for me."

"Oh, that's it," Evie said politely. "We were afraid he was sick."

"No, he's not sick. He's not sick at all."

Abruptly the woman backed away, spare-lipped mouth moving as if to utter further words of explanation that would reduce the unusual to the commonplace. Then she turned, stepped through her back door and locked it behind her.

"The man next door is out of town," Evelyn told Ed that evening.

He smiled. "So you went over, after all."

"No."

"Oh? You talked to her, though?"

"Yes. I talked to her." Evelyn bent over the knitting. "She took the car and went away this afternoon."

Rustling the paper, Ed settled to read.

"She wasn't gone long. When she came back, she had two big dogs in the car with her."

He lowered the paper. "She did?"

"Two big thin dogs," described Evelyn. "She tied them in the back yard using the clothesline to tie them to the clothes pole. She had a big wash this morning and after it dried, she went and got the dogs and tied them with the clothesline."

"Maybe she's scared while her husband's gone. And she got them for watchdogs."

"Maybe."

Now Evelyn felt ready to give up the nembutal she had used to get her to sleep all these months. Pushing the little bottle of sleeping tablets far back on the bedside table, she lay down. She thought of the woman next door, the dogs and the car in the driveway . . . the woman, the dogs and the car . . .

At last, she rose to pace through the darkened house.

Standing at the kitchen window, she looked out at the night to see a button of light cross the yard next door. Her eyes followed it. She heard a plop, a snarl and a growl—then the gulping, snuffling sound of hunger being satisfied. The light made an arc and moved back to the house and was lost.

For a long time she stood at the window, then she went to her bedroom, took a nembutal and fell asleep . . .

"She doesn't like the dogs," Evelyn told Ed several days later.

"She doesn't have to. They're watchdogs, not pets."

"She walks them every day. She unties their ropes from the clothes pole and goes off with them. When she comes back, she's tired and the dogs are tired. Then after dark she gives them a big dinner."

Evie thought of them, the slip-slap drag of the animals, their lolling tongues—the fatigued tread of the woman, her face drained of everything but lassitude. Of the way she re-tied them to the clothes pole, knotting, knotting and re-knotting the ropes while they lay, eyes closed, panting, satiated.

"What does she say about her husband? Seems to me that convention is lasting awfully long."

"She doesn't say anything. She just walks the dogs. Walks them and feeds them."

Ed laid down his paper. "Evie," he said, "Don't you talk with her any more?"

Holding the needles tightly, Evelyn looked at him. "I don't see her to talk with her. She just walks the dogs. She doesn't hang anything on her line any more because she doesn't have any line. She doesn't seem to do anything in the yard except untie the dogs and tie them up again."

"Well, that's too bad. I wanted you to have some company. Maybe you could walk . . ."

"No! I don't want to walk with her or the dogs." Evelyn dropped the knitting on the chair as she left for bed . . .

Filled with torpor, the dogs were quiet now, lazy, growing fat as they ambled reluctantly at the end of their rope leashes, to crawl back and lie somnolent.

Evelyn was knitting quietly. The sweater was almost finished; the drab, uninteresting sweater with the bright little pattern of scarlet she had added. "She took the dogs away in the car today," she told Ed on Friday.

Ed looked at her over his glasses. "She did?"

"And she came back alone. Then she went in the house, got two suitcases, came out, put them in the car and drove off."

"Maybe that's why she took the dogs away—she's going on a trip."

"She's going on a trip all right."

"Or perhaps the upkeep was too high." Ed yawned, and polished his glasses, fitted them carefully on his nose. "She shouldn't have exercised them so much. It made them too hungry." He opened his paper and placed it across his knees. "Must have cost her plenty to feed the brutes."

Evie pulled the needles from the yarn and folded the sweater. She stood. The thing was a pattern, its design all finished.

"I don't think it did," she said. "I don't think it cost her hardly anything at all."

D-DAY

Robert Trout

COLUMBIA BROADCASTING SYSTEM
CBS WORLD NEWS—Robert Trout
April 12, 196—
2:07 a.m.

TROUT: Columbia's News Headquarters in New York, Bob Trout speaking. It's a little more than two hours after midnight here in New York, and we still don't have much real news on the Pittsburgh explosion but—standing here beside the teletypewriters in the news room with the portable microphone—I'll summarize briefly for you what we do have. Just thirty-six—no, forty-six, just forty-six minutes ago, the United Press and the Associated Press almost simultaneously flashed the news that the great steel and iron city had been rocked by a tremendous explosion. Strangely—and of course we hope *not* ominously—there have been almost no details, since the flash, from Pittsburgh. What we have had is a flood of bulletins and dispatches from places as far as a hundred and eighty miles from Pittsburgh telling of brilliant lights in the sky and the huge roar of the explosion.

In a few moments we'll go over these dispatches that have come in during the past quarter of an hour. But first, I can see that—I can see through the glass wall on the other side of this news room that Paul White, Columbia's Director of Public Affairs, is at last in contact with our correspondent in Washington, so we take you now to Washington, Bill Henry reporting.

TROUT: Back in New York again. As you could hear, we are still unable to bring you a report from Washington, although—despite the lateness of the hour—that city is certainly not asleep. In fact, it was no more than half an hour ago that the International News Service reported from Washington that the lights were going on in the White House and the State Department, but there has been no dispatch of any kind from Washington since that short one from INS. I've been walking about the news room, with this portable microphone, while talking to you, and now, back at the International News Service tele-typewriter—looking back over some of the tape that has come in since we took the air—but nothing at all from Washington. However, there should—just a second, here comes a bulletin. (Bells) . . .

Over at the United Press machine now, those five bells you heard mean a bulletin just being tapped out on the UP machine. I'll read it as it comes. DETROIT, APRIL 12, U.P. Detroit was shaken by a heavy blast at 12:58 this morning. Extent of the damage is not yet known but the indications are it will be heavy and it is feared that a number of persons lost their lives. Although the exact location and nature of the accident have not been revealed, city officials state that an investigation is under way to ascertain whether the blast might have any connection with the explosion reported earlier from Pittsburgh. MORE. There is more coming, as the—more coming from Detroit, but not at the moment, for, after printing that one word "more" the United Press machine has gone back to transmitting the continuation of a story on ladies' fashions—the usual kind of thing that can be expected normally at this hour of the night. Hats, too, will be more extreme with the accent on devastating allure this summer—that's enough of that at this moment of suspense and tension.

This is a good time to repeat that we are not sure yet just what has happened, and while, unfortunately, it does seem that a disaster has occurred, still, no good purpose would be served by becoming excited prematurely. At any rate, there is nothing to do at the moment except wait for the news.

Our Columbia news staff is being assembled as rapidly as possible. Major George Fielding Eliot, who used to be known as Columbia's *military analyst* back in the days when men still fought wars, should be with us here in the news room very shortly. Perhaps he has been delayed by the rather unseasonable thunderstorm that seems to be rolling in from the direction of New Jersey. You have probably been able to hear, above the clatter of the news machines, the loud booms of thunder that have been resounding across the Hudson River into this news room and this microphone.

As we are still unable—I beg your pardon. Yes? I have just been informed that, according to the Associated Press, an emergency call has gone out to all fire-fighting equipment and ambulances in towns as far north as Havre de Grace, Maryland. I'd better repeat that—towns as far north as Havre de Grace, Maryland. That's the wording of the message just handed me. I can't be sure just what it means, but I am told now that this information—incomplete, as you can see—was telephoned to us by the AP offices in New York. Something wrong with the AP wires where?—south of Trenton? Yes, the Associated Press sent over that brief report by telephone as there is some trouble with the regular wire circuit between New York and Philadelphia. That one sentence doesn't tell us much but there will be more to follow as soon as the AP gets it; I don't know exactly *how* they are getting it. We shall see, later. Until a few moments ago, the teletype here, which is connected with the AP building right in New York City, was ticking away—it seems to have stopped now. In fact, there is a general lull. The other machines have fallen silent also, temporarily; not often that it is so quiet in this office.

Perhaps, at this point, I should read you the accumulation of earlier dispatches from places *outside* Pittsburgh. Mostly, they are extremely vague, very few hard facts, and in none of them is there any hint of—any hint of hostilities; I started to say "war," but even the word "hostilities" sounds completely out of place—fantastic, utterly unbelievable in these modern times.

Still, without wishing to cause any unnecessary alarm, still there is something odd about this unusual quiet in this usually noisy room. Accidents—train wrecks, floods, and explosions—don't usually cut off the flow of news; on the contrary. Every news machine in the entire room remains silent, which I report as a fact, not to cause any —well, panic. That is a harsh word, "panic," but perhaps not too strong judging from the fashion in which our telephone switchboard, here at Columbia, has been tied up since the first flash at—at exactly twenty-one minutes past one o'clock New York time. Apparently, many of those who heard the first news on Columbia were not listening carefully, for there has been no official word—no unofficial suggestion, even—that any kind of war might have begun.

The Second World War ended a good many years ago, and since then mankind has progressed in many fields, until . . . (several sentences missing—broadcast interrupted) . . . and the jagged edges of girders . . . windows smashed and the smoke pouring in now. As soon as the lights stop flickering . . .

THE MAN WHO LIKED DICKENS

Evelyn Waugh

ALTHOUGH Mr. McMaster had lived in Amazonas for nearly sixty years, no one except a few families of Shiriana Indians was aware of his existence. His house stood in a small savannah, one of those little patches of sand and grass that crop up occasionally in that neighborhood, three miles or so across, bounded on all sides by forest.

The stream which watered it was not marked on any map; it ran through rapids, always dangerous and at most seasons of the year impassable, to join the upper waters of the River Uraricuera, whose course, though boldly delineated in every school atlas, is still largely conjectural. None of the inhabitants of the district, except Mr. McMaster, had ever heard of the republic of Colombia, Venezuela, Brazil or Bolivia, each of whom had at one time or another claimed its possession.

Mr. McMaster's house was larger than those of his neighbours, but similar in character—a palm-thatch roof, breast-high walls of mud and wattle, and a mud floor. He owned a dozen or so head of puny cattle which grazed in the savannah, a plantation of cassava, some banana and mango trees, a dog, and, unique in the neighbourhood, a single-barrelled, breech-loading shotgun. The few commodities which he employed from the outside world came to him through a long succession of traders, passed from hand to hand, bartered for in a dozen languages at the extreme end of one of the longest threads in the web of commerce that spreads from Manáos into the remote fastness of the forest.

One day, while Mr. McMaster was engaged in filling some cartridges, a Shiriana came to him with the news that a white man was approaching through the forest, alone and very sick. He closed the cartridge and loaded his gun with it, put those that were finished into his pocket and set out in the direction indicated.

The man was already clear of the bush when Mr. McMaster reached him, sitting on the ground, clearly in a bad way. He was without hat or boots, and his clothes were so torn that it was only by the dampness of his body that they adhered to it; his feet were cut and grossly swollen, every exposed surface of skin was scarred by insect and bat bites; his eyes were wild with fever. He was talking to himself in delirium, but stopped when Mr. McMaster approached and addressed him in English.

"I'm tired," the man said; then: "Can't go on any farther. My name is Henty and I'm tired. Anderson died. That was a long time ago. I expect you think I'm very odd."

"I think you are ill, my friend."

"Just tired. It must be several months since I had anything to eat."

Mr. McMaster hoisted him to his feet and, supporting him by the arm, led him across the hummocks of grass towards the farm.

"It is a very short way. When we get there I will give you something to make you better."

"Jolly kind of you." Presently he said: "I say, you speak English. I'm English, too. My name is Henty."

"Well, Mr. Henty, you aren't to bother about anything more. You're ill and you've had a rough journey. I'll take care of you."

They went very slowly, but at length reached the house.

"Lie there in the hammock. I will fetch something for you."

Mr. McMaster went into the back room of the house and dragged a tin canister from under a heap of skins. It was full of a mixture of dried leaf and bark. He took a handful and went outside to the fire. When he returned he put one hand behind Henty's head and held up the concoction of herbs in a calabash for him to drink. He sipped, shuddering slightly at the bitterness. At last he finished it. Mr. McMaster threw out the dregs on the floor. Henty lay back in the hammock sobbing quietly. Soon he fell into a deep sleep.

"Ill-fated" was the epithet applied by the Press to the Anderson expedition to the Parima and upper Uraricuera region of Brazil. Every stage of the enterprise from the preliminary arrangements in London to its tragic dissolution in Amazonas was attacked by misfortune. It was due to one of the early setbacks that Paul Henty became connected with it.

He was not by nature an explorer; an even-tempered, good-looking young man of fastidious tastes and enviable possessions, unintellectual, but appreciative of fine architecture and the ballet, well-traveled in the more accessible parts of the world, a collector though not a connoisseur, popular among hostesses, revered by his aunts. He was married to a lady of exceptional charm and beauty, and it was she who upset the good order of his life by confessing her affection for another man for the second time in the eight years of their marriage. The first occasion had been a short-lived infatuation with a tennis professional, the second was a captain in the Coldstream Guards, and more serious.

Henty's first thought under the shock of this revelation was to go out and dine alone. He was a member of four clubs, but at three of them he was liable to meet his wife's lover. Accordingly he chose one which he rarely frequented, a semi-intellectual company composed of publishers, barristers, and men of scholarship awaiting election to the Athenæum.

Here, after dinner, he fell into conversation with Professor Anderson and first heard of the proposed expedition to Brazil. The particular misfortune that was retarding arrangements at the moment was defalcation of the secretary with two-thirds of the expedition's capital. The principals were ready—Professor Anderson, Dr. Simmons the anthropologist, Mr. Necher the biologist, Mr. Brough the surveyor, wireless operator and mechanic—the scientific and sporting apparatus was packed up in crates ready to be embarked, the necessary facilities had been stamped and signed by the proper authorities but unless twelve hundred pounds was forthcoming the whole thing would have to be abandoned.

Henty, as has been suggested, was a man of comfortable means; the expedition would last from nine months to a year; he could shut his country house—his wife, he reflected, would want to remain in London near her young man—and cover more than the sum required. There was a glamour about the whole journey which might, he felt, move even his wife's sympathies. There and then, over the club fire he decided to accompany Professor Anderson.

When he went home that evening he announced to his wife: "I have decided what I shall do."

"Yes, darling?"

"You are certain that you no longer love me?"

"*Darling*, you *know*, I *adore* you."

"But you are certain you love this guardsman, Tony whatever-his-name-is, more?"

"Oh, yes, *ever* so much more. Quite a different thing altogether."

"Very well, then. I do not propose to do anything about a divorce for a year. You shall have time to think it over. I am leaving next week for the Uraricuera."

"Golly, where's that?"

"I am not perfectly sure. Somewhere in Brazil, I think. It is unexplored. I shall be away a year."

"But darling, how ordinary! Like people in books—big game, I mean, and all that."

"You have obviously already discovered that I am a very ordinary person."

"Now, Paul, don't be disagreeable—oh, there's the telephone. It's probably Tony. If it is, d'you mind terribly if I talk to him alone for a bit?"

But in the ten days of preparation that followed she showed greater tenderness, putting off her soldier twice in order to accompany Henty to the shops where he was choosing his equipment and insisting on his purchasing a worsted cummerbund. On his last evening she gave a supper-party for him at the Embassy to which she allowed him to ask any of his friends he liked; he could think of no one except Professor Anderson, who looked oddly dressed, danced tirelessly and was something of a failure with everyone. Next day Mrs. Henty came with her husband to the boat train and presented him with a pale blue, extravagantly soft blanket, in a suède case of the same colour furnished with a zip fastener and monogram. She kissed him good-bye and said, "Take care of yourself in wherever it is."

Had she gone as far as Southampton she might have witnessed two dramatic passages. Mr. Brough got no farther than the gangway before he was arrested for a debt—a matter of £32; the publicity given to the dangers of the expedition was responsible for the action. Henty settled the account.

The second difficulty was not to be overcome so easily. Mr. Necher's mother was on the ship before them; she carried a missionary journal in which she had just read an account of the Brazilian forests. Nothing would induce her to permit her son's departure; she would remain on board until he came ashore with her. If necessary, she would sail with him, but go into those forests alone he should not. All argument was unavailing with the resolute old lady who eventually, five minutes before the time of embarkation, bore her son off in triumph, leaving the company without a biologist.

Nor was Mr. Brough's adherence long maintained. The ship in which they were travelling was a cruising liner taking passengers on a round voyage. Mr. Brough had not been on board a week and had scarcely accustomed himself to the motion of the ship before he was engaged to be married; he was still engaged, although to a different lady, when they reached Manáos and refused all inducements to proceed farther, borrowing his return fare from Henty and arriving back in Southampton engaged to the lady of his first choice, whom he immediately married.

In Brazil the officials to whom their credentials were addressed were all out of power. While Henty and Professor Anderson negotiated with the new administrators, Dr. Simmons proceeded up river to Boa Vista where he established a base camp with the greater part of the stores. These were instantly commandeered by the revolutionary garrison, and he himself imprisoned for some days and subjected to various humiliations which so enraged him that, when released, he made promptly for the coast, stopping at Manáos only long enough to inform his colleagues that he insisted on leaving his case personally before the central authorities at Rio.

Thus while they were still a month's journey from the start of their labours, Henty and Professor Anderson found themselves alone and deprived of the greater part of their supplies. The ignominy of immediate return was not to be borne. For a short time they considered the advisability of going into hiding for six months in Madeira or Teneriffe, but even there detection seemed probable; there had been too many photographs in the illustrated papers before they left London. Accordingly, in low spirits, the two explorers at last set out alone for the Uraricuera with little hope of accomplishing anything of any value to anyone.

For seven weeks they paddled through green, humid tunnels of forest. They took a few snapshots of naked, misanthropic Indians, bottled some snakes and later lost them when their canoe capsized in the rapids; they overtaxed their digestions, imbibing nauseous intoxicants at native galas; they were robbed of the last of their sugar by a Guianese prospector. Finally, Professor Anderson fell ill with malignant malaria, chattered feebly for some days in his hammock, lapsed into coma and died, leaving Henty alone with a dozen Maku oarsmen, none of whom spoke a word of any language known to him.

They reversed their course and drifted down stream with a minimum of provisions and no mutual confidence.

One day, a week or so after Professor Anderson's death, Henty awoke to find that his boys and his canoe had disappeared during the night, leaving him with only his hammock and pyjamas some two or three hundred miles from the nearest Brazilian habitation. Nature forbade him to remain where he was although there seemed little purpose in moving. He set himself to follow the course of the stream, at first in the hope of meeting a canoe. But presently the whole forest became peopled for him with frantic apparitions, for no conscious reason at all. He plodded on, now wading in the water, now scrambling through the bush.

Vaguely at the back of his mind he had always believed that the jungle was a place full of food, that there was danger of snakes and savages and wild beasts, but not of starvation. But now he observed that this was far from being the case. The jungle consisted solely of immense tree trunks, embedded in a tangle of thorn and vine rope, all far from nutritious. On the first day he suffered hideously. Later he seemed anæsthetized and was chiefly embarrassed by the behavior of the inhabitants who came out to meet him in footmen's livery, carrying his dinner, and then irresponsibly disappeared or raised the covers of their dishes and revealed live tortoises. Many people who knew him in London appeared and ran round him with derisive cries, asking him questions to which he could not possibly know the answer. His wife came, too, and he was pleased to see her, assuming that she had got tired of her guardsman and was there to fetch him back, but she soon disappeared, like all the others.

It was then that he remembered that it was imperative for him to reach Manáos; he redoubled his energy, stumbling against boulders in the stream and getting caught up among the vines. "But I mustn't waste my breath," he reflected. Then he forgot that, too, and was conscious of nothing more until he found himself lying in a hammock in Mr. McMaster's house.

His recovery was slow. At first, days of lucidity alternated with delirium; then his temperature dropped and he was conscious even when most ill. The days of fever grew less frequent, finally occurring in the normal system of the tropics between long periods of comparative health. Mr. McMaster dosed him regularly with herbal remedies.

"It's very nasty," said Henty, "but it does do good."

"There is medicine for everything in the forest," said Mr. McMaster; "to make you well and to make you ill. My mother was an Indian and she taught me many of them. I have learned others from time to time from my wives. There are plants to cure you and give you fever, to kill you and send you mad, to keep away snakes, to intoxicate fish so that you can pick them out of the water with your hands like fruit from a tree. There are medicines even I do not know. They say that it is possible to bring dead people to life after they have begun to stink, but I have not seen it done."

"But surely you are English?"

"My father was—at least a Barbadian. He came to British Guiana as a missionary. He was married to a white woman but he left her in Guiana to look for gold. Then he took my mother. The Shiriana women are ugly but very devoted. I have had many. Most of the men and women living in this savannah are my children. That is why they obey—for that reason and because I have the gun. My father lived to a great age. It is not twenty years since he died. He was a man of education. Can you read?"

"Yes, of course."

"It is not everyone who is so fortunate. I cannot."

Henty laughed apologetically. "But I suppose you haven't much opportunity here."

"Oh, yes, that is just it. I have a great many books. I will show you when you are better. Until five years ago there was an Englishman—at least a black man, but he was well educated in Georgetown. He died. He used to read to me every day until he died. You shall read to me when you are better."

"I shall be delighted to."

"Yes, you shall read to me," Mr. McMaster repeated, nodding over the calabash.

During the early days of his convalescence Henty had little conversation with his host; he lay in the hammock staring up at the thatched roof and thinking about his wife, rehearsing over and over again different incidents in their life together, including her affairs with the tennis professional and the soldier. The days, exactly twelve hours each, passed without distinction. Mr. McMaster retired to sleep at sundown, leaving a little lamp burning—a hand-woven wick drooping from a pot of beef fat—to keep away vampire bats.

The first time that Henty left the house Mr. McMaster took him for a little stroll around the farm.

"I will show you the black man's grave," he said, leading him to a mound between the mango trees. "He was very kind to me. Every afternoon until he died, for two hours, he used to read to me.

I think I will put up a cross—to commemorate his death and your arrival—a pretty idea. Do you believe in God?"

"I've never really thought about it much."

"You are perfectly right. I have thought about it a *great* deal and I still do not know . . . Dickens did."

"I suppose so."

"Oh yes, it is apparent in all his books. You will see."

That afternoon Mr. McMaster began the construction of a head-piece for the negro's grave. He worked with a large spokeshave in a wood so hard that it grated and rang like metal.

At last when Henty had passed six or seven consecutive days without fever, Mr. McMaster said, "Now I think you are well enough to see the books."

At one end of the hut there was a kind of loft formed by a rough platform erected up in the eaves of the roof. Mr. McMaster propped a ladder against it and mounted. Henty followed, still unsteady after his illness. Mr. McMaster sat on the platform and Henty stood at the top of the ladder looking over. There was a heap of small bundles there, tied up with rag, palm leaf and raw hide.

"It has been hard to keep out the worms and ants. Two are practically destroyed. But there is an oil the Indians know how to make that is useful."

He unwrapped the nearest parcel and handed down a calf-bound book. It was an early American edition of *Bleak House*.

"It does not matter which we take first."

"You are fond of Dickens?"

"Why, yes, of course. More than fond, far more. You see, they are the only books I have ever heard. My father used to read them and then later the black man . . . and now you. I have heard them all several times by now but I never get tired; there is always more to be learned and noticed, so many characters, so many changes of scene, so many words. . . . I have all Dickens's books except those that the ants devoured. It takes a long time to read them all—more than two years."

"Well," said Henty lightly, "they will well last out my visit."

"Oh, I hope not. It is delightful to start again. Each time I think I find more to enjoy and admire."

They took down the first volume of *Bleak House* and that afternoon Henty had his first reading.

He had always rather enjoyed reading aloud and in the first year of marriage had shared several books in this way with his wife, until one day, in one of her rare moments of confidence, she remarked that it was torture to her. Sometimes after that he had thought it might be agreeable to have children to read to. But Mr. McMaster was a unique audience.

The old man sat astride his hammock opposite Henty, fixing him throughout with his eyes, and following the words, soundlessly, with his lips. Often when a new character was introduced he would say, "Repeat the name, I have forgotten him," or, "Yes, yes, I remember her well. She dies, poor woman." He would frequently interrupt with questions; not as Henty would have imagined about the circumstances of the story—such things as the procedure of the Lord Chancellor's Court or the social conventions of the time, though they must have been unintelligible, did not concern him—but always about the characters. "Now, why does she say that? Does she really mean it? Did she feel faint because of the heat of the fire or of something in that paper?" He laughed loudly at all the jokes and at some passages which did not seem humorous to Henty, asking him to repeat them two or three times; and later at the description of the sufferings of the outcasts in "Tom-all-alone" tears ran down his cheeks into his beard. His comments on the story were usually simple. "I think that Dedlock is a very proud man," or, "Mrs. Jellyby does not take enough care of her children." Henty enjoyed the readings almost as much as he did.

At the end of the first day the old man said, "You read beautifully, with a far better accent than the black man. And you explain better. It is almost as though my father were here again." And always at the end of a session he thanked his guest courteously. "I enjoyed that very much. It was an extremely distressing chapter. But, if I remember rightly, it will all turn out well."

By the time that they were well into the second volume, however, the novelty of the old man's delight had begun to wane, and Henty was feeling strong enough to be restless. He touched more than once on the subject of his departure, asking about canoes and rains and the possibility of finding guides. But Mr. McMaster seemed obtuse and paid no attention to these hints.

One day, running his thumb through the pages of *Bleak House* that remained to be read, Henty said, "We still have a lot to get through. I hope I shall be able to finish it before I go."

"Oh, yes," said Mr. McMaster. "Do not disturb yourself about that. You will have time to finish it, my friend."

For the first time Henty noticed something slightly menacing in his host's manner. That evening at supper, a brief meal of farine and dried beef eaten just before sundown, Henty renewed the subject.

"You know, Mr. McMaster, the time has come when I must be thinking about getting back to civilization. I have already imposed myself on your hospitality for too long."

Mr. McMaster bent over his plate, crunching mouthfuls of farine, but made no reply.

"How soon do you think I shall be able to get a boat? . . . I said how soon do you think I shall be able to get a boat? I appreciate all your kindness to me more than I can say, but . . ."

"My friend, any kindness I may have shown is amply repaid by your reading of Dickens. Do not let us mention the subject again."

"Well, I'm very glad you have enjoyed it. I have, too. But I really must be thinking of getting back . . ."

"Yes," said Mr. McMaster. "The black man was like that. He thought of it all the time. But he died here . . ."

Twice during the next day Henty opened the subject but his host was evasive. Finally he said, "Forgive me, Mr. McMaster, but I really must press the point. When can I get a boat?"

"There is no boat."

"Well, the Indians can build one."

"You must wait for the rains. There is not enough water in the river now."

"How long will that be?"

"A month . . . two months . . ."

They had finished *Bleak House* and were nearing the end of *Dombey and Son* when the rain came.

"Now it is time to make preparations to go."

"Oh, that is impossible. The Indians will not make a boat during the rainy season—it is one of their superstitions."

"You might have told me."

"Did I not mention it? I forgot."

Next morning Henty went out alone while his host was busy, and, looking as aimless as he could, strolled across the savannah to the group of Indian houses. There were four or five Shirianas sitting in one of the doorways. They did not look up as he approached them. He addressed them in the few words of Maku he had acquired during the journey but they made no sign whether they understood him or not. Then he drew a sketch of a canoe in the sand, he went through some vague motions of carpentry, pointed from them to him, then made motions of giving something to them and scratched out the outlines of a gun and a hat and a few other recognizable articles of trade. One of the women giggled, but no one gave any sign of comprehension, and he went away unsatisfied.

At their midday meal Mr. McMaster said: "Mr. Henty, the Indians tell me that you have been trying to speak with them. It is easier that you say anything you wish through me. You realize, do you not, that they would do nothing without my authority. They regard themselves, quite rightly in most cases, as my children."

"Well, as a matter of fact, I was asking them about a canoe."

"So they gave me to understand . . . and now if you have finished your meal perhaps we might have another chapter. I am quite absorbed in the book."

They finished *Dombey and Son;* nearly a year had passed since Henty had left England, and his gloomy foreboding of permanent exile became suddenly acute when, between the pages of *Martin Chuzzlewit,* he found a document written in pencil in irregular characters.

Year 1919.

I James McMaster of Brazil do swear to Barnabas Washington of Georgetown that if he finish this book in fact Martin Chuzzlewit I will let him go away back as soon as finished.

There followed a heavy pencil *X,* and after it: *Mr. McMaster made this mark signed Barnabas Washington.*

"Mr. McMaster," said Henty, "I must speak frankly. You saved my life, and when I get back to civilization I will reward you to the best of my ability. I will give you anything within reason. But at present you are keeping me here against my will. I demand to be released."

"But, my friend, what is keeping you? You are under no restraint. Go when you like."

"You know very well that I can't get away without your help."

"In that case you must humour an old man. Read me another chapter."

"Mr. McMaster, I swear by anything you like that when I get to Manáos I will find someone to take my place. I will pay a man to read to you all day."

"But I have no need of another man. You read so well."

'I have read for the last time."

"I hope not," said Mr. McMaster politely.

That evening at supper only one plate of dried meat and farine was brought in and Mr. McMaster ate alone. Henty lay without speaking, staring at the thatch.

Next day at noon a single plate was put before Mr. McMaster, but with it lay his gun, cocked, on his knee, as he ate. Henty resumed the reading of *Martin Chuzzlewit* where it had been interrupted.

Weeks passed hopelessly. They read *Nicholas Nickleby* and *Little Dorrit* and *Oliver Twist*. Then a stranger arrived in the savannah, a half-caste prospector, one of that lonely order of men who wander for a lifetime through the forests, tracing the little streams, sifting the gravel and, ounce by ounce, filling the little leather sack of gold dust, more often than not dying of exposure and starvation with five hundred dollars' worth of gold hung round their necks. Mr. McMaster was vexed at his arrival, gave him farine and *passo* and sent him on his journey within an hour of his arrival, but in that hour Henty had time to scribble his name on a slip of paper and put it into the man's hand.

From now on there was hope. The days followed their unvarying routine: coffee at sunrise, a morning of inaction while Mr. McMaster pottered about on the business of the farm, farine and *passo* at noon, Dickens in the afternoon, farine and *passo* and sometimes some fruit for supper, silence from sunset to dawn with the small wick glowing in the beef fat and the palm thatch overhead dimly discernible; but Henty lived in quiet confidence and expectation.

Some time, this year or the next, the prospector would arrive at a Brazilian village with news of his discovery. The disasters to the Anderson expedition would not have passed unnoticed. Henty could imagine the headlines that must have appeared in the popular Press; even now probably there were search parties working over the country he had crossed; any day English voices might sound over the savannah and a dozen friendly adventurers come crashing through the bush. Even as he was reading, while his lips mechanically followed the printed pages, his mind wandered away from his eager, crazy host opposite, and he began to narrate to himself incidents of his home-coming—the gradual re-encounters with civilization; he shaved and bought new clothes at Manáos, telegraphed for money, received wires of congratulation; he enjoyed the leisurely river journey to Belem, the big liner to Europe; savoured good claret and fresh meat and spring vegetables; he was shy at meeting his wife and uncertain how to address . . . "*Darling,* you've been much longer than you said. I quite thought you were lost. . . ."

And then Mr. McMaster interrupted. "May I trouble you to read that passage again? It is one I particularly enjoy."

The weeks passed; there was no sign of rescue, but Henty endured the day for hope of what might happen on the morrow; he even felt a slight stirring of cordiality towards his gaoler and was therefore quite willing to join him when, one evening after a long conference with an Indian neighbour, he proposed a celebration.

"It is one of the local feast days," he explained, "and they have been making *piwari.* You may not like it, but you should try some. We will go across to this man's home to-night."

Accordingly after supper they joined a party of Indians that were assembled round the fire in one of the huts at the other side of the savannah. They were singing in an apathetic, monotonous manner and passing a large calabash of liquid from mouth to mouth. Separate bowls were brought for Henty and Mr. McMaster, and they were given hammocks to sit in.

"You must drink it all without lowering the cup. That is the etiquette."

Henty gulped the dark liquid, trying not to taste it. But it was not unpleasant, hard and muddy on the palate like most of the beverages he had been offered in Brazil, but with a flavour of honey and brown bread. He leant back in the hammock feeling unusually contented. Perhaps at that very moment the search party was in camp a few hours' journey from them. Meanwhile he was warm and drowsy. The cadence of song rose and fell interminably, liturgically. Another calabash of *piwari* was offered him and he handed it back empty. He lay full length watching the play of shadows on the thatch as the Shirianas began to dance. Then he shut his eyes and thought of England and his wife and fell asleep.

He awoke, still in the Indian hut, with the impression that he had outslept his usual hour. By the position of the sun he knew it was late afternoon. No one else was about. He looked for his watch and found to his surprise that it was not on his wrist. He had left it in the house, he supposed, before coming to the party.

"I must have been tight last night," he reflected. "Treacherous drink, that." He had a headache and feared a recurrence of fever. He found when he set his feet to the ground that he stood with difficulty; his walk was unsteady and his mind confused as it had been during the first weeks of his convalescence. On the way across the savannah he was obliged to stop more than once, shutting his eyes and breathing deeply. When he reached the house he found Mr. McMaster sitting there.

"Ah, my friend, you are late for the reading this afternoon. There is scarcely another half-hour of light. How do you feel?"

"Rotten. That drink doesn't seem to agree with me."

"I will give you something to make you better. The forest has remedies for everything; to make you awake and to make you sleep."

"You haven't seen my watch anywhere?"

"You have missed it?"

"Yes. I thought I was wearing it. I say, I've never slept so long."

"Not since you were a baby. Do you know how long? Two days."

"Nonsense. I can't have."

"Yes, indeed. It is a long time. It is a pity because you missed our guests."

"Guests?"

"Why, yes. I have been quite gay while you were asleep. Three men from outside. Englishmen. It is a pity you missed them. A pity for them, too, as they particularly wished to see you. But what could I do? You were so sound asleep. They had come all the way to find you, so—I thought you would not mind—as you could not greet them yourself I gave them a little souvenir, your watch. They wanted something to take home to your wife who is offering a great reward for news of you. They were very pleased with it. And they took some photographs of the little cross I put up to commemorate your coming. They were pleased with that, too. They were very easily pleased. But I do not suppose they will visit us again, our life here is so retired . . . no pleasures except reading . . . I do not suppose we shall ever have visitors again . . . well, well, I will get you some medicine to make you feel better. Your head aches, does it not. . . . We will not have any Dickens to-day . . . but tomorrow, and the day after that, and the day after that. Let us read *Little Dorrit* again. There are passages in that book I can never hear without the temptation to weep."

THE IRON GATES

Margaret Millar

1

THE dream began quietly. She and Mildred were in a room and Mildred was curled up in a chair, writing.

"What are you writing, Mildred?" Lucille said. "You are writing, what are you writing?"

Slowly, dreamily, Mildred smiled, "Nothing, I have finished, I have quite finished," and she rose and walked through the window into the snow.

"You mustn't go out just in your dress like that, Mildred, you'll catch cold."

"No . . . I'm going away. . . . I've quite finished. . . ."

"No, it's dark, it's snowing."

But she walked away inexorably, leaving no tracks, casting no shadow.

"Mildred, come back! The back of your head is open!"

"No . . . "

"You're bleeding. You'll make the park untidy."

"I'm going away," Mildred called back, softly. "Good-bye, dear. Good-bye, Lucille."

She walked on, between the trees, and up and over the hills. With each step she became smaller and smaller, yet more and more distinct, as if neither time nor space had the power to blur her details. Now and then she turned around and she was always smiling, like a little doll.

315

"Little doll!" Lucille cried. "Little doll . . ."

"Away," came the answer, soft as a whisper but so clear. "Good-bye—good-bye, dear . . ."

Eternally she walked and bled and smiled and grew clearer and clearer.

Lucille awoke, suffocating, sick with horror at this tiny thing moving across her mind, no bigger than a finger, a match, a pin. She sprang from her bed and pulled aside the curtains that shrouded the windows. She looked out, and there was the park, there were the trees, the hills, the trackless snow. But Mildred had been dead for sixteen years.

Somewhere in the distance a church bell rang out the Sunday sound of a city. She became suddenly conscious of how grotesque she would appear if Andrew should walk in and find her like this, crouched beside the window, scanning the snow for his dead wife.

She rose and turned, and caught sight of herself in the mirror. She had forgotten the mirror was there, and for an instant, before she had time to set her face, she seemed a stranger, a lady in a mirror, no longer young, wearing a blue nightgown, with her red-gold hair swinging against her shoulders in two long thick braids. She paused to look at the stranger, smiling faintly because it was only a game, yet uneasily because games were never just games, Andrew said, there had to be some motive behind them. Perhaps even after fifteen years that was how she still felt, like a stranger in the house, visiting someone else's husband and someone else's children.

"Oh, nonsense," she said aloud, and walked quickly toward the mirror and the stranger moved and grew and became herself. "What utter nonsense!"

Her tone was the one she used with Andrew and the children, half-severe, half-humorous, completely understanding. The I'm-smiling-but-I-mean-it voice. The sound of it was so familiar that automatically the accompanying facial pattern sprang into place. Her eyes lost the strained anxious look and became kindly and intelligent, her full firm mouth softened, one eyebrow rose a little.

That's better. This is how I really am. This is me. Lucille Morrow.

Mildred wasn't important any more, though her portrait still hung on the living-room wall, and now and then she bobbed up in dreams. A fat kewpie doll carved out of soap, Lucille thought. Something doughy and sticky you couldn't get off your hands . . .

She picked up a brush and began to brush her hair vigorously.

With each stroke the dream receded and the doll blurred and melted.

Her moment of insecurity had passed and left her with a more conscious sense of possession. This was her hand, her brush, her house, her husband whistling in the adjoining room. Only the children could never belong to anyone but Mildred. For Andrew's sake Lucille had tried to like them and make them like her in return. But they remained Mildred's children and she was uneasy with them and the most she ever achieved was an armed truce.

Still, they were no longer children. Polly was getting married this week, and some day Martin would marry, and she and Andrew would be left alone in the house. With Edith, of course, but she didn't count.

Her hand paused. She gazed into the mirror and saw the future stretching out in front of her, a length of red-velvet carpet covered with a marquee.

She dressed quickly and coiled her hair in a coronet around her head. Like a queen she moved out into the hall, proudly but cautiously, as if she must test the red-velvet carpet and measure the height of the marquee. She walked down the stairs enjoying the sound of her taffeta morning coat following her with obsequious little noises like a genteel servant.

Upstairs, a door slammed and Andrew's voice shouted, "Lucille! Wait a minute, Lucille!"

She paused at the bottom of the steps.

"What is it, Andrew?"

"What's happened to my scarf?"

Lucille checked an impulse to say, "What scarf?" She said, "All your scarves are in your bureau drawer."

"All except this one and this is the one I want to wear."

"Naturally."

"What did you say?"

Lucille raised her voice. "I said, naturally, the one you want to wear is the one that isn't there."

"It's the other way around," Andrew shouted. "The one I want to wear is the one . . ."

"All right," Lucille said, smiling. "What does it look like?"

"Blue. Dark blue with little gray things on it." He came to the head of the stairs and gesticulated. "Little gray things like this."

He was a tall, gray-haired man, nearly fifty now, but he was still slim and he had the quick vigorous movements that characterized his son Martin and his sister Edith. His features were thin, almost delicate, but he had large soft brown eyes which gave his face an oddly guileless expression and caused him trouble now and then with his women patients. Like many really good-natured men, when he tried to look cross he overdid it. He sent a ferocious scowl down the steps at his wife.

"Somebody gave it to me for Christmas last year," he said.

"I did," Lucille said serenely. "And it's not blue, it's black. Have you looked under your bed?"

"Yes."

"Andrew, why? Why do you always look under beds for things first?"

"It's the logical place. So much room. Lucille, you wouldn't come up and . . ."

"I wouldn't," Lucille said. "If I came up and found it for you it would only make you crosser."

"I promise."

"No." She turned calmly and walked away, flinging over her shoulder, "Try the cedar closet in the hall."

Ignoring Andrew's noises of distress she went into the dining room. Edith and Polly were already at breakfast. Edith was buttering a piece of toast with the precise contemptuous movements of one who despises food as a necessary evil to be gotten over with as quickly as possible. Polly, a cup of coffee in front of her, was smoking and gazing dreamily out of the window.

"Good morning, Edith," Lucille said. She bent over Edith's chair and the cheeks of the two women touched briefly. It was a routine of long standing. They were fond of each other, in a dry expedient way, for they were of the same age and they were interested in the same thing, Andrew. "Good morning, Polly."

"Morning," Polly said, without taking her eyes from the window.

"Good morning," Edith said. "Sleep well?"

"Fine."

"More than I did." Her voice was so high and sharp that it seemed ready to break into hysteria, or snap with a death twang like a violin string. Every year it seemed to Lucille that Edith's voice got higher, that the string was pulled more and more taut and played a thin sinister obbligato over the most ordinary remarks.

"What is all the shouting about?" Edith said. "If you want fresh toast, ring for Annie. I told her to have it ready. Sometimes I think Andrew likes to shout simply for the sake of shouting."

Lucille sat down, smiling, and unfolded her napkin. "Perhaps."

"I've seen him at the office simply oozing quiet charm, and when he gets home he howls, he does, he really *howls*."

"He couldn't find a scarf he wanted," Lucille said.

She felt suddenly and absurdly happy. She wanted to laugh out loud, she felt the laughter forming in her throat and she had to force it down. She couldn't explain to Edith or Polly that she wanted to laugh because this room was warm and bright, because it had begun to snow outside, because Andrew couldn't find something and had looked under the bed. . . .

She looked at Edith and Polly and for a minute she loved them both utterly, because she was so pleased with herself and the beautiful quiet life she had built out of nothing. *I love you, my dears, my dears. I can afford to love you because I have everything I want and neither of you can take anything away from me.*

"Andrew never could find anything," Edith said. "And the closer it is to him, of course, the more trouble he has finding it. I suppose it's psychological."

Polly stirred slightly. "What is?" she said. "No, don't tell me. . . ."

"Finding things," Edith said. "I expect Freud would say that you find only the things you really want to find. Some people have the most wonderful gift for finding money. There's a man in New York . . . Polly, it would be *nice* if you sat up *straight*."

"What for?" Polly said.

"You look as if you have curvature of the spine all huddled up like that."

"I'm not huddled, I'm relaxed."

"The table is no place to relax."

"O.K.," Polly said without resentment, and uncoiled herself from the chair. For a minute she remained upright, and then she propped her elbows on the table and supported her head in her hands. Her long black hair swung silkily over her wrists.

"Honestly," said Edith, in affectionate exasperation.

Lucille remained quiet. She no longer made any attempts to discipline her stepchildren, and even when she was especially annoyed with one of them she had enough self-control to refrain from comment. She had always tried to be fair to them and when they disagreed with their father she often forced herself to take their side against him. But in spite of her efforts they had remained aloof and careful.

Perhaps it's because they were at a difficult age when I married

Andrew, Lucille thought. Polly was only ten, and Martin twelve, and they were both so fond of Mildred.

Mildred, Lucille thought, and found that the laughter in her throat had evaporated like the bubbles in a stale drink.

"Though I never relax myself," Edith said, sitting very upright, "I don't mind others relaxing in the proper place. It depends on the personality whether you can or can't."

"Mildred," Lucille said, "Mildred had a very relaxed personality."

She hadn't said the name aloud for years, she didn't want to say it now, but she forced the words out. Her moment of complete happiness had gone, and it was as if the warm bright room had led her on and deceived her and she must cast a corpse into it for revenge.

"Yes, she had," Edith said shortly. "Though I think you should have enough sense not to . . ."

"Yes, I know," Lucille said in confusion, conscious of Polly's hard steady stare. "I'm very sorry."

"Today of all days," Edith said.

"I'm sorry, Edith."

"I'm glad you are. Today of all days we don't want to be reminded of unpleasant things. We must make a good impression on Mr. Frome."

"Lieutenant Frome," Polly said. "And you needn't bother about the impression. I made that weeks ago."

"Still, we *are* your family, my dear."

"He's not marrying you."

Edith blushed and said sharply, "I realize that he's not marrying me and that no one ever has, if that's what you're getting at."

"Please!" Polly said, and got up and planted a quick kiss on her aunt's cheek. "I didn't mean that, silly. I meant I hate fusses, and so does Giles. I don't want this to be a today-of-all-days. Giles'd curl up and die if he thought he was putting anyone out by coming here."

"Then he's too sensitive," Edith said crossly.

"I know he is. That's why I'm glad he's got me. I'm not." She put her arm around her aunt's shoulders and whispered in her ear, "It's lucky I'm not sensitive or how could I have stood all your crabbing?"

"Crabbing?" Edith's mouth fell open. "Really, Polly! As if I'd ever stoop to crabbing!"

"You do crab," Polly said, laughing. "And you make speeches."

"Well, I never! The nerve of . . ."

"Confess it, confess it now or I'll tickle you."

"Oh! You sit down right this minute and behave yourself." Edith smoothed her ruffled hair and feelings. "You and your jokes. You're worse than Martin. As if I ever made speeches. Do I, Lucille?"

"Never," Lucille said, with a smile.

"You see, Polly?"

But as soon as Lucille was brought into the conversation Polly's mood changed. Her face became a blank, her eyes fixed themselves coldly on Lucille and Lucille read in them: "See how nicely we get along without you? This is how you've been spoiling things for us all these years."

"I don't believe in making speeches," Edith said. "I think the tongue is a much overrated organ."

"Isn't it," Polly said absently, and strolled over to the window, her square shoulders outlined in the light.

Lucille glanced at her and was struck again by the difference between Polly and the rest of the family. There was something compact and uncompromising and stubborn about even the way she was built. She was rather short, and though slim, she gave the impression of sturdiness and durability. She did not expend her energy haphazardly and aimlessly like Martin and Edith. She moved with a kind of lazy competence and she did nearly everything well, and was at home anywhere.

Her features had the soft roundness of her mother's, and she was, like her, fundamentally a tranquil person. But where Mildred's tranquillity had been deepened by happiness and security, Polly's had been warped and hardened by years of implacable hatred of her stepmother.

Perhaps with Martin alone I would have been successful, Lucille thought. He's a man, and more pliant. But Polly . . . Polly seemed already grown-up at ten. She distrusted me, as a grown woman distrusts another woman whose house she has to share.

Edith had finished her coffee and her long thin fingers drummed restlessly on the tablecloth. She had finished one thing, breakfast, therefore she must start another thing at once. Whether the activity was her own or someone else's did not matter. She was constantly on the move and setting other people in motion.

"I wish Andrew would hurry," she said. "I expect Martin to be late, of course. I think I'd better go up and see what's keeping them."

"Lots of time," Polly said. "Giles' furlough doesn't begin officially until noon and it won't take us over an hour to drive out to the camp."

"I understand," Lucille said, rather shyly, "that officers have 'leaves' and enlisted men have 'furloughs.' "

Polly shrugged, and said, without turning around, "Oh, do you?"

"I think I—I heard it somewhere."

"Really?"

"Of course, so did I," Edith said hurriedly. "Though I prefer to call it 'furlough.' It sounds so much more important, Polly. Why Andrew and Martin insist on driving out with you I don't know."

"They want to look him over first," Polly said, "and then if he doesn't measure up they can dispose of the body some place and bring me on home, teary but intact."

Edith tried to look shocked. "I'm sure such an idea never entered Andrew's head."

"I was joking, darling."

"What a way to joke!"

"But the main idea, I suppose, is to give Giles the impression of male solidarity behind me. 'None of your funny work, Frome, or else . . .' 'Be good to our little Polly'—that sort of thing."

"I consider it quite touching," Edith said.

"Yes, isn't it? And so redundant. They both know that since I have decided on Giles, nothing in this world can stop me from marrying him." She glanced briefly at Lucille.

"I'm glad you feel like that," Lucille said quietly. "It's bad policy to interfere with marriages."

The girl flushed and turned away again.

"There's altogether too much fuss made about marrying," Edith said. "When I was young I naturally had some experience with moonlight and roses, but the roses nearly all turned out to be the crepe-paper ones from the dime store, and the moonlight no better than a street lamp, not so good for seeing purposes." She smiled affectionately at Polly's back. "But I expect you've known that for years."

"Off and on," Polly said. "I lapse. This is my nicest lapse."

"I'm really very anxious to see him," Edith said with a break in her voice. "It's so hard to believe you're old enough to be getting married. It seems like yesterday . . ."

"I never thought you'd get sentimental about me."

"As if I'd ever get sentimental," Edith said and briskly pushed back her chair. "I'm going up to hurry Andrew along. If he looks for the scarf much longer he'll have the whole house torn up."

She went out in a flutter of silk and sachet.

Left alone with her stepmother, Polly came back to the table and poured herself another cup of coffee.

Because she felt embarrassed with Lucille she focused her eyes carefully on the objects on the table, examining and appraising them as if she were at an auction—the silver coffee urn with the little gas flame under it, the red cups on white saucers, the remains of Edith's breakfast, two pieces of toast sagging against the toast rack, a bald and imperturbable boiled egg in a red bowl, and a corner of Lucille's blue sleeve.

"I'm glad Giles could get his—his furlough," Lucille said politely.

Polly did not look up. "So am I, naturally."

"Three weeks, is it?"

"Yes."

"And you're being married on Friday—five more days."

"We have to wait for the license. Then we'll go down to the registry office and get the mumbo-jumbo over with and be off."

"Where are you going?"

Polly shrugged. "Here or there. It doesn't matter."

"No, I guess not," Lucille said, and the two were silent again.

In the hall there were sounds of laughter and running footsteps, and a few seconds later Martin came bursting into the room. His hair was rumpled and his tie wasn't tied but he had the self-assurance and smiling arrogance of a man who has achieved success early and easily. He had had his back broken when he was a child and sometimes his walk was stiff and painful; but he never talked about it and he was almost always smiling, and if he lived a secret bitter life of his own behind the smile he never let on.

He looked so much like his father that Lucille's lips curved involuntarily when she saw him and her eyes were soft as a lover's.

"Edith just flung me down the stairs," Martin said cheerfully. "What in hell's the hurry? It's only nine-thirty and the Big Four don't meet until noon."

He pulled out a chair and sat down, and ran his two hands over his hair to smooth it. In the process he knocked over a cup on the table and narrowly missed Polly's head with his elbow.

"I don't think Giles is going to like you, Martin," Polly said crisply. "You're too violent."

"Of course Giles will like me. I'm going to give him lots of advice. I'll tell him everything a young man in his condition should know."

"He's twenty-nine, darling. A year older than you are."

"But totally lacking in experience."

Polly made a face at him.

So far Martin hadn't even looked at Lucille but she knew the omission was not deliberate as it would have been in Polly's case.

She did not want to call attention to herself by speaking, so she watched the two of them in silence, forgetting Mildred and taking pride in the fact that these were Andrew's children and both of them so good-looking and dark and clever. Martin was literary editor of the Toronto *Review,* and very young for his job. Polly had taken her degree in sociology at the university, and for four years had worked in various settlement houses doing everything from investigating cases to helping deliver babies.

"Is that my egg?" Martin said, pointing to the red bowl.

"Nobody can own an egg," Polly said. "They're so impersonal."

"I can."

"Don't take it," Lucille said, laughing. "It's not very warm. Annie will make you another."

But Martin had already sliced the top off the egg, and was choosing a piece of stale toast from the rack. Lucille poured his coffee for him and then rose to leave. She would have liked to stay on at the table as she usually did on Sundays, but she knew she'd be in the way. Martin and Polly were already deep in a discussion of how Martin should and should not behave to Giles.

"Do *not* be funny," Polly said. "And above all do *not* slap him on the back or ask him what his officer's swagger stick is for. Everyone asks him that and it's very embarrassing because he doesn't *know*. And above all . . ."

Lucille closed the door softly behind her.

She stood for a moment in the hall, uncertain of herself and her position, not sure what to do or where to go. She had a sudden shock of recognition.

I've been here many times before, she thought. Alone in a hall with the doors closed against me, a stranger, a tramp.

She had a vision of herself, her body bent forward in lines of furtiveness like a thief about to tiptoe past a sleeping policeman.

Then from upstairs she heard Edith's voice raised in angry solicitude, "I do believe you've given yourself a fever, Andrew!" and abruptly everything became normal again, the policeman woke, the thief was caught and put neatly behind bars, and Lucille's thoughts folded and packed themselves into their proper files.

"My dear Edith." Andrew's voice was raised too, and he sounded nervous and irritable. He doesn't want Polly to get married, Lucille thought. He still thinks of her as a little girl. "How can anyone *give* himself a fever?"

"You know very well what I meant," Edith said. "You're coming down with a cold, and it's a lot of nonsense anyway, this dashing out into the snow to meet . . ."

"My dear *Edith*. I am not dashing out into the snow. I intend to conduct myself in a dignified manner in a *closed* car with a *heater,* providing . . ."

"You know very well . . ."

". . . providing I am allowed enough privacy to get dressed."

"All right, *get* double pneumonia."

"Dear heaven!" Andrew said, and a door slammed.

Lucille walked down the hall, thinking, with a smile, of Edith. Poor Edith, she thrives on imminent catastrophes and likes to think of herself as the great Averter of them. . . . I could do the menus and make out the shopping list for tomorrow. . . . I wonder if Giles is allergic to anything. . . .

She went into the small book-lined room that Andrew called his den. The sun hadn't reached this side of the house yet and the room was gloomy and smelled of unused books.

She turned on a lamp and sat down in Andrew's chair and stretched out her hand for a memo pad and a pencil. She began to plan the menus for the week, with one eye on rationing and the other on Annie's limitations in the kitchen. Lobster, if available, and a roasting chicken. Mushrooms, or perhaps an eggplant.

She bent over the pad, frowning. She wanted everything to be perfect for Giles, not because he was Giles and about to marry Polly, but because she was Lucille. She had the subtle but supreme vanity that often masquerades under prettier names, devotion, unselfishness, generosity. It lay in the back of her mind, a blind, deaf and hungry little beast that must always be fed indirectly through a cord.

While she planned she drew pictures absently on the back of the memo pad. Vaguely through a sea of lobsters and shrimp she heard Edith's voice calling her.

"Lucille, where on earth are you?"

"In here. In the den."

Edith came rushing through the door with an air of challenging a high wind.

"I think Andrew's caught a cold," she said with a tragic gesture. "Today of all days. His face is quite flushed."

"Excitement," Lucille said. Edith was smoking, and her pallor, seen through a veil of smoke, reminded Lucille of oysters.

"Oysters," she said.

Edith looked a little surprised. "I loathe oysters. Unless they're covered with something and fried."

"Yes."

"I don't like the *color* of the things."

"Neither do I," Lucille said calmly, and added oysters to the list.

"Though I wasn't, as a matter of fact, talking about oysters," Edith said with a certain coldness. "I was talking about Andrew. I think he should be sensible and stay home today."

"Oh, leave him alone, Edith." Seeing her sister-in-law's color rise she added quickly, "Andrew hates to be babied. The best thing you and I can do is to stay out of everyone's way. Leave the three of them together. In a way it's their morning, we mustn't interfere. For the present—we're—we're outsiders."

Edith looked as if she were about to continue arguing, then with a sudden twist of her shoulders she turned and sat down on the edge of the desk.

"You're so reasonable, Lucille," she said, almost complainingly. "I don't know how you do it, always putting yourself in some other person's place and coming out with exactly the right solution. It's extraordinary."

"I've had a lot of practice." Contented and smiling she leaned back and touched her hair lightly with the tips of her fingers. The little beast had been fed and had stopped gnawing for a moment.

A few minutes later Edith went out, and Lucille sat with the memo pad on her knee, patiently waiting for Andrew to come in and say good-bye to her. But he didn't come.

He's forgotten you.

Well, of course he has. He's with his children. It's their day, after all. I said it myself.

But he has forgotten you.

Well, of course. I'm not a dewy-eyed bride any more. . . .

She got up and went to the window and stood waiting to catch a glimpse of him as he left the house. She saw the three of them going up the driveway, close together, arm in arm. With the snow whirling around them they seemed like a compact unit, indivisible and invulnerable.

While she watched, a squat dark cloud moved across the sun like a jealous old woman.

Lucille stood, wanting to cry out, "Andrew! Andrew, come back!" as she had cried out to Mildred in the dream.

But no sound came from her lips, and after a moment she went back to her chair and lighted a cigarette and picked up the memo pad again.

She looked down at the pictures she had drawn while she was planning the menus. They were women's faces, the faces of fat silly kewpie-doll women. They smirked and simpered at her from the paper and tossed their coy ringlets and fluttered their eyelashes.

Detachedly, almost absently, she burned out their eyes with the end of her cigarette.

2

AROUND noon on Sunday, December fifth, the Montreal Flier was derailed about twenty miles from Toronto. The cause of the derailment was not known but it was hinted in the first radio reports that it was the work of saboteurs, for the train had been passing a steep bank at the time and the number of people killed and wounded was very high. Volunteer doctors and nurses were asked to come to Castleton, the nearest hospital.

Edith heard the news on the radio but paid little attention to it beyond thinking fleetingly that death and catastrophe were so common these days that one had to be personally involved to get excited over them.

"All volunteer doctors and nurses report at once to Castleton Hospital, King's Highway number . . ."

She rose, yawning, and turned the radio off, just as Lucille came in.

"What was that?" Lucille asked.

"Some train wreck."

"Oh. Lunch is ready. Any calls for Andrew this morning?"

"Two." Years ago Edith had appointed herself to answer Andrew's calls on Sunday. She said wistfully, "Remember the old days when I used to spend nearly the whole day at the phone?"

"Andrew is sensible not to work so hard," Lucille said. "His assistant is perfectly capable."

"Still it was rather fun to be so busy."

"Not for Andrew." She smiled, but she was annoyed with Edith for bringing the subject up. She and Edith, between them, had made the decision that Andrew was to retire, at least partially. Now that he had, Lucille was beginning to doubt her own wisdom. Andrew's health was better but he had spells of moodiness.

"Doctors are too hard on themselves," she said, as if to convince herself. "That's why so many of them die young."

"Don't talk about dying young. It upsets my digestive tract." She turned away, biting her lower lip. "It makes me think of Mildred. . . . I can't help wishing you hadn't referred to her this morning, especially in front of Polly."

"I'm really sorry. It just slipped out."

"You'll have to be careful. She might not want Giles to know how—how Mildred died."

"She's probably told him already."

"No, no, I don't think so. Such a terrible thing." Edith closed her eyes and Lucille saw that the lids were corpse-gray with the blue veins growing on them like mold.

"So bloody," Edith said. "So—*bloody*. I—really . . ."

"Edith, you mustn't." Lucille put out her hand and touched Edith's thin pallid arm. "Come along and have your lunch."

"I couldn't eat a thing."

"Certainly you can."

"No. Just remembering it upsets me. . . ."

"We'll see," Lucille said, a trifle grimly.

She walked out, leaving Edith to wander wispily behind her like a little unloved ghost.

Lucille estimated the situation and acted as usual with good sense. Given any sympathy or encouragement Edith would mope herself into indigestion or a migraine.

"Sweetbreads for lunch," Lucille said cheerfully.

Edith brightened at once. In spite of the tug of her conscience she saw Mildred floating away out of her mind and the blood frothed into yards and yards of beautiful pink gauze trailing Mildred down the years.

"I adore sweetbreads," she said.

She ate too heartily and had indigestion anyway, and by two-thirty she had begun to fidget because Andrew and the children hadn't returned. Lucille tried to calm her and succeeded only in making herself nervous and impatient.

At four o'clock Lucille built a fire in the living-room grate to cheer them up. But the wood was damp and the flames crept feebly up along the log like dying fingers beckoning for help.

"They should *be* here," Edith said. "They should *be* here. I can't think what has happened."

"Probably nothing at all," Lucille said and poked the log again and turned it.

"I told you that wood wouldn't burn."

"My dear Edith," Lucille said, "it *is* burning."

"Not really burning. I'm surprised at Andrew worrying me like this, I'm surprised at him. He should know better."

"How could Andrew know you were going to eat too much and make yourself nervous?"

"You're going too far, Lucille."

"I should have said that two hours ago."

"It carries a nasty implication," Edith said coldly. "As if I would not worry about Andrew if I hadn't eaten too much, which I'm not admitting in the first place. I think you might . . ."

The telephone in the hall began to ring. The two women looked at each other but did not move.

"Aren't you going to answer it, Edith? It's probably a call for Andrew."

Edith didn't hear her.

"An accident," she whispered. "I know—an accident . . ."

"Don't be silly," Lucille said and went out to answer the phone herself.

The operator's nasal voice twanged along the wire.

"A collect call from Castleton for Mrs. Andrew Morrow. Will you accept the call?"

"This is Mrs. Morrow. Yes, I'll take it."

"Here is your party. Go ahead."

"Hello," Lucille said. "Hello?"

For a moment there was no reply but a confused background of sound. Then, "Hello, Lucille. This is Polly."

"What's happened?"

"There's been an accident."

"Polly . . . "

"No, not ours. We sort of happened into it and Father and I are staying to help. There's a little hospital here, that's where I'm phoning from."

"Polly, you sound funny."

"Maybe I do. I've never seen a train wreck before. Anyway, I'm in a hurry. There aren't enough doctors and nurses. Tell Edith not to worry. Good-bye."

"Wait—when will you be home?"

"When they can spare us. Martin and Giles are helping get the bodies out. Good-bye."

"Good-bye," Lucille echoed.

Edith was tugging at her sleeve. "What is it?"

"Nothing much," Lucille said. "There was a train wreck and Andrew's helping."

"How awful!" Edith said, but the words meant nothing to Lucille. She was looking over Edith's shoulder, smiling. Andrew was safe, her world was safe. All the trains on earth were of no importance if Andrew wasn't on them.

She hurried back into the living room to stir up the fire. . . . Andrew would be tired when he came home, he would like a fire and a hot toddy.

But no matter how hard she worked, the wood refused to burn. She rose to her feet, dusty and defeated. Slowly she moved her head and her eyes met Mildred's. Mildred, whole and happy and done in oils, and changeless; Mildred, still a nuisance after sixteen years, having to be dusted once a day and sent away to be cleaned when her plump white shoulders showed scurf.

Lucille looked at her bitterly but Mildred's soft sweet mouth did not alter, and her blue eyes undimmed by time or tears or hate stared forever at a piece of wall.

"It's all coming back to me," Edith said.

"What?" Lucille said. "What?"

"The wreck I was trying to remember. It was when Andrew and I were practically children. I don't remember how it happened exactly but the train was derailed in some way not a mile from the house. And of course we had to go over as soon as we heard about it."

She went on and on, and Lucille heard only snatches. "Hundreds of bodies, yes, hundreds . . . very unpleasant for children . . . soldiers to help because the other war was on then . . ."

In the excitement Edith's indigestion disappeared, and Lucille acquired a headache.

"You're becoming more moderate with the years," she said sharply. "The last time you told me, it was thousands of bodies."

"Oh, it was not," Edith said, offended. "I'm very accurate at numbers. You're not yourself today, at all, Lucille. You're quite critical."

"I have a headache."

"Go up and lie down then. You're not yourself today," she repeated.

"I don't want to lie down," Lucille said and was surprised to hear how childish she sounded.

Edith and I are not friends, she thought. We get along and laugh together and understand each other but with only a little less control we might rail at each other like fishwives.

"Very well, I'll lie down," she said. She walked abruptly to the door hoping that if she hurried she might defeat Edith by having the last word.

But she was not quick enough.

"Well, I should *think* so," Edith said.

Breathing hard, Lucille went to the staircase and began to ascend. She wanted Edith to hear how briskly and youthfully she went upstairs, but the deep carpet and her own weariness betrayed her and the sounds she made were the soft treacherous sounds of a panther moving across the uncertain floor of a jungle.

She had intended to pass the hall mirror without looking at herself but now that she had reached it she couldn't bear to turn her head away and slight an old friend.

"Hello," she said, quirking an eyebrow to show herself how whimsical she was being saying hello to herself. "Hello, stranger."

She passed down the hall into her own room.

As far as anything in the house could be free of Mildred, this room was. In Mildred's day it had been the guest room because the windows looked out over the park. Mildred had draped the windows herself with yards of suffocating ruffles and net and visitors saw the park only through a pink fog.

Lucille's first act had been to strip off the ruffles and replace them with crisp tailored drapes. There was a chair beside the windows and here Lucille often sat watching the people in the park, in the winter the skiers and the children with sleds and toboggans, in the summer the parade of prams and picnickers and cyclists.

There was one very steep hill that hardly any cyclist ever managed to get up, and Lucille found pleasure in estimating at just what point the bicycles would falter and the riders dismount and trudge up the rest of the hill.

She enjoyed the people who used the park. They were so tiny

and harmless and always making things difficult for themselves by going up and down hills. But she especially loved the cyclists, the ones who never reached the top. Cruelly she enjoyed their endless and futile activity while the clock on her bureau ticked away the minutes and the years.

Outside it had stopped snowing. The park lay like a silent lolling woman softly draped in white with hints of darkness in its hollows.

Lucille turned from the window. She did not like the park at dusk. For a long time after Mildred died nobody had gone into the park after nightfall. There were rumors of a man who roamed the hills with an axe in his hand, there were tales of ghosts and half-human animals. But Mildred and the man were soon forgotten, and intrepid children and impatient lovers had driven away the ghosts.

Only Lucille remembered the man with the axe. She had never believed in him for an instant, yet some perverse part of her mind had kept him for her in storage. When she was disturbed and restless he came out from hiding, gently at first so that she would think he was an old friend. His face was smiling and familiar and she never saw the axe in his hand or the blood on his clothes until it was too late. Then gradually his face would change and distort into something so grotesque and hideous that she could never describe it in words or even remember it when she was feeling calm again.

Lucille laughed suddenly, thinking of Edith.

"Edith would say I have repressions," she said aloud. "Poor Edith."

She went to the mirror and began to make up her face for Andrew.

"If you're tired," Martin said, "why not let me drive?"

Andrew did not take his eyes off the road.

"Gravel and snow," he said. "I think I'd better keep the wheel."

Polly's voice came from the back seat, "You should know by this time, Martin, that Father thinks nobody can drive as well as he can."

"Never saw one," Andrew said.

"The trouble with you . . ." Polly said.

"The trouble with you," Andrew said, "is you talk too much, my dear. You're likely to give Giles the right impression."

"Giles," Polly said, "do I talk too much?"

The young man beside her stiffened in order to show her that he was alert and listening to her. But he hadn't heard the question at all. A combination of circumstances had made him so ill at ease that he was aware only of his own problems and discomfort.

In the first place he didn't feel quite at home yet in his officer's uniform. He didn't know what to do with his swagger stick, and though he felt that he should put his arm around Polly he didn't want to lose the stick, or break it.

He was, moreover, nervous with Polly's family. How could they talk like this after seeing the wreck and the bodies?

The wreck had affected him more than the others because he was not used to death and sickness and because it was a little bit like war and he was going to see a lot of things worse than this. The knowledge clutched his stomach like an iron hand.

He sat up straighter. In the headlights of an approaching car his face was stern and white, and the small fair moustache he was growing only emphasized his youth and helplessness.

"Forget about it, Giles," Polly said, seeing the misery in his eyes.

"Forget about what?" he said stiffly.

"Everything."

"Oh."

She squeezed his hand. "You look awfully nice in your uniform."

"Thank you."

"I'm sorry we had to run into this today, darling."

"Don't be sorry," Giles said. "I mean, it's all right. I mean, it's not your fault."

"True," Martin said dryly.

He rather liked Polly's young man, but he was in no mood to go easy on him. He himself had been stirred by the wreck to pity and anger which, in Martin, turned at once into sarcasm.

"Martin doesn't want anybody to know he's human," Polly said, "so he'll be biting and snarling for a week now."

"Like the cur I am," Martin said.

"Martin loves snarling."

"Don't you both?" Andrew said, suddenly irritated with the road and his children and their endless wrangling and the young lieutenant who wasn't good enough for Polly.

"I don't," Polly said. "I get along with everybody."

"Lack of taste," Martin said, slumping further on the seat. "Your chief fault."

More uneasy than ever, Giles cleared his throat and tried to think of something very correct to say. By the time something occurred to him Polly and Martin were talking again. Frustrated, he began to beat his stick rhythmically against his knee.

The car glided over the treacherous road. On a curve the wheels slipped and lurched ahead and the car sprawled sideways in the middle of the highway.

"Better reconsider," Martin said. "I'm a heller on snow and gravel."

"Kindly shut up, Martin," Andrew said, twisting the steering wheel furiously.

"I'm trying to save trouble," Martin said. "Lucille will blame me if I don't deliver you cosy and safe at the door."

"See?" Polly said to Giles. "Now he's biting Father. I think we should feed the poor mutt and walk him past a hydrant."

"What?" Giles said, and blushed. "Oh. I see."

Martin grinned into the darkness. "You can't blame Polly for being earthy now and then. She's had such a wide range of experience. Tell him the case of Mrs. Palienczski, Polly."

"Not until after we're married," Polly said calmly.

Married, Andrew thought, and his fingers dug into the steering wheel. Polly getting married, staking her life on the chance that this young man was clean and decent and responsible and healthy . . .

I don't like him, Andrew decided.

Once the words had formed in his head, the feeling which had been vague before became definite and irrevocable. "I don't think I like him," had become "I'm determined I'll never like him."

Andrew was not given to introspection or self-analysis—he had been too busy for it all his life—and so he thought his judgment of Giles was perfectly impartial and well-considered, and, of course, correct.

"It's nearly midnight," Martin said.

"Nearly midnight," Giles echoed, and was conscious of a feeling of relief that the day was amost over and tomorrow could be no worse.

For the rest of the journey he was silent. Every now and then when they passed a lighted village he would glance down at Polly's dark fur coat. He had never seen her wearing it before and it looked very expensive, like the car, and Martin's hat, and Andrew's watch. In addition to his other fears he began to be afraid that the Morrows were rich, that they might have servants who would intimidate him, that he wouldn't know which fork to use. Or he might slip on a waxed floor, or break an antique chair . . .

Anyway, I'm a soldier, he thought. Anyway, that's more than Martin is. I'm a lieutenant with a whole platoon of my own.

He closed his eyes and wished that he could be back where he belonged, with his platoon. . . .

"Giles," Polly said. "Darling, wake up. We're here."

He was awake immediately and reaching instinctively for his swagger stick. But his mind was confused and when the car jerked to a stop he had the impression that Andrew had driven right up onto a veranda, a spacious veranda with huge white pillars. He blinked slowly and looked out the window and saw that the car had stopped under a portico. Between the pillars he could see the dim sprawling hills of the park.

"You take the car in, Martin," Andrew said wearily and climbed out of the car.

Martin slid over on the seat. "All right. Remove yourselves back there."

"Come on, Giles," Polly said. "We'll get out here."

He was still staring out the window at the park. A park, he thought, their park, a whole damn park in the middle of a city.

"Come *on*," Polly said. "You can moon over the scenery some other time. I'm cold."

Giles got out. There was a brisk clumsiness in his movements as if he hadn't quite got used to his own size.

"Is it yours?" he said. "All that?"

"Of course not," Andrew said brusquely.

"Really, Giles," Polly said, laughing. "That's High Park. We happen to live next to it. You'll love it, Giles. Tomorrow we'll walk through it. . . ."

"No, you won't," Andrew said. He turned his back to them and pressed the doorbell. He spoke over his shoulder and his voice sounded thin and distant. "I don't want to be tyrannical about this but I must insist that you stay out of the park."

"I'm afraid you've caught a cold, Father," Polly said.

"You must stay out of the park," Andrew said. "It isn't a nice place."

"Of course, sir," Giles said stiffly. "Of course, sir. I don't like parks."

"I'm afraid Father is overtired," Polly said. "Martin and I often go into the park, especially in the winter to ski."

"It isn't a nice place," Andrew said, and pressed the bell again.

Martin came running up the driveway. He had his hat off and his dark hair was feathered with snow. He threw his hat up in the air and caught it, and let out a shout that was an exultant challenge to the weather.

Giles stood, shaken with envy and wistfulness. *I'd* like to do that, he thought. I could do that.

"Martin is always uninhibited," Polly said, "but especially in the first snow of the year."

The portico light went on suddenly, and the door opened.

Giles had a confused impression that several women were rushing out at him all talking at once. . . . "We didn't hear the car . . ." "Andrew, you didn't tie your scarf. . . ." "You're not chilled, Andrew?"

Polly's voice rose above the babble, clear and cold.

"Come on, Giles. I'll fix you a drink while they're taking Father's temperature."

The talk died down and Giles was able to see now that there were only two women. One of them was tall and thin and looked like Martin, with her dark curly hair cropped close to her head. She had bright birdlike eyes and a wide mobile mouth and it surprised Giles to hear how high and tight her voice was and how anxious her laugh. This must be Edith, Giles thought.

The other woman was taller, and seemed at the same time younger and more mature than Edith. She had the controlled subdued beauty that plain women sometimes acquire when they have achieved happiness and success and security. Her red-gold hair was coiled in a braid around her head.

She came toward Giles, holding out her hand and smiling apologetically.

"We've been terribly rude," she said. "You're Giles, of course. I'm Lucille Morrow."

He shook her hand, very embarrassed because he still had his gloves on and because Polly had flounced ahead into the house without looking back.

"How do you do?" Giles said.

"And this is Edith, Polly's aunt. Edith dear, come over and meet Giles."

Edith darted at him. She was wearing something that fluttered in the wind and it seemed to Giles that she was entirely fluid and never stopped moving, talking, smiling, having ideas.

"Hello, Giles," she said. "What a pretty uniform, don't you think so, Lucille? We are so glad to have you here, Giles. Andrew, please go into the house at once, though you probably have pneumonia already."

"Nothing I'd like better," Andrew said and stamped ahead into the house.

"What a way to talk!" Edith slipped her hand inside Giles' arm. "Polly is always rude, don't mind her. One of the first things you have to do is teach her some manners. We've never been able to."

Giles found himself being guided expertly and firmly into the house and down a hall. He had no time to look around or even to think. Edith did not once pause for a breath or an answer.

Her hand on his arm was like a bird's claw, helpless and appealing, yet somehow grotesque. He thought if he moved his arm the claw would tighten from fear and the harder he tried to shake it off, the tighter it would cling.

"Here we are," Edith said, and thrust him neatly into the living room.

Lucille was pouring out the hot toddies. Martin and Polly were sitting on the chesterfield talking, and Andrew stood in front of the fire warming his hands.

"Attention, everybody," Edith said. "And Polly, this means you as well as everyone else because I'm going to make a speech."

"I knew it," Polly said tragically. "I knew it."

"How could you know it when I just decided myself?" Edith said. "Besides, it's a very short speech, and I consider this an occasion."

"And occasions deserve speeches," Martin added. "Preferably by Edith. Come on over here, Giles. We may be up all night."

"You will if you keep interrupting me," Edith said. "Anyway, I want to welcome you to the house, Giles. We are glad you could come and we think you will find us a—a happy family." She blushed and gave Giles an embarrassed and apologetic smile. "I know how sentimental that sounds but I think it's true, we are a happy family. Of course we have our lapses. Polly is invariably rude and Martin's high spirits are a trial . . ."

"And Edith gets maudlin," Polly said.

"Oh, I do not," Edith said. "And Andrew can never find anything and then he gets cross. Don't you, Andrew?"

"I may become justifiably irritated," Andrew said, "but never cross."

"As for Lucille," Edith said and smiled across the room at her sister-in-law.

There was a pause and the room seemed to Giles to become static. It was no longer a real room but a picture, the man standing warming his hands at the fire, the two women smiling and smiling at each other, the three figures on the chesterfield relaxed and yet unnatural. Happy family, Giles thought. An ambitious picture painted by an amateur. The smiles of the women were set and false, and the figures on the chesterfield sprawled ungracefully like stiff-jointed dolls.

"As for Lucille," Edith said, "I don't believe she has any lapses."

Lucille laughed softly. "Don't you believe her, Giles. I'm the worst of the lot."

His eyes met hers and he felt suddenly warm and understood and contented. The rest of the family with their constant jokes and squabbles were a puzzle to him, but he felt that he knew and liked this quiet beautiful woman.

Something stirred in her eyes like mud at the bottom of a pool. "I haven't seen you before," she said. "Have I?"

"No," Giles said uncertainly.

"For a moment you reminded me of someone."

"There!" Edith said triumphantly. "That's Lucille's lapse. Someone is always reminding her of someone."

Lucille said, "Life is an endless procession of faces for me. I am always trying to match them up."

She picked up her glass and looked into the murky liquid. It seemed to come alive and surge with millions of little faces, winking, frowning, sly, puckered, brooding, bitter, smiling little faces, incredibly mobile and knowing. She could not close her eyes and blot them out. She knew that then they would appear behind her eyelids and that she must walk alone through this delicate, soundless hell.

When Giles said good night to her she was still holding the glass, looking into it with bewildered melancholy, like a child trying to comprehend the universe.

"Good night, Mrs. Morrow," he said.

She raised her head, and in her quick nervous smile he saw a flutter of questions: You? Where do you fit in? Have you a place? Have I?

"Good night, Giles," she said in a composed voice. She glanced across at her husband. "Coming, Andrew? It's very late."

Very late, too late, later than you think . . . I mustn't let my nerves bother me like this, or I'll dream of Mildred again.

3

IN THE late afternoon of December the sixth Lucille Morrow disappeared.

The house had been quiet all day. Martin and Andrew were working, and Edith had gone on a shopping tour with Polly and Giles.

In the kitchen the two young servants, Annie and Della, were cleaning silverware. When the front door-bell rang Annie snatched up a clean apron, tying it as she ran along the hall.

As soon as she opened the door she regretted this waste of energy. It wasn't a real caller but a dark shabby little man in a battered trench coat.

"Mrs. Morrow?" he said hoarsely.

Annie, who admired Lucille, was both flattered and angry at the mistake.

Mrs. Morrow is resting," she said, in a voice very like Lucille's own. "She cannot be disturbed."

The little man blinked, and shifted his feet. "I got something for her. I got to give it to her. You go and get her." He turned up his coat collar and then slowly and patiently put his hands in his pockets. "Special delivery like."

"I'll take it," Annie said. "And why you can't use the back door is more than I can say."

"Very special delivery," the man said, but his voice lacked conviction. He seemed to have lost all interest in the matter and wasn't even looking at Annie any more. "What the hell, you give it to her, I give it to her, what's the odds. Here."

He brought one hand out of his pocket, and thrust a parcel at Annie. Then he turned with a jerk and walked away, his head lowered against the wind.

Annie closed the door and looked at the parcel. It was a small rectangular box wrapped in plain white paper. Perfume, Annie thought, and shook it to see if it gurgled. But the parcel remained noncommittal and neither gurgled nor rattled.

Briskly Annie mounted the steps and knocked on Lucille's door.

"Come in," Lucille said. "Yes, Annie?"

"A parcel for you," Annie said. "A funny little guy brought it."

"Man," Lucille said.

"A funny little man, then," Annie said. "Don't you think my grammar is getting swell, Mrs. Morrow? Della noticed today, I sound just like you."

"Yes," Lucille said. "You're a very clever girl."

"Oh, I'm not really clever," Annie said modestly. "I just figure, here is my chance to get cultured so I try to get cultured."

"That will be all, Annie."

"I figure, chances don't grow on trees. I could be making more in a war plant but what would I be learning, I tell Della."

Lucille waited in silence and after a time the silence penetrated into Annie's consciousness and she turned, with a small sigh, and went out.

She had barely reached the kitchen when she heard the scream. It rushed through the house like a wind and was gone.

"My goodness," Della said. "What was that?"

The two girls looked at each other uncertainly.

"I guess it was her," Annie said. "I never heard her scream before. Maybe she twisted her ankle. Maybe I better go up and see."

But when Annie went up Lucille's door was locked.

"Mrs. Morrow," Annie called. "Mrs. Morrow. You hurt yourself?"

There was no answer, but Annie thought she heard breathing on the other side of the door.

"Hey," Annie said. "Mrs. Morrow!"

"Go away," Lucille said in a harsh whisper. "Go away. Don't bother me."

"Della and me, we figured you twisted your ankle or something. . . ."

"Go away!" Lucille screamed.

Her spirit bruised, Annie returned to the kitchen.

"Well, I like that," she told Della. "You hear her? She *yelled* at me."

"And her usually so quiet," Della said. "But then she's just at the age. Sometimes they go off like that." Della snapped her fingers.

"Who?" Annie said.

"Women," Della said mysteriously. "At that age. Hysterics and fits over nothing. Maybe she didn't like what was in the parcel. Say it was jools, emeralds, say, and she didn't like them. Say she gives them to us."

"To us," Annie breathed. "Oh, Lordy."

"A necklace, say."

The silverware was forgotten. The emeralds were sold, except two. ("We should keep one apiece," Della said.) The money was invested in war bonds ("I believe in war bonds," Annie said), and flowered chiffon dresses and mink coats ("Exactly alike," Della said. "Wouldn't that be cute?" "Except you're fatter than I am," Annie said).

The argument over a red roadster was interrupted by the ringing of the telephone.

"Red," said Annie, "is vulgar," and picked up the telephone.

"Yes, Dr. Morrow. Yes, I'll call her, Dr. Morrow."

She turned and hissed at Della, "Him. For her. You go and tell her."

"Well, I won't," Della said. "Nobody can call me vulgar and expect favors all the time."

Stubbornly, she turned her back, and Annie, seeing that nothing short of a sharp pinch would move her, decided to go herself.

When she arrived upstairs the door of Lucille's room was open and Lucille was missing. Annie called out several times, and then, in a fit of exasperation, she searched Lucille's room and the adjoining bathroom, and the room beyond that, which belonged to Andrew.

Della was called, and the two girls looked through the entire second floor, now and then calling, "Mrs. Morrow." The silence made them nervous and each time they called their voices were shriller and higher.

Clinging together they came down the stairs and switched on all the lights. The house ablaze with light no longer seemed so quiet, and Annie moved almost boldly ahead into the living room.

"Wait," Della said. "I thought I heard something. I thought I heard a—a footstep."

"You heard no such thing," Annie said, shaken.

"Oh, I don't like this," Della moaned. "She's done away with herself. Things like that happen at her age. Oh, I wish people would hurry up and come home."

"She didn't do away with herself, we would've found the corpse."

Once the idea of death had entered their heads the girls became too frightened even to talk. Silently they went through all the rooms on the first floor.

There was no trace of Lucille Morrow or the box she had received.

The girls returned to the kitchen and the more familiar scene loosened their tongues.

"Maybe it was really emeralds," Della said, "and instead of giving them to us she's gone out to throw them away, say, or have them reset."

"How could she go out?" Annie said. "Weren't we sitting here in these very chairs? Did anybody ever come in or go out that I don't know about, I ask you."

"We could go up again and see if any of her coats are missing."

"I don't want to."

"I was just saying we could."

Annie's curiosity was whetted. A minute later the girls were on their way upstairs again.

In the clothes closet Lucille's dresses hung, ready to be worn, and the shoes lay on the racks ready to be stepped into.

"It's like looking at a dead person's things," Della whispered. "You know, after they're dead when you sort out their clothes and there they are all ready only nobody to wear them."

"Oh, shut up," said Annie, intent on studying the coats.

"I got a funny feeling, Annie."

"Oh, you and your feelings. It would serve you right if she walked in here right this minute and fired us both for getting into her things."

Dreading this possibility, and yet feeling that it would be an improvement on their present situation, they cast longing fearful glances toward the doorway.

But Lucille didn't walk through the door and neither of the girls ever saw her again.

They returned to the kitchen and Della suddenly noticed that the telephone receiver was still dangling on its wire. Instead of merely presenting this fact to Annie, Della, true to her nature, opened her mouth, put one hand over it and with the other hand pointed toward the telephone.

Annie, whose back was to it, gave a shriek and swung round to meet whatever doom Della's open mouth and quaking finger indicated.

Seeing only the telephone she whispered, faint with relief, "I thought—I thought you saw—something."

"Him," Della said. "You forgot *him*."

"Oh, Lordy."

"You better phone him back."

"Oh, Lordy, he'll be mad."

But Annie did not give him a chance to be mad. She told him immediately and bluntly that his wife had disappeared.

"Have you gone crazy, Annie?" Andrew demanded.

"Plumb disappeared, Dr. Morrow, honestly."

"Annie, kindly . . ."

"Oh, I know how it sounds, Dr. Morrow, nobody can tell me how it sounds. Della and me, we're *scared*. We been through all the rooms except ours and there ain't a trace of her, I tell you."

"Where's my sister?" Andrew said. "Let me speak to her."

"She didn't come back yet."

"Then you two incompetents are there alone?"

"Della and me," Annie said huffily, "we may not have an education but we got eyes and Mrs. Morrow has plumb disappeared. Right after the man brought the box we heard her scream and I went up and she told me to beat it. And that's the last thing she said to me on this earth."

"I'll be right home," Andrew said. "Meanwhile don't get hysterical. Mrs. Morrow very likely went out for a walk."

"Without a *coat*?" Annie said, and paused slyly.

"What's this about a coat?"

"Her coats are all in her closet. Della and me, we looked and they're all there."

"See here, Annie," Andrew said in a calm voice, "don't get excited. You know Mrs. Morrow fairly well by this time. Has she ever done anything that wasn't practical and reasonable?"

"N-no, sir."

"Then hold the fort until I get there."

"Maybe it wasn't something she done, maybe it was something somebody done *to* her."

But Andrew had already hung up. Slowly Annie did the same and turned to face a feverish-looking Della.

"But there's nobody here," Della said.

"Maybe not."

"Oh, you're trying to scare me again! What'd he say?"

"He's coming home."

"Right away?"

"That's what he said. He don't believe us. He says she went

for a walk. A walk in this weather in a short-sleeved dress, I ask you. And anyway does she ever go for walks?"

"Not that I know of," Della agreed. "But you can't tell at her age."

"I'm sick of hearing about her age."

They were silent a moment. Then Della said wistfully, "We could talk about the emeralds again. You want to?"

"Sure."

"We'd keep one apiece. How many do you think there was in the first place?"

"Fifty," Annie said listlessly.

"Fifty, imagine that! They'd be worth a million. What'd be the very *first* thing you'd buy, Annie?"

"A dress, I guess."

"I'd buy a black-chiffon nightgown."

The game went on, but the emeralds had turned into green glass.

Shortly before six o'clock Andrew arrived home with Martin. Hand in hand, for moral support, the two girls came out into the hall.

"Well?" Andrew said, with a trace of irritation. "Mrs. Morrow back yet?"

Annie shook her head. "No, sir."

"You said over the phone that you looked through the whole house except your own rooms?"

"We didn't look there because what would she be doing up there? You think we should go up there now?"

"Don't bother," Andrew said and turned to Martin. "Run up to the third floor, will you, just as a precaution."

"All right." Martin flung his coat and hat on the hall table and ascended the steps, two at a time.

Andrew took off his own coat in a leisurely manner. "What are all the lights on for?"

"Della and me, we felt better with them on," Annie said. "Della's got bad nerves."

"It wasn't just me," Della muttered.

"Turn off some of the lights," Andrew said.

His refusal to get excited made the girls calmer. Della's mind began to function again and she went out to the kitchen to start preparing dinner, leaving Annie to tell about the man with the parcel.

Annie couldn't remember whether the man was short or tall,

dark or fair, young or old. She knew only that he was sinister.

"By sinister no doubt you mean shabby?" Andrew said dryly. "Go on."

"The light was dim and I didn't notice him much because he should've come to the back door."

Andrew listened patiently as she described the box and the conversation. But Annie noticed that he kept one eye on the steps waiting for Martin to return.

Martin came back, looking partly amused, partly exasperated. "Crazy as it sounds," he said, "she's gone."

His father silenced him with a look and turned to Annie. "All right, Annie, you may go. It's simply a matter of waiting for Mrs. Morrow to come back."

"What gets me," Annie said, "is the coats."

"What coats?" Martin said.

"You may go, Annie," Andrew repeated sharply.

Annie left, and remarked to Della that never ever until today had Dr. Morrow or Mrs. Morrow spoken roughly to her.

Left alone in the hall Andrew and Martin glanced uneasily at each other.

"Crazy as hell, isn't it?" Martin said. "A grown and capable woman goes out of the house and everyone begins to imagine things."

"If she went, she went without a coat. Annie says there is none missing. Come in here. I don't want those two to hear us."

They went into Andrew's den and closed the door.

"She might have slipped over to a neighbor's house," Martin said, avoiding his father's eye.

"She doesn't know the neighbors. Lucille's not like that."

"How do you know? She might do some calling that she doesn't tell you about."

Andrew blinked. "What are you implying?"

"Nothing. Just that you can't know everything about a person."

"That's true. But in fifteen years you get a fairly accurate impression, you can anticipate reactions." He reached for the decanter on his desk. "Drink?"

"Thanks," Martin said.

"This is practically the first time I've ever come home without having Lucille greet me. No doubt that sounds dull to you, Martin."

"Pretty dull," Martin said, and at the mere mention of dullness and constriction and boredom he felt incredibly vital and alive.

He wanted to fling himself out of the chair, to stretch, to jump, to run, to make noises. He felt his muscles go taut, and he had to force himself to keep his feet still.

Andrew noticed the tension but misunderstood the cause.

"What did you mean, that Lucille might do some calling that she doesn't tell me about?"

"Good Lord, I wasn't slandering her. I simply meant that she wouldn't tell you every little thing she did for fear of boring you. She's a quiet person anyway."

"Yes. Annie said she screamed."

"Screamed?" Martin said. "Lucille? What about?"

"She wouldn't tell Annie." Andrew leaned his head on his hands. He looked grayer and more tired than Martin had ever seen him look before.

How old he is, Martin thought, how old and settled. Intolerant of age and inactivity, Martin began impatiently to move the stuff about on Andrew's desk. He emptied and then filled a pen, he rearranged some books, he scribbled his name on the blotter and he folder a page from the memo pad into a fan.

"Being a doctor's wife," Andrew said, "is a hard job. Being a second wife doesn't make it easier. Yet Lucille has never complained. What's that you're staring at?"

"Nothing," Martin said. "A piece of paper. Somebody's burned holes in it with a cigarette."

"Put it down then, and don't fidget. You're as jumpy as Edith."

"Odd."

"What?"

"These pictures. They look like my mother. Somebody's burned the eyes out."

"What? Give it to me." Andrew took the paper and looked at it briefly. "Nonsense. Not a bit like your mother."

"I think so."

"More implications, Martin?"

"Not at all," Martin said politely, and tossed the paper aside as if it suddenly bored him.

"You believe," Andrew said, "that Lucille drew pictures of Mildred and then mutilated them?"

"Oh, what does it matter?"

"It matters to me. If you like, when Lucille comes back home I'll ask her."

"Good Lord, no!"

"I insist on asking her," Andrew said.

Martin pounded his fist on the desk. Nearly all of his arguments with his father left him with this feeling of helpless rage against Andrew's naïvete. After twenty-five years of being a doctor Andrew seemed never to have lost his faith in human nature. Martin, who had no faith in anyone but himself and no religious convictions beyond the basic one that he was God, alternately respected and despised his father.

The two men watched each other across the width of the desk. The return of Lucille was now an issue between them, and their faces had a waiting look.

At six-thirty Edith arrived. She had left Polly and Giles dining at the Oak Room and had rushed home in the conviction that everything would go wrong in the house if she didn't.

The fact that everything had already gone wrong was explained to her vividly by Annie as soon as she opened the door. After the first shock was over Edith plunged into the mystery and upset the whole house with her splashing and churning.

It was Edith who discovered that Lucille's black-suede purse and the housekeeping money for the rest of the month were missing. Della and Annie vigorously denied going near the drawer where Lucille kept her purses. Edith believed them.

"So," she told Andrew, "Lucille must have taken it herself."

"But why?"

"I don't know. Perhaps she wanted to go out and buy something, that's the simplest explanation."

"She wasn't wearing a coat."

"Nonsense," Edith said. "I'm not pretending to know *why* she went out but I refuse to believe any sensible person would go out in this weather without a coat. She may have worn one of mine."

Edith's coats, however, were all found in her closet.

It was Della who backed up Edith's belief in what a sensible woman would do. Della had gone up to her room on the third floor to change her uniform. Her discarded one, tear-stained because Edith had called her a moron, she tossed into the closet. She saw that someone had disarranged the clothes.

A few minutes later she came down the stairs wailing.

"My money," she screamed at Edith. "My coat and money! She took it! She's a thief, a common thief!"

Twenty dollars and a reversible raincoat had been taken from Della's closet. The coat, beige gabardine on one side and red-plaid wool on the other, was practically new and not even a fifty-dollar check mended Della's broken heart.

Though the manner of Lucille's departure now seemed to be explained, for Edith the taking of Della's coat merely deepened the mystery.

"Why Della's coat?" she said. "Why not one of her own? It's as if—as if she was escaping and didn't want anyone to recognize her."

"No," Andrew said. "No, I don't believe it."

"And the money . . . Yes, Andrew, she ran away."

"The girls swear they didn't hear her go out. They went upstairs and looked for her."

"That was when she got out," Edith said. "She ran up to hide in Della's room while they were looking through hers. When they went downstairs again and were searching the living room she came down with the coat and the purse and the money. . . ."

She put her hand over her eyes to blot out the picture. How vivid it seemed, how grotesquely easy it was for the mind to twist Lucille's placid smile into a crafty grin, to add slyness to the quiet eyes, and furtiveness to the sure slow movements of her body.

Perhaps I look like that to someone, Edith thought. We are all protected by a veil of trust. I must think of her as she was.

But the veil was already torn and the crafty grin and the furtiveness became clearer. Suspicions grew in Edith's mind like little extra eyes.

"And then," Edith said, "she simply went out the back door while the girls were in the living room."

"Simply," Andrew said with a sharp mirthless laugh. *"Simply!"*

Edith flushed. "I'm terribly sorry, Andrew."

"Sorry! Another magnificent understatement, my dear. I don't want you to be sorry for having spoken your mind. If you believe that my wife is a thief and perhaps worse, you can't help it. Any more than Martin can help it."

"I haven't said anything," Martin said. "Yet."

"Keep quiet, Martin," Edith said. She went over to Andrew and placed her hand on his shoulder. "Andrew, I'm sorry, I don't know what to think."

He smiled up at her, wryly. "Then why think? If Lucille went away she had a reason to go. She'll be back."

Edith and Martin exchanged glances over his head.

"And if she had a reason," Andrew continued, "she had a right to go. People should be allowed a certain freedom of movement. They shouldn't get the feeling that they are constantly required to be some place at some specific time. They should have certain periods when nothing whatever is expected from them."

"This is very like a lecture," Edith said coldly, "directed against me."

"Perhaps deservedly, Edith. You're a driver. You can't help it, I know, any more than I can help allowing myself to be driven, for the sake of peace."

"What has all this to do with Lucille?"

"Nothing," Andrew said. "Nothing at all. I was just talking."

"You aren't usually so talkative."

"I keep thinking," he said with a vague gesture, "I keep thinking, suppose when she was up in her room she had a feeling that she was in prison, that she must suddenly escape, that the very walls were a weight on her. When I feel like that I escape to my office, I run like a hare back to my pregnant women, my neurotic young girls, my ladies with cysts and sorrows and headaches and backaches and constipation. . . ."

"Really, Andrew!" Edith said, frowning.

"Women," Andrew said. "I don't know how many there are in the world, but I think I've seen half of them and they're all constipated."

"Father had a couple of drinks before you came," Martin said.

"You *know* you can't drink, Andrew," Edith said, annoyed. "It goes to your head."

"Please go away, Edith. Please go away back and sit down some place."

But Edith refused. She was as incapable of sitting down as she was of keeping quiet. Pacing the room she went over all the facts again, returning in the end to the unanswerable question, *why?*

"Why?" Martin echoed. "Perhaps Father's right. She felt like that, and off she went."

Edith shook her head. "No, that's quite incredible. You know what a thoroughly sensible person Lucille is. If she felt like that she would simply have gone for a nice long walk or something."

"People aren't always capable of making sense," Andrew said in a strange voice. "There are forces—forces in the mind . . ." He leaned forward and fixed his eyes on her. "Look, Edith. See, it's like a jungle, the mind, dark and thick, with a million little paths that the light never reaches. You never know the paths are there until something pops out of one of them. Then, Edith, you might try to trace it back looking for its spoor and tracks, and you go so far, just so far, but the path is too twisted, too lightless, soundless, timeless . . ."

Edith was standing with her mouth open, and quite suddenly she began to cry. She cried not for Andrew's sake or Lucille's, but from sheer exasperation, because two people in whom she had placed her trust had betrayed her by stepping out of character. She saw Andrew as a dear little boy who suddenly and incongruously grows a long gray beard.

She brushed away her tears with the back of her hand, angrily conscious that Martin was looking at her with dismay, and Andrew with a kind of detached interest.

She averted her face and said stiffly, "You're implying that Lucille has gone crazy?"

"No," Andrew said, his voice mild again, and a little tired. "No, I think she . . ."

"It would be far more to the point to investigate the man who brought the parcel to her. However dark a jungle my mind is, Andrew, I am still capable of logic. Whatever prompted Lucille to go away, the man with the parcel is connected with it. That's the only out-of-the-ordinary thing that's happened to her."

"No," Andrew said, "there's one other, isn't there? Giles Frome."

"What on earth would Giles have to do with it?"

"Probably nothing. Like yourself I'm simply being logical."

"Good Lord," Martin said. "I haven't been able to get a word in. I agree with Edith about the man with the parcel. The trouble is finding him."

"What are the police for?" Edith said.

"The police," Martin said dryly, "are for finding people."

4

"MY WIFE," Andrew said, "has disappeared."

"Ah," Inspector Bascombe said, and folded his big square hands on the desk in front of him. He was a heavy, sour-looking man with bitter little eyes that seemed to fling acid on everyone they saw.

He was thinking, so your wife has disappeared. Yours and a couple of thousand others'. Including mine. With an electrician from Hull.

"The details, please," he said without inflection.

"They're rather peculiar."

Why, sure they are, Bascombe thought. The details are always peculiar. What isn't peculiar is how the wives turn up again when they're left flat and broke. Except mine.

He said, "Sit down, Dr. Morrow, and make yourself comfortable. There's rather a long form to be filled out, her description and so forth."

Bascombe watched him as he sat down. He felt very glad that Morrow's wife had disappeared because Morrow was the kind of man he hated most, next to electricians. Goddam whiskey ad, he thought. Men of achievement, men of tomorrow. Even the top drawer have women troubles, what a goddam shame.

Thinking of whiskey ads reminded him of the bottle of Scotch he had hidden in the files. He tried to forget it again by being extra crisp and businesslike.

"Name?"

"Lucille Alexandra Morrow."

He wrote rapidly. Lucille Alexandra Morrow. Female. White. Age forty-five. Red-gold hair, long; blue eyes, fair skin, no distinguishing marks.

The red-gold hair reminded him of the Scotch again. His hand jerked across the paper leaving a spray of ink.

He looked up to see if Morrow had noticed, but Morrow wasn't watching him. He had his eyes fixed on the lettering on the glass door—Department of Missing Persons.

"Kind of fascinates you, doesn't it," Bascombe laughed. "I read it a million times a day."

Make it two million, and every time, I get a cold wet feeling in the gut. The Missing Persons. Some of them will never be found, some will come back by themselves, drunk or sick or broke or just tired. And some of them will come up from the mud at the bottom of the river in April or May, the ladies on their backs, and the gentlemen face down.

He got up abruptly, and the pen rolled across the desk. Muttering something under his breath he went into the next room and closed the door behind him.

Sergeant D'arcy, a small rosy-cheeked young man who looked a little too elegant in his uniform, glanced up from his desk.

"Yes, sir?" he said.

"Get the hell in there," Bascombe said thickly. "Some guy's lost his wife. Take it all down. I feel rotten."

"Yes, sir" D'arcy said, riffling some papers efficiently. "Is there anything I can do, sir?"

"What I've already told you to do."

"I meant aside from . . ."

"Scram, lovely."

When D'arcy had gone Bascombe removed the bottle of Scotch from the back of the Closed Cases M to N file. D'arcy, who was listening, heard the gurgle of liquid, and thought, poor Bascombe, he had a truly great brain but he was drinking on duty again and would have to be reported.

To Andrew, D'arcy presented his fine teeth, brushed for five minutes in the morning and five at night.

"Inspector Bascombe had a slight touch of indigestion. He asked me to continue for him."

He picked up the form, noticing at once the spray of ink. *Poor Bascombe.*

"Now, of course," he said, "we require a few more details. Has Mrs. Morrow ever gone away like this before?"

"Never."

"There is no evidence of coercion?"

"None," Andrew hesitated, "that I know of."

"Did she have any reason for leaving, to your knowledge, any domestic upsets and the like?"

"None."

"No other man involved, of course?"

Andrew looked at him with cold dislike. "There has never been any other man involved in her life except her first husband, George Lanvers. He's been dead for nearly twenty years."

"We have to ask certain questions," D'arcy said, flushing. "We really do."

"I understand that."

"We . . ." D'arcy paused and looked hopefully toward the door.

He wished Bascombe would come back. He didn't like asking people questions, he didn't even like the Department. Or Bascombe.

He cocked his head, listening for sounds in the outer office. As soon as he heard one he excused himself and went out.

Bascombe had gone, but three people were waiting on the benches along the wall. One of them, an elderly well-dressed woman, D'arcy was able to dismiss immediately. She had come every day for nearly six months looking for her son.

"Sorry, Mrs. Granger," D'arcy said.

She seemed quite cheerful. "No news from Barney yet? He'll turn up. One of these days he'll be turning up and surprising me."

She went out briskly. The two men rose and came over to D'arcy. They were in the fur business and they had sold a mink coat to a man named Wilson for cash. The cash had turned out to be counterfeit and Wilson and the coat were missing.

D'arcy referred them, with a superior smile, to another department. But he wasn't feeling superior. He had the sinking sensation that he always got when he was required to do any thinking for himself.

The door opened and Bascombe came back in.

"The doctor still here?" he asked.

"Yes, sir. It seems to be a very interesting case."

"Aren't they all."

"I wish—I think you should talk to him personally."

Bascombe's face was flushed and his eyes were a little glassy. "Thanks for the advice, D'arcy."

"Well, but I really mean it, sir. Dr. Morrow looks as if he might have considerable influence."

"The only kind of influence I care about comes in quart bottles," Bascombe said, but he laughed, almost good-naturedly, and went back into his own office.

It was nearly noon when he came out again with Dr. Morrow. Morrow left immediately, looking, D'arcy noticed, pretty grim.

Bascombe was smiling all over his face. "A very nice case. The lady disappeared with all the money she could get her hands on, wearing one of her maid's coats. A reversible coat. Get it?"

"No, sir."

"Plaid on one side, beige on another. She can switch them around and make it harder for us to find her. Inference, she's not coming back and she doesn't want to be found. So just for the hell of it we'll find her. Get your notebook."

"Yes, sir."

"All right. The usual checkups first, hospital and morgue and her bank—Bloor and Ossington Branch of the Bank of Toronto. I think you'll draw blanks there. Morrow's going to send over a couple of studio portraits by messenger. Meanwhile, start calling beauty parlors."

"All of the beauty parlors?" D'arcy said faintly.

"Use your noodle and you won't have to. If the woman is really in earnest about disappearing, she'll probably try to disguise her most distinctive feature, her hair, and then grab a train or bus for out-of-town."

"And the bus terminals and stations being mostly in the south and west I'm to try those sections first?"

"Amazing," Bascombe said. "Beauty *and* brains you have, D'arcy. I'm going out to lunch. Be back later."

When he had gone D'arcy did a little checking-up on his own and discovered that the bottle of Scotch was missing from the file.

"Poor Bascombe," he said sadly. "I'll have to report him. It's my duty."

He didn't want to report Bascombe, who was a fine figure of a man, really.

He sat down at his desk and picked up the telephone directory. D'arcy was at his best on a telephone, he could forget how small he was and how the other policemen didn't like him and kept shunting him back and forth from one department to another.

While he was working Kirby came in. He was a big loose-jointed young man who spent half his time around the morgue and the hospitals.

"It's about time someone appeared," D'arcy said. "I haven't had my lunch. I'm hungry."

"Too bad." Kirby took off his hat and stretched and yawned. "Where's Bascombe?"

"I'm sure I don't know. He doesn't confide in me."

"He owes me five bucks on the Macgregor girl. I found her this morning. She's in a ward at Western with a nice case. Says she got it in a washroom."

"People," D'arcy said primly, "should behave themselves."

Pointedly, he returned to the telephone. He worked nearly all afternoon with one eye on the door, waiting for Bascombe to come back.

At four-thirty he became quite excited by a telephone conversation he had with Miss Flack, who owned and operated the Sally Ann hairdressing parlor in Sunnyside. He tried to get Bascombe's apartment on the wire. Nobody answered.

"I'll report him," D'arcy whispered. "I really will. It's *high time*."

He went up to Sands' office.

The Allen Hotel is on a little street off College. A red-brick building, caked with soot, it has passed through many phases in its long life. It has been, in turn, a private hospital, a barracks, an apartment house, and a four-bit flophouse. The Liquor Act was passed just in time to save it from the wreckers. A few licks of paint, extra chairs and tables, a new neon sign and a license to sell beer and wine transformed the old building into the Allen Hotel, a fairly prosperous tavern with a dubious clientele. The clientele was kept under control by a large tough bartender and a number of printed prohibitions which were strictly enforced: No checks cashed. No credit. No spitting.

There were other prohibitions also, but these were not printed on signs. The bartender attended to them himself. He would sidle up behind a customer and say gently, "No pimps," or sometimes, "No fairies."

Not that he gave a damn about them but he was afraid of the health and liquor inspectors that came around. He didn't want the place to close up. With his salary and the rakeoff he got from the beer salesmen he was buying a house out in the east end for his family.

Through his efforts the Allen Hotel got quite a good name with the various inspectors. They didn't bother much about it any more. The word was passed around, and a number of people who didn't want to come in contact with the law began to use the rooms upstairs. It was ironical, but in one way it wasn't so bad. The bartender soaked up information like a blotter. Some of it he sold, some of it he gave away to his friend Sands. From Sands, in return, he got the pleasant feeling that he was on the good side of the law, and that if a time came when he wasn't, there was at least one honest policeman in the world.

He took personal pride in Sands and followed all his cases in the newspapers. Whenever Sands came in for a drink or some information the bartender's face would take on a sly, conspiratorial smile because here were all these bums drinking side by side with a real detective and not knowing it. Sometimes he was so pleased he had to go into the can and roar with laughter.

Today he wasn't so pleased. He leaned across the counter and spoke out of the side of his mouth.

"Mr. Sands."

"Hello, Bill," Sands said, sitting on the bar stool.

"Mr. Sands, there's a friend of yours in the back booth. Been here nearly all day. I would sure like to lose him."

"Bascombe?"

The bartender nodded. "This is no kind of place for a policeman to get drunk in. I wouldn't want anything to happen to Mr. Bascombe." He grinned suddenly. "Not unless it was fatal."

"I'll talk to him," Sands said. "Bring me a small ale."

He got off the bar stool, a thin tired-looking middle-aged man with features that fitted each other so perfectly that few people could remember what he looked like. His clothes blended in with the rest of him, they were gray and rather battered and limp. He moved unobtrusively to the back of the room.

Bascombe was sitting alone in the booth with his head in his hands.

"Bascombe."

No answer.

"Bascombe." Sands knocked away Bascombe's elbows. Bascombe's head lolled and then righted itself. His eyes didn't open.

"Don't mind if I do," Bascombe said huskily. "Make it double."

Sands sat down on the other side of the booth and sipped his ale patiently. Pretty soon Bascombe blinked his eyes open and looked across the table at him.

"Oh, for Christ's sake," he said, "it's you. Go away, Sands, go away, my boy. You have this elfin habit of appearing suddenly. I don't like it. It's upsetting."

"D'arcy's been looking for you," Sands said.

"Trouble with D'arcy is his brassiere's too tight."

"You'd better come to and listen. D'arcy's got his knife in you."

"Sure, I know," Bascombe said. "I got sick of him following me around and maybe I talked a little rough to him."

"He reported you for drinking on duty."

Bascombe blinked again. "Who to?"

"To me."

"As long as it was to you."

"Maybe next time it won't be," Sands said. "How many times is this that Ellen's left you?"

"Five," Bascombe said, his face twisting. "Yeah. Five. In three years."

"I suppose it's no use my pointing out that Ellen is a little tramp?" Sands said dryly. "She isn't housebroken. You can't do anything with that kind but leave them. Get a divorce, Bascombe." Bascombe didn't answer. "If it'll make it easier for you, I could have you transferred to another department. That's D'arcy's suggestion."

"That goddam little . . ."

"Sure, but even D'arcy hits it on the button sometimes. I think he's right. He said you were fussed up this A.M. over some doctor whose wife is missing."

"I can't help thinking of Ellen."

"That's what I mean. Incidentally D'arcy thinks he's traced the doctor's wife as far as some hairdressing shop down near Sunnyside."

"How do you know so much about it?"

"Oh, I've been interested in the Morrow family for a long time," Sands said, and picked up his glass again. "For about sixteen years, I guess. Get your coat on."

"What for? I'm not going any place."

"Yes, you are. I spent an hour and a half looking for you. I told D'arcy that you were out doing some work for me and that I'd pick you up and take you down to Sunnyside. Get your coat."

"You're an easy guy to hate, Sands. You're so goddam right all the time, aren't you, so goddam sure of yourself."

Sands said nothing. He never talked about himself, and he didn't like to listen to other people talk about him. It seemed unreal to him, as if they must be talking about someone else.

He left Bascombe struggling with his overcoat and went ahead to the bar.

The bartender was rinsing glasses. He stopped work and wiped his hands.

"He going with you, Mr. Sands?"

"Yes."

"Jesus," Bill said. "You must be a regular one of those guys that the rats followed."

"A nice description," Sands said. Great rats, small rats, lean rats, brawny rats . . .

"Human nature is sure a funny thing," Bill said. "Take me, how big I am, and take you, how small you are, and here I couldn't do a thing with Mr. Bascombe, and he follows you like a lamb. You must have plenty muscle that don't show."

"Any eight-year-old could knock me off my pins."

"Jesus, Mr. Sands, you shouldn't talk like that." Bill was offended. "It might get around."

Bascombe came up. He had his overcoat buttoned wrong but he walked straight and his voice had lost its thickness.

"Bye, Billy-boy," he said to the bartender. "When they kick me off the force let's make a date in a dark alley."

"I'd like that fine," the bartender said thoughtfully.

When the two policemen had gone Bill returned to the glasses. Officially the Allen Hotel had been open all day but it was after dark that business got heavy. Bill had a couple of waiters who came in around seven. When there was a rush on he helped serve but most of the night he spent sizing up the customers and easing out drunks and keeping an eye on the money. At the Allen any bill over five dollars was automatically considered phony until Bill had passed on it.

Tuesday night was the slowest of the week and only one thing happened that Bill felt Sands should know about. A little ex-con and hophead called Greeley came in with a red-headed fat woman. The woman Bill recognized as a floozie from a house down the street. But it took him several minutes to recognize Greeley. He had on a brand-new topcoat and a new green fedora. But the newest thing about Greeley was his expression. He acted like a millionaire who had to rub shoulders with a rough mob.

"Well, well," Bill said. "*Mister* Greeley. Pardon me while I catch my breath. And is this charming lady Mrs. Greeley?"

The woman giggled, but Greeley gave him a sour look and led the woman to one of the tables. Bill followed them.

"If I'd known you was coming, Mr. Greeley, I'd have got out my Irish-lace tablecloth, sure as hell."

"Champagne," Greeley said, and sat down without taking off his hat and coat.

"Teaspoon or tablespoon?" Bill said. The woman giggled again.

Greeley laid a fifty-dollar bill on the table.

Bill did everything to the bill but chew it up, and it still looked good.

When the bottle of champagne was gone Greeley had lost his sour look and was beginning to talk big. Bill stood as near the table as he could and now and then he caught a snatch of Greeley's talk.

"I don't want to spend the rest of my life bouncing in and out of Kingston for rolling drunks and picking pockets. Listen, Sue, I'm on to something. You climb on the wagon with me, baby."

"Sure," the woman said. "Sure. Anything you say."

"The kinda life we lead we don't get respect for ourselves. Something high class, that's what I got, something classy and steady. Look around this dump, look at it."

The woman obliged.

"Ain't it a dump?" Greeley said. "Couple of days ago this was my idea of a big night, getting tanked in a dump like this with a chance to get fixed up after."

"Well, what are we sitting here for if you're so high class?"

"Saying good-bye," Greeley said solemnly. "Saying good-bye to a crappy life like this. From now on you'll be covered with diamonds."

"The hell with diamonds. I want a square meal."

Greeley ordered a couple of hamburgers and another bottle of champagne.

The woman ate the hamburgers, biting on them as if her teeth hurt.

Three soldiers at the bar began to sing and Bill couldn't hear what Greeley was saying now. But he guessed it was the same kind of stuff. Greeley was leaning across the table being very intense while the woman chewed and watched him with a where-have-I-heard-this-before expression in her eyes.

Around ten they got up to go out and Bill noticed that Greeley's pants were badly frayed at the bottom. He hurried over to the till to test the fifty-dollar bill again.

Greeley saw him and flung him a contemptuous smile. Bill followed him to the door.

"Good night, *Mister* Greeley," he said. "You'll be back, we hope not."

The woman giggled and said, "Honest, you're a scream."

Greeley grabbed her arm. "You never laugh at nothing *I* say."

The woman pushed him away coolly. "At you I'm laughing all the time. I just gotta stop myself or I'd die."

"Good-bye, Wisenheim," Greeley said to Bill, opening the door. "Come and see me at the Royal York."

"They still taking on dishwashers? I bet you look cute in an apron."

A final giggle from the woman and then the door slammed.

Wish my wife would laugh like that at everything I say, Bill thought. She's got no sense of humor.

He went over to the soldiers. "Better quiet down, boys. I just saw a couple of M.P.s go past the door."

The soldiers quieted, and Tuesday night went on.

5

ON Tuesday Edith quarreled with nearly everyone in the house. She began with Andrew, who told her at breakfast time that he was going to report Lucille's disappearance to the police.

Edith raged and wept. It was too humiliating, it was too shameful. How would they ever hold their heads up again?

Andrew had left without even bothering to argue. Frustrated, Edith turned her anger on Martin. How *could* Martin go to the office when they needed him? He must stay home, it was his duty . . .

Directly after breakfast Martin too left the house.

The most violent quarrel was in the evening. Edith was in the living room with Polly and Giles. She suggested that the wedding be postponed.

Polly gave her a long hard stare. "What for?"

"It wouldn't look right if you were married at a time like this."

"It wouldn't look right to whom?" Polly said. "You? Lucille?"

"People will talk."

"People always do. This is Giles' last furlough before he goes overseas."

"I know," Edith said tragically. "I know it's a terrible thing to have it spoiled like this. But couldn't you wait just a few days? Perhaps Lucille will be back then."

"I don't care a damn about Lucille," Polly said. "I never have. The only way I've been able to live in the same house with her was to ignore her, not to let her spoil things for me. Well, she's not going to spoil them now."

Giles tried not to listen to the two women. He looked down

at his hands, hardly recognizing them as his own he felt so unreal
and formless. He seemed to be moving through a nightmare, without the power to wake up and without the strength to protect
himself against the dim shapes of danger. Sometimes the house
was like a box and he was alone in it and on the ceiling of the
box there were shadows without cause and the walls moved slightly,
in and out, as if the box were breathing. Sometimes he stopped
to listen to it, and he heard his own breathing, surely it must be
his own, but it sounded as if someone were breathing along with
him in rhythm that wasn't quite perfect.

When he went into a room it always seemed that someone had
just left it. The air was stirring, and the door quivered.

"She's been very good to you," Edith was saying shrilly. "You
shouldn't talk like that about her in front of Giles."

"I talk the way I want to. I don't fake things."

"Nobody listens to me in this house! I won't have it! I forbid
you to be married until we find out about Lucille."

"I don't need permission," Polly said. She turned her back, but
Edith's voice clawed at her ears.

"What do you know about Giles? What do you know about
him?"

"I guess there isn't much to know," Giles said, and attempted
to smile. "I mean, I realize how queer it looks that Mrs. Morrow
should disappear the day after I arrive. But I assure you . . ."

"You must be crazy, Edith," Polly said in a cold flat voice.
"It's bad enough that Giles should have to be here at such a time,
without being accused by you."

"She said he reminded her of someone," Edith cried, flinging
herself violently into this new idea. "You can't tell about people,
you can't believe anyone, you can't trust . . ."

Her voice snapped. She turned abruptly and ran out of the
room, the sleeves of her dress fluttering. She looked like a great
flapping bird with broken wings.

"Giles."

"Yes?"

"Let's get out of here. Now. Tonight."

"Can we?"

"No one can stop us. We'll just leave. Giles, go up and pack.
We can go to a hotel."

"All right." The ceiling of the box seemed to open and clear
cool air rushed in. "All right, we'll just leave."

"Oh, Giles."

The telephone in the hall began to ring.

"It surely looks like her," said Miss Betty Flack. "It surely does. But I can't be sure. I mean if it's important, with the police in it and all, then I can't be sure." Miss Flack handed back the photographs and added thoughtfully, "But it surely looks like her."

Over Miss Flack's platinum curls Bascombe and Sands exchanged glances.

"What I mean is," said Miss Flack with an elegant gesture, "I *think* it's her, all right. She came in just when I was closing the shop up and wanted to know if I did hair-cutting. Well, naturally I do, though my real specialty is cold waves."

"You cut her hair?" Sands said, gently guiding Miss Flack's mind back from the cold waves.

"I gave her a feather cut. Did you see *For Whom the Bell Tolls?* Well, like that. The girl in it, I mean. Mrs. Smith, she said that was her name, she didn't seem to care how I cut it, just sat there holding her purse. I noticed her shoes were wet and I like to make a little joke now and then with my customers, so I asked her, laughing-like, if she'd been in swimming down at the lake. She didn't think it was funny," Miss Flack said, adding fairly, "Maybe it wasn't."

"Didn't she say anything at all?" Sands asked.

"Just about how cold it was. I surely felt sorry for her with such a flimsy little coat on. She was such a *lady,* if you know what I mean, and so sort of *desperate* looking. I thought to myself at the time, maybe her husband drinks or something." Miss Flack had another of her thoughtful pauses. "He certainly *looked* as if he drank."

"Oh," Sands said, and Bascombe's hands twitched as if they wanted to get around Miss Flack's throat and choke something out of her. "Her husband came with her?"

"Not exactly. I mean, I don't know if he *came* with her, but when she went out I stood at the door getting a breath of fresh air and I saw this man waiting across the street. Mrs. Smith stopped and talked to him for a minute and then she walked ahead and he followed her. I remember thinking to myself at the time, isn't it a caution what women marry sometimes. She was so tall and handsome and he was just a little fellow."

"A little fellow," Sands said, and thought back sixteen years to the last time he'd seen Andrew Morrow. Morrow was about six foot three. Even making allowances for the fact that the light had been dim and Miss Flack's memory was of the vague and romantic order, Sands was sure that the man Mrs. Morrow met across the street had not been her husband.

It was easy enough to check. Sands asked Miss Flack for a telephone and while he was sitting in the booth looking in the directory for Morrow's number, he heard Miss Flack tell Bascombe that she herself was single, had a half-interest in the beauty parlor and liked great big men.

Sands dialed.

The door into the hall was still open and Polly and Giles heard Della answer the phone and then trot down the hall. A minute later Andrew came to the phone. They heard him say, "Hello. Yes, this is Dr. Morrow."

"Well," Polly said sharply, "do we listen or do we talk? Or do you go up and pack?"

"I will if you want me to."

"*If!*" Polly said bitterly. "Oh, well, nothing like a telephone ringing for breaking up moods, is there, Giles?" She clenched her hands and began to swear in an undertone. "Damn, damn, damn, damn."

Andrew's voice crept into the room. "Sands? No, I'm sorry I don't think I do remember. Sands." A pause, a change of tone. "Oh. Oh, yes." He cleared his throat. "I'm—I'm very glad you were able to—to get that far. S-sunnyside? No, I was at home. The maids were frightened and called me home from the office. Will you hold the line, please?"

Gray-lipped, he came to the door of the living room and shut it without saying anything.

"It's the police," Giles said. "I suppose they've found out something. I—Polly, what's the matter?"

Her shoulders were shaking and a film had spread over her eyes like ice over a river.

"Giles, it's that man, it's that same one. Sands. He came with a lot of men and I could see them from my window going over the snow. Parts of it were like red slush."

"I don't understand . . ."

"One of them, Sands, came in the house and sat over there,

in that chair. He just sat and looked at us, at Martin and me, for a long time. Martin kept laughing. I don't know why, but he kept on laughing and laughing."

She rose unsteadily and walked across the room and stood in front of Mildred's portrait. For a minute the implacable brown eyes stared into the mild and vacuous blue eyes.

Giles looked after her, puzzled. "Who is that?"

"My mother."

"Oh."

"She was quite young when she died." Polly turned around. Her face was hard and merciless. "Probably it's just as well. She was the type who would have run to fat."

Giles didn't want to look at her. He was always a little frightened of her. In their relationship it was Polly who was the realist, he the dreamer; she was the leader, he the follower.

"I'd better go up and tell Martin," she said. "He'll want to know."

"Do you still want to leave? Do you want me to go up and pack?"

"What?" she said, as if she had forgotten about it, had even forgotten him and who he was and why he was there. "I'll have to tell Martin."

"It was in the winter," Sands said. "For a couple of months there'd been stories of children being chased in the park on their way home from school. The stories were vague and nobody was ever arrested. Then one night Mildred Morrow was out visiting a friend. She didn't come home."

Sands paused. "The friend was a widow who lived in the next house. Her name was Lucille Lanvers. Her statement was that Mildred had left her house before eleven o'clock, ostensibly to go home. Dr. Morrow was at the hospital on a confinement case and when he returned at one o'clock Mildred Morrow still hadn't come home. He called his sister Edith who was in bed and they went over to Mrs. Lanvers' house. The three of them looked around the park for an hour or so and then called in the police.

"About six o'clock the next morning we found Mildred Morrow lying against a tree with her head split open. Her purse and some valuable jewels were missing. The weapon wasn't found but we were pretty sure it was an axe. There was a heavy snowfall during the night, the body was almost completely covered and while there were indentations in the snow where foot tracks had been they were useless to us."

"Who had the case?" Bascombe said.

"Inspector Hannegan. I was a patrolman at the time. I rode a motorcycle."

"Oh, for Christ's sake," Bascombe said. "A motorcycle."

Sands smiled quietly. "Sure. Hannegan figured the case was simple robbery and he had a great time hauling in all the boys who'd ever stolen a balloon from the dime store. As a favor, he let me fool around with the case from another angle. I got nowhere. There seemed to be no motive for the crime except robbery. I talked to the family and to Mrs. Lanvers, but I had no official standing. Then Hannegan got tired of the case and closed it after a few weeks."

"What was your verdict?"

"I had none. Dr. Morrow had an alibi. His sister Edith puzzled me, she's one of these rather unstable people, and I had an idea that she was jealousy fond of her brother and probably preferred him without a wife. Mrs. Lanvers was a quiet restrained woman, quite plain-looking, not as pretty as she is now, if her photographs don't lie. She was Mildred Morrow's best friend, and here again there was no motive but the vaguely possible one that she wanted Mildred's husband."

"And got him."

"Yes, but it's not unusual for a man to marry his wife's best friend. It's happening all the time, especially in cases like this where the man was profoundly in love with his wife. Morrow was crazy about Mildred. He was very sick for a long time after she was killed."

"And Lucille nursed him, I suppose," Bascombe said with a cynical smile.

"I don't know," Sands said. "But it was the children who worried me most. I don't know much about children and I found their reactions very queer. The girl was ten or eleven at the time. She acted as though nothing had happened and whenever I asked her a question she would stare at me and pretend she hadn't heard. The boy was a couple of years older, going to Upper Canada College at the time; he acted wild and crazy. He laughed a great deal and offered to fight me. He said he'd take me on with one hand tied behind his back provided I promised to keep clear of his spine which he'd had broken once in a football game."

"What happened to him?"

"He's now literary editor of the *Review*."

"My God!"

"The only one of the family I've seen since is the girl, Polly.
I came across her three years ago in court. She was testifying in
some charity case. She recognized me and turned her head away."

"Funny she remembered you."

"Yes. Funny. Her father didn't when I phoned. Anyway, Hannegan closed the investigation and I was called off. Now I think it's
opening again." He looked across at Bascombe. "Don't you?"

"Yeah," Bascombe said.

Miss Flack emerged from the small cubicle where she'd been
gilding the lily.

"It surely is nice of you to offer to drive me home." she said.
"To tell the honest truth I was scared to death when you said
you were policemen. Now I'm not a *bit* scared."

"Good for you," Sands said.

Miss Flack was deposited at her apartment.

"What now?" Bascombe said.

"We look around."

"I think somebody told me once that Toronto was fifteen miles
east and west and nine miles north and south."

"Is that a fact," Sands said.

"What I want to know is who's holding the baby, you or me?"

"We're sharing it until it's old enough to choose." The car shot
ahead almost as if it knew what direction to take, like a well-trained
horse. "I want to get to Mrs. Morrow first."

Mr. Greeley and his lady friend were at a dime-a-dance hall out
on the pier. Neither of them felt at home. The place was too
classy. Greeley was ashamed to take off his overcoat and show his
old suit. By the end of the second dance the sweat was pouring
down his neck and the effects of the champagne were wearing off.
Greeley needed something stronger than champagne.

"Let's get the hell out of here," he said.

"What for?" the woman said. "I'm having a swell time."

"Hell, if it's rear-bumping you want you can get it in a street
car and cheaper."

"We just get some place and then you want to go."

"I got a date, anyway. Come on."

He walked out, not even looking around to see if she followed.

When they were outside she said, "You got no manners, Eddy."

She buttoned her coat. The lake slapped at the pier with cold contemptuous hate.

"Jesus, Eddy, let's go home."

"Quit crabbing."

"I don't like it here."

"Well, for Christ's sake, wait a minute."

He pushed aside the flap of his overcoat, and stabbed something into his thigh through his clothes. His thigh felt sore but his mind began to see things right again, he had the right perspective now. Life was a stinker, but he, Greeley, had it licked.

Me, Greeley.

It was two o'clock in the morning when Sands called up again. Andrew hadn't gone to bed, he was sitting in his den with a book in his lap.

"Yes?" he said into the phone.

"Dr. Morrow? Inspector Sands. Could you get dressed . . ."

"I am dressed. What's happened?"

"I'm at the Lakeview Hotel. It's on Bleacher Street, right off the Boulevard, west of Sunnyside. Your—your wife is here."

"Yes . . . yes . . ." It was as if something had split inside his head and he had to talk above a terrible roaring. "Is she—she's all right?"

"She's alive," Sands said.

"She's sick, then? You say she's *sick?* I . . ."

Edith appeared at the door of the den, wrapped in an old plaid bathrobe. "What is it, Andrew? Tell me this instant! What is the matter?"

"I'm coming right away," Andrew said and laid down the phone.

"I'm going with you," Edith said. "Whatever it is I'm going with you, you can't face it alone."

Andrew looked at her, but he couldn't see her properly. She was just a blur of colors, a whirling chart of colors without form or meaning or substance. He didn't even feel his own hand pushing her aside, and though his legs moved, his feet didn't seem to touch the floor.

His eyes functioned but only if he looked at one thing at a time, one separate stationary thing, the door, the instrument bag packed and ready in the front seat of the car, a street lamp, a house, a tree.

She sat upright in a chair. Beside her the steam radiator was turned on and gave off blasts of noise and heat that smelled of paint. But her face remained cold and waxy and her eyes frozen.

"Mrs. Morrow . . ."

(There is a man in my room. Is it my room? No. Yes, my room. One man and another man. Two men.)

". . . I've phoned your husband. He's coming right away."

(What a lot of men in my room and so much talk.)

"If there's anything I could get you . . ."

(They might be talking to me.)

Bascombe shifted uneasily. "I don't think she hears you."

(But I do. You're making a mistake, young man. Young man? Old man? Two, anyway. Two, two.)

"Mrs. Morrow, I'd like to help you. If you can remember what happened to you . . ."

An expression moved across her face, softly, like a cat walking. She knew she must be clever now, these were her enemies.

(She was in the lake, she was swimming, and the water was cold and dark and the waves passionate against her and so strong. She saw a hand stretched out to help her, she reached for the hand and it pushed her savagely away, down, down, down, so black, so dying, dying.)

"Mrs. Morrow, here is your husband."

"Lucille—Lucille, darling . . ."

He came into the sweltering room. She turned her head very slowly and saw him hold out his hand to her.

She began to scream. The screams came out of her throat smoothly, almost effortlessly, like a song from a bird.

When the ambulance came she was still screaming.

The ambulance neglected to pick up Mr. Greeley. The headlights just missed him.

He was sitting in the alley behind the hotel propped up against the wall. The wind from the lake stabbed at his face but Greeley didn't mind it. Life was a stinker but he, Greeley, had it licked. The night was dark but full of bright dreams—warm women, silk, thick soft fur, velvet hills and soft snug places.

Dreaming, he passed into sleep and sleeping into death.

6

SHE felt safe again. Behind her there was an iron gate and a hundred doors that locked with a big key. One of the nurses kept the key in the palm of her hand all the time.

There were no steps, only inclines that you walked up with someone beside you talking pleasantly and impersonally, and then finally the last door, the last clink of a key and the enemy was shut out. The room had windows but no one could get in through them. On both sides there was steel mesh.

She went immediately to the windows and felt the mesh, knowing that the nurse was watching her and would report it to the superintendent. But she had to know the room was safe and the feel of the mesh under her fingers was reassuring.

"It's strong, isn't it?" she said.

"Oh, yes," the nurse said cheerfully. She was young, with blonde curls and a pretty smile. She looked trim and efficient, but her eyes seemed to be laughing as though they lived a secret giddy life of their own. "I'm Miss Scott."

"Miss Scott," Lucille repeated.

"We'll just unpack your clothes now and put them away, Mrs. —Morrow."

"Mrs. Morrow."

"You'll be sharing this room with Miss Cora Green. Miss Green is down in the library at the moment. I'm sure you'll like her very much. We all do."

She began to unpack Lucille's clothes, keeping the key flat in the palm of her left hand. She did not turn her back to Lucille or take her eyes off her, but her vigilance was unobtrusive. She talked pleasantly and steadily. When Lucille finally noticed how closely she was being watched she did not resent it. Miss Scott was so smooth. She gave the impression that she was being merely careful, not suspicious, cautious but not in the least mistrustful.

"What a pretty blue dress," Miss Scott said. "Almost matches your eyes, doesn't it? I think we'll save that one for the movie night."

"I didn't know I was to share a room."

"We find it's better to have two people in a room. It's not so lonely. And you'll love Miss Green. She makes us all laugh."

"I wanted to be by myself."

"Of course you may feel like that at first. Would you mind handing me another hanger, Mrs. Morrow?"

Lucille moved automatically. The familiar act of hanging up one of her own dresses made her feel more at home. She picked up another hanger.

Miss Scott observed her. "Perhaps you'd like to finish up by yourself, Mrs. Morrow? Then you'll know where everything is."

"All right."

"We let everyone help herself as much as possible. We like to feel that each suite is a little community . . ."

"I don't want to see the others." The others, the crazy ones. "I want to be by myself."

"You'll feel a little strange at first, but we find our system is the best."

It was Lucille's first contact with the dominant "we." We, the nurses; we, the doctors, the brass keys, the steel mesh; we, the iron gate, the fence; we, the people, society; we, the world.

"There are four rooms to each suite," Miss Scott said. "Two to a room. We try to put people of similar background together."

From somewhere outside the door a woman began to moan, "Give me more food and more clotherings." The voice was weak but distinct.

"That's Mrs. Hammond," Miss Scott said briskly. "Don't pay any attention to her, she has plenty to eat and to wear."

"Give me more food and more clotherings."

"That's all she ever says," Miss Scott added.

"Give me . . ."

Lucille bent over the suitcase, as if her body had flowed suddenly out of her dress and the dress itself was ready to fold itself up in the suitcase and go home.

"Do you feel ill, Mrs. Morrow?"

There was a blur in front of her eyes and beyond the blur words dangled and danced, and beyond the thickness that clothed her ears voices spoke, out of turn, out of time.

Give me more food. People of similar background. Mrs. Morrow, here is your husband. More clotherings. What a pretty blue dress. Do you feel ill, Mrs. Morrow? Do you feel ill? Ill? Ill?

"No," she said.

"Just a little upset, eh?" Miss Scott said. "We expect that. Perhaps you'd like me to leave you alone for a minute or two until you get used to the room. I'll go down to the library and get Miss Green. Here, you'll find this blue chair very comfortable."

"Are you going to lock my door? I want my door locked."

"We never lock individual doors during the day."

"I want my door . . ."

"Tonight, when you're all tucked in, we'll lock your door."

Miss Scott reached the door without exactly walking backward but without turning her back to Lucille. She hooked the door open and stepped into the hall.

Mrs. Hammond was standing just outside, her arms folded across her flat chest. She was a handsome young woman with thick black hair and somber brown eyes, but her skin was yellowish and stretched taut over the bones of her face. She wore a black skirt and a heavy red sweater.

"Give me more food and more clotherings."

"A little quieter, please, Mrs. Hammond," Miss Scott said. "We have a new guest today. Tell Miss Parsons to give you an apple."

Miss Parsons herself appeared in the corridor. She was younger than Miss Scott and less sure of herself.

"Well, she's already had two apples and a banana, Miss Scott."

"Goodness," Miss Scott said. "You don't want to get a pain in your tummy, Mrs. Hammond."

"Give me more food . . ."

"I could give her a milk shake," Miss Parsons said nervously.

"There," Miss Scott said cheerfully, "if you're good and behave yourself Miss Parsons will give you a milk shake. You go back to your room, Mrs. Hammond. Rest period isn't over yet."

Majestically, Mrs. Hammond went down the corridor and disappeared into her room.

"Where does she put it?" Miss Parsons said in a worn voice. "Where *does* she *put* it?"

"Go down for Miss Cora. She's in the library." She lowered her voice. "I don't think Mrs. Morrow is going to be any trouble at all, except that Dr. Goodrich wants everything she says put on her chart."

Miss Parsons looked desperate. *"Everything?"*

"It's all right. She doesn't say much. Here's the key to get Miss Cora."

Miss Scott returned to her desk. It was in the center of the short corridor and from it she had a view of the open door of each room and the locked door that led to the incline.

She looked at her watch. Two-forty. That left her twenty minutes to introduce Miss Cora to her new roommate, get the ward ready for their walk and persuade Mrs. Morrow to leave her room, peacefully, and see Dr. Goodrich in his office.

She sighed, but it wasn't from weariness. It was the contented sigh of someone who has a hundred things to do and knows she can do them well.

The incline door opened and Miss Parsons came in with Miss Cora Green.

Miss Green was a small sprightly woman in her sixties. Her black silk dress was immaculately clean and pressed and her white hair was combed in hundreds of tiny pincurls with a pink velvet bow perched on top of them. She moved quickly and delicately as a bird.

"Is she here?" Miss Cora said.

"Is *who* here?" Miss Scott said, quite severely. She had to be severe with Miss Cora in order not to laugh. Miss Cora was so sharp, she knew almost as much about the patients as Dr. Goodrich, and she was continually trying to wheedle more information from the nurses.

"You *always* send me to the library when I'm getting someone new in my room," Miss Cora said. "What's the matter with her? What's her name?"

"Mrs. Morrow," Miss Scott said. "Come along and make a good impression."

"Well, the *least* you could do is to tell me what's the matter with her."

Miss Parsons and Miss Scott exchanged faint smiles.

"I don't know," Miss Scott said.

"Well, the least you could do is tell me how *bad* she is. Is she as bad as Mrs. Hammond?"

"No."

"Thank heaven! I find Mrs. Hammond a *dull* woman. If I were the superintendent I'd feed her and feed her and feed her, just to see what happens. I wonder how much she could *really* eat."

Miss Scott, who had wondered the same thing herself, looked pleasantly blank. She took Miss Cora's arm and they went together into the room.

"Here is Miss Green, Mrs. Morrow."

"Miss Green?" Lucille looked up. The fear that had sprung into her eyes slid away slowly. "Miss Green?" A tiny old woman, no threat, no danger. "How do you do, Miss Green?"

"How do you do, Mrs. Morrow?" Miss Cora said. "What perfectly beautiful hair you have!" She glanced back at Miss Scott with a sly smile that said: that's the kind of thing *you* say but you're not fooling *me*.

Miss Scott pretended not to notice. "It is lovely, isn't it? Such a pretty color. I'm sure you and Miss Green will get along splendidly, Mrs. Morrow. I'll be right out in the corridor if you want me for anything. You remember my name?"

"Miss Scott," Lucille said.

"That's fine," Miss Scott said, sounding very very pleased. She went out.

"She says a lot of silly things," Miss Cora said. "They're *trained* to say silly things."

"Are they?" Lucille said.

"They underestimate our intelligence, especially mine." She studied Lucille for a minute and added pensively, "Perhaps yours too. Is there anything special the matter with you?"

"I don't know." She had felt cold and detached before, but now she had a sudden wild desire to talk, to explain herself to Miss Green: there is nothing the matter with me. I am afraid, but it is a real fear, I didn't imagine it. I am afraid I am going to be killed. I am going to be killed by one of them. Andrew, Polly, Martin, Edith, Giles, one of them.

She whispered, "I came here to be safe."

"Are people after you?"

"Yes."

"Oh dear, they all say that," Miss Cora said, disappointed. "You mustn't tell that to Dr. Goodrich, you'll simply *never* get out of here. They have such *suspicious* minds around this place."

Miss Scott stuck her head in the door. "Get your coat on, Cora. Time for a walk."

"I am not going for a walk today," Miss Cora stated firmly.

"Come on, that's a good girl."

"No, my neuritis is bothering me this afternoon."

"You haven't been outside for a week," Miss Scott said. While it was impossible for Miss Cora to prove she had neuritis it was equally impossible for anyone to disprove it. Miss Cora's neuritis was hard to pin down. It skipped agilely from limb to limb, it settled in the legs if a walk was necessary, in the arms if Miss Cora didn't feel like doing occupational therapy, and in the head under any provocation.

"There is also," Miss Cora pointed out, "my weak heart."

"Nonsense," Miss Scott said brusquely. "Gentle exercise is good for heart patients."

"Not for me."

Miss Scott retreated without further argument.

"The walks are very boring," Miss Cora explained to Lucille. "They do very naïve things like gather leaves. The level of sophistication in this place is very low."

Miss Scott appeared again, a navy-blue cape flung over her uniform. "Good-bye, Cora. You'll be sorry you didn't come. We're going to build a lovely snow man."

"Isn't she *absurd?*" Miss Cora cried, shaking her head. "A lovely snow man. Really!"

Mrs. Hammond strode past the door muffled in an immense fur coat, with a woollen scarf tied around her head. Behind her came two stout middle-aged women who looked and were dressed exactly alike. They walked arm in arm, and in step.

"The Filsinger twins," Miss Cora said, without bothering to lower her voice. "I can't tell which is which any more. A while ago you could tell which was Mary because she was crazier. Now Betty's as bad as she is."

Miss Cora waved her hand at them and the twins disappeared, scowling.

"Mary was in here first," Miss Cora explained. "Betty used to come to see her, and was all right till a few months ago when she began to copy Mary's symptoms. Now they're both here. Mary looks after Betty, she even gives her baths." Miss Cora sighed. "It's all very Freudian. I have a sister myself but the mere thought of giving her a bath is abhorrent to me. She's quite stout, and rather hairy."

She paused, looking down at her own white delicate hands. Her movements were a little too brisk and her talking a little too fast for a woman of her age. But Lucille felt that here, of all the people she had known, was one who was entirely sane.

"I know what you're thinking," Cora said, "and of course you're quite right. I am far too sensible to cope with a nonsensical world. I'd rather stay here." She laughed. "I in my small corner and you in yours."

Somewhere in the building a gong began to ring. In a sudden panic Lucille started out of the chair but even before she was on her feet the gong had stopped again.

"That's Mary Filsinger," Cora said wryly. "Every time she goes out for a walk she runs to the fence and touches it to see if the escape alarm is still working. She never misses."

"Why?" Lucille said.

"Why? No one ever asks *why* at Penwood, it's too futile. Concentrate, instead, on the beautiful consistency and order of things —Mary Filsinger and the fence, Mrs. Hammond and her solitary sentence. There's a pattern of divine illogic about it, and the pattern doesn't change. It's what I miss in the real world, some kind of pattern that doesn't change."

"The fence," Lucille said. "If someone tried to get in here—the alarm would ring?"

"To get *in?*" Cora's voice was sharp with disappointment. She had wanted to go on talking about patterns. She had felt that she had at last acquired a roommate capable of appreciating her, a woman, like herself, who could observe life but was utterly bewildered in the living of it. "Who on earth wants to get into Penwood? The more common desire is to get out."

"I want to stay here," Lucille whispered.

"Hush." Cora jerked her head around toward the open door. "Miss Scott will be coming back in a minute. Don't let her hear you. Why do you want to stay here?"

"I don't know—I'm—afraid . . . " She felt the words pressing on her throat like bubbles ready to break. *If I told someone, I could get help, someone might help me . . . Help me, Cora. . . .*

Then she saw Cora's eyes, bright with a wild unreasonable excitement. She shrank back in the chair, pressing her fists against her breasts.

"Don't say anything," Cora said. "If you want to stay here don't tell Dr. Goodrich anything. Don't answer him at all, not a word. Even one word might give you away."

"Give me—away?"

"You don't belong here. But if you want to stay that's your business. Don't tell Dr. Goodrich *anything.*"

"Good afternoon, Mrs. Morrow."

(Don't answer him at all.)

"I hope you're settled comfortably in your room. Sit down here, please. You may go, Miss Scott."

(Silence. Eyes. Surely he had more than two eyes?)

"Please sit down, Mrs. Morrow."

(Should I sit down? Would that be giving myself away?)

"That's better, that's fine. Perhaps you'd like a cigarette. I'm sorry we can't allow smoking in the rooms, you can understand why."

(Of course. We're children, you can't trust us with fire.)

"Can't you?"

(What is he holding out to me? A cigarette? No, a pen. Why a pen?)

"I have a few routine questions to ask you. If you'll take the pen and sign your name right here . . . What is your full name, please? . . . What date is this anyway?"

(December 9th, but I won't tell you, you can't catch me.)

"Your full name?"

(Can't catch me.)

"What year were you born? Do you know where you are? Can you see this? Can you hear this? What color is your dress?"

The questions continued. Lucille said nothing. Dr. Goodrich was entirely unperturbed at her silence. He seemed intent on what he was writing and barely looked at her any more.

She felt secure in her silence, and suddenly triumphant. It was easy, after all; it was the easiest thing in the world to fool him. Almost boldly she glanced across the desk to see what he was writing. She saw with a shock that he wasn't writing anything; he was drawing pictures, and he'd been waiting for her to find it out, deliberately.

In that instant he looked up and their eyes met. His were kindly but a little cynical. *You're not putting anything over on me,* they said.

"All right, Mrs. Morrow," he said pleasantly. "We don't want to overdo things the first day. Miss Scott will show you back to your room."

Through a haze she saw Miss Scott gliding across the room toward her. She put out her hands, blindly, to clutch at something safe.

Miss Scott caught her as she fell.

"She's fainted," Miss Scott said in a surprised voice.

"Put her on the couch and get a stretcher. Don't send her to the dining room tonight for dinner unless she asks to go. And send Miss Green down here, please."

Fifteen minutes later Cora arrived, flanked by a blushing Miss Parsons.

"Why on earth you have to have *her* bring me is more than I can say," Cora said. "I know my way around this place better than *she* does. And it isn't as if I'd try to escape."

Miss Parsons made a hurried exit. Cora bounced across the room toward Dr. Goodrich.

"That's what I wanted to talk to you about, Cora," Goodrich said with a faint smile.

Cora sat down. She was breathing heavily and her lips had a bluish tinge that Goodrich noted with concern.

"How do you feel, Cora?"

"Fine."

"You should learn to move more slowly."

"I've never been cautious," Cora said with a toss of her head. "It's too late to learn now."

"Tomorrow's visitors' day. Your sister is coming. I thought it would be a good idea for you to be all packed ready to go home with her."

She stared at him. "Did you tell Janet?"

"She suggested it herself. You haven't been home for quite a while."

"I don't want to go. I'm too old to be shunted back and forth like this all the time."

"You may come back whenever you feel like it. You're much better than you were."

"You know that's a lie, doctor," Cora said. "Why do you want me to go home? Because I'm not going to last much longer, is that it?"

"Nonsense. Your sister thought you might like to come. It's up to you. If you'd rather stay here, well, you know we like to have you."

It was true. Miss Green was the favorite of the hospital. It was difficult to imagine this bright cheerful little woman getting wildly drunk whenever the opportunity presented itself. On these occasions her moral barriers were all swept away. Twice she had been arrested for stealing, and several times for disorderly conduct. Usually she remembered nothing of what she had done. After the second offense, her sister Janet had sent her to Penwood and from here she made periodic visits home. But they were not successful. Under the vigilant and worried eye of her sister, Cora felt far more irresponsible and restless than she did at Penwood. After a few days of this constant watching Cora felt impelled to escape from it. She had the subtle cunning of the superior drunkard, and Janet, an unimaginative and successful businesswoman, was no match for her. Cora always managed to get out, to get money, to get drunk. Her heart made these excursions increasingly dangerous.

"You know what would happen," Cora said. "You know very well I'm not cured."

Goodrich, who knew it very well, said nothing.

"How many of us *ever* are?" she demanded.

"Not many."

"I used to think that once I knew *why* I drank I could stop, just like that." She snapped her fingers. "But nothing is so simple as it seems. I know, and you know, why I drink."

He let her talk, though he knew her history in every detail. She had been fifteen when both her parents died, leaving her with a five-year-old sister to look after. For twenty-five years she had done her job thoroughly and unselfishly. As Janet began to succeed in business Cora began to go downhill. Her memory often failed her and she became almost scatterbrained in dealing with situations and people. She was throwing off the weight of a responsibility that had been too heavy for her. Now, though the weight was gone, the mind remembered, guiltily, the feel and contours of it.

"The responsibility is still there," Cora said. "It will be there until I die. . . . Oh, Lord, I'm getting heavy, aren't I? I don't like heavy people."

She rose, pulling herself up by clinging to the arms of the chair.

Goodrich noticed. "Better drop in on Dr. Laverne for a checkup tomorrow, Cora."

"I don't need a checkup. I feel fine."

"I'll arrange it."

"All this silly fussing," Cora said. "It would hardly be a tragedy for an old woman of sixty to die."

"Don't cheat, Cora. Sixty-six."

She turned away, laughing. "All the less of a tragedy."

Cora Green died two days later.

During the week the Morrow family visited Lucille, a small boy called Maguire found a parcel washed up on the beach and took it home to his mother. And on the same day an inquest was held on the body of Eddy Greeley.

7

BOTH in life and in death Mr. Greeley was a public nuisance. Alive, he had cost the province his board and room for several years, and by dying in an alley he was responsible for the cost of an inquest and the loss of the valuable time of the coroner, the jury and the police surgeon.

Edwin Edward Greeley, the police surgeon stated, was a morphine addict of long standing. The body was in an emaciated condition and both thighs had hundreds of hypodermic scars and several infected punctures. Examination of Mr. Greeley's trousers (not on exhibit) showed that he was in the habit of injecting the morphine through his clothing with a home-made syringe (exhibited to the jury who eyed it with interest and disgust).

An autopsy proved the cause of death to be morphine poisoning.

The coroner went over the evidence, implying strongly that he himself had no doubt that Greeley had miscalculated and given himself an overdose (and no loss to the world, his tone made clear); however, if the jury wanted to make fools of themselves they were perfectly welcome to do so and bring in a verdict of homicide or suicide.

The jury was out twenty minutes. Miss Alicia Schaefer summed up the opinions of the other jurors when she stated that anybody who would use a syringe like that instead of going out and buying a proper one, and using it through his clothes, imagine! instead of having it properly sterilized, well, anybody like that could make any kind of mistake.

Miss Schaefer's compelling logic carried the day, and it became part of the court records that Edwin Edward Greeley had died by misadventure.

The bartender at the Allen Hotel read the news in the *Evening Telegram*. He called Inspector Sands' office and left a message for him.

Shortly after seven o'clock on Thursday night Sands came in and sat in the back booth and ordered a beer.

"You wanted to see me?" he said to Bill.

"Yeah," Bill said. "I see by the papers that Greeley got his."

"Friend of yours?"

"Not so's you'd notice. He was in here couple nights ago. Must have been the night he conked. Tuesday."

"Well?"

"He had a tart from down the street with him. He ordered champagne and paid for it with a fifty."

Sands didn't look impressed, and Bill added anxiously, "I guess maybe that don't sound like much, but I had a kind of idea he was onto something big. He shot off at the mouth about how from now on he's got a steady income. I figured you'd like to know."

"Thanks."

"Jesus, he's got a steady income now, all right. Laying gold bricks."

"Who was the hooker?"

"Susie. She's from Phyllis's house down the street, a big redhead. Nice girl. I figure there's nothing against her. Maybe she gets a case now and then but she ain't mean."

"Does she come in here often?"

"Now and then."

"I'd like to talk to her. How would you like to dig her up for me?"

"Aw, now, Mr. Sands," Bill said. "What the hell. I got a wife and family. I don't whore, you know that. If my wife'd hear about it . . ."

"Use a phone."

"Sure. I never thought of that. Why, sure, Mr. Sands." He got up. "It'll probably cost you some money. I figure I'll say it's a business appointment."

"Good idea."

"You got five bucks to waste?"

"Yes."

Bill went into the office. After assuring the manager of the house that he meant business, five bucks' worth, he was allowed to speak to Susie.

"Susie? This is Bill, up at the Allen."

"Well, what do you want? Or is that too personal?"

"There's a guy here. Five bucks."

"I don't want to come out on a stinking night like this for five bucks."

"You see in the papers about Greeley? He got his wings. And I don't mean the kind that lets you fly a plane."

"Well, well," Susie said thoughtfuly and hung up.

Fifteen minutes later she was at the Allen. She had dressed in a hurry and hadn't combed her hair and her lipstick was blurred around her mouth.

Bill took her to the back booth and introduced her to Sands. She looked Sands up and down very slowly.

"Who are you kidding?" she said.

"Jesus, you can't talk to Mr. Sands like that," Bill said. "Why, Mr. Sands . . ."

"Sit down, Susie," Sands said. "You're right, I'm harmless."

"I didn't mean that," Susie said. "Holy God, I wouldn't say a thing like that to any guy. I meant, you're not the type."

"How do you know?" Bill said, scowling. "Mr. Sands has a hell of a lot of muscle under those clothes, ain't you, Mr. Sands?"

"Blow," Sands said, without looking at him.

"Sure," Bill said. "Sure, I'm on my way."

When he had gone Susie sat down. "What's the gag?"

"Questions. About Greeley."

"I get it. Policeman?"

"Yes."

Surprisingly, she leaned back and smiled. "That's a relief. I'm kind of tired tonight. And I got nothing on my conscience you don't know about."

"Known Greeley long?"

"Not so long. Two months maybe, just in the line of business. He was a cheapskate. You could have knocked me over with a feather when he came in Tuesday night and paid ten bucks for the whole night and didn't even stay. We came here and stayed for a couple of hours and guess what we drank."

"Champagne," Sands said.

"Yeah, can you beat it? Poor Eddy, it must have been too much for his system. Bill told me he died."

"Yes."

"Did you know him?"

"Not personally."

"He was a hophead. He gave himself a dose after we left the pier."

"What time?"

"Twelve, or so."

"And then?"

"Then he sent me home in a taxi," Susie said dryly. "Believe it or not. He said he had to meet someone. He'd been talking big stuff all night. It made me laugh. The only thing Eddy was good for was rolling drunks, like he must have done to get that fifty."

Sands gave her five dollars. She took it with a wry smile.

"Easy money. Wish to hell I could always get paid for talking. You couldn't see me for mink."

Sands got up and put on his hat. "Good night, and thanks."

"Too bad you got to go."

"Yes. I have an appointment."

He didn't mention that the appointment was at the morgue, with the mortal remains of Mr. Greeley. Nobody had claimed Greeley and he was due for a long cold wait before someone did.

The morgue attendant slid out the slab like a drawer out of a filing cabinet.

"You want me to stick around, Inspector?"

"No," Sands said. His face looked gray and when he reached out to take the sheet off Greeley his hands were shaking.

The morgue was intensely quiet. None of the street sounds penetrated the walls and the harsh white ceiling lights emphasized the silence. Light should have motion and sound to go with it, but there was no motion except the fall of the sheet and no sound but Sands' own breathing.

Mercilessly the lights stared down at Greeley like cold impartial eyes, examining the protruding bones, the misshapen feet, the broken grimy toenails, the legs skinny and hairy and slightly bowed. Whoever had washed Greeley had done a poor job, and whoever had stuffed his chest with sawdust and sewed him up after the autopsy had been equally careless.

Greeley, a nuisance from first to last, and even yet a nuisance for nobody wanted to pay for his burial.

"Greeley," Sands said.

It was the only epitaph Greeley got and he wouldn't have liked it if he'd known it came from a policeman.

Sands bent over, forcing himself to touch the cold flesh.

Later he telephoned Dr. Sutton, one of the coroner's assistants.

"I just had a look at Edwin Greeley," he said.

"Greeley? Oh yes. Accident case."

"Did you notice a puncture on his left upper arm?"

"Can't recall it. He was so full of punctures it's a wonder he could walk."

"This one's on his arm, barely noticeable."

"What of it? The inquest is over. The evidence was perfectly clear. It was either accident or suicide and I can't see that it makes much difference at this stage of the game. Are you thinking of *murder*?"

Sutton sounded incredulous and quite irritated. "You know me, Sands. I'm always on the lookout for homicide. There's not a chance of it in this case. I knew Greeley, had to testify that he was an addict a couple of years ago. He was a damned suspicious man. If you think he'd stand around while somebody shot a lethal dose of morphine into him . . ."

"How would he know it was lethal?" Sands asked softly. "Here's something else for you. I just found out that Greeley took a shot of morphine around twelve Tuesday night. He was found the next morning around six, and had been dead about three hours or so, is that right?"

"Right."

"Well, think about it a minute. There's no hurry, Greeley won't run away."

There was a long silence.

"Yeah," Sutton said at last. "I catch it. The times are wrong. If the shot that killed him was the one he took at twelve, he didn't die soon enough. So it wasn't the twelve o'clock one."

"And carrying the time element further," Sands said, "why would Greeley take another dose some two hours later? Addicts don't throw the stuff around. Greeley had an appointment some time after twelve. It looks as though he hopped himself up for it, and then someone gave him a little extra."

The case of Mr. Greeley was unofficially re-opened on Friday morning.

On Friday morning, too, Dr. Goodrich made his second report to Andrew by phone.

"It's difficult for me to give you any definite statement at this stage," Goodrich said. "As a gynecologist you've had plenty of experience with the mental disturbances of women during the menopause period. Usually the disturbances are fairly light—insomnia, bad dreams with a latent sexual content, periods of hysteria or depression . . ."

"You think that's what's the matter with her?" Andrew said.

"Frankly, I don't. It's intensified the situation, of course. But she seems to be suffering the after-effects of a very severe shock. She is dazed and badly frightened, so frightened that I get the impression that she wants to stay here because it is safe. That's not uncommon, we have quite a few patients here who refuse to leave, but they're ones who've been here for a long time and who can't bring themselves to give up their changeless routine and face a changing world again. But your wife is a newcomer; they usually fight to get out. . . . Are you sure you've been entirely frank with me about the preceding events?"

"I've told you everything I know," Andrew said, listlessly. "She was alone in the house with the two maids and a man delivered a parcel. No one knows what was in it. She took it with her when she left."

"There was no difficulty between the two of you? At Mrs. Morrow's age, sometimes . . ."

"No difficulty at all. We've been married fifteen years and Lucille has been the best possible wife. And I—I don't know what kind of husband I've been, but she seemed happy." He paused and added quietly, "Very happy, I think."

"This fear of hers," Goodrich said. "It's not the wild irrational type we find here so often. I was wondering if it might do any good to have you and the rest of your family come here this afternoon. Some frank talking might clear the air somewhat. On the other hand, you understand it might do some harm?"

"I understand. Will she—will she want to see us?"

"We might have a little trouble there, but so far she's been co-operative about doing things and she can probably be persuaded."

"Of course we'll come. We want to do everything possible to help her."

"Her difficulty seems to have started with that parcel. I'd like to know what was in it. I haven't asked her, naturally, since she has refused to answer even my ordinary questions. But my own idea is that it was some token from the past, and that, coming when it did, it's caused some exaggerated guilt complex."

"We'll do everything we can," Andrew said. "We—feel it very keenly. My daughter was to have been married this afternoon."

"What a pity," Goodrich said. "Three o'clock would be the best time. I'll see you then."

The taxi came up the driveway and Giles leaned over and picked up his suitcase.

"Well, good-bye, Giles," Polly said. "Nice to have known you."

"Oh, for God's sake." He let the suitcase fall again. It sent up a little cloud of snow as it landed. "Are we going into it right from the beginning again?"

"I don't like people who run out on things."

"I'm not running very far. To the Ford Hotel, in strict fact. I can't stay here any longer, I'm in the way and you know it."

"You've changed quite a bit in the last few days." She scuffed the snow with the toe of her shoe, scowling at it. "You didn't used to be rude *all* of the time."

"I can't stay here," he repeated. "I feel like the worst kind of fool. The expectant bridegroom out on a limb and the fire department out to lunch." He looked down at her, helplessly. "Damn it, you shouldn't stand out here without a coat."

The taxi driver honked the horn.

"You'd better hurry," Polly said flatly.

"Polly, I'll phone you when I get there."

She looked at him coldly. "What for?"

He leaned down to kiss her but she turned her head away. He put his hands on her shoulders and swung her around again.

"Look," he said. "You've made a mistake about me. I'm not a man like your father."

"Leave my father out of this. He's a better man than you'll ever be."

"That's what I'm saying," he told her quietly. "He's big enough not to resent being bossed around by the women in his family. But I can't take it like that. If I could I'd make my peace and agree to stay here and take whatever comes. You can't have it *all* your own way, Polly."

"Can't I?"

He picked up his suitcase again. "You know where I am if you want me."

"Certainly."

She turned and walked toward the house without looking back. With a savage bewildered, "Damn," he strode to the taxi and opened the door.

Slowly Polly went into the living room and stared for a minute, her eyes hot with rage, at the small photograph of Lucille on the mantle.

"She did it," she said through clenched teeth. "She did it, it's her fault. She's always spoiled everything for me."

The occupational-therapy department consisted of two large cheerful rooms with wide windows through which the sun was pouring. There were two nurses in the room as well as the teacher, but they wore bright-colored smocks over their uniforms and the place had the atmosphere of a friendly informal workshop.

In one corner fibers of willow-wood were soaking in a tub of water and standing beside the tub was Mrs. Hammond weaving the wood on an upright frame. She paid little attention to detail but seemed to enjoy flipping the strands violently around.

"Come, come, Mrs. Hammond," the teacher said. "Let's take it a little more slowly." She turned to Lucille. "Mrs. Hammond is making a lampstand. Isn't she doing well?"

"Yes," Lucille said.

Mrs. Hammond went on flipping.

"If you see anything you'd especially care to work at, Mrs. Morrow . . ."

"No. No—anything—anything at all."

"Come, Cora," the teacher called across the room. "Let's get to work now. Show Mrs. Morrow your lovely picture. Perhaps she'd like to do one like it."

"I'm sure she would," Cora said primly.

Cora had a small niche of her own occupied by a wooden frame with a piece of burlap stretched across it. On a table beside it lay little bowls of macaroni, barley, rice and similar foods.

"We glue these to the burlap," the teacher said to Lucille. "And when the whole thing is done, it is painted. Some of the work is really amazing, though Cora, I'm afraid, is not very diligent."

"It isn't diligence that counts," Cora said with a wink. "It's the artistic impulse, and scope."

"It certainly has a great deal of scope," the teacher said and glanced at the odd pieces of rice and barley scattered haphazard over the frame. "I'm still not *quite* sure what it's going to be."

"It's a pictorial representation of James Joyce's *Ulysses*. I believe I told you that before. The medium is perfect for the work."

The teacher hesitated. "Well, in that case . . . Would you care to do something along this line, Mrs. Morrow?"

"She could work on this with me," Cora said.

"Let Mrs. Morrow answer for herself, Cora. We must be polite."

"All right," Lucille said. "I don't care."

Mrs. Hammond had stopped work and was staring at the bowls of food with somber eyes. Unobtrusively, one of the nurses moved across the room and stood beside her.

"Give me more food and more clotherings," Mrs. Hammond intoned. "Give me . . ."

"Now, Mrs. Hammond, you've just had your breakfast. We'll give you a little lunch later on. What a really good job you're . . ."

". . . more food and more clotherings."

The nurse picked up a strand of willow and handed it to her. Mrs. Hammond flung it down again. It whistled through the air and struck the nurse's leg.

"Give me more food and more clotherings."

"All right. Come along."

The two went out, the nurse's arm tucked inside Mrs. Hammond's in a firm friendly way.

"She's always worse on visitors' day," Cora explained. "Her husband comes to see her. Here, pretend you're working and the teacher won't interrupt us talking."

Lucille selected a piece of macaroni from the bowl. She held it up between her fingers and gazed at it dully. It seemed to expand before her eyes, to become the symbol of her future life.

All of my life, she thought, all of my life, while Cora's voice tinkled on: "Mrs. Hammond came from a very wealthy Jewish family. Then she married this man, a clerk of some kind, and her family cut her off because he wasn't Jewish. They were very poor, and then she lost her baby at birth. Since they told her she's never said a word but that one sentence. On visitors' day her husband comes and talks to her, but I don't think she hears anything. She's been here for a long time."

A long time? Lucille thought. So will I.

"You aren't listening," Cora said.

"Yes, I am."

"Well, then, Mrs. Hammond must feel that her husband starved her and killed the baby. And at the same time she must blame herself too, for renouncing her religion."

The Filsinger twins came in with Miss Scott. Mary identified herself immediately.

"I have told the superintendent a thousand times that when Betty doesn't feel well she shouldn't have to come down here." She threw back her head and shouted, "Superintendent. Super—in—ten—dent!"

"Hush, Mary," Miss Scott said, and turned to Betty. "How do you feel, Betty?"

"I feel fine," Betty said vacantly.

"She's putting on a brave front!" Mary cried. "She doesn't look well—oh, any simpleton could see how pale she is."

She stroked her sister's rosy cheek.

The teacher appeared from the other room.

"Mary, Miss Sims is going to have her washrag finished before you if you don't hurry. She's tatting the edge right this minute."

Mary snorted. "Come on, Betty, come on, Betty. Watch you don't fall. Oh, you shouldn't be allowed to come down here in your condition. Don't fall, Betty."

"I feel fine," Betty said.

"Oh, you're so brave, dear. If it wasn't for Miss Sims beating me, I'd go right to the superintendent this minute. Oh, dear. Oh, Miss Scott, am I doing right?"

"Perfectly right," Miss Scott said.

The morning went on. Except for Mary Filsinger's occasional cries for the superintendent, there were no disturbances. Lucille and Cora were skillfully separated by the teacher and Lucille found herself becoming genuinely interested in Mrs. Hammond's abandoned lampstand. She liked the feel of the willow fibers, smooth and pliant, and for the first time in years she felt the satisfaction of actually constructing something with her hands. When the luncheon bell sounded she had almost forgotten where she was and that she was to stay there the rest of her life.

"I won't go down." Lucille stood by the window in her room, her hands clenched against her sides. "I don't want to see anyone."

"Oh, come now," Miss Scott said. "We all have visitors today, even the twins. You'll be all alone up here. And after your family sent you those lovely roses . . ."

"I don't want the roses. Give them to someone else."

She had never dreamt that the family would come to see her, openly and casually like this. She had imagined one of them sneaking in, in the dead of night, to find her, to make her suffer. Yet they were here now, all of them, waiting downstairs to see her as if nothing had happened, sending her roses, and pretending this was an ordinary hospital and she herself was merely a little ill.

"We know it's always hard to see your family for the first time," Miss Scott said, "but if you could make the effort we feel it will do you worlds of good."

"Like Mrs. Hammond," Lucille said.

Miss Scott looked almost cross for a moment. "Cora does a great deal too much talking. You want to see your husband, don't you?"

Lucille pressed her hands to her heart. *I want to see Andrew, to go home with him, to live with him all of my life, never even bothering to see anyone else.*

"No, I don't," she said.

"Very well, I'll tell Dr. Goodrich. You may stay up here."

When she had gone Lucille sat down on the edge of the bed. She was barely conscious. Though her body was upright and her eyes open, it was as if she were almost asleep and her mind in labor and heaving with dreams, little faces, willow fingers, roses of blood, clotherings and a pellet of rice, did you count the spoons, nurse? hard dead flesh of macaroni, doing as well as can be expected, are these roses for me, for *me*, for *me*?

Willow drowned in a tub. Soft dead willow floating hair and headache in a tub.

Superintendent!

How smooth, how dear, how dead. Come Cora Cora, come Cora. Super—in—ten—dent!

Grape eyes mashed, rotten nose splashed on a wall, I'm sure you'll love the soup today, it floats the willow, nursie, nursie . . .

Suddenly she leaned over and began to retch.

Miss Scott came running. "Mrs. Morrow! Here. Head down. Head down, please."

She pressed Lucille's head down against her knees and held it. "Breathe deeply, that's right, that's better. We'll be fine again in a minute. It must have been something you ate."

Miss Scott took her hands away, and slowly Lucille raised her head. She knew Miss Scott was there, she could see her and hear her, but Miss Scott wasn't really there, she was a cloud of white smoke, you could wave her away with your hands, blow her away, she didn't matter, she couldn't do anything, she wasn't there.

"Would you like a glass of water, Mrs. Morrow? Here, let me wipe your mouth, you've bitten your lip. There now do we feel better?"

(Didums bitums ittle ip?)

"There, drink this. I'm sure you're upset because you didn't go down to see your family. They're awfully worried about you, you know. You wouldn't want to upset them, would you now?"

Miss Scott expected no answer. She went to the dresser and picked up a comb and began to comb Lucille's hair. Then she brushed off Lucille's dress and straightened the belt. Passive, indifferent, Lucille allowed herself to be guided through the door.

"We felt it was better for you to meet your family in Dr. Good-

rich's office, not in the common room. Here we are. Would you like
to go in alone?"

Lucille shook her head. She meant to shake it just once, but she
couldn't seem to stop, she felt her head shaking and shaking. Briskly,
Miss Scott reached up and steadied it.

The door opened and Dr. Goodrich came out into the corridor.
Miss Scott frowned at him and tipped her head almost imperceptibly
toward Lucille.

"I see," he said. "Come in, Mrs. Morrow. Here is your family."

Andrew came over to her and kissed her cheek. The others sat
stiffly on the leather couch, as if they didn't know what was expected
of them.

Then Edith, too, rose and came toward her.

"Lucille, dear," she said, and their cheeks touched for an instant
in the old familiar gesture.

Lucille stood, rubbing and rubbing her cheek.

(Here is your family. At least they *said* it was your family, and
there was some faint resemblance to Andrew in the tall man. But
the girl, who was she? And the young man? And the scraggly hag
who'd kissed her? Ho, ho, ho, ho. What a joke! But she knew.)

"Hello, Lucille."

"It's nice to see you again, Lucille."

"Hello, Lucille. I like your hair-do."

"Will you sit down, Mrs. Morrow?"

"We've been so worried about you, Lucille, not letting us know
or anything . . ."

(That was the hag who wasn't Edith. Her voice was Edith's, high,
piercing, thin as a wire, but Edith had never looked like this, a dried
and shriveled mummy with sick-yellow skin. Yet—yet . . .)

"Edith?" she said, her face wrinkling in pain and bewilderment.
"Is that you, Edith?" She looked slowly around the room. "And
you, Andrew? And you, Polly—Martin . . . ? This is a surprise.
I didn't know you were coming."

(There was something wrong about that, but it wasn't important,
she would figure it out later.)

"This *is* a surprise. I feel so confused."

Andrew brought her a chair, and when she sat down he stood
beside her, his hand on her shoulder, strong and steady.

"If you have any troubles, Lucille," he said gently, "share them
with us. That's what a family is for."

"So confused—and tired."

"You can trust us, darling. Whatever is bothering you, it's probably not nearly as bad as you think it is." He looked over at Polly and Martin. "Tell her, tell her, Polly. Martin, tell her we're all behind her, whatever . . ."

"Of course," Polly said stiffly. "Of course. Lucille knows that."

"Sure," Martin said, but he didn't look across the room at her.

"If you'd tell us what happened," Edith said shrilly. "There's been so much mystery. I'm worried half to death. What did the man . . .?"

"I'm so tired," Lucille said. "I'm sure you'll excuse me."

She moved slightly.

"Please!" Andrew said and tightened his grip on her shoulder. "Please!"

With a sudden cry she wrenched herself out of his grasp and ran to the door. An instant later Dr. Goodrich was in the corridor beside her.

Edith clung to Andrew. Her body was shaking with silent sobs and her hands clawed desperately at his coat sleeve. "Take me home, Andrew, please take me home, I'm frightened! She is—she really is *crazy*! I'll be like that some day, I know it, she's just my age. . . ."

"Behave yourself," Andrew said, and looked down at her with an ugly smile. "People with as little sense as you have rarely lose it. Law of compensation, Edith."

Martin was lighting a cigarette. He seemed absorbed in the flare of the match, as if by watching it he could learn something vital.

"I hate to be wise after the fact," he said, "but I think we've underestimated Lucille. We shouldn't have come. She knows that Polly and I have never been friendly to her. It's not anybody's fault, it just happened like that. If she ran away from the lot of us on Monday what reason had we for thinking she was going to break down and confess all on Friday?"

He glanced over at Polly who was staring sulkily down at the floor. "Certainly the sight of Polly's sunny little face isn't going to do anyone any good."

"Take a look at your own," Polly said.

"I have. I grant it doesn't measure up. Still, I try. A for effort."

"Oh, it's so terrible!" Edith cried. "There they are wrangling again as if—as if they didn't care where they were—and poor Lucille—she doesn't *matter* to them!"

"She matters a great deal," Polly said with a dry little smile. "Or haven't you noticed? She matters so much that I wasn't married today, that my fiancé couldn't even stay in the same house with me. . . . She's managed to mess things up very nicely for me."

"Don't be mawkish," Martin said. "Giles was polite enough to leave until things were settled."

"Sure." Polly shrugged. "Very polite of him."

"You sound like the deserted bride."

"How should I sound? He might have stood by me for a while until . . ."

Martin's voice sliced her sentence. "Since when are you the type that asks to be stood by? Or even wants it?"

"Stop it!" Edith said. "Stop your wrangling. It's indecent."

Dr. Goodrich returned to the room.

"I'm sorry," he said. "I thought it was advisable for Mrs. Morrow to go to her room. She seems far more irrational this afternoon than she did this morning." He glanced, with sympathy, at Andrew. "I'm sorry things didn't work out better. But there is a good deal of trial and error in these cases, it's the only way we learn. In its present stage psychiatry has many classifications and rules, but far more exceptions. What I am trying to tell you is not to expect results too soon."

"I see," Andrew said slowly.

"And for the present I think your wife should have no visitors."

"I'm not to come again?"

"I'll let you know when I think it's advisable. Meanwhile it would be a good idea to send her gifts, flowers and fruit and little things. She must be given the feeling that her family care for her and are thinking of her."

"We are," Polly said. "We think of very little else."

Odd girl, Dr. Goodrich thought fleetingly. He shook hands with Andrew. "By the way, Dr. Morrow, if you're driving back to town, perhaps you'd give a lift to someone here."

"Certainly."

"He's had a bad time. His—one of his relatives is here and became disturbed. His face is scratched. I'd like to feel he'll get home all right."

"We'll be glad to take him."

In the corridor a nurse was standing talking to a thin shabby man. The man had his hands in his pockets, and his head was bent over as if he were too tired to hold it up any longer.

"Mr. Hammond," Dr. Goodrich said. "Dr. Morrow is going into town and will be glad to give you a lift."

Hammond raised his head. His face was very pale, the only color in it was in the red-rimmed eyes and the three long scratches down his cheek.

"Thanks," he said huskily. "Very nice of you."

He didn't look at anyone. When he walked down the corridor he moved as if his whole body was in pain.

8

THERE'S a man and woman and kid down here," the desk sergeant told Sands on the phone. "They've got the damnedest story I ever heard. I don't know exactly where to send them."

"You have every intention of sending them up here," Sands said.

"Seems up your alley, Inspector, but I don't know."

"Send them up."

The Maguire family was escorted into Sands' office. The boy was about ten, and looked intelligent and thoroughly awed by his surroundings. He had to be prodded into the office by his mother's large competent thumb.

The Maguires looked respectable lower-middle-class, and uncertain, and the combination, Sands knew, would merge into belligerence unless he could restore their self-assurance.

"I'm sure I don't know whether I'm doing right or not," Mrs. Maguire said loudly. "I told John, I said, maybe we should just phone, or maybe we should come right down."

"Personal interviews are so much more satisfactory," Sands said. "Few people are intelligent enough to do as you've done."

It was broad, but so was Mrs. Maguire. She relaxed far enough to sit down, although giving the impression that she considered all chairs booby-traps.

"It's like this. Tommy was out playing this morning; it's Saturday and no school, and sometimes he goes down to the lake. I don't know, he just seems crazy about water, he can swim like a fish, and his father and me don't take to the water at all."

"Let me tell it," Tommy said. "Let *me* tell it."

"That's a fine way to behave in front of a policeman! You hold your tongue." Mrs. Maguire opened her purse and brought out a parcel wrapped in newspaper. She laid it on the desk, as if she were reluctant to touch it. "I put the newspaper around it myself. After I saw what was in the box I couldn't hardly bear to wrap it up again."

"You're telling it wrong," the boy said.

"Show some respect to your mother," Mr. Maguire said.

"I found it on the beach," the boy said, ignoring both his parents. "I often find things there, once fifty cents. So when I found this box I thought there'd be something in it, so I took it home."

"First, I could hardly believe my eyes," Mrs. Maguire said in an agitated voice. "I didn't even recognize what it was. It was sort of swollen, being soaked in the water and all."

Sands removed the newspaper and revealed a water-soaked cardboard box which almost fell apart under his hands. Mrs. Maguire turned her head away, but the boy watched, fascinated.

A few minutes later Sands was in Dr. Sutton's office.

"Take a look at that."

Sutton looked. "Been robbing graves?"

"What is it?"

"A finger. To be exact, a forefinger, probably male, and sliced off by an expert. The bones are badly crushed, probably had to be amputated." He grimaced. "Hell-of-a-looking thing. Take it away. The joke's over."

"It's just beginning," Sands said.

"Where did you get the thing?"

"A boy found it on the beach. I think someone flung it into the lake last Monday, but the waves washed it up. It couldn't have been in the water long, the box would have fallen apart."

"Got a corpse to fit it?"

"Not yet," Sands said. "Possibly it doesn't belong to a corpse."

"Maybe not," Sutton said. "Maybe the guy that owns it is going around looking for it."

"Your humor is nauseous stuff, Sutton."

"Can't be helped. Leave the thing here and I'll examine it in the lab."

"Don't die laughing about it, will you?" Sands said and went out of the room. He felt unjustly irritated with Sutton who was, he knew, a kind and simple young man. Perhaps too simple. To Sutton the finger was merely a finger, bones and skin, gristle and ganglia. To Sands it was part of a man, once warmed and fed by flowing blood, articulated and responsive to a living brain, knowing the feel of wind and grass, the touch of a woman.

He went back to his office and put on his hat and coat, slowly, because he dreaded the job he had to do.

Ten miles west of Toronto stand the iron gates of Penwood, protecting its inmates against the world and the world against its inmates. At the ornamental apertures in the gates society could press a cold peering eye, but inside, the little colony carried on, undisturbed and uncaring. It grew most of its own food, ran a dairy farm, handled its own laundry, and sold samples of needlework, watercolors, and wicker baskets to a curious public. ("Made by a crazy person, imagine! Why it's just as good as I could do!")

The colony was fathered by its superintendent, Dr. Nathan, a psychoanalyst turned business executive, and mothered by its host of nurses, chosen for their quality of efficient and cheerful callousness. No nurse who confessed to daydreaming, or sentimentalism, or an interest in art, was accepted on the staff. A surplus of imagination could be more dangerous than stupidity, and a weakness for emotionalism could destroy the peace of a whole ward.

Miss Scott had none of these undesirable qualities. In addition to her vital lacks she had a sense of responsibility and a detached fondness for all of her charges. Miss Scott listened and observed and because she had a poor memory she committed her observations to paper, thus doubling her value. She pitied her patients (while impersonally noting that there were lots of people worse off than they were) but when she went off duty at night she was able to forget the day entirely and devote herself to her succession of boy friends.

Incapable of a grand passion, she was the kind of woman who would one day make an advantageous marriage, stick to it, and produce curly-headed and conveniently spaced offspring.

Though he didn't admire the type, Sands liked Miss Scott at once.

"I'm Miss Scott," she said in her warm bright voice. "Dr. Goodrich is doing his rounds right now. I understand you wanted to see Mrs. Morrow."

"I do," Sands said. "My name is Sands, Inspector Sands."

Miss Scott gave him a well-what-do-you-inspect? glance.

"I'm a detective. Homicide. I'm afraid I have to see Mrs. Morrow."

"I'm sorry, I don't think Dr. Goodrich will allow it," Miss Scott said. "She was quite disturbed last night. She's still N.Y.D., I mean not yet diagnosed, and Dr. Goodrich . . ."

"If I could possibly get out of seeing Mrs. Morrow, I'd be glad to do it. I rarely pinch children or attack the sick, but sometimes it's necessary."

What a queer man, Miss Scott thought, and was dumbfounded into temporary silence.

"In this case it is," Sands said. "What I have to say to Mrs. Morrow may, remotely, help her. More probably it will disturb her further. I wanted this to be clear before I see her."

"Under those conditions, I'm sure Dr. Goodrich will refuse to let you see her."

"Perhaps not." He turned his head and seemed to be contemplating the brown-leather furniture of the waiting room. But perhaps he will refuse, Sands thought, and in that case I'll have to tell him what I know. But what to tell?

The picture wasn't clear, the only real figure in it was Lucille herself haunted by dreams and driven by the devils locked up in her own heart. The rest of the picture was in shadow, blurred stealthy shapes merging into darkness, a face (Greeley's?), a finger, a hump in the snow (Mildred?).

"Well, Dr. Goodrich will be here any minute," Miss Scott said and moved toward the door, glad to return to the world of unreason where everything was, in the long run, much simpler.

She stopped at the parcel desk to pick up the gifts for her suite. Everything, even the flowers, had been opened, inspected, and done up again.

Chocolates for Cora. Flowers and a basket of fruit and a bed-jacket for Mrs. Morrow, the morning newspaper, no longer a newspaper but merely selected items clipped and pasted on a piece of cardboard. Mrs. Hammond's daily box of food from her family. The Yiddish delicacies looked very tempting and Miss Scott had often wanted to taste some but Mrs. Hammond always grabbed the box and disappeared with it into the bathroom.

It was an unwritten rule that Cora should get the newspaper first and complain of it.

"Why I can't have a decent ordinary paper is more than I can say," Cora said.

"Now, Cora," Miss Scott said, "look at the goodies you got."

"I loathe chocolates. Will Janet never learn?"

"We're a little cross this morning, aren't we?"

"Oh, really!" Cora said, half-laughing in exasperation. "What are the other parcels?"

"For Mrs. Morrow. Here you are, Mrs. Morrow."

"Thank you," Lucille said in a frozen polite voice. "Thank you very much."

She didn't put out her hand to take the parcels, so Miss Scott herself opened them, making happy noises as she worked.

"Hm! A bed-jacket. Look, Mrs. Morrow. It matches your eyes almost exactly. We're going to look lovely in it."

"Certainly," Cora said. "You in one sleeve and Lucille in the other."

"Now, Cora," Miss Scott said in reproof.

"If I were running this place I would insist on some form of intelligent communication."

Quite unruffled, Miss Scott unwrapped the flowers, and the basket of Malaga grapes. "Shall I read the cards to you? Well, the bed-jacket is from Edith. 'Lucille dear, I know this is your favorite . . .' "

"Don't bother," Lucille said.

" '. . . color and how it becomes you. Love from Edith.' The grapes are from Polly, with love. And your husband sent the flowers. 'Remember we are all behind you. Andrew.' Aren't they sweet little mums?"

"Yes," Lucille said. Sweet little mums, little secret faces with shaggy hair drooping over them, sweet flowers, a rosebud of cancer on a breast, a blue bloated grape, drowned woman, bile-green leaves, cold, doomed, grow no more.

"Yes," Lucille said. "Thank you very much."

But Miss Scott was gone, and so was Cora. How had they gotten out without her seeing them go? She was watching and listening, wasn't she? How long ago was it? How long had she been alone?

Her eyes fell on the flowers. The flowers, yes. She didn't like them looking at her. She may have missed Cora and Miss Scott leaving the room, but she was perfectly rational about this. The roses had squeezed-up sly little faces. You couldn't see the eyes but of course they were there. Weren't they? Look into one. Take it apart and you will find the eyes.

The torn petals fell softly as snowflakes.

"Why, Miss Morrow, you're not going to tear up your lovely flowers," Miss Scott said. "My goodness, I should say not."

Had she been gone and come back again? Or had she never left at all? No, she must have left, I'm quite rational; it's perfectly sensible to look for eyes if you think they're there.

Miss Scott was moving the flowers, taking away the rosebuds and the shaggy-haired chrysanthemum children. Miss Scott was talking.

Was she saying "We mustn't tear our lovely children"? What silly things she said sometimes. As if anyone would tear a child.

"Come along, Mrs. Morrow. Miss Parsons will take you down to Dr. Goodrich's office. That's right, dear, come along."

Docile, a bruised petal still between her fingers, Lucille moved out into the hall.

Cora looked coldly across the room at Miss Scott.

"Is it possible to talk sense to you?"

"Oh, come off it, Cora," Miss Scott said. "None of that."

"I wondered."

"Talk if you want to."

"I shall," Cora said. "In the meager hope that something will get across. Mrs. Morrow is deathly afraid."

"Yes, she is, isn't she?" Miss Scott said thoughtfully.

"She's afraid of her family. She told me last night. One of them is trying to kill her."

"Oh, come, Cora. I thought you had too much sense to believe . . ."

"I believe her," Cora said.

"Don't worry your pretty head about it. She's in good hands, she's safe here, even if it's true. Come, cheer up. The superintendent will be around in a few minutes and you wouldn't want him to see you down in the dumps like this."

"Have you ever been afraid, really afraid?"

"I don't remember. Besides, why would anyone want to kill Mrs. Morrow?"

"I've been afraid," Cora said. "For Janet's sake. When the epidemic of flu was on after the last war . . ."

"Get your hair combed, dear. You look a sight. Dr. Nathan will be disappointed in you."

Lucille knew that Sands' face was one of the thousands of little faces that pursued her with silent shrieks through dreams and half-dreams. But she could not remember where he fitted in, and even when he told her his name she merely felt, vaguely, that he was a part of fear and death. Yet it didn't frighten her. She knew that he was on her side—more than Dr. Goodrich, or the nurses—he looked at her evenly, without embarrassment, and his face seemed to be saying: I know fear and I respect its power, but I am not afraid.

She looked into his eyes and quite suddenly he began to recede, to get smaller and smaller until he was no bigger than a doll. She remembered this happening to her as a child, when she was looking at something she especially loved or feared. The experience had always filled her with terror. ("*I am awake, I am truly awake, it can't be happening, I haven't moved, nothing has changed.*" "*It was only a dream, dear.*" "*I am really awake.*" "*Only a dream.*")

Sands. Ugly little old doll. How wonderfully he was made. Almost human, the way he moved.

"I am not feeling very well," she said in a strong clear voice.

"Did you hear me, Mrs. Morrow?"

"Oh, yes . . . Oh, yes."

"We've found the parcel you threw into the lake."

"Oh, yes."

"Did you throw it away, or did Greeley?"

He came back, life-size.

"Greeley?" Lucille said.

"He may not have used that name. Will you look at this, please, Mrs. Morrow? Is this the man?"

He held out a picture and she looked at it, blinking slowly, trying to control the expression of her face. Her mind seemed to be working with extraordinary clarity. (I could pretend not to recognize the picture. But perhaps they can prove I knew him. I'll admit I know him, but nothing else, nothing else . . .)

"This is Greeley," Sands said. "He was the man who waited for you across the street from the hairdressing shop. He is dead."

"Dead?"

She had a sudden wild surge of hope. If this man was dead she had a chance. She would get out of here, she would *fight*.

"He was murdered," Sands said.

The hope drained out of her body like blood from a wound. Her hands were icy, and her face had a stupid dazed expression.

"I am not trying to harry you, Mrs. Morrow, but to protect you. Someone has taken the trouble to kill Greeley on your account. Greeley was in the way—of something. Greeley was between you—and someone." His voice pressed, relentless, on her ears. "Who wants you dead?"

To frighten her, Sands thought, enough, but not too much . . .

"If I knew," Lucille said. "If I knew . . ."

"You know why."

"No."

"You gave Greeley fifty dollars?"

("Here, take this, it's all I've got." The little man grinning as if the bitter wind had swept up the corners of his mouth. "I figured on more, I figure it's worth it." "I'll get it for you." The wind piercing her thin coat. "Now wait a minute, I ain't been standing around here for my health. I know what was in that box. I looked." "Who gave it to you? Who told you to bring it to me?" "Offhand like this I can't remember." The grin again, though he looked cold and sick and ready to drop in his tracks. "I'll get more for you.")

"No," she said.

"One of your maids has already identified Greeley as the man who brought the box to your house. If I am to help you, Mrs. Morrow, I must know what was behind this thing. It is too crude and grotesque for a joke. And too dangerous to lie about."

She shivered. She could still feel the wind. It seemed to be blowing at her back, pushing her along toward the water, into the water. She felt an icy wave roll against her leg, and her forehead was bathed in sweat. Her head lolled and her mouth opened, sucking in the rush of water.

There was a movement in the room, a hand touching her lightly on the shoulder, Dr. Goodrich's voice saying, "That will be all, I think, for today," and Miss Parsons wiping off her forehead with a cloth.

At the door Lucille turned around. Sands was still watching her.

"Good-bye," she said clearly.

She gave him an intelligent, almost apologetic glance, as if she felt even yet the strange alliance between them. You and I—we both have secrets—there isn't time to tell them.

"Good-bye," Sands said.

She moved, heavily, out into the corridor. Beside her Miss Parsons chattered, trying to imitate Miss Scott and doing it badly.

Up the incline, past an old man bundled in a wheelchair who peered at her suspiciously over his blankets. A door. A girl sweeping the corridor, moving the broom in perfect unfaltering rhythm over the same spot of floor.

"Come, Doris," Miss Parsons said. "Let's do *this* corner now."

But Miss Parsons lacked Miss Scott's assurance. The girl Doris didn't look up or pause a second in her sweeping.

Miss Parsons hesitated and walked on. I'll go crazy if I have to stay here, she thought, I'll go *crazy*.

She locked the last door behind her and led Lucille into her room. Breathing hard, she came out again and handed the big key over to Miss Scott.

"Everything all right?" Miss Scott said.

"Fine."

"What's the matter with you? You look done in."

"Jitters," Miss Parsons said. "Creeps. Whatever you want to call them."

"Cheer up. We all get them."

"When I think how many nurses actually end up here . . ."

"Well, for that matter," Miss Scott said practically, "look at how many of everything end up here, doctors, teachers, lawyers . . ."

"But more nurses."

"Oh, nuts," said Miss Scott. "Count your blessings. This is the nicest ward in the hospital to work in. Should be, at the prices they pay and with me in charge."

"Even so."

"Oh, cheer up, Parsons." She smiled kindly, and instantly became businesslike again. "I'll get the word down to O.T. Mrs. Hammond stays up here. Dr. Nathan says she may have to be put in the continuous bath. Next week they're going to try metrazol on her."

Miss Parsons bit her lip. "Gosh, I hope—I hope I don't have to assist. Last year I saw a woman break both her legs in a treatment— the noise . . ."

"That's all changed now," Miss Scott said. "They use a curare injection to relax the muscles. It's quite marv—" She turned her head suddenly. Her alert ears had picked up a sound from Mrs. Morrow's room, like a retch or a low grunt.

Pushing Miss Parsons out of her way she ran noiselessly down the corridor. Mrs. Morrow might be sick again, as she was yesterday . . .

But Lucille was not sick. She was standing just inside the door, saying over and over again in a blank voice, "Cora? Cora? Cora?"

Cora Green was lying on the floor. She had fallen forward on her face with her hands outstretched, and spilled around her were blue grapes like broken beads.

"Why, Cora," said Miss Scott.

She knelt down.

Why, Cora, you're dead.

9

QUIETLY and quickly Miss Scott walked back to Lucille, thrust her out into the hall and locked the door.

"Come along, Mrs. Morrow. Let's find another room, shall we?"

(A door opened in Lucille's mind, and out popped Cora, giggling, "Really! Isn't she absurd?")

"Cora's not feeling well." There was a lilt in Miss Scott's voice, but the pressure of her fingers was businesslike. "She's had these attacks before. They always pass off."

(*Absurd, absurd,* screamed the little Cora, hilariously. *Really, oh, really, really.*)

"Oh, Miss Parsons, would you mind calling Dr. Laverne? Miss Green is ill."

In fact, said Miss Scott's wriggling eyebrow, Miss Green is deader than a doornail but let's keep it from the children.

"Oh," said Miss Parsons, paling. "Of course. Right away."

She fumbled for the telephone.

"Now, let me see, Mrs. Morrow," Miss Scott said. "It's just about time for O.T., isn't it? Are we all ready to go down?"

(The little Cora doubled up with mirth, her hands at her throat, choking with laughter. Choking . . . "Cora! Cora, you're poisoned— Cora." Cora went right on choking.)

"She was poisoned. In the grapes. They killed her," Lucille said. The words were clear cut in her brain, but they had lost their outlines in traveling to her tongue, and came out as a muffled jumble of syllables.

Miss Scott bent her head attentively, and looked as if she quite understood everything.

"You didn't hear me," Lucille said.

"Pardon?"

"You didn't hear me. She was killed. The grapes were for me."

"Now, now, nobody's going to take your nice grapes away from you. Don't you worry your pretty head about the grapes."

Lucille drew in her breath. If she spoke very very slowly and tried to control her tongue they would understand her. "Cora—Cora— was . . ."

Miss Scott smiled blankly. "Why, of course, Cora will be all right."

Lucille turned her anguished eyes to Miss Parsons, pleading. Miss Parsons tried to smile at her, like Miss Scott. Her lips drew back from her teeth but her eyes were stirred with panic. You're crazy, why, you're crazy as a bedbug, I'm afraid of you.

Dr. Laverne came in the door. He walked softly on his rubber-soled shoes but he had a big booming voice.

Lucille saw him lock the door behind him. He was carrying his instrument bag in one hand and he didn't palm the key as the nurses did, but put it in his coat pocket. It was so large that one end of it stuck out at the top of the pocket.

Lucille couldn't take her eyes off it. The key that would unlock everything. Escape from the hounds, set up a new trail. They have holed you up here, but if you can get the key . . .

Carefully she looked away. She must be very canny, not let them suspect anything. She knew that Cora had been poisoned but no one would ever believe her. They thought she was insane because she couldn't say the right words.

They didn't realize how clever she was. One more look at the key, to make sure it was there. Then she would pretend to be sick, or to faint, that was better. And when the doctor bent over her she would take the key. Through the doors and down the slopes and past the iron gate.

Clever, clever, she thought, and fell back against Miss Scott's arm, and heard the doctor padding softly toward her.

"Watch your key, doctor," Miss Scott said pleasantly.

She didn't actually faint then, but she felt too tired to get up. She sagged against Miss Scott's knees. They were talking about her, but she was too tired to listen. They were urging her to do something, to move her legs, go through a door, behave yourself, lie down, room of your own. We feel that, we know that, we want you to, we are convinced, we, angels of mercy stepping delicately around the blood, so tenderly bathing the dead unfeeling flesh.

Time for lunch, time for rest, time to take a walk, time for Dr. Nathan, time for Dr. Goodrich, time for dinner.

Music, therapy, color movies, church, a dance, bridge.

So much time and never any of it your own, so many people and such shadows they all were. Only sometimes did a scene or a person seem real to her—the Filsinger twins, pressed close together, dancing dreamily to a Viennese waltz, Mrs. Hammond carefully dealing out a bridge hand and as carefully strewing the cards on the floor, Dr. Goodrich talking.

"The report on the autopsy is perfectly clear, Mrs. Morrow. Miss Green died of heart failure."

No, no, no.

"Do you understand me, Mrs. Morrow? Miss Green has had a heart condition for some time. Her death was not a surprise to us. The autopsy was performed by a police surgeon and there was not the faintest evidence of poison."

"The grapes."

"The grapes were all tested, Mrs. Morrow."

Liar.

"Miss Green, Cora's sister, is perfectly satisfied with the report. Cora was apparently eating some of the grapes and a bit of skin got caught in her throat. She became panicky. You must have come into the room just then, and perhaps the sudden entrance, and the blockage in her throat . . ."

"Filthy sonofabitch lying cur," Lucille said distinctly. "Filthy stinking whoremaster . . ."

He waited patiently until she had finished, a little surprised, as always, by the secret vocabulary of women.

"There was no trace of any poison," he repeated. "I arranged for Cora's sister to come and see you. She's in the waiting room now."

Miss Janet Green had been reluctant to come to Penwood. She had been there so often, always to see Cora, always with a little bit of hope in her heart that this time Cora would be better, would actually want to come home. But three days ago Cora had died, and her death had had the same enigmatic quality as her life. Everything was perfectly clear on the surface but there were strange undercurrents.

Janet Green had attended the inquest, a little puzzled, a little bovine.

Quite incredible that Cora should panic over a bit of grape-skin. Her heart was bad, of course, and there was no evidence of anything else, but still . . .

After the inquest Dr. Goodrich had come over and spoken to her and told her about a woman called Mrs. Morrow who thought Cora had been poisoned.

"What nonsense!" Janet said, dabbing at her eyes with a damp handkerchief. "Poor Cora, everyone loved her."

"It is, of course, pure imagination on Mrs. Morrow's part, but that doesn't make it any easier for her. I want you to come to Penwood and talk to her."

"I? There's nothing I can do."

"It's possible that you can convince her you're perfectly satisfied with the inquest. Cora told her a great deal about you. I think she'll look upon you as being on her side. That is, you are Cora's sister and would be most interested in the fact of Cora's death."

"As indeed I am," Janet said dryly. "I'm not quite satisfied. Are you?"

"Perhaps not. The only person who knows the facts is Mrs. Morrow."

"I see. So I'm to see her for two reasons, to talk, and to listen?"

"I have no right to ask you to do this, of course."

"That's all right," Janet said brusquely. "I'll do what I can."

She was a good-hearted woman. She liked to help people, and since Cora was dead and in no need of anything, she would help Mrs. Morrow.

She went at it firmly, telling Lucille in a calm kind voice that she was Cora's sister, that Cora had died of heart failure, she herself had attended the inquest. She was used to the hospital and not at all nervous, but there was something in Lucille's expression that made her uncomfortable. Lucille's mouth was twisted as if she were tasting Janet's words and finding them bitter.

And those eyes, Janet thought. Really quite hopeless.

She went on, however, and out of pity even invented a lie, though inventions of the sort were foreign to her nature and very difficult for her.

"Cora was always afraid of choking, even when she was a child."

"She was ten years older than you," Lucille said. Her tongue felt thick but the words were audible.

Janet flushed. "I can remember hearing her tell about it."

"You mustn't treat me as if I'm stupid. Cora wasn't stupid. She knew right away that she'd been poisoned."

"I'm certain you're wrong. No one would want to harm Cora."

"Not Cora. Me. They were meant for me. She ate some when I was out of the room. When I came back she was sitting on her bed eating them."

"Slower, please, Mrs. Morrow. I can't understand you."

"I ran to her and told her the grapes were poisoned and tried to get them away from her, but it was too late. She was dead, instead of me."

The picture became suddenly clear to Janet. Cora had been sitting on the bed, eating the grapes, when Mrs. Morrow came in. Cora had looked up, smiling impishly, apologetically, because they weren't her grapes, after all. . . . The smile fading as Mrs. Morrow lunged across the room to grab the grapes away from her . . . "They're poisoned!"

Cora had been frightened to death.

It was all clear. It even accounted for so many of the grapes being spilled around the room. It was one of the things that had worried her—why Cora should have plucked so many of the grapes off the stem, if she had just been sitting there eating them in the ordinary way. But it was perfectly clear now. Everything was settled.

She explained it all to Dr. Goodrich, who seemed relieved, and then set out for home.

Off and on throughout the following week she thought of Lucille Morrow. She was sorry that she had not been able to do more for her, but also a little resentful because if it hadn't been for Lucille, Cora might still be living.

On Friday morning, the day after Cora's funeral, Janet returned to the office. She was head buyer for the French Salon at Hampton's, a department store, and she had a good deal of work to do before she went to New York for the spring clothes preview. But she didn't get as much work done as she'd hoped to, for about eleven o'clock a policeman came to see her.

Her secretary brought her his card, and Janet turned it over in her hand, frowning. Detective Inspector Sands. Never heard of him. Probably something about parking or driving through a red light. Still, an inspector. Perhaps my car's been stolen.

"Send him in." She leaned back in the big chair, filling it comfortably. She looked quite calm. It wasn't the first time she'd been visited by a policeman. Cora's misdemeanors had made her acquainted with a number of them.

But surely, she thought, even Cora couldn't be raising hell in hell. One corner of her mouth turned up in a regretful little smile.

"Miss Green? I'm Inspector Sands."

"Oh, yes. Sit down, will you?"

"I've come about your sister's death."

"Well." Janet raised her thick black eyebrows. "I thought that was settled at the inquest."

"The physical end of it, yes. . . . There is no doubt at all that your sister's death was accidental. It's Mrs. Morrow's connection with your sister that I'd like to know more about."

He sat down, holding his hat in his hands. Janet looked at him maternally. He seemed very frail for a policeman. Probably they had to take just anybody on the force nowadays, with so many able-bodied men drafted. Probably he doesn't get proper meals and rest, and certainly somebody should *do* something about his clothes.

Sands recognized her expression. He had seen it before, and it always caused him trouble.

Tomorrow I enroll with Charles Atlas, he thought.

"Dr. Goodrich and I talked it over," Janet said. "It wasn't the poor woman's fault that she killed Cora. Dr. Goodrich said she was actually very fond of Cora, and in telling her the grapes were poisoned she was trying to save Cora's life."

"That's why I'm here. On Saturday Miss Green died. On Friday you'd been to visit her. Did she say anything about Mrs. Morrow to you then?"

"Oh, she said a few things, I guess. Cora was such a chatterbox sometimes I didn't pay much attention. She did say that she liked her new roommate and felt sorry for her."

"Tell me, how many years was your sister at Penwood?"

"Off and on, for nearly ten years. She really liked it there. She was quite sane, you know, and very interested in the psychology of the patients."

"And not at all nervous about being with them?"

"Not at all."

"Isn't it odd, then, that she should have actually believed Mrs. Morrow when Mrs. Morrow told her the grapes were poisoned? She was accustomed to the fancies and vagaries of the other patients. Why did she take Mrs. Morrow seriously?"

"I never thought of that," Janet said with a frown. "Of course you're right. Cora would have said, 'Oh, nonsense,' or something like that. Unless—well, unless the grapes were really poisoned?"

"They weren't."

"I'm very confused. I thought everything was settled, and now—well, now, I don't know what happened."

"What happened is clear enough. Your sister died of shock. And why? Because I think she *believed* Mrs. Morrow, she was convinced that Mrs. Morrow was not insane, that someone was really trying to kill her."

"You sound," Janet said, "you sound as if you believe that too."

"Oh, yes. I do, indeed."

Janet looked skeptical. "Some of the patients at Penwood can be very convincing, you know."

"Yes. But your sister isn't the first of Mrs. Morrow's associates to die. She's the third."

"The—third?"

"Miss Green's death is the third. I believe it was accidental. The other two were deliberate murders. They remain unsolved."

He waited while Janet registered first shock at the murders, and then indignation that they were still unsolved. In his mind's eye he could see the three who had died: Mildred Morrow, young and plump and pretty; Eddy Greeley, a diseased and useless derelict; Cora Green, a harmless little old woman.

Each so dissimilar from the others, all having only one thing in common—Lucille Morrow.

"Well, I don't know what I can do to help," Janet said. "I'm sorry I can't remember more of what Cora said about Mrs. Morrow."

Sands rose. "That's all right. It was a slim chance, anyway."

"Well, I really am sorry," Janet said, and rose, too, and offered him her hand. "Good-bye. If there's anything more I can do . . ."

"No, thanks. Good-bye."

They shook hands and he went out, into the subdued whispering atmosphere of the French Salon. As he passed through the store the air became warmer, the people noisier, the counters garish with Christmas. Perfume, gloves, specialty aisles, slightly soiled and marked-down underwear, clerks in felt Dutch bonnets, "The Newest Rage," "Anything on this table 29¢," "Give her—Hose!"

Throngs of housewives and college girls, harassed males and bewildered children, prams and elbows and tired feet and suffocating air.

He paused beside a tie counter to get his breath. That's what you see with your eyes open, he thought. The tired feet and shoulder-sag, the faces lined by pain or by poverty, the endless hurry not to get to some place, but to get out of some place.

But you could stand back and almost close your eyes and see only the happy bustling throng, joyous with Christmas spirit, happy, happy people in a happy, happy world.

Happy. Silly word. Rhymes with sappy and pappy.

The clerk came up. "Is there anything I can do for you?"

"No, thanks," Sands said. "Everything's been done for me."

He fought his way to the door, aware that he was being childish and neurotic, that his own failure condemned him to see at the moment only the failure of others.

He passed through the revolving door on to Yonge Street and drew the cold air into his lungs. He felt better almost immediately, and thought, tomorrow I enroll with Charles Atlas *and* William Saroyan.

The street crowd was more purposeful in its bustling than the store crowd. The stenographers, bank clerks, truss-builders, type-setters, lawyers and elevator operators were all in search of food. The elevator operators picked up a hamburger and a cup of coffee at a White Spot. The stenographers ate chicken à la king jammed knee to knee in a Honey Dew, and the lawyers, with less drive and perhaps a more careful use of the privilege of pushing, headed for the Savarin on Bay Street.

On the corner a newsboy about seventy was urging everyone to read all about it in the *Globe and Mail*. About two o'clock he would be equally vociferous about the *Star* and *Tely* and around midnight he would appear again, this time with the *Globe and Mail* for the following day.

Heraclitus' state of flux, Sands thought. Not a flowing river, but a merry-go-round, highly mechanized, with the occasional brass ring for a free ride.

He bought a paper, and with it folded under his arm he walked to the parking lot to get his car.

While he was waiting for the attendant he opened the newspaper and read the wants ads. Later he would read the whole thing, but the want ads were the most fascinating part to him. He could, offhand, tell anyone how much it cost to have facial hair per-manently removed, how many cocker spaniels were lost and mechanics were needed, the telephone number of a practical nurse and what you did, supposing you owned a horse and the horse died.

Bird's-eye view of a city.

The attendant returned. Folding the paper again, Sands tipped him and climbed into his car. He forgot about lunch and drove back to his office instead.

The first person he saw when he opened the door was Sergeant D'arcy.

"Good afternoon, sir," D'arcy said.

When he talked, his prim little mouth moved as little as possible.

"Oh," Sands said. "What do you want?"

"Well, sir, as a matter of fact I'm not happy in Inspector Bascombe's department."

"That's too damn bad."

D'arcy flushed. "Well, I mean it, really. Mr. Bascombe is a truly intelligent man, but he is uncouth. He doesn't understand me. He keeps picking on me."

"And?"

"I told the Commissioner that my qualifications, educational and otherwise, were of more specific use in your department." The Commissioner was D'arcy's uncle by marriage. "I told him I'd be much happier working with you because you don't pick on me."

"Then it's about time I started," Sands said.

D'arcy took it as a joke and began to giggle. When he giggled the air whistled through his adenoids and the general effect was so unlovely that Sands' contempt turned momentarily into pity.

"Why you want to be a policeman, I don't know," he said.

"I feel that my qualifications, educational and . . ."

"Stop quoting yourself. Why doesn't uncle set you up in an interior-decorating business or something? You'd look all right lugging around bolts of velvet."

"That's the kind of remark that Mr. Bascombe makes," D'arcy said stiffly. "My uncle wouldn't like it if he heard you say that."

"Your uncle isn't going to hear," Sands said pleasantly. "Because if I ever catch you sniveling and taletelling while you're in this office . . ."

"Then I'm really in?" D'arcy said. "This is very good of you, sir. I'm just terribly pleased."

"Get to work," Sands said, and went into his private office and slammed the door.

He picked up the inter-office phone and called Bascombe.

"Bascombe? D'arcy's changing hands again."

"What a shame," Bascombe said with a spurt of laughter. "I'll certainly miss him when I go to the can. Had your lunch?"

"No."

"I'll stand you to a blueplate special."

"What's behind this?"

"Nothing. I had a letter from Ellen yesterday."

"Oh."

"She's still in Hull but she's sick of the electrician, she wants to come home."

"I see. Yeah. You buy me a lunch to pay for my advice which you won't take?"

"What the hell, I don't need advice," Bascombe said. "I wired her the money to come home."

"That's swell," Sands said. "That's dandy. Pardon me if I'm not hungry."

"She swears that this time she's learned her lesson."

"She's working her way nicely through grade school. They say the work is tough, but no doubt she likes it."

"What the hell, what else could I do, but send her the money? She's my wife."

"That's a technicality," Sands said and quietly put down the phone.

Things were normal again. D'arcy was back, Ellen was back. Ellen had caught the brass ring. Some day someone would put it through her nose, but in the meantime she was seeing the world and a hell of a lot of different kinds of bedroom wallpaper.

The phone rang. It was Bascombe, sounding more uncertain now.

"All right," he said. "So what do you think I should do, smarty pants?"

"Lock the apartment and disappear. See a lawyer, make some arrangements to give her an allowance if your conscience bothers you. The essential fact is not that Ellen is a tramp, but that she wouldn't be one if she gave a damn about you or ever had. It's not a physical thing, she's not insatiable. She's just one of these lowgrade morons who wants love as it is in the movies. Romance, soft lights and sweet music. All of the trimmings and none of the repercussions. Can be done, but not by Ellen. She's not bright enough."

There was a silence. Then Bascombe said, "The blueplate offer still holds."

"All right. I'll pick you up on my way down."

During lunch they didn't mention Ellen. They talked about the Morrow case. Bascombe's department had had nothing to do with it since Lucille Morrow had been found. But he had a professional interest in the case, and he listened intently to the story of Cora Green's death.

"Three of them," he said when Sands had finished. "Damn odd."

"Miss Green's death was, of course, an accident. It wasn't planned or even imagined by the person responsible for the other two. But the hellish part of it is, her death is serving a purpose. It's driving Mrs. Morrow past the borderline of sanity. And that, I believe, is the ultimate motive—to get Mrs. Morrow. The driving power behind it is hate. Mrs. Morrow must be made to suffer, perhaps eventually she must be killed. But the present setup may stand. Someone is getting an exquisite pleasure in seeing Mrs. Morrow trying to cling to the wreck of her mind."

"Jes—us," Bascombe said. "Damn funny the mere sight of an amputated finger would send her crazy, though."

"It didn't. It wasn't the finger itself, but her own state of mind at the time and the *implications* of the finger. A dead finger meant to her a dead woman—Mildred, the first wife; and a death warning to her, the second wife. Who can tell, if she doesn't? Perhaps to her it was a sexual symbol, a token of her marriage." He looked at Bascombe and added softly, "And perhaps it meant more, much more than that.

"Of course it's a member of her family. No one else could hate her so thoroughly, or know enough of her weaknesses to attempt such a refined sport as driving her insane. Greeley did his share in helping. To a woman who has lived a cultured, quiet, comfortable life the mere contact with a man like Greeley must have been a shock. And the sending of the finger was a piece of mental sadism that I've rarely seen equaled."

"Who in hell would even *think* of sending a finger? And where did it come from?"

"The Morrow family can offer no suggestions. They are united on one thing—that the police have no right to bother them, that they are having enough trouble as it is. I questioned them at their house. When I was leaving, Dr. Morrow took me aside and asked me everything about the finger. He looked frightened, as if he knew quite a lot that he wasn't telling."

"The Morrow women," Bascombe said dryly, "have bad luck."

"But the method is getting more genteel. From axes to suggestion. I've gone through all the police files and press clippings on Mildred Morrow. The first person to check in a wife-murder is, of course, the husband. Dr. Morrow not only had a complete alibi but the news of his wife's death put him in a hospital with brain fever. There's nothing phony there. The hospital records and charts stand, and the woman whose baby he was delivering at the time Mildred was killed is still living and remembers the night very well. All this, and the fact that he had no possible motive, puts Dr. Morrow in the clear."

"Morrow seems to have bad luck too." Bascombe finished a piece of pie and pushed the plate away. "Don't we all?"

"You picked yours."

"Don't labor the point. Coming?"

Sands said he was not going back to the office. He had an appointment at the Ford Hotel.

Fifteen minutes later he was facing Lieutenant Frome across a small writing desk at the Ford.

Frome was very stiff and very military. In clipped tones he told Sands that he had recently finished his Transport Officer's course at the Canadian Driving and Maintenance School at Woodworth. He was now waiting to be transferred overseas. It was his last furlough and he had intended to spend it getting married. How he actually was spending it was sitting around this dreary hotel waiting for Polly Morrow to make up her mind.

As he talked Frome became less a soldier and more an ordinary man with a grievance.

"I can't understand it," he told Sands. "She's got some idea in her head that I've walked out on her. What I did was come down here. The rest of the family didn't want me there. Why should they? I'm a stranger to them." He forgot that Sands was a policeman on official business. Sands let him talk uninterrupted. He liked listening to people's problems, it was a little more personal than the want ads.

"Martin's been O.K.," Frome said. "He says Polly likes to boss people around until there's an emergency and then she has to be bossed. I don't understand women. I'm from the West, Alberta. Women don't act like this out there."

"Don't they," Sands murmured.

"In fact, the whole thing has been a mess from the time I met her family. Practically before we said hello we had to run into a train wreck."

"Oh? Who was with you?"

"Polly and her father and Martin. I was so damn nervous anyway about meeting her family—I'd only known *her* for three weeks. And then running into that mess and ending up by picking up bodies . . ." He looked bitterly at Sands, as if Sands had engineered the whole thing. "All right. What did you want to ask me?"

Sands smiled. "Nothing. Not a thing. Just dropped in to see how you were."

Still smiling, he walked across the lobby, pausing at the door to wave his hand cheerfully.

"Everybody's crazy," Lieutenant Frome told the bartender some time later. "Everyone's crazy but me."

"Sure," the bartender said. "Sure."

10

ON THE day of Cora's death Lucille was transferred to a room of her own and put in the charge of a special nurse.

Miss Eustace had a highly specialized and difficult job. She called herself a free-lance psychiatric nurse. She worked in institutions and private homes, taking over twenty-four-hour-a-day care of violent or depressed patients to prevent them from doing harm to themselves or to others.

Her reputation and her wages were high, and she was regarded with awe by the other nurses, who felt the strain of even eight-hour duty on a disturbed ward. Over forty now, Miss Eustace considered herself a dull woman and was always surprised when she was praised for her skill and endurance and patience. In addition to these qualities Miss Eustace had a firm belief in God, a working knowledge of judo, and the ability to sleep and awaken as quickly as a dog. Only once had she been injured on a case, and that had been with one of her own knitting needles. She subsequently gave up knitting, and for amusement she played solitaire and wrote letters or simply talked.

Lucille refused food for nearly a week and on the fourth day Miss Eustace force-fed her by tube.

When it was over Miss Eustace said calmly, "It's very undignified, isn't it? Especially for a pretty woman like you."

Almost unconsciously Lucille turned her head toward the mesh-covered mirror. Pretty? Me? Where is my hair?

"Tonight we'll have a bit of soup together," Miss Eustace continued. "You can't possibly starve yourself to death, you know. It takes too long."

Miss Scott, trained in a different tradition, would have been horrified to hear Miss Eustace speaking of "death" or "starving" to a patient. On the level of pure theory Miss Scott may have been

right, but Miss Eustace got results. For supper Lucille had a bowl
of soup and a custard, and some faint trace of color returned to
her pallid drawn face.

But she was losing weight rapidly. Her clothes sagged on her
body, and there were hollows beneath her cheekbones and a little
sac of flesh under her chin. She never bothered to comb her hair
and had to be told when to wash her hands. Though she seemed
to listen quite attentively when Miss Eustace was talking, she rarely
answered, and what talking she did was at night after she had
been given a sedative. At these times she was like a person who,
after a certain number of drinks, feels he is thinking and talking
very clearly and brilliantly, with no consciousness of his blurred
speech.

Miss Eustace went on playing solitaire and marking down her
score. Out of one hundred and forty-nine games she had only won
eleven. (But then it was, she wrote to her mother, a very difficult
type of solitaire.)

"All of it is Mildred's fault," Lucille muttered into the shadows.
"Mildred . . ."

("My case is just popping off to sleep," Miss Eustace wrote,
steadily. "So please excuse the writing as just the floor light is on
and it isn't very bright in here.")

"Miss Eustace!"

"Here I am," Miss Eustace said pleasantly. "Would you like a
drink?"

"I keep thinking about Mildred."

"Turn over and think about something else."

"What have they done with my hair?"

("She wants to know what they've done with her hair," Miss
Eustace wrote. "They do think of quite the oddest things to say
sometimes.")

Lucille turned over in the bed. Think about something else. Not
about Mildred. But look, see Mildred's hair. How coarse it looked,
each hair as thick as a tube, moving, writhing like snakes, oh, Miss
Eustace, oh, please God.

("I really feel sorriest of all for the family. After all, they're
still sane. My case's family came today, visitors' day, but they
couldn't see her, Dr. Goodrich's orders.")

The snakes writhed and bled in spurts, covering Mildred's face
with their blood—go away, go away—I won't look at you. . . .

"Bloody, bloody," she said, softly.

("The language some of them use! I declare, for a Christian woman, I do know some of the awfullest words. I'd blush to repeat them. It even disturbs me when someone refers to our darling Lassie as a 'bitch.' I just can't get used to it. Give Lassie a bone for me and tell her I'll be coming home soon.")

"I can't sleep," Lucille said.

"You're trying too hard. Just close your eyes and think of someing nice and soothing, like rain or grass waving or trees."

Grass. I am thinking of grass and trees. The park, late at night, black, but moving, astir with shapes and shadows—be careful, look over your shoulder, there is something there—careful! Ah. It's only Martin, don't be afraid. Martin? Is it Martin, or Edith? It's too dark, I don't know. But it's a friend, I can tell. Such a nice face, so wide and frank and candid.

Suddenly it closed up like a fist. Where the eyes and mouth had been there were only folds of skin, and two holes for a nose and little buds of ears.

"I can't stand it! I can't stand it!"

"What can't you stand? You just tell me and we'll fix it in a jiffy."

"I see—things . . ."

"How about some nice warm milk? I find warm milk puts me off just like that."

"No—no . . ."

The warm milk was sent for, but when it arrived Lucille couldn't drink it.

"It smells bad."

"Why, it smells perfectly all right to me. Look, I'll take a sip first, how would that be?"

"It's bad."

Miss Eustace took a number of sips to encourage her and pretty soon the milk was gone. Refreshed, Miss Eustace returned to her letter.

The smell of the milk lingered in the room, very faint and subtle, like the smell of blood or fresh snow.

"The poor woman really thinks someone is trying to poison her." Miss Eustace's pen moved in slow rhythm across the page. "I have found the best thing to do is to take a taste of everything before she does. It reassures her. Perhaps it's not very sanitary, *but!*")

The scratching of the pen was barely audible but Lucille's ears magnified the sound. The sedative was wearing off, leaving her nerves raw and her senses too acute. Though she hadn't drunk the milk, the taste lingered on her tongue, a furry gray-white sickness. The giant claws of the pen dug deep into the paper, and Miss Eustace's quiet breathing was loud as a wind.

She turned over again. The blankets were heavy on top of her, painful and suffocating. She flung them off, and cool air struck her bare legs, and she began to shiver.

Silently Miss Eustace crossed the room and lowered the window.

"Do you want me to rub your back?"

"No."

"It might help. Can't have any more sedatives tonight, you know."

In a sudden fury Lucille told her what she could do with all sedatives.

Miss Eustace remained calm. "Now, now."

"You drank all my milk. *I* wanted it!"

"We'll get you some more."

"I wanted *that* milk."

Miss Eustace walked briskly into the bathroom and came back with a box of talcum powder.

"Roll over. We'll try a back rub."

"No!" Like a child she kept saying "No!" even while she was complying.

Miss Eustace turned back her sleeves, revealing the highly developed forearm muscles that mark an experienced nurse.

Up and down. Across and around. As she worked Miss Eustace talked in a monotone about her mother, her dog Lassie, her pretty sister who had just been married.

At first the pain of her hands was unbearable to Lucille, but gradually she relaxed and flung herself on the mercy of her dreams.

Miss Eustace opened the window and sat down on the edge of her cot to take off her slippers. The last thing she did before she went to bed was to cover Lucille.

Lucille tossed and turned in her sleep under the light blankets that seemed to bind her legs and waist. Her sleeping mind was alive and sentient in her fingers, her nipples, her hips, her thighs, the sensitive palms of her feet; but it seemed to lie caught in a net of words. *Miss Eustace my father and my murther flusttering in the aviary tower in vanity all inanity ah night my sweethurt take me out of the dunjuan through the griefclanging door to the godpeace of sir night.* She struggled in the web of words, the blankets fell to the floor, and the web parted.

Her dreaming mind moved in images across the unforgotten fields of the unconscious, seen forever for the first time. Across the footstippled snow she moved like a gull, like a ghoul, leaving no track, casting no shadow. The iron gate stood ajar behind her, the sky curved over her head, poised and ponderous like an unclosed trap. Along the highway which ran like a ruler to the house where she must go, a line of cars went by, their wheels mourning on the road. Their drivers were faceless with grief and doubt and malice: Polly, Martin, Andrew, Edith, faceless things passing to nothingness on the straight and narrow assembly-line of doom.

A man in gray clothes whose facelessness looked four ways stopped his car by the gate, and the line of cars extending to the horizon stopped. He stretched out a gray aspen-quaking hand to assist her and the door of the car closed behind her softly like a mouth. The gray car moved on the gray road and the line of cars began to hurry hurry. The driver scanned the road ahead, and the woman in the back seat, and the bloody snow in the ditch, with omniscient eyelessness.

The car dissolved around her like a mist and the funereal procession went on forever over other hills, white rising hills pimpled with blood. She was alone among the pines, walking in a tunnel of dark-dripping pines which led to the house which led to the house the house. She could see its white portico like a grinning mouth with long teeth, grinning in pain or menace. Behind the smiling pillars the doors and windows blazed with light, but she knew there was nobody home.

As she approached, the lights faded slowly like recognition in dying eyes, and the portico grinned alone like a jawbone bared by worms. Passing a pillar she touched it with her hand and felt the rotting plaster. Within the house a faint stench of mold hung in the air like a souring regret. Moving in the earthy darkness she knew it was a tomb she had entered. It was terrible to step into a tomb, but she must find what she had come to get. The book of life which was the book of death.

Suddenly the house was as friendly and multiform as a large family spawned suddenly like mushrooms. As she climbed the hunched stairs the walls nudged her with obscene expectancy, the threads creaked like the malicious cackle of children, the curtains on the landing curved outward and divided like fingers to pinch her buttocks and stroke her thighs. She took a knife from her bosom and cut them away, and the severed fingers fell down and danced like babies at her feet.

I must find the book, her fear said, and she went to her room and opened the bureau drawer. The Sangraal radiance of the book lit the room, and she saw it as she remembered it and knew she was remembering it, knew she was dreaming. *Thank God,* she said or dreamed, with the diary in her hands. *Thank God, no one has taken it.* She opened the book, the cover came off like the lid of a box, and the finger wriggled and squirmed inside like a mangled worm.

Out of the grinning tomb the gravestench house she ran with her hair coiling on her head like snakes like long dead nervous hands. The gray car came up to the door and the gray man led her into the little room behind the gathered curtains, where the dead slept on rollers under gravestench flowers. The long gray-curtained car moved away on rollers through the maze of streets cast over the city like a concrete net, along the gelid lake, the hill-flanked forests, beyond the triune towers, the many-nippled mountains into space which expanded utterly as they moved into bright anguished light beyond through the hard and alien blaze to the extreme edge. The bleak and brilliant sword-edge of death.

The lights at Penwood are never out. At night they are dimmed to give the illusion that darkness and sleep come naturally here as they do in the other world, but even at midnight and from a distance you can see the glow of Penwood.

There were always night noises. Someone screamed, someone wanted to go to the bathroom; or someone died, and the stretcher rolled softly up and down the inclines.

In the morning the roosters crowed, the cows made their sad sounds, the night nurses washed their patients and went off duty, and another day began. Breakfast, doctors' rounds, occupational therapy, lunch, rest, walk outside or in gym, private talks in doctors' offices, dinner, music and card games, bed.

The routine was subject to sudden changes. Wet packs or continual baths had to be given, or Miss Sims might obey her hidden voice and defile herself with food at the table, or Miss Filsinger might get out of the dining room with a forbidden spoon.

Miss Eustace woke early, and was immediately alert. Lucille

was stirring but she hadn't opened her eyes, so Miss Eustace used the bathroom first. She washed her face and hands, cleaned her teeth thoroughly, and put on a fresh uniform.

Returning, she found Lucille awake.

"Good morning. Have a nice sleep?"

"Is it morning?" Lucille said.

"Oh my, yes. But it doesn't seem like it, does it? That's the one thing I don't like about winter, getting up before the sun."

While she talked she glanced with a professional eye at Lucille. She seemed rested and quite calm. Though Miss Eustace knew the calmness wouldn't last, she always considered it a good idea to take advantage of even a momentary improvement.

"Let's go down to breakfast this morning," she said cheerfully. "Some new faces would be good for you. Certainly you must be pretty tired of mine."

Lucille looked a little surprised. She hadn't, until this moment, been conscious that Miss Eustace had a face. Miss Eustace was uniform and authority, a starched white impersonalized symbol of "we."

"Let's wear the red dress. There's something so cheery about red on a winter morning, I find."

Lucille had no answer to this. None was possible. Miss Eustace had made up her mind that she, Lucille, in a red dress on a winter morning, should go down to breakfast.

"It's like a nursery school," she said.

"What is?"

"This place."

Miss Eustace laughed. "I suppose it is. Here's your toothbrush."

While Lucille was dressing, Miss Eustace made the two beds, timing herself by her watch. Two minutes for Lucille's bed, one minute, thirty-seven seconds for her own. With pride she marked the times down on her solitaire score pad.

Before she left she opened two windows wide to give the room a good airing, hung up Lucille's nightgown in the closet, and put her own wrinkled uniform in a laundry bag. Then, with a clear conscience and a good appetite, she went down to breakfast.

The dining room was quiet and orderly. The patients ate at small round tables in groups of three or four.

Automatically Lucille walked to the table where she had sat before with Cora and the Filsinger twins.

Miss Eustace said "Good morning," to the twins, and then seated Lucille and herself.

"We personally don't want you here," Mary Filsinger said. "We like a table to ourselves. I've told the superintendent so a dozen times, haven't I, Betty?"

"I don't know," Betty said, with her mouth full.

"Don't stuff your mouth so. It's disgusting. Chew one hundred times."

"I can swallow everything whole," Betty explained proudly to Miss Eustace.

"Don't talk to her," Mary said. "She's a spy."

Smiling and calm Miss Eustace began to talk about her house in the country and what she had for breakfast there and how her tulip tree first blossomed in the spring and when the blossoms fell off the leaves appeared.

"What color blossoms?" Mary asked, suspiciously.

"Pale pink, almost white, really."

"That's very funny about the leaves. I don't believe it for a minute."

"It's true," Lucille said suddenly. "I had a tulip tree, too."

"I wish I had one," Betty said.

Her sister touched her hand. "I'll buy you one."

"You always say that and you never do."

"Ungrateful liar."

"I'll swallow something whole if you call me that."

"Oh, Betty, don't! Darling, please don't!"

A maid arrived with orange juice, oatmeal cooked with raisins and a covered dish of eggs on toast.

Lover-like, the twins quarreled, while Miss Eustace talked about dogs. Collies were nice, and so were cocker spaniels, but she preferred Airedales, really. They were very faithful.

"Cats are best," said Mary, unable to resist Miss Eustace's dangling bait. "We like cats best of all."

"Well, cats are nice too," Miss Eustace agreed. "What do you like best, Mrs. Morrow?"

"Oh, I don't know," Lucille said. "Dogs, I guess."

"Dogs are vicious," Mary said, and closed her mouth decisively on a piece of toast.

"Some of them are, of course," Miss Eustace went on. "It depends mostly on the training and to a certain extent on heredity. I personally have never been able to quite trust a chow, for instance."

"I'd rather have a tulip tree," Betty said.

Mary leaned over and muttered something in her ear but Betty tossed her head and looked scornful.

Miss Eustace watched Lucille out of the corner of her eye to see if the scene interested her or upset her. She noted with approval that Lucille had eaten half of her oatmeal, and, though she didn't talk voluntarily herself, except for the remark about her tulip tree, she seemed to be following the conversation.

We should have quite a good day, Miss Eustace thought, and felt pleased with herself.

The twins were fighting again, in low voices but with a great many flashing glances and passionate gestures. Finally Mary retreated into cold silence, and it was then that Miss Eustace saw her pick up her spoon and tuck it carefully into the bun of hair at the back of her head.

With a furtive glance around the room Mary rose and made for the door. Miss Eustace rose too.

"We're not supposed to take spoons out of the dining-room," she said kindly. "Put it back please."

"Spoon?" Mary cried in great surprise. "What spoon?"

"Put it back."

"I don't know what you're talking about."

The nurse in charge of the dining-room was making her way toward them between the tables. She had the spoon out of Mary's hair before Mary was aware it was missing.

"Now, Mary," she said. "You know better than to do that. This is the second time this week."

"I'm running away," Mary cried. "I'm leaving her flat. She can't treat me like that and get away with it! I'm running away so she'll know what it's like to be left with no one to look after her!"

"I'll swallow something," Betty said calmly, and before anyone could stop her she had removed her ring from her finger and popped it in her mouth. Gulping and gasping she was dragged out of the room and pounded vigorously on the back by the nurse. But it was too late, the ring had already joined the collection of other articles in Betty's stomach.

The twins departed in disgrace with Miss Scott.

"Her insides must be a regular museum," the dining-room nurse said to Miss Eustace. "I'm going to catch it for this."

"It wasn't your fault at all," Miss Eustace said and returned to the table to finish her breakfast.

The episode had apparently made no impression on Lucille. She was intent on her toast, breaking it up into small pieces and arranging them symmetrically around the plate.

She's being very co-operative, Miss Eustace thought, she's really trying to eat.

Aloud she said, "Sugar for your coffee?"

"Yes, thanks."

The fat pink sugar bowl was passed. Lucille would not touch it, its flesh was too pink, too perfect. Not real flesh at all, she thought, but she knew it was because she could see it breathing.

Miss Eustace's spoon clanged against the grains of sugar. "One or two?"

"One."

"There. Stir it up before you drink it. No, dear, stir it up first." She picked up her spoon, dreading the feel of it. Everything was alive, everything hurt. She was hurting the spoon, and though it looked stupid and inert it was hurting her in return, digging into her fingers.

"Not so *hard,* Mrs. Morrow."

Round the cup the spoon dashed in fury and pain, stirring up the hot muddy waves and all the little alive things. She swallowed them, in triumph because she had won, and in despair, because, swallowed and out of sight, they would take vengeance on her.

Everything was alive. The floor that hurt your shoes that hurt your feet. The napkin that touched your dress that pressed against your thighs. Pain everywhere.

No privacy. You could never be alone. You always had to touch things and have them touch you. You had to swallow and be swallowed, have things inside you—alive things . . .

Her shoulders began to twitch.

She's impatient to leave, Miss Eustace thought. A good sign. Usually she just wants to stay where I've put her.

Miss Eustace rose. Callously her feet struck the floor, roughly she folded the napkins.

"Come along and we'll get the mail."

She put out her hand as if to help Lucille up. Lucille stared at the hand, and a shriek began to rise up inside her, making her throat raw and thick.

Miss Eustace saw the screaming eyes and began to talk fast and at the same time to coax her with gentle fingers out into the corridor.

The mail—push—what did she suppose she'd get this morning?—push—you never could tell with mail—parcels were the best, though . . .

Arm in arm, close, intimate, they strolled down the corridor.

They stopped at the mail desk. Andrew's daily box of flowers had arrived, but the incoming mail had not come yet and the girl behind the wicket was looking over the patients' outgoing mail. She picked up an envelope labeled in red crayon, "Wother."

"Look at this," she said, and passed the letter through the wicket to Miss Eustace. "He writes dozens of them every day."

"Wother? What's that?"

"He inverts his M's. He means his mother. I can't let his letters go out, I have to take them in to Dr. Nathan. They upset his mother terribly because all the boy does is complain."

"Hush," said Miss Eustace with a frown toward Lucille

But Lucille hadn't heard anything. She was standing with her arms tight around the box of flowers. Brutally, the box hugged her breasts, and she embraced the pain.

"Though I just hate to suppress any letters," the girl said. "It's against my principles."

"Dear Wother," Miss Eustace read. "I can't stand it any longer the inflationary bargains of the state of the world, wother they are cruel to we they hate we and hardly any consequence could eventuate under the status quo of"

It was not signed but there was a row of X's at the bottom.

"Such a pity," said Miss Eustace, sighing. "I always say, it's the family that suffers most." She raised her voice. "Mrs. Morrow, you're crushing the box. Shall we go back up now or do you want to wait for the mail?"

"I don't know," Lucille said.

"Then I suppose we might as well wait. Shall we open the flowers?"

Lucille's grasp on the box tightened for an instant and then quite suddenly her fingers relaxed and the box fell on the floor. The lid came off and there was a spill of violets.

"Oh, the darlings," said Miss Eustace, picking them up. "Aren't they grand? Such an earthy smell, somehow." She nuzzled them while Lucille watched, suffering in silence for the violets, the long-limbed delicate children, too delicate to breathe and so, dead, and blue in the face, giving off the smell of earth, earth-buried coffins.

The live floor quivered under her feet, the air touched her

cheeks and arms, its caress a warning and a threat, and the violets returned to life. They had only been holding their breath like Cora, and their little bruised faces puckered in pain! *Oh, I hurt, I hurt, and what have I done? Oh, what have I done?*

So tight and sad did the little faces become that they turned into eyes, damp blue eyes dragging their limp and single legs behind them into the box.

"Here you are," Miss Eustace said, passing the box to her. "Why, they're just the color of your eyes."

Lucille felt the sharp corner of the box touch her arm. The pain was so intense and unbearable that she had to reach out and grab the box and thrust the corner of it into her breast like a knife.

I have died. I am dead.

She smiled, and clutching the symbol of death, she moved silently and swiftly down the corridor.

"Mrs. Morrow, wait for me!" Miss Eustace caught up with her, panting. "Well, I declare, I didn't know you were in that much of a hurry. Were you going somewhere?"

"Out."

"Out where?"

"I want some fresh air."

"Oh, you do?" Miss Eustace said, half-pleased, half-suspicious.

"I want some fresh air."

"Well, let's wait a bit until the sun gets stronger, then we'll go out on the roof garden, there's such a pretty view from there. Wait here a minute and I'll go back for the mail."

Miss Eustace returned to the wicket, moving in a kind of sideways fashion so that she could keep Lucille in sight. Lucille made no attempt to get away from her. She stood, straight and alert, as if she was standing guard over something precious to her.

Miss Eustace came back. "Here's a letter for you, dear. Now aren't you glad we waited?"

Lucille wouldn't take the letter so Miss Eustace put it in the pocket of her uniform. So *unnatural* not to be interested in mail, she thought, and tried again when they reached the room.

"Here's your letter. You can read it while I'm doing the chart. Sit down right there. I'll put the flowers in water."

She settled Lucille in a chair and placed the letter on her lap. Then, humming softly, she went into the bathroom and filled a Monel vase with water. She was always excited by mail, other people's as well as her own. Even the most commonplace observations on the weather were glamorous when sealed and postmarked, with privacy protected by His Majesty, King George VI.

I wonder who it's from, she thought, and returned to the room. "Do you want me to read it to you?"

"I don't care."

Miss Eustace, thrilled, slit the envelope with an efficient thumbnail.

"It's signed 'Edith.' I always peek at the end of a letter just to see who it's from. Well, here goes. 'Dear Lucille: I hope you received the chocolates and pillow rest I sent day before yesterday.' Well, of course, we did, didn't we? Those back rests are very comfy. 'It is very difficult to get chocolates these days, one has to stand in line.' Wasn't it silly of you to destroy them when she went to so much trouble to buy them?"

Lucille turned her head and looked deliberately out of the window. *It is very difficult to get poisoned chocolates these days, one has to stand in line.*

" 'We all miss you a great deal, though I feel so hopeless saying it because I know you won't believe it.' "

I feel so hopeless.

" 'Everything is such a mess. The policeman Sands was here again, talking about the train wreck. You remember that afternoon? I don't know what he was getting at, but whoever did anything to you, Lucille, it wasn't me, Lucille, it was not me! I don't know, I can't figure anything out any more. I have this sick headache nearly all the time and Martin is driving me crazy.' "

"She isn't very cheerful, is she?" said Miss Eustace in disapproval. "Shall I go on?"

"Go on."

"Very well. 'They have always seemed like my own children to me, the two of them, and now, I don't know, I look at them and they're like strangers. Meals are the worst time. We watch each other. That doesn't sound like much, but it's terrible—we watch each other.' "

Silly woman, thought Miss Eustace, and turned the page.

" 'I know Andrew wouldn't like me to be writing a letter like this. But, Lucille, you're the only one I can talk to now. I feel I'd rather be there with you, I've always liked and trusted you.' "

I've always loathed and been jealous of you. We watched each other.

" 'Everything is so mixed up. Do you remember the night Giles came and I said, God help me, that we were a happy family? I feel this is a judgment on me for my smugness and wickedness. I don't know how it will all end.

This is a judgment on me for my wickedness. It will all end.

"That's all," said Miss Eustace.

That is all. It will all end and that is all.

Miss Eustace returned the letter to its envelope, her movements brisk because she was annoyed. People shouldn't write problem letters. Letters should be nice and homey and rather dull.

"Let's bundle all up and get some nice fresh air, shall we?"

Lucille didn't move. She sat, heavy and inert, while Miss Eustace lifted her arms into her coat and tied a scarf around her head and put on her gloves.

The roof garden glittered in the sun. Snow clung to the high fence, and where the strands of barbed wire ran around the top, there were globules of snow caught on the barbs.

Slowly Lucille walked over to the fence and put her hand on it. Snow sifted down on her upturned face, touching her eyelids lightly and coldly. She looked down through the fence and saw little people walking, their tracks behind them in the snow the only sign that they were real. So tiny and futile they seemed from a distance, like the skiers in the park.

Futile, futile, she thought and pressed her forehead hard against the fence, branding her flesh with a diamond.

"Goodness, I just can't look down from high places," Miss Eustace said. "It makes me quite dizzy."

She looked down anyway, shivering with cold and dread delight. Then she stepped back, and squinted her eyes against the sun. She breathed deeply because she didn't get much fresh air in her job and she had to get as much of it as she could when the chance came.

In—hold—out—hold—in—hold . . .

Miss Eustace felt glad to be alive.

Lucille remained pressed against the fence. She did not feel the cold, the pain, the heat of the sun. She was not aware of Miss Eustace behind her. She looked down, her eyes strained. The snow burst into orange flame, the sharp black shadows pointed at her, the smoke curled up at her, the windows stared at her, the wind went past whispering, It will all end.

In and out Miss Eustace breathed. She was beginning to wheeze a little but when she spoke she sounded triumphant.

"One hundred. Phew! I didn't realize just *breathing* was such hard work. Still, I always say there's practically nothing the matter with anybody that one hundred deep breaths won't cure. Shall we walk a bit now?"

Lucille didn't answer, but Miss Eustace was feeling too invigorated to care. She strode away, planting her feet firmly, making nice clear tracks in the snow.

Twenty strides north, twenty strides south, in the rising wind.

It will all end.

"If you don't move around a bit, Mrs. Morrow, you'll be cold."

I will be burned in the snow they are waiting for me it will all end.

"No, really, you mustn't take your gloves off, dear, your hands will freeze."

She could feel Miss Eustace coming up behind her, but she didn't hurry with the second glove, she didn't even look to see what she was doing. She was filled with a great power because for the first time in weeks she knew now what she must do. Miss Eustace, no one, could stop her.

Her hands clung to the fence like eagle's claws, and she began to climb. Slowly. There was no hurry. She braced herself by catching the heels of her shoes in the fence holes, and up she climbed, bent double, her coat flapping around her.

Miss Eustace screamed "Stop!" and caught hold of one of her ankles and pulled. The heel of the other shoe came down viciously on the bridge of her nose and there was a crunch of bone and a spurt of blood. Miss Eustace lurched back screaming and wiping the blood out of her eyes.

"Come back! Come back!"

No—no—this is a judgment on me for my wickedness . . .

The barbed wire tore her hands and her face, but she felt nothing, made no sound. At the top she hoisted herself over, clumsily, but with great strength. Her coat caught on a barb and for a second she hung suspended in the air, a grotesque thing, bleeding and flapping.

Then the threads of the coat broke and she fell. Her big black shadow slid quietly down the wall of the building.

11

"MR. SANDS?"

"Yes. Sit down, Miss Morrow."

"Mr. Sands, is this the end of it? It *must* be the end of it. She's dead now—the inquest is over—she's going to be buried this afternoon. . . ."

"Why not sit down?" Sands said and waited while Polly let herself drop into a chair.

She wore a black dress and a dark fur coat and the brim of her black hat shaded her eyes. She looked thinner than he remembered her, and more vulnerable. She kept her head down when she talked as if she were trying to hide behind her hat.

"I don't know why I came here. To get away from the family, I guess, and the smell of those damned flowers. Calla lilies. I feel as if they're sprouting out of my ears."

"They aren't."

She gave a tight little smile. "Nice to know. Anyway, I haven't any reason for being here, I haven't anything to tell you. I guess—well, I wanted someone to talk to."

"Normal."

"It is? Most people would say it's very abnormal to be dashing around town on the morning of your stepmother's funeral. Especially after the way she died. Dr. Goodrich said it's humanly impossible for anyone to scale that fence. Yet she did it." She bit her underlip.

"Isn't that just like Lucille? A surprise to the very end. Not one of us really knew a damn thing about her because she didn't talk about herself. How *can* you know anything about a person without the evidence of her own words? And even then . . ."

"Yes, even then," Sands said.

"What a mess." She stared moodily at a corner of the desk. "What a filthy mess."

"You sound as if you're about to say, what have I done to deserve all this?"

"Well, I *do* say it. What have I?"

"I wouldn't know. But if you're looking for any system of logic in this world, in terms of human justice, you're younger than I thought."

"Twenty-five. But I've never been young."

"Women are notoriously fond of that cliché," Sands said. "Possibly there's some truth in it. Girls are usually held more responsible for their behavior than boys, and any sort of responsibility is aging."

Perhaps mine most of all, he thought. The collection of an eye for an eye. A mind for a mind.

She raised her head and looked at him. "You've changed quite a bit since I saw you years ago."

"So have you. And what have we done to deserve all this?"

He smiled but she continued to regard him soberly. "I really meant that."

"I know you did. Charming."

She began to put on her gloves. "I guess I'm just wasting your time, I'd better be going. You don't take me seriously."

"I don't take you seriously?" He raised his eyebrows. "Four people dead and I don't take you seriously? It's four now. The grand total. As you say, this *must* be the end of it. The finale—the climbing of a fence that can't be climbed, smash, bang, zowie."

"You needn't . . ."

"No, I needn't, but I will. She died a hideous death and one of you is responsible. You, or your father, or your brother, or your aunt. It's that simple, and that complicated. She wasn't killed cleanly, she was hounded to death. As by-products, there were two other deaths."

"You make us out a lovely family," she said dully. "Perfectly lovely. I'll be going now. Thanks for cheering me up, you and the calla lilies."

"It's not my business to cheer you up. Lieutenant Frome is at the Ford Hotel."

"What of it?"

"He seems a pleasant young man, though a little distraught. Having girl trouble. Once he's overseas I expect he'll forget about it."

She rose, drawing her coat close around her. "I've sent him back his ring. It would be useless to drag him into this mess. As you were kind enough to point out, it's a family matter and we'll keep it in the family."

"Why not let him decide that?"

"I make my own decisions and always have."

"Oh, sure. You have what is known as a lot of character, meaning you can be wrong at the top of your lungs." He got up and held out his hand to her across the desk. "Well, good-bye. It was nice seeing you."

She ignored his hand, recognizing the gesture as ironic. "Goodbye."

"See you at the funeral."

She paused on the way to the door and turned around. "Must you come?"

"Hell, I like funerals. I like to give my clients a good send-off. I'm having a wreath made: Happy Landing, Lucille."

Her face began to crumple and she put out one hand as if to balance herself. "I have never—met—a more inhuman man."

"Inhuman?" He walked toward her slowly. "Do you realize that not one of you has given me a scrap of information to help me solve these murders? I might have saved Cora Green and your stepmother, and Eddy Greeley."

"Two insane people," she said in a bitter voice. "And a dope fiend. It was practically euthanasia. They were all old and hopeless. It's the young ones, Martin and me, who have to live on and suffer and never be able to forget or lead happy normal lives. It was Martin and me who had to live without a real mother. It was I who had to give up the only person I've ever really loved because I couldn't bear to have him disgraced too. Officers in the army can't afford to get mixed up in a scandal."

"That's his business."

"No, it's mine. If he lost his commission, all through our marriage every time we quarreled he would fling it up to me."

"If he's the flinging-up type he won't need any excuse."

"I didn't say he was that type! He isn't!"

"What you're saying is, that's what *you'd* do if you were he. Well, I'm not Dorothy Dix, I don't give a damn what you do as long as it doesn't come under homicide."

He thought she was on the verge of walking out and slamming the door. Instead she went back and sat down and took off her gloves again.

"All right," she said calmly. "What can I do to help you find out the truth?"

"Talk."

"About what?"

"It was on a Sunday, wasn't it, that you and your father and brother went to get Lieutenant Frome. And on Monday your stepmother ran away. Tell me everything that happened on those two days, what was said and who said it, even the most trivial things."

"I don't see how that will help."

"I do. Up to that point you were a fairly normal family group. You had made the adjustments to your real mother's death, and were living along with the normal trivial quarrels and jokes and affection . . ."

"That's not true. Not for me, anyway. I never adjusted to my mother's death and I had no affection for Lucille. I have never forgiven my father for marrying again."

"In any case you managed to live with her, like the rest, and even found her useful and competent sometimes, perhaps?"

"Yes."

"What I'm getting at is that something must have happened on that Sunday to precipitate matters. It doesn't look to me as if someone had been brooding for years about sending Lucille an amputated finger and waiting for a convenient train wreck. No, I think that on Sunday someone received a revelation, and the wreck itself suggested a means of getting back at Lucille."

"That leaves Edith out. She was at home."

"Yes."

"And that Sunday was just the same as other Sundays. I got up the same time as I always do and was the first one down for breakfast. Is that the sort of thing you want to hear?"

"Yes."

"Annie gave me orange juice and toast and coffee. The other maid, Della, was at church. Then Edith came down. She was a little fluttery about Giles coming and I remember she kept saying 'today of all days,' which annoyed me. I don't like fusses."

She paused, frowning thoughtfully down at her hands. "Oh, yes. Then father couldn't find something, as usual, and I heard Lucille talking up the stairs to him in the way she had—as if the rest of us were a bunch of children and she the well-trained nursemaid. She said something about trying the cedar closet and then she came in and had breakfast, and she and Edith talked. I expect Edith said the usual things to me, about my manners and my posture—she always did. After that Edith went up to get Martin and he came down and began to kid me about Giles. As soon as Martin came in Lucille left. I remember that because it was so pointed."

"Pointed?"

"Yes. Now that father and Edith weren't there she didn't have to put up with us and our chatter, she could get up and leave. When father was there she was all sweet and silky. No, I'm not being imaginative, either. You should have seen her face when I told her I was getting married. She positively beamed. One out, two to go, see? Perhaps Martin would get married too, and Edith might die, and then she could be alone with father. That's what she wanted. She never fooled Martin and me for an instant—even before . . ."

She stopped.

"Even before your mother died?" Sands said.

"Yes. Even then. She could hide it in front of grown-ups but not in front of us. Not that we were so perceptive and subtle, but because adults are so stupid about hiding things from children. They overdo it and you can smell the corn miles away. Well, that's why we didn't like her—because she was in love with my father. And she—stayed that way."

"And he?"

"Oh, he loved her," she said grudgingly. "Not in the same way that he loved my mother—Lucille was so different from her. Father always had to look after Mildred, but when he married Lucille she was the one who looked after him. She and Edith. Poor Father."

"Why poor?"

"Oh, I don't know. Because—well, I guess not many people understand my father. He's a very good doctor, there's no better gynecologist in the city. All day and half the night he'd be at his office or one of the hospitals or making his calls—very skillful and authoritative and all that—and then he'd come home and be gently and unobtrusively forced into taking aspirins and lying down for a rest and eating the right food. Sort of a schizophrenic existence. And all through it he's remained good-natured and kind and—well, a good egg. A couple of years ago Edith and Lucille pressed him into retiring from full practice. Maybe they were right, I don't know. He's never had very good health and a doctor's life is a hard one. Still—it's a thing for a man to settle by himself."

"Like marriage."

She flushed and said coldly, "That's different."

"All domineering women resent domineering women."

"A directly domineering woman is one thing, a sly managing female is another."

"Very feministic."

"And I didn't come here to argue."

"Then back to Sunday."

"I've told you everything. It was the most ordinary day in the world until we ran into the train wreck. From then on it became very confused. We all worked steadily until late that night. I hardly saw any of the others. I helped undress and wash the wounded and make beds and things like that. I haven't had much real hospital training, that's all I could do. I took time off to phone home because I knew Edith would be worried." Again the grudging note in her voice. "Lucille, too, I suppose, though not about us. That's really all I can tell you."

She got up, a stocky, healthy-looking girl with a direct and somewhat defiant gaze.

"I've talked too much," she said curtly, pulling on her gloves.

"You've been very helpful."

"I—I'd rather you didn't tell the others I came here this morning. They wouldn't like it." She raised her head proudly. "Not that I'm in the least frightened."

"It might be wise to be a *little* frightened."

"If I admitted, in words, that I was even a little frightened, I'd never go home again."

She went out, the echo of her own words ringing in her ears: never go home again, never go home again.

But she could not resist a challenge, especially one that she presented to herself. And so she drove straight home.

She let herself in with her own key. As soon as the door opened she could smell the flowers, the heavy cloying calla lilies and the poisonously sweet carnations. Funeral flowers.

With Deepest Condolences—With Sincerest Sorrow.

Please omit flowers, the notice in the paper had read. But some of their friends thought a funeral just wasn't a funeral without flowers. And so they kept arriving by personal messengers and florist vans, to be unwrapped by Annie, and stacked up haphazardly in the living room by a distraught and red-eyed Edith.

"Idiots," Polly said through clenched teeth. "Idiots, idiots."

Edith came out of the living room. She looked old and tragic and she kept pressing one hand to her head as if to press away the pain.

"I'm so tired. I don't know what to do with all these flowers."

"Throw them out."

"It wouldn't look right. Someone might see us. It seems so silly, sending flowers when she isn't even here."

Her words ended in a sob. "I have this blinding headache, I can't seem to think."

"Ask Father to give you something."

"No, I can't bother him. He didn't sleep all night."

The front door opened and Martin came in. A blast of cold air swept down the hall.

"Hello," Martin said cheerfully. "You've been out, Polly?"

Edith turned away and went quickly up the stairs without speaking to him.

Martin frowned at her back. "What's the matter with her lately? As soon as I come she goes."

"You get on her nerves, which doesn't surprise me. Give me a cigarette."

He tossed a package of cigarettes toward her. "Well, why do I get on her nerves?"

"Respect for the dead. That sort of thing."

"She's been doing this for two weeks. Lucille wasn't dead two weeks ago."

"If you're worried, why not ask her?"

"No, thanks. My policy is to stay away from the rest of the family as much as I can."

"Mine too," Polly said dryly. "And isn't that a coincidence?"

Martin looked at her with detachment. "Pretty long in the tooth and claw this morning, aren't you? Where have you been?"

"Here and there."

"Well, well." He looked amused but she could tell from the way his eyes narrowed that he was angry. "I don't seem to be much of a success with the ladies today. One walks out, the other shuts up."

"It's just pure envy. We'd like to be able to bury ourselves in books too."

"My work has to be done."

"Come hell or high water. You've made that clear."

"Oh, Lord." He put his hand out and caught her arm and smiled suddenly. "Look, there's no sense in the two of us fighting. We're the ones that have to stick together—aren't we?"

For a minute she couldn't speak. She felt the tenseness in his voice and in his eyes, crinkled at the corners with smiling lines, yet cold because they were always turned in upon himself.

"Oh, sure," she said calmly, and shrugged away his hand. "We'll all stick together. There's not much else we can do."

"I'll be away this afternoon," Janet Green told her secretary. "See that these are ready for me in the morning and that Miss Lance gets the samples, and . . ." Her eyes settled vacantly on the desk. "Oh, that's all."

The secretary picked up the samples, frowning. Miss Green had been very absent-minded for the past few days. She was always forgetting things and breaking off sentences in the middle. In the secretary's opinion, Miss Green had been working too hard and should have had a holiday after the death of her sister.

As she passed across the front of the desk she gave Miss Green a sharp glance. Janet caught it.

"Damn," she muttered when the door closed. "I'll have to keep my mind on business. I shouldn't go there this afternoon. It's not my affair."

But it is, she answered herself silently. I have every right to go to her funeral; Cora died because of her.

Since she had read of Lucille's suicide in the paper, Janet's conscience had been troubling her. She felt that she had not done enough to help Lucille and that she was, in a sense, responsible for what happened. Twice she had begun to call Sands on the telephone seeking reassurance and explanations, but each time she had hung up again. Then the urge had seized her to go and see the Morrow family. She felt vaguely that once she had seen them, things would be clearer and the whole business less mysterious and frightening.

Since she did not want an actual encounter with the family she decided to go to the cemetery where Lucille was to be buried. There would be a crowd of curiosity-seekers there; no one would notice her.

But Janet's hope of remaining unnoticed was dispelled almost as soon as she arrived. Bad weather had kept most of the curiosity-seekers away; and to make it worse, she arrived late and the first person she saw was Sands.

He was standing apart from the little group of people clustered around the open grave. He had his hat off and the driving snow had whitened his hair. She began to walk around to the other side, conscious of the crunching noise her feet made in the snow.

He heard it, and looked up and nodded at her.

Janet hesitated and stood still. What bad taste to come here, she thought, what idiocy. If I could only get away quietly . . .

But it was too late, she couldn't get away. The minister was praying, and one of the group around the grave had turned around and was looking at her. It was an older woman, heavily draped in black, with a pale pinched face and dark tired eyes which said, without anger, without bitterness: *What are you doing here? Leave us alone.*

Ashes to ashes.

"Edith Morrow," Sands' voice said in her ear. Janet jumped. She hadn't heard him approaching and there was something sinister in the way he said, "Edith Morrow."

Dust to dust.

"Dr. Morrow's sister," Sands said. "Why did you come?"

"I wanted to see the Morrows."

"Well, there they are. Standing together, as usual. They do it well."

As if to disprove his statement, Edith Morrow turned and began walking toward them.

"You have no right to be here," she said to Sands in her high desperate voice. "Trailing us even to the grave—despicable . . ." She made a nervous gesture with one black-gloved hand. "And these others—why did they come? Why can't they leave us alone?"

"This is Miss Green," Sands said quietly. "Cora Green's sister."

"C—Cora Green . . . ?"

Janet flushed. "I agree, I shouldn't have come. I'll leave immediately."

"It's all over anyway," Edith said harshly.

"I'm sorry. I thought of calling on you—but then I'm a stranger to you."

"Why did you want to call?"

"Oh, I don't know. I thought I could help, perhaps. I met Mrs. Morrow at the hospital. . . ." She knew she was saying all the wrong things and turned to Sands for help. But he had slipped away. She couldn't see him anywhere.

She turned back and met Edith's gaze.

"I was rude," Edith said. "The apology should be mine."

"No, not at all."

"It was your sister who died?"

"Yes."

"We—one of us . . ."

"Oh, I don't look at it like that at all," Janet said in embarrassment. "I just thought I'd—like to see you all."

"To judge us?"

"Yes, I suppose."

"You've seen us now." Edith leaned closer and her voice was a whisper. "Tell me, which one of us? Look at us and tell me, which *one* of us?"

There was a silence. Then Janet said, with warm deep sympathy, "You poor woman. It must be terrible for you!"

She no longer felt uncomfortable herself because here was someone who needed comforting.

"Mr. Sands could be wrong, you know," she said in her rich voice. "Policemen often are. Very likely it'll turn out that he's been far too imaginative, and someday perhaps you'll all be laughing about how suspicious you were of each other."

"If I could think that . . ."

"Well, I *do* think it. We're all inclined to take things too seriously, all except Cora. She was a great laugher. Sometimes when I'm alone at night and feeling mopey I remember some of the jokes she made and get to laughing myself. I haven't any real friends, you know, there was just Cora."

"Nor have I."

"I've always been too busy to make friends, and now when I could use some I don't know how to go about it."

"I wouldn't know either," Edith said. She was astonished to find herself talking so personally and at such an odd time to a total stranger. The wind had whipped a little color to her cheeks, and she felt her rigid neck relaxing and the hard dry lump in her throat dissolving. She had stepped temporarily outside the walls of her own world and was reluctant to go back. They were waiting for her, she knew, but she kept her eyes fixed deliberately on Janet, a stranger, and so one who could be trusted.

"What do you do?" Edith said. "I mean, suppose you want to have a—a good time, what do you do?"

"Oh, I dress all up and take myself to dinner," Janet said, smiling. "And then to a concert or a movie, perhaps."

"I'd like that."

"There's no reason why we couldn't go together sometime."

"You wouldn't mind having me along?"

"I'd like it very much. We could get really silly and buy a bottle of champagne."

"Do you ever do that?"

"Once. I felt very frivolous and giggled through a whole performance of *Aïda*."

Champagne, Edith thought, a gay giddy drink, for weddings, for youth, not for two lonely aging women . . .

"Yes, I'd like that," she said, without hope. "I guess—they're waiting for me. I'd better go."

"No, wait. I really mean it, about having dinner together. We'll make it a definite day."

"Any day. They're all the same."

"How about next Tuesday?"

"Tuesday. That would be fine."

"I could meet you in the Arcadian Court and we'll go to see *The Doughgirls* if you like."

She had the uncomfortable feeling that Edith was no longer listening to her, that the two of them had, in a few minutes, gone through the emotional experience of months or years—from antagonism through friendship to mutual boredom.

"See you Tuesday then," she said with extra heartiness to compensate for her thoughts. "In the meantime don't worry too much. We and our troubles aren't so important as we think." She laid her hand for an instant on Edith's arm. "Good-bye and good luck."

"Good-bye," Edith said, and turned and stepped back into her own world.

Janet's eyes followed her, full of pity and understanding. The little group beside the grave was waiting for her. When Edith had almost reached them she stumbled and the younger man put out his hand to steady her. Edith shrank away from him and pulled the black veil down over her face.

It was only a gesture, yet Janet felt ashamed to have witnessed it. She walked quickly back to her car.

On the way home she began to make further plans for Tuesday. Perhaps the Arcadian Court was too stuffy. They might try Angelo's if Edith liked spaghetti—or some place down in the village where you saw such queer people, sometimes. . . .

By the time she got home she had everything planned, but she never saw Edith again.

12

WHO was that?" Martin said.

"A friend of mine," Edith replied, pressing her lips together tightly behind the veil. "Someone you don't know."

"In brief, none of my business?"

"Exactly."

"All right. I was just trying to be pleasant."

He opened the car door and she got in the back seat. She was breathing fast, as if she were excited.

"You should take it easier, Edith," Andrew said, and sat down beside her and shut the door. "There's no hurry. Is there?"

"No."

He raised his voice. "Martin, you might stop and pick up some cigarettes some place." He spoke easily and naturally, as master of the house setting the tone and pace for a new set of circumstances.

Edith looked at him gratefully and covered his hand with hers. "That was kind of you, Andrew."

He professed not to understand. "What was?"

"Oh, you know, just being ordinary."

He closed his eyes wearily. "I'm always ordinary."

"No, I mean . . ."

"Now don't be silly, Edith."

They fell into a companionable silence while in the front seat Polly and Martin discussed a book he was reviewing.

At the first drugstore Martin stopped the car and got out to buy the cigarettes. When he came out of the store he was whistling, but as soon as he saw the car he became silent and adjusted his face self-consciously as if he'd just caught sight of himself in a mirror, wearing the wrong expression.

It was a small thing and no one noticed it but Edith. Behind the veil her eyes glittered. Martin flung her a mocking glance and slid behind the wheel.

We watch each other, she thought.

The phrase echoed in her mind. *We watch each other*. Someone had said that recently. Who was it?

She remembered with a shock that she herself had written it to Lucille. It was the first time she'd thought of the letter since she'd sent it, and she flushed with shame at her own stupidity. She should never have written it. Where was it now? Destroyed, surely. But suppose it wasn't destroyed? Suppose it was in the bundle of clothes and things that the hospital had sent back this morning?

Her mind set up a wild clamor: I must get the letter, Andrew mustn't see it—no one . . .

As soon as they arrived home she excused herself with a headache and went upstairs. She had intended to go straight to Lucille's room to look for the bundle and make sure the letter had been destroyed. But Annie was in the hall, vacuuming the rug.

When Annie saw her she shut off the motor and the vacuum bag deflated with a drawn-out whine.

"This isn't the time to be doing the rugs, is it?" Edith said.

Annie looked surprised, and a little sulky. "Maybe not, but I figured I might as well be doing something if you wouldn't let me go to the funeral." She was gratified to note that her subtle counter-attack made Edith ill at ease, and she pressed her advantage. "If it wouldn't be too much trouble, Miss Morrow, I figured you'd look at the food grinder in the kitchen. It's not working and Della accuses me of losing one of the parts which I never did."

"Some other time—not now."

"Well, I just thought, I was thinking I needed it to make the stuffing for the veal."

I'll teach you, her eyes said, for keeping me away from the funeral of someone who had more class than all the rest of you put together.

"I just thought it'd be nice," she said blankly. "You can't buy food grinders any more."

"All right, I'll see it," Edith said.

She passed the door of Lucille's room without looking at it, and went down the stairs again with Annie following her. She had a sudden wild notion that Annie had opened the bundle from the hospital and seen the letter, that she must be placated.

"About Mrs. Morrow's clothes," she said, and tried to keep the agitation out of her voice.

"I put them in Dr. Morrow's room," Annie said. "Naturally he'll want to look over it, I figured. I didn't touch a thing."

"I didn't say you had."

"Over here's the grinder. See? Here's where the screw's missing."

Edith bent over it. Her body drooped with weariness, it seemed that it would never have the strength to right itself again.

"It's so—so complicated," she whispered.

"If Mrs. Morrow was here, she'd know about it. She was real handy around the house."

"I'm sorry, I . . ."

"You look real bad, Miss Morrow. Maybe you'd like a cup of tea? You go up and lie down and I'll bring you a cup of tea. I don't really *have* to stuff the veal."

Then why didn't you say so? Edith screamed silently, why didn't you say so?

"It's just as nice *not* stuffed," Annie said. "The tea'll be up in a jiffy."

"Thank you," Edith said, and turned, and dragged herself back up the stairs. There was no use arguing with Annie, and no use getting excited. The letter wasn't important. It was probably not there anyway, and even if it was, there was nothing in it except a record of her own fears and her own folly.

I'll see about it later on, she thought, and lay down on her bed, with one arm shielding her eyes from the light.

Annie brought the tea in and left again. Edith lay without moving. She could feel her migraine coming on, the beat of the blood on one side of her neck and up along the artery behind the ear. Pretty soon the actual pain would be there, and after that the nausea. She began to massage the side of her neck gently, the way Andrew had told her to do when she felt the first symptom.

But it was no use. By dinnertime the pain was intense, and immediately after dinner she came back to her room and lay listening to the sounds that filtered through the house, Annie and Della washing up in the kitchen and then going up to their rooms on the third floor. A little later they came down again, whispering, and the back door opened and closed.

They're going to a movie, Edith thought and remembered Janet Green and Tuesday, and the funeral, and then the letter again.

In the darkness she got off the bed and crept to the door and out into the hall. She could hear people talking down in the living room, and she waited until she could distinguish all their voices, Polly's and Martin's and Andrew's, so she would know she was alone upstairs.

She hesitated, suddenly appalled by her own secretiveness. Why, they were her own family, down there. And she, herself, had every right to go into Andrew's room and sort out Lucille's clothes—every right, it was her duty, in fact, she must spare Andrew—there was no need to be afraid.

But in silence and in secret her slippered feet crossed the hall. It was only when she had switched on a lamp in Andrew's room that some of her fear left her. For the room was like Andrew himself, it was familiar and comfortable and getting old, but it had worn well. Even the smell was reassuring—polished leather and books and tobacco.

She glanced toward the smoking stand beside the leather chair and saw that Andrew had left the lid of the humidor off. Automatically she walked over and replaced it. His pipe lay across the ash tray, and an open book straddled one arm of the chair.

He must have been up all night, she thought. Walking around and smoking and trying to read and then pacing the room again. She felt suddenly overwhelmed with pity for him and her knees sagged against the chair.

The book slid limply to the floor. It made only a faint noise, yet she went rigid, and a trickle of ice water seemed to ooze down her spine. Her ears moved a little, like an animal's, waiting for some sound, some signal . . .

But there was no sound. Hurriedly she bent to pick up the book. It was a diary.

Funny, I didn't know Andrew kept a diary, she thought. No, it can't be his. The writing's different, very round and big, and the ink's faded. I mustn't look at it . . . None of my business . . . I must find my letter. . . .

She closed the book and put it on the arm of the chair again. She had already turned to walk away before the name on the cover penetrated to her mind.

Then she became aware that someone was walking along the hall outside. The blood pounded against her ears, and unconsciously she began to rub her neck.

"What are you doing in here, Edith?" Andrew said, and the door clicked in place behind him.

Her hand paused. "I—I was looking for Lucille's clothes."

"They're in the closet. We thought you were asleep."

"No—no—I—couldn't sleep."

She saw his eyes go toward the chair and falter.

"I didn't read it," she said. "It fell, I just picked it up. But I didn't read it."

"Don't talk like a child. What difference would it make if you had read it?" He closed his eyes for a second. "Mildred never wrote anything that other people couldn't see."

"You read it—last night?"

"Yes."

"You've kept it all these years?"

"All these years, yes."

Her hand began to move again up and down the cord of her neck. "But I thought—wasn't it missing after she died? Didn't the police-man . . . ?"

"Yes, it was missing. I had it. I didn't feel justified in handing my wife's diary over to a policeman. You were the one who told the police that the only things missing after she died were the jewels she had on and her diary?"

"Yes, I told them, I was the one."

"Silly of you, Edith," he said gently. "Did you think there might be a clue in it?"

"Perhaps—for a while . . ."

He picked up the book and handed it to her. "Take it with you."

"No, no, I wouldn't want to read it! It will just upset me. . . . I have this headache."

"It won't upset you. It's a very ordinary diary, just the little things that happened to her day by day, about the children, and us."

He was still holding the book out to her and now she took it, almost without volition.

"Don't show it to the children," he said. "They're not old enough yet to get any comfort from the past."

"You look tired," Edith said with a return of her old crispness. "You'd better go to bed."

"I'll sit up and smoke for awhile."

"You have to take better care of yourself, Andrew, keep more regular hours. I noticed you didn't touch your salad tonight."

"Don't nag, Edith."

"I wasn't nagging."

"Go to bed yourself."

"I would, if I could sleep," she said gratingly. "You'll never give me anything to make me sleep."

"It's a bad habit."

"It can't be a habit if you do it once!" She knew that she was getting shrill and tried to stop herself, but too many things had happened to her today—the funeral, Janet, the diary, the migraine—she felt her control slipping away. "Other doctors give sleeping prescriptions! I'm your own sister and I have to lie awake night after night . . ."

"You're the type who forms habits too easily," he said quietly. "But rather than see you hysterical like this I will set aside my better judgment."

Even though she was getting her own way she couldn't stop talking at him. Her voice pursued him into the closet where he kept his medical supplies locked up, and into the bedroom where he poured out a glass of water.

"Here. Take this. It will begin to work in an hour or so. Now go to bed."

He half-pushed her toward the door, glad to be rid of her finally, to be able to enjoy the peace and darkness of his own room.

At ten o'clock the maids came home, and went, twittering, up to the third floor. Shortly afterward Martin came to bed, and last of all, Polly. She had locked the house and put out the lights, and now she paused in front of Edith's door and rapped softly.

"Who is it?"

"Me. Polly."

"Oh. I'm in bed."

"I saw your light on."

"Well, come in. Don't shout at me through the door!"

Edith was sitting up in bed. Her cheeks were flushed and her eyes had a glaring sightless look. She wore a bed-jacket.

"I was just sitting here a moment before turning off the light," she said.

One of her arms jerked nervously and the sleeve of the bed-jacket slid back and showed an inch or so of the black dress she'd been wearing. She covered it again quickly, but Polly had already seen.

"Well, I didn't have anything special to say," she said, her voice carefully blank. "Guess I'll turn in. How's your headache?"

"Headache? Oh, it's all right."

"Well, good night."

"Good night."

Their eyes met for an instant and passed on, like strangers on a dark street.

The door closed and Edith got out of bed and tore the bed-jacket from her shoulders. She put on a coat and tied a black scarf over her head and picked up the diary from underneath the bedclothes.

Then, a black shadow, she moved through the house, and went out into the street.

13

GOOD morning, Mr. Bascombe," D'arcy said. "Mr. Sands has just come in. I was terribly sorry to hear you're leaving us."

Bascombe stopped, looked him up and down. "Yeah, I know."

"We were all thrilled to hear you got a commission. I bet you'll look swell in your uniform."

"Ask me to take it off for you sometime and see where it gets you."

D'arcy looked pained. "That's no way to talk. I thought you'd be nice to me at least on your last day."

Smiling grimly, Bascombe strode into Sands' office.

Sands looked up and said, "Good morning. How's the Military Intelligence this morning?"

Bascombe saluted smartly. "I beg to report, sir, that A-56 of the Division of Lawns and Gardens, that is, myself, has discovered the existence of a pansy in your own office. A-56 recommends fertilization of the roots or complete extermination."

Sands laughed. "Sit down. When do you leave?"

"It's a military secret, even from me."

"Ellen back?"

"Yeah. She's pulling the gag about how-can-I-live-without-you-my-hero. I've signed the papers for her allotment, now I'm forgetting the whole thing." He sat on the edge of the desk, swinging one foot. "I hope."

"Got the jitters?"

"Some. Afraid I'll pull a boner. What I've been doing around here seems like kid stuff compared to what's in store for me."

"I don't think you have to be afraid. D'arcy says you have a *truly great* brain."

"What the hell!" Bascombe swung himself off the desk, embarrassed. "Well, good-bye." He held out his hand. "It's been damn nice having a decent guy in this dump."

Sands, too, was embarrassed. He got up, and they shook hands across the desk. "Good-bye and good hunting."

"Thanks."

Bascombe went out. In the outer office he saw D'arcy talking to a middle-aged woman. He noticed the woman especially because she was carrying an enormous leather handbag.

Well—what the hell—women, to hell with them . . .

"There now," D'arcy said to the woman. "Now you can go in."

She seemed distraught. "Thank you. I—it's really urgent."

"Just step in." D'arcy opened the door of Sands' office with a flourish. "Miss Green to see you, sir."

"Good morning, Miss Green," Sands said, and was surprised to see how agitated she looked. "What brings you here?"

"I can't make head nor tail of it. Look." She opened the big handbag and drew out a paper bag.

"Shut that door, D'arcy."

"Oh, yes, sir."

Janet Green put the paper bag on the desk. It had been stamped and postmarked, and Janet Green's name and address had been written shakily in pen and ink.

"I just don't know what to make of it," she said. "This came this morning, a while ago. It's a diary, and why anyone should send me a diary . . ."

Sands took the book carefully from the bag. The cover was tooled leather and across it, in gold letters, was printed "Mildred Scott Morrow." He opened it. The ink was faded but still legible. "July 3, 1928. Today is my birthday and Edith has given me this lovely diary. I told her, what would *I* put in a diary, I never have anything interesting to say . . ."

"Why to *me*?" Janet cried in exasperation. "I thought, of course, as soon as I saw the name Morrow that Edith Morrow herself must have sent it. I don't know any of the others at all. And yet I only met her yesterday."

"Perhaps that's why."

"What is?"

"She could trust you because you have no ax to grind."

"Yes, but there's nothing in the book that I can see! And why not keep it herself? The strange thing is that someone has marked passages in it here and there. They're mostly about Lucille."

"Go on."

"Well, as soon as I looked into the book I rang up Edith Morrow. At least I rang the house and whoever answered the phone sounded very peculiar. They said that Miss Morrow couldn't come to the phone. Then they hung up, just like that."

Before she had finished speaking Sands had risen. "Thanks for coming. I'll keep this. I'm in a hurry."

"You can't leave me . . ."

"Sorry. D'arcy will see you out. I've got to leave."

He went to the coat rack and slipped the diary into the pocket of his overcoat. Then with the coat over his arm he walked out.

When he reached the Morrow house the doorbell was answered by Annie.

She recognized him and said, "Oh!" and put her hand over her mouth.

"I'd like to speak to Miss Edith Morrow," he said.

"Well, you can't."

"Why not?"

"She's dead. And it's none of your business this time. It happened natural. She died in her sleep."

She opened the door a little wider, not wide enough for him to walk in comfortably, but just enough so that he could squeeze through the opening if he really had the nerve to come calling on people at a time like this. . . .

"I'm very sorry," he said, and Annie was impressed by his sincerity. Her face lost its guarded look.

"I've been real miserable about it," she said. "I wasn't very nice to her yesterday and now I'll never have a chance to make it up to her. That's the first thing I thought of when I found her this morning. There she was lying on the bed, all stiff and peaceful, and I thought, now it's too late, now I'll never have a chance to make it up to her."

"Where is the family?"

"They're up there with her."

"I don't want to intrude on them." Too late now. Edith was stiff and peaceful, at home with her family. "I'll wait some place. Don't bother telling them I'm here. I'll just wait."

"They wouldn't like it if I didn't tell them. They don't like having a policeman around. There's a fire in Dr. Morrow's den, you can go in there, I guess, but I don't really think they'll like it."

"I'll take a chance."

She left him then, and when he heard her go upstairs he took the diary from his coat pocket and began to read.

In the first few pages there was nothing marked, no reference to Lucille. Mildred Morrow had been chiefly concerned with her family and the details of the home. He read at random:

August 4.

Raining today and Polly is pestering me to let her get her curls cut off. I suppose I'm old-fashioned, I don't really want her to do it. But if I say no she'll just go to Andrew and twist him around her little finger. What a Daddy's girl she is! I told Andrew, it's a shame he can't see more of the children. But then he is doing so *much good* for the world I feel selfish.

August 31.

Edith looks so pretty today! She's got on a new dress, so I told her, we must do something *special*. So we had a picnic in the park! Lucille came along. I think Lucille could be very beautiful if she would only have some vitality. (Like Edith) She is still far too young to go on grieving for her husband. He was a lot older than

she, and what we saw of him, not a nice person like her. The
children came on the picnic too but they don't seem to like Lucille.
She is too shy.

The last sentence was underlined in fresh ink.

September 6.
   Well, I finally got Lucille and Andrew together! Andrew had a
whole evening off, and though we've been Lucille's neighbors for
ages, why, Andrew hardly knows her he's away so much! We played
cards (*not* bridge!) and I told Andrew, here you are with three
women, after seeing women all day you must be tired of them. He
said no, they whetted his appetite, and we all laughed.

In the entries for the next two months there were various short
references to Lucille.

   We went shopping today. Lucille doesn't buy much, which puzzles
me, because she certainly needs clothes.
   I am getting very fond of Lucille. Once you know her she is
really delightful, though Andrew and Edith don't believe me! Martin
is getting to that smart-alecky stage and he calls Lucille "the blondy."
Martin is very *hard* to handle. Though he's awfully good in his
studies I think he's very sensitive about not being able to join in
games and things since he had his back broken. Lucille says he
is "compensating," whatever that means. She is much cleverer than
I am.

Much cleverer, Sands thought. Far too clever for you, Mildred.
He felt a strange pity for this woman who had been dead for sixteen
years and had come to life again on paper, in all her guilelessness
and sweet stupidity.

November 12.
   I started my Christmas shopping today and tonight Edith went
to her club and Andrew is working, of course. So I am sitting in
Lucille's living room writing this while she knits. She knits with
her eyes shut, imagine! I asked her what she was thinking and she
told me that she was thinking she wasn't going to celebrate Christmas
this year. Not celebrate Christmas! I told her, why not? She was
very annoyed for a minute. She told me, look around you, look at
my house and my clothes, can't you figure it out by yourself? Well,
of course I could *then.* It was very embarrassing and I asked her
if she wanted some money, a loan or a gift or *anything.* But she

refused. I think she refused on account of Andrew, she knows he doesn't much like her.

December 2.

Polly found out today (isn't that just like her! She is a minx!) that Lucille's car, which we all thought was stored in her garage, has really been sold.

December 4.

I took my portrait down to Morison's for a good cleaning today. Lucille came along and afterward we went to a movie and then to Child's for a cup of chocolate (which I should *not* drink). She is so quiet and patient, it's nice to go places with her. Edith is always in so much of a hurry!

Quiet and patient, Sands thought. Biding her time, thinking out the plan that was, in the end, to destroy not only Mildred and herself, but three others. How did the plan start? At what particular moment did she begin to covet Mildred's husband and Mildred's money?

December 5.

Well, here I am over at Lucille's again tonight. I told her, this is getting to be practically a tradition! But it is nice (and I *mean* it!) to have someone to drop in on after the children are in bed and when Andrew is on a case and Edith is out. Edith is having quite a rush from this George Mackenzie, but Lucille says she doesn't think Edith will marry him because she's too wrapped up in Andrew. I was quite surprised at this! I mean, I know Edith *adores* Andrew and harries the life out of him, but I always thought it's because she hasn't a man of her own. I told Lucille this and she just smiled. But I still think I'm *right*! You don't know everything, I told her, just in fun, of course!

Sands had nearly reached the end now, and with each page he turned, the picture of Mildred became clearer. Mildred, smiling and secure, never questioning, never looking behind her to see the inexorable fate that was creeping up on her. Happy Mildred, proud of her husband and his work, secure in the knowledge that her life was to be a series of repetitions, of Andrew and Edith, and the children and new dresses and cups of chocolate; and, like a child herself, never tiring of repetitions.

December 7.

Lucille and I took a walk through the park this afternoon. We talked about marriage. I guess it started when I said something about how attractive Andrew was to women. My goodness, every once in a while one of them makes a big scene at his office and poor Andrew is so completely bewildered by the whole thing. He considers himself an old fogy. At thirty-four! Anyway, I told Lucille this and for some reason she lost her reserve and began to talk about her own marriage. Both her parents died in a hotel fire when she was seventeen, and quite soon afterward she married one of her father's friends, years older than she was. She said she hated him from the very first day. (And the way she said it! I couldn't believe it was really my own friend talking!) Imagine living in hate for ten years! No wonder it's left its mark on her. I *do* wish she would let me help her in some way. You really should get married again, I told her.

December 10.

I bought Lucille's Christmas present today, a gorgeous rawhide dressing case, and of course now Polly wants one too. Andrew phoned to say he won't be home until late tonight because Mrs. Peterson's time is up and she absolutely refuses to go to a hospital. So I guess I'll drop over to Lucille's for a while. I want to show her the new earrings Andrew bought me. Later. Well, here I am. Lucille has the living room beautifully decorated for Christmas with clusters of pine tied with ribbon. I was quite envious. I asked her where she got it and she said she'd simply gone out into the park and cut it, and we both laughed. I think I'll try it too! The pine smells so fresh and clean, and think of the fun cutting it for oneself!

It was the last entry. The pictures kept forming in Sands' mind, though there were no more words to hang them on.

Mildred, pink and pretty against the pine.

"Oh, I love it! It smells so fresh and clean."

"Yes, doesn't it. I cut it myself."

"How exciting!"

"We could go out and cut some for you. It's snowing, the night is dark, and I have an ax."

"An ax? Oh, goody!"

"Yes, an ax . . ."

Had the details of the plan occurred to her suddenly at that point? Or had she plotted it carefully beforehand, using the pine as the bait for Mildred to swallow, more innocent than any trout? No one would ever know now. Lucille's secrets had been buried with her in a closed coffin.

They went, laughing, out into the snow.

"Oh, this is fun! Wait'll I tell Andrew."

"Here, let me cut it for you. I'm bigger than you are."

"Do be careful. It's rather frightening out here alone, isn't it?"

"I'm not frightened."

"I just meant, the dark. I can hardly see you, Lucille! Lucille! Where are you? Lucille!"

"Why, I'm right here. Behind you. With an ax."

The ax swung and whistled. The snow fell soundlessly and covered Mildred and the tracks.

What had Lucille done with the ax? Put it in the furnace, Sands thought. The handle would burn, and if the fire was high enough the blade itself might be distorted beyond recognition. And Mildred's jewels—had she put them in the furnace with the ax, or did she hide them, hoping to sell them later? Perhaps she had never intended to sell them and had taken them only in the hope that Mildred's death would be construed as a robbery.

As it was, Sands thought grimly. Thanks to Inspector Hannegan's precious bungling.

He returned to Lucille. He could see her destroying the ax, and hiding the jewels and then coming, suddenly, upon the diary Mildred had left behind in the sitting room. If she hadn't been pressed for time she might have read the diary then and there and realized that it would have to be destroyed. But she didn't have time to read it and she was cautious enough not to want to destroy it if it should prove harmless to her.

Where has it been all these years? Sands thought.

At one o'clock Andrew Morrow had come home.

"Edith! Edith, wake up! Mildred isn't home yet. Something must have happened to her."

"Why, she was just over at Lucille's."

"I'm going over to get her."

They had gone over to Lucille's but they didn't get Mildred.

"She left here ages ago, before eleven o'clock. I thought she was going straight home."

"She's not there."

"She may have decided to go for a walk, and stumbled and fell."

"Come on, Edith, we'll look for her."

"Wait and I'll get dressed and help you look."

She had helped them look, guiding them firmly away from the tree that sheltered Mildred.

Hers had remained the guiding hand. She soothed Edith and nursed Andrew through his illness and got the children off to school; and when she had become indispensable, he married her.

Sands closed the diary and put it in his pocket. He thought of Edith creeping downstairs with the diary, finding only a paper bag to wrap it in, and sending it not to him, Sands, but to her new friend, Janet Green.

To send it to me would have been too final and definite an act, he thought. She wasn't sure, she wanted only to get the diary in some safe place outside the house until she could decide what to do about it.

He felt a sudden terrible pity for Edith, not because she was dead but because in her childish impulsiveness and indecision she had sent the diary to Janet Green.

Polly came in and found Sands slumped in the chair, holding his head with one hand.

He rose when he saw her, but for a minute neither of them spoke. He noticed that she had not been crying but her face had the strained set look that told of deep and bitter tears inside.

"I was—we were just going to phone you. My father will be down in a minute. He thinks—he thinks Edith killed herself."

"Why?" Sands said, and had to repeat it. "Why?"

"It wasn't natural." She turned her face and gazed stonily out of the window. "My father thinks it was morphine."

"Why morphine?"

"I don't know. He just thinks so. She was in his room last night, half-hysterical, begging him to give her something to make her sleep. He unlocked his cupboard and then went into the bathroom to mix her a bromide. It must have been then when it happened."

"What did?"

"When she—took the morphine."

"Why?"

She turned and looked at him. "You keep asking why and I don't know."

"Can you take advice?"

"I don't know what you mean."

"Get out of this house right away. Walk out the door and don't look back."

"Are you—crazy?"

"Go to your lieutenant. Don't stop to pack or think. Pick up your coat and get out."

"I—can't."

"Don't argue."

Her eyes widened. "I don't understand you. You're frightening me. I can't leave my father. And there's no reason—no reason . . ."

He reached out and grasped her shoulder savagely.

"Get out of this house. Run. Don't let anything stop you."

Neither of them had heard Andrew approaching. He spoke from the doorway. "Mr. Sands is right. I advise you to go."

He sounded tired but perfectly under control. "Lieutenant Frome's leave is up Sunday, isn't it? Today is Thursday, you haven't much time."

She looked from one man to the other, her mouth open in bewilderment.

"I don't understand. You know I can't leave you here alone, Father."

"Why not? Has it occurred to you that I might prefer to be alone?"

Sands stepped back and watched the two of them. It might have been an ordinary family argument except that the girl's eyes had too much fear in them, and there was too much acid in the man's voice.

"I think I'm old enough to be allowed some freedom, Polly. Edith is dead now, the whole business is ended. Do you know what that means to me, in plain realistic terms? It means I'm no longer phone-ridden."

The girl's face moved, and it seemed for an instant as if she were going to cry or laugh at the ridiculous word.

"It means," he said, "that wherever I choose to go, at whatever time, I won't be required to phone home and give my exact location, the nature of my companions, and the state of my health. I am now a free agent, an emancipated man. I've had to suffer to get to this point, but I'm there now. *Nothing whatever is expected of me.*"

"I'm not the type who interferes," Polly said. She tried to sound cold and scornful but her voice trembled. "I don't require ten-minute reports, you wouldn't have to be phone-ridden. I'm not—I'm not Edith."

"No. But Edith wasn't always Edith either. Years ago Edith too was engaged to a young man. But when Mildred died she broke her engagement, she said it was her duty to stay with me. The fact was that she didn't love the young man enough to take a chance on marriage, so she eased herself out of it by that word *duty*. As the years passed Edith closed her mind to the real facts. She blamed me for her frustrated love affair. She took it out on me, not overtly, but by kind and gentle and loving nagging."

She looked at him, stubborn and mute.

"I'm wasting my time pointing out analogies. I'll have to give you a direct order, Polly. Leave this house."

"I won't. This is ridiculous."

"Leave this house immediately, do you hear?"

"You might at least keep your voice down. The maids . . ."

He saw that she had no intention of going. Even though she might have wanted to, her own obstinacy was in the way.

"I'm sorry," he said, and struck her on the cheek with the flat of his hand.

Her face seemed to break apart under the blow. With a sudden whimper she turned and ran out of the room holding her hand to her cheek.

The two men stood in silence. They heard the front door open and slam shut, a car engine racing, the blast of a horn, and then just quiet again.

"I'm sorry," Andrew repeated. "I—I don't really believe in violence."

"No," Sands said. "It boomerangs."

"The poor child, she was frightened to death."

"She'll get over it. Edith won't."

"Edith—yes. You want to see Edith, of course?"

"Yes."

"Very peaceful. Morphine is a peaceful death. You go to sleep, you dream, you never know where the dream ends."

Where the dream ends—for Greeley in an alley and Edith in her soft bed.

14

SHE had not undressed. She lay on the bed, a blanket covering her to the waist, her head resting easily on two pillows.

"She didn't go to bed," Andrew said softly, as if she might wake at any minute and be displeased to find him in her bedroom talking about her. "She wouldn't have liked to be found in a nightgown."

"You think that's it?"

"Perhaps. I'm only guessing. It's all we can do now."

Sands moved closer to the bed. Edith's hands were folded and he saw that one of her fingers had a smudge of ink on it. His eyes strayed to the night table beside the bed. It held a glass of water and a pitcher and a lamp. At the base of the lamp lay a fountain pen with the top jammed carelessly on.

Sands thought, she sat here marking the passages in the diary. She worked quickly—why? Was she fighting against time, or was she in a hurry to go to sleep, to dream, to die?

"Why?" he said aloud. Why go to all the trouble of marking the diary and seeing that it got in neutral and therefore safe hands?

"Why kill herself?" Andrew said, quietly. 'Because she'd written a letter. When I came upstairs last night she was in my room trying to find it. It was in the bundle of Lucille's clothes that came from the hospital. She was afraid that I might read it and find out that she had driven Lucille to suicide."

"I see."

"Here it is. I read it last night."

He brought the letter from his pocket and handed it to Sands.

Sands read the agitated scrawl:

"Dear Lucille: I hope you received the chocolates and pillow rest I sent day before yesterday. It is very difficult to get chocolates these days, one has to stand in line. We all miss you a great deal, though I feel so hopeless saying it because I know you won't believe it. Everything is such a mess. The policeman Sands was here again, talking about the train wreck. You remember that afternoon? I don't know what he was getting at, but whoever did anything to you, Lucille, it wasn't me, Lucille, it was not me! I don't know, I can't figure anything out any more. I have this sick headache nearly all the time and Martin is driving me crazy. They have always seemed like my own children to me, the two of them, and now, I don't know, I look at them and they're like strangers. Meals are the worst time. We watch each other. That doesn't sound like much but it's terrible —we watch each other. I know Andrew wouldn't like me to be writing a letter like this. But, Lucille, you're the only one I can talk to now. I feel I'd rather be there with you, I've always liked and trusted you. Everything is so mixed up. Do you remember the night Giles came and I said, God help me, that we were a happy family? I feel this is a judgment on me for my smugness and wickedness. I don't know how it will all end. Edith."

It had all ended now, for both of them. Edith's calm cold face denied all knowledge. *Whoever did anything to you, Lucille, it wasn't me, Lucille, it was not me!* The words rang clear and true in Sands' mind.

"She had to get the letter back," Andrew said. "She knew that Lucille killed herself soon after it was read to her, and she realized that if other people read it they would know the letter was mainly responsible for Lucille's death."

Sands barely heard him. He was looking at Edith, seeing the cold denial on her face. The diary felt large and heavy in his pocket, as if it had grown since he'd put it there.

He turned suddenly and walked back to the door. The diary swung against his side, and when he passed Andrew he saw Andrew's eyes on his coat pocket.

"Do you carry a gun?" Andrew said.

"No."

"What's that?"

"A book."

"If you don't carry a gun, what do you do in an emergency?"

"I plan for emergencies. Then they are no longer emergencies." He smiled, very faintly. "Do *you* carry a gun?"

"No."

"You are against violence, I had forgotten. Excuse me, I have to phone in a report. Your sister—must be attended to."

"Yes, of course. You know where the phone is."

Sands was gone for ten minutes. When he came back Andrew was standing in the hall outside Edith's room, waiting for him.

"That book in your pocket," he said, "that's my wife's diary, isn't it?"

"Yes."

"I thought it would be. I couldn't find it. I gave it to Edith last night to read."

"Why?"

"She found it in my room when she came to look for her letter. I thought it was the natural thing to do, to let her read it."

"Natural," Sands repeated. "Everything's been pretty natural all down the line, hasn't it? Everything has more or less just *happened*."

"I'm glad you see that. I feel it very strongly myself."

"Yes, I know."

"The only really unnatural thing is where you got my wife's diary."

"Your sister wrapped it in a paper bag and mailed it to Janet Green last night before she died." Seeing Andrew's frown he added, "She was at the funeral yestday. Cora Green's sister."

"Oh, yes. The little old woman who ate the grapes." He flung a quick uncertain glance at Sands. "Well, at least nobody could claim that was anything but an accident."

"Nobody has."

"And Lucille herself, and the Greeley fellow, and now Edith—all accidents."

"If you plan accidents," Sands said grimly, "then they are no longer accidents."

Andrew laughed. "Ah, yes. Like the emergency." He sobered at the look on Sands' face. He felt that he must somehow deflect that cold direct gaze. "What were we talking about?"

"Accidents."

"And the diary, yes. I didn't imagine Edith would do anything so preposterous as sending it to Janet Green."

"Why did you give her the diary to read?"

"I told you, she found it in my room, I thought she would be interested in it."

"No. I think you were making one of your experiments. On Edith's mind, this time. When you first read the diary it threw you completely. You wanted to see what it would do to Edith."

"When I first read the diary?" Andrew repeated. "Why, I've had it for years, as I told Edith."

"But once she'd read it she didn't believe you. Any more than I do. I think you found the diary two weeks ago last Sunday."

They were both silent. The words spun between them—two weeks ago last Sunday—and Sands could picture Polly sitting in his office yesterday morning, saying blankly: "It was the most ordinary Sunday. . . . Father couldn't find something, as usual, his scarf, I think it was. . . ."

"You couldn't have had the diary all this time," Sands said, "without knowing that Lucille had killed your first wife. And having that knowledge you could never have lived with her for fifteen years. It is humanly impossible."

A door opened at the end of the hall and Martin came out. Though he walked slowly Sands had the impression that he was holding himself back, that if he thought no one was looking he would bound along the hall, as buoyant and unfeeling as an animal.

"Oh, there you are, Father," Martin said, and his voice too gave the impression of carefully imposed restraint. His eyes strayed to Edith's door and then back to his father. "Conference in the hall?"

"Mr. Sands and I are talking," Andrew said.

Martin raised his brows. "Not by any chance about me? You're looking very guilty."

"Guilty?" Andrew laughed, but one of his hands crept up toward his face as if to smooth away the lines of guilt. "It's difficult for you to believe, Martin, but people frequently talk about other things than you."

"Granted."

"I . . . Polly is not here. She's gone down to meet Lieutenant Frome. I expect they'll be married this afternoon."

Martin flickered another glance toward Edith's door. "Nice day for it."

"My suggestion entirely," Sands said.

"Don't bother with explanations," Andrew told him curtly, and turned back to Martin. "I want you to go down there now—where is it?—the Ford Hotel?"

"Yes."

"Go down there now. I—well, I forgot to give Polly some money. I'll write a check and you can take it down to her and—and wish her luck. Wish her luck for me, Martin."

"This is a damn funny time to ask me to go traipsing around with checks and touching messages."

"I'm not asking you, I'm telling you. Come downstairs and I'll write the check."

He went to the staircase, and after a moment's hesitation Martin followed him, frowning at Sands as he passed him. If Sands had not been there he would have made an issue of it and insisted on an explanation from his father. But Sands was there and in some strange way allied with Andrew, and together the two men had a personal ascendancy that Martin would not defy.

Besides, he was a sophisticated young man and dared not show surprise. In the study he accepted the check from Andrew docilely, but with a quirk of his mouth to show that he was not in any way impressed.

"Wish her luck," Andrew said again.

"Sure," Martin said, and departed with a debonair wave of his hand.

The sophisticate, Sands thought, the man about town, the babe swaddled by Brooks Brothers.

"Sit down and make yourself comfortable, Mr. Sands," Andrew said. "We have quite a lot to talk about. Cigarette?"

"Thanks."

"Do you mind if I close this door?"

"Not at all."

"I wouldn't want the maids to hear me talking about my murders. It might destroy their faith in doctors." He closed the door. "Murders, I don't know how many, or how many causes . . . Faulty diagnosis, too much pressure on the scalpel, bad timing, sheer ignorance and lack of experience. . . . Every time I lost a case I used to brood about it. Then I began to believe that sometime between now and the end of time everything would be put right again. In the forever-ever land the dead baby lifted by Caesarean section would have its second chance, would breathe again, and live, and grow beautiful. Mildred called it *having faith*."

The smoke from his cigarette slid up his face. "You used the phrase, humanly impossible. Practically nothing is that. A man can endure anything if he believes in ultimate justice, if he believes that somewhere dangling in space is justice and the wicked shall be punished and the good shall be rewarded. That is the working principle of the religion of the people I know. Revenge and reward."

He leaned forward. "Think of it! Somewhere dangling in space justice, great impartial justice built like a monstrous man straddling the universe. A big fellow, a strong fellow, a kind fellow, but still like us, with sixteen bones in each wrist and his pubic hair modestly covered with a bit of cloth."

Sands thought, another fallen idealist, the man who expects too much and loses his faith not all at once but gradually and with suspense and bitter doubts.

"Don't be boyish," he said, and glanced at his watch. "My friends will be here in five minutes."

"And then?"

"And then," Sands said carefully, "I will try to prove that you are a murderer."

"You have no proof?"

"Circumstantial evidence only. Quite a bit of it in Greeley's case. You had the means of committing the murder and you were around at the crucial time."

"So were a lot of other people."

"True. Then Miss Green's death offers no problem to you. You can only be charged there with moral guilt, moral irresponsibility. Evil and fear grow like cancer cells, inexorably, aimlessly, destroying whatever they touch. Cora Green was one of its victims." He blinked his eyes, dreamily. "Circumstantial evidence only," he repeated. "Perhaps we'll have to wait for that big fellow straddling the universe to get you."

"I'm not afraid of him."

"What?" Sands said in an exaggerated drawl. "And him so big and full of vitamins?"

They both smiled but there was a glint of rage in Andrew's eyes and he crushed out his cigarette with a gesture that was almost savage.

"You are making me out a fool and a villain. I am neither. I am an ordinary man, and if out-of-the-ordinary things occurred to me, they occurred naturally. You understand? They just *happened*. You said it yourself. I was not looking for that diary when I found it, I had forgotten there was such a thing. I was looking for the scarf Lucille gave me last Christmas, a black scarf with little gray designs on it."

"Black? With little gray designs? It sounds terribly cute."

He leaned back, watching Andrew lazily as if the whole episode was a mildly amusing joke.

A flush of anger rose slowly up Andrew's face. He knew that Sands was baiting him, that he must control himself. But he felt too that he must impress the man and make him realize that he was not a child to be laughed aside.

"The scarf was not in the cedar closet where Lucille said it was. I looked in my own room and then in hers. The diary was in one of her bureau drawers. It wasn't even hidden properly, it was just there. As if she took it out now and then to read . . ." He stopped, sucking in his breath. "Think of it! She murdered my wife. And all these years she's kept the evidence to convict her, casually, in a bureau drawer."

"It may not have been there all the time," Sands said. "Perhaps she'd hidden it well, and came across it and wanted to read it again." Why? To re-live it, and by reliving it to lay the ghost that haunted her mind?

"I think you're right. She'd been thinking of Mildred that day, Sunday. Martin and I found the sketches she made of Mildred. She had burned out the eyes with a cigarette." He paused again, shaking his head half in sorrow, half in bewildered rage. "The systematic illogic of women. A man cannot believe it. When they are angry they are cold and merciless. When they have a grievance they tuck it up their sleeve and it comes out at some inexplicable and unconnected moment as tears. They can live, almost happily, with a man they hate, and harry a man they love to death."

"Like yourself?"

"Like myself, yes. All my life I've been fair prey for any woman, because I value peace. I gave up my independence for the sake of peace. I've hired myself out to a series of managers—my mother, Edith, Lucille. A man has no redress against the soft lilting command, no refuge at all from the voices of the women who love him and are doing everything 'for his own good.' "

He was no longer angry. He even seemed bored with his own words, as if he had said them to himself a great many times and was now reciting a piece of memory work.

"I killed Edith," he said.

Sands did not reply.

"I killed her because she started to nag at me. She wanted a sleeping prescription, so I gave her one. I hadn't planned anything, hadn't thought of it. But suddenly there she was, wanting to be put to sleep. You understand? It was so simple, so predestined. She asked for it."

"Yes."

"I went in after she was dead, to find the diary and destroy it. But it wasn't there. I didn't worry about it, however."

"You should. It might help to hang you."

"No, it won't. This talk is confidential between the two of us. And the evidence against Edith is too strong. Your friends will find morphine in Edith's glass, and I will supply the letter she wrote to Lucille at Penwood."

"Edith was the only one who couldn't possibly have sent the amputated finger to Lucille."

"You can't fool me like that," Andrew said. "You will have to bring me to trial one case at a time. You can't try to prove that *perhaps* I killed Greeley, and *perhaps* I killed Edith, and have the two *perhaps*'s make a certainty."

"That's right."

"Why do you want to hang me, anyway? Revenge? Punishment? To teach me a lesson or teach other people a lesson?"

"It's my job," Sands said wryly.

"Purely impersonal?"

"No, not quite."

"Why, then?"

"I think you might do it again."

"That's ridiculous," Andrew said. "I have no reason to kill anyone else."

"Perhaps you had no reason to kill Greeley?"

"He was interfering, getting in my way. I hadn't planned on killing him or anyone else. I hadn't really planned anything. I was pretty dazed after reading the diary, I hardly remember driving out to meet Giles. All I could think of was Lucille's two faces—the one she showed to me and the one I saw in Mildred's diary. I thought I would keep quiet until after Polly was married and then I would confront Lucille with the diary. But what then? Would she confess? Would she lie? Would she even try to kill me perhaps, to save herself? Then we came upon the train wreck and the situation solved itself. I knew how I could test Lucille. I saw the finger in a slop pail and I picked it up and wrapped it in my handkerchief."

The grotesque picture formed in Sands' mind. The man bending furtively over a slop pail, wrapping the finger carefully in his handkerchief, like a jewel.

"You know how it makes you feel when you do something like that?" Andrew said. "It makes you feel a little crazy."

"It would."

"It was only a test for her, you understand. I had to know whether she was guilty. I didn't foresee the actual results—it wasn't even her own guilt that drove her crazy, it was the knowledge that someone else *knew* of her guilt, and was pointing it out, that someone had tracked her down. She, who had lived a placid, happy life for sixteen years now found herself a criminal." He paused. "I keep thinking of what she did when she opened the box. She screamed, we know that, and then she must have run to the bureau drawer to find the diary. When she saw it was gone, she knew one of us must have taken it."

"A pretty symbol, that finger."

Andrew shrugged away the implications.

"I carried it in my pocket for the rest of the night. In the morning I bought a box in the dime store on my way to the office, and wrapped it. I thought of sending it through the mail, but then I saw this shabby-looking little man standing beside the newsstand. I asked him if he'd deliver a parcel for two dollars and he said he would."

"You could have saved yourself trouble by lowering it to fifty cents. A parcel worth a two-dollar delivery is worth opening. Childish of you."

"I—it just didn't occur to me not to trust him. I've had no experience with such things."

"The first thing he did, of course, was take it to a washroom and open it. Maybe he was a little surprised by it, but I don't think so. Greeley had seen a lot of things in his life. What interested him was the smell of money, and he got a big whiff when he opened that parcel. He delivered it, all right. Then he waited around to see what would happen. He followed Lucille down to Sunnyside and waited outside while she was in the beauty parlor. When she came out he confronted her. She gave him a fifty-dollar bill to keep him quiet. She took a room at the Lakeside Hotel, and when he was pretty sure she was going to stay there for a while he went out and had what for Greeley was a big evening. Life was all right for Greeley that night. He had champagne, even if it was in a third-rate joint; he had a girl, no matter how many other people had had her; he danced, though his legs must have hurt him; he had a shot of morphine for a cheap dream, but most of all he had a future.

"Lucille must have promised him more money, for he told the girl he was with that he had a date, and then he returned to the Lakeside. He got there about the same time as Inspector Bascombe and I did. Men like Greeley have a sharp nose for two things— money and cops, and he probably recognized us right away. He didn't know what we were there for. Maybe it was Lucille, maybe not. He hung around the alley for a while, and then you came along. He recognized you immediately."

"It was a shock," Andrew said, "it was a terrible shock to me to meet him again. I'd almost forgotten about him. Then I saw what I should have seen the preceding afternoon if I hadn't been intent on my plan—he was a morphine addict. I could see his eyes clearly in the light of the hotel sign, they were pupil-less, blind-looking. The tragedy of it was that I was carrying my instrument bag in case I'd have to give Lucille a sedative."

"Tragedy?"

"He saw I was a doctor."

"I see."

"Yes, a doctor means only one thing to an addict—a chance for more dope. We're all pestered by them at one time or another. The first thing the man said was, "A sawbones, eh?" I told him I wasn't, but he didn't believe me. He seemed to be burning up with triumph.

I could see then what I had let myself in for. I had committed no crime, but I had done what most people would consider a revolting thing—and I wanted it kept secret. But Greeley, you understand, thought I *had* committed a crime.

" 'Some parcel,' he said. 'Where's the rest of the guy?' I didn't answer him. Then he asked me for some morphine. He told me he had a hard time getting any and what he did get was diluted. 'I haven't got any extra,' I told him. 'Just a quarter grain, not enough for you.'

"The crazy part of it is that if I hadn't refused to give it to him at first, he would have been suspicious. But because I refused, he said, 'What do *you* know about me? That'll do—for *now.*'

"He didn't need it then, he was pretty full of the stuff already. But he couldn't pass up the chance, you see. They all have that same senseless greed because they know what it's like to be without it. Anyway he led me around to the alley. It was dark and intensely cold. I put my bag on the ground and opened it. Greeley lit a match and cupped it in his hands, and then we both squatted down beside the bag. Bizarre, isn't it, and somehow obscene?

"I could tell you it was then that I decided to kill him, but I couldn't tell you why. There was no one reason, perhaps there never is for a murder. Perhaps I killed him because I was afraid of him, and because he hadn't long to live and would be better off dead anyway, and because he had betrayed my trust, and because of the very ugliness of the scene itself.

"It was no trick to kill him. He had no way of knowing how much I was giving him. Besides, he kept watching the end of the alley and urging me to hurry up. I prepared the syringe and told him to take off his coat. He said, 'What the hell, nothing fancy for me,' and shoved out his arm.

"I gave him two grains. The whole incident didn't take ten minutes."

Two grains, ten minutes, the end of Greeley, Sands thought.

"Simple," he said. "Natural. Practically an accident."

"I told you that."

"Sure. Any logical sequence of events ends in murder just as the logical sequel to life is death."

"Irony doesn't affect me," Andrew said. "I was trying to present my story sincerely and honestly. I feel that you are a civilized man and can understand it."

"It's easy enough to be civilized in a vacuum. The mouse in an airless bell jar can't be compared to ordinary mice. In the first place he's dead."

"Quite so."

The doorbell began to ring.

"Your friends are here," Andrew said politely.

While the policemen were there Andrew remained in his study with the door shut. Overhead, the men worked very quietly, and only by straining his ears could he hear them moving about.

What are they doing up there?

Nothing. Don't listen.

What have I overlooked?

Nothing. It is all arranged. Poor Edith killed herself in remorse.

Poor Edith, how like Greeley she'd acted after all, both so greedy for a little death and so surprised at getting the real thing.

He didn't worry about either of them. About Greeley he had no feelings at all, and while he felt sorry for Edith because she had made her own death necessary, he did not wish her back. He had turned a corner in his life. Looking back he could see only the sharp gray angle of a nameless building, and ahead of him the road was a nebula of mist swirling with forms and shapes, faces that were not yet faces, sounds that were not yet sounds. As he walked along the mist would clear. But right now it was frightening. It stung his eyes and muffled his ears and curled down deep into his lungs and made him cough. He could taste it in his mouth, fresh like the snow he had eaten when he was a child.

I don't feel very well.

Andrew dear, have you been eating Snow?

I don't feel very well.

The child is Ill. Call the doctor Immediately.

Calling Dr. Morrow. Calling Dr. Morrow. Dr. Morrow is wanted in . . .

Andrew my Dear. Snow is full of Germs. It may look pretty but it is not to Eat because it is full of Germs. I'll buy you a microscope for your birthday so you can see for Yourself how many Germs there are Everywhere.

Many many many many Germs. Everywhere.

He became aware, suddenly, that the noises overhead had ceased. The house was empty. Mildred had gone, with the children, Edith was gone, and Lucille—only the maids were left and they must go too. He had to be alone, to think.

He rose painfully. His legs were cramped, he had been sitting too tensely. He must learn not to look back or look ahead. Where, then, could you look? At yourself. Turn your eyes in, like two little dentist's mirrors, until you saw yourself larger than life, in great detail, each single hair, each pore of skin a new revelation, wondrously crawling with germs.

But the silence, the appalling silence of the man in the mirrors; the brittle limbs, the face mobile but cold like glass . . .

He crossed the hall, quickly, to escape his own image.

He found the maids in the kitchen. They had been quarreling. Della's eyes were swollen from weeping and Annie's mouth had a set stubborn look. She didn't change her expression when she saw Andrew.

"I say we're leaving," she said. "I say there's too much going on around this place that don't look right."

"Of course," Andrew said. "If you feel like that."

"She don't want to go. Afraid she won't get another job. Why, in times like these they get down on their knees and beg you to take a job. She's too dumb to see that."

"It's different with you!" Della cried. "I got to send money home every month!"

"Don't I got to live too? And am I scared?"

"I'll give you both a month's wages," Andrew said quietly. "You may leave today if you like."

Della only wept harder, and Annie had to do the talking for both of them. It was real kind of Dr. Morrow, really generous. Not that they couldn't use the money. Not that they *wanted* to leave him in the lurch like this. But what future was there in housework?

"What future indeed?" Andrew said. "You may leave at once. I'll make out your checks."

They went upstairs and began to pack.

"Remember the emeralds?" Della said wistfully.

"What emeralds?"

"You remember. The parcel."

"Oh, hell," Annie said and jerked open the closet door savagely. "We're too old to play games like that. You're eighteen and you talk like you were ten. Imagine *us* with an emerald."

"Maybe—some day we'll find something. Money or something.

Or maybe radium. They say if you find just a little bit of radium you get to be a millionaire."

"Will you shut up?" Annie banged her fist against a suitcase. "Will—you—shut—up?"

They hadn't many clothes to pack. Within half an hour they were on Bloor Street waiting for a streetcar, their purses tight beneath their arms. They were still quarreling, but there was a softer look on Annie's face and now and then she scanned the sidewalk and the gutter. Just in case.

Andrew stood at the door, watching, long after they were out of sight. They were gone, the last remnants of the old life, and now he must begin his new one. But he felt curiously tired, reluctant to move from the door, as if any movement at all might bring on a new situation, a new series of complications that he would have to deal with. He wanted to see and hear nothing, to feel nothing, to be alone in a vacuum, like the mouse in the bell jar.

But the mouse was dead. *In the first place he's dead.*

He heard someone coming down the stairs behind him. He had thought the house was empty, but now that he found it wasn't, he was too weary to feel surprise. He turned slowly, knowing before he turned that it was Sands.

"I thought you were gone." He had to drag the words out of his mouth.

"I'm leaving in a minute. Everyone else has gone. You'll be alone."

Alone. The word had a solemn sonorous sound that struck his ears with a thud.

"That's what you wanted," Sands said. "Isn't it?"

"Yes."

"Well, now you have it. You'll be alone. And you'll be lonely."

"No, no, I—Martin—Martin will come back."

"But he won't stay. There's nothing left for him here in this house."

"He'll stay if I ask him to, if I . . ."

"No, I don't think so. You'll be quite alone."

Andrew closed his eyes. He saw the mist on the road ahead suddenly sweeping back toward him in gusts of fury.

"No—no . . ." he said, but how faint and suffocated his voice was, with the mist smothering his mouth. "I'm not—not afraid of being alone."

"You're afraid of the big fellow. You don't want justice any more, you want mercy."

Andrew bowed his head. Mercy. A terrible and piteous word that conjured up all the lost people wailing to their lost gods.

"I want nothing," he said.

"But it's too late now. You already have what you wanted. Don't you recognize it?" Sands smiled. "This is *it*, Morrow."

"Is this it?" He heard in his own voice the wailing of the lost men.

"The role of avenger is not for a little man like you. You dispensed justice to Lucille, now you must await it, in turn. You even asked the police to help you hunt her down. You couldn't wait, could you? . . . You enjoyed seeing her suffer, didn't you?"

"No—no—I'm sorry . . ."

"Too late, it's all over."

"And now?"

"Now, nothing." He smiled again. "Doesn't that amuse you? You're like Lucille, after all. You have nothing left to live for."

Andrew was propped up against the wall like a dummy waiting for someone to come along and move it into a new position.

Sands took out his watch, and in the silent house the ticking seemed extraordinarily important.

He put his watch back and began buttoning his overcoat. "I've got to leave now."

"I am afraid," Andrew said, but the door had already opened and closed again, softly, and he knew he must die alone.

Sands stepped out into the keen sparkling air.

He stood on the veranda for a moment and looked across the park where the phallic points of the pines were thrust toward the sun. He felt outside time, naked and frail and percipient. Evergreens and men were growing toward decay. Time was a mole moving under the roads of the city and imperceptibly buckling the asphalt. Time passed over his head in a thin gray rack of scudding clouds, as if the sky had fled away and its last remaining rags were blowing over the edge of the world.